GODSGRAVE

THE NEVERNIGHT CHRONICLE
BOOK II

JAY KRISTOFF

HARPER
Voyager

Harper*Voyager*
An imprint of HarperCollins*Publishers* Ltd
1 London Bridge Street
London SE1 9GF

www.harpercollins.co.uk

This paperback edition 2018
8

First published by HarperCollins*Publishers* 2017

A catalogue record for this book
is available from the British Library

ISBN 978-0-00-818006-5

This novel is entirely a work of fiction.
The names, characters and incidents portrayed in it are
the work of the author's imagination. Any resemblance to
actual persons, living or dead, events or localities is
entirely coincidental.

Set in Adobe Garamond Pro 10/11.5 pt by Palimpsest Book Production Limited,
Falkirk, Stirlingshire

Printed and bound by CPI Group (UK) Ltd, Croydon CR0 4YY

MIX
Paper from
responsible sources
FSC™ C007454

This book is produced from independently certified FSC™ paper
to ensure responsible forest management.

For more information visit: www.harpercollins.co.uk/green

for my enemies
I couldn't have done it without you

THE REPUBLIC OF ITREYA

NALIPSE

STORMWATCH

DAWNSPEAR

WHITEKEEP

SEA OF SILENCE

CITY OF GODSGRAVE

SEA OF S

TALIA

FARROW

SEAWALL

ISLES OF DWEYM

TSANA

N

N

THE SWORD ARM

THE SPINE

THE HEART

THE SEA OF SILENCE

GODSGRAVE
CATHEDRAL

MERCURIO'S
CURIOS

LIISIAN MARKET

THE BAY OF
BUTCHERS

WESTERN NETHERS

THE BRIDGE OF FOLLIES

IN THE REPUB

THE SHIELD ARM

THE AQUEDUCT

THE RIBS

THE WHITE PALAZZO

THE PHILOSOPHER'S STONE

ORKERY

EASTERN NETHERS

N

GODSGRAVE

THE CITY OF BRIDGES AND BONES

IC OF ITREYA

CROW'S NEST

Good turn to you, gentlefriends. It's lovely to see you again.

I confess, I missed you in our time apart. And now, reunited, would that I could simply greet you with a smile, and let you be about the business of murder and revenge and occasional lashings of tastefully written smut. But before we slip back between the pages together, I should impart a warning true.

Memory is a traitor, and a liar, and a good-for-nothing thief. And though our drama's cast is doubtless inked indelibly on your psyche, we must sometimes make allowances for the lesser among you mortals.

So, perhaps a refresher is in order?

DRAMATIS PERSONAE

Mia Corvere – assassin, thief, and heroine of our tale – if our tale can be said to have one at all. Her father, Darius, was executed under order of the Itreyan Senate and, vowing vengeance, she became a disciple of the Republic's most feared cult of assassins, the Red Church.

Though she failed the Church's trials, Mia was inducted as a Blade (aka assassin) after rescuing the Church's ministry during an assault by Luminatii legionaries.

Mia is of mixed Itreyan-Liisian blood. She is also darkin – one who controls the darkness itself. She has little understanding of her powers, and the only other darkin she has ever met died before he could give her the answers she desired.

Tragic, I know.

Mister Kindly – a daemon, passenger, or familiar (depending on who one asks) made of shadows, who eats Mia's fear. He saved her life as a child, and claims to know very little about his true nature, though he's been known to lie from time to time.

He wears the shape of a cat, though he is nothing close to a cat at all.

Eclipse – another shadow daemon, who wears the guise of a wolf. Eclipse was passenger to Lord Cassius, former head of the Red Church. When Cassius died during the Luminatii assault, Eclipse bound herself to Mia instead.

Like most dogs and cats, she and Mister Kindly do not get along.

Old Mercurio – Mia's trainer and confidant in the time before she joined the Red Church. Mercurio was a Church Blade himself for many years, but is now retired in Godsgrave. The old Itreyan runs a store named Mercurio's Curios and serves as an information broker and talent scout for the servants of the Black Mother.

A grumpier old bastard was never found under any of the three suns.

Tric – an acolyte of the Red Church, also Mia's friend and lover. Tric was of mixed Itreyan-Dweymeri heritage. He was poised to be inducted into the Blades, but Ashlinn Järnheim stabbed him repeatedly in the heart and pushed him off the side of the Quiet Mountain.

As a promise to Tric, Mia assassinated Tric's grandfather, Swordbreaker, king of the Dweymeri Isles, after the boy's death.

Which wasn't all that sensible, when you think about it . . .

Ashlinn Järnheim – an acolyte of the Red Church and formerly one of Mia's closest friends. Ash was born in Vaan, and is the daughter of Torvar Järnheim, a retired Blade of the Church. As vengeance for a maiming he received in the Mother's service, he and his children hatched a plot that almost brought the entire Church to its knees, though their conspiracy was finally foiled by Mia.

Ash's brother, Osrik, was killed in the process, but Ashlinn escaped.

Ash's feelings about Mia are best described as . . . complicated.

Naev – a Hand (aka disciple) of the Red Church and close friend of Mia, who manages supply runs in the desolate Whisperwastes of Ashkah. Naev was disfigured by Weaver Marielle out of jealousy, but as reward for Mia's assistance during the Luminatii assault, Marielle restored Naev's former beauty.

Naev never forgets and never forgives – one of the reasons she and Mia get along.

Drusilla – Revered Mother of the Red Church and, despite her apparent old age, one of the deadliest servants of the Black Mother alive. Drusilla failed Mia in her final trial, and it was only after the intercession of Cassius, Lord of Blades, that the girl was inducted.

To put it kindly, she is not Mia's greatest fan.

Solis – Shahiid of Songs, trainer of Red Church acolytes in the art of steel. Mia cut his face during their first sparring session. Solis hacked off her arm in retaliation.

They get along swimmingly now, as you can imagine.*

Spiderkiller – voted 'Shahiid Most Likely to Murder Her Own Students' five years running, Spiderkiller is mistress of the Hall of Truths. Mia was one of her most promising acolytes, but after she failed Drusilla's final test, Spiderkiller's fondness for the girl has all but evaporated.

Mouser – Shahiid of Pockets and master of thievery. Charming, witty, and as fond of larceny as he is of wearing ladies' underthings. The Itreyan has no strong enmity towards Mia, which practically makes him the leader of her fan club.

Aalea – Shahiid of Masks and mistress of secrets. It is said there are only two types of folk in this world: those who love Aalea, and those who've yet to meet her.

She actually seems quite fond of Mia.

Shocking, aye?

Marielle – one of two albino sorcerii in the service of the Church. Marielle is a master of the ancient Ashkahi magik of flesh weaving, capable of sculpting skin and muscle as if it were clay. However, the toll she pays for her power is a steep one – her own flesh is hideous to behold, and she has no power to change it.

Marielle cares for no one save her brother Adonai, and he, perhaps too much.

Adonai – the second sorcerii who serves the Quiet Mountain. Adonai is a blood speaker, capable of manipulating human vitus. Thanks to his sister's arts, he is handsome beyond compare.

Though, I do recall a saying about books and covers . . .

Aelius – the chronicler of the Quiet Mountain, charged with maintaining some semblance of order in the Red Church's great athenaeum.

Like everything else in Niah's library, Aelius is dead.

He seems a little ambivalent about the fact.

---

*Yes, gentlefriends, that was sarcasm. Admit it, you missed me, didn't you?

Hush – a former acolyte of the Red Church, now a full-fledged Blade. Hush never speaks, instead communicating through a form of sign language known as Tongueless.

The Itreyan boy assisted Mia in her final trials, though he'd insist they are not friends.

Jessamine Gratianus – a Red Church acolyte from Mia's crop who failed to become a Blade. Jessamine is the daughter of Marcinus, an Itreyan centurion executed for his loyalty to Mia's father, Darius 'the Kingmaker' Corvere. Jess blames Darius, and by extension, Mia herself, for her father's death – though in truth, the girls have much in common.

The desire to see Consul Julius Scaeva gutted like a pig, for example.

Julius Scaeva – thrice-elected consul of the Itreyan Senate. Scaeva has maintained sole consulship since the Kingmaker Rebellion six years ago. The position is usually shared, and consuls sit only one term, but with Scaeva, the rules seem not to apply.

He presided over the execution of Mia's father, and sentenced her mother and baby brother to die in the Philosopher's Stone. He also ordered Mia drowned in a canal.

Yes, he's something of a cunt.

Francesco Duomo – grand cardinal of the Church of the Light, and the most powerful member of the Everseeing's ministry. Along with Scaeva and Remus, he was responsible for passing sentence on the Kingmaker rebels.

Duomo is the right hand of Aa upon this earth. The mere sight of a holy relic blessed by a man of his conviction is enough to send Mia writhing in agony.

Stabbing the bleeding fuck out of him may prove problematic as a result.

Justicus Marcus Remus – former justicus of the Luminatii Legion, and leader of the attack on the Quiet Mountain. During his climactic confrontation with Mia, Remus made several cryptic remarks about Mia's brother, Jonnen.

Mia stabbed the Itreyan to death before he could fully explain himself.

He was not pleased.

Alinne Corvere – Mia's mother. Though she was born in Liis, Alinne rose to prominence in the halls of Itreyan power. She was a political genius, and a dona of no little esteem and will. Imprisoned in the Philosopher's Stone with her infant son after her husband's failed rebellion, she died in madness and misery.

Yes, I quite liked her, too.

Darius 'the Kingmaker' Corvere – Mia's father. Former justicus of the Luminatii Legion, Darius forged an alliance with General Gaius Maxinius Antonius that would have seen Antonius crowned as king. Together, the two Itreyans raised an army and marched on their own capital, but were both captured on the eve of battle. Without leadership, their army shattered. Their troops were crucified, and Darius himself was hanged with his would-be king Antonius beside him.

So close they could almost touch.

Jonnen Corvere – Mia's brother. An infant at the time of his father's rebellion, Jonnen was imprisoned with his mother in the Philosopher's Stone at the order of Julius Scaeva. He died there before Mia ever had a chance to rescue him.

Aa – the Father of Light, also known as the Everseeing. The three suns, known as Saan (the Seer), Saai (the Knower), and Shiih (the Watcher), are said to be his eyes, and one or more is usually present in the heavens, with the result that actual nighttime, or truedark, occurs for only one week every two and a half years.

Aa is a beneficent god, kind to his subjects and merciful to his enemies. And if you believe that one, gentlefriends, I've a bridge in Godsgrave to sell you.

Tsana – Lady of Fire, She Who Burns Our Sin, the Pure, Patron of Women and Warriors, and firstborn daughter of Aa and Niah.

Keph – Lady of Earth, She Who Ever Slumbers, the Hearth, Patron of Dreamers and Fools, and secondborn of Aa and Niah.

Trelene – Lady of Oceans, She Who Will Drink the World, the Fate, Patron of Sailors and Scoundrels, thirdborn daughter of Aa and Niah, and twin to Nalipse.

Nalipse – Lady of Storms, She Who Remembers, the Merciful, Patron of Healers and Leaders, fourthborn of Aa and Niah, and twin to Trelene.

Niah – the Mother of Night, Our Lady of Blessed Murder, also known as the Maw. Sisterwife of Aa, Niah rules a lightless region of the hereafter known as the abyss. She and Aa initially shared the rule of the sky equally. Commanded to bear her husband only daughters, Niah eventually disobeyed Aa's edict and bore him a son. In punishment, she was banished from the skies by her beloved, allowed to return only for a brief spell every few years.

And as for what became of their son?

As I said last time, gentlefriends, that would be spoiling things.

The wolf does not pity the lamb,
And the storm begs no forgiveness of the drowned.

— RED CHURCH MANTRA

BOOK 1

THE RED PROMISE

CHAPTER 1

PERFUME

Nothing stinks quite like a corpse.

It takes a while for them to really start reeking. O, chances are good if you don't soil your britches before you die, you'll soil them soon afterwards – your human bodies simply work that way, I'm afraid. But I don't mean the pedestrian stink of shit, gentlefriends. I speak of the eye-watering perfume of simple mortality. It takes a turn or two to really warm up, but once the gala gets into full swing, it's one not soon forgot.

Before the skin starts to black and the eyes turn to white and the belly bloats like some horrid balloon, it begins. There's a sweetness to it, creeping down your throat and rolling your belly like a butter churn. In truth, I think it speaks to something primal in you. The same part of you mortals that dreads the dark. That *knows*, without a shadow of a doubt, that no matter who you are and what you do, even worms shall have their feasts, and that one turn, you and everything you love will die.

But still, it takes a while for bodies to get so bad you can smell them from miles away. And so when Teardrinker caught a whiff of the high, sweet stink of decay on the Ashkahi whisperwinds, she knew the corpses had to be at least two turns dead.

And that there had to be an awful lot of them.

The woman pulled on her reins, bringing her camel to a stop as she raised her fist to her crew. The driver in the train behind her saw her signal, the long, winding chain of wagons and beasts slowing down, all spit and growls and stomping feet. The heat was brutal – two suns burning the sky a blinding blue and all the desert around them to rippling red. Teardrinker reached for the waterskin on her saddle, took a lukewarm swig as her second pulled up alongside her.

'Trouble?' Cesare asked.

Teardrinker nodded south along the road. 'Smells like.'

Like all her people, the Dweymeri woman was tall – six foot seven if she was an inch, and every inch of that was muscle. Her skin was deep brown, her features adorned with the intricate facial tattoos worn by all folk of the Dweymeri Isles. A long scar bisected her brow, running over a milk-white left eye and down her cheek. She was dressed like a seafarer: a tricorn hat and some old captain's frock coat. But the oceans she sailed were made of sand now, the only decks she walked were those of her wagon train. After a wreck that killed her entire crew and all her cargo years ago, Teardrinker had decided that the Mother of Oceans hated her guts, arse, and the ship she sailed in on.

So, deserts it was.

The captain shielded her eye against the glare, squinting into the distance. The whisperwinds scratched and clawed about her, the hair on the back of her neck tingling. They were still seven turns out of the Hanging Gardens, and it wasn't uncommon for slavers to work this road even in summersdeep. Still, two of three suns were high in the sky, and this close to truelight, she was hoping it'd be too hot for drama.

But the stench was unmistakable.

'Dogger,' she hollered. 'Graccus, Luka, bring your arms and come with me. Dustwalker, you keep up that ironsong. If a sand kraken ends up chewing on my cunny, I'll be back from the 'byss to chew on *you*.'

'Aye, Cap'n!' the big Dweymeri called. Turning to the contraption of iron piping bolted to the rearmost wagon in the train, Dustwalker hefted a large pipe and began beating it like a disobedient hound. The discordant tune of ironsong joined the maddening whispers blowing in off the northern wastes.

'What about me?' Cesare asked.

Teardrinker smirked at her right-hand man. 'You're too pretty to risk. Stay here. Keep an eye on the stock.'

'They're not doing well in this heat.'

The woman nodded. 'Water them while you wait. Let them stretch their legs a little. Not too far, though. This is bad country.'

'Aye, Cap'n.'

Cesare doffed his hat as Dogger, Graccus, and Luka rode up on their camels to join Teardrinker at the front of the line. Each man was dressed in a thick leather jerkin despite the scorch, and Dogger and Graccus were packing heavy crossbows. Luka wielded his slingblades as always, cigarillo hanging from his mouth. The Liisian thought arrows were for cowards, and he was good enough with his slings that she never argued. But how he could stand to smoke in this heat was beyond her.

'Eyes open, mouths shut,' Teardrinker ordered. 'Let's about it.'

The quartet headed down through rocky badlands, the stench growing stronger by the second. Teardrinker's men were as hard a pack of bastards as you'd find under the suns, but even the hardest were born with a sense of smell. Dogger pressed a finger to his nose, blasting a stream of snot from each nostril, cursing by Aa and all four of his daughters. Luka lit another cigarillo, and Teardrinker was tempted to ask him for a puff to rid herself of the taste, accursed heat or no.

They found the wreck about two miles down the road.

It was a short wagon train: two trailers and four camels, all bloating in the sunlight. Teardrinker nodded to her men and they dismounted, wandering through the wreckage with weapons ready. The air was thick with the hymn of tiny wings.

A slaughter, by the look. Arrows littered on the sand and studding the wagon hulls. Teardrinker saw a fallen sword. A broken shield. A long slick of dried blood like a madman's scrawl, and a frantic dance of footprints around a cold cooking pit.

'Slavers,' she murmured. 'A few turns back.'

'Aye,' Luka nodded, drawing on his cigarillo. 'Looks like.'

'Cap'n, I could use a hand over here,' Dogger called.

Teardrinker made her way around the fallen beasts, Luka beside her, brushing away the soup of flies. She saw Dogger, crossbow drawn but not raised, his other hand up in supplication. And though he was the kind of fellow whose biggest worry when slitting a man's throat was not getting any on his shoes, the man was speaking gently, as if to a frightened mare.

'Woah, there,' he cooed. 'Easy, girl . . .'

More blood here, sprayed across the sand, dark brown on deep red. Teardrinker saw the telltale mounds of a dozen freshly dug graves nearby. And looking past Dogger, she saw who it was he spoke at so sweetly.

'Aa's burning cock,' she murmured. 'Now there's a sight.'

A girl. Eighteen at most. Pale skin, burned a little red from the sunlight. Long black hair cut into sharp bangs over dark eyes, her face smudged with dust and dried blood. But Teardrinker could see she was a beauty beneath the mess, high cheekbones and full lips. She held a double-edged gladius, notched from recent use. Her thighs and ribs were wrapped in rags, stained with a different vintage than the blood on her tunic.

'You're a pretty flower,' Teardrinker said.

'S-stay away from me,' the girl warned.

'Easy,' Teardrinker murmured. 'You've no need of steel any more, lass.'

'I'll be the judge of that, if it please you,' she said, voice shaking.

Luka drifted to the girl's flank, reaching out with a swift hand. But she turned quick as silver, kicked his knee and sent him to the sand. With a gasp, the Liisian found the lass behind him, her gladius poised above the join between his shoulder and neck. His cigarillo dangled from suddenly dust-dry lips.

She's fast.

The girl's eyes flashed as she snarled at Teardrinker.

'Stay away from me, or Four Daughters, I swear I'll end him.'

'Dogger, ease off, there's a lad,' Teardrinker commanded. 'Graccus, put up your crossbow. Give the young dona some room.'

Teardrinker watched as her men obeyed, drifting back to let the girl exhale her panic. The woman took a slow step forward, empty hands up and out.

'We've no wish to hurt you, flower. I'm just a trader, and these are just my men. We're travelling to the Hanging Gardens, we smelled the bodies, we came for a look-see. And that's the truth of it. By Mother Trelene, I swear it.'

The girl watched the captain with wary eyes. Luka winced as her blade nicked his neck, blood beading on the steel.

'What happened here?' Teardrinker asked, already knowing the answer.

The girl shook her head, tears welling in her lashes.

'Slavers?' Teardrinker asked. 'This is bad country for it.'

The girl's lip trembled, she tightened her grip on her blade.

'Were you travelling with your family?'

'M-my father,' the girl replied.

Teardrinker sized the lass up. She was on the short side, thin, but fit and hard. She'd taken refuge under the wagons, torn down some canvas to shelter from the whisperwinds. Despite the stink, she'd stayed near the wreck where supplies were plentiful and she'd be easier to find, which meant she was smart. And though her hand trembled, she carried that steel like she knew how to swing it. Luka had dropped faster than a bride's unmentionables on her wedding night.

'You're no merchant's daughter,' the captain declared.

'My father was a sellsword. He worked the trains out of Nuuvash.'

'Where's your da now, flower?'

'Over there,' the girl said, voice cracking. 'With th-the others.'

Teardrinker looked to the fresh-dug graves. Maybe three feet deep. Dry sand. Desert heat. No wonder the place stank so bad.

'And the slavers?'

'I buried them, too.'

'And now you're waiting out here for what?'

The girl glanced in the direction of Dustwalker's ironsong. This far south, there wasn't much risk of sand kraken. But ironsong meant wagons, and wagons meant succour, and staying here with the dead didn't seem to be on her mind, buried da or no.

'I can offer you food,' Teardrinker said. 'A ride to the Hanging Gardens. And no unwelcome advances from my men. But you're going to have to put down that sword, flower. Young Luka is our cook as well as a guardsman.' Teardrinker risked a small smile. 'And as my husband would tell you if he were still among us, you don't want me cooking your supper.'

The girl's eyes welled with tears as she glanced to the graves again.

'We'll carve him a stone before we leave,' Teardrinker promised softly.

The tears spilled then, the girl's face crumpling as if someone had kicked it in. She let the sword drop, Luka snatching himself loose and rolling up out of the dirt. The girl hung there like a crooked portrait, curtains of blood-matted hair about her face.

The captain almost felt sorry for her.

She approached slowly across the gore-caked earth, shrouded by a halo of flies. And taking off her glove, she extended one callused hand.

'They call me Teardrinker,' she said. 'Of the Seaspear clan.'

The girl reached out with trembling fingers. 'M—'

Teardrinker seized the girl's wrist, spun on the spot and flipped her clean over her shoulder. The lass shrieked, crashing onto the dirt. Teardrinker put the boot to her, medium style – just enough to knock what was left of her fight loose from her lungs.

'Dogger, set the irons, there's a lad,' the captain said. 'Hands and feet.'

The Itreyan unslung the manacles from about his waist, bolted them about the girl. She came to her senses, howling and thrashing as Dogger screwed the irons tighter, and Teardrinker drove a boot so hard into her belly she retched into the dirt. The captain let her have another for good measure, just shy of rib-cracking. The girl curled into a ball with a long, breathless moan.

'Get her on her feet,' the captain commanded.

Dogger and Graccus dragged the girl up. Teardrinker grabbed a fistful of hair, hauled the girl's head back so she could look into her eyes.

'I promised no untoward advances from my men, and to that I hold. But keep fussing, and I'll hurt you in ways you'll find all manner of unwelcome. You hear me, flower?'

The girl could only nod, long black hair tangled at the corners of her lips. Teardrinker nodded to Graccus, and the big man dragged the girl around the ruined wagon train, threw her onto the back of his growling camel. Dogger was already looting the wagons, rifling through the barrels and chests. Luka was checking the cut he'd been gifted, glancing at the girl's gladius in the dust.

'You let a slip like that get the drop on you again,' Teardrinker warned, 'I'll leave you out here for the fucking dustwraiths, you hear me?'

'Aye, Cap'n,' he muttered, abashed.

'Help Dogger with the leavings. Bring all the water back to the train. Anything you can carry worth a looting, snag it. Burn the rest.'

Teardrinker spat into the dirt, brushed the flies from her good eye as she strode across the blood-caked sand and joined Graccus. She slung herself up onto her camel, and with a sharp kick, the pair were riding back to the wagon train.

Cesare was waiting in the driver's seat, his pretty face sour. He brightened a little when he saw the girl, groaning and half-senseless over the hump of Graccus's beast.

'For me?' he asked. 'You shouldn't have, Cap'n.'

'Slavers hit a merchant caravan, bit off more than they could chew.' Teardrinker nodded to the girl. 'She's the only survivor. Luka and Dogger are bringing back water from the wreckage. See it distributed among the stock.'

'Another one died of heatstroke.' Cesare motioned back to the train. 'Found him when we let the others out to stretch. That's a quarter of our inventory this run.'

Teardrinker hauled off her tricorn, dragged her hand along her sweat-drenched scalp. She watched the stock stagger around their cages, men and women and a handful of children, blinking up at the merciless suns. Only a few were in irons – most were so heat-wracked they'd not the strength to run, even if they had somewhere to go. And out here in the Ashkahi Whisperwastes, there was nowhere to get except dead.

'No fear,' she said, nodding at the girl. 'Look at her. A prize like that will cover our losses and then some. One of the Daughters has smiled on us.' She turned to Graccus. 'Lock her in with the women. See she's fed a double ration 'til we get to the Gardens. I want her looking ripe on the stocks. You touch her beyond that, I'll cut off your fucking fingers and feed them to you, aye?'

Graccus nodded. 'Aye, Cap'n.'

'Get the rest back in their cages. Leave the dead one for the restless.'

Cesare and Graccus set about it, leaving Teardrinker to brood.

The captain sighed. The third sun would be rising in a few months. This would probably be the last run she'd make until after truelight, and the divinities had been conspiring to fuck it to ruin. An outbreak of bloodflux had wiped out an entire wagon of her stock just a week after they left Rammahd. Young Cisco had got poleaxed when he slipped off for a piss – probably took by a dustwraith, judging by what was left of him. And this heat was threatening to wilt the rest of her crop before it even got to market. All she needed was a cool breeze for a few more turns. Maybe a short spell of rain. She'd sacrificed a strong young calf on the Altar of Storms at Nuuvash before she left. But did Lady Nalipse listen?

After the wreck years ago that had almost ruined her, Teardrinker had vowed to stay away from the water. Running flesh on the seas was a riskier business than driving it on land. But she swore the Mother of Oceans was still trying to make her life a misery, even if it meant getting her sister, the Mother of Storms, in on the torment.

Not a breath of wind.

Not a drop of rain.

Still, that pretty flower was fresh, and curves like hers would fetch a fine price at market. It was a stroke of luck to have found her out here, unspoiled in all this shit. Between the raiders and the slavers and the sand kraken, the Ashkahi Whisperwastes were no place for a girl to roam alone. For Teardrinker to have found her before someone or some-*thing* else did, one of the Daughters had to be smiling on her.

It was almost as if someone wanted it this way . . .

The girl was thrown in the frontmost wagon with the other maids and children. The cage was six feet high, rusted iron. The floor was smeared with filth, the reek of sweating bodies and carrion breath almost as bad as the camel corpses had been. The big one named Graccus hadn't been gentle, but true to his captain's word, his hands had done nothing but hurl her down, slam the cage door and twist the lock.

The girl curled up on the floor. Felt the stares of the women about her, the curious eyes of the boys and girls. Her ribs ached from the kicking she'd been gifted, the tears she'd cried cutting tracks down through the blood and dirt on her cheeks. Fighting for calm. Eyes closed. Just breathing.

Finally, she felt gentle hands helping her up. The cage was crowded, but there was room enough for her to sit in a corner, back pressed hard to the bars. She opened her eyes, saw a young, kindly face, smeared with grime, green eyes.

'Do you speak Liisian?' the woman asked.

The girl nodded mutely.

'What's your name?'

The girl whispered through swollen lips. '. . . Mia.'

'Four Daughters,' the woman tutted, smoothing back the girl's hair. 'How did a pretty doll like you end in a place like this?

The girl glanced down at the shadow beneath her.

Up to those glittering green eyes.

'Well,' she sighed. 'That's the question, isn't it?'

CHAPTER 2
FIREMASS

Four months earlier

King Francisco XV, sovereign ruler of all Itreya, took his place at the edge of the stage. He was decked in a doublet and hose of purest white, cheeks daubed with rose paint. The jewels in his crown sparkled as he spoke, one hand to his chest.

'Ever I sought to rule both wise and just,
But kingly brow as beggar's knees now must;
To kiss the dirt and—'
'Nay!' *came a shout.*

Tiberius the Elder entered from stage left, surrounded by his Republican conspirators. A silver dagger gleamed in the old man's hand, his jaw set, eyes bright. Without a word, he lunged across the stage, sinking his blade deep into his monarch's chest, once, twice, three times. The audience gasped as bright red blood sprayed, splashing onto the polished boards at their feet. King Francisco clutched his ruptured heart, sinking to his knees. And with a last groan (a little overcooked, some said afterwards), he closed his eyes and died.

Tiberius the Elder held aloft his dagger, delivered his fateful, final lines.

'Heart's blood is spilled, and what shall be, shall be,
No price too steep to stand 'gainst tyranny.
But know, I struck this blow, friends, not for me,
But drenched my blade in name of liberty.'

Tiberius looked among the audience, bloody knife in his hands. And as he dropped into a low bow, the curtains closed, heavy red velvet falling across the scene.

The guests cheered as the music swelled, signalling the drama's end. Arkemical chandeliers in the ceiling glowed brighter, banishing the darkness that had accompanied the final act. Applause rippled across the crowded room, over the mezzanine above, out to the back of the room. And there, it found a girl, with long raven hair and pale, perfect skin, and a shadow dark enough for three.

Mia Corvere joined in with the guests' applause, though in truth, her eyes had been anywhere except the play. A cool chill flitted across the back of her neck, hidden in the shadows thrown by her hair. Mister Kindly's whisper was velvet soft in her ear.

'. . . that was mind-bendingly awful . . .' the shadowcat said.

Mia replied softly, adjusting the ill-fitting masque on her face.

'I thought the chicken blood was a nice touch.'

'. . . that was thirty minutes of our existence we will never have again, you realize . . .'

'At least they've turned the bloody lights back on.'

Letting the crowd clap a while longer, the curtains finally parted, revealing King Francisco hale and whole, the punctured bladder that had contained his 'heart's blood' just visible under his soaked shirt. Joining hands with his murderer, spring-loaded dagger clutched between them, Tiberius the Elder and Francisco XV took a long bow.

'Merry Firemass, gentlefriends!' the murdered king cried.

The applause slowly died as the actors left the stage, chatter and laughter resuming now the play was done. Mia took a sip of her drink, peered around the room. Now the house lights were back up, she could see a little better.

'All right, where is he . . .' she muttered.

She'd arrived fashionably late and the ballroom was crowded, but that was no surprise – the soirées of Senator Alexus Aurelius were always popular affairs. With the play concluded, the twelve-piece orchestra took up a bright tune on their gilded mezzanine at the back of the room. Mia watched as marrowborn gentry in crisp frock coats stepped onto the dance floor with graceful donas in their arms, gowns of crimson and silver and gold shimmering in the light of the arkemical chandeliers.

Their faces were hidden behind a dizzying array of masques, a hundred different shapes and themes. Mia could see square-faced voltos and laughing punchinellos and half-cut dominos, bejewelled paint and gleaming ivory and fans of peacock feathers. The most common design among the salon crowd was the triple-sun of Aa, or beautiful variants of the Face of Tsana. It was Firemass, after all, and most folk at least tried to make some attempt *to venerate the Everseeing and his firstborn daughter before the inevitable hedonism of the feasteve got into full swing.**

Mia was clad in an off-the-shoulder gown of blood-red, layers of Liisian silk flowing to the floor. Her half-cut corset was cinched tight, a string of dark rubies spilling into her cleavage, and while she appreciated the effect the corset and jewels had of emphasizing her assets, the admiring glances she'd been getting all nevernight didn't make it any easier to bloody breathe. Her own features were covered by a Face of Tsana – a masque depicting the warrior-goddess's helm, a plume of firebird feathers about the edge. Her lips and chin were bare, which made it a little easier to drink. And smoke. And swear.

'*Byss and fucking blood, where is he?*' she muttered, eyes roaming the crowd.

She felt that chill again, the soft whisper in her ear.

'. . . the booths . . .' Mister Kindly said.

Mia looked over the swaying throng to the walls above the dance floor. Senator Aurelius's ballroom had been built like an amphitheatre, with the stage at one end, seats arranged in concentric rings, and smaller private booths overlooking the main floor. Through the smoke and long sheaves of sheer silk strung from the ceiling, she finally saw a tall young man, decked in a long white frock coat and black cravat, the twin horses of his familia embroidered in golden thread upon his breast.

'. . . gaius aurelius . . .'

Mia lifted her ivory cigarillo holder, took a thoughtful drag. The young man's face was half-hidden behind a golden domino with a triple-sun motif, but she could see a strong jawline and a handsome smile as he whispered into the ear of a beautiful young woman in a stylish gown beside him.

'Looks like he's made a friend,' Mia whispered, grey spilling from her lips.

---

*Firemass is a celebration that marks the turn towards summersdeep in the Itreyan calendar. Dedicated to Tsana, the Lady of Fire, it falls on the eighth month before truelight – the holiest of Aa's feasts, when all three suns burn in the sky.

Tsana is Aa's firstborn daughter, a virgin goddess who serves as patron of both warriors and women. Firemass is marked by a four-hour cathedral mass, and is meant to be a turn of reflection and chaste contemplation. Of course, most of the Republic's citizenry use it as an excuse to don masques and hold a raucous piss-up, indulging in precisely the kind of behaviour Tsana frowns upon.

But, as with spouses, so with goddesses, gentlefriends; it is often better to beg forgiveness than seek permission.

'. . . well, he *is* a senator's son. he is unlikely to spend the nevernight alone . . .'

'Not if I can help it. Eclipse, go tell Dove to be ready. We may need to leave in a hurry.'

A soft growl came from the shadows beneath her dress.

'. . . DOVE IS AN IDIOT . . .'

'All the more reason to make sure he's awake. I think I'll go say hello to our esteemed senator's firstborn. And his friend.'

'. . . two is company, mia . . .' Mister Kindly warned.

'True enough. But there's plenty of fun to be had in a crowd.'

Slipping from her corner, Mia drifted through the ballroom like the smoke from her lips. Smiling at the compliments, politely declining entreaties to dance. She strode blithely past two guards in fine-cut coats at the bottom of the stairs, pretending she belonged and thus, appearing to do just that. There was no one else in the room who shouldn't have been there, after all. The invitation had taken her five patient nevernights to steal from the house of Dona Grigorio.* And the masques these marrowborn fools insisted on wearing every feasteve made it easy to walk among them unmarked. Especially with her curves strangled in a fashion designed to draw the eye away from her face.

Mia checked her paint in a small silver mirror case, applied another dark red coat to her lips. And taking one last drag from her cigarillo, she crushed it under her boot heel and stumbled past the velvet curtains into Aurelius's booth.

'O, apologies,' she said.

Don Aurelius and his companion looked up in mild surprise. The pair were sat on a long divan of crushed velvet, half-empty glasses and a bottle of fine Vaanian red on the table before them. Mia pressed her hand to her breast in faux alarm.

'I thought this one empty. Forgiveness, I beg you.'

---

*The three drams of the toxin known as 'Mishap' that Mia had slipped into the dona's tea yestereve ensured she'd not be up to attending Senator Aurelius's soirée – suffering explosive discharge from every orifice does tend to put a damper on one's ability to hobnob. Mia normally would have used a smaller dose, especially on someone so elderly. But in the five turns she'd been casing Grigorio's palazzo, the old woman had proved herself to be a battleaxe of the first order, whose only pleasure seemed to be shouting at a portrait of her dead husband and beating her slaves. So, Mia found it hard to feel too guilty about giving the old bitch an extra-large serving.

Though she did feel sorry for whoever had to clean up the mess afterwards.

The young don gave a small nod. His handsome smile was dark with wine. 'Think nothing of it, Mi Dona.'

'Do you . . .' Mia heaved a sigh, uncertain. Reaching up, she unfastened her masque, used it to fan her face. 'Apologies, might I trouble you to sit for a moment? It's hotter than truelight in here, and this dress makes it frightfully hard to breathe.'

Aurelius ran his eyes over Mia's unmasqued features. The black eyes framed with artful smudges of kohl. The milk-pale skin and pouting, dark red lips, the necklet of jewels at her slender throat, a fox-quick glance to the bare skin below as Mia made a show of adjusting her corsetry.

'By all means, Mi Dona,' he smiled, motioning to the spare divan.

'Aa bless,' Mia said, sinking down onto the velvet, fanning herself again. 'Allow me to introduce myself. I am Don Gaius Neraus Aurelius, and my lovely accomplice here is Alenna Bosconi.'

Aurelius's companion was a Liisian beauty around Mia's age – probably the daughter of local administratii, by the look. Dark of hair and iris, her skin olive, the gold chiffon of her gown accented by metallic powder on her lips and lashes.

'Four Daughters, I adore your dress,' Mia gasped. 'Is it an Albretto?'

'A fine eye,' Alenna replied, raising her glass. 'My compliments.'

'I've a fitting with her next week,' Mia said. 'Presuming my aunt lets me out of the palazzo again. I've a suspicion she'll have me sent to a convent amorrow.'

'Who is your aunt, Mi Dona?' Aurelius asked.

'Dona Grigorio. Stuffy old cow.' Mia pointed to the wine. 'May I?'

Aurelius watched her fill a glass and finish it just as swift, bemusement in his eye. 'Forgive me, I didn't know the dona had a niece?'

'Colour me distinctly unsurprised, Mi Don,' Mia sighed. 'I've been in Galante almost a month and she doesn't let me out of the palazzo. I had to sneak out to be here this eve. Father sent me to summer with her, insisting she'd teach me how to behave like a god-fearing daughter of Aa should.'

'Meaning you don't behave like one should now?' Aurelius smiled.

Mia made a face. 'Honestly, you'd think I'd bedded one of the stableboys, the way he goes on about it.'

Aurelius raised the bottle to Mia's glass with an enquiring tilt of his head.

'Another?'

'Most generous, sir.'

Aurelius poured, passed the full glass. Mia took it with a knowing smile, let her fingertips brush the young don's wrist, arkemical current prickling between their skin. Alenna raised her glass to golden lips, faint annoyance in her voice.

'There's not much left, Gaius,' *she warned, glancing at the bottle.*

Mia looked to the girl, tucking a stray lock of hair behind her ear. Any fear she might have felt was swallowed by the shadows at her feet. She rose from her seat with silken grace, sank down on the divan beside the golden beauty. Looking into Alenna's eyes, she took a small sip of the wine. It was rich, velvet smooth, dancing dark upon her tongue. And taking away her empty glass, Mia pressed her own into Alenna's hand, fingers entwined, lifting it to those golden lips.

She looked over her shoulder to Aurelius, saw him watching, enraptured. She smiled as she whispered, loud enough to be heard over the music below.

'I don't mind sharing.'

*A*urelius *stood behind her, hands roaming her bare arms, across her breasts. Mia felt his lips at her ear, brush the edge of her jaw, reaching back to tangle her fingers in his hair. Leaning into the hardness at his crotch she sought his mouth, sighing as he left a trail of burning kisses down her throat, stubble tickling her skin. Finding the silken ribbon lacing the back of her corset, he pulled it loose with slow, steady hands.*

Alenna was behind him, unbuttoning his jacket and letting it fall to the floor. Her cheeks were flushed from more than drink, long fingernails tearing his silken shirt and leaving his torso bare. Mia reached back to the hardness of his chest, fingers slipping down the troughs and furrows of his abdomen. His lips were at the nape of her neck, she felt the press of his teeth, sighing yes as he bit harder, seeking his mouth again. But with his free hand, he took hold of her long tresses, easing her head back, back, goosebumps thrilling along her skin as he pulled her corset away.

The music was faint and far above, near lost beneath the song of their sighs. They'd stumbled down the stairs, Aurelius ushering Mia and Alenna before him with playful slaps on their backsides. House guards pretended to pay no mind as the trio had stumbled past, Mia pressing her lips to Aurelius's throat as he'd stopped to give the Liisian beauty a long kiss. He'd pushed Mia against the wall and reached between her legs, setting to work with clever fingers right there in the hallway. They'd barely made it to his room.

Like most marrowborn palazzos, the bedchambers were underground – all the better to shield them from the suns' relentless light. The air was cooler down here, the light from the arkemical globes low and smoky. Mia's corset fell to the floorboards as Aurelius slipped his hands inside her gown.

She sighed as she felt his hands cupping her breasts, pinching one swollen nipple hard enough to make her gasp. He peeled her dress off, letting it fall in a rumpled heap about her ankles. She sought his belt, found Alenna's hands there also, their fingers entwined as they worked the buckle loose. Mia felt Aurelius's hands roam lower, arkemical current dancing on her skin as his fingers slipped over her belly, down through her soft curls to her aching lips beyond.

She groaned as his fingers went to work, weakening her knees. Turning her head, she sought his mouth with her own, but his grip on her hair pulled her up short, left her gasping, moaning as she pushed her arse back, grinding against his crotch with the same rhythm he was strumming on her.

His belt finally loose, the beauty tore the buttons on his britches free, Mia's fingers slipping inside. She found her mark after a moment, smiling at his groan as she took his heat in her hand. She felt Alenna's hands also, the pair of them working his length as his finger slipped inside her, stars bursting behind her eyes, almost bringing her legs out from under her.

Aurelius turned, his mouth finding Alenna's, their tongues entwined. Mia untangled his hand from her hair, curled her fingers in his own, desperate to kiss him. But her skin prickled as she sensed him step aside, as she felt warm lips on her shoulder, the back of her neck, warm hands slipping about her waist.

Not his . . .

Alenna's fingertips were dancing up her arms, flitting across the swell of her breasts. Her breath came quicker as she felt the girl's hand at her chin, turning her slow. Heart hammering, Mia came about to face her.

The girl was beautiful, bee-stung lips parted, dark eyes welling with desire in the smoky light. Her chest was heaving as she pressed closer, still clothed against Mia's near-naked body. Aurelius began kissing the nape of Alenna's neck as she smoothed back a lock of long dark hair from Mia's cheek, Mia feeling a thrill run all the way to her toes as the beauty leaned in to kiss her. Close. Closer. Clos—

'No,' Mia said, pulling away.

Alenna's eyes clouded with confusion, and she glanced over her shoulder to Aurelius. The young don quirked an eyebrow in question.

'Not on the mouth,' Mia said.

The beauty's golden lips curled in a knowing smile. Dark eyes roamed Mia's naked body, drinking her in.

'Everywhere else, then,' she breathed.

Alenna ran her hands down Mia's cheeks, the jewels at her throat, *making her shiver. And slow as agony, she leaned in and pressed her lips to Mia's neck.*

Mia sighed, goosebumps prickling, no fear inside her. Leaning her head back, surrendering, eyelashes fluttering as Alenna's hands cupped her heaving breasts, floating over her hips, caressing her arse. Mia couldn't feel anything but those hands, those lips, teeth nipping, breath warm on her skin, the beauty's mouth roaming down to the swell of her breast. She groaned as the girl took her nipple into her mouth, tongue flickering over the swollen tip, all the room spinning.

Alenna's fingernails sent shivers up Mia's spine as they skimmed her skin, guiding her backwards. She felt the bedframe behind her knees, bending like a sapling before the storm and tumbling back with a gasp onto the furs.

Alenna sighed as Aurelius nuzzled her neck from behind, working the ties of her corset loose. Slipping her dress off her shoulders, the young don let the golden chiffon tumble away in a shimmering wave, underthings following, stripping her bare.

Mia's eyes roamed the girl's body as she climbed onto the bed on hands and knees, prowling like a cat. Alenna knelt above her, sighing as the young don sank to his knees behind her, kisses trailing down her back, over her arse. Mia felt the girl's hands trail the insides of her shivering thighs, breath coming fast as those fingers brushed her lips. Alenna was breathing quick too, groaning as Aurelius pressed his mouth between her legs, went to work with his tongue. Her eyes were bright with lust as she leaned in close, seeking Mia's mouth again.

Mia turned away, one hand to the girl's lips.

'No.'

She reached out across Alenna's skin, finding Aurelius's hand at the girl's hip. Entwining her fingers with his own, the beauty sighed in protest as Mia dragged him away from his prize. Eyes on his. Breathless.

'Kiss me,' she begged.

Aurelius smiled as Alenna descended, the girl's kisses like ice and fire across Mia's throat, breasts, belly. The young don crawled up the mattress as the girl sank farther down, licking the cusp of Mia's navel, the divots at her hips. Mia felt gentle teeth on the inside of her thighs, hands roaming her skin, whimpering as Alenna blew on her softly, lips just a whisper away from her own. Mia reached up with one hand, down with the other, tangling her fingers in their hair. She dragged Aurelius towards her, pleading, pulling Alenna in. And the don's mouth closed over her own, smothering her breathless moan as she felt the first touch of the beauty's tongue.

They went to work, the pair of them, Mia writhing on the fur as they adored her. A heat like she'd never known burned between her legs as Alenna kissed her like no man ever had, back arching, fingers knotted in the girl's tresses. She could taste the girl on Aurelius's tongue, the salt and sweetness of it. She kissed him fiercely, biting his lip hard enough to split the skin, dark red paint mixing with the blood on their mouths. Her lips smothered his gasp of pain, her tongue found his, teasing, tasting, dancing in some pale semblance of the beauty's between her legs.

Time stopped turning, the world stopped spinning. Breaking away from her mouth, the don left a trail of bloody kisses down her neck. Mia gasped as he descended, licking, suckling, biting, eyes fluttering closed as Alenna began her work in earnest, lapping at her swollen bud.

Aurelius lifted his head.

A quick shudder ran through him.

A soft groan slipped past his lips.

And drawing in a ragged breath, the young don coughed a mouthful of bright red blood all over Mia's breasts.

'F-four Daughters . . .'

Aurelius stared in horror at the scarlet on Mia's skin, on his hands. Mia pulled herself up on her elbows as he fell back with another red cough, fingers at his throat. Alenna realized what was happening, her face spattered with crimson. Rearing back, she drew breath to scream as Mia lunged across the bed and seized her throat, dragging her into a choke hold.

'Hushhh, now,' she whispered, lips brushing the beauty's ear.

The girl struggled in Mia's grip, but the assassin was stronger, harder. The pair toppled to the floorboards, into the tangle of their clothes as Aurelius began thrashing, fingernails clawing his neck as he coughed up another lungful.

'I know it's hard to watch,' Mia whispered to the beauty. 'But it only lasts a moment.'

'Th-the wine . . . ?'

Mia shook her head. 'Not on the mouth, remember?'

Alenna stared at the split Mia had bitten in Aurelius's lip, the red paint smeared with the blood around his mouth. The young don flopped on the bed like a landed fish, every muscle seizing tight, face twisted. Alenna's lips parted to scream as a shadow moved on the headboard, another at the foot – two shapes cut from the darkness itself. Mia's hand closed about the girl's mouth again as Mister Kindly and Eclipse coalesced, staring enraptured as the young don groaned in agony, blood bubbling between his teeth. And with eyes wide, lips peeling back in a silent cry, the first and only son of Senator Alexus Aurelius exhaled his final breath.

'Hear me, Niah,' *Mia whispered.* 'Hear me, Mother. This flesh your feast. This blood your wine. This life, this end, my gift to you. Hold him close.'

Mister Kindly tilted his head, watching the young don die.
His purr almost sounded like a sigh.

Mia was thirsty.

That was the worst part. The cage, the heat, the stink, she could stomach it all. But no matter how much her captors gave her to drink, in this bastard desert it was never enough. When Dogger or Graccus shoved the ladle through the bars of her cage, that lukewarm water seemed a gift from the Mother herself. But between the swelter and the sweat and the wagon's crush, her lips were soon cracking, her tongue swollen and dry.

The captives were jammed together like strips of salt pork in a barrel, and the smell was sickening. The first turn she'd spent baking inside that kiln-hot cage, Mia had begun to think she'd made an awful mistake.

Think it. But not fear it.
Never flinch.
Never fear.

Mia tried not to talk much. She didn't want to grow too close to the other captives, knowing what was coming at the Hanging Gardens. But she watched how they cared for each other, an elderly woman comforting a lass crying for her mother, or a girl giving her own meagre ration to a boy who'd puked his own meal down the front of his rags. Little kindnesses that spoke of the biggest hearts.

Mia wondered where her own might be.
No place for it out here, girl.

Her captors were a motley bunch. Their captain, Teardrinker, looked to be bedding her second, Cesare, though Mia had no doubt who'd be holding the reins on that particular ride. No woman got to lead an outfit of cut-throat slavers in the Ashkahi wastes unless she had the sharpest of teeth.

The Itreyans, Dogger and Graccus, both seemed the typical brand of bastard you'd find in any one of a hundred fleshpeddler outfits operating out of Ashkah. As per Captain's orders, they didn't lay a finger on the women. But from the hungry looks they threw her way, Mia imagined they resented it no end. They spent their downtime playing

Spank with a dog-eared set of playing cards, betting with a handful of clipped beggars.*

The big Dweymeri, Dustwalker, seemed a more careful sort. He played the flute, and he'd treat the captives to a melody when he had no other work to do. The last of them was Luka – the young Liisian Mia had kicked into the dust. Short locks and a dimpled smile. The slop he cooked tasted worse than a pig's arsehole, but Mia had seen him sneak some extra bread to the children at evemeal.

And that was it. Six leather-clad slavers and a row of locked iron bars between her and the freedom any of the captives around her would have killed to taste. All was sweat and puke. Shit and blood. At least half the women in her wagon cried themselves to what little sleep they could find. But not Mia Corvere.

The girl sat against the door and waited. Ragged bangs hanging in deep, dark eyes. The reek of sweat and filth was inescapable, the press of the bodies around her enough to make her ill. But she swallowed her vomit along with her pride, pissing in the road when commanded and keeping her mouth on the right side of shut. And if the shadow pooled beneath her was too dark – dark enough for two, perhaps – then the covered wagon's innards were too gloomy to notice.

It was only four more turns to the Hanging Gardens. Four more turns of this awful heat, this godless stink, this sickening, trundling sway. Four more turns.

Patience, she'd tell herself, whispering the word like a prayer.

If Vengeance has a mother, her name is Patience.

It was maybe an hour 'til nevernight's end, and the caravan was pulling over to the side of its long, dusty road. Peering out through the tear in the wagon's canopy, Mia could see a tumble of sandstone bluffs throwing shadows on the desert sand. It was an obvious – and therefore, dangerous – spot to shelter, but best to stop here in shade than press on for another hour and spend the entire turn baking in the suns.

Mia heard Dustwalker in the supply wagon as always, banging out an occasional peal of ironsong to scare off any sand kraken daring

---

*You'll remember the coinage of Itreya is nicknamed for the folks most often found handling them, gentlefriends. Coppers are called 'beggars'. Silvers are called 'priests'. Depending on the social standing of the person you ask, gold coins are either called 'tossers' or 'get away from me, you filthy pleb, before I have my man here break your fucking legs'.

enough to travel this far south.* She caught a glimpse of Graccus, scouting the rocky outcroppings from atop his snarling, shit-machine of a camel. He looked salty, face dripping as he squinted up at the suns and cursed the Everseeing for a bastard.

The first arrow took him in the chest.

It whizzed out of the sunlight, piercing his jerkin with a thud. A stupid frown darkened Graccus's brow, but the next two arrows flying out of the rocks wiped it off his face, sent him tumbling backwards off his beast in a spray of bright red.

'Raiders!' Teardrinker bellowed.

The women in Mia's wagon screamed as a hail of arrows rained down on the caravan, punching through the canopy. Mia heard a gasp, felt the flesh around her shift. A young lass sank down in the crush, an arrow in her eye. One of the sprats took a shaft to the leg, started howling, the entire mass of bodies around her shifting like the sea in a storm and crushing her against the bars.

''Byss and blood . . .'

Mia heard galloping hooves, the sound of black-feathered rain. Somewhere distant, Dustwalker was roaring in pain, Teardrinker shouting orders. The ring of steel rose over the bellow of wounded camels, the hiss of spraying sand. Mia cursed again as she was shoved face-first against the bars, the folk around her boiling to a panic.

'Right, fuck this,' she spat.

Reaching down to her boot, Mia twisted the heel, retrieving her trusty lockpicks. In a moment, she was free of her manacles, reaching between the rusted bars. She set to sweet-talking the lock, tongue poking out in concentration. An arrow sheared through the canopy just shy of her head, another thudded into the wood near her hand.

'. . . *you may wish to hurry . . .*'

---

*Typically, the predators of the Ashkahi Whisperwastes don't travel much past the Great Salt, and the biggest sand kraken are only found in the deep deserts. Occasionally, smaller specimens will range south when game grows scarce, and in recent years, several enterprising outfits operating out of southern Ashkah have set about capturing these roaming kraken, selling them for use in spectacle matches during the *Venatus Magni* – the great games held in honour of Aa during the Feast of Truelight.

The masters of the *venatus* are constantly looking for ways to outdo the spectacle (and attendance) of previous games, and if the thought of watching a favourite gladiatii battling a horror from the Ashkahi Whisperwastes doesn't get arses on seats, very little will, gentlefriends.

The whisper was soft as baby's breath, intended for her ears only.

'You're not helping,' she whispered back.

'... *i am offering moral support* ...'

'You're being an annoying little shit.'

'... *that too* ...'

The lock sprung open in her hand and Mia kicked the door aside, tumbled out in the blazing light. She rolled beneath the wagon as the other women realized their cage was open, falling over themselves in their bid to escape.

Mia could see a half-dozen raiders circling the caravan. They were clad in dark leather and desert colours, a mix of sexes and skin tones. Cesare was dead, punctured with black-feathered arrows. Mia saw no sign of Luka, but Dogger was crouched behind the aft wagon, Dustwalker's corpse beside him. Teardrinker's camel had taken an arrow to the throat, and the captain was hunkered behind its body, crossbow in hand.

'Stinking whoresons!' she roared. 'Do you know who I am?'

The riders only jeered in response. Riding in that incessant circle, driving the escaping women back towards the wagons, and the captives in the other cages into a frothing panic.

'Diversion,' Mia realized.

'... *from what* ... ?'

Dogger ducked out from cover, loosing a quick shot with his crossbow. From somewhere among the rocks, a black-feathered arrow flashed, striking him in the chest. Dogger fell, scarlet bubbles bursting on his lips.

'From that sharpshooter up there,' Mia muttered.

The girl reached out to the shadows beneath the wagon, gathering them up like a seamstress pulling thread. It was so bright out here, so different from the belly of the Quiet Mountain. But ever so slowly, she stitched the shadows together, weaving them into a cloak. And beneath it, she became little more than a smudge, like a greasy fingerprint on a portrait of the world.

Of course, she could barely see a bloody thing. She'd always thought it cruel that the Goddess of Night would give her the gift to remain unseen but make her almost blind while doing it. Still, blind was better than butchered.

Mia crept closer to the wheel, moving by feel, preparing to dash from cover.

'... *try not to get shot* ...'

'That's excellent advice, Mister Kindly. My thanks.'

'... *moral support, as i said*...'

Then she was moving. Crouched low, hands out before her, away from the wagons and towards the outcropping ahead. All the world was a blur, coffee black and milky white. The dark shape of a horse and rider loomed out of the nothingness, clipped her hard as it rode by. She staggered, wobbling blind until she hit a low outcropping of rock with her shins and tumbled into cover with a curse.

'Ow, fuck it.'

'... *o, poor child, where does it hurt*...?'

The girl pulled herself up with a wince, slapped her rump.

'Kiss it better?'

'... *perhaps a bath is in order first*...'

The girl was off again, groping her way up the rocky slope, moving by feel and sound alone. She could still hear Teardrinker roaring challenge, but the girl was listening for the telltale hiss of arrows, the whip-snap of a bowstring. And there it came... and there again, Mia circling up and around, quiet as a particularly quiet dormouse who'd just been appointed Master of Quiet at the Iron Collegium.*

Another arrow. Another snap of the bowstring. Mia could hear soft whispering between each shot, wondering if there was more than one shooter up there. She was behind them now, hidden among a tumble of boulders. And throwing aside her shadows, she peered over her cover to find out how many bowmen she'd have to murder.

Turned out, there was none at all.

O, there was an archer, no doubt. But she was no more a bowman than Mia was a swordsman. A woman, clad in grey leathers and mottled brown, her blonde hair cropped short. Whenever a shot presented itself, she'd press an arrow to her lips, whisper a prayer, then let fly. Whatever divinity she prayed to seemed to be listening, too – as Luka dashed for one of the camels, the archer put an arrow in his shoulder, another in his shin as he scrambled back into cover.

The rock crushed her head with the first blow, but Mia smashed it

---

*You may recall the Ironpriests of the Collegium have their tongues removed at a young age to preserve the secrets of their order. Technically, there is no 'Master of Quiet' at the Collegium – that was simply puffery on my part. But I was concerned you wouldn't get the joke otherwise.

... o, never mind.

Bastards.

What do you know about funny anyway?

twice more into the back of her skull, just to be sure. The archer fell with a bubbling gurgle, fingers twitching. And picking up her bow, Mia drew the string to her lips, took aim, and put a black-feathered arrow into the spine of one of the raiders below.

The woman twisted in her saddle, fell with a bloody cry. A comrade saw her fall, turned to the bluffs above and tumbled back off his horse with an arrow in his throat. Another raider cried warning, '*Ware the rocks! The rocks!*' as Mia's shot took him in the thigh, her second in his belly. A slingblade glittered as it flew out from the cover of the middle wagon, near taking the man's head off his shoulders.

The raiders were all a confusion now, their sharpshooter gone, and their plan along with her. Teardrinker took a shot with her crossbow, killing a horse and sending its rider to the dirt. Mia killed another rider with two shots to the chest. The last few raiders broke, scooping up their horseless comrade and galloping away as fast as their steeds could take them.

'*. . . fine shooting . . .*'

Mia looked to the shadow sitting atop the archer's corpse. It was small, wore the shape of a cat, cleaning a semitranslucent paw with a semitranslucent tongue.

'My thanks,' Mia bowed.

'*. . . that was sarcasm . . .*' Mister Kindly replied. '*. . . you let four of them get away . . .*'

Mia made a face, raised the knuckles at the shadowcat.

'*. . . while we're still alone, i should probably take this opportunity to point out the insanity of this scheme of yours again . . .*'

'O, aye, Daughters forbid you let a turn pass without riding my arse about it.'

Mia wiped her bloody hand on the dead archer's britches, slung her quiver of arrows over her shoulder. And bow in hand, she made her way carefully down the slope to the carnage around the 'van.

The women captives were still huddled around their cage. Graccus, Dogger, Dustwalker and Cesare were all dead. Luka was slumped near the middle wagon, arrows in his shoulder and shin. Mia watched him try to get to his feet, settling instead for one knee. His eyes were locked on hers, his second slingblade in hand.

Teardrinker had taken an arrow to the leg somewhere in the fray. Her face was spattered with blood, but she still aimed her crossbow with steady hands right at Mia. The girl stopped forty feet away, raised her bow. It was finely crafted – horn and ash, graven with prayers to the Lady of Storms. It'd put an arrow through an iron breastplate at this range. And Captain Teardrinker was wearing nothing close to iron.

'That father of yours taught you well, girl,' the captain called. 'Fine shooting.'

'. . . *pfft* . . .' whispered her shadow.

Mia kicked the dark pooled around her feet, hissing for silence.

'I've no wish to kill you, Captain,' Mia called.

'Well, there's a stroke of fortune. I've no wish to fucking die, either.'

The captain looked at the corpses around her, the wreckage of her crew, the arrow in her leg, down the long road to the Hanging Gardens.

'I suppose we could call this even,' she called. 'I was planning on fetching a fine price for you at market, but saving my life seems fair tithe. What say you ride up front with me for the rest of the trip, see us safe to the Gardens? I can cut you in on some of the profit? Twenty per cent?'

Mia shook her head. 'I don't want that, either.'

'Well, what *do* you want?' Teardrinker spat, stare locked on the bow in Mia's grip. 'You're holding decent cards, girl. You get a say in how this hand is played.'

Mia looked to the other women huddled around the forewagon. They were filthy and haggard, clad in little more than rags. The dusty road stretched out across the blood-red sand, and she knew full well the fate that awaited them at the end of it.

'I want back in the cage,' Mia said.

Teardrinker blinked. 'You just broke out of the cage . . .'

'I chose you very carefully, Captain. Your reputation is well known. You don't let your men spoil your goods. And you have an accord with the Lions of Leonides, neh?'

'Leonides?' Exasperation crept into Teardrinker's voice. 'What in the name of Aa's burning cock does a gladiatii stable have to do with any of this?'

'Well, that's the rub, isn't it?'

The girl lowered her bow with a small smile.

'I want you to sell me to them.'

CHAPTER 3

SHADOWS

Mia lay naked on the floor, spattered in red, Alenna in her arms. Music still swelled faintly from the ball upstairs, none of the senator's guests any the wiser that his only son had been murdered right below their heels. Mister Kindly sat on the headboard, staring at the young don's corpse. Eclipse licked her lips with a translucent tongue, the shadowwolf's sigh rumbling through the floor.

The girl in Mia's arms shivered at the sight of them.

'I'm going to take my hand away now, love,' *Mia whispered.* 'I'm not going to hurt you. I'm going to tie you up, put my clothes back on, and then slip out into the sunlight and you're never going to see me again. Does that sound fair?'

Alenna nodded frantically, blinking the tears from her eyes.

Eclipse's soft feminine voice seemed to come from below the floorboards.

'. . . THAT IS FOOLISH . . .'

'. . . and you would be the expert on foolishness, pup . . .' *Mister Kindly sneered.*

'. . . BETTER TO BE RID OF HER. WE HAVE NO REASON TO LET HER LIVE . . .'

'And no reason to end her,' *Mia replied.* 'Unless someone is paying me. Now, shouldn't one of you be watching the hallway in case a guard comes down here?'

'. . . i kept watch last time, when you ended that magistrate . . .'

'. . . LIAR, I KEPT WATCH OUTSIDE THE WHOLE TIME. YOU WERE FEEDING LIKE A SOW AT TROUGH . . .'

'. . . and how would you know that, if you were keeping watch outside the whole time . . . ?'

If you two are quite finished? I give less than no fucks for who does it, but one of you better get out there, because someone's go—

A soft knock sounded at the door. A deep voice calling beyond.
'Mi Don?'

Mia cursed beneath her breath, grip tightening on Alenna's throat.

'Mi Don,' said a second voice. 'Your father requests your presence.'

Guards, by the sound. At least two of them . . .

'. . . IT WAS YOUR TURN . . .' *Eclipse whispered fierce.*

'. . . lying mongr— . . .'

Mia hissed for silence, her mind racing. With guards outside the bedchamber door, her chances of slipping out unnoticed were aflame. Dove was waiting with the carriage upstairs, but he wouldn't be any use to her down here. She could fight easily enough, but she was buck naked, all but unarmed, and the noise would only bring more guards. The shadows down here were deep, but with the bedchambers in the basements, there weren't any windows for her to climb out o—

Mia gasped as Alenna's elbow collided with her ribs, and with a black curse, the girl cracked her head back into Mia's nose. Her grip momentarily loosened, Alenna drew breath and screamed, only partially muffled by Mia's fingers.

'Murder!' she cried. 'Help me!'

Mia slammed her fist into the side of the girl's head, once, twice, knocking her senseless. She heard a curse, a heavy thump as something crashed into the door.

'Mi Don?' someone shouted. 'Open up!'

'. . . it was your turn . . .'

'. . . LIAR . . .'

'Will the pair of you shut up!'

Mia slung her dress over her head as the door shuddered on its hinges. Fishing about in her abandoned corset, she retrieved her gravebone dagger, the crow on the hilt rebuking her with its glittering amber stare. And reaching to the shadows around her, she dragged them over her head, throwing all the world into black and disappearing utterly beneath it.

The door crashed open, two blurred shapes silhouetted against the light. One of them cried Aurelius's name, moving in what Mia hoped was the direction of the bed. The other saw the naked, blood-spattered Liisian girl on the floor and crouched beside her. And with the door now clear, Mia slung aside her cloak of shadows and ran.

The guards bellowed for her to stop, but Mia paid no mind, sprinting down the plush hallway towards the broad stairs. Two more guards appeared above, frowning in confusion at the bloodstained girl barrelling up the stairs towards them. One held up a hand to stop her as Mia's dagger flashed, in and out, hilt-deep in his belly. The man gasped and fell, tumbling down the stairs as his comrade cried warning, hefting his shortsword. Mia twisted sideways, gasping as his blade cut deep into her shoulder and upper arm, her whistling counterstrike slicing his neck clean through.

The man collapsed, gurgling, and Mia was already gone, up out of the stairwell and onto the ground floor. She burst into the main hall, the marrowborn dons and donas crying out in alarm at the sight of her – bloodied blade in one hand, dark hair strewn around darker eyes, wide with fury.

'Pardon me, Mi Dona,' she begged, smashing some pretty young thing aside as she tore through the hall. More guards burst into the room, unsure who to chase or why. The pair from Aurelius's bedchamber appeared at the top of the stairs, scanning the confused crowd, finally spotting Mia as she pushed her way through the mob.

'The girl in red!' one bellowed. 'Stop her!'

'Assassin!' the other cried. 'The senator's son, slain!'

The hall dissolved into chaos, some folk reaching for Mia, others fleeing before her. She cut some well-heeled administratii from thigh to crotch as he made a grab for her, elbowed another gent in the face and dropped him cold. The knife in her hand and the look in her eye dissuaded the other do-gooders in the crowd, and with a sidestep, a shove, and a rolling tumble, she was through the double doors, sprinting down the plush entry hall. Snatching a tumbler off the drinks tray of a gobsmacked servant, she belted down the goldwine inside before hurling it at the guard rushing at her, bouncing the heavy crystal off his head and sending him sprawling.

Bursting through the doors, out into the courtyard outside Aurelius's palazzo. The cries of 'Assassin!' echoed behind her, three guards rushing up the stairs to meet her, the twin suns in her eyes almost blinding.

'Shit . . .'

The guards each had a short, double-edged gladius and a murderous stare. Her shoulder was bleeding freely, her gown soaked with blood. Mia was forced into defence; reaching out to the leader's shadow and fixing his boots to the floor, rolling past their blades, kicking out at a pair of legs as she tumbled, scrambling to her feet. She dashed towards the horses and carriages parked around Aurelius's front yard, spying one amid the crowd.

'Dove!' she roared.

A teenaged boy among the throng raised his head. He was dressed in a simple rectangular volto masque, servant's finery, dark hair cropped short. A cigarillo hung from one corner of his mouth. Three bloody tears crawled down his masque's right cheek. He didn't much look the part of a Hand in the Church of Our Lady of Blessed Murder, but at the sound of Mia's second cry, he stood suddenly in the driver's seat.

'All right?' he called.

'Do I look all-fucking-right?' Mia shouted, sprinting towards him.

Mia's Hand took in the sight of his wounded Blade, the guards on her tail. Spitting out his cigarillo, the boy reached into his greatcoat and produced two small crossbows. Taking careful aim, he felled the guards closest to Mia with two swift shots.

'Run!' he called, beckoning.

'O, aye, you reckon?'

A whistling sound by Mia's ear told her more guards had arrived with crossbows of their own, and as she barrelled past the astonished coach drivers, a burst of white-hot pain in her backside told her at least one of them was a halfway decent shot.

She stumbled, falling with a curse and grating her palms and knees like cheese on the flagstones. Hissing in pain, she scrambled back to her feet, clutching the crossbow bolt protruding from her backside.

'Maw's teeth, did they just shoot you in th—'

'Just shoot them back, you fucking nonce!'

Dove fired again, dropping another guard with a quarrel in his throat. The boy ducked to reload, and a flurry of quarrels flew over Mia's head, perforating two of the panicking drivers and one particularly annoyed stallion. Sadly, as Dove rose with his own bows reloaded, one of the bolts caught him in the chest, toppling him back into the carriage roof in a spray of blood. Mia watched her Hand try to rise, lips painted blood, but the boy finally collapsed with a bubbling moan.

'. . . I DID WARN YOU HE WAS AN IDIOT . . .'

'. . . for once, we are in complete agreement . . .'

Mia was on her feet, seeking cover amid the milling horses and panicked drivers. But with her arm cut to ribbons, there was no way she could steer a carriage and work the whip at the same time, and Aurelius's guards were closing fast.

Her gravebone dagger flashed, severing leather straps and couplings about a tall white stallion. Wincing at the pain, she dragged herself onto the stallion's back.

'. . . have you forgotten how much horses hate you . . . ?'

'Apparently so.'

'. . . RIDE . . . !'

Mia kicked the horse's flanks, the stallion bolted, hooves kicking up

the packed gravel of the senator's yard as the guards roared at her to halt.*
Crossbow bolts flew past her head, grazing her horse's flank, one bolt
thudding into its hindquarters. The beast screamed, tried to throw her,
but Mia clung on like a shadow to its owner's feet. The stallion put on
a burst of speed, dashing past the front gate and out into the broad thor-
oughfares of the city of Galante. Bells tolled in the distance, echoing from
dozens of different cathedrals, domes, and minarets. The streets were
crowded for Firemass, revellers shouting curses as Mia galloped past on
her bleeding stallion.

The Blade glanced behind, saw half a dozen guards riding in pursuit.
The blood pouring from her shoulder was sticky across her back, her sodden
dress clinging to her skin. She was starting to feel light-headed from the
loss. With a colourful curse, she snapped off the crossbow bolt in her backside, head swimming with agony. She needed to get off the streets, somewhere
dark, hide until the noise died down.

Galante's streets were packed even here in the marrowborn district –
too crowded to run a high-speed chase through much farther. Her stallion's
burst of terrified speed was coming to an end, the horse now limping from
the quarrel in its own hindparts. Mia slid off the hobbling beast, down
into a crowd of drunken revellers, the cries of the pursuing guards ringing
in her ears. She limped down an alley between one of the city's countless
cathedrals and a looming administratii building, twisting into the warren
of the Galante backstreets. Gasping for breath, vision swimming, blood loss
making her hands shake. Her left arm was entirely numb, Mister Kindly's
voice in her ear urging her on. Finally, she found a wrought-iron fence, a
crowded sea of headstones and tombs beyond it, run through with dark
weeds and bright flowers.

Galante's necropolis.

She limped through the gate, stumbled down the tightly packed rows of
marble and mossy granite, looming mausoleums, packed with generations
of marrowborn dead. Finally, she ducked beneath the eave of a tomb
belonging to some rich bastard, long ago forgotten. And reaching out to
the shadows, Mia plucked them with clever fingers, weaving them about
her shoulders.

As it always did, all the world fell to black beneath Mia's cloak. But
she still heard Aurelius's guards as they entered the necropolis, boots tramping
on the flagstones. Their captain barked an order and the group split up,

---

*A note for would-be members of the law-enforcement community: this *never*
works.

weaving into the overcrowded labyrinth of crypts and vaults and tombs, cries of 'Assassin!' ringing on the pale stone.

But one guard remained.

Mia could only dimly see him through her veil of shadows, but she could tell from his vague silhouette the man was huge. His boots echoed on the flagstones as he slowly prowled the mausoleums, muttering softly. Mia held her breath as he walked closer to her hiding place, head moving side to side. She felt a warm trickle down her back, her flash of dread swallowed by her passengers as she realized that, despite her shadowcloak, her blood would have left a trail, and would now be pooling at her feet.

The guard prowled towards Mia's crypt. And rather than pray he'd pass her by, the girl simply threw aside her cloak and lunged, stiletto in hand.

The guard was wearing mail beneath his finery, but her gravebone blade pierced the steel rings as if they were butter. Her blow sank to the hilt, but striking blind, she'd landed shy of the fellow's heart. The big man cried aloud as she struck again, this time slicing his jugular. A spray of red hit her face, warm and wet, the guard seizing her wrist and delivering a crushing hook to her jaw. Mia was flung back against the tomb wall, lashing out at the hand that held her, the pair of them going down in a tumble.

His windpipe was still intact, and the guard was bellowing, the girl snarling, stabbing again and again. They rolled about on the flagstones, Eclipse and Mister Kindly both whispering warning that the other guards were returning. But her foe was huge, and for all her training, Mia was wounded, bleeding, and anyone who believes there's no advantage in being twice as big as your opponent has never fought a foe half their size.

She heard thundering boots, face twisted as the guard grabbed a fistful of her hair. Her blade finally found his neck again, sending him back onto the ground in a frothing red spray. Mia scrambled upright, saw another four guards approaching.

'. . . run . . . !'

'How?' she gasped.

'. . . HIDE . . . !'

'Where?'

'Halt!'

The guards fanned out around her, four clad in Senator Aurelius's finery. She could hear whistles in the distant street, the tramp tramp *of legionaries' boots. Fearless, even staring into the eyes of death, she glared at the tallest guard and twirled her stiletto through her fingers. She thought of Consul*

Scaeva and Cardinal Duomo. Her familia unavenged. But regret came ultimately from fear, and even there at the finish, she could find none inside her. Only rage that it could end like this.

'Who dies first?' she asked, glaring at the assembled men.

The most sensible of the guards aimed a loaded crossbow at her chest. 'That'd be you, bitch,' he spat.

A chill stole over her, dark and hollow. Goosebumps rippling on her bloodied skin. The suns burned high overhead, but here in the necropolis, the shadows were dark, almost black. A shape rose up behind the guards, hooded and cloaked, blades of what could only have been gravebone in its hands. It lashed out at the crossbow guard, hacked his head almost off his shoulders. The other guards cried out, raised their blades, but the figure moved like lightning, striking once, twice, three times. And almost faster than Mia could blink, all four guards were dead on the dirt.

'Maw's teeth,' she whispered.

The shadows at her feet shivered, Eclipse coalescing with a growl. Mister Kindly was on her shoulder, puffed up and spitting. Mia felt the chill in her bones, her passengers swallowing her fear as her saviour turned to face her.

Not human. That much was clear. O, it was shaped like a man beneath that cloak – tall and broad-shouldered. But its hands . . .' byss and blood, the hands wrapped about its sword hilts were black. Tenebrous and semi-translucent, fingers coiled about the hilts like serpents. Mia couldn't see its face, but small, black tentacles writhed and wriggled from within the hollows of its hood, pulling the cowl lower over its features. And though it was near summersdeep, two suns burning high in the sky, its breath hung in white clouds before its lips, Mia's whole body shivering at the chill.

'. . . Who are you?'

'ASK THAT OF YOURSELF,' the figure replied. Its voice was hollow, sibilant, tinged with a strange reverberation. 'MIA CORVERE.'

The girl blinked.

'. . . You know me?'

The figure moved closer, in a way Mia could only describe as . . . slithering. A rime of frost creeping across the tombs and crypts around them.

'I KNOW THAT YOU ARE MEANT FOR MORE THAN THIS,' it said. 'YOUR TRUTH LIES BURIED IN THE GRAVE. AND YET YOU PAINT YOUR HANDS IN RED FOR THEM, WHEN YOU SHOULD BE PAINTING THE SKIES BLACK.'

'. . . o, joys, a cryptic one . . .'

'YOUR VENGEANCE IS AS THE SUNS, MIA CORVERE. IT SERVES ONLY TO BLIND YOU.'

'What the fuck are you talking about?'

Mia heard shouts, turned towards the sound of approaching boots.

'SEEK THE CROWN OF THE MOON.'

Turning back, she found the thing gone, as if it had never been. Her breath still hung white in the air, the chill receding slow from her bones, its voice ringing in the black behind her eyes. She looked about the grave-yard, seeing only corpses and crypts and wondering if she were dreaming awake.

'. . . mia, they are coming . . .'

'. . . WE MUST GO . . .'

More whistles. Boots coming closer. Blood on her face and skin. Mia snatched up one of the guard's cloaks – the least bloody of the lot. And pulling the cowl over her head, she limped through the necropolis, quick as she could, struggling over the wrought-iron fence and disappearing into the warrens of the Galante backstreets.

Only bodies in her wake.

The Hanging Gardens of Ashkah are a sight unlike any under the suns.

In Godsgrave, the vast rooftop gardens of Little Liis overflow with sunsbride and honeyrose, helping to smother the sewer reek of the Rose River in their wondrous perfume. In Whitekeep, the garden mazes that King Francisco III built to entertain his mistresses stretch for miles, and an army of slaves toils to keep them trim, even a century after the monarchy's fall. The Thorn Towers of Elai stand seventy feet high, covered in vast tangles of razorvine. When the vines bloom just before summersdeep, the towers are covered in blossoms than can be seen across the city. But no garden in all the Republic can match the Hanging Gardens of Ashkah, gentlefriends.

Not for their grandeur, nor their horror.

The smell struck Mia first. It rose over the stench in her cage miles from the city. Blood and sweat and blackest misery. She stared at the metropolis rising out of the haze ahead, chewing her lip. Some of the children in her wagon began to cry, younger women alongside them. Mia felt her shadow surge as she looked to their destination.

Never fear.

The Hanging Gardens had been settled by Liisian explorers after the Ashkahi Empire's fall. In the centuries since the collapse, the port had grown into the largest metropolis on the coast, and now served as the greatest hub in the south seas for the fuel that drove the Itreyan Republic's heart.

Slavery.

The cityport was red stone, nestled on the edge of a natural bay. The architecture was a blend of old Ashkahi ruins and graceful spires and domes of Liisian design built atop the old city's remains. And all around the city walls hung thousands of iron gibbets, filled with thousands of human bodies.

Some were decades old, only tattered bones inside. Some were fresh dead. But from the piteous wails rising over the bustling metropolis beyond, Mia knew hundreds still lived. Left to hang in their cages 'til they perished.

The Hanging Gardens of Ashkah. Its flowers made of flesh and bone.*

And Mia was here at last.

The wagon train trundled through broad wooden gates, the stench rising with the heat. The streets were crowded, the harbour beyond filled with ships from all over the Republic, some off-loading, some shipping out laden with stock for resale. This was market season, when the slaver

---

* The history of the Hanging Gardens is drenched in blood. Founded as a trade city, it quickly became a hub of flesh commerce after the rise of the Itreyan kings. But the port was originally named Ur-Dasis, meaning 'Walled City' in the tongue of old Ashkah, and it was only after a revolt during the reign of Francisco II that the city received its new moniker.

With slave labour serving as the backbone of his kingdom, Francisco couldn't afford any sort of rebellion. When a group of slaves revolted against their captors and seized Ur-Dasis, the king sent an entire legion under the infamous general Atticus Dio to quash the revolt. Though the besieged rebels fought bravely, they were ultimately starved out, agreeing to surrender if Atticus promised mercy. The general agreed, vowing that the rebels would only be returned to captivity.

Predictably, Atticus didn't keep his word. When the rebels laid down their arms, they were strung up from the city walls in their thousands as a warning to any who'd dare revolt in future. Some of the original iron gibbets still decorate the city, and rebellious slaves meet the same fate even now – caged upon the walls to die in the blazing suns.

Francisco was so pleased with his general's performance, he renamed Ur-Dasis the Hanging Gardens in his honour.

Interestingly, Atticus himself was to lead a revolt against Francisco's grandson, the boy king Francisco IV, nearly twenty years later. And when said revolt failed, the general was transported to Ashkah and hung upon the same walls he had liberated two decades earlier.

History, gentlefriends, is not without a sense of irony.

crews returned from their runs up the Ashkahi coast and farther east, their holds laden with fresh meat. Itreyan legionaries rubbed shoulders with Liisian merchants, and the din of coin and sorrow filled the air.

Mia felt someone push up beside her. Turning, she saw a thin woman staring out at the streets, her face pale.

'Everseeing help us . . .'

Mia squinted at the two suns above.

'I don't think he's listening,' she murmured.

The wagon pulled to a halt at the market square's seething edge. Teardrinker hopped down from the driver's seat, limping to the rear of the women's wagon, pulling back the cover and pointing at Mia.

'All right, girl,' she said. 'Off to the Pit we go.'

The captain unlocked the cage, stepped back with crossbow in hand. Merchants were already crowded around the wagon, prodding the stock inside and appraising their worth. Thugs in the market's employ began off-loading men from the rear wagon, shackles singing a rusted song as the captives hopped down on the hard-packed earth. Mia climbed out of the wagon, watching the crowd around them.

I'm here.

She hid her smile behind the matted locks of her hair.

One step closer.

The Pit was dug at the other end of the marketplace, and Mia could hear it well before she laid eyes on it. Ragged cheers and grunts of pain, the clink of coin and the crack of bone. As they made their way across the crowded square, Teardrinker was stopped at least a dozen times by merchants enquiring about Mia's sale. It took all the girl's will to keep her temper in check as she felt them pawing her curves, checking her teeth with dirty hands. But Teardrinker declined all offers for Mia's purchase, indicating she'd be for sale in the Pit soon. The captain's refusals were met with disbelief or dismay, one merchant declaring it a 'waste of good tits.' But Teardrinker held firm, and the pair walked on.

The Pit was exactly that – a hole dug ten feet deep, fifty feet wide, hemmed with limestone walls. A broad stockyard was built beside it, rusted iron bars holding back a multitude of muscular slaves. It was encircled by limestone bleachers, packed with cheering gamblers and shouting bookmakers. And on the innermost ring, attended by the seconds and servants, she saw over a dozen sanguila.*

---

*Literally, 'blood masters'. Keepers of human stables, who fight their stock in the various gladiatii arenas across the Republic.

Mia stood with head bowed at the Pit's iron gates. Itreyan legionaries in plumed helmets were inspecting another slaver's stock before allowing him to pass. The girl whispered from beneath her tangled curtains of hair.

'Can you see Leonides?'

'Aye, there.' Teardrinker nodded across the stockyard. 'The fat bastard.'

'. . . They're *all* fat bastards.'

'The fattest bastard, then.'

Mia squinted, finally spying an Itreyan man seated under a broad parasol. He was dressed in a long frock coat despite the heat, his cravat knotted tight, pierced with a pin in the shape of a lion's head. His face was swarthy, his body pudgy from too many years of too much food and wine. Beside him sat another Itreyan, broad and muscular, watching the Pit with a keen eye.

'That's Titus,' Teardrinker said. 'He serves as executus, trains all of Leonides's stock.'

'I know what an executus does,' Mia muttered.

'Are you certain? Because if I was a betting woman, I'd wager my last beggar you had *no* fucking idea what you're about.'

'I told you,' Mia replied. 'Leonides has trained two of the last three champions of the *Venatus Magni*. He has qualifying berths in all the arenas. He bribes the right officials, owns the right people. If I'm to win my freedom, my best chance is training under him.'

'But *why*, girl?' Teardrinker demanded. 'You could've walked away free in the desert! 'Byss, I'll let you walk free *now*! You saved my hide from those raiders, and I pay my debts. Why in the Everseeing's name do you want to be gladiatii?'

'I made a promise,' Mia said. 'And I mean to keep it.'

'What kind of promise could be kept in a place like this?'

'A red promise.'

Teardrinker sighed and shook her head. 'This is madness.'

'. . . *she is wiser than she looks* . . .'

The whisper came from the shadow under Mia's matted hair, too

---

Successful sanguila have popularity to rival the most beloved Itreyan senator, though they lack the noble blood that would allow them to stand for political office.

Most content themselves by crying themselves to sleep in the arms of beautiful concubines on vast piles of money.

soft for the captain to notice. Teardrinker pulled off her tricorn and dragged her hand over her scalp. She looked at Mia sidelong and sighed.

'A girl like you has no place in this sort of business.'

'Believe me, Captain,' Mia replied. 'You've never met a girl like me.'

Teardrinker cursed, but true to her word, the slaver made her way to the legionaries at the entrance. Both men nodded greetings, raised eyebrows at the scrawny slip shuffling along in chains beside her.

'You lost, Captain?' the big one asked.

'Pleasure pens are yonder,' the bigger one nodded to the bay.

Teardrinker sniffed hard, spat into the dirt. 'Step aside, you stinking whoresons. I've a trueborn fighter to hock and no time to jaw unless you're slinging coin.'

The bigger one blinked at Mia. '. . . You plan on selling this slip to a sanguila?'

The legionaries burst into uproarious laughter, holding their sides like bad actors in a pantomime. Mia kept her head bowed as Teardrinker squared up to the first guard. Big as he was, the woman could look the man eye to eye.

'Have I ever sold chaff in here, Paulo?' She looked to the next man. 'Don't tell me my business, you cocksure wanker. I know it well, and it's in the fucking Pit.'

The soldiers looked at each other, a little abashed. And with small shrugs, the pair stepped aside and let Teardrinker and Mia out into the stockyard. A greasy man with a wax tablet took Teardrinker's name, a young boy with a crooked eye marked Mia's arm and the back of her tunic with a number in blue paint. She watched him while he worked, wondering where he came from, how he'd come to be here. Staring at the single arkemical circle tattooed on his cheek.*

---

*Slavery in the Itreyan Republic is a highly codified affair, with an army of administratii devoted to overseeing it. Slaves are broken into three main categories, and branded with an arkemical symbol on their cheek to indicate their standing.

Slaves with one circle are the rank and file: chattel who serve as housebodies, labourers, brothel fodder, and the like. Two circles denote a person trained in military matters: gladiatii, houseguards, and members of the Itreyan slave legion – the infamous Bloody Thirteenth. Folk marked with three circles are the rarest and most valuable, their brand indicating they're possessed of an education or some exceptional skill: scribes, musicians, majordomos, and some highly prized courtesans.

And if you're wondering why skilled prostitutes are so valued in the Republic,

Taking Mia by the shackles, the boy started dragging her towards the other slaves. The girl resisted for a moment, looked Teardrinker in the eye.

'One more thing, Captain,' she said softly.

'O, aye?' The captain raised an eyebrow. 'Owed so many favours, are you?'

'You owe me your life. I'd call that the Largest Kind of Favour There Is. One turn, I might call in that marker. And it'd be lovely if I didn't have to ask you twice.'

Teardrinker breathed deep. 'As I said, girl, I pay my debts.'

Satisfied, Mia let herself be dragged away, standing in the sweltering heat with the other human livestock. Looking around, she realized she was one of only two females, and the other woman was a Dweymeri with hands the size of dinner plates. She kept her eyes straight ahead, watching proceedings out in the Pit and avoiding the curious stares of her pen-mates.

It seemed a simple enough process. fleshmongers like Teardrinker wandered the bleachers, spruiking their wares to the sanguila. And one at a time, their offerings were handed a wooden sword, and thrown face-first into a fight for their lives.

There were half a dozen professional fighters at work in the Pit's centre, each a mountain of muscle and scars. When a new prospect was pushed into the ring, a random fighter would promptly heft a wooden sword and set about trying to bash their head in. Bets would be placed, the crowd would bay and howl, and if the competitor was still standing after a few minutes, the sanguila were given the opportunity to bid for their purchase. Those who fought with promise were snatched up. Those who failed were dragged away for resale somewhere else in the Hanging Gardens.

Mia glanced at Sanguila Leonides. The man was considering matches the way spiders consider flies, but he never made a bid. The Lions of Leonides were the finest gladiatii in the Republic, and Leonides spent six months a year trawling coastal markets, handpicking the finest. If Mia wanted to call him Domini, she'd need to impress.

Fortunately, one didn't become a Blade of the Red Church by being a slouch with a sword.

The ledgerman called Mia's number. The holding pen door opened. The crook-eyed boy unlocked her shackles, handed her a dented wooden

gentlefriends, you've obviously never spent the night with a skilled prostitute.

gladius that she wouldn't have used for firewood under normal circumstances. And without ceremony, Mia found herself shoved into the middle of the Pit.

Jeers rang across the bleachers, choking guffaws and fountains of abuse. The sight of the skinny, black-haired girl standing knock-kneed in the centre of the ring didn't seem to be impressing the plebs in the crowd, let alone the blood masters.

'Aa's burning cock, is this a joke?' one yelled.

Spit and curses rained into the Pit, the various sanguila turning disinterested eyes to their ledgers – whatever this jest was, it was clear not a one of them found it amusing. One of the pit fighters raised an eyebrow at the ledgerman, who simply nodded. The man shrugged and hefted his wooden sword, striding towards Mia. He was a Dweymeri, broad as bridges, brown skin glistening with sweat.

'Hold still, lass,' he growled. 'This won't hurt long.'

Mia did as she was bid, standing motionless as the big man closed. But as the giant raised his blade to stove her skull in, the girl moved. Quick as shadows.

A sidestep, the blade whistling past her head. Mia cracked her wooden gladius down on the man's wrist, shattering bone. Several sanguila turned to stare as the big man screamed. Mia kicked savagely at his knee, rewarded with a nauseating crunch as the joint bent entirely the wrong way. The big man dropped with a bellow, and with deliberate brutality, Mia slammed her wooden blade directly into his throat, smashing his larynx to sauce.

Red froth spattered the man's lips as he turned astonished eyes to Mia. The girl slung her hair over her shoulder, whispering soft.

'*Hear me, Niah,*' she whispered. '*Hear me, Mother. This flesh your feast. This blood your wine. This life, this end, my gift to you. Hold him close.*'

And with a gurgle, the pit fighter toppled dead into the dirt.

Bewildered murmurs rippled among the crowd. Mia curtseyed to the sanguila, like a new dona at her debut ball. Then she turned to the next fighter in the row and levelled her wooden sword at his head.

'You're next, prettyboy.'

The fighter (who *was* rather pretty) looked to his fellows, the corpse on the ground, and finally to the ledgerman. The greasy fellow glanced up at the sanguila, who were now staring at Mia intently. And turning back to the swordsman, he nodded.

The fighter stepped forward, Mia skipped up to meet him. Their match lasted less than ten seconds, ending with Mia's bootprint embedded in the man's crotch and her wooden sword shoved down his pretty throat, all the way to the hilt. The girl turned to the crowd and curtseyed again.

'A hundred priests,' came the call.

'One hundred and ten.'

Mia smiled behind her hair as sanguila began bidding. Within moments, her bid was two hundred silver coins – a decent sum by anyone's measure. But as she looked up into the bleachers, she saw Leonides and Titus hadn't uttered a word. Though the sanguila watched her intently, though Teardrinker was whispering in Titus's ear and he was nodding slow, Leonides didn't raise his voice to bid.

Time to stoke the flame.

Mia retrieved her wooden blade from the dead fighter's throat, turned to the third and spoke loud enough for the bleachers to hear.

'You. Next.'

The big man looked at the two corpses at Mia's feet.

'Fuck that,' he scoffed.

'Bring your friends.' Mia smiled at the fighters beside him. 'I've always wanted to try three at once.'

The girl tossed her wooden sword onto the dirt.

'Or are you cowards all?'

The crowd hooted and jeered, and the fighters rankled. To be bested on their own soil was one thing, but to eat a plateful of shit from an unarmed girl half their size was another. With flashing eyes and swords raised, the men stepped out into the Pit.

With a dark smile, the girl stepped up to meet them.

CHAPTER 4

OFFERING

'Maw's teeth, are we going to be here 'til truelight?' Mia snarled.

Pietro raised an eyebrow, poured another measure of goldwine onto her bloody shoulder. Mia winced in pain, took a drag of her cigarillo with a shaking hand. She was sat on a low stone bench, Pietro behind her, swathed in his customary black robes. The Hand was busy sewing up the bloody gouge in her shoulder, and he'd padded a wad of gauze about her backside, soaking through with red.

The chamber was sparse, dark stone walls and dim arkemical globes. Like most rooms in the Galante Chapel, it was perfumed with the faint stench of shit. The servants of Our Lady of Blessed Murder here in the Cityport of Churches* had built their hideaway among the vast network

---

*Galante proudly boasts the greatest number of churches and temples in all the Republic, besting even Godsgrave in the tally.

Before the Great Unifier, King Francisco I, conquered the nation, the people of Liis worshipped a holy trinity known as the Father, the Mother, and the Child. But once assimilated by the Itreyan monarchy, worship of the God of Light caught on among the common folk like a fire in a well-stocked brewery.

One wily fellow, a merchant named Carlino Grimaldi, decided the best way to distinguish himself in the new world order was to chuck wagonloads of money at the Itreyan church. He built the first cathedral to Aa in all of Liis; a towering structure known as Basilica Lumina, right in the heart of Galante. Sculpted of rare purple marble and beautiful stained glass, construction almost bankrupted its patron. However, so impressive was the final result, Galante's cardinal had Grimaldi appointed as governor of the entire city. Galante nobles were soon falling over themselves to curry favour among Aa's ministry, and churches to the Everseeing and temples to his four daughters began springing up over Galante like a rash on a sugargirl's nethers after the navy hits town.

of sewers beneath Galante's skin, and it was hard to escape the smell. In the eight months she'd served here, Mia had become accustomed to it, but as a preference spent as little time down here as possible. Unless she needed stitching up or resupply, she really only visited when she needed to speak to—

'Well, bugger me all the way backwards,' said a familiar voice. 'Look what the shadowcat dragged in.'

Mia looked up, saw a woman standing in the doorway, dressed in leather britches, long boots, and a black velvet shirt. She was finger-thin, light brown hair cut in a distinctly masculine style, dark shadows under her eyes. She walked with a singular swagger, and wore more knives than anyone in her right mind would know what to do with.

'Bishop Tenhands,' Mia said, inclining her head. 'I'd stand and bow, but the crossbow bolt in my backside isn't too agreeable.'

'An interesting nevernight, then,' the woman smirked.

'Some coul— Ow, fuck!' Mia glared over her shoulder again. ''Byss and blood, Pietro, are you stitching me up or sewing a dress?'

'All right, all right, bugger off,' Tenhands told the beleaguered surgeon. 'I'll finish her up. I'd like a word with our Blade alone.'

'My Bishop,' Pietro nodded, slapping a bundle of gauze none too gently on Mia's bleeding shoulder and leaving the room. Tenhands sauntered around behind Mia, pulled away the bandage, the girl wincing as the blood stuck it to her skin.

Tenhands was a figure of infamy in Red Church lore, a long-serving Blade of the Mother with near twenty sanctified kills to her name. Old Mercurio had told Mia tales about the woman when she was younger, and Mia had grown up as something of an admirer.* Serving in the Cityport of

---

Though he was later crucified for tax evasion, Carlino still went down in Liisian history as an Exceptionally Clever Bastard. Even to this turn, to curry favour among men of the cloth in Liis is known as 'pulling a Grimaldi'.

*Tenhands began her career as a thief on the streets of Elai, and even after she became a Blade of the Mother, she never lost her knack for the art of stealth. She was said to move like the dark itself, and was capable of dislocating both shoulders at will, allowing her to squeeze through the tightest of places with little difficulty.

Her most infamous offering was a senator named Phocas Merinius – a man so astonishingly paranoid about assassination, it was said he kept a retinue of half a dozen guards on hand at his bedside when he made love to his wife. Tenhands reportedly gained access to Phocas's villa by crawling in through the sewer and up the privy spout – an ingress eight inches wide at best – and lying

Churches, she'd learned its bishop wasn't much for civility. Or frivolity. But she liked results, so fortunately, Tenhands liked her.

'This looks like it hurts,' Tenhands muttered, eyeing the horrid wound across Mia's back and shoulder.

'It's far from ticklish.'

The bishop took up the bone needle, began sewing Mia's wound with steady fingers. 'I trust the pain was worth it?'

Mia winced, taking a long drag of her clove cigarillo. 'Senator Aurelius's son is being fitted for his death masque as we speak.'

'You used the lament?'

Mia nodded. 'On the lips, just as you suggested.'

'I shan't ask how you got access to the young don's mouth, then.'

'Never kiss and tell.'

'And where's young Dove?'

'Sadly,' Mia sighed, 'my young Hand won't be back for supper. Ever.'

'Shame, that.'

'He was never the sharpest blade on the racks, Bishop.'

'Beggars can't be choosers.' Tenhands dug the needle in for another stitch. 'Since the Järnheims gutted us, quality around here is in short supply. Present company excepted, of course.'

Mia chewed her lip and sighed. Bishop Tenhands spoke truth – good Hands and Blades were hard to find in the Red Church these turns. Galante was never a glamorous appointment, and most of the servants of Niah posted here dreamed of grander things. But matters were worse than ever since the Luminatii attack.

Eight months on, Our Lady of Blessed Murder's congregation was still bleeding from the blow Ashlinn Järnheim and her brother had inflicted at the behest of their father. It wasn't simply Lord Cassius's murder that had the Church reeling, although the loss of the Black Prince would have been grievous enough. But Torvar Järnheim hadn't merely had his children serve up the Ministry to the Luminatii – the old assassin had also revealed the location of every Red Church chapel in the Republic.

And so, while Justicus Remus was invading the Quiet Mountain, the Luminatii had launched simultaneous assaults across greater Itreya. The

---

in wait right there inside the pipe. When poor Phocas heard the call of nature in the middle of the nevernight, he sat down on the privy seat and found both his femoral arteries severed before he could even commence his business.

Tenhands reportedly spent the next seven turns in the chapel's baths trying to wash off the stink.

The things we do for our Mothers . . .

chapels in Dweym and Galante remained unscathed.* But every other chapel had been destroyed.

Worse, Torvar had supplied names. Aliases. Last known residences. Between Torvar's treachery and the Luminatii attacks, Our Lady of Blessed Murder had lost near three-quarters of her assassins in a single nevernight.

As the bishop said, the Red Church had been gutted; that was probably the only reason a Blade as young as Mia was even entrusted with offerings like the one on Gaius Aurelius. In the eight months since her posting to Galante, she'd ended three men and one woman in the Black Mother's name. Most Blades her age would be lucky to have been sent on their first kill.

Mia was thankful for the chance to show her worth. But problem was, her list of throats to slit was growing longer, not shorter. She'd killed Justicus Remus, but Consul Scaeva and Grand Cardinal Duomo still lived. Her familia were still unavenged. And with Tric's murder at Ashlinn's hands during the Luminatii attack, she now had one more windpipe to open before her vengeance was done.

And stuck here in Galante, she was no closer to any of them.

Mia clenched her jaw as the bishop continued to stitch her, thinking about . . . that . . . thing that had accosted her in the necropolis. Truth was, it had saved her life. Her near-death should have left her shaken, but as ever, her passengers ate any sense of fear inside her, twice as swift now as when she carried Mister Kindly alone. She felt nothing close to afraid. And so, she was only left with questions.

What was it?

What did it want with her?

---

*The Luminatii raids had missed both: the Galante Chapel was only recently constructed, and unbeknownst to the Järnheims, the old Dweym Chapel had been relocated the previous winter, when, due to unusually heavy rains and some dodgy plumbing, its cellar (and thus, its blood pool) had flooded.

Instead of refilling the pool, the Ministry decided to build a new structure on higher ground in the cityport of Seawall, and abandoned the ruined one in Farrow. If constructing an entirely new chapel to Our Lady of Blessed Murder, in secret, in the middle of a major metropolis, seems a costly and cumbersome affair, consider the following:

1. Two thousand-odd cubic feet of vitus fills every Church blood pool.
2. There are approximately seven and a half gallons of liquid per cubic foot.
3. The average pig holds approximately one gallon of blood in its body.

Do the maths, gentlefriends. And ask yourself if you ever want to be filling one of these damn pools twice.

'The Crown of the Moon'?

She'd seen that particular phrase before, buried in the pages of—

'Heard about some trouble with Aurelius's guards,' Tenhands remarked, *ceasing her needlework long enough to take a pull of the medicinal goldwine.*

'Nothing I couldn't handle,' *Mia replied.*

'You normally operate with a little more discretion.'

'Beg pardon, Bishop, but you didn't ask for discretion,' *Mia said, faint annoyance in her voice.* 'You asked for a dead senator's son.'

'One doesn't necessarily preclude the other.'

'But given the choice, which would you rather?'

Mia hissed as the bishop poured more alcohol onto her now closed wound, bound it in long strips of gauze.

'I like you, Corvere,' *Tenhands said.* 'You remind me of me in my younger turns. More balls than most men I've ever met. And you get your killing done, so you've earned a little ego. But word to the wise: you'd best leave that lip of yours behind when you head back to the Mountain. The Ministry aren't as fond of you as I.'

'And why would I head back to the Mountain? I'm posted to—'

'Speaker Adonai sent a blood missive just now,' *Tenhands interjected.* 'You've been recalled by the Ministry.'

Mia's eyes narrowed in suspicion. Goosebumps on her skin.

'. . . Why?' *she asked.*

Tenhands shrugged. 'All I know is they're leaving me a killer down, and a pile of throats that need slitting. If I could use Blades on more than one offering at a time, that'd be something. But that'd breach the Promise.* So

---

*It is commonly known among folk who employ hired killers that the Red Church operates under a code of, if not outright *honour*, then at least *conduct*, known as the Red Promise. The strictures are thus:

- Inevitability – no offering undertaken in the history of the Church has *ever* gone unfulfilled.
- Sanctity – a current employer of the Church may not be chosen as a target of the Church.
- Secrecy – the Church does not discuss the identity of its employers.
- Fidelity – a Blade will only serve one employer a time.
- Hierarchy – all offerings must be approved by the Lord/Lady of Blades or Revered Father/Mother.

The first three strictures were loosely in place at the Church's inception, but the strictures of Fidelity and Hierarchy were codified after an infamous event in Church history, told to acolytes as 'The Tale of Flavius and Dalia'.

when you see that bastard Solis, be a love and knee him in the codpiece for me, will you?'

Mia's mind was turning, suspicion and excitement entwined in her belly. Being recalled by the Ministry could mean anything. Reassignment. Rebuke. Retribution. She'd served the Black Mother well in the past eight months, but every Shahiid in the Mountain knew she'd failed her final trial, refusing

---

Take a pew, gentlefriends.

Flavius Apullo was an Itreyan general who stood among the conspirators who overthrew King Francisco XV and forged the Republic. He went on to become a senator, and as one does, immensely wealthy.

The period around the collapse of the Itreyan monarchy was a busy time in the art of professional murder, and authority was being granted to individual bishops of local chapels to accept offerings. Senator Flavius Apullo began fearing assassination around the same time his rivals got serious about bumping him off, and in an embarrassing turn, the Red Church undertook to murder Flavius the very same nevernight as he employed a Church Blade on retainer as his bodyguard.

Red faces all around, gentlefriends.

In a further cluster of fuckery, the Blade designated for *both* these offerings was a woman named Dalia. Beautiful, manipulative, and peerless with a punching dagger, Dalia served as Flavius's bodyguard for three years. In that time, the pair became lovers, and Dalia eliminated a slew of Flavius's rivals – all save his most vocal opponent, Tiberius the Elder. Tiberius was the senator who'd employed the Church to murder Flavius, and under the Law of Sanctity, he was off-limits until said murder was complete. Tiberius, however, was dying of Old Mother Syphilis, and in quite a hurry to see Flavius necked before he shuffled off this mortal coil.

The Red Church was on the brink of a political embarrassment that could have ended their reputation.

Cleverly, Flavius proposed marriage to Dalia to cement her place at his side – he assumed a fiancée would keep him safer from any would-be assassins than a mere employee. Not so cleverly, he let his patronage with the Red Church lapse the same turn that Dalia accepted his marriage proposal.

Dalia stabbed her husband to death on their wedding night. Rumour conflicts whether she wept as she did the deed. She brought Flavius's head to the sickbed of Tiberius the Elder to prove the contract was fulfilled. And content the Church's reputation was intact, but more, that Tiberius was no longer a Church employer protected by the Law of Sanctity, Dalia raised her punching dagger and saved Old Mother Syphilis the trouble.

Rumours about whether she was weeping at the time are quite clear.

After this incident, it was decided to write some actual bloody rules about how things would be run around here.

to kill an innocent. The only reason she became a Blade at all was because Lord Cassius had baptized her as he lay dying on the sands of Last Hope. Perhaps the good grace his endorsement had given her had finally run out . . .

Who knew what awaited her when she arrived?

'When do I leave?' Mia asked.

Tenhands lifted her bone needle, looked meaningfully at Mia's backside. 'As soon as you can walk.'

Mia sighed. No sense fretting on what she couldn't change. And getting back to the Mountain, she could speak to Chronicler Aelius again, see Naev. Maybe find some of the answers she sought.

'Bend over,' the bishop ordered. 'I'll try to be gentle.'

Mia took the bottle of medicinal goldwine and took a long, deep pull. 'I'll bet you say that to all the girls.'

I t turns out three men at once was almost more than Mia could handle. The battle had started well enough. The pit fighters had advanced, spurred on by the jeering crowd and the fact that Mia had thrown her wooden sword into the dirt. The first – a burly Itreyan – had bellowed a war cry and swung his blade at her head. And with a glance, Mia had reached towards the dark at his feet.

Out here in the light of two suns, the shadows were sluggish and heavy. But Mia was stronger now, in herself, in what she was, and she'd been playing this particular trick for years, after all. With a glance, she affixed the big Itreyan's boots in his own shadow, stopping his charge short. Weaving close as he lost balance, she'd kicked him hard in the knee, punched him square in the throat, and as he toppled backwards, she'd pirouetted and caught the sword flying from his hand to the tune of the cheering crowd.

'*. . . you are showing off now . . .*' came a whisper in her ear.

'That's the bloody poin—'

The blow caught her on the back of the head, sent her reeling. She barely managed to turn and block the next flurry, staggering back into a semblance of guard. The remaining pit fighters – a broad Liisian with a pockmarked face, and a taller Dweymeri with only seven fingers – advanced, giving her no time to catch her breath. She was forced back across the Pit, warm blood dripping down the back of her neck.

Sevenfingers stepped up, swung at her face, throat, chest. Mia countered, locking him up and slipping inside his guard, but Pockface's sword cracked across her ribs before she could strike, and an elbow sent her sprawling into the dirt.

She kept her grip on her sword, rolling aside as the pair tried to stomp her head in. Scrabbling on the ground, she slung a handful of red sand into Pockface's eyes, lashed out with her boot and sent Sevenfingers to the ground. Rolling to her feet, she planted her boot in the now-blinded Pockface's bollocks, hard enough to elicit a groan of sympathy from every man in the crowd. And to their cheers, she smashed her sword hilt into his face, smearing his nose across his cheeks.

'. . . *behind* . . .'

She turned, barely blocking a blow that would've caved her skull in. The burly Itreyan was back on his feet, chin smeared with vomit and spit. She danced with him in the dust, strike and riposte, weave and flurry. Burlyboy was huge, twice as strong as she. But what Mia lacked in size, she made up for in speed and sheer, bloody ferocity. The Itreyan swung hard, snapping her gladius in half as she blocked. But with a shapeless cry, she danced inside his follow-through, crouched low and smashed her broken sword up beneath his chin. The splintered wood punctured his throat, gouts of blood coating Mia's hands as Burlyboy fell.

'. . . *left, left* . . . !'

Mister Kindly's whisper brought her around, but too late – a gladius caught her across the shoulder, sent her reeling as the crowd roared. Sevenfingers swung again, struck her in the ribs, Mia gasping in agony. She locked up his swordarm, pulled him close. Smelling sweat, dirty breath, blood. Sevenfingers punched her in the face, once, twice, and with a ragged cry she reached out to the shadows, locking up his feet as she pushed backwards with all her strength. With his feet rooted, the man toppled backwards, Mia falling on top of him, fingers finding his mouth, slipping inside his cheeks and twisting like fishhooks before ripping outwards.

The man screamed as his lips split, the crowd baying. The girl began pounding on his jaw with her fists, once, twice, three times. Hands red. Teeth gritted. Blood in her mouth. Picturing a smiling consul with dark, pretty eyes. A grand cardinal with a beard like a hedgerow and a voice like honey. Their faces pulped as she pounded, again

'. . . *mia* . . .'

and again, picturing her mother, her brother, her father, everything she'd lost, everything they'd *taken*, and this man beneath her just one more enemy, just one more obstacle between her and the turn she'd spit on all their fucking grav—

'. . . *mia* . . . !'

She fell still. Drenched in sweat. Breath burning. Covered in warm, sticky red. She could feel Mister Kindly's chill, mixed with the blood on the back of her neck. The world came back into focus, its volume swelling in her ears. And beneath the thundering pulse and echoes of her past, she heard it. Swelling in her chest and tingling her fingertips.

Applause.

She stood, painted to the elbows in red. The crowd in the bleachers were on their feet, Teardrinker tending a flurry of bids rolling in from the sanguila at the Pit's edge. *Three hundred silver. Three hundred and fifty. Four.* And on trembling legs, the girl walked across the Pit and stood before Leonides. She looked her would-be master in the eye, and dropped into a perfect curtsey before him.

'Domini,' she said.

The sanguila regarded her with narrowed eyes. His executus whispered in his ear. And as a storm of butterflies took wing in Mia's belly, Leonides raised his hand and spoke in a voice that rang across the entire Pit.

'One thousand silver pieces.'

A low murmur rippled across the audience, Mia's heart thrilling. Such a sum! Truth told, it was an overbid – the man could have probably knocked out most of his fellows with half that. But Mia knew the domini of the Lions of Leonides was fond of theatre, and his bid told everyone in the Pit that he was in no mood to haggle.

Leonides wanted her. And so, he would have her. Price be damned.

It had gone perfectly. If Mia fought among the Lions of Leonides, she was almost assured a place in the *Venatus Magni*. And when the games were over, when she stood victorious upon the dais—

'One thousand and one,' came a call.

Mia's belly turned cold. She glanced up to the stands, saw a figure step forward from the crowd. Wrapped in a long cloak despite the heat, pulling back the hood to reveal a young pretty face, long auburn hair, pale Itreyan skin.

A woman.

'. . . *who is that* . . . ?'

'No bloody idea,' Mia whispered.

'One thousand and one silver pieces,' the woman repeated.

Mia's eyes narrowed. She'd never heard of a female sanguila – though there had been a few famous female gladiatii, the stage of the *venatus* was ever managed by the careful hands of men. Maybe the newcomer was an agent for another domini? A foil from the ledgerman to drive up her price?

Mia looked to Leonides expectantly. Whoever this woman was, the greatest sanguila in the history of the games wasn't going to be outbid by a single silver coin.

Titus's face was a mask. Leonides glanced to his executus, back to the newcomer, speaking as if the words soured his mouth.

'This is somewhat childish, don't you think, my dear?'

The woman's smile was splashed across her face like poison.

'Childish? Whatever do you mean?'

'I hear tell you have but a handful of coppers to rub together,' Leonides said. 'If your intent is to embarrass the *patriis familia* of your own House, are there not less expensive ways to do so?'

The woman smiled wider, and Mia's stomach sank.

'My thanks for your concern,' she said. 'But this is just business, Father.'

'. . . o, dear . . .'

'I have told you before, Leona,' Leonides warned. 'The *venatus* is no place for women. And the sanguila's box is no place for you.'

'Frightened my Falcons might eclipse your Lions, dear Patriis?'

Leonides scoffed. 'One victor's laurel in a backwater stoush does not a collegium make.'

'You won't mind if I take the bloody beauty, then?'

Leona glanced at Mia. Leonides also turned to stare. Mia stepped forward, pleas roiling behind her teeth. But Mister Kindly's whisper held her still.

'. . . *remember who you are. and who you are supposed to be* . . .'

The not-cat was right. This was *her* script, after all, and she had the hardest role to play. If she was to fight on the sands in service to a gladiatii collegium, she could only do so as its property. And property didn't speak unless spoken to. It certainly didn't wade into a public pissing contest between father and daughter . . .

Shit.

Mia stared at Sanguila Leonides. Eyes pleading. She'd calculated it so well. She'd fought like a daemon, won the approval of every blood master in the Pit. She was only a single word, a *single bid* away from entry into the greatest collegium in the Republic. One step closer to Consul Scaeva's and Cardinal Duomo's throats. All Leonides need do was speak . . .

'Very well, Leona.'

Leonides feigned a shrug, turning his back on his daughter.

'Take her, then. For all the good she will do you.'

Leona smiled, sharp and bright. Mia's shoulders sagged. Legionaries marched into the ring, the crook-eyed boy slapping shackles around her wrists. She could've run then. Hidden beneath her cloak of shadows, slipped from the Pit with only dismayed shouts and prayers to the Everseeing in her wake.

But then she'd be right back where she started. It had taken weeks to orchestrate a clandestine trip to Ashkah, the broken caravan, her sale in the Gardens. She'd waste weeks more in trying to get sold to a mightier collegium, and with the grand games so close, they were weeks she simply didn't have to spare.

She'd ended too many lives, risked so much to be here to simply abandon her plan altogether. And though Leona was an unknown factor, Mia still had faith in her own abilities, and no real fear she could fail. Behind her lay only blood and a Mountain full of treachery. Ahead lay the sand of the *venatus*, and vengeance.

This was her course now. For good or ill, she had to walk it.

The legionaries parted. Mia looked up to see Dona Leona standing before her. This close, she could see the woman was in her early twenties. Bright blue eyes and auburn hair coiled in gentle ringlets, lightly freckled skin. She wore gold jewellery, a ruby wedding band. Beneath her cloak, her gown was cut of soft Liisian silk. Every part of her screamed 'wealth', save her eyes. As Mia risked a glance into those kohled pools of brilliant blue, she could think of only one word to describe them.

Hungry.

'My bloody beauty,' she smiled. 'What a pair we shall make.'

Mia hung still, unsure what to say. Leona glanced at the soldiers, annoyance in her gaze. One of the men drew a truncheon, struck Mia across her legs. The girl cried out, fell to her knees. Teeth clenched, bloodstained hands in fists. But she could feel Mister Kindly, prowling cool inside her shadow, his whisper in her ears.

'*. . . who you are, and who you are supposed to be . . .*'

And so, she stayed there in the dust, eyes downturned, silent and still.

'I am Dona Leona,' the woman said. 'Though you will call me Domina.'

The woman extended her hand. Mia saw a golden ring on Leona's signet finger – a falcon, wings spread, crowned with a victor's wreath.

The truncheon cracked across her shoulder blades. Mia gasped in pain.

'Show your respects, slave!' a soldier barked.

Mia stared at that bird of prey in its wreath of gold. Just as proud and fierce and wild as she. And yet here she was, kneeling in the dirt like a whipped kitten.

Patience, she thought.

If Vengeance has a mother, her name is Patience.

Mia drew a deep breath.

Closed her eyes.

'Domina,' she murmured.

And leaning forward, she kissed the ring.

CHAPTER 5

DEVOTION

Pig's blood has a very peculiar taste.

The blood of a man is best drunk warm, and leaves a hint of sodium and rust clinging to the teeth. Horse's blood is less salty, with an odd bitterness almost like dark chocolate. But pig's blood has an almost buttery quality, like oysters and oiled iron, slipping down your throat and leaving a greasy tang in its wake.

Mia fucking hated it, truth told.

She burst from the pool of red with a gasp, a thudding pulse still ringing in her ears, head spinning. She was naked save for a gravebone stiletto at her wrist, a gravebone sword at her waist, long black hair glued like ropes of weed to bloody skin. A rectangular package wrapped in oilskin was clutched in her fingers. Two Hands in dark robes stood in the pool beside her, helping her to her feet as she gasped and sputtered and pawed the gore from her lashes.

Blinking around the room, she found herself waist-deep in a triangular marble pool of blood, thirty feet at a side – Speaker Adonai's chambers within the Quiet Mountain. The room was carved with sorcerii glyphs, the heavy scent of butchery in the air. Maps of every city in the Republic were painted on the wall in blood.

Mia licked her teeth and spat, dragged her hair from her eyes.

Looking to the head of the pool, Mia saw Blood Speaker Adonai, knelt on the stone. Though she'd not admit it to any, her belly thrilled a little at the sight of him. Weaver Marielle could make a portrait of any face, but her brother was her masterpiece – high cheekbones and a chiselled jaw. His skin was ghostly pale, his tousled hair snow white. He wore a red silk robe, open at the chest, the troughs and valleys of his chest carved in marble. His leather britches rode so low on his hips they were almost indecent, and the V-shaped cut of his abdom—

'Good turn to thee, Blade Mia,' the sorcerer said.

Mia dragged her stare back up to eyes the colour of blood.

'And you, Speaker.'

Adonai's pretty lips twisted in a knowing smile, but Mia kept her face like stone. The speaker was a picture, no doubt. And Mia had entertained her share of fantasies; lying in bed and picturing his pale, clever fingers as her own roamed ever lower. She'd even saved his and his beloved sister's lives during the Luminatii attack. But Mia couldn't fool herself into thinking of him as anything but a blackhearted bastard.

Still. A fuckable bastard . . .

'The Ministry await thee in the Hall of Eulogies,' Adonai said.

Mia waded out of the pool, still limping from her wounds, careful of slipping on the bloody tile. She was conscious of the speaker's stare on her naked body, the blood sloshing like a gentle sea. Mia looked down the hall to the stairwell leading up to the waiting Ministry. Wondering why the 'byss she'd been called here.

With a final glance to the speaker, Mia walked from the room. Washing off the drying blood and changing silently; black leathers and wolfskin boots, a shirt of dark linen. She hid her gravebone stiletto in her sleeve, hung her beautiful gravebone longsword from the scabbard at her waist. The former had belonged to her mother, the latter to her father, taken from the dead hand of Justicus Remus. Both blades had hilts fashioned like crows in flight, eyes of red amber. They were all she had left of her parents, aside her name.

She supposed there was a metaphor in there somewhere . . .

Unwrapping her oilskin package, she took the beaten leatherbound book inside under her arm and trudged up the stairs.* The voice of a ghostly choir hung in the black, and Mia couldn't help but smile at the familiar song. After months in Galante, she'd returned to the hallowed halls of the most feared assassins in all the Itreyan Republic.

At last, she'd come home.

After an interminable climb, she stepped out into the Hall of Eulogies. The space was vast, circular, carved into the Quiet Mountain's granite

---

* Mia often counted stairs in the Mountain as she climbed them. She was never surprised when the tally changed. Some of the more 'temperamental' flights, such as the one leading to the Hall of Songs, shifted constantly, whereas the flight leading to the Sky Altar seemed almost lazy by comparison. Interestingly enough, the stairs leading up to the chambers of the Hall of Eulogies remained constant in number.

Three hundred and thirty-three.

heart. A beautiful statue of Niah, Mother of Night and Our Lady of Blessed Murder, loomed forty feet above Mia's head. A set of scales hung in her right hand, a wickedly sharp sword in her left. Wherever Mia stood in the room, Niah's eyes seemed to follow.

The space was ringed with pillars thicker than ancient ironwoods. The walls were lined with tombs, scarlet light washing through huge stained-glass windows. On the flagstones, Mia could see the names of every one of the Red Church's victims – thousands of lives claimed in their Black Mother's name. In contrast, the tombs were unmarked. They contained bodies of servants of the Mother and in death, only the Mother mourned them.

Mia's eyes drifted to a tomb in the western wall. The four small letters she'd scratched into the stone with a gravebone blade eight months ago.

'Blade Mia,' said a deep voice. 'Welcome home.'

Mia turned to the foot of the statue. The entire Red Church Ministry was assembled, watching with expectant gazes.

All except Revered Father Solis, of course.

The big Itreyan stood with blind eyes turned to the soaring gables. He was clad in a robe of fine grey cloth, his hood pulled back. Pale blond stubble dusted a scarred scalp, his beard set in four resin spikes. His ever-empty scabbard hung at his side, the leather embossed with concentric circles.

To Solis's right stood Spiderkiller, Shahiid of Truths. The elegant Dweymeri was clad in emerald green, gold at her throat. Her saltlocks were artfully coiled atop her head. Hands and lips stained black from poisoncraft.

To Solis's left stood Mouser, Shahiid of Pockets, his handsome face belying the years in his twinkling eyes. An Ashkahi blacksteel blade hung as his side, two naked figures with feline heads entwined on the hilt. He was rolling a coin across the knuckles of his right hand, his left clutching an ornate cane – his legs had been badly broken during the Luminatii invasion, and the Shahiid would limp for the rest of his life.

Third was Aalea, Shahiid of Masks. Milk-white skin and blood-red lips, curtains of black hair framing a face that made the word 'beauty' hang its head in shame. She smiled at Mia as if the whole world were a secret and only she knew the answer. Promising to share it as soon as the pair were alone.

To date, there had been no new Shahiid of Songs appointed – Solis was still teaching fresh acolytes the art of steel until a suitable replacement could be found. Wounds from the Järnheims' assault were fresh, and even here, in the seat of the Church's power in the Republic, the scabs remained.

'Shahiids,' Mia said, bowing low. 'I return, as requested.'

'As commanded,' Solis growled.

'. . . *Forgiveness, Revered Father. Commanded.*'

The title tasted strange on Mia's tongue. After Cassius's death, it was fitting that Revered Mother Drusilla become the Lady of Blades, but Drusilla's decision to appoint Solis as Revered One had vexed Mia more than a little. Solis still bore the tiny scar on his face from where Mia had bested him in the Hall of Songs, and her arm still sometimes tingled where he'd hacked it off in retaliation. Truth told, Mia hated him like poison, and the idea of taking orders from him sat about as well with her as a collar on a cat.

Solis glowered, white eyes turned to the ceiling, his robe straining against the span of his shoulders. He dwarfed the other Ministry members, making them look like children. Mia supposed she should feel intimidated, but she found it all just another reminder of how ill-suited for his role Solis seemed.

He doesn't even fit the robe he's supposed to wear . . .

'So?' Spiderkiller asked, without preamble. 'Gaius Aurelius is dead?'

'. . . Aye, Shahiid,' Mia replied.

'Word has it you were almost killed in the process,' Mouser mused.

'A scratch, Shahiid.' She shrugged, wincing at the pull of the stitches in her shoulder. 'Though I'll not be dancing for a while.'

'You can barely walk, Acolyte,' Solis growled.

'All due respect, Revered Father,' Mia said, temper fraying. 'But I was anointed by Lord Cassius with his dying breath. I'm not an acolyte. I'm a Blade.'

Solis sneered. 'That remains to be seen.'

'I've four kills to my name already.'

Mouser tilted his head. 'Don't you mean five?'

'Surely you haven't forgotten murdering a king of the Dweymeri in his own keep without our permission?' Spiderkiller asked.

Mia bit down on her response. Glancing again at the name she'd carved into the unmarked tomb on the western wall.

TRIC.

They'd made a promise. Him to her and her to him. If she were to fall, Tric had sworn to murder Scaeva and Duomo for her. And if he fell, she swore she'd kill his wretched bastard of a grandfather, Swordbreaker. In truth, she thought she was owed a death after saving the lives of every man and woman in this room. But perhaps here was the reason she'd been sent to a backwater like Galante?

Silence rang in the hall, Mia stewing within it.

'May I ask why I am here?' she finally ventured.

Solis's lip curled. 'You have a devotee, little Blade.'

The girl raised an eyebrow at the Revered Father. 'If it's someone in this hall, they hide it very well.'

Aalea smiled, lips dark as blood. 'Perhaps "patron" is a better word. The last three offerings you performed – the son of Senator Aurelius, Magistrate Phillip Cicerii, and the mistress of Armando Tulli – were all requested by the same client of the Church. They specifically requested the services of "she who slew the justicus of the Luminatii Legion and his finest centuries beside him." And they paid handsomely for you.'

'Who is this patron, Shahiid?'

'Irrelevant,' Solis scowled. 'All you need know is that, miracle of miracles, they are pleased with your results. You are being sent after bigger game.'

Mia looked Solis up and down, considering. From the scowl at his brow, the tension in his jaw, she'd wager her last coin the Revered Father had violently objected to her assignment. But despite that, she'd been appointed anyway. Which meant this patron was powerful. Or rich. Or both.

Well, that narrows it down . . .

'So what new backwater does my illustrious patron send me to?' Mia asked. 'Last Hope? Amai? Sto—'

'Godsgrave,' Mouser replied.

Mia's tongue cleaved to her teeth, her heart running quicker.

Maw's teeth. The 'Grave . . .

The capital of Itreya. Only the Church's finest Blades served in the City of Bridges and Bones. Grand Cardinal Duomo lived there, as did Consul Scaeva. If Mia wanted revenge for her familia, her first step was getting close to the men who murdered them.

If she'd somehow lucked into a dream posting . . .

'I know your mind,' Solis growled. 'I know why you came to this Church and what it is you seek. So, while I am sending you to the capital against my better judgement, I am telling you this now, and I am telling you once.' Solis towered over her, blind eyes boring into Mia's own. 'Consul Julius Scaeva is not to be touched.'

Mia scowled. 'Wh—'

'I will not tolerate you pursuing your own vendettas while serving this Ministry,' Solis said. 'You already murdered a bara of the Dweymeri out of some misplaced sympathy for the boy you were bedding. I'll not have another unsanctioned kill wrought by your hand. Or your quim.'

'Who I bed is my concern. And you don't get to dec—'

'I do decide!' Solis roared. 'I am Revered Father of this congregation! I give not a beggar's cuss for who you wet the furs with, but Swordbreaker was a fucking king! What if he'd been a patron of this Church? We'd have breached Sanctity! Our reputation shattered over a child's whim.'

'It wasn't a whim, it was a promise!'

'Let us speak of promises, then, girl,' Solis spat. 'Disobey me, and I promise you an ending from which even the Goddess herself would avert her gaze. Scaeva is not to be touched!'

'And why not?' Mia looked among the Ministry, her anger finally getting the better of her. 'The Luminatii killed Lord Cassius, almost killed all of you! You think Scaeva didn't order it? Remus was a fucking lapdog. You think he took a piss without asking the consul's permission first?'

'Hear me now!' Solis raised a finger in warning, blind eyes flashing. 'Scaeva will be dealt with. But in our own way. In our own time. You are a servant of Our Lady of Blessed Murder, and in the Mother's name, that means you fucking serve!'

Mia felt her cheeks flush with rage. She stared into Solis's blind eyes and imagined drawing the gravebone stiletto in her sleeve. Cutting his throat. Spilling his steaming guts onto the floor. But amid the outrage, a single, ice-cold thought took her by the scruff of the neck and shook her 'til she was still.

. . . He's right.

She had been childish.

She had risked the Church's reputation in killing Swordbreaker.

She had thought to kill Duomo and Scaeva if she got back to the 'Grave.

Her knuckles were white on the book in her grip. But she forced her fingers to unclench, speaking words that rang heavy in the quiet dark.

'In the Mother's name. I will serve.'

Solis's huge frame slowly relaxed – Mia realized he was actually hoping she'd buck. But after a long heavy silence, the big man reached into his robe, produced a leather scroll case sealed with black wax.

'One kill. A woman who calls herself "the Dona". Leader of a braavi gang who run in the streets of Little Liis. You grew up there, neh?'

'. . . Aye.' Mia reached for the case.

'One stipulation,' the big man said, holding up his finger. 'An item of import to your patron. A map, written in Old Ashkahi and set with a seal shaped like a sickle's blade. The Dona is brokering an exchange with the map's current owner. You must take the map, along with her life.'

'. . . What's the map of?'

'It provides detailed directions to the Empire of None of Your Fucking Concern.'

'The exchange will take place in the headquarters of the Toffs,' Spiderkiller said. 'Before month's end.'

'That's eight turns from now,' Mia said.

'Black Mother be praised,' Solis replied. 'The girl can count.'

'On both hands, Revered Father.'

Solis gave over the scroll case with a scowl. Mia sucked her lip, mind spinning. Eight turns wasn't long to plan a kill like this. She needed backup she could trust.

'Can I bring my own Hand to the 'Grave?' she asked. 'My last one met a crossbow bolt he didn't like.'

'I fear not,' Aalea said, as if reading her mind. 'Naev is needed here. With most of our blood pools destroyed, our supply situation is critical. A new chapel has been built in the necropolis beneath Godsgrave. The local bishop will provide you with a Hand. Adonai has already sent a blood missive informing him of your arrival.'

Solis tilted his head, milk-white eyes aimed somewhere over Mia's shoulder.

'You have eight turns to end this Dona and recover the map. Your patron may have more offerings for you, presuming you do not perish in pursuit of this first.'

'I'm too pretty to perish.' Mia tossed her fringe from her eyes.

Solis sneered. 'Marielle will tend to your wounds. Adonai will prepare your transportation to Godsgrave. Say your farewells and be in his chambers by midbells.'

Questions bounced around inside her skull. Who was this patron? Why kill a member of the braavi? Why did they request her specifically? What's on this map?

It doesn't matter, she realized.

It wasn't her place to ask. It was her place to serve. The sooner she proved herself, the sooner she'd earn a permanent posting in the Godsgrave Chapel. And from there, no matter what Solis might say, she'd be one step closer to her revenge.

The wolf did not pity the lamb.

The storm begged no forgiveness of the drowned.

'I'll not fail,' Mia vowed. 'In the Black Mother's name, I swear it.'

Solis folded his arms, his face unreadable in the gloom.

'Go,' he finally said. 'May Our Lady be late when she finds you. And when she does, may she greet you with a kiss.'

Mia took the scroll case, tucked it under her arm along with her beaten book. Bowing low, she backed slowly out of the hall. As she stalked away down the darkened corridors, past beautiful stained-glass windows and grotesque bone sculptures, two shapes slipped from the darkness and fell into step alongside her.

A cat made of shadows. And beside it, a wolf of the same.

'*Can you believe him?' Mia hissed. 'Calling me "acolyte," the bastard.'*

'*. . . you act as if solis's bastardry is some kind of revelation . . .' Mister Kindly replied.*

Eclipse's growl came from somewhere beneath the floor.

'. . . CASSIUS ALWAYS THOUGHT OF HIM AS AN ARROGANT THUG. OF ALL THE MINISTRY, HE LIKED SOLIS LEAST. ONE TURN, WE SHOULD TEACH HIM A LESSON IN MANNERS . . .'

'*. . . there are less dramatic forms of suicide, pup . . .*'

'. . . SO LITTLE FAITH IN OUR MISTRESS, LITTLE KITTEN . . .'

'*. . . she is not yours, you w—*'

'*Black Mother, enough,' Mia snapped, rubbing her temples. 'The last thing I need to hear right now is you two bickering like a pair of old maids.'*

Her passengers fell quiet, leaving only a disembodied choir to echo in the dark. Mia took a deep breath, tried to pull her notorious temper into check. They were still treating her like a novice. Despite all she'd done. But if nothing else, she was headed to Godsgrave. The patronage of this mysterious benefactor was unexpected, but in truth she was glad somebody was recognizing the talent it took to murder a justicus and a hundred of his men. If it got her closer to Scaeva and Duomo, all the better.

But still, her mind swam with images of her fight in the necropolis. That thing and its gravebone blades, the tentacles writhing at the edges of its cowl. Though she couldn't find it in her to be afraid with the shadows so thick at her feet, she knew there was something grander at play here.

She looked at the book under her arm, running her fingers across the timeworn cover. The tarnished brass clasp.

'*Seek the Crown of the Moon,' she muttered.*

'*. . . we have until midbells . . .*'

The girl hooked her thumbs into her belt.

Realized she was dying for a smoke.

'*Time enough to take my library books back.*'

H er cell smelled like piss and stale misery.

The straw was musty, the bucket in the corner crusted in filth and flies. Mia had been escorted from the Pit, Teardrinker nodding farewell as she was taken out through the gates. Four heavyset legionaries had marched her across the roiling marketplace, finally locking her in a holding pen inside a large administratii building. Though her price was settled, coin had yet to be paid. She had a few hours before her new domina took full possession. A few hours to pull together the tattered threads of her plan.

'. . . *we must inform the viper . . .*'

Mia scowled at Mister Kindly. He was only a darker shape against the shadows thrown by the bars across the floor. The cells beside Mia's were empty, but she kept her voice a whisper.

'I wish you wouldn't call her that.'

'. . . *you have another term less flattering . . . ?*'

'You could use her bloody name.'

The not-cat made a sniffing sound; impressive for a creature without lungs.

'. . . *we were supposed to be purchased by leonides. leonides's daughter bought you instead. the viper has no way of knowing this. she and eclipse will be waiting for us at leonides's collegium in whitekeep as planned . . .*'

'That *was* something of an oversight,' Mia admitted.

'. . . *this entire plan is oversight and folly, stitched together by jiggery-fuckery . . .*'

'I know what I'm doing.'

'. . . *a pity, then, that the viper does not . . .*'

Mia sighed. 'You'll have to go tell her. Can you make your way to Whitekeep?'

'. . . *i am certain i can find a ship to stow aboard. but what will you do . . . ?*'

'What else can I do?' Mia shrugged. 'Train in Leona's stable. Fight. Win. The destination hasn't changed, just the starting point.'

'. . . *and where do i tell the viper to meet you? where is your new dona's collegium . . . ?*'

'I've no fucking idea.'

'. . . *o, aye. you certainly know what you're doing . . .*'

Mia flipped the knuckles at the shadowcat, dragged her matted hair behind her ears. She was still covered in dried blood, old sweat, dust. Sitting in the straw, she tried not to picture the faces of the men she'd killed in the Pit. She'd needed to impress, and she'd done so . . . after a fashion. She'd killed dozens who'd stood in her way before now. But still, those pit fighters had only been doing as they were bid . . .

'I feel like shit,' she sighed.

'. . . *you do not smell particularly pleasant either . . .*'

'That's not what I—'

'. . . *you cannot afford to pity those men, mia. swimming this deep, your*' *compassion will only serve to drown you. you must be as hard and as sharp as the men you hunt . . .'*

'If not for the pity I took in my final trial at the Red Church, I'd have been at the initiation feast when Ashlinn and Osrik poisoned the Ministry. We'd *all* be dead.'

'*. . . you're just going to keep rubbing that in, aren't y—*'

Footsteps echoed down the corridor, and the not-cat faded away like smoke. Mia looked up to see an administratii unlocking her cell. The man was stocky, bearded, clad in white robes marked with the three suns of the Itreyan Republic. Beside him stood a young boy in a short-sleeved novice frock, carrying a tall chair and a mahogany box.

Dona Leona walked softly into the cell, followed by one of the most well-built men Mia had ever seen. He was Itreyan, perhaps in his mid-thirties, thick beard going grey at the edges, thick hair swept up and back in a long tail. His skin was like leather, and a particularly vicious scar bisected his brow, cheek, and lip, twisting his features into a perpetual scowl. His stare was bloodshot, and he leaned heavily on a walking stick, its handle shaped like a lion's head. Looking down, Mia saw he was missing his left leg below the knee, an iron pin affixed there instead.

He scowled at Mia with steel-blue eyes, his voice like cracking stone.

'She's a girl.'

Dona Leona raised one perfectly manicured brow. 'I noticed.'

''Byss and blood, Dona, you dropped a thousand silver on this slip? I'm not a miracle worker. I need good clay to work with.'

'She killed five men in five minutes,' Leona said. 'She was worth every coin.'

'A bloody good thing, then. Since we've not a beggar left to our names.'

'We've two other purchases this trip, both fine stock. And you've no cause to rebuke me, Executus. If you weren't out drinking the Gardens dry yestereve, you'd have been with me this morn when I made purchase.'

The big man grunted, looked again at Mia.

'On your feet, slave.'

Mia complied mutely, stood with hands clasped. The man limped in a circle around her, iron leg clanking on the stone. He poked the muscle at her gut, squeezed her biceps with massive hands, checked her teeth. Mia endured the inspection silently, eyes downturned. She could smell goldwine on his breath.

'She's too short,' he declared. 'No reach in these arms.'

'She is fast as the wind,' Leona replied.

'She's too young. It'll be years before she's ready for the sand.'

'Five men,' Leona repeated, 'in five minutes.'

'She's a *girl*,' the big man growled.

'So was I,' the dona replied softly. 'And you never thought lesser of me for it.'

'One sniff of her and the men will lose their fucking minds.'

'Did my father not say the same about me when I'd visit the collegium? And was it not you who asked that I be allowed to stay? To learn?'

'A different tale, Mi Dona. You were the domini's daughter. This slip's going to be down in the barracks with the rest of them.'

'And until she proves herself in the Winnowing, you will ensure my investment comes to no harm,' Leona said coolly.

'She'll never survive the Winnowing.'

'Then you will have the distinct pleasure of saying "I told you so," Executus.'

The big man scowled at Mia. She met his stare, just for a second. Fury burned in the blacks of her pupils as a silent vow echoed in her mind.

You'll be eating those words come truelight, bastard.

'What's your name?' he asked.

'They call me Crow, Mi Don,' she replied, eyes once more to the floor.

'Do I look like a fucking don to you, girl? You will address me as Executus.'

It was all Mia could do not to bury her knee in his bollocks. Punch his teeth loose from his jaw and dance on his head.

'Yes, Executus,' she replied.

The man glowered, his expression turned all the darker by his scar. Bladework, she reckoned. Probably earned somewhere on the sand. He moved like a fighter. Graceful and powerful, despite the missing leg.

'We sail on the morrowtide,' Leona said. 'The sooner we return to Crow's Nest and begin her training, the better.'

Mia's heart surged in her chest.

'. . . Crow's Nest?' she whispered.

The slap knocked her back into the wall. Her head cracked on the stone and she collapsed to her knees, gasping. She was back on her feet in a moment, eyes flashing with hatred as she glared at the man who'd slapped her. But quick as silver, the executus's fist crashed into her belly, sending her to her knees once more.

He's fast . . .

Mia felt a brutish hand in her hair, dragging back her head as she gasped in pain.

'You forget your place, girl,' the big man said. 'If ever again you speak in presence of your domina without being spoken to, I'll set my blade to your tongue and feed it to my fucking dog. Do you hear me?'

Patience . . .

'Yes, Executus,' she whispered.

The man grunted, released his hold. Mia glanced up at Leona, saw the woman regarding her with a cool, imperious gaze. Whatever her opinion of Mia's martial skills, it was clear her new domina had no issue with her man's brutal methods.

After a moment's tense silence, Dona Leona turned to the administratii, still waiting patiently in the corridor.

'Come, then, be about your work.'

The administratii shuffled into the cell, his novice beside him. The boy plonked the tall chair down beside Mia, opened the mahogany box he carried and proffered it to the administratii. Inside Mia saw a collection of iron needles. Powders in stoppered phials, small bottles of ink. Her shadow surged, fear swelling in her belly. She knew this was coming. It was all part of the game. But still . . .

'Sit,' the administratii said.

Mia dragged herself up from the floor, glanced at the buckles and straps on the chair's armrests. They obviously intended to bind her for what came next. She knew if she spoke again, she'd only earn herself another blow. And so she fixed her stare on the small barred window, the blue sky beyond. And she remained standing.

The executus growled deep, raised his hand to strike.

'Do as you're—'

'No,' Dona Leona said, watching Mia with curious eyes. 'Let her stand.'

'All respect, Dona Leona,' said the administratii, 'but this is no simple inkwerk. The process is arkemical. The pain immense. She is likely to swoon.'

Mia thought back to her scourging at Weaver Marielle's hands and almost laughed at the word. That same laughter twinkled in Dona Leona's eyes.

'A hundred silver says she does nothing of the sort.'

The executus groaned softly. The administratii looked taken aback.

'I am not a gambling man, Mi Dona.'

'But you *are* a man who insists on telling me what I already know?' Leona's tone turned razor-sharp. 'I grew up in the finest gladiatii collegium in all the Itreyan Republic. I know how a damned slave brand works. Now proceed.'

The administratii almost succeeded in stifling his sigh. He turned to the box, set about unstopping phials, mixing components into a shallow glass bowl. The poisoncrafter in Mia watched with interest, noting the way the arkemical concoction came together, bubbling and hissing and spitting black.*

The administratii dipped his needle, raised it to Mia's face. The novice stood behind her, held her head steady. The girl forced herself to be still, grit her teeth. Lining up the steel against Mia's cheek, the administratii hefted a thin jeweller's hammer. The girl held her breath. And without further foreplay, the administratii smacked the needle through Mia's cheek and straight into the bone beyond.

Black fire. Burning agony. Mia's eyes grew wide, pupils dilated, the pain lancing through her skull and stealing her breath away. Her knees buckled, black stars bursting in her eyes. The administratii stepped back, obviously expecting her to fall. But with her shadow swelling, chest heaving, the girl remained on her feet.

Mia looked at Leona. The dona was watching her with a growing smile.

'Well?' the woman asked the administratii. 'Proceed!'

The man shrugged, and with no more pause for drama, began hammering the needle into Mia's cheek, over and over again. Small series of three tiny blows, each like a thunderclap in her head.

tapTAPTAP

---

* The arkemy of slave brands is a secret tightly guarded by the Itreyan administratii. The process not only marks a person's skin, but also the bone beneath, and the tattoo will bleed through scar tissue and reassert itself should the recipient decide to remove their brand through knifework or flame.

There are only four ways to remove an arkemical brand.

First, at the hands of the administratii, after one's freedom is purchased or earned. Second, by Ashkahi sorcery. Third, by hacking out pieces of one's own skull, but since wandering about with a missing cheekbone is something of a giveaway of one's fugitive status, the agony is hardly worth it. And lastly, by dying – through some rude semblance of Old Ashkahi bloodmagik, the arkemical brand is tied to the recipient's own life, and once it ends, the mark on their cheek will slowly dissolve over the course of the next few minutes.

Thus, the only freedom most slaves ever achieve is in the arms of death.

tap TAP TAP
Fingernails digging into her palms.
White spots swelling before her eyes.
The room rolling beneath her like a ship in a storm.
tap TAP TAP
tap TAP TAP
The anticipation was the worst of it. The moment between one sequence and the next. That tiny respite that seemed an eternity, waiting for the pain to begin again. Adonai's scourging, Marielle's weaving . . . nothing she'd ever felt in her life had come close, made all the worse by the bitter thought that in this moment, to the world outside this cell, her life was no longer her own.
tap TAP TAP
If not for Mister Kindly, she thought she might have broken.
tap TAP TAP
But at the end
after all the pain
all the praying
cheek bleeding
legs trembling
Mia still stood.
'A good thing,' Dona Leona declared, 'that you are not a betting man, sir.'
The administratii packed up his gear without a word. Aiming a poison glance at Mia, he gave a curt bow to the dona, and with his novice trailing behind, swept from the cell with a rustle of white cloth. Leona turned to her executus with a triumphant smile.
'You ask for clay to work with, Executus? I give you steel.'
The big man looked at Mia with narrowed eyes. 'Steel breaks before it bends.'
'Four Daughters, you're never happy, are you?' Leona sighed. 'Come. We should let her rest. She will need her strength in turns to come.'
The dona cupped Mia's face, wiping her wounded cheek with a gentle thumb. Sapphire-blue eyes burning into her own.
'We will bleed the sands red, you and I,' she said. '*Sanguii e Gloria.*'
Gifting her a final smile, Leona swept from the room in a flurry of blue silk. The executus limped after her, locked the door behind him. The clank of his iron leg faded with his dona down the corridor.
Mia sank to her knees. Her cheek was swollen, throbbing with pain. Her palms were bleeding from the press of her nails. She ran her

fingertips over her skin, feeling the raised ridges of the two interlocking circles branded just below her right eye. But beneath the remembered agony, her mind was racing, the dona's words tumbling inside her skull with the echoes of the hammer blows.

They're taking me to—

'. . . *crow's nest* . . . ?'

She glanced up at the not-cat, once more cleaning his not-paw with his not-tongue. Licking at parched lips, she tried to find her voice.

'It was the home of the Familia Corvere. *My* familia. Consul Scaeva gave it to Justicus Remus as reward for ending my father's rebellion against the Senate.'

'. . . *and now leona owns it* . . . ?'

Mia shrugged mutely. The not-cat tilted his head.

'. . . *are you well* . . . ?'

Her father, holding her hand as they walked in fields of tall sunsbell flowers. Her mother standing atop battlements of ochre stone, cool wind playing in her long dark hair. Mia had grown up in Godsgrave – her father's role as justicus meant he could never stay away from the City of Bridges and Bones for long. But every few summersdeeps, they'd travelled to Crow's Nest for a week or two, just to be with one another. Those had been the happiest turns of Mia's life. Away from Godsgrave's crush, its poison politics. Her parents seemed happier there. Closer somehow. Her brother Jonnen had been born there. She remembered visits from General Antonius, the would-be king who'd hanged beside her father. He and her parents would stay up late into the night, drinking and laughing and O, so alive.

All of them gone now.

'. . . *i should go. find a ship bound for whitekeep. tell the viper to seek you in crow's nest* . . .'

'. . . Aye,' she nodded.

'. . . *will you be all right while i am gone* . . . ?'

The thought should have terrified her. She knew if Mister Kindly weren't there, it would have. For seven years, ever since her father died, the shadowcat had been beside her. She knew he had to leave, that she couldn't do this all by herself. But the thought of being alone, of living with the fear he usually drank to nothing . . .

'I'll be well enough,' she replied. 'Just don't dawdle.'

'. . . *i will be swift. never fear* . . .'

She sighed. Pressed her hand to the brand on her throbbing cheek. 'And never, ever forget.'

CHAPTER 6

MORTALITY

The athenaeum opened at the touch of Mia's finger, the colossal stone doors swinging wide as if they were carved of feathers. And taking a deep breath, clutching her tome to her breast, she limped out into her favourite place in the entire world.

Looking out over the mezzanine to the endless shelves below, the girl couldn't help but smile. She'd grown up inside books. No matter how dark life became, shutting out the hurt was as easy as opening a cover. A child of murdered parents and a failed rebellion, she'd still walked in the boots of scholars and warriors, queens and conquerors.

The heavens grant us only one life, but through books, we live a thousand.

'A girl with a story to tell,' came a voice from behind her.

Smiling, Mia turned to see an old man standing beside a trolley piled high with books. He wore a scruffy waistcoat, two shocks of white hair trying to flee his balding scalp. Thick spectacles sat on a hooked nose, his back bent like a sickle. The word 'ancient' did him as much justice as the word 'beautiful' did Shahiid Aalea.

'Good turn to you, Chronicler,' Mia bowed.

Without asking, Chronicler Aelius plucked his ever-present spare cigarillo from behind his ear, lit it on his own and offered it to Mia. Leaning against the wall with a wince as her stitches pulled, she puffed and sighed a shade of contented grey.

Aelius leaned beside her, his own cigarillo bobbing on his lips as he spoke.

'All right?'

'All right,' she nodded.

'How was Galante?'

Mia winced again, the pain of her sutures twinging in her backside.

'A pain in the arse,' she muttered.

The old man grinned around his smoke. 'So what brings you down here?'

Mia held up the tome she'd brought with her across the blood walk. It was bound in stained leather, tattered and beaten. The strange symbols embossed in the cover hurt her eyes to look at and its pages were yellowed with age.

'I supposed I should return this. I've had it eight months.'

'I was starting to think I'd have to send out a search party.'

'That'd be unpleasant for all concerned, I'd bet.'

The old man smiled. 'The late fees are rather exorbitant in a library like this.'

The chronicler had left the book in Mia's room, right before she was posted to Galante. In the intervening months, she'd pored over the pages more times than she could count. The pity of it was, she still didn't understand the half of it, and truth told, in recent turns, she'd become more than a little disillusioned about it. But her encounter in the Galante necropolis had renewed her interest tenfold.

The book was written by a woman named Cleo – a darkin like Mia, who spoke to the shadows just as she did. Cleo lived in a time before the Republic, and the book was a diary of sorts, detailing her journey through Itreya and beyond. It spoke of meetings between her and other darkin – meetings that ended with Cleo apparently eating her fellows. The strange thing was, from Cleo's writing, she'd encountered dozens of other darkin in her travels. And from the look of the woman's scribbled self-portraits, she was accompanied by dozens of passengers, wearing a multitude of different shapes – foxes, birds, serpents, and the like. An entire shadow menagerie at her command.

In all her life, the only darkin Mia had met was Lord Cassius. And the only two daemons were Mister Kindly and Eclipse.

So where the 'byss were the rest of them?

Amid nonsense scrawl and pictograms that spoke of her ever-growing madness, the latter half of the book concerned Cleo's search for something she called 'the Crown of the Moon' – just as that shadowthing in the Galante necropolis had told Mia to do. And flipping through the illustrations after her encounter, Mia had seen several that bore an uncanny resemblance to the figure that had saved her life.

Sadly, Cleo made no mention of who or what this 'Moon' might be.

The book was written in an arcane language Mia had never seen, but

Mister Kindly and Eclipse were both able to read it. Strangest of all, it contained a map of the world in the time before the Republic, but the bay of Godsgrave was missing entirely. Instead, a landmass filled the sea where the Itreyan capital now stood. This peninsula was marked with an X, and an unsettling declaration:

Here he fell.

'Did you read this before you gave it to me?' Mia asked.

The old man shook his head. 'Couldn't make out a bloody word. Only thing that made me think of you was the pictures. Make any sense to you?'

'. . . Not half as much as I'd like.'

Aelius shrugged. 'You asked me to look for books on darkin, and so I did. Didn't promise you'd be any more enlightened when you were done.'

'No need to rub it in, good Chronicler.'

Aelius smirked. 'I'm always on the lookout for more. If I find anything else of interest down here, I'll send it to your chambers. But I'd not hold my breath.'

Mia nodded, dragging on her smoke. Niah's athenaeum was actually a library of the dead. It contained a copy of every book that had ever been destroyed in the history of the written language. Moreover, it also held other tomes that had never been written in the first place. Memoirs of murdered tyrants. Theorems of crucified heretics. Masterpieces of geniuses who ended before their time.

Chronicler Aelius had told her new books were appearing constantly, that the shelves were always shifting. And though Niah's athenaeum was a wondrous place as a result, the downside was plain: finding a particular book in here was like trying to find a particular louse in a dockside sweetboy's crotch.

'Chronicler, have you heard of the Moon? Or any crowns said Moon might be partial to?'

Aelius's stare turned wary.

'Why?'

'You answer questions with questions an awful lot,' Mia sighed. 'Why is that?'

'Do you remember what I said that turn you first came down here?'

'See, there you go again.'

'Do you remember?'

'You said I was a girl with a story to tell.'

'And what else?'

Smoke drifted from the girl's lips as the old man stared her down.

'You said maybe here's not where I'm supposed to be,' she finally replied. 'Which stank like horseshit at the time, and smells even worse now. I proved *myself. The Ministry would all be nailed to crosses in the 'Grave if not for me. And I'm sick and bloody tired of everybody around here seeming to forget that.'*

'You don't find any irony in earning your place in a cult of assassins by saving half a dozen lives?'

'I killed almost a hundred men in the process, Aelius.'

'And how do you feel about that?'

'What are you, my nursemaid?' Mia snapped. 'A killer is what I am. The wolf doesn't pity the lamb. And the—'

'Aye, aye, I know the tune.'

'And you know why I'm here. My father was executed as a traitor to entertain a mob. My mother died in a prison, and my baby brother beside her. And the men responsible need a fucking killing. That's how I feel about it.'

The old man hooked his thumbs into his waistcoat. 'Problem with being a librarian is there's some lessons you just can't learn from books. And the problem with being an assassin is there's some mysteries you just can't solve by stabbing fuck out of them.'

'Always riddles with you,' Mia growled. 'Do you know about this Moon or no?'

The old man sucked on his cigarillo, looked her up and down. 'I know this much. Some answers are learned. But the important ones are earned.'

'O, Black Goddess, now you're a poet, too?'

The chronicler frowned, crushed his cigarillo out against the wall.

'Poets are wankers.'

Aelius dropped the murdered butt of his smoke into his waistcoat. He looked down at the book in Mia's hand. Back up into her eyes.

'You can keep that. Nobody else can read it anyways.'

With a small nod, he took hold of his RETURNS trolley.

'What, that's all the explanation I get?' Mia asked.

Aelius shrugged. 'Too many books. Too few centuries.'

The old man wheeled his trolley off into the dark. Watching him fade into the shadows, the girl took a savage drag of her cigarillo, jaw clenched.

'. . . well, that was enlightening . . .'

'. . . AELIUS HAS ALWAYS BEEN THAT WAY. BEING CRYPTIC MAKES HIM FEEL IMPORTANT . . .'

Mia scowled at the shadowwolf materializing beside her.

'Are you sure Lord Cassius never learned anything of this, Eclipse? He was head of the entire congregation. You're telling me he knew nothing about what it was to be darkin? Cleo? The Moon? Any of it?'

'. . . I TOLD YOU, WE NEVER LOOKED. CASSIUS FOUND ENOUGH MEANING IN LIFE BY ENDING THE LIVES OF OTHERS. HE NEEDED NO MORE THAN THAT . . .'

Mister Kindly snorted. '. . . small things and small minds . . .'

'. . . HAVE A CARE, LITTLE GRIMALKIN. HE WAS MY FRIEND WHEN YOU WERE STILL SHAPELESS. HE WAS AS BEAUTIFUL AS THE DARK AND AS SHARP AS THE MOTHER'S TEETH. SPEAK NO ILL OF HIM . . .'

Mia sighed, pinching the bridge of her nose. She couldn't understand how Cassius had never sought the truth of himself. She'd wondered on it since she was a child. Old Mercurio and Mother Drusilla had said she was chosen of the Goddess.

But chosen for what?

She remembered fighting in the streets of Last Hope with Ashlinn. Her attack on the Basilica Grande when she was fourteen. On both occasions, simply looking at the trinity – the holy symbol of Aa – had caused her agony. The Light God hated her. She'd felt it. Sure as the ground beneath her feet. But why? And what the 'byss did this 'Moon' have to do with any of it?

And Remus.

Fucking Remus.

He was dead by her hand on a dusty Last Hope thoroughfare. His attack on the Mountain failed. His men slaughtered on the sands all around him. But before she'd plunged her gravebone blade into his throat, the justicus had uttered words that turned her entire world upside down.

'I will give your brother your regards.'

Mia shook her head.

But Jonnen is *dead*. Mother told me so.

So many questions. Mia could taste frustration mixed with the smoke on her tongue. But her answers were in Godsgrave. And Black Mother be praised, that was exactly where this mysterious patron of hers was sending her.

Time to stop moaning and start moving.

Mia limped out from the athenaeum. Down the winding stair towards the Church's belly. Through the puddles of stained-glass light, Mister Kindly on her shoulder and Eclipse prowling before her. The Church choir rang as they trod the winding stairs, the long and twisting halls, until finally, they reached Weaver Marielle's chambers.

She took a breath, rapped on the heavy door. It opened after a moment, and Mia found herself looking into scarlet eyes, down to a beautiful, bloodless smile.

'Blade Mia,' Adonai said.

The Blood Speaker was clad in his indecent britches and red silk robe, open as ever at his chest. The room beyond was lit by a single arkemical lamp, the walls adorned with hundreds of different masques, all shapes and sizes. Death masques and children's masques and Carnivalé masques. Glass and ceramic and papier-mâché. A room of faces, without a single mirror in sight.

'Thou art here for a weaving,' Adonai said.

'Aye,' Mia nodded, meeting those blood-red eyes without fear. 'Wounds heal in time, but I'll not have much of it where I'm headed.'

'The City of Bridges and Bones,' the speaker mused. 'No place more dangerous in all the Republic.'

'You've not seen my laundry basket,' Mia replied.

Adonai smirked, glanced over his shoulder.

'Sister love, sister mine? Thou hast company.'

Mia saw a misshapen form shuffle into the arkemical glow. The woman was albino pale like her brother, but what little Mia could see of her skin was swollen and cracked, blood and pus leaking through the bandages about her hands and face. She was clad in a black velvet robe, her lips splitting as she looked at Mia and smiled.

'Blade Mia,' Marielle whispered.

'Weaver Marielle,' Mia said, bowing.

'To the 'Grave she goes. At Father Solis's word, to a new patron's arms. And though stitched, still she bleeds.' Adonai shivered slightly. 'I smell it on her.'

'All thy hurts shall be mended, little darkin,' Marielle lisped. 'Sure and true.'

The weaver nodded to the dreaded stone slab that dominated her room. It was set with leather straps and buckles of polished steel – though Marielle could weave flesh like clay and mend almost any wound, the process itself was agony. Mia hated the thought of being bound for the process, truth told. Trussed up like some hog at the spit, britches around her ankles. But, resigning herself to the pain, feeling the shadows within her shadow drink down her fear, Mia limped into the chamber.

As he closed the door behind her, Speaker Adonai caught her arm.

Mia looked up into his glittering eyes, snow-pale lashes. He leaned close, closer, and for a terrible, thrilling moment, she thought he might kiss her. But instead, Adonai spoke with lowered voice, lips brushing her ear, barely a whisper.

'Two lives ye saved, the turn the Luminatii pressed their sunsteel to the

Mountain's throat. Mine, and my sister love's. Marielle's debt to thee was repaid the turn she gave Naev back her face. But my debt, little Blade, is still owed. Know this, in nevernights to come. As deep and dark as the waters ye swim might turn, on matters of blood, count upon a speaker's vow, ye may.'

Adonai fixed her in his scarlet stare, voice as sharp as the gravebone at her wrist.

'Blood is owed thee, little Crow,' he whispered. 'And blood shall be repaid.'

Mia glanced to Marielle. Back up into Adonai's glittering red eyes. Her mind swimming with thoughts of Godsgrave. Braavi. Stolen maps and hidden patrons and a Ministry that seemed to feel nothing but ire towards her.

'. . . Do you know something that I don't, Speaker?'

A beautiful, bloodless smile was her only reply. With a swish of his scarlet robe, Speaker Adonai motioned to his sister. Mia turned to the Room of Faces and its mistress, looming above that awful slab. Marielle beckoned her with twisted fingers.

No matter what was to come, it was too late to turn back now.

And heaving a sigh, Mia lay down on the stone.

She almost wept when she saw it.

It rose from the clifftops and pierced the sky, ochre stone bleeding through to gold in the light of two burning suns. A keep carved out of the cliffs themselves, once home to one of the twelve finest familia of the Republic.

Crow's Nest.

Mia knelt on the deck of the *Gloryhound* and stared, overcome with memories. Walking in the bustling port, hand in hand with her mother. The shopkeeps calling her 'little dona' and bringing her sweets. Her father striding the battlements above the ocean, sea breeze playing in his hair as he stares across the waves. Dreaming, perhaps, of the rebellion that would be his undoing.

She'd been too young to understand, too small to—

Crack!

The whip snapped across her shoulder blades, bright red pain tearing her from her reverie.

'I gave no permission for you to stop! Chin to the boards!'

Mia risked a hateful glance at the executus, looming over her with a long stock whip in hand. Sweat was dripping down her face, hair clinging to her skin. A second strike across her back was her reward for her hesitation. Arms burning with fatigue, she dropped into another push-up and rose again. Black spots swam in her eyes. The two men beside her did the same, grunting with exertion.

The journey from the Hanging Gardens had taken almost three weeks. Every turn, she and the two other slaves Leona had purchased at market were taken up on deck and run through exercises, and the sound of the executus's stock whip was starting to haunt her dreams.

Her first comrade in captivity was a hard Liisian boy named Matteo. He looked a few years older than Mia, with softly curling hair, strong arms and a pretty smile. Despite his impressive physique, Matteo had been sick as a dog for the first week they'd been at sea – Mia guessed he'd never set foot on a ship in his life.

Her second bedfellow was a burly Itreyan named Sidonius. He was in his late twenties and looked hard as a coffin nail. Bright blue eyes and a shaven head. He seemed the meaner of the pair, and looked at Mia like he wanted to fuck and/or kill her. She wasn't quite sure in which order. She wasn't sure Sidonius was either. Strangest of all, the man had a rough brand that looked to have been burned into his skin with a red-hot blade. A single word, carved right across his chest.

COWARD.

He offered no explanation for it, and Mia didn't like him enough to ask.

After another thirty-two push-ups, the executus signalled the three to stop, and Mia collapsed face-first onto the deck, arms trembling.

'Your upper body strength is a jest,' the big man growled at her. 'And yet, my lips are absent laughter.'

'Enough for the turn, Executus,' called Dona Leona from her seat on the foredeck. 'They'll need to be able to walk when they meet their new familia.'

'On your feet.'

Mia stood slowly, staring out at the ocean. The welts on her back tickled with the sting of her sweat. The executus's salt-and-pepper hair whipped about in the ocean breeze, his beard bristling as he glared. Long minutes ticked by in silence, only the calls of gulls and the sounds of the distant port for company.

'Drink,' the executus finally grunted.

Mia turned and practically dashed for the water barrel lashed to the main mast. The big Itreyan, Sidonius, shoved her aside with a curse, snatching up the ladle and drinking his fill. Mia seethed, half-tempted to knock the thug on his arse as she waited her turn, but the sensible part of her brain counselled patience. When Sidonius finished drinking, Matteo flashed her his pretty smile, waved to the barrel.

'After you, Mi Dona.'

Crack!

The boy winced as the executus's whip found his back.

'I gave no permission for you to speak!'

The boy gritted his teeth, bowed apology. Mia nodded thanks, turned to the water barrel, gulping down mouthful after sweet mouthful.

It chafed her almost to screaming, bowing down to these people. Told when to eat, when to drink, when to shit. The executus's contempt for them was matched only by Dona Leona's ambivalence. On the one hand, the woman treated them with a sort of affection, and spoke of the glory to come on the sands of the *venatus*. But on the other, she had them whipped for the smallest slight. They weren't allowed to look her in the eye. They spoke only when spoken to. Performing on command.

Like favoured dogs, Mia realized.

Mia's parents had slaves when she was a little girl – every noble familia in the Republic did. But Mia's nanny, Caprice, was practically treated like blood, and her father's majordomo, a Liisian named Andriano Varnese, stayed on to serve the justicus even after he'd purchased his freedom.*

Even on the run for her life as a child, even sworn into the service of the Black Mother, Mia had never really understood what it was to not belong to herself. The thought of it burned her, like the memory of that needle being hammered into her skin. Again and again. The indignity. The shame.

But you cannot win if you do not play.

---

*In marrowborn houses and some well-established places of business, it is not uncommon for slaves to be paid for their labour – the notion being, a slave with the ability to buy back their freedom with enough hard work will work fucking hard indeed.

The rate of pay is totally unregulated, however, and many slaves earn a pittance. Unscrupulous masters will often charge a slave for their upkeep and deduct the cost from their 'earnings,' with the result that a lifetime of labour will not earn back the sum paid for their initial purchase.

Unfair? Absolutely. But if the system were fair, it wouldn't be much of a system, gentlefriends.

The *Gloryhound* dropped anchor in the harbour, and a short row later, Mia stood with her fellow captives on the bustling docks of the cityport beneath Crow's Nest, known as Crow's Rest. Her wrists were manacled and chafed, her clothes filthy, her hair a matted mess. Mister Kindly's absence was a knife wound in her belly, bleeding all the warmth right out of her. She looked down to her shadow, once dark enough for two, even three. Now, no different than any other around her. Fear hovered about her on black wings, and for the first time in a long time, she had to face it alone.

What if she failed?

What if she wasn't strong enough?

What if this gambit was just as foolish as Mister Kindly had warned?

'Move!' came the cry, punctuated by the sting of knotted leather on her back.

Gritting her teeth, as was now the custom, Mia did as she was told.

A wagon ride later, she was trundling into the courtyard of Crow's Nest, heart aching inside her chest. The keep seemed so familiar, the sights, the sounds, Black Mother, even the smells were unchanged. But decorating the ochre stone of the courtyard walls where the Crow of Corvere once flew, she saw the familia crest of Marcus Remus – a red falcon on a crossed black-and-white field.

I have a decidedly sinking feeling about this . . .

Memories of her childhood were awash in her head, mingled with images of her parents' end. Her father executed along with General Antonius before a howling mob. Her mother and brother dead in the Philosopher's Stone. Some part of her had always known this castle was no longer hers, that her home was not her home. But to see that bastard Remus's colours still on the walls, even after she'd buried him . . . she felt as if the whole world were shifting beneath her feet. A sickness swelled in her belly, greasy and rolling. And still, she had no time to muse on the end of her old familia.

Her new one was waiting for her.

They stood in a row, like legionaries awaiting inspection. Thirteen men and two women, dressed in loincloths and piecemeal leather armour – spaulders, padded shin guards, and the like. Sweat-soaked skin gleamed in the light of two burning suns, giving them the look of statues cast in bronze. Men and women who fought on the sands of the *venatus*, who lived and died to the cheers of a blood-drunk crowd.

Gladiatii.

As Dona Leona climbed down from the wagon, each of them slammed a fist to their chest and roared as one.

'Domina!'

Leona pressed her fingers to her lips, blew them kisses.

'My Falcons.' She smiled. 'You look *magnificent.*'

The executus cracked his whip, barked at Mia and her fellows to get out of the wagon. Sidonius pushed his way out first as usual. Matteo again smiled, motioned she should go before him. Mia climbed down onto the dirt, felt fifteen sets of eyes appraising her every inch. She saw lips curl, eyes narrow in derision. But the gladiatii were as disciplined as any soldier, and none breathed a word in the presence of their mistress.

'I will leave you to introductions, Executus,' Dona Leona said. 'I have an appointment with a ledger and a very long, very deep bath.'

'Your whisper, my will,' the big man bowed.

The woman disappeared beneath a tall stone archway and into the keep beyond. Mia's eyes followed, watching the way she spoke with the servants, the way she moved. The girl was reminded a little of her mother. Leona w—

Crack!

The snap of the executus's lash caught her full and complete attention.

The big man stood before them, whip in one hand. In the other, he held a handful of ochre earth from the ground at his feet, slowly letting it trickle through his fingers. He looked Mia and the other newcomers in the eye, spoke with a voice like breaking rock.

'What do I hold in my hand?'

Mia saw the ruse right away. Felt it in the hungry eyes of the gladiatii assembled behind the executus. She was new to this game, but not fool enough to fall for—

'Sand, Executus,' said Matteo.

Crack!

The whip flashed across the air between them, left a bleeding welt across Matteo's chest. The boy staggered, his pretty face twisted in pain. The assembled gladiatii sneered as one.

Mia studied the fighters, assessing each in turn. The eldest couldn't be more than twenty-five. Each wore the twin interlocking circles of a fighter's slavemark branded into their cheek. Each was a stunning physical specimen – all hard muscle and gleaming skin. But apart from that, they were each as different as iron and clay.

She saw a Dweymeri woman, with saltlocks so long they almost touched the floor. Her tattoos, which normally marked a Dweymeri's face, covered her entire body, flowing over her deep brown skin like black waterfalls. A Vaanian girl around Mia's age stood beside her, blonde topknot and bright green eyes. She was barefoot, almost slight compared to her fellows. Mia looked to these women to see if she'd sense some sort of kinship or sympathy, but both stared through her as if she were made of glass.

'What do I hold in my hand?' Executus repeated.

Mia remained silent, that sickness swelling in her belly. She doubted there was a right answer, or that the executus would acknowledge it even if it was given. And she was sure one of the two she'd ridden in with were stupid enough to—

'Glory, Executus,' said Sidonius.

Crack!

The assembled gladiatii chuckled as Sidonius dropped to the floor, clutching split and bloody lips. Executus could wield that whip like a Caravaggio fighter wielded a rapier, and he'd gifted the big Itreyan a blow right across his fool mouth.

'You are nothing,' Executus growled. 'Unworthy to lick the shit from my boot. What do you know of glory? It is a hymn of sand and steel, woven by the hands of legends and sung by the roaring crowd. Glory is the province of gladiatii. And you?' His lip curled. 'You are naught but a common slave.'

Mia turned her eyes back to the line, studying the men behind their smiles.

They were a motley bunch, all of them bears. A handsome blond caught her attention – he looked so similar to the Vaanian girl, they were almost certainly kin. She saw a huge Dweymeri man, his beard plaited the same as his saltlocks, his beautiful facial tattoos marred by his brand. A burly Liisian with a face like a dropped pie rocked on his heels as if unable to stand still. And standing first in the row, she saw a tall Itreyan man.

Belly turning cold.

Breath catching in her chest.

Long dark hair flowed about his shoulders, framing a face so fine it might've been sculpted by the weaver herself. He was fit and hard, but lither than some of his fellows, the whisper of a frightening speed coiled in the taut lines of his arms, the rippling muscle at his abdomen. He wore a thin silver torc about his neck – the only jewellery among the multitude. But when Mia looked into his dark, burning eyes, she felt the illness in her belly swell, innards growling as if she were suddenly, desperately hungry.

I've felt this before . . .

When she stood in the presence of Lord Cassius, the Prince of Blades . . .

Executus turned to the assembled warriors, let the sand spill from his fingers.

'Gladiatii,' he asked. 'What do I hold in my hand?'

Each man and woman roared as one.

'Our lives, Executus!'

'Your lives.' The man turned back to the newcomers, hurling his fistful of sand to the ground. 'And worthless as they be, one turn they may be sung of as legend.

'I care not what you were before. Beggars or dons, bakers or sugar-girls. That life is *over*. And now, you are less than nothing. But if you watch like bloodhawks and learn what I teach, then one turn, you may stand among the chosen, upon the sands of the *venatus*. As gladiatii! And *then*' – he pointed at the bleeding Sidonius with his whip – 'then, you may learn the taste of glory, pup. Then you may know the song of your pulse as the crowd roars your name, as they do Furian, the Unfallen, primus of the *Venatus Tsana* and champion of the Remus Collegium!'

'*Furian!*' The gladiatii roared as one, raising their fists and turning to the tall Itreyan standing first in the line.

The raven-haired man still stared at Mia, unblinking.

'Gladiatii fear no death!' Executus continued, spittle on his lips. 'Gladiatii fear no pain! Gladiatii fear but one thing – the everlasting shame of defeat! Mark my lessons. Know your place. Train until you bleed. For if you bring such shame upon this collegium, upon your domina, I swear by almighty Aa and all four of his holy fucking Daughters, you will rue the turn your mother shit you from her belly.'

He turned to his fighters, fist in the air, scar twisting his face as he roared.

'*Sanguii e Gloria!*'

'*Blood and glory!*'

The gladiatii answered as one, thumping their fists against their chests.

All except one.

The champion they called Furian.

The man was looking right at Mia, fury or lust or something in between in his stare. Her breath came quicker, skin prickling as if she were freezing. Hunger churned inside her, her mouth dry as dust, her thighs aching with want. Mia looked to the ground at his feet, saw his shadow was no darker than the rest. But she knew this feeling, sure as she knew her own name.

And looking into his eyes, she knew he felt it too.

This man is darkin . . .

CHAPTER 7

HUNGERS

A thudding heartbeat. A sea of red. A rush of vertigo, filling her head.

Mia burst from the blood pool, rising to her feet. The hurts in her shoulder and backside were mended, but she still lost her footing, saved only by the two Hands beside her. The pair helped Mia up, holding one arm apiece until they knew she was steady. Mia spat the blood off her tongue, pawed the gore from her eyes with a sigh.

Looking about, she found herself in a triangular pool brimming with blood – identical to the one she'd just left in the Quiet Mountain. The walls were patterned with sorcerii glyphs, and a map of Godsgrave was painted on the wall in blood. The archipelago sprawled across the stone, shattered isles run through with traceries of canals, looking for all the world like a headless giant laid upon its back.

Mia took a deep breath, found her feet, slung her bloody hair over her shoulder.

'Maw's teeth, I'll never get used to this,' she croaked.

'Stop whining, Corvere. It beats the britches off travelling by ship.'

Mia's stomach flipped as she recognized the voice. Turning to the head of the pool, she found a slender redhead staring back at her. The girl was around her age, but taller, sharper. Her eyes were green, twinkling with a feral, hunter's cunning. Her face was lightly freckled, arms folded inside the voluminous sleeves of a long black robe.

A Hand's *robe*.

Mia would recognize her anywhere – the girl who'd been a thorn in her side all throughout her training at the Quiet Mountain. The girl who blamed Mia's father for the death of her own. The girl who'd vowed to kill her.

'Jessamine,' Mia breathed, climbing out of the pool on unsteady legs.

The redhead inclined her head. 'Welcome to the City of Bridges and Bones.'

'You were posted to Godsgrave?' Mia asked. 'After initiation?'

'Brilliant observation, Corvere,' the redhead replied. 'What gave it away?'

Mia simply stared, the shadows beneath her seething. Jessamine looked her up and down, threw a bundle of linen at Mia's chest.

'Baths are this way.'

The bundled fabric was a robe, and Mia dragged it around her blood-sodden body, leaving sticky red footprints as she followed Jessamine down a twisting hallway. The temperature was stifling, the stench of iron and gore almost overpowering.

Mia saw the walls and ceiling were made of thousands upon thousands of human bones. Femurs and ribs, spines and skulls, forming a dark maze run thick with shadows – whoever thought to construct the new chapel to Our Lady of Blessed Murder inside Godsgrave's vast necropolis obviously had a deep appreciation of the value of ambience. Dim light was provided by arkemical globes, held in skeletal hands on the walls. But despite being surrounded by the remains of untold thousands, Mia's eyes were fixed on the girl in front of her. Spitting the greasy blood off her tongue, she watched Jessamine as if the girl were about to sprout a second head.

After initiation, Mia knew Jessamine had been anointed as a Hand, but she'd been so caught up in her work in Galante that she'd never found out where. It seemed of all cities in the Republic, her old nemesis had been sent to work in Godsgrave.

Fucking typical . . .

The hallway ended at a door made entirely of spines, which Jessamine opened with a gentle touch. Mia saw three baths beyond, the air hung faint with ashwood smoke and honeysuckle perfume. Mia scratched at the drying blood on her face, eyes never leaving the redhead's. Adonai's cryptic warning echoing in her head. The gravebone blade she kept ever strapped to her forearm was just a flick of the wrist away.

'I'll be out here.' Jessamine nodded to the baths. 'Don't take too long. The bishop is waiting, and he's of a darker mood than usual.'

Mia stood her ground, staring into the redhead's eyes.

'You're wondering if I'm going to try to drown you, aye?' Jessamine's lips twisted in a smile. 'Put a knife in you as soon as your back is turned?'

'What makes you think I'm going to turn my back, Red?'

Jessamine shook her head, her voice hard and cold.

'There's still blood between you and me. But the turn I come for you,

*you won't be naked in a tub with soap in your eyes. You'll be wide awake,
blade in hand. I promise you that.' Jessamine smiled, ear to ear. 'So never
fear, Corvere.'*

Mia looked to the steaming baths. Down to the shadow at her feet. And
then she smiled back.

'I never do.'

A n hour later, Mia was standing outside the chambers of the bishop of
the Godsgrave Chapel. She was dressed in knee-high boots and black
leathers, a doublet of crushed black velvet, hair neatly combed. Her father's
gravebone longsword hung at her side, her mother's stiletto sheathed inside
her ruffled sleeve.

The bishop's chambers were hidden away in a twist of bone tunnels – the
chapel's innards were a labyrinth, and Mia had lost her bearings quickly. If
not for Jessamine, she doubted she'd be able to find her way back to the
blood pool again, which made her all the warier about being in the girl's
presence.

The chamber door opened silently, and a slender young man stepped out
into the shadows of the hall, dressed in dark velvet. His face had been woven
since last Mia saw him, but he was still too thin, and Mia would recognize
those piercing blue eyes anywhere. Dark hair, ghost-pale, lips slightly pursed
against his toothless gums.

'Hush,' Mia smiled.

The boy stopped, looked Mia up and down as if surprised to see her. A
small smile curled his lips as he signed to her in Tongueless.

hello

She signed back, hands moving quickly.

you serve here? in godsgrave?

Hush nodded.

eight months

it's good to see you

is it

we should have a drink

The boy looked at Jessamine, then gave a noncommittal shrug.

'Listen, I hate to break up this heartwarming reunion,' Jess said. 'But
honestly, I'm about to start weeping at the emotion, and the bishop is
waiting.'

Hush nodded, looked to Mia.

mother watch over you

With a small bow, the boy pressed his fingertips together and walked away down the hall, silent as a shadow. Mia watched him go, a touch saddened. She'd been an acolyte with Hush. He'd helped her in her final trials, and in turn, she'd saved his life during the Luminatii attack. But as ever, the strange boy held himself distant.

A killer *first*, and always.

Jess knocked on the door three times.

'Fucksakes, what?' demanded a haggard voice from within.

Jessamine opened the door, motioned Mia inside. The girl entered the bishop's chamber, looked about the room. Bone walls were lined with bookshelves, laden with haphazardly stacked paperwork. Sheaves of vellum and scrolls in boxes or simply piled atop one another, hundreds of books stacked without care or scattered across the floor – it looked like a globe of wyrdglass had exploded inside a drunkard's library. Along one wall was a row of weaponry from all corners of the Republic: a Luminatii sunsteel blade; a Vaanian battleaxe; a double-edged gladius from some gladiatii arena; a rapier of Liisian steel. All gleaming in the low arkemical light.

Seated at a broad wooden desk, almost hidden behind a tottering pile of paperwork, Mia saw the bishop of Godsgrave, a quill held between his liver-spotted fingers.

'Maw's teeth,' she breathed. '. . . Mercurio?'

The old man looked up from his paperwork, pushed his spectacles up his nose. His shock of thick grey hair seemed to have got unrulier since she last saw him, ice-blue eyes framed by his perpetual scowl. He obviously hadn't slept well in months.

'Well, well,' Mercurio smirked. 'I thought you were the Quiet One, come back to complain some more. How do, little Crow?'

Mia looked at her former mentor with astonishment.

'What the 'byss are you doing here?'

'What's it bloody look like?'

'They made you bishop of Godsgrave?'

Mercurio shrugged. 'Bishop Thalles got ventilated when the Luminatii purged the city. Fuckers never hit the Curio Shop for some reason, but I couldn't ever risk going back there. So, once the chapel got rebuilt, Lady Drusilla lured me out of retirement. Without the shop, I had bugger all else to do.'

'Why didn't you tell me?'

'You were in Galante. And in case your bloody eyes have stopped working, I've been a trifle busy. So, without further foreplay, Adonai sent missive you'd be arriving. You got the particulars?'

Mia was a little taken aback. Mercurio had never quite got over the fact that she'd failed her final trial. Though he'd always be fond of her, he still seemed . . . disappointed somehow. Like everyone else in the Ministry, her old master could carry a grudge. It saddened her, no doubt – the old man had taken her in, looked after her for six long years. Though she'd admit it to no one, she loved the old bastard.

But still, she was a Blade and he was now her bishop, and his tone reminded her sharply where she was. Mia produced the scroll case Solis had given her. It was leather, so it could cross the blood walk – nothing that hadn't once known the pulse of life could travel via Adonai's magiks. Mia watched Mercurio unroll the parchment, pore over it with narrowed eyes.

'The Dona,' he murmured.

'Leader of the Toffs,' Mia replied. 'They run down by the Bay of Butchers.'

The bishop nodded, picked up the character sketch of Mia's mark. It showed a woman with a dark scowl, darker eyes. She wore a frock coat of a fine cut, hair styled into artful ringlets, as was the fashion among marrow-born ladies in recent seasons. A monocle was propped (rather ridiculously, Mia thought) on her right eye.

Mercurio dropped the parchment on his desk.

'Shame to bury a knife that sharp.' The old man took a long sip of his tea. This close, Mia could smell the goldwine in it. 'Right. The particulars are detailed, you know where to start looking. You've got eight turns to end her and snaffle this map, and the hourglass is running. What do you need from me?'

'A place to sleep. Wyrdglass. Weapons. A Hand who knows the 'Grave as well as me and can move as fast as I do.'

'You've got your Hand, she's standing right behind you.'

Mia turned to look at Jessamine. Back to Old Mercurio. The bishop was obviously unaware of the enmity that lay between the girls, and to bring it up seemed on the south side of petty. But Mia trusted Jessamine like she trusted the suns not to shine, and enjoyed her company the way eunuchs enjoy looking at naughty lithographs.

How best to broach this . . .

'Perhaps there's someone with more . . . experience?'

Mercurio peered at Mia over his spectacles, his expression sour.

'Blade Mia. Godsgrave is the only Red Church chapel we've managed to rebuild in the eight months since the Luminatii attack. Thanks to Grand Cardinal Duomo and his god-bothering shitheels, I'm one of two bishops servicing the whole fucking Republic, in fact, and with Scaeva running for a fourth term as consul and Godsgrave politics all aflutter, *there's no end of bastards who need killing. So, given that I'm busier than a whorehouse running a two-for-one special, do me the honour of saying thank you, and taking what you're bloody given.'*

Mia looked her former mentor in the eye. She recognized his tone – the same one he'd use when she was a little girl and he'd caught her stealing his cigarillos. She glanced over her shoulder at Jessamine. Softly sighed.

'Thank you, Bishop.'

'My fucking pleasure.'

'May the Moth—'

'Aye, aye, black kisses all around. Now sod off, will you?'

Mia backed out of the room with a bow, trying not to take Mercurio's mood too personally. He'd always been a sour old cur, and running the Godsgrave Chapel at a time like this couldn't be doing his humours any favours.

Jessamine led Mia down a twisting passage, the Blade following close on her heels. Once they were safely out of the bishop's earshot, Mia took Jessamine by the arm, turned the Hand to face her.

'Are we going to have problems, you and I?'

'Whatever do you mean, Corvere?'

'I mean it's no secret we hate each other like fucking poison. But you're my Hand now. I need to be able to trust you, Jess.'

The redhead's green eyes sparkled as she spoke.

'I don't like you, Corvere. You think you're clever. You think you're special. You poisoned Diamo and cheated me out of my spot as top of Songs. But I serve the Mother, I serve the Ministry, same as you. Don't question my devotion again.'

The redhead turned and stalked off into the dark.

The shadows at Mia's feet rippled, a cold whisper in her ear.

'. . . you always had a talent for making friends . . .'

'. . . well, I am quite fond of you, if that makes a difference . . .'

'. . . thank the mother i am not actually capable of vomiting . . .'

'. . . shut up . . .'

'. . . such a witty riposte . . .'

'. . . wit is wasted on the witless . . .'

'If you two are quite finished?' Mia asked.

'. . . mongrel . . .' *came a soft whisper.*

'. . . cur . . .' *came a softer reply.*

Mia folded her arms, tapping her toe on the stone. Silence fell in the corridor, punctuated only by Jessamine's receding footfalls.

'Hurry up, Corvere,' the Hand called. 'The hourglass isn't getting any fuller.'

Thumbs in belt, Mia had no choice but to follow Jessamine down the hall.

D*arkin* . . .
     Mia stared across the courtyard at the gladiatii called Furian. The man met her stare, warm breeze blowing his long dark hair about his face. His eyes burned right through her with an intensity that . . .

Well, truth told, without Mister Kindly at her side, it frightened her.

But Black Mother, what might this mean? Mia had only met one of her kind before now, and Lord Cassius had died before he gave her any answers about who or what she was. Perhaps Furian knew something more? Perhaps he held all th—

The executus cracked his whip.

'Gladiatii! Return to training!' He turned to Mia, Sidonius, and Matteo. 'You three. Attend me.'

The gladiatii fell out, holding perfect formation as they marched down to the courtyard at the building's rear. The executus limped after them, leaning on his lion-headed cane. As Mia followed, she saw him take a sip from a metal flask at his belt.

In the rear yard, where Mia's father had once kept a stable of proud horses, she saw the grounds had been completely refitted. The ochre sands were set with training dummies, racks of shields and wooden weapons. The ground was uneven, scaffolds and pits dividing the space into different levels, from ten feet high to ten feet deep. A broad circle was marked with white stones, and sigils of the Familia Remus flew proudly upon the battlements.

The gladiatii paired off to spar. Mia saw different combinations of weapons, different fighting styles. The Vaanian girl hefted an ironwood bow and began peppering targets at the other end of the yard. Furian took up twin swords, began beating one of the training dummies as if it had insulted his mother.

The executus limped to the verandah, greeting a huge dog sitting in the shade. It was a mastiff, male, with dark fur and a studded collar. The dog was clearly overjoyed, and the big man knelt with a wince so it could slobber on his face.

'Good to see you again, old friend,' he murmured, patting the dog. 'Been guarding the collegium while I was gone?'

Mia and her fellows sweated in the boiling suns while Executus finished making a fuss of the dog. It was the first time she'd seen the bastard smile in a month, though with that scar at his face, it was still a little hard to tell. Once he was done, Executus limped out into the stone circle, snapped his fingers.

'Maggot!' he barked. 'Sword and board.'

Mia caught movement from the corner of her eye, saw a girl dash out from the shade of a small building in the corner of the yard. She was Liisian; skinny and tanned, with dark hair growing wild. She couldn't have been more than eleven, but three arkemical circles branded on her cheek marked her as the highest tier of slave.

What skill is a girl that age prized for?

The girl ran to the weapon racks, picked up a wooden practice blade and a broad oaken shield, fetched them to the executus. The big man pointed the blade at Matteo.

'Come. Show me what you're made of, boy. Maggot, fetch the lad a cock and something to hide behind.'

The girl nodded, ran back to the racks and returned with another wooden sword and shield. Matteo squared up, adopted a halfway-decent fighting stance.

'Attack!' Executus roared.

Matteo swung his wooden blade with a cry, but the executus blocked the assault with ease.

'I didn't ask for a fucking kiss, I said attack!'

The boy scowled, launching a series of blows, head, chest, belly. The executus was strong as a bull, but he moved slow on that iron leg of his, and Matteo's footwork proved surprisingly good. The boy pushed the older man back, sword cracking against sword, dust rising from their shields as they clashed. Mia noted the gladiatii were only sparring half-heartedly, watching the bout with interest.

Matteo grew more aggressive – like Mia, he'd obviously expected the executus to be a master bladesman. But in the face of the boy's furious attacks, Executus was on full defence. Matteo landed blow after blow against the big man's guard, utterly dominating, until the executus was pressed against the circle's edge.

And then, like a bear too early from its slumber, the man came awake.

He shifted from back to front foot in the blink of an eye, moving swift and graceful despite his iron leg. And in the space of a few seconds, he'd knocked the sword from Matteo's hand, cracked his blade into the lad's gut, and left him sprawled in the dust.

Executus loomed over the gasping boy, only a thin sheen of sweat on his brow.

'What did you learn?'

Matteo grasped his bruising belly, too breathless to speak.

'The sand is no place for brawlers,' Executus said, his scar creased in a scowl. 'It is a chequered board. And on it, we play the greatest game of all. A wily opponent may feign weakness. Allow you to exert yourself and learn your patterns, all without breaking a sweat. Overconfidence has ended a thousand fools who'd name themselves gladiatii. Mark this, or it will be the end of *you*. Now get off my fucking sand.'

Executus turned to Mia, pointed his wooden blade.

'You next, girl. Show me how many of those thousand priests you're worth.'

The girl named Maggot handed Mia a practice blade and shield with a shy smile. But Sidonius snatched the weapon from the little girl's hand, shoved Mia aside.

'Fuck that,' he growled. 'No bitch steps onto the sand before me.'

Perhaps it was the heat, or three weeks of eating shit from this man at sea. Perhaps her legendary temper coming out to play without Mister Kindly to keep her in check, or Furian's dark eyes following her across the yard. Whatever the reason, Mia found her hands on the big man's shoulders, and her knee buried in his bollocks.

'Bitch, am I?' she whispered.

Sidonius's eyes bulged as he doubled up. Mia locked her fingers behind his head and brought his face down into her knee. She was on top of him in a heartbeat, fists pounding his jaw, teeth clenched, blood in her—

Crack!

The whip etched a line of agony across her shoulder blades. Another blow sent her scrambling away with a gasp, twisting out of range. Laughter rang among the assembled gladiatii. Executus glared at her, lash unfurled in his hand.

'That is your domina's property you just damaged, cur. If he falls now in the Winnowing, will you pay her the forfeit of his life?'

Mia rubbed the welt on her shoulder, growling. 'No man speaks to me that way.'

'He is not a man!' Executus spat. 'He is a *slave*. As are you. And *both* of you forget your places. Until you survive the Winnowing at next *venatus,* you are less than nothing. Now pick up those weapons and show me a scrap of the promise your domina sees in you, before you truly test my patience.'

The girl called Maggot helped Sidonius to his feet, and with gentle hands, led him out of the circle. Executus coiled his lash at his belt, took another swig from his flask as Mia scooped up the sword and shield with a black scowl. Fury burned in her belly, teeth clenched tight. Mia could feel Furian watching her with those dark glittering eyes, that hunger and sickness coiled in her gut.

And without a word, she struck.

Her attacks were vicious, blinding. Dancing across the ochre sands, sliding between the executus's blows. But during her training in the mountain, she'd spent most of her time learning Caravaggio style, fighting with a sword in each hand. It wasn't likely a Blade of the Mother would be traipsing about with a great bloody shield strapped to her arm, and so in all her time, Mia had never trained how to use one.

It was deadweight. Each impact jarring her elbow, her shoulder. And as desperate to make an account of herself as she was, she was still aware enough to know that the executus was toying with her. Letting her dodge and weave and grow wearier by the moment, all the while studying her patterns and setting her up for the kill.

But she was no worthless punching bag or training dummy. She'd be damned if she'd let him treat her like one. And so, looking to show this man what she was truly capable of, she narrowed her eyes and reached out to the shadows at his feet.

None would have marked it – the executus's shadow barely rippled. Mia couldn't quite grasp the iron peg; the suns out here were too bright, her grip on the shadows too weak. But she held the sole of his boot well enough, just as she'd done in the Pit and the Mountain and a hundred times before. The executus's eyes widened as his stance failed him. Mia swung at his throat, tightening her hold on the shadows and preparing to teach this man who thought her less than nothing exactly what she was worth.

And then she lost her grip.

The shadows slithered from her hold like sand through her fingertips, releasing the big man's boot. Executus slammed his shield into her face, knocking her backwards. Mia tried to twist aside, cried out in pain as his sword smacked across her back, sending her into the dust. The wooden sword crashed down beside her head as she rolled aside, slinging a handful of dirt. But the executus raised his shield with casual ease, countering with a vicious kick from that iron peg, right into her belly.

Mia doubled up and retched, blinded by the pain. Executus skewered the sand beside her head with his practice blade, looked down at her and growled.

'A thousand silver pieces? I'd not have paid a one.'

Mia clawed her way to her knees, dusty hair stuck to the vomit on her chin. The other gladiatii dismissed her with sneers on their lips, returned to their training. Mia slung the shield off her arm, spat blood into the dust.

'Again,' she demanded.

'No,' Executus said. 'I sought your measure. And now I have it in spades. Go wash off your defeat. The hour grows late. Your training begins amorrow.'

Matteo walked forward slowly, helped Mia up from her knees. Standing with a wince, she stared across the dusty yard, rage burning inside her. She'd had a grip on the executus's footing, sure and true. A trick she'd performed countless times before – she should have bested him easily. But something . . . no, some*one*, had wrested control of the shadows, and saw her bested instead.

Furian looked up from beating the stuffing from his hapless training dummy, sweat gleaming on his beautiful face. Long dark hair blowing in the warm breeze. Silver torc glittering. Dark eyes fixed on hers.

'Bastard,' she whispered.

The Unfallen returned to his training without another glance.

CHAPTER 8

PRAYERS

'Well, this is going to be tricksy.'

Mia took a long drag of her cigarillo, looking down on the pleasure house from their room in the taverna opposite. Jessamine stood at the window beside her, eyes narrowed as she watched the brothel door.

'You were expecting the leader of a braavi gang to just wander down the street with the map in her hand and fall onto your sword, Corvere?'

'You know I love your sarcasm more than anyone, Jess,' Mia sighed. 'But we've been cooped up in this room a week and I could use a change of tune.'

'I know we've been up here a week, I'm the one who has to put up with your incessant fucking smoking.'

'. . . WELL, PERHAPS WE COULD QUARREL 'TIL THE MORROW AND MISS OUR OPPORTUNITY ENTIRELY . . . ?'

Mia glanced to Mister Kindly, licking at his translucent paw on the bed.

'Your commentary is always appreciated.'

'. . . and freely given . . .'

'You're a little prick, you know that?'

'. . . o, well and truly . . .'

Seven turns had passed since she'd arrived in the City of Bridges and Bones, and the only thing keeping Mia's belly from dissolving in a puddle of nerves were the passengers riding her shadow. Asking around her old haunts in Little Liis, Mia and Jessamine had tracked down their mark after a turn – the Toffs' headquarters was known to most of the lowlifes who peopled Little Liis. But finding their lair wasn't the problem. It was getting inside that was going to be the riddle.

The Toffs' stronghold was a well-appointed five-storey palazzo named the Dog's Dinner. The bottom levels seemed a regular taverna, full of bawdy *song and a crush of people. The third floor looked to be an ink den, and the top two, a brothel. Thugs the size of small houses guarded the front doors, dressed up in expensive frock coats and powdered wigs that did little to hide the scars on their faces or the muscle beneath the fabric. Though no signage distinguished the building from its neighbours, this was braavi turf, and all the locals knew exactly what went on behind those doors.*

Their reconnaissance had gone flawlessly – being able to send two wisps of living darkness into the building to listen to every conversation and study every nook meant they knew everything that was set to happen this eve. But that didn't mean pulling this off was going to be easy.

Mia felt a tremble in her shadow, the kiss of a cool breeze. Eclipse coalesced from the darkness at her feet, shaking herself from head to tail.

'News?' Mia asked, cigarillo bobbing at her lips.

'. . . SHE IS ON THE TOP FLOOR, CORNER OFFICE. SHE SPENT THE TURN ISSUING ORDERS, DRINKING, SMOKING, AND HAVING A GREAT DEAL OF SEX . . .'

'Fine work if you can get it,' Jess said.

'The map is still being delivered here?' Mia asked.

'. . . THE SELLER IS DUE TO ARRIVE SOMETIME WITHIN THE NEXT HOUR. THE EXCHANGE WILL TAKE PLACE IN THE DONA'S OFFICE . . .'

'So we have two options,' Mia muttered. 'We intercept the map before it arrives and end the Dona later, or wait for the seller and do them both at once.'

'. . . WE DO NOT KNOW WHAT THE SELLER LOOKS LIKE . . .'

'Presumably a dodgy bastard carrying a map case.'

'. . . you would still need to get into that office to end the dona regardless . . .'

'And therein lies the problem.'

'You could steal inside?' Jessamine suggested. 'Hidden in your shadows?'

---

*The braavi are a loose collective of gangs that run much of the criminal activity in Godsgrave – prostitution, larceny, and organized violence. Though a thorn in the side of Itreya's kings and Senate for centuries, the city's history is replete with bloody episodes where various city leaders tried (and failed) to dislodge them from their traditional roosts in Godsgrave's nethers.

It was Consul Julius Scaeva who first proposed the idea of paying the more powerful braavi an official stipend, and the first payment to them was made from his own personal fortune. Since then, the city has enjoyed a long tenure of peace and stability, and Scaeva a tremendous upswing in popularity.

As Mia so memorably stated in our first adventure, the so-called People's Senator is an unspeakable cunt, gentlefriends.

But he's not a stupid cunt.

Mia shook her head. 'I can't see a thing under them. Groping around blind inside a braavi den sounds a splendid way to get a sword in the tits. And the weaver did a particularly good job on these two. It'd be a shame to ruin them.'

Jessamine squinted across the way.

'You could throw a grapple from this roof to the neighbouring building. Jump the alley, get in through the Dinner's roof, work your way down.'

'It's weeksend. Lots of people in the street. If one looks up . . .'

'Front door, then?'

Mia stared out across the street, muttering, 'I'm terrible at the front door.'

'. . . you are getting better . . .'

'Liar.'

'. . . o, ye of little faith . . .'

'Faith never kept a drowning man from sinking.' Mia dragged long on her cigarillo. 'But admittedly, we don't have many options.'

'. . . we could stay up all nevernight and plait each other's hair and talk about boys . . . ?'

'. . . MUST YOU ALWAYS PLAY THE FOOL, LITTLE MOGGY . . . ?'

'. . . it is part of my charm . . .'

'. . . THIS MUST BE SOME NEW DEFINITION OF CHARM WITH WHICH I AM UNACQUAINTED . . .'

'If you two are done,' Mia growled, 'go keep a lookout, aye?'

Emptiness filled her as her passengers departed, butterflies replacing them. Mia tried to shush her nerves, staring across at the braavi den and wondering what awaited her there. Close-quarter fighting. An inn full of hardened criminals. And whoever was selling the map would presumably bring muscle of their own. Bad odds.

Pushing aside her questions, Adonai's warning ringing in her head, she crushed her cigarillo under her heel.

'Right,' she nodded. 'I need a dress.'

M ia walked across the crowded street as if she owned it, over the broken cobbles right towards the door of the Dog's Dinner.*

---

*A well-established taverna on Godsgrave's lower west side, which has undergone an astonishing number of name changes over the years. Originally called 'the Burning Bush', its first owner was a retired brothel madam with a rather cheerful outlook on the ailments her many years in the saddle had given her.

Nevernight had fallen, wind howling down the thoroughfare. A summer storm had rolled in with it off the ocean, lukewarm rain coming down in thin curtains, the two suns hidden behind a mask of grey. But inclement weather was rarely a reason for folk in Godsgrave to stay inside on a weeksend, and the streets still bustled with folk on their way to their revels.

Little Liis was one of the more squalid sections of the 'Grave, but Liisian folk had flair, and growing up here as a girl, Mia had always found the colours and styles of their dress beautiful. They reminded her of her mother, truth told, and something in the music and aromas of this place called to the blood in her veins. Her outfit had been purloined from the chapel's wardrobe to fit in with the locals; leather britches and knee-length boots, a corset over a velvet shirt, a glittering necklet, all various shades of blood-red. If she got murdered in there, at least she'd leave a fine-looking corpse.

Up close, the doormen looked even more intimidating. They were under cover of the Dinner's front awning, but both still looked a little damp and more than a little surly. The gentle on the left was almost as wide as he was tall, and his comrade looked like he'd eaten his own parents for breakfast.

Wideboy held up a hand, stopping Mia short. 'Hold there, Mi Dona.'

'Merry nevernight, my lovely gentles,' Mia smiled, dropped into a small curtsey.

'Can't come in 'ere,' said Orphanboy, shaking his head.

Purchased by a staunch monarchist years later, it was renamed 'the Golden King' shortly before the overthrow of Francisco XV. After the good king's brutal murder, the pub was renamed 'the Slaughtered Tyrant' in what most locals considered a fucking smart move.

Decades after, a slew of successive owners renamed the taverna 'the Drunken Monk,' 'the Daughter's Bosom', the amusing if inexplicable 'Seven Fat Bastards' (there were only two owners at the time, and neither was particularly obese). It was finally purchased by a braavi leader named Guiseppe Antolini and his new bride, Livia, and redubbed 'the Lover's Vow'.

Guiseppe disappeared soon after the pub's purchase, however, and Livia took over sole proprietorship of the hotel and leadership of the gang, renaming herself 'the Dona' and the taverna 'the Dog's Dinner'. Rumour had it she'd discovered her beloved was diddling one of the serving girls, and according to the fireside gossip, she'd chopped off his wedding tackle and fed it to her dog, Oli.

Whether or not the rumour is true, it must be noted that the first sights to greet a newcomer to the establishment will be a well-fed pooch sitting by the hearth and a razor-sharp cleaver hanging over the bar.

'No riffraff,' Wideboy agreed.

Mia looked down at her outfit, sounding mildly wounded. 'Riffraff?'

Four drunken sailors who'd sit comfortably next to the definition of 'riffraff' in Don Fiorlini's bestselling Itreyan Diction: the Definitive Guide stepped up to the door.

'Good eve, gentlefriends,' said Wideboy. 'Welcome, welcome.'

The man opened the doors, a burst of flute and laughter rang within, and the mariners stepped inside without a backward glance.

Mia smiled sweetly at Wideboy. 'I've friends waiting insid—'

'Can't come in 'ere this eve,' the big man said.

'Not serving your kind,' Orphanboy nodded.

'. . . My kind?'

The thugs grunted and nodded in unison.

'Let me understand this,' Mia said. 'You're a band of thieves, pimps, stand-over men and murderers. And you're telling me I'm not good enough to drink here?'

'Aye,' said Wideboy.

'Fugoff,' said his partner.

Mia adjusted her corset as meaningfully as possible. The braavi thugs stared at her without blinking. Finally, she folded her arms and sighed. 'How much do you want?'

Orphanboy's eyes narrowed. 'How much you got?'

'Two priests?'

The doorman looked up and down the street, then nodded. 'Give it over, then.'

Mia fished around in her purse, and flipped one coin apiece to the doormen. They disappeared into their pockets quicker than a smokehound into the pipe on payday.

Mia stared at the pair, eyebrows rising. 'Well?'

'Can't come in 'ere this eve,' said Orphanboy.

'Not serving your kind,' Wideboy agreed.

The pair stood aside for a second group of revellers (carrying a street sign and a somewhat troubled-looking sheep), bidding them good eve as they stepped inside. Every one of them was a man. Peering into the room beyond, Mia saw every single one of the clientele was also male. And somewhere in her head, Realization tipped its hat.

'Ohhhh,' she said. 'Riiiiight.'

'Right,' said Wideboy.

Orphanboy stroked his chin and nodded sagely.

'Well,' she said.

'. . . Well what?'

'Well, can I have my money back?' the girl asked.

'You're terrible at this,' said Wideboy.

'Just awful,' agreed Orphanboy.

Mia pouted. 'Mister Kindly said I'm getting better.'

'Whoever he is, Mister Kindly's a bloody liar.'

The doormen folded their arms like a pair of synchronized dancers.

Mia sighed. 'Merry nevernight, my lovely gentles.'

And giving another bow, she marched back into the rain.

D on't you say a fucking word,' she warned Mister Kindly.
          She was crouched on a rooftop opposite the Dinner, staring out at a fourth-floor balcony. The not-cat sat beside her, tail swishing side to side.

'. . . considering your childhood, it's little wonder you lack people skills . . .'

'Not. A. Fucking. Word.'

'. . . meow . . .'

'. . . STRICTLY SPEAKING, THAT IS STILL A WORD . . .' Eclipse growled.

'Aye.' Mia held up a warning finger. 'One more, and I officially enter your name in the Book of Grudges.'

Mister Kindly lifted a translucent paw, placed it over the spot his mouth might've been. The rain was still spattering, warm and wet on her skin. Jessamine finished securing a length of silk line to an iron grapple, handed it dutifully to her Blade.

'Don't forget the map,' the redhead warned. 'And wait 'til I'm down on the street before you make your crossing. Nobody will look up if they're looking at me.'

'I know. This was my idea, Jess.'

'Were those britches your idea too?' Jessamine looked Mia up and down. 'Because they're not doing that arse of yours any favours.'

'O, stop, I fear my sides shall split.'

'That's j—'

'Just what the britches said?' Mia rolled her eyes. 'Aye, aye. Bravo, Mi Dona.'

'I'll be waiting back here on the roof when you come out. And try not to get killed, neh?' Jess warned. 'I'd be ever so disappointed I didn't do it myself.'

Mia raised the knuckles. The redhead smirked, slipped down the stairwell without further insult. The crowd had thinned from the rain, but gentles *were still spilling out of the Dinner, others staggering home after a merry nevernight. Mia watched Jessamine march across the street, straight for a young man just leaving the pleasure house.*

'*Youuuu* bastard!' *she cried, an accusing finger aimed at his face.*

'*Eh?*' *the young man blinked.*

'*You told me you were headed to your cousin's!*' *Jessamine shouted.* '*And here I find you, drinking and whoring behind my back!*'

The gentle in question frowned in confusion. '*Mi Dona, I ha—*'

'*Don't you "Mi Dona" me!*' *Jessamine stepped closer, building up a head of steam.* '*Is this the example you wish to set for our son? O, Four blessed Daughters, why didn't I listen to Mother? She warned me about you!*'

The revellers and braavi doormen watched as Jess launched into a scathing tirade, the fellow she was howling at barely able to get a word in edgeways. And with all eyes on the wronged paramour and her drunken beau, Mia took her chance.

Hurling her grapple across the fifteen-foot gap, she snagged it in the wrought-iron railing and tied it off tight. It was a four-storey plunge to a sticky end on the cobbles below, and the railing was slick with rain. Yet, quick as silver, she stepped out into the void between buildings and began stealing across.

Fearless.

Reaching the rooftop of the bordello beside the Dinner, she peered over a chimney stack, not entirely surprised to find two miserable-looking braavi under a single umbrella, guarding the rooftop door. Mia was certain she could take the pair with the white wyrdglass in her pouch – hurling the arkemical globes at the men's feet would produce a cloud of Swoon big enough to knock both unconscious. But wyrdglass made a noteworthy bang when it popped, and the noise might raise an alarm.

'. . . mpphgglmm . . .' *said Mister Kindly.*

'*What?*'

'. . . HE SAID MPPHGGLMM . . .'

'*Daughters, all right, all right, you can speak.*'

The not-cat cleared its throat.

'. . . which room is the dona's . . . ?'

Eclipse nodded to the corner windows on the top floor. The curtains were drawn, no sign of what might be going on inside.

'. . . SHE HAD FIVE MEN IN THERE WITH HER, WHEN LAST I LOOKED . . .'

'*I don't like the idea of bursting in blind,*' *Mia muttered.* '*And the map might not be here yet.*'

'. . . start in the ink den, work your way up, hide until it arrives . . . ?'

'That sounds suspiciously like a plan.'

Mia dropped onto a narrow ledge on the bordello's third floor, and leapt across the rain-soaked gap to the balcony on the Dinner. Waiting a moment to listen for any commotion, she peered through the keyhole to the bedchamber beyond. Four figures in various stages of undress were passed out in a tangle of limbs on a four-poster bed, empty ink needles on the furs beside them. Dead to the world.

Quiet as shadows, Mia retrieved her lockpicks from her boot heel, sweet-talked the balcony door and slipped inside. The quartet didn't stir from their inkdreams. She shook off the rain and was sneaking past the bed when a soft knock sounded. Mia was across the room in a flash, hiding behind the door as it opened gently.

'Service?' a young voice said. 'Mi Dons? I have your sugarwater.'

A girl stepped inside, a golden courtesan's masque on her face. She looked barely a teenager, but dressed as a woman – crushed black taffeta and cheap chiffon. She carried a silvered tray, four fine goblets and a decanter of sea-blue liquid. Lowering her voice as she saw the slumbering inkfiends on the bed, she turned to push the door closed and silence the celebrations downstairs.

Lightning flashed across the skies outside. A hand reached from behind her, holding her tray. Another about her mouth.

'Hush now,' Mia whispered.

The lass stood still as a statue in Tyrant's Row.

'I mean no harm, love,' Mia said. 'You've my word. I'll take my hand away if you promise not to cry out?'

The girl nodded, chest heaving. Mia edged her hand from the girl's lips, stepped back, hand on her gravebone sword. The girl turned slowly, looked her up and down – the blades, the black, the stare – her breath coming even quicker as she realized what Mia was about. Glancing towards the bed, looking for marks of murder.

'I'm not here for them,' Mia promised.

'Are you . . . here for me?'

Mia looked her over – the low neckline, the tightly cinched corsetry, the golden masque. A woman twice her age might find herself comfortable in such an outfit. Might revel in the power it gave. But this one was barely more than a child.

. . . Barely more than a child?

Daughters, what am I?

She should be away about her business, she knew it. The Dona was upstairs, the map was on its way, and Mia needed to end one and steal the *other by the morrow. But there was something about this girl. Just one of dozens working inside these walls. Could she have ended in a place like this if Mercurio hadn't found her? If her life had been just a little different?*

This was softness, she knew it. She should be steel. But still . . .

'How old are you?' she found herself asking.

'Fourteen,' the girl replied.

Mia shook her head. 'Is this what you want?'

A blink. 'What?'

'Is this what you dreamed of being?' Mia asked. 'When you were younger?'

'I . . .' The girl's eyes were locked on the sword at Mia's belt. Her voice turned cold with self-mockery. 'I used to pray Aa would make me a princess.'

Mia smiled. 'None of us get to be princesses, love.'

'No,' the girl said simply. 'No, we don't.'

Silence hung in the room like morning fog. Mia only stared, as she often did, letting the quiet ask her questions for her.

'Horses,' the girl finally said, tugging her dress higher. 'I used to dream of working with horses. A little merchant's wagon, perhaps. Something simple.'

'That sounds nice.'

'I'd have a black stallion named Onyx,' the girl said. 'And a white mare named Pearl. And we'd ride wherever the wind blew, nobody to stop us.'

'So why don't you do that?'

The lass looked around the room, the bordello beyond it. The light dying in her eyes as she shrugged helplessly. 'No choice.'

'You could choose the purses at their waists.' Mia pointed at the trio of marrowborn on the four-poster. 'The jewels at their throats. I know a man called Mercurio who lives in the necropolis. If you told him Mia sent you, he could help set you up. Someplace with horses, maybe. Someplace you want to be.'

A glance upstairs. Fear in shadowed eyes. 'They'd catch me.'

'Not if you're quick. Not if you're clever.'

Thunder rolled beyond the window.

'I'm not,' the girl said.

'That's Fear talking. Never listen to him. Fear is a coward.'

The girl looked Mia up and down, shaking her head. 'I'm not like you.'

Mia could see her reflection in the serving girl's stare as lightning arced across the skies outside. Death-pale skin. Gravebone at her side. Shadows in her eyes.

'I'm not sure you want to be like me,' she said. 'I just doubt this' – she reached out and untied the golden masque – 'is anything like you.'

The face behind the gold was thin. An old bruise at her lip. Tired, pretty eyes.

'But it's your choice. Always yours.'

The girl looked to the inkfiends. Back to Mia's eyes.

'Are there many of them upstairs?' Mia asked.

The girl nodded. Licked the bruise at her mouth. 'The worst of them.'

'There's a package being delivered here this eve. Do you know anything of it?'

The girl shook her head. 'They don't tell me much.'

Mia looked down at the crystalware goblets, the decanter and the silver tray. Up at the girl and her tired eyes. The girl was staring at a purse among the inkfiend's scattered clothes. A golden ring on another's finger.

'What's your name?' Mia asked.

The girl blinked. Looked back at Mia. 'Belle.'

'Could you do me a favour, Belle?'

Sudden wariness dawned in the girl's eyes. 'What kind of favour?'

Mia walked a slow circle around her. Nodded once.

'Can I borrow that dress?'

M ia and Matteo were escorted from their sparring session by two guards wearing tabards of the Familia Remus. Staring at that falcon sigil on their chests, Mia felt that sinking feeling in her belly growing worse. Sidonius limped out from an infirmary at the keep's rear. The big man's nose had been set with a wooden splint after Mia's beating, fresh stitches at his brow. The girl called Maggot followed him, wandering over to the big mastiff and letting him lick the man's blood from her fingers. She looked at Mia, again gifting her that small, shy smile.

Not knowing quite what to make of the girl, and despite the bitter sting of her defeat at the hands of the executus, Mia smiled back.

The guards collected Sidonius, and the new recruits were marched up to the great double doors at the keep's rear. There, they were met by a slender woman with long grey hair and three circles branded into her cheek. She was in her late forties, and carried herself with an almost regal air. A flowing dress of fine red silk hugged her body, and her neck was encircled with a silver torc, similar to Furian's.

'I am Anthea, majordomo of this house,' she said. 'I manage the domina's affairs in these walls. You will refer to me as Magistrae. You are to be bathed and fed before being locked down for the nevernight. If you have questions, you may speak.'

Sidonius rubbed a hand across his bloody chin, looked the woman up and down.

'Will you wash my back for me, Dona?'

The magistrae glanced at the guards. The men drew wooden truncheons and proceeded to beat the bleeding shit out of Sidonius right there in the foyer. Mia rolled her eyes, wondering how the Itreyan could be so dense. After a hard drubbing – his second of the turn – Sidonius lay on the tiled floor in a spatter of his own blood.

'That's a n-no . . . I take it . . . ?'

'Mistake me not for some simple servant, cur,' Magistrae said, her dark eyes roaming the *COWARD* burned into his chest. 'I have known our domina since she was a child, and when she is absent, I am her voice in this house. Now cease your bleeding upon my tiles and follow.'

Sidonius wobbled to his feet, brow and lips dripping red. Mia watched the magistrae from the corner of her eye. The woman reminded her of her father's majordomo – Andriano – who was head of this household back when the Corvere colours still flew upon the walls. He too lived in bondage, but carried himself like a freeman. Anthea seemed cut from the same cloth.

The more things change . . .

'May I ask a question, Magistrae?' Mia asked.

Anthea looked her over with a careful eye before replying. 'Speak.'

'I see falcons hanging on the courtyard walls.' Mia winced, massaging her bruised ribs. 'But is our domina not of the Familia Leonides?'

'The falcon is the sigil of Marcus Remus,' the woman nodded. 'Aa bless and keep him. This was his house, awarded for his service to the Republic after the Kingmaker Rebellion. Now he is gone to his eternal rest by the Hearth, the estate passes to his widow, your new domina.'

The sinking feeling in Mia's belly reached all the way down to her toes.

I fucking knew it . . .

Mia had no idea where he might be, but she could almost hear Mister Kindly's rebuke in her ears. She hadn't just failed to win a place with the collegium she'd intended, she'd also fallen into servitude to the wife of the justicus she'd *murdered*? Her scheme was drifting farther down the sewer with every passing turn . . .

Be still. Be patient. Leona will never know.

Mia bowed her head, followed the magistrae obediently. They were escorted through a broad hall at the keep's rear, the trio all limping after their beatings. Mia was reeling from the news about Leona, about the presence of another darkin, but somewhere in the back of her mind, the child who'd walked these halls was struck by how much Crow's Nest had changed. The layout was untouched, but the decor . . .

Dona Corvere had favoured an opulent look, but now the halls were plain – the beautiful tapestries and carpets replaced by suits of armour and weapons of war. Mia wanted to see her old room, the view of the ocean from the balconies, but she and her fellows were led down a winding stair to an antechamber outside the cellar. An iron portcullis blocked them from going any farther, a complex mekwerk device on the wall beside it. A guard inserted an odd key, worked a series of levers. The portcullis rose, and Magistrae ushered Mia and the others inside.

Darius Corvere had used the vast sublevel as a living area for the brutal summer months, but Mia could see it had been refitted as a barracks. The space had been partitioned into six-by-six cells, lined with long rows of heavy iron bars.

Very generous of the dona to let her pets live underground . . .

Walking past the cages, Mia noted the fresh straw, the thick chains. Arkemical globes glowed on the wall. The barracks smelled of sweat and shit, but at least they were cool. The guards kept them moving, marching to the end of a long corridor, where they found a large bathhouse, hung thick with steam. Mia and her fellows were ushered in by Magistrae, the guards left outside. The older woman looked at them expectantly.

'Off with your clothes,' she ordered.

Another girl her age might have blushed. Trembled or simply refused. But Mia saw her body as just another weapon, as dangerous as any blade. Weaver Marielle had gifted her curves sharp enough to almost kill a man if she wished it, and Mia had murdered more men than she could rightly count.

What matter now to show a little skin?

And so, she stripped off her rags and boots without hesitation, stood naked in the steam. Sidonius was still too shaky from his beating to take much notice, but she saw Matteo drinking in her body from the corner of his eye. Magistrae pointed to a stone bench near the pool. Mia saw razors, combs, a bevy of soaps.

'Gladiatii bathe together, eat together, fight together,' the woman explained. 'But until you survive the Winnowing, you will tend to your own ablutions. Mark me well; I'll not tolerate filth beneath this roof. And have a care with that hair of yours, girl.' Magistrae looked at Mia's long, dirty locks. 'If I find a single flea in it, I'll have the lot chopped off.'

The woman raised one grey, sculpted eyebrow, inviting questions. After a moment's silence, she nodded curtly.

'I will return in twenty minutes. Keep me waiting, taste the lash as your reward.'

Magistrae stalked away, the guards remaining stationed outside the door. Mia waded into the bath, sinking down with a long sigh. The temperature was glorious, and she luxuriated in the sensation, running her hands over her skin. Pushing back her hair, she finally surfaced, blinking the water from her lashes. She fixed Matteo in her stare, let herself rise in the water just enough that her breasts showed above the surface. The boy had his hands at his crotch, unsuccessfully trying to cover his growing erection as he stepped into the bath.

'Four Daughters, you'll have someone's eye out with that,' Sidonious growled. 'Anyone'd think you'd never seen a pair of baps before.'

Matteo raised the knuckles and Mia found herself laughing. She reached for a cake of honeysoap, wondering how a peace offering might fare. Thugs often stood down once you stood up to their bullshit . . .

'If you weren't such a pig, I'd find you more amusing, Sidonius.'

'Aye, well, if you weren't such a cunt, I'd find you more attractive, little Crow.'

'I think I'll learn to live with the heartache.'

The Itreyan smirked, gingerly touched his broken nose. Though she'd given him a drubbing, he seemed not to take it personally, and Mia decided Sidonius was one of those fellows who worked out his feelings through the application of violence. The kind who'll walk into a taverna and beat the wailing shit out of the first man to look at him crossways, but the moment the fight is done, will be calling his foe 'brother' and buying him drinks. Now that she'd given him a walloping, he seemed more kindly disposed. Though watching Sidonius prod his new sutures, she still wouldn't be willing to bet whether he'd rather fuck or murder her.

'Who stitched you?' she asked, blinking suds from her eyes. 'That young girl?'

'Aye,' Sidonius nodded. 'Maggot they call her.'

'What kind of name is that?'

The big man sank up to his chin in the water. 'No clue. But she's swift with a needle. Good thing, too. She'll have more stitching to do after the Winnowing.'

Matteo finally dragged his eyes away from Mia's breasts, frowning.

'What is this Winnowing they speak of?'

Sidonius scoffed. 'Where you from, boy?'

'Ashkah. Down near Dust Falls.'

'They got no arenas down there?'

Matteo shook his head. 'I'd never seen the ocean until a month ago. Never even left my village. And now I'm here. Locked up with Itreyan pigs and Dweymeri brutes.'

'Watch your mouth.' Sidonius raised an eyebrow. 'I'm Itreyan.'

'Aye,' Mia said. 'And the most brilliant boy I ever met was Dweymeri.'

Sidonius nodded. 'I'd leave that shit in the sewer if I was you, countryboy.'

Matteo mumbled apology, fell silent. Minutes passed, the boy fumbling with the soap, finally dropping the cake and fishing about for it in the water.

'How'd you end up here?' Mia asked.

The boy shrugged, steam sticking those dark curls to his skin. 'My da sold me. Gambling debts. Foisted me off for want of coin.'

'Aa's cock,' Sidonius growled. 'And I thought *I* was cold-blooded.'

'You're half decent with a blade,' Mia said. 'Where'd you learn to fight?'

'My uncle.' Matteo ran a hand through his hair, Mia idly watching the muscles at play in his arm as she combed her knots. 'I was going to join the legion. I hoped I might get posted to a big city one turn. I always wanted to see the City of Bridges and Bones.'

'Perhaps you will,' Mia said. 'They hold the *Venatus Magni* in Godsgrave.'

'What's that?'

'The greatest games in the calendar,' Sidonius replied. 'Held at truelight, when all of Aa's eyes are open in the sky. The purses are fortunes to the sanguila who win them. And to the gladiatii who wins the *magni*? He knows the greatest prize of all.'

Hope gleamed in Matteo's deep brown eyes. 'Freedom?'

The big Itreyan nodded. 'A gladiatii can buy his way free if he wins enough coin. But the gladiatii who wins the *magni* has freedom handed to him by God himself.'

The boy frowned in confusion, obviously oblivious. Sidonius rolled his eyes.

'You heard the tale of the beggar and the slave?'*

---

*A parable from the Gospels of Aa. In his wisdom, one fine weeksend, the Light God sought to test the worthiness of his subjects. And so, dressed as a

'Aye.'

'Well, to honour the God of Light during truelight, every beggar in the 'Grave is fed from the Republic's coffers. And the winner of the *magni* is given his freedom by the grand cardinal himself. Clad in naught but rags, just like Aa was in the gospel.'

Sidonius leaned forward, eyes glittering.

'And then, if that weren't enough, the bloody *consul* hands you your victor's laurel. Imagine it. Crowd going berserk. That god-bothering bastard Duomo dressed like a beggar, and that marrowborn wanker Scaeva kissing your arse in front of the entire arena.' Sidonius grinned like a madman. 'Every woman in the 'Grave would know your name. You'd be swimming in cunny for the rest of your life, countryboy.'

Mia looked to the ripples on the water before her. Imagining it, just as she'd imagined it for months now. Grand Cardinal Duomo, standing within arm's reach, dressed in nothing but his beggar's robes.

No cathedral around him.

No holy vestments around his shoulders.

And no trinity hanging around his neck . . .

And beside him, Consul Scaeva, victor's laurel waiting in his hand . . .

'And all I need do is win the *magni*?' Matteo asked.

---

beggar, he sat outside the grand temple to his name, dressed in rags with an alms bowl before him.

The king walked by in his golden crown, and the beggar pleaded for a coin. But the king told him nay.

The cardinal strode past in his silken robe, and the beggar pleaded again. But the cardinal gave him none.

Then a slave came by, and in his wisdom, Aa asked nothing, for the man had naught to give. But seeing the beggar's plight, the slave took his cloak – his only possession in the world – and wrapped it around the old beggar's shoulders. And Aa threw off his guise and stood, and the slave fell to his knees, amazed.

'Stand, I pray thee,' said almighty Aa. 'For even in thy poverty, thou hast dignity. And I say thou shalt kneel to no man again.'

And the Light God granted the slave his freedom. And the slave was mighty pleased. And nobody stopped to ask what the slave was planning to give the *next* beggar he found if the first one hadn't been a god, or how it's not really sound economic policy for kings to wander about giving taxpayer money to the destitute when public infrastructure is in such dire need of overhaul, or why the creator of the universe had nothing better to do on a weeksend afternoon than come down to earth to fuck with people.

Pfft.

Parables.

Sidonius guffawed. 'All? Aye, that's *all* you have to do. Just win the greatest games in the Republic. Against the finest gladiatii under the suns. This collegium hasn't even *won a berth* in the great games yet.'

'Well, how do we do that?'

'With difficulty,' Mia sighed. 'A collegium that earns enough laurels leading up to truelight can send gladiatii. But apparently this is our domina's first competitive season, and it seems she's but one victor's laurel to her name.' Mia scowled. 'Furian's.'

'And we three are a long way from the sands just yet,' Sidonius growled. 'Before we're even counted among the gladiatii, we must survive the Winnowing.'

'So come to explanation, then,' Matteo demanded. 'What *is* this Winnowing?'

'A cull,' Sidonius said. 'They hold them before every major games in the lead-up to the *magni*. Separate the wheat from the chaff.'

'Nobody knows what shape the Winnowings take,' Mia explained. 'The editorii change the format each time. But the next one is in two weeks. At Blackbridge.'

Matteo swallowed thickly, muscle in his jaw twitching.

'But if we don't know what the format will be, how do we prepare for it?'

'Do you pray?' Mia asked.

'. . . Aye.'

Mia shrugged.

'I'd start there if I were you.'

CHAPTER 9

STEPPING

Mia walked slowly, service tray balanced on her upturned palms. Other girls passed her in the hallway, carrying drinks or bowls of purple slumberbloom or phials of ink. Her shirt had been left behind in her room, but she still wore her britches beneath the corset and gown, sword and stiletto and a pouch of wyrdglass strapped to her thighs. She proceeded up the hallway carefully, hoping she portrayed an image of poise, rather than that of a girl with a small armoury bumping against her nethers.

She reached the stairs at the end of the hall, made to breeze past the two lumps of muscle there without a word. One spoke as she passed, freezing her in her tracks.

'Good eve, Belle.'

She'd tied the golden courtesan masque over her own, propped Belle's powdered wig atop her head. She was a good inch or two taller than the serving girl, and harder muscled, but her curves were around the same, and that was where the bruiser was spending most of his eye time.

'Lazlo,' *she said, giving a small curtsey.*

'A stupid one,' *Belle had told her.* 'Just give him a flirt and he'll let you past.'

'You're looking dashing as ever,' *Mia smiled.*

'Where you goin' with that?' *the second man asked, eyeing the tray.*

'Dario,' *Belle had warned.* 'A mean one. But even stupider than Lazlo.'

Mia nodded upstairs. 'Toliver and Vespa ordered a bottle for the Dona.'

Dario looked to Lazlo, muttering. 'We're not supposed to let anyone up 'til—'

'Aa's cock, man, leave her to it,' *Lazlo said. He trailed one finger gently down Mia's arm, and the girl had to steel herself from taking his hand off at the shoulder.* 'You head on upstairs, little dove.'

Skin crawling at the thought of a grown man calling a fourteen-year-old his 'little dove', Mia trod carefully up the stairs. From what Dario had said, the map still wasn't here yet, but the seller had to be arriving soon. She could hear rain on the roof now, walking down a polished hallway hung with nudes of beautiful men and women. A double door flanked by two guards waited for her at the corridor's end, and thanks to Eclipse's scouting, she knew the Dona's office was beyond it.

'... FIVE MEN AND YOUR MARK INSIDE ...' *came a soft growl at her feet.*

'... though one of them will prove little trouble ...'

Four men, plus the Dona, plus whoever the map dealer brought with them.

Black Mother, they don't make it easy, do they?

Mia had thought perhaps to wait in a side room until she heard the seller arrive, but the guards on the office door were staring right at her.

'Eclipse,' *she whispered.* 'Head downstairs and look for our seller.'

Feeling her shadow ripple, she adjusted her wig and walked blithely up to the office, greeted both men with a smile.

'Maxis, Donato, pleasant eve,' *she said, curtseying.*

'Belle, you shouldn't b—'

Before Donato could finish his objection, Mia rapped on the door with her foot. After a moment, it swung wide, and she looked up into the face of a tall Dweymeri man, his features inked with artful tattoos, his broad chest wrapped in a fine waistcoat with gold buttons. He scowled at the pair of guards beside the door.

'Thought I said no visitors 'til she arrives.'

'I tried to stop 'er, blame fucking Laz—'

'Who is it?' *called a low, musical voice from inside.*

With one last black scowl at the guards, the Dweymeri replied over his shoulder.

'Belle. And booze.'

'Four Daughters, send her in. I could drink the Sea of Stars.'

The braavi thug stared at Mia a moment longer, then stepped aside.

Mia breezed past, noting the rapier and stiletto sheathed at the thug's belt. The room beyond was a grand boudoir, three other braavi thugs waiting around the periphery. Though all were dressed like marrowborn dandies, each carried a small armoury. Fine art hung on the walls and red silk

---

*Well, as breezy as one can get with a gravebone longsword and a bag of arkemical explosives pressed against one's crotch.

was draped on every surface. A large bed dominated the setting, and a pretty young man lay sleeping upon it.

'*Set it over there, Belle. And be quick about it, there's a love.*'

A figure in the shadows spoke, a low and dusky voice Mia finally identified as female. As the speaker stepped into the light, Mia saw dark hair, dagger-sharp cheekbones. She wore a monocle on a silver chain about her neck, and was slipping a fine-cut silk shirt over her head. Mia recognized her from the sketch in Solis's scroll case immediately – the Dona, leader of the Toffs.

'*Don't mind him, he's down for a while.*' *The Dona smiled, nodding to the snoozing figure on the bed.* '*Lads today. No stamina at all.*'

Mia offered what she hoped was a polite laugh, set the tray down where she was bid. The guards were barely paying attention to her – two were close enough to get caught in a wyrdglass blast, and her shadow could hold at least one other in place. The sweetboy on the bed would be no drama. Five short steps and she could have the Dona's throat open. It would all depend on who the map seller brought wi—

'*. . .* SHE COMES *. . .*' *came a whisper in her ear.*

'*Dona,*' *called one of the door guards.* '*Company.*'

The braavi leader nodded, motioning Mia towards the corner.

'*Plant yourself over there and look mysterious, love. But plants don't talk, aye?*'

Mia nodded, slinking back into the shadows. She heard brief murmurs at the boudoir door, thunder cracking outside the window. A figure walked past the guards – short, decidedly feminine – clad in a loose outfit of mortar grey, slightly damp from the storm outside. Her face was cowled, covered, a pair of sparkling blue eyes visible between the folds. An assortment of blades was strapped to her body, and Mia's heart beat quicker as she spied a wooden map case slung over her shoulder.

'*Well, well,*' *the figure said.* '*This is nice and dramatic, isn't it?*'

'*You came alone,*' *the Dona mused.*

'*That's the way I work,*' *the newcomer replied, strolling into the room. Her words were muffled under her cowl, but there was something . . .*

Those eyes.

That voice . . .

It couldn't be . . .

The newcomer glanced at the naked young man on the bed, Mia with her too-tight corset. '*Nice view. But it's a touch crowded, don't you think?*'

'*That's the way I work,*' *the Dona replied.* '*And I've two golden rules in this life, little one – never trust a man who speaks of his mother without kindness, and never trust a woman who wears a masque without cause.*'

The newcomer rolled her eyes, but nevertheless pulled her cowl down, releasing long warbraids of golden blonde. And as Mia's belly flipped sideways and all the way around, the newcomer pulled away the fabric, revealing a face Mia knew almost as well as her own.

Thunder crashed, Mia's fingernails biting her palm.

Black fucking Mother . . .

It was Ashlinn Järnheim.

When last they'd seen each other, they'd been facing down across a dusty thoroughfare in Last Hope. The Luminatii invasion had failed, the justicus was slain. But a trinity around Ashlinn's neck had held Mia at bay long enough for Ash to escape.

And now she was here in Godsgrave.

Carrying the very item Mia had been sent to steal . . .

What the 'byss is going on here?

'You have the map?' the Dona asked.

'You have the money?' Ashlinn replied.

The Dona nodded to a guard, who tossed a clinking pouch in the girl's direction. Ashlinn snatched it from the air, opened the drawstring and took out a single coin. Not a copper beggar, not a silver priest, but . . .

Gold.

Mia shook her head.

Goddess, a fortune . . .

'Now,' the Dona said. 'Your half of the bargain, if it please you.'

Ashlinn slung the map case off her shoulder, tossed it to the Dona. The woman opened one end with a soft click, pulling a rolled piece of vellum a little way out of the case. Mia caught a glimpse of strange writing, a sickle-shaped symbol in the corner.

'Well,' Ashlinn sighed. 'Pleasant as this is, I spied a pretty redhead downstairs so I'll just be . . .'

Ashlinn's sentence trailed off as the guards at the entrance pushed the door closed with all due drama. Mia shook her head, calculating whether she should reach for her wyrdglass or longsword first. Deciding on the arkemy, she cursed Ashlinn for a fool – marching into a braavi den and mouthing off like she owned it. Did she honestly think this was going to end another way?

The fool in question glanced over her shoulder, blue eyes narrowed.

'Could you ask your fancylads to step out of my way, please, Dona?'

'I'm afraid not,' the braavi leader replied. 'The grand cardinal was rather specific about what we were to do with you after coin changed hands.'

Mia's heart surged at the Dona's words.

Cardinal Duomo? How is he mixed up in all this?

Thunder crashed outside the window again, lightning flickering through the curtain cracks. The Dona leaned against her desk and smiled.

'I confess, I'm surprised you made this so easy, little one. Duomo warned me you and your father were as sharp as razors.'

'I'd heard the same about you,' Ashlinn said, eyes on the braavi thugs now slowly fanning out around her. 'Imagine my disappointment.'

'Fear not, it shan't last long,' the Dona smiled.

Ashlinn nodded to the map case in the Dona's hands.

'Do you even know where that leads?'

'No. I don't stick my nose into what doesn't concern me.'

'You might want to work on that,' Ashlinn smiled. 'Because a nosy person might have spied the false bottom in the case they'd been handed. And a person not so fond of her own voice might have heard the flint that sparked the fuse on the tombstone bomb inside.'

The Dona's eyes widened. Ashlinn threw herself aside, Mia barely having the presence of mind to hurl herself behind the bed before the map case exploded with an ear-splitting boom. The Dona was blasted across the room, dead before she hit the floor. Three guards were caught in the arkemical fireball, the Dweymeri smashed through the doors, his waistcoat aflame, the other thugs tossed about like burning straw.

The room was filled with choking smoke, Mia's skull pounding from the blast.

'Maw's teeth,' she spat, trying to rise.

'... MIA ...!'

'... are you well ...?'

Ashlinn uncovered her ears, picked herself off the ground. She snatched up her sack of gold, and drawing a short blade from her belt, plunged it into the braavi groaning on the floor beside her. Satisfied that the Dona was already dead, she quickly perished any guard who was still moving, then turned towards the serving girl in her smoking chiffon lying beside the bed.

'Apologies, Mi Dona, but I ...'

Mia rolled over onto her back. Her masque had been knocked clear in the blast, her ears ringing, her vision blurred. Mister Kindly coalesced on her shoulder, Eclipse at her feet, translucent fangs bared in a snarl that could be felt through the floor.

''Byss and blood,' Ashlinn breathed.

Eyes as blue as empty skies were fixed on the shadowcat on Mia's shoulder. Focusing now on his mistress herself.

'. . . Mia?'

'Four fucking Daughters . . .' came another voice.

Mia squinted through the haze, saw Lazlo, Dario and three other Toffs at the office door, staring in horror at the carnage beyond. Dario clapped eyes on the corpse of their leader. Lazlo, the figure swathed in grey.

'Kill 'er!' one of the thugs roared.

Without a word, Ashlinn was dashing towards the window, hurling a dagger and shattering the glass. The Toffs charged in a mob, and more out of instinct than forethought, Mia reached under her dress and threw one of her white wyrdglass globes at their feet. The arkemical sphere burst with a loud bang, a cloud of thick white Swoon engulfing the thugs.

Ashlinn climbed through the window, grabbed a silk line tied to a stone gargoyle above. Without a backward glance, she was up the wall and gone.

Mia staggered to her feet, head still ringing, swaying to the windowsill. She was in a tight corset and long gown; not the easiest gear to be scaling brothel walls in, even without a concussion. But, fearless as ever, she seized hold of the line and swung out over the five-storey drop, scrambling onto the roof just in time to see Ashlinn leap across to the bordello next door.

'Eclipse, go get Jessamine!' she barked. 'Mister Kindly, with me!'

The shadowwolf disappeared, Mister Kindly flitted across the roof after their quarry. Shaking her head to clear the ringing, Mia followed hard. Truth was, her boots weren't made for a chase scene, and the rain had made the roof tiles as treacherous as the snake she was chasing. As Ashlinn dropped off the bordello roof, Mia skidded to a cursing halt, hacking at her skirts with her gravebone stiletto so she could run faster.

Mia's mind was reeling. It'd been eight months since she'd laid eyes on Ashlinn Järnheim, and she could scarce believe the girl was here now. She and her father had been in alliance with Justicus Remus to bring down the Red Church. Now she was in league with the grand cardinal?

Mia pushed the questions from her mind, tore away the rest of her sodden skirts and ran on. Peering over the bordello roof, she saw Ashlinn dropping to the cobbles below, too far away to reach her shadow. Fearless of the fall, she flipped over the edge, scaling from window to window, fingers white on the rain-slick stone. Reaching the cobbles, she dashed off through the Godsgrave streets, and over the Bridge of Tears.*

---

*Situated near the bordellos and pleasure houses of Little Liis, the Bridge of Tears is supposedly named for the sorrows of a thousand jilted lovers, who over the years have stood upon the bridge and wept upon discovery their beloved had sought the company of a sweetboy or sugargirl in the brothel district.

Ashlinn ran like the Mother herself was on her tail, weaving in and out of the crowd like smoke. Mia sprinted in pursuit, losing sight of her at least twice, turned aside in the maze of canals and dogleg alleys. But Mister Kindly flitted from rooftop to rooftop, leaping across awning and gable like the wind and calling above the summer storm.

'. . . left, left . . .'

'. . . alley beside the chandler's . . .'

'. . . no, the other left . . .'

Mia broke out onto a main drag, sliding beneath the axle of a galloping horse and cart and skirting the handfuls of limping jacks Ashlinn was throwing behind her.* Row after row of houses, temples with windows like empty eyes, thin bridges and winding canals. They were headed towards Godsgrave's marrow-born district now, the Ribs rising into the storm-washed skies. Ashlinn dashed down a dead-end alley, kicked left then right up the stonework, scrabbling over the broken glass at the top.

Mia followed, cutting her palms bloody. Ash was running across the rooftops again now, the terracotta treacherous with the rain. Leaping over the gap between one roof and another, Mia almost slipped as a tile cracked beneath her sodden boots. If she fell, it'd be a broken leg at best, a shattered spine at worst.

Where the fuck are Eclipse and Jessamine?

Mia saw the Basilica Grande looming ahead – a gothic masterpiece of marble spires and stained glass. The trinity of three suns glittered in every window, gleamed atop every steeple. Mia couldn't help but recall the truedark when she was fourteen – the dozens of men she'd murdered here in her failed attempt to kill Consul Scaeva. Ash knew Mia's weakness for the Everseeing's holy symbols – she was obviously hoping the basilica grounds were hallowed enough to repel the darkin on her heels.

Clever girl. But it doesn't work that way . . .

Ash reached to her belt, gathered another thin line and grapple. Throwing it across to the basilica's gutters, Ash swung across the gap and scrambled onto the roof. Mia ran harder, hoping to leap the distance, but even with

---

In truth, the bridge earned its moniker long before the surrounding borough became a den of iniquity, and is actually named for the tear-shaped stonework supporting its main arch.

Still, never let the truth get in the way of a good yarn, gentlefriends.

*Limping jacks: Godsgrave streetslang for caltrops, so named because of their similarity to jumping jacks, and the fact that people who decide to run through clusters of them tend to end up . . . O, you get the gist.

Mister Kindly eating her fear, she knew the gap was too wide. Skidding to a halt at the edge, she watched Ashlinn clamber up the tiles. Gasping for breath. Heart hammering in her chest.

Mia drew a throwing knife from her boot, took aim. She'd poisoned her blades with Swoon, and even a scratch would be enough to drop the girl like a bag of bricks. But, much as she wanted to, Mia realized . . .

I need her alive.

She lowered the blade, looked to the cobblestones thirty feet below. A novice wandering the cathedral grounds looked up and saw her, jaw dropping in surprise.

'Shit . . .' she breathed.

'. . . a distance like that should not trouble you . . .'

Mia looked to the shadowcat at her feet. Down to the gap again.

'I can't jump that far, it's impossible.'

'. . . not so long ago, you stepped from the top of the philosopher's stone all the way to the isle of godsgrave to this very cathedral. skipping across the city like a child over puddles . . .'

'That was during truedark, Mister Kindly.'

'. . . you did so again in the quiet mountain . . .'

'Aye, and the suns have never seen inside that place.'

'. . . it is raining. aa's eyes are hidden behind the clouds . . .'

'I'm not strong enough out here, don't you see?'

The not-cat sighed, shaking his head.

Ashlinn had reached the apex of the cathedral's roof, turning to look at Mia. Her blonde hair had grown longer, damp with rain and plastered to her tanned skin. Her pretty eyes were the blue of sunburned skies. Mia felt her fingers curl to fists, remembering what she'd done to Tric.

Ashlinn smiled. Holding two fingers to her eyes, pointing at Mia across the gap and speaking in the wordless sign language of Tongueless.

I see you.

And with a small smile, the Vaanian girl blew Mia a kiss.

Rage came then. Watching Ash scuttle away towards the basilica's bell tower. Mister Kindly could still follow; Mia could scramble down to street level and give chase. But the lead Ash now had was a long one, and truth was, all the cigarillos she'd been smoking lately weren't doing Mia's constitution any favours.

She was sick of running.

All right, fuck it then . . .

Mia reached out across the gulf, beneath that muddy grey sky. The shadows were indistinct with the sunlight veiled, but she could still sense two of Aa's eyes, burning in the heavens. A thin film of cloud and rain wasn't enough to rein in the rage of a god, and Mia could feel it scorching the back of her neck. But still . . .

But still . . .

She knew the dark. Knew its song. Remembering the way she'd felt it at truedark. Seeped into the cracks of this city's pores, puddling in the catacombs under its skin. The dark she cast at her feet, the dark that lived inside her chest, her womb, all the places the light had never touched. And teeth gritted, trembling, she reached into those warm and hollow places, stretched out her hand to the shadow of the bell tower

        and Stepped
               across
                      the hollow space
                                  between.

Mia reeled, vertigo swelling in her belly, vomit in her throat. Swaying backwards, she tottered as all the world shifted beneath her, almost toppling to her death on the wrought-iron fence below. She realized she was on the basilica roof, rain slicking the shingles beneath her feet, blinking hard and trying to regain her balance as Ashlinn loomed out of the blinding light, dagger in hand.

'. . . mia . . . !'

She barely dodged, bending backwards as the blade sliced the air. Mia raised her gravebone sword, trying to regain her footing. Bile in her mouth. Sweat in her eyes.

'. . . mia . . . !'

Ash struck again, forcing Mia's back against the bell tower's wall. Mia raised her longsword into guard, gasping and blinking and trying to stop the world from spinning.

'Learned a few new tricks, love?' Ashlinn smiled, dagger in hand.

The girl reached down her leg, fishing about inside her boot. It took her a moment, but finally she found what she sought, drawing out a long golden chain with a blazing kick to Mia's belly spinning at the end of it.

Aa's trinity.

Mia hissed like she'd been scalded. Mister Kindly yowled, slithering away across the rooftops. The basilica bells started tolling the hour, joined by the countless other cathedrals across the City of Bridges and Bones. Mia dropped to her knees, puking. The agony of it almost made her scream, the sight of those three suns — white gold, rose gold, yellow gold — was blinding. She scrambled back against the bell tower, hands up to shield her eyes from that awful, burning light.

'Looks like the old tricks still work, then,' Ashlinn said.

The bells fell silent, the rain still falling overhead. Ash looked about them, over the basilica's gutter to the drop below. Another novice of Aa was down in the courtyard now, pointing with his fellow at the girls on the roof.

'It's good to see you, Mia,' Ash said softly.

'F-fuck . . . y-y—'

'I wondered if Drusilla would send you after me. I think out of all of them, you knew me best.' Ash twirled the holy symbol around her finger. 'Kept this, just in case. But you tell that crusty old bitch if she wants me dead, she can come herself. Because I'm surely coming for her. Her and all her merry fucking band.'

Ash hung the medallion around her neck, rendered in silhouette against that awful, blistering hatred. The fury of a god, burning Mia blind.

'I'm sorry it was you, Mia,' Ash sighed. 'I always liked you. You're better than that place. Those murd—'

The dagger struck Ashlinn's shoulder. Blood sprayed, bright red between the raindrops. Ash twisted aside, another blade whistling past her cheek and chopping off a lock of her hair.

'Traitor!'

And as the blonde curl fell, tumbling, turning towards the tiles, Jessamine dragged herself up over the guttering and flew at Ashlinn with her rapier drawn.

T he smell of hot food met them as they emerged from the cellar.

Magistrae had met them in the bathhouse in exactly twenty minutes, carrying a bundle of new clothes. Not even Sidonius was fool enough to keep her waiting.

Once Mia had dressed in all she'd been given, she was tempted to ask where the rest of her outfit was. She wore a loincloth of padded grey linen, a leather belt to keep it in place. Her breasts were strapped with another strip of padded grey, leather sandals laced halfway up her shins. Her comrades wore even less – just loincloths and sandals for Sidonius and Matteo, with heavy leather cups to protect their dangles from the worst training might offer. The weather approaching truelight was so hot, the lack of material wouldn't bother anyone. But very little was being left to the imagination . . .

Sidonius wiggled his codpiece side to side. 'I hear it's what all the marrowborn gentry are wearing in the 'Grave this year.'

In a flash, a guard whipped out his truncheon and cracked it across the back of Sid's legs. The big man collapsed to his knees with a cry.

'For the last time, you will speak only when spoken to in my presence,' Magistrae said. 'Forget your place again, and I'll fashion you a worthy remembering. You can die on the sands just as well without a tongue in your head.'

Sidonius grunted apology, and Mia helped the big man to his feet with a sigh. The big Itreyan wasn't the sharpest sword she'd ever met, but when living like a dog, you don't get to pick your fleas.

The houseguards escorted the trio upstairs to the verandah. The gladiatii were gathered at long benches, shovelling bowls of porridge home with all the appetite of folk who'd spent the turn sweating under the boiling suns. Magistrae nodded to a stick-thin man in a leather apron serving food. He had a crooked eye, a single circle marked on his cheek, and very few teeth in his head. Mia's mother had warned her never to trust a thin chef. But again, when living like a dog . . .

'Eat,' Magistrae ordered, tossing her long grey braid over her shoulder. 'You will need your strength amorrow.'

Sidonius stalked towards the cook like a man at purpose, Mia and Matteo following. The girl realized she hadn't eaten since yestereve, but beneath her hunger, she still felt that cold queasiness from earlier in the afternoon. Scanning the faces of the gladiatii, she found Furian at the head of the first bench. The man had tied his long black hair back in a braid, speaking to the Dweymeri man between mouthfuls.

He glanced up as she entered, turned his gaze away just as swift. Questions burned in Mia's mind, backing up behind her teeth.

Patience.

She followed Sidonius to the porridge pot and snatched up a wooden bowl, almost drooling at the aroma. The thin man served a great, sloppy spoonful to Matteo.

'Oi, I was here first, you scrawny shit,' Sidonius growled.

A meaty paw pushed the chef aside. Mia recognized the big Liisian gladiatii with a face like a dropped pie as he snatched the ladle. His head was shaved, only a tiny crop of dark hair remaining, like a cock's comb on his scalp. His face was pockmarked, his smile crooked – and not in the roguishly handsome sort of way. More in a dropped-one-too-many-times-on-his-head-as-a-babe kind of way.

'Pleasant turn to you, gentlefriends,' he bowed. 'Welcome to Remus Collegium.'

Sidonius nodded greeting. 'My thanks, brother.'

Mia noted the other gladiatii all watching. Her hackles rising.

'O, think nothing of it,' the pieman said. 'Butcher, they name me. The Butcher of Amai.' The Liisian looked them over with a smile. 'Long journey from the Gardens? You must be hungrier than a breadline strumpet on the rag, neh?'

'Aye,' Sidonius nodded. 'We've not eaten since yesterturn.'

'O, you'll find your needs well fixed presently. No better pigswill in all the Republic than's served by our domina.' He rubbed his chin, thoughtful. 'The porridge *can* be a touch bland, though. But no fear, I've just the spice.'

The big Liisian reached into his loincloth with a grin. And without further ado, he whipped out his cock, and took a long noisy piss into the porridge pot.

The gladiatii erupted into howls of laughter, thumping the tables and calling Butcher's name. The big Liisian looked Mia square in the eye and he milked the last drops from his bladder, then turned back to Sidonius. His grin had evaporated utterly.

'You call me "brother" again, I'll piss in your dinner and fucking drown you in it. My brothers and sisters under this roof are *gladiatii*.' Butcher thumped his chest. 'Until you last the Winnowing, you're *nothing*.'

Butcher strode back to his meal, slapped on his back by several others. Mia stood with bowl in hand, the stench of fresh urine in her nostrils.

'I find myself not as hungry as I first thought,' she confessed.

'Aye,' Sidonius said. 'We're of like mind, little Crow.'

The trio found an empty bench, Mia and Sidonius staring while the other gladiatii ate their fill. After one look at their mournful expressions, Matteo scooped a spoonful of his own meal into Sidonius's bowl, another into Mia's. The big Itreyan watched in disbelief, Mia stared into Matteo's eyes.

'Are you certain?'

'Eat, Mi Dona,' he smiled. 'You'd do the same for me.'

Mia shrugged, and she and Sidonius scoffed down the food without pause. The big mastiff wandered into the mess area, sniffing around on the floor for scraps. He mooched up to Matteo, eyeing his now empty bowl and wagging his stubby tail.

'Sorry, friend,' Matteo sighed. 'If I had a crumb left, I'd share it.'

Mia watched the boy sidelong as he patted the big dog, scruffing him behind his ears and grinning as his hind leg began thumping on the floor.

'His name is Fang,' said a voice.

Mia looked up, saw the little girl named Maggot sitting in the rafters above their heads. Mia could remember climbing those some gables when she was a little girl, her mother scolding, her father applauding. That had ever been their way – Justicus Corvere indulging her tomboyish impulses, and the dona trying to sculpt her into a prize fit to marry off one turn. Mia wondered how her life might look if things had been different. Where she'd be if General Antonius had become king by her father's hand. Probably nowhere with a brand on her cheek and the stink of piss in her nose . . .

'Fang,' Matteo smiled, patting the dog's shoulders. 'A fine name.'

'He likes you,' the little girl said.

'I had hounds at home. I've a way with them.'

He smiled wider, dark eyes sparkling. Too pretty for this place by far. But Maggot seemed to approve, ducking her head to hide her blush as she scrambled away.

With the meal finished, the gladiatii were marched down to the cellars. Mia, Sidonius, and Matteo shuffled along in the rear, no word spoken to them that wasn't an order, no attention paid that wasn't a shove or a sneer. After only a handful of hours living at the bottom of the barrel, Mia found the novelty wearing thin. She wondered where Mister Kindly was, if he'd yet made it to Whitekeep and met—

'Looks like our champion is too good to sleep with the rest of us plebs,' Sidonius muttered. 'Effete wanker.'

Mia followed the Itreyan's stare, saw Furian being escorted farther into the keep, instead of down to the barracks.

The Vaanian girl turned on Sid with a scowl.

'I'd watch that tongue of yours, Itreyan.'

'Normally women offer to buy me a drink first,' Sidonius grinned. 'But, aye. You can watch it if please you, Dona. Where would you like me to put it?'

Mia rolled her eyes and sighed. The girl thrust her hand into Sidonius's codpiece, squeezing tight as he squeaked.

'Up your arsehole, you dopey fuck,' she spat. 'Furian the Unfallen is champion of this collegium. He sleeps apart from us, as is his right. You can speak ill of him when you best him in the *venatus*. Until then, shut your mouth, lest I shut it for you.'

'Move!' barked the guard behind them.

The girl released her grip on Sidonius's jewels, stomped down the stairs. The big Itreyan sagged against Mia, and since she'd already kneed him in the dangles today, she was charitable enough to help him walk.

'You've certainly got a way with women, Sid,' Matteo sighed, propping up the big Itreyan's other shoulder.

'J-just what your mother said,' the big man winced.

The gladiatii gathered in the antechamber, and with a twist of that odd key in the mekwork on the wall, the portcullis opened to the barracks beyond. Mia was led into a wide cell littered with fresh straw, Sidonius and Matteo behind her. Once each gladiatii was in their allotted cage, the guard in the antechamber outside flipped a lever. Each door slammed closed, the mekwerk locks thudded home, and in a moment, every warrior was secured behind a lattice of iron bars over three inches thick.

Now Mia saw the reason behind the dona letting her property sleep down here in the dark and the cool. It seemed for all her love of her precious 'Falcons,' Leona didn't want any of them flying their coop.

The arkemical lights burned low, the gladiatii talking among themselves out in the gloom. Mia listened to the warriors murmur, noting the blend of accents and timbres. The Dweymeri woman with the extensive tattoos had her own cell across the corridor, with genuine stone walls that offered some small privacy. Beneath the door, Mia could hear soft singing.

Without warning, the talk died, silence falling like fog. Mia heard a familiar *clink* thump, *clink* thump on the stone. She saw the towering figure of the executus limping among the cells, that hateful whip in his hand. His long salt-and-pepper hair was arranged about his shoulders like a mane, his beard freshly combed. That awful scar cut down his face, casting a long shadow across his features.

'I've been away from these walls too long, it seems,' he growled. 'If you've strength to sit up and chatter like maids at loom, you've obviously not been worked hard enough.'

Passing by Mia's cell, he barely deigned to look at her. Executus limped back to the portcullis, blue eyes twinkling in the gloom.

'Rest your heads, Falcons,' he called. 'Tomorrow will be a long turn. I vow it.'

The portcullis slammed shut with a mekwerk whine. Mia shook her head, mumbling under her breath. Sidonius grumbled too, voice thickened by his broken nose.

'I hope I get a chance in the circle with that bastard on the morrow. I'll knock his block off and fuck his corpse before it's cold.'

'You'd need a cock for that, coward.'

The barb came from across the corridor. Mia looked up to see Butcher, the Ruiner of Porridges, watching them from between the bars of his cage. His face was all bent nose and pockmarked skin, his body a patchwork of scar tissue.

Sidonius scowled at the gladiatii. 'Call me coward again, I'll kill you and your whole fucking family.'

'Talk, talk, little one,' Butcher's lips twisted in an ugly smirk. 'You'll see how much it avails you when you step into the circle with Executus.'

'Pfft, you think I can't dance with a lame old dog like that?'

Butcher shook his head. 'You're talking about one of the greatest gladiatii to walk the sand, you ignorant fool. He'll chew you up and use your bones for toothpicks.'

Sidonius blinked. 'Eh?'

'You never heard of the Red Lion of Itreya?'

''Byss and blood.' Mia looked to the gate Executus had left by. '*That's* Arkades?'

Matteo rubbed his eyes, sat up a little. 'Who's Arkades?'

Butcher scoffed. 'Clueless, the lot of them . . .'

'The Red Lion, they called him,' Mia said.

'. . . Executus used to be a slave like us?' Matteo asked.

'Not like you, you worthless shit,' Butcher snarled. 'He was fucking gladiatii.'

'Victor of the *Venatus Magni* ten years back.' Mia spoke softly, voice hushed with awe. 'The Ultima was a free-for-all. Every gladiatii who'd been signed up for the games was released onto the sand for that final match. One warrior sent out every minute until the killing was done. Must've been almost two hundred.'

'Two hundred and forty-three,' Butcher said.

'And Executus killed them all?' Matteo breathed.

'Not by himself,' Mia said. 'But he was the last standing when the butchery was done. They say the sand in Godsgrave arena has never been the same colour since.'

'So they named him the Red Lion,' Butcher said. 'He won his freedom under Leonides's colours, see? Standing on a leg so badly broken, they had to cut it off afterwards.' He sneered at Sid. 'Still want to dance with him, little man?'

Sidonius scowled, remained silent.

'I commanded you to *sleep!*' came the bellow from the portcullis.

Butcher sniffed, rolled over on his straw. Matteo did likewise, and after a few choice curses, Sid curled up with his back to them all. Mia sat brooding in the gloom.

The arkemical globes faded, their glow dying slow. Darkness fell in the barracks, only the faintest chinks of sunlight falling across the threshold from the stairs above. Mia felt it crawling across her scalp, goosebumps rising on her skin. The air down here was stifling, the stink of straw and sweat thick in the air. But at least it was dark.

It almost felt like home.

She waited an hour, until every chest rose and fell with the rhythm of slumber. Matteo murmuring. Sidonius snoring softly. Mia looked around the gloom, making sure each of her fellows was still. She closed her eyes. Held her breath

and Stepped
                out of the shadows
                                in her cell
                                        and into the shadows
                                                of the antechamber.

The room swam and she steadied herself against the wall. She could feel the heat of those two blazing suns in the sky above. Crouching low, she peered through the portcullis, back to the cells. And content her absence was unmarked, she stole like a whisper up into the keep.

Without Mister Kindly or Eclipse in her shadow, her heart was pounding, her palms damp with fear. She knew the building's layout like she knew her own name, but with no eyes to see except her own, she felt utterly alone. She could have waited until the shadowcat returned from Whitekeep with news, but her questions couldn't. Since the turn her father died, she'd wondered what she was. Now, all the answers might be only a heartbeat away . . .

She moved swift, all Shahiid Mouser's lessons ringing in her head. Listening for the tread of the houseguards who walked the lower levels. There was only one pair patrolling inside and it was easy enough to avoid them, sneaking through the silken curtains and ducking out of sight, making her way towards the kitchens.

She found them empty, the starving chef nowhere to be seen. But there was food aplenty in the larder and Mia dived in face-first, eating her fill. If she was to survive the Winnowing, she'd need every ounce of strength she could muster. She stole two steel forks, then slipped from the kitchens without a sound.

She dodged the patrol again, listening to the sickness in her belly and working her way by feel. She passed a long tapestry depicting the *venatus* – gladiatii clashing with fantastical beasts. Sets of gladiatii armour lined the hallway, sunslight glinting on crested helms and breastplates of polished steel. Fear rising now, churning in her belly as she reached a room with a barred slit, an iron lock.

And beyond it . . .

She took the two forks from her loincloth, bent the tines against the wall. Turning her ear for the guards, she knelt before the keyhole and set to work. Soon enough, it popped open, the door came next, and with a glance over her shoulder for the guards, she stole inside.

Hands around her neck, twisting tight, flipping her over a broad shoulder and sending her crashing to the floor. Stars burst in her eyes as her skull cracked on the flagstones, an elbow jammed into her throat. She blinked up into a pair of glittering brown eyes, a handsome face framed by flowing locks of raven black.

Furian, the Unfallen.

He sat atop her, crushing the air from her lungs. This close, the gnawing sickness she felt in his presence was all-consuming, becoming less an illness and closer to a terrible hunger. But more pressing still was the need to breathe.

Mia pricked one of her forks into the champion's armpit. One good thrust and it'd slip over his ribcage and into the heart beyond. She tapped it against the hollow, trying not to sputter as Furian pressed his elbow farther into her larynx.

She pushed her steel harder, glaring wordlessly. And finally, Furian eased off, leaning back just enough to allow her to breathe.

His voice was deep and melodic. His eyes the brown of dark chocolate, delicious but edged with bitterness. Mia tried very hard not to notice that the body he pressed against her was utterly naked.

'What are you doing in here, slave?'

She put her free hand on his elbow, slowly pushed it aside.

'We need to talk,' she replied. 'Brother.'

CHAPTER 10

SECRETS

Thunder split the skies as Ash and Jessamine clashed on the cathedral roof.

Both were soundless. No war cries or curses. No razored quips. Both had been trained in the art of death by the finest killers in the Republic, and both had marked their lessons well. Ashlinn drew two stilettos from her sleeves and met Jessamine's charge. Mia blinked through the falling rain, that awful burning light, noticing that Ash's weapons were discoloured with poison. Though Jessamine had advantage with a longer blade, one scrape from Ash might be enough to end her.

Mia groped towards her longsword, tried to stand. But she could manage neither — not with that accursed trinity around Ashlinn's throat. Every time Ashlinn moved, the muted sunlight caught the medallion's face, lancing Mia's eyes. Clenching her teeth, it was all she could do to hold back her whimper, let alone stand and fight.

Mister Kindly had fled, and Eclipse couldn't approach the trinity either. Mia was alone. Awful fear swelled in her belly, terror in the face of this god and his hatred.

All her power. All her training. All her gifts.

And she was utterly helpless.

Jessamine lunged across the slick tiles, the speed and feral cunning that had made her Solis's favoured pupil on display. Ash backed away, fear shining in her eyes as she realized she was outmatched. But her voice was steady and cold.

'Nice to see you again, Jess. How's being second in line treating you?'

The bright notes of steel on steel.

The percussion of thunder.

'Tell me' — Ashlinn narrowly ducked Jessamine's strike — 'how did it

taste when they teamed you up with the girl who cheated you out of becoming a Blade?'

Jessamine remained silent, refusing to be goaded. Pushing Ashlinn back, lunging as her foe slipped on the rain-slick tile. Ashlinn scrambled back to her feet, losing her grip on one of her knives. The poisoned dagger skittered down the roof's slope, caught itself on the gutter's lip.

'How did it taste when Mia killed Diamo?'

Jessamine faltered for a moment, renewing her attack with furious intensity. Ashlinn smiled, backing up closer to where Mia lay helpless. She held her poisoned blade in front of her, deadlier poison dripping from her lips.

'Were you fucking him?' Ash asked. 'I never found out. How did it taste bending the knee to the girl who murdered him?'

'Shut up,' Jessamine whispered.

'He died messy, Jess,' Ashlinn said. 'Puking blood. Shit in his britches. Could you smell it from the testing circle? I got a whiff from up in the bleachers.'

'Shut up!'

Jessamine lunged, face twisted with rage. Ashlinn spun aside, and with her foe off-balance, found time to reach into a belt pouch. Grasping a handful, flinging out her hand, a bright flash of arkemical powder bursting in Jessamine's eyes. The redhead staggered back, sputtering and blinded. Ashlinn closed for the kill, but with her stomach seething, Mia lashed out with her boot, knocking Ashlinn's feet out from under her.

Jessamine and Ashlinn went down together, rapier and poisoned blade both clattering to the tiles. The girls fell to brawling, clawing at each other's faces, punching and kicking and cursing. They tumbled down the sloping roof, rolling to a halt on the gutter's edge. Ashlinn lay underneath Jessamine, hands wrapped around the redhead's throat. Jessamine punched hard, splitting Ash's lip. Still half-blinded, she groped for Ash's collar, wrapping up the gold chain in her fist and strangling back. The chain snapped clean, the trinity dropping thirty feet onto the cobbles below. Thunder rolled, lightning tearing across the skies as the medallion fell out of sight, the pain in Mia's skull, the sickness in her belly slowly fading.

'You fucking traitor,' Jessamine spat, punching Ash in the jaw.

'Get . . . off m-me!'

'I'll show you what dying messy looks like.'

Jessamine wrapped her fingers around Ash's throat, punched her again with her free hand. She was raising her fist to strike again when a voice rose above the storm.

'Jess, th-that's enough.'

The redhead refused to look over her shoulder, bloodshot eyes locked on Ashlinn. Mia was on her feet, not looking anything close to steady, but slowly making her way down the roof with her gravebone longsword in hand.

'Fuck you, Corvere,' Jessamine spat.

'We n-need her alive.' Mia spat the taste of vomit off her tongue. 'She double-crossed the braavi. But they p-paid a fortune. There's no way she just incinerated a map that valuable. Presuming she even has it, we can't find it if she's dead.'

'I don't take orders from you.'

Mia sighed. 'You're my Hand, Jess. That's exactly what you do.'

Jessamine turned to glare at Mia, sodden hair in her eyes. Her frustration, the rage of the past seven nevernights in Mia's company finally getting the better of her.

'I should be delivering this offering. I should be the Blade here, not you.'

'Nobody said life was fair, Red.'

'Fair?' Jessamine laughed. 'Who the f—ckkkg . . .'

Jessamine reeled backwards, blood gushing from her throat. Ashlinn stabbed the girl again, the poisoned blade that had fallen into the gutter flashing in her hand. Jessamine gasped, hands to her punctured neck, arterial red spraying between her fingers and down her sodden tunic. Ashlinn stabbing again. And again.

Mia roared Jess's name as thunder crashed, as Ashlinn grabbed the Hand's collar and slung her forward. Jessamine clutched Ash's wrist in desperation, trying to stop her fall. But with a sickening crunch, the girl toppled off the roof and onto the fence bordering the basilica grounds, impaled on the wrought-iron spikes below.

The novices below cried out in horror, ran screaming for the Luminatii, for the cardinal, for anyone. Arcs of jagged blue white lit the skies as Ashlinn dragged herself to her feet, soaked with Jessamine's blood.

'You bitch,' Mia whispered.

Ashlinn wiped her knuckles across split lips. Pawing at her throat, she realized the trinity was gone.

'Mia, you don't understand what's happening here . . .'

Mia raised her blade. 'You killed her.'

Blood soaking Ashlinn's hands.

Rage swimming in Mia's eyes.

Lightning reflected on the pale edge of her longsword, in the empty gaze of the dead girl hanging on the wrought-iron fence below their feet.

The basilica bells started ringing again – a warning this time. Acolytes were gathered in the courtyard below, howling, 'Murder! Murder!' Mia stepped forward, blade poised. With the trinity over the edge of the building, Mister Kindly and Eclipse had returned, filling the terrifying emptiness she'd felt with the strength of cold steel. Ash's feet were snared in her own shadow – she had nowhere to run. But Mia had spoken truth to Jessamine; if she killed the girl now, she'd not see that map. And after her last flaying before the Ministry, she'd be damned if she'd return to them empty-handed.

But if she returned with the girl who'd brought the Ministry to their knees?

Black Mother, imagine the look on Solis's face . . .

So, Mia drew back her sword and cracked the crow hilt across Ashlinn's jaw. The girl tumbled onto her backside, half-senseless. Mia set about searching Ash's clothing, boots, sleeves, finding blades and toxins and arkemical powders and hurling them off the roof. Ashlinn sat up, dazed, and Mia pressed her sword tip into the flesh above the girl's heart. She could hear the faint sound of heavy boots over the thunder.

'. . . luminatii, mia . . .'

'. . . GOD-BOTHERING CURS. LET THEM COME . . .'

'. . . so eager for blood, dear mongrel . . . ?'

'. . . SO EAGER TO RUN, LITTLE MOGGY . . . ?'

'I appreciate the sentiment, Eclipse,' Mia whispered. 'But living to fight another turn is probably the goal here.'

The shadowwolf growled grudging assent, and Mia turned to Ashlinn. 'Right. You can get off this roof two ways. Feet or face first?'

'Is . . . this a t-trick question?'

Mia dug the razored point of her blade into Ashlinn's skin. Gravebone was harder than steel, sharp enough to bleed stone. One soft push . . .

'You try to make a break, or even breathe in a way I don't like, we paint the cobbles an interesting shade of Ashlinn. Are we clear?'

'. . . mia, we must go . . .'

The blade twitched. 'Clear?'

Ash winced. *'As Dweymeri crystal.'*

Mia slipped her belt from around her waist. 'Hold out your wrists.'

'Didn't know you were so inclined,' Ash smirked. 'Honestly, all you n—'

The blade sank deeper, and Ashlinn winced in pain. With a hurt glance, she offered her wrists. Mia looped the belt around them, cinching tight. She could hear the legionaries clearly now, a multitude of citizens gathered beyond the cathedral gates, looking in horror at Jessamine's dangling corpse.

Mia stood, pulled on the leather strap.

'*Move.*'

She led Ashlinn to a downspout behind the bell tower. A gargoyle spewed rainwater from its mouth into the churchyard two storeys below.

'*Traitors first,*' Mia insisted.

'*Going to be hard climbing with my hands tied, neh?*'

'*You'll manage. And don't even think about running when you hit the floor. Throwing knives run quicker than you, and I'm carrying six in your size.*'

Ash scowled, but for all her moaning, shimmied down the spout without much trouble. Mia followed, Mister Kindly whispering urgent warnings in her ear. The girls ran across the basilica grounds, past a necropolis littered with familia tombs. They vaulted the iron fence as a troop of Luminatii rounded the cathedral, shouted, '*Halt!*' Mia snatched the belt around Ash's wrists, dragging her captive into the streets.

The legionaries were wearing steel breastplates and carrying burning sunsteel longswords, but they vaulted that fence quicker than Mia would've given them credit for – a murder on Aa's holy ground was no chucklefest for his faithful. Mia looked at the crowd around her, pausing to snatch the full braavi purse from Ashlinn's belt.

'*Corvere, don't you fucking d—*'

Mia slung the bag in a wide arc, scattering a shower of glittering gold into the mob. The reaction was instantaneous, astonishingly violent, the people around them erupting as they realized the sky had somehow rained a living fortune. People flocked into the street from the taverna and stores all around, beggars, bakers, butchers, cutting off the cadre of Luminatii and punching and shouting and kicking over Ashlinn's gold.

Ashlinn wailed as Mia dragged her away through the driving rain. They dashed over a broad bridge, into the warrens behind the administratii buildings, and there, finally, Mia pulled Ashlinn into a small alcove.

'*Do you realize how much—*'

'*Shut up,*' Mia hissed. Reaching out to the shadows around them, Mia plucked them with clever fingers, twisting and weaving them into a mantle about her shoulders. With a flick of her wrist, she enveloped Ashlinn as well, just as she'd done the turn they stole into Speaker Adonai's chambers. Memories of their turns in the Red Church made Mia think of Jessamine; the sight of the Hand's body dangling from those wrought-iron spikes burned in her mind's eye.

Jess, Tric, every Blade murdered in the Luminatii pogrom, the capture of the Ministry . . . Ashlinn was responsible for all of it. The girl in her arms might as well have been a snake, coiled and ready to strike.

'*Not a sound,*' Mia whispered, pressing her gravebone blade to Ash's throat.

All the world was black beneath Mia's cloak, but she still heard the legionaries shouting to each other as they searched the Godsgrave backstreets. The girls waited, pressed against each other beneath Mia's shadows for endless minutes.

A whisper finally rose over the pattering rain.

'. . . they are gone, mia . . .'

Ashlinn swallowed against the blade at her throat. 'You kill me now, I swear by the Mother you're never going to see that map they've got you chasing.'

'*Good thing I'm not going to kill you, then,*' Mia said. 'Mister Kindly, you check the rooftops. Eclipse, you scout ahead, make sure the way back to the chapel is clear.'

'. . . SO BE IT. BUT IF YOU MURDER ANYONE WHILE I AM GONE, I WILL BE MOST UPSET . . .'

She felt the shadows about her ripple, the not-cat and not-wolf slipping from the dark at her feet. Mister Kindly flitted up the wall, shadow to shadow, Eclipse spilling across the cobbles and off into the street. She could feel Ash's heart beating, smell a faint perfume of lavender and fresh sweat on her skin.

'You're taking me back to the chapel?' the girl asked.

'There's a dose of Swoon on the blade at your throat, Ash. I don't much fancy knocking you out and carrying you back, but I will if I must. Now, shut the fuck up.'

'They've been hunting me for eight months. They get their hands on m—'

'You can count the shits I give on no hands, Ashlinn.'

'I didn't want to kill Tric, Mia.'

Ashlinn winced as Mia pushed her gravebone stiletto up under her chin. 'Don't you dare say his name.'

Ashlinn raised her hands, spoke slow and careful. Mia could hear the fear in her voice, the slight tremble that told her that, for all Ash's front, the girl didn't want to die.

'I wanted the Ministry, Mia. Anyone else was just wrong place, wrong time.'

'Including your own brother?'

'So. It was *you* that killed Osrik.'

'No,' Mia replied. 'But only because Adonai ended him before I got the chance. The pair of you killed Tric. You betrayed your vows. You betrayed the Church.'

'*To avenge my father! You of all people should understand that.*'

'*Don't push your luck, Ashlinn.*' Mia tightened her grip. '*My father is dead.*'

'*Aye?*' Ash snarled. '*Well, so is mine.*'

That gave Mia pause. Unspoken questions hanging in the air. The rain was dying now, the skies still a sullen grey. Ashlinn drew a long ragged breath.

'*We dodged the Church and their Blades for eight months,*' she murmured. '*They finally caught us in Carrion Hall. My father was good. One of the finest Blades to ever serve the Black Mother. But everyone's luck runs out eventually.*'

Mia simply shook her head, refusing to bite. Ashlinn Järnheim was made of lies. She'd lied all through their training at the Church. She'd lied to the Ministry, to Mia, to everyone she ever met. She'd struck at the heart of Jessamine on the basilica roof, she was striking at Mia's heart now. Every word she spoke was poison.

'*I'm not going to tell you to shut up again, Ash.*'

Ashlinn sighed, her temper fraying. '*You have no fucking idea what's going on here, do you? I know you, Mia. Do you have any idea what the Red Church actually is? Do you think they're ever going to let you kill Scaeva when he pays their wages?*'

Mia felt the consul's name like a fist in her belly.

'*You're full of shit.*'

'*Why do you think Scaeva isn't dead already? Half the Senate want him in the ground, you think they couldn't afford to hire a Blade to do him over if he wasn't protected by Sanctity? Julius Scaeva is a fucking bastard, but he's not a fucking fool. He's been a patron of the Church for years.*'

'*They'd never—*'

'*They're assassins, of course they would! There's no sanctity to what the Red Church does. They murder people for money. Half of them are psychopaths and the rest are just sadistic bastards. They're not servants of some divine Goddess of Night, they're fucking whores.*'

Mia's mind was racing. She knew nothing Ash said could be trusted . . . but somewhere in her words, Mia could hear the ring of truth. People who posed a threat to Scaeva either got killed like her father, or bought like the braavi. Wouldn't it make sense he'd buy the Church, too? Why else would they order her Scaeva wasn't to be touched?

'*How do you know all this?*' she asked.

'*Because I'm a sneaky bitch, Mia.*'

'*You're a lying cunt is what you are.*'

'*There's an obsidian vault inside the Revered One's chambers,*' Ash spat. '*And inside that vault, they keep a ledger of every offering the Church has undertaken. All their patrons. All their shit. When I poisoned the Ministry at the initiation feast, I stole the ledger, Mia. That's the reason they've been hunting me and my da for the past eight months. Not because we betrayed them. Because we know all their dirty little secrets.*'

Ashlinn turned her head a little, despite the blade at her throat. Just so she could look into Mia's eyes.

'*Including the one about you and your father.*'

Ashlinn fell silent as Mia pressed her blade back against her throat. Ash killed Jessamine. She'd killed Tric. Mia knew she'd do anything, say anything to avoid being taken back to the chapel.

'*You're a liar,*' *Mia said.*

'*I am at that. But not about this, Mia. If you take me back to the Church, they're going to kill me, and you'll never know the truth of what they did.*'

'*And I'm just supposed to take you at your word on all this?*'

'*You can see for yourself.*'

'*. . . You have the ledger?*'

'*Something tells me names on a page aren't going to sway you. But I can tell you exactly where you need to go to find proof written in something more than ink.*'

'*O, aye? And where would that be exactly?*'

Ashlinn looked up at Mia, blue eyes glittering like broken sapphires.

'*Back to Church.*'

W e have nothing to talk about,' Furian spat.

Mia was still sprawled underneath the Champion of the Remus Collegium, his forearm against her throat. Muscle rippling in his arm, across his chest. She pressed her fork into Furian's armpit again, hard enough now to break the skin.

'I'm not sure about the other women you've known,' she said softly, 'but I don't much fancy it on my back. Let me up.'

'I should knock your teeth out for even talking to me. How did you get in here?'

'Let. Me. Up. Fucker.'

Furian glanced to his now-unlocked door. Mia had no idea of the consequences if they were discovered in each other's company, but she doubted they'd be pleasant. She could hear the guard patrol, slowly coming closer.

With a curse, Furian twisted off Mia, pushed the door closed. He listened for a moment, ear to the wood as the guards passed by. Mia looked the champion up and down, skin prickling in spite of herself. She'd never seen a man quite like him, all hard tanned skin and rippling muscle. But there was a speed to him, also. Lithe and fierce, like a big cat. His body was utterly hairless – shaved, she supposed, to show off his physique to the adoring crowds. His jaw was strong, the rivers and valleys of his abdomen leading her eyes down, chewing her lip as she drank in the sight of him.

She'd no idea what had come over her. Though she'd found Lord Cassius attractive, her reaction to his presence hadn't been quite as . . . carnal. Perhaps because she'd never been quite this close to the Lord of Blades? Perhaps because she'd been younger? Whatever the reason, looking at Furian now, she found her breath coming quicker. Thighs aching. Waves of butterflies thrilling her belly.

His chamber was sparsely adorned. A small barred window looked out over the ocean, a simple bed stood against the wall, a practice dummy and wooden swords in another corner. A small shrine to Tsana, First Daughter of the Everseeing and patron of warriors, sat beneath the window, and the three interlocking circles of Aa's trinity were scribed on the wall in charcoal. Though it was only trinities blessed by Aa's truest believers that made her feel ill, the sight of the holy symbol was still a little unsettling.

All in all, Furian's accommodations were hardly a marrowborn villa. But compared to the barracks, they were positively palatial. And better, private.

When the guards had passed beyond earshot, the champion turned to Mia. His jaw was clenched. Long dark hair framing those delicious chocolate eyes.

'You feel it, don't you?' Mia breathed.

Furian stalked across the room and snatched up a strip of grey linen from the bed, wrapped it around his waist to make himself decent.

'Feel what?'

Mia pulled herself up off the floor, dragged her hair behind her ear. She saw movement from the corner of her eye, glanced to the shadows cast on the wall by the shrine's candlelight. Hers. His.

'Maw's teeth,' she breathed. 'Look . . .'

Their shadows were moving of their own accord.

Hair blowing as if in some hidden breeze, ebbing and flowing towards each other like waves on a lonely shore. Mia's shadow reached towards Furian's, though in the flesh, the girl hadn't moved a muscle. The Unfallen reached out and touched the wall, as if to test if his shadow were real. But his shadow didn't move as he did, instead reaching out towards Mia's.

The champion stumbled back, held up three fingers – Aa's warding sign against evil. And at that, the shadows fell still, trembling only for the candle flame.

'You're like me,' Mia said.

Furian blinked, turned away from the shadows to look at Mia.

'I am nothing like you,' he growled. 'I am gladiatii.'

'I mean you're *darkin*,' Mia said. 'Just as I am.'

'I say again, I am nothing like you, girl.'

'Where is your passenger?'

'. . . My what?'

'Your daemon,' Mia said. 'I have two who live in my shadow. Usually, anyway. What shape does yours wear? And where is it?'

'I know of no daemon,' he growled, 'save the one standing before me now.'

He looked her up and down, something close to disgust on his face. But she could see goosebumps rising on his skin, just as they did on hers. He was breathing harder, his pupils dilated – all the telltale marks Shahiid Aalea had taught her to recognize in a man. Or woman.

Want.

'How did you escape your cell?' he demanded.

Mia shrugged. 'I Stepped between the shadows.'

'Witchery,' he spat.

'It's not witchery. It's what we *are*. Can you not do the same?'

'I'll hold no truck with the darkness.' Furian raised the warding sign again.

'But you already did,' she said, stepping towards him. 'This very turn on the sands, when I fought Executus. You stopped me from—'

'Get out of here, girl. I am champion of this collegium, and a god-fearing son of Aa. Gladiatii do not mix with chaff, and I do not mix with heretics.'

Mia glanced at the shrine to Tsana, the trinity of Aa on the wall.

Could it be?

'. . . You're of the faithful? How can you—'

'Get *out*,' he hissed. He dared not raise his voice lest the guards overhear, but Mia could see the fury in his clenched fists, the tendons taut at his neck. 'If the guards find you in my cell, Executus will see the skin peeled off both our backs. And I'll not bleed for the likes of you. Now begone before I snap your neck and take my chance with the domina's mercy.'

His shadow seethed across the wall, hands extended towards her own shadow's throat. Mia stepped back, but her shadow remained unmoved, its hair twisting and coiling like a nest of snakes. The hunger surged inside her again, the sickness, mixed now with a dull, seething anger.

This man didn't know anything about darkin. Didn't know anything about himself. There were no answers here. Only more questions.

And the longer she stayed in his room, the more likely she'd be caught.

Mia retreated slowly, not turning her back, listening for the guards at the door. Hearing nothing, she opened it without a sound, checking that the corridor beyond the chamber was clear. Satisfied, she looked back over her shoulder to the champion of the collegium, his shadow flickering upon the wall.

She reminded herself of why she was here. To stand as victor in the *magni*, she'd have to best this man, darkin or no. And whatever dark kinship she might have with him came second to the knowledge that he stood between her and victory.

Her and vengeance.

So be it.

'This is a nice room,' she noted, looking about the chamber.

'What of it?' Furian spat.

Mia shrugged.

'I'd not get too comfortable in it if I were you.'

The girl slipped out the door, closing it behind her.

It took a few heartbeats for her shadow to follow.

C*rack!*

    'Gladiatii fear nothing, save defeat!'

Crack!

'Gladiatii thirst for nothing, save victory!'

Crack!

'Gladiatii live for nothing, save glory!'

Such was the tune of Mia's hours, sweltering beneath the blistering suns. Executus's voice was the verse, the snap of his whip the beat, and the grunts and sighs and curses of the men and women around her the chorus.

A week had passed since she'd arrived at Crow's Nest, but those seven turns had seemed long as years. Executus showed no mercy, drilling her and Matteo and Sidonius in every weapon, every fighting form, every trick and twist his years in the games had taught him. They sparred in the circle, on the uneven levels across the yard, in their sleep. Every stumble was met by his whip. Every misstep. Every slight.

Crack!
Crack!
Crack!

They'd been kept apart from the gladiatii, bathed and fed last. Butcher had spoiled at least three more of their evemeals, twice with piss, and once with a handful of dogshit he'd fetched after Fang had done his business in the yard. Mia had stolen food every nevernight in shadow jaunts to the kitchens, once had even managed to sneak some bread to Sidonius and Matteo with the excuse she'd found it in the mess hall. But she was still worn thin. Her fellow recruits were in even worse shape.

'You worthless whorespawn!' Executus roared at the trio. 'In a few turns, you step onto the sands of the *venatus* under the colours of this collegium. If you think the crowd will not howl for more when they see the first drop of your blood, you are greater fools than I gave credit for. Now, attack with purpose!'

'Executus?' came a call from above.

Mia looked up, saw Dona Leona standing on the broad balcony above. She was dressed in rippling white silk, gold at her wrists, auburn hair plaited down her back.

'Attend!' Executus roared.

The gladiatii fell still, thumping fists to chest.

'Domina?' Executus asked.

The woman crooked a finger and beckoned.

'Your whisper, my will,' the big man bowed.

He turned to Mia and her fellows.

'Sidonius, work the woodmen.' He glared at Mia and Matteo. 'You two, spar in the circle. You still carry a shield like a parcel of posies, girl. And Matteo wields a sword like a three-year-old swings his pecker. If you want to keep those pretty heads on your shoulders during the Winnowing, the pair of you had best get to toiling.'

Executus stroked his beard, limped away into the keep. Sidonius set to work on the training dummies, Maggot fetched Mia and Matteo some wooden swords and shields, and they set to sparring, clashing in the dust and dancing around the circle.

'Get to toiling?' Matteo spat. 'What the 'byss does he think we've been doing all week?'

Mia made no reply, intent on training. Despite being an utter bastard, now that she knew the executus was Arkades, she hung on his every word. If the Red Lion told her to work her shield arm, then Black Mother, she was going to work her fucking shield arm.

'Strike harder,' she growled. 'Press me.'

'I am!' Matteo spat, stabbing at her with his blade.

Mia fended off his blows with ease, and a flurry of strikes sent the boy skipping back across the sand. She battered his shield again, spitting dust off her tongue.

''Byss and blood, you're swinging at me like I'm made of glass. Hit me!'

Matteo blocked another blow, countered with a weak riposte. Wooden blades cracked against wooden shields, their feet dancing to the frantic percussion.

'I don't want to hurt you, Crow,' Matteo said.

'And why not? Because I might hurt you back?'

'Because . . . you're a girl,' he said.

Mia's eyes widened at that. Gritting her teeth, she wove past Matteo's strike, sandals scuffing in the dust. Spinning on the spot, she smacked him hard across his shoulder blades, sent him staggering. As he turned to face her, she clocked him in the face with her shield, blood spraying as he toppled onto the dirt.

Mia stood over him, pressing her wooden blade to his throat.

'Take hold of your fucking jewels,' she said. 'Maybe your mother raised you to treat us all as delicate flowers, maybe you're just thinking with your cock. But there *are* no girls on the sand. No mothers or daughters. Sons or fathers. Only *enemies*. You spend a moment worrying about what's between your opponent's legs, you'll find your head parted from your body. And what good will your fool cock do you then?'

The boy wiped the blood from his face, swallowing thick.

'Forgiveness,' he muttered. 'I d—'

'Gladiatii! Attend!'

Mia turned from Matteo's bloodied face to the balcony. She saw

Executus Arkades, Dona Leona beside him. The woman smiled like the suns, spoke with a loud, clear voice.

'My Falcons! Tomorrow we set out for Blackbridge and the grand games held in honour of Governor Salvatore Valente! This is the second official event of the *venatus* season, and all eyes will be upon it. Remus Collegium now stands in high regard, thanks to the victory of our champion in Talia last month.'

Here she took in Furian with a wave of her hand. The gladiatii roared his name, pounded swords upon shields.

'But Furian's triumph has not assured our berth in the *magni*!' Leona continued. 'The crowds are ever hungry for blood, and the editorii seek only the finest for their grand spectacle. We must have victory. We *will* have victory!'

'Victory!' they cried.

'The following gladiatii have earned the right to attend the Blackbridge *venatus* and fight for the Falcons of Remus. Step forward, Butcher of Amai!'

The Ruiner of Porridges stepped forward with his dropped-as-a-babe smile, raising the knuckles to the men behind him.

'Bladesinger, the Reaper of Dweym!'

The woman with the full-body tattoos stepped forward and bowed.

'Our equillai, Byern and Bryn, shall once again thrill the crowd!'

The blond Vaanian siblings bowed low. Looking closer at the pair side by side, Mia marked them for twins – they were simply too alike to be otherwise.

'Our legend of the sands, the mightiest Falcon in this collegium, victor of Talia, Furian, the Unfallen!'

The champion strode forward to the cheers of his fellows, twin blades in hand. His eyes were fixed on the balcony as he bowed deep, long black hair spilling around his high cheekbones, his square jaw. Mia looked to his shadow and saw nothing of note. But her own rippled slightly, like still water when a stone is dropped into it.

'And finally,' Leona called. 'Our three new recruits will wager their lives in the Winnowing, earning their place among you or perishing in the attempt. Pray that Aa grants them favour, that Tsana guides their hands to victory.' Leona looked among her flock, opened her arms. '*Sanguii e Gloria!*'

'*Sanguii e Gloria!*' came the cry.

Mia listened to them call, fists raised high, crying out for blood and glory. In truth, she wanted nothing to do with the latter. Blood was her intent, her dream, her only prize. Cardinal Duomo and Scaeva within arm's reach on the victor's podium. But to stand before them, she needed to accrue victories enough to secure a place in the *magni*. And somehow, in the midst of that bloodbath and butchery, she had to win.

The gladiatii around her looked to the sky, called to Aa and his firstborn to bring them victory. But Mia had no use for the Everseeing, nor his warrior daughter. Aa had only ever proved her enemy, and Tsana had never helped her before.

Why would she start now?

And so, Mia turned her eyes to the sand. To the shadow, black and pooled around her feet. Wondering if the goddess would answer after all she'd done.

All she'd undone.

Wondering if prayers would help her at all.

'Black Mother,' she whispered, 'give me strength.'

CHAPTER 11

THUNDER

Mia emerged from Adonai's pool with a gasp.

Blood in her eyes and on her tongue, thudding in her temples. Standing naked in the pool, she looked at the speaker at its apex. Pale skin and paler hair, his lips twisted in a small smile. He opened his eyes, the whites slicked with red.

'Thou hast returned, Blade Mia. Thy quarry dead, thy offering complete?'

'Not yet.'

Adonai tilted his head, smiling wider. 'Missed me then, didst thou?'

Mia turned her back, waded up out of the pool, feeling the speaker's eyes roaming her curves. Dripping red on the stone, she headed to the baths to wash the gore off, sinking below the water with a sigh.

'. . . i do not like this, mia . . .'

Mister Kindly sat at the corner of her bath, watching with his not-eyes. 'Nor I. But what choice do I have?'

'. . . ashlinn is a liar, and we are fools to trust her . . .'

'We don't trust her. Eclipse is watching her.'

'. . . i do not trust eclipse, either . . .'

She dried off, wrapped herself in black leathers and velvet, picturing Ash as she'd left her; chained to a four-poster bed in a cheap Godsgrave inn, a wolf made of shadows poised over her, translucent fangs bared. Eclipse couldn't actually touch the girl, of course. But Mia didn't feel any particular need to tell Ashlinn that . . .

'. . . she is leading you by the nose, mia . . .'

'You think I don't suspect that? I'm not a fucking idiot, Mister Kindly. But what if she's telling the truth?'

'. . . then we will find ourselves in interesting waters . . .'

'I have to know . . .'

The shadowcat sighed.

'. . . i know. and i am with you, mia. do not be afraid . . .'

She checked the gravebone blade at her belt, the other in her sleeve.

'Not with you beside me.'

She stole out from the bathhouse, into the Red Church's gloom. The hymns of the ghostly choir hung in the air as she made her way up winding stairs and down corridors of black stone, carved with patterns of endless spirals. Naev had once told her the patterns in the walls were a song about finding her way in the dark. Thinking about all Ashlinn had told her, she found herself wishing she knew the words. If the girl had spoken true, Mia would be utterly lost.

It can't be true.

On through the hungry dark.

It *can't* be . . .

Up coiling stair and down twisting spiral until she reached it.

The Hall of Eulogies.

She looked up at the towering statue of Niah, her sword and scales in her hands. It might have been a trick of the light, but the goddess looked grimmer than usual.

Mia's footsteps echoed in the silent hall as she walked the periphery, brushing her fingertips over the empty tomb marked with Tric's name. She thought of her friend then. The counsel he'd given. The comfort she'd found in his arms. He'd been a rock in a world growing more uncertain by the nevernight . . .

'You miss him,' came a voice.

Mia turned, saw Shahiid Aalea standing in the archway, dark eyes glittering. She was dressed in sheer, bloody red, the same colour as her lips. Black curls tumbled about her shoulders, her skin alabaster pale. A woman like her could have seemed cold as wintersdeep in the wrong light. But Aalea's smile was as warm as a glass of goldwine.

'Shahiid,' Mia said, bowing low.

'You return.' Dark eyes flitted over Mia's face. 'Absent victory, by the look.'

'I needed a nevernight back in my own bed,' Mia said. 'But the Dona is dead. And the map is almost within my grasp.'

'You'd rather the boy there instead, I'll wager?'

Aalea nodded to Tric's empty tomb. Mia stared too, saying nothing. The Shahiid ran fingertips over Tric's name, carved in the stone.

'You miss him?' she asked.

Mia saw no sense in denying it.

'Not like a piece of me is gone.' She shrugged. 'But aye. I do.'

Aalea pursed her lips, as if uncertain to speak.

'I loved someone once,' she finally said. 'Thinking this place, this life I chose, could not sully what I knew to be so pure.' The Shahiid ran her fingers across her lips. 'I loved that man as the Night loved the Day. I promised him we'd be together for ever.'

'What happened?' Mia asked.

'He died,' Aalea sighed. 'Death is the only promise we all keep. This life we live . . . there is room in it for love, Mia. But a love like autumn leaves. Beautiful one turn. A bonfire the next. Only ashes the remainder.'

Mia was quietened by the picture Aalea conjured. Eyes to the tombs. She'd no wish to raise suspicion, but the last thing in the world she wanted was to stand here talking about love and loss with a mass murderer. Not if what Ashlinn had told her was anything close to true . . .

'Did you think one turn you might find yourself beside a happy hearth?' Aalea asked. 'With a beau at your side and grandchildren on your knee?'

'. . . I'm not sure what I supposed any more.'

'Such is not the lot of a Blade,' Aalea took Mia's hand, pressing it to her lips. 'But there is beauty in knowing all things end, Mia. The brightest flames burn out the fastest. But in them, there is warmth that can last a lifetime. Even from a love that only lasts the nevernight. For people like us, there are no promises of for ever.'

Mia looked to the statue above. Those eyes that followed wherever she walked. 'My father used to say the art of telling a good story lies in knowing when to stop. Keep talking long enough, you'll find there's no such thing as a happy ending.'

Aalea smiled. 'A wise man.'

Mia shook her head. Remembering the way he died. What he died for.

'Not that wise.'

Ashlinn's words ringing in her ears. Her jaw clenched.

Aalea looked again to Tric's empty tomb.

'He would have made a fine Blade,' she sighed. 'And he was a beauty. But he is gone. Do not allow your sorrows to stray you from your path, Mia.'

Mia looked Aalea deep in the eye. Her voice was iron.

'I know my path, Shahiid. Sometimes, sorrow is all that keeps me on it.'

Aalea smiled, sweet and dark as chocolate.

'Forgive me. An old teacher's habits die hard, I suppose. You are a Blade, for now. And a woman. And a beauty at that.' Aalea leaned closer, eyes locked on Mia's, lips just a breath from her own. 'I have been ever fond of you. Know if ever you seek counsel, it is yours. And if ever you wish to build a bonfire to keep you warm one nevernight, I am here.'

Mia's pulse ran quicker, skin prickling. This close, she could smell the rose and honey of the Shahiid's perfume. Staring into those dark, kohl-smudged eyes, she wondered if there was some arkemy at work in Aalea's scent, or if . . .

Eyes on the prize, Corvere.

Mia slipped her hand free of Aalea's. Licked at suddenly dry lips.

'My thanks, Shahiid,' she murmured. 'I'll think on it.'

'I am certain you will, love,' Aalea said, her smile deepening. 'But now, I will leave you to your memories. Do not let the Revered Father find you here absent quarry, unless you actually enjoy hearing him bluster.'

The Shahiid of Masks inclined her head and drifted out of the room, leaving her perfume hanging in the air. Mia watched her go, the pull of the woman almost dragging her off-balance. But knowledge of why she was here tempered all, crushing the butterflies in her belly. She felt her shadow ripple, the dark swelling at her feet.

'. . . dangerous, that one . . .'

'The same could be said of every woman I know.'

'. . . where to begin . . . ?'

'You start at this end and head inwards. I'll begin at the Mother's feet. Keep an ear out for company. We've need of none.'

'. . . you do not honestly expect this search to bear fruit . . .'

'I don't know what to expect any more. Let's be about it.'

Mia crouched at the foot of Niah's statue, and in the light of that bloody stained glass, she began searching the names carved into the stone. One by one. Thousands of them. A spiral, coiling out from the goddess's feet. The names of kings, senators, legates, lords. Priests and sugargirls, beggars and bastards. The names of every life taken in the service of the Black Mother.

The choir and Mister Kindly were her only company, and she worked in silence. Wondering what she would do if all Ashlinn had told her was true. Once or twice she was forced to hide herself beneath her cloak of shadows as a Hand or new acolytes wandered through the hall. But for the most part, she was uninterrupted, on her knees in the dark as the names of the dead blurred together inside her head.

She remembered the turn he died. Her father. Standing before the noose and the baying mob. Cardinal Duomo on the scaffold, hedgerow beard and broad shoulders. Julius Scaeva standing above, with his jet-black hair and his deep, dark eyes and his consul's robes dipped in purple and blood. There to watch the leaders of the rebellion executed for their crimes against the great Itreyan Republic. Justicus Darius Corvere and General Gaius Antonius had gathered an army, set to march it upon their own capital. But on the eve of the invasion had come salvation, the rebel leaders delivered into the Republic's hands.

Mia had been too young to ask. And then, too blinded to wonder.

But how?

How had the leaders of the rebellion fallen into the Senate's clutches, when they were safely ensconced within an armed camp? Antonius was no fool. Mia's father, neither. It would have taken God himself to breach their defences and steal them away.

God. Or perhaps someone in service to a goddess . . .

'. . . mia . . .'

She looked up at the tone in Mister Kindly's voice, pupils dilating in the dark.

'. . . o, mia . . .'

She scuttled across the floor to where the shadowcat stood. Searching the names carved in the granite. Her father and Antonius had been hanged before the Godsgrave mob – even if the Red Church had something to do with their capture, they hadn't actually killed them. But if others fell during their capture, then perhaps . . .

Mia's belly turned to greasy ice.

''Byss and blood,' she whispered.

Carved in the stone, just as Ashlinn promised. A single name among the thousands. The name of a slave who purchased his freedom, and yet remained by her father's side afterwards. Darius Corvere's right hand. His majordomo. A man who would have been with his justicus as he prepared to march on his own capital. A man who would have been with her father until the end.

Andriano Varnese.

'. . . it is true, then . . .'

Cold ice in her belly as her fingers traced the name in the stone.

Ashes and dust in her mouth.

The Red Church had a hand in her father's capture. The rebellion's failure. Why else would the name of her father's majordomo be carved here on the stone? How else would a general and his justicus be captured in the middle of ten thousand men?

All this time, she'd been training in a den of murderers to avenge herself on the men who'd executed her father. Never imagining for a moment that the murderers she trained with played a role in that same execution.

And all at the behest of the man she wished to murder most of all.
Ash had spoken truth.
All of it. Everything.
Undone in a moment.
'O, Goddess,' Mia breathed.
She looked to the statue above her. The sword and scales in her hands.
The jewels sparkling in her robe, like stars in the still of truedark. Those
black, pitiless eyes.
'O, Black Mother, what do I do now?'

T he crowd was thunder.
It reverberated through the stone around her, echoed on the sweat-slick walls. Dust drifted down from the wooden beams above, the rumble of thousands of feet, the tremor of their applause, the deafening peals of their adulation all around her, crawling on her skin and vibrating in the pit of her belly.

Mia had never heard anything like it in all her life.

She stood in the holding cell beneath the arena, peering out through the bars to the sands beyond. Matteo stood beside her, dark eyes wide in wonder. Sidonius paced up and down their little cell, like a caged beast longing to be unleashed. Or perhaps, longing to run. Mia looked at the word COWARD branded into his chest. Wondered what exactly he'd done to earn it.

'You ever attended a *venatus*, little Crow?' he asked.

'My father would never allow it. He thought the games were barbaric.'

Sidonius looked out to the mob and nodded. 'A wise man.'

'Not *that* wise . . .'

The wagon ride from Crow's Nest to Blackbridge had taken almost a week. As ever, Mia, Matteo and Sidonius had been kept apart from the true gladiatii, and none of them deigned to speak a word to her. They'd been well fed, however, and perhaps out of some sympathy for what was to come, Butcher had refrained from pissing in any more dinners. After six turns, they'd arrived in the shadows of the Drakespine Mountains, and rolled into the sprawling metropolis of Blackbridge.*

---

*A city situated in the Drakespine Mountains, Blackbridge was the site of one of the most infamous sieges in Itreyan history.

Set on forging the greatest kingdom the world had seen, the Great Unifier, Francisco I, first set his sights on the Kingdom of Vaan. When word reached

Now, they waited under the city's great arena. The first exhibitions were under way – public murders sponsored by the local administratii. Mia watched as the sands were baptized with blood, convicted criminals and heretics and escaped slaves being executed *e gladiatii*, whetting the crowd's appetite for the bloodshed to come.

The Blackbridge arena was huge, elliptical, four hundred feet long. It seated at least twenty thousand people, the sunslight kept off the crowd by moving mekwerk canvases overhead. The stalls and bleachers were packed, folk travelling from miles around to witness the blood and glory of the *venatus*. Mia could see vendors selling salted meats and wine. Wives sitting with husbands, children riding on their parents' shoulders for a better view.

Nothing brings the familia together like a nice afternoon of slaughter.

As common chattel, Mia and the other recruits were scheduled to fight first. The Winnowing was always a bloody spectacle, and the editorii

---

the Vaanian king, Brandr VI, that Francisco was marching his War Walkers towards his kingdom, he sent two of his most loyal captains – Halfstad and Ulfr – to hold the line at Blackbridge.

Nestled in a valley in the Drakespine, the city was shielded on all sides by great granite peaks, and accessible from the south by a single stone bridge for which the city was named. Halfstad, who was elderly at the time, gave command of the walls to his daughter, the shield-maiden Eydis. Ulfr, a much younger man, commanded the guerilla troops that harried Francisco's troops in the field. The siege was hard and tempers among the Vaanians were stretched, but still, they managed to fend off the Itreyan assault for six months. With wintersdeep setting in, Francisco's great general, Valerian, declared Blackbridge to be impregnable.

Sadly, the same could not be said of Halfstad's daughter, Eydis.

In the six months cooped up in the city, Eydis and Ulfr had grown rather fond of each other, you see. But when Eydis informed her father she was pregnant by his ally, old Halfstad took the news worse than anyone had expected. Declaring Ulfr had besmirched his daughter's honour, he attacked his fellow hüslaird in the city square. Ulfr's men leapt to their laird's defence, Halfstad's men joined the fray to protect their own, and before anybody knew what was happening, the Vaanian forces were venting six months' frustration and murdering each other by the hundreds.

Both hüslairds perished in the fracas. Blackbridge fell to the Itreyans shortly afterwards, which opened the entire country for invasion. Within two years, Vaan became the first vassal state of the great Kingdom of Itreya.

And if you can find me a better endorsement for the rhythm method, gentlefriends, I shall eat my pen.

always tried to put on a good show for the mob. But the crowd still favoured bouts between their heroes over the mass slaughter of nameless wretches, no matter how impressive their murders. The bouts featuring *true* gladiatii would be fought afterwards, once the Winnowing was done.

Staring out at the blood-soaked sand, Mia felt herself trembling. The long-forgotten sensation of fear was swelling in her gut, turning her legs to water. The absence of Mister Kindly and Eclipse was a gnawing emptiness. An almost physical pain. She gripped the bars to still her shaking hands, cursing herself a coward.

You fought to be here. All this, your design. And now you stand there, trembling like a fucking child . . .

She pictured Duomo and Scaeva presiding over her father's execution in the forum. The baying crowd, howling for her father's blood. Looking out into the arena seats, she saw those same faces, that same awful delight. The same kind of people who cheered for her father's death.

But not for mine, you bastards. This is not where I die.

She curled her fingers into fists.

I've far too much killing to do.

'Recruits,' came a voice.

Mia turned, saw Executus at the cell door. Instead of his usual leather armour and whip, he was dressed in britches and a fine doublet, set with the red falcon of the Familia Remus and the golden lion of the Familia Leonides. His long grey hair was braided, his beard combed – if not for the scar slicing down his face and the iron leg, he might have been mistaken for a wealthy don out for an afternoon's sport.

'Now is the hour,' he said, his voice grave. 'Death or glory awaits. It shall be for you to decide which is given, and which received.'

Matteo spoke with a trembling voice. 'What shape will the Winnowing take?'

'The editorii will announce once you are in position. But no matter the challenge, the way to victory is always the same.' He gave a soft shrug. 'Don't get killed.'

Matteo looked ready to spew his mornmeal all over his sandals. Sidonius was pacing again, running his hand over his stubbled scalp. Mia shifted her weight, one foot to another, sick to her stomach.

The executus looked among them, and for the first time, Mia thought she saw the tiniest hint of softness in his eyes.

'Every gladiatii once stood where you stand now,' he said. 'Myself among them. No matter what you face on those sands, fear is the only enemy in your path. Conquer your fear, and you can conquer the world.'

He placed his hand on his chest. Nodded once.

'*Sanguii e Gloria.* I will see you after the Winnowing as blooded gladiatii, or by the Hearth when I go to my eternal sleep. Aa watch over you, and Tsana guide your hand.'

Arena guards in black armour marched into the cell, escorted Mia and the others down a long corridor. She heard trumpets signalling the end of the executions. A roar echoed above their heads in response. Through the walls and beneath her feet, Mia heard the creak and groan of metal on metal, the grinding of mighty gears.

'What *is* that?' Matteo whispered.

'Mekwerk beneath the arena floor,' Mia replied. 'The editorii control everything that happens on the sands from the underbelly.'

'You know an awful lot about the *venatus* for a girl who's never attended one,' Sidonius muttered.

Mia tried to smile mysteriously in reply, but couldn't quite manage it for the butterflies in her belly.

They were marched into a larger holding pen, sealed with a great iron portcullis. Beyond, Mia could see the blistering sunslight, and the waiting arena. The sands daubed in crimson. The crowd swaying and rolling like water.

The room was filled with perhaps forty others, lined up in orderly rows. Each was handed a heavy iron helm with a tall crest of scarlet horsehair, a short steel gladius and a broad rectangular shield daubed with a red crown. No armour. Nothing to protect the rest of her skin but the strips of fabric around her hips and chest. Mia looked among the mob, saw folk of every colour and size, mostly men, a handful of women. In their eyes, she saw fervour, she saw fury, she saw fatalism.

But most of all, she saw fear.

'When the doors open,' bellowed a guard in a centurion's plume, 'take your place upon the sands and upon the stage of history! *Sanguii e Gloria!*'

'Four Daughters, I'm not ready for this . . .' Matteo whispered.

'Stay staunch,' Mia said, squeezing his hand. 'Stay beside me.'

'You have a plan, little Crow?' Sidonius murmured.

Trumpets sounded again, the crowd roaring in answer.

'Aye.' She swallowed thickly. 'Don't get killed.'

A voice rang out across the arena, loud as the bellowing crowd.

'Citizens of Itreya! Honoured administratii! Senators and marrow-born! Welcome to the forty-second *venatus* of Blackbridge!'

The roof above Mia's head shook, dust falling as the folk on the bleachers overhead thundered in reply.

'In honour of Governor Salvatore Valente, we present an epic contest between heroic gladiatii of the finest collegia in the Republic! But first, those who seek glory upon the sands must be proved worthy before the eyes of the Everseeing! The time is nigh! The hour has come! The Winnowing is here!'

Mia pushed her helm down onto her head, checked her gladius, missing Mister Kindly like a hole in her chest.

Conquer your fear, and you can conquer the world . . .

'Behold!' came the cry. 'As we present to you, the Siege of Blackbridge!'

Applause came then, almost deafening. But beneath the crowd's fervour, Mia heard the great grinding under the floor rising in pitch. A commotion broke out in the front ranks, men and women pushing forward against the portcullis to see. Before Mia's wondering eyes, the arena floor split apart, and a small keep made of stone began rising from the mechanism in the stadium's underbelly.

'Four Daughters,' Matteo breathed. 'Is that a . . . castle?'

Other parts of the floor split asunder, hidden platforms rising as the great mekwerk gears in the depths churned and rolled. Mia saw siege towers made of wood, a battering ram covered with a pavilion of thick hide, a heavy ballista, and two catapults stocked with barrels of burning pitch. Scarlet banners unfurled on the stone keep's walls, set with the sigil of the old Kingdom of Vaan. Mia looked at the red crown daubed on her shield, the scarlet plumes on the helms around her.

'O, shit,' she breathed.

'. . . What?' Matteo asked.

'They're reenacting the Siege of Blackbridge,' she realized. 'The battle between Itreya and Vaan that marked the beginning of King Francisco's empire.' Mia tapped the red crown on Matteo's shield, the scarlet plume on his helm. '*We're* the Vaanians.'

The boy tilted his head. Mia inwardly sighed.

'The Vaanians *lost,* Matteo.'

'. . . O, shit.'

The mekwerk gears slowly ground to a halt, all the pieces of the battle to come laid out on the field. The editorii's voice rang across the sands.

'Behold! The troops of King Brandr VI, the besieged defenders of Vaan!'

The portcullis shifted, rolled up. Guards shoved Mia and her fellows, prodding them with spears until they emerged blinking into the sunlight. They were met with jeers, the mostly Itreyan crowd roaring with disapproval at the sight of their ancient foes.* The guards marched the competitors across the arena floor, towards the open gate of the small keep. And ushering them inside, they sealed it behind them.

The keep stood perhaps twenty feet high, fifty feet square. Taller towers loomed on every corner, crenellated battlements crested the walls. From the inside, Mia saw the structure wasn't stone at all, but a thick plaster façade reinforced with a heavy timber frame. The group milled about in confusion, most unsure what came next.

'Man the walls, for fucksakes!' someone hollered.

'Get up there, you bastards!'

Trumpets rang across the arena as Mia, Matteo, and Sidonius scrambled up a wooden ladder and claimed their place on one of the towers. She saw two shortbows made of ashwood, two quivers full of arrows.

'Can either of you shoot?' she asked her fellows.

'I can,' Matteo replied.

Mia took up one bow and slung a quiver over her shoulders, handed the other to Matteo. She squeezed his hand as he took it, looked him in the eye.

'Don't be afraid,' she said. 'This is not where we die.'

The boy nodded. All around them, an ocean of people were on their feet in the stands. The arena walls stood fifteen feet high, boxes containing the marrowborn and politicians studded around the edges. In one, Mia saw Dona Leona, seated with other sanguila. She was dressed in a golden gown, her long auburn hair coiled around her brow like a victor's laurel. But for all her beauty, the legacy of her name, her property had still wound up playing the roles of the conquered.

Not the politician your father is by half, Mi Domina.

In a great booth on the western edge, Mia saw a man she presumed was the city governor, surrounded by officials, administratii, pretty women in beautiful gowns. The games' editorii stood at the edge of this booth, clad in a blood-red robe, the waist and sleeves trimmed with dozens of small golden daggers. A white capuchin monkey sat on his

---

* The Vaanians in the audience kept their mouths on the safe side of shut.

shoulder. He spoke into a long curling horn, his voice amplified by other horns around the arena's edge.

'Citizens!' he cried. 'Behold the noble legions of Itreya!'

A portcullis at the other end of the arena yawned wide, and the guards escorted in another cadre of competitors. They were armed and armoured the same as Mia and her fellows, but the plumes on their helms were golden, the three eyes of Aa painted on their shields. The crowd roared in approval at the sight of them, stamping their feet and shaking the floor. Most of the group took up position by the wooden siege towers, others manned the ballista and catapults on the arena's edge.

'The contest ends when only one colour remains!' cried the editorii. 'To the victors, the right to stand as fully fledged gladiatii upon the sands of the *venatus*! To the defeated, the eternal sleep of death! Let the Winnowing . . . begin!'

Roars from the crowd. Movement from the golden troops, dozens of them bracing against the base of the siege towers and pushing them forward. Mia looked about the red troops manning the walls, searching for a leader and finding none. Turning her eyes back to the approaching towers, she called above the mob.

'Any of you fine gentles serve in the legion?'

'Aye,' said a burly man on the tower opposite.

'You wouldn't be experienced in siege warfare by any chance?'

'I was a fucking cook, lass.'

Mia looked at the approaching army. Down to the little sword in her hand.

'Well, shit,' she sighed.

'Archers, lay down fire on those incoming towers! I need six of you ready at the gate for that battering ram, the rest of you on the walls to repel their troops! Two men to a station, lock your shields and keep your backs to each other, clear?'

Mia raised an eyebrow, looked about to see who was shouting.

It was Sidonius. But not the smart-mouthed, lecherous Sid she'd kicked in the bollocks and punched in the jaw. This man was fierce as a whitedrake, his voice booming, radiating an aura of command that brooked no dissent.

'O, aye?' someone yelled. 'And who the fuck are you?'

'Aye,' Mia murmured. 'Who the fuck *are* you?'

'I'm the bastard who's going to save your miserable lives!' Sid bellowed. 'Unless one of you pathetic sheepfuckers have a better plan?

Now see to your swords and send these bastards to the 'byss where they belong!'

Mia stared a moment longer, eyebrow raised. But seeing Sid was in no mood to argue, and being counted among the pathetic sheepfuckers with no better plan, she aimed her bow at the incoming towers. Matteo nocked an arrow beside her, speaking from the corner of his mouth as he smirked at Sid.

'Well, *that* was unexpect—'

The ballista bolt hit him like an anvil. Blood spattered Mia's face as Matteo was flung off the tower with a *'whufff'*, toppling headfirst into the sand below. The boy hit the ground with a sickening crunch, two feet of steel and wood in his chest, neck twisted the entirely wrong way around.

''Byss and blood,' Mia breathed.

A shattering boom shook the castle as one of the catapults flung a barrel of burning pitch. The projectile shattered on the wall, liquid fire raining down on the men and women inside. The crowd roared approval as the second catapult fired, the barrel smashing into the façade and setting the wooden gate ablaze. Men fell from the battlements covered in flaming oil, screaming as they tried to douse themselves on the sand. Mia and Sidonius ducked low, looking at each other with wide eyes.

'Four fucking Daughters,' the big man breathed.

'Suggestions, General?' Mia asked.

'Archers! Have at those towers!'

Mia and a few of her fellows rose up from cover, unleashed a volley into the approaching siege towers. Several of the gold troops fell, the crowd howling as a second volley dropped a handful more. Black smoke billowed from the rising flames, clawing at Mia's eyes and throat as she fired again.

'Battering ram!' she shouted. 'Coming hard.'

'Brace the doors!' Sidonius roared.

Half a dozen of the Golds rushed forward between the troop towers, the battering ram between them. Mia fired again, but the team were protected by a cover of thick hide. The walls shook as they hit the front gate, shaking further as another barrel of blazing oil hit one of the keep's rear towers to the crowd's delight. The explosion bloomed, bright and fierce, immolating another three Reds on the walls. They fell screaming, a fourth among them tumbling back with a ballista bolt through her chest.

'Those siege weapons are killing us!' Mia shouted.

'Well, we've little to throw at them but harsh language!' Sidonius roared. 'The Vaanians lost the siege of Blackbridge, little Crow! These dice are rigged!'

The gate boomed again as the ram struck home. Mia twisted up from cover, firing through the rolling smoke and putting an arrow through the foot of one of the battering team. It was all she could see of them under that blasted hide, but it had the desired effect; the man dropped, howling, and Mia ducked a ballista bolt as she loosed another shot, her arrow striking him clean through the throat.

Another barrel exploded, the crowd now howling drunk with fury. The castle was ablaze, the gate coming off its hinges. The first siege tower struck the battlements, spilling half a dozen men onto the defences with bloodthirsty cries. Sidonius charged along the wall and put his sword through a man's belly with a roar. Mia rose without a sound, reaching out to one Gold's shadow and fixing him in place, battering aside another man's sword and slamming him off the wall with her shield before burying her blade in the first man's chest. Blood spattered, warm and copperish on her lips. She'd wondered how she might use her gifts without the crowd getting wise, but in all the chaos and smoke and flame, nobody could see a thing of her shadow-werking.

The gate shuddered again, the wood splitting. One more good thrust and they'd be home. Another Red sailed off the battlement with a ballista bolt through his belly, another barrel burst on the ground in front of the keep, spraying the walls with burning oil. It was all well and good to stay here and defend the walls – Mia cut down another Gold, slicing his belly wide open and spilling his guts across the deck as he fell screaming – but those catapults would eventually set the whole place ablaze.

Conquer your fear, and you can conquer the world.

She thought back to her lessons in the Hall of Masks with Shahiid Aalea. The assassin inside her rising to the fore. She could swing a sword with the best of them, she knew that true, but the advantage she truly had over the people fighting and dying around her was her training in the Red Church. Her wits. Her guile.

Don't think like a gladiatii. Think like a Blade.

She looked at the faces around her. The face of the man she'd just killed, sealed inside his helm. And tearing the helm off the dead Gold's head, she shoved her hand into his sundered guts, and pulled out a great, steaming handful. Pulling off her own headgear, she slammed on the golden-crested helmet and shouted to Sidonius.

'Don't let them shoot me on the way back!'

Mia smeared blood down her neck and chest, slapped her handful of ruptured intestines against her belly, and taking a deep breath, dropped off the wall. She hit the sand outside the keep with a grunt, wobbled and fell onto her side. Black smoke boiled all around her, timbers breaking and folk roaring as the gate shattered. A boom echoed across the arena as another barrel exploded against the wall, Mia curling up tight to shield herself from the flaming globules of oil.

She rose to her feet, holding her fistful of torn guts against her own stomach. And with her sword dangling from her other hand, she staggered towards the first catapult.

The crowd paid her little mind – from the look of her wound across the arena, she was a dead girl walking. The crew on the catapult paid no heed either; her golden helm marked her as one of their own, but each of them was fighting to save their own skins. And so, nobody ran to help her or stop her as she staggered across the sand, blood and guts drenching her front, dripping at her feet.

She stumbled to sell it better, rising with a gasp. Closer now, the catapult and the three men manning it just a few feet away. She dragged herself up with a groan, limping ever closer. And a few feet from the team, she came to life, slinging her handful of guts into the first Gold's face and plunging her gladius into his chest.

The man fell back with a cry. Before the other two could process what had happened, Mia had gutted one, his insides spraying across the sand as he fell with a blood-curdling scream. The last fumbled for his blade but Mia smashed it aside, weaving left, right. And with a flash of her blade, she gifted him to the Maw.

'*Hear me, Mother,*' she whispered, snatching up one of the fallen men's swords.

'*Hear me now,*' she breathed, sprinting towards the second catapult.
'*This flesh your feast.*'
One of the team saw her coming out of the smoke
'*This blood your wine.*'
opening his mouth, perhaps to cry warning
'*Hold them close.*'
but her blow severed his throat all the way to the bone, lodging in his spine. She tore it free, chopped another's legs out from under him, hurling her second blade at the last man's chest. The sword punched through flesh and ribs, knocking the man off his feet in a spray of red, and the second catapult fell silent.

The crowd began to notice something amiss. The Golds had broken through to the keep, a bloody brawl now erupting at the gate, upon the walls. But more and more were pointing at the short, pale girl, drenched in red among the now-silent machines. She knelt by the bodies of those she'd killed, took off her helm and dipped the gold plume in the blood pooled on the sand, staining it red. And slamming it back on her head, she dashed with swords in hand, right at the ballista crew.

They saw her coming, swivelling the weapon and firing off a bolt at her. But smoke was rolling across the sands from the burning keep, and after all, she was only a little thing, fast and sharp as knives. Mia tumbled aside, rolling back up to her feet as one of the crew charged her down. He was a giant of a man: a Dweymeri with long saltlocks, two feet taller than she. Mia met his blades with her own, taking a glancing blow to her helm, and being so much shorter than him, slipped her blade lower than his shield could reach. His hamstring was sliced through to the bone, Mia grabbing a handful of his saltlocks as he fell to one knee. She twisted him around as the ballista fired at her again, shielding herself behind her foe as the bolt punched through his shield and into the chest beyond.

The crowd roared as she climbed up on the falling man's shoulder and sprang at the two women crewing the machine, twisting the shadows at the first one's feet as she sliced the second's chest open. The woman fell with a scream, her own strike cutting deep into Mia's arm, blood spraying. The girl staggered, crowd and pulse and thunder deafening in her ears as she hurled her second sword at the other woman's head.

With her boots fixed to the floor, the woman could only fall backwards to dodge the blow, landing on her backside in the dust. She cursed, eyes wide with fear as she pulled at her boots, still stuck fast in the sand. Mia loomed up over her, one arm hanging limp, drenched head to foot in blood, second sword raised.

'No,' the woman breathed. 'I have a baby girl, I—'

No mothers.

No daughters.

Only enemies.

Her sword silenced the woman's plea. The crowd around her bellowed. With a pained wince for her wounded arm, she loaded another bolt into the ballista, ratcheted back the drawline to fire another shot. But the battlements behind her were now clear, the only fighting seemed to be going on inside the keep walls.

Mia picked up a sword with a weary sigh. Her right arm was bleeding freely from a deep gash in her bicep, her head swimming. Adjusting her helm on her head and slinging a shield onto her wounded arm, she stalked back across the bloodied, burning sands to face whoever was left alive in there. The crowd were chanting, stamping their feet in time with her tread – though the girl wore the colour of the enemy, the fancy of the reenactment had given way to a purer kind of bloodlust, and this small slip of a girl had just murdered almost a dozen people in a handful of minutes.

She stopped twenty feet before the gate in a veil of smoke, the stench of sundered bowel and burning blood. She saw four figures in the haze, marching towards her. Drawing a deep breath, picturing all she stood to lose if she failed, she raised her sword. And squinting through the smoke, she made out the colour of their plumes.

Blood red.

Mia dropped her shield, laughing loud as she saw Sidonius, battered and bleeding among the men. Beyond them, Mia could see the bottle-neck at the gate had become a slaughterhouse, Golds and Reds lying dead by the dozen. She saw Matteo among them, pretty eyes open wide and seeing nothing at all.

She tried to push the sorrow aside, knowing she had no use for it. This was her world now. Life and death, with just a sword stroke between them. And with every stroke, she stood one step closer to revenge.

No room for anything but enemies.

'Citizens!' cried the editorii. 'Governor Valente presents to you, your victors!'

The crowd bellowed in answer, a fanfare of trumpets splitting the air. Smeared head to foot in blood, Mia limped forward, held out her hand to Sidonius. The big man grinned, clasped her forearm, then dragged her into a crushing hug.

'Come here, you magnificent little bitch,' he laughed.

'Let me go, you great fucking lump!' she grinned.

Sidonius raised the knuckles into the air, roared at the crowd. 'Take that, you bastards! No man can kill me, you hear? NO MAN CAN KILL ME!'

Mia looked to the marrowborn boxes, saw Dona Leona on her feet applauding. Beside her stood Executus, his arms folded, glowering as always. But ever so slightly, the man inclined his head. The closest thing to praise he'd ever given.

She turned in a circle, taking in the ocean of faces, the blood-drunken cheers, the thundering feet. And for a tiny moment, she ceased being

Mia Corvere, the orphaned girl, the darkin assassin, the embodiment of vengeance. She held her arms wide, dripping red onto the sand, and listened to the crowd roar in response. And just for a breath, she forgot what she had been.

Knowing only what she'd become.

Gladiatii.

CHAPTER 12
EPIPHANY

'Did you know?'

The bishop of Godsgrave leapt near three feet out of his chair. His teacup of goldwine slipped from his fingers, spilled across the parchment on his desk. Heart rattling about his chest, Mercurio turned and found his old pupil behind him, swathed in the shadows of his bookshelves.

''Byss and bl—'

His heart stilled as he saw the gravebone stiletto in his former protégée's hand. A blonde girl was standing in the gloom behind her, dressed in dark leathers. She looked vaguely familiar, but damned if Mercurio could place her . . .

A low growl made him turn, and he saw a wolf made of shadows coalescing near his open chamber door. As if in a soft breeze, it slowly creaked shut.

'Did. You. Know?' Mia repeated.

Mercurio turned his eyes back to his former pupil.

'I know lots of things, little Crow,' he said calmly. 'You'll have to be m—'

She moved in a blur, across the space between them in a blinking. He hissed as she seized his throat, pressed her blade to his jugular.

'Get that bloody pigsticker off my neck,' the old man demanded.

'Answer me!'

Mercurio tapped his own blade – which he'd drawn as he dropped his goldwine – against Mia's femoral artery.

'One good twitch and you'll be bled out in moments,' he said.

'That makes two of us.'

'I gave you that knife,' he said, swallowing against the gravebone blade.

'No, Mister Kindly gave it to me.'

Mercurio eyed the not-cat now coalescing on Mia's shoulder.

'. . . you just gave it back, old man . . .'

'Still. Never thought I'd find it against my own throat, little Crow.'

'I never thought you'd give me a reason,' the girl said.

'And what would that be?'

'They killed my father, Mercurio,' she said, voice trembling. 'Or as good as. They handed him over to Scaeva and let him hang!'

'Who did?' the old man scowled, glancing over Mia's shoulder at the blonde.

'The Ministry!' Mia spat. 'Drusilla, Cassius, the rest of them. My father and Antonius were captured in the middle of a camp of ten thousand men. Who could do that if not a Blade of Niah?'

'That makes no blo—'

'Did you know?'

The old man looked at his pupil, saw no fear of the blade in his hand. No fear of dying reflected in her eyes. Only rage.

'Six years, I trained you for the Church's trials,' he said quietly. 'Why in the Black Mother's name would I do that, if I knew the Church helped Scaeva murder your da?'

'Well, why would the Church train me at all if they helped kill him, Mercurio?'

'That's what I mean about this not making sense, Mia. Think on it.'

Mia hand trembled on her stiletto, and she stared into his eyes. He could see the Blade in her, the killer they carved from the girl he'd given them. He knew that was what she'd become, sending her there. He knew the mark it would leave. You don't gift someone to the Maw without gifting a piece of yourself, also. But beneath, he could still see her. The waif he'd saved from the Godsgrave streets. The girl he'd sheltered beneath his roof, taught everything he knew. The girl who, even after she failed, he'd still thought of as his kin.

'I'd never hurt you, little Crow. You know that. On my life, I swear it.'

She stared a moment longer. The killer she'd become warring with the girl she'd been. And slowly, ever so slowly, Mia withdrew the knife. Mercurio lifted his blade away from her leg, slipped it back into his armrest, and leaned back in his chair.

'You want to tell me what all this is about?' he asked.

The blonde girl produced a book from beneath her cloak, placed it on the desk before him. It was black. Leather. Unadorned.

'The fuck's this?' he asked.

'*The Red Church ledger,*' Blondie replied.

His eyes grew wide. Suddenly, it made sense. Suddenly . . .

'*I recognize you now,*' *he breathed.* '*We met at the Church, when I came to get Mia. You're Torvar's girl. You're Ashlinn fucking Järnheim.*'

'*Well, my middle name's actually Frija, but—*'

'*We've been hunting you for eight bloody months!*' *Mercurio turned to Mia, voice rising.* '*Have you taken complete leave of your senses? Thanks to this traitor and her da, most of our Blades are in the fucking ground!*'

Ashlinn shrugged. '*Live by the sword . . .*'

'*It was a miracle they never got me!*'

'*Bullshit,*' *the girl replied.* '*When the Luminatii purged Godsgrave, they never kicked in the door of your little Curio Shop, did they?*'

'*O, and why's that, pray tell?*' *the old man growled.*

Ashlinn looked towards Mia. Back to the red-faced bishop.

'*Because I didn't want her hurt.*'

Silence fell in the room, Mia looking anywhere but into Ashlinn's eyes. After a long, uncomfortable quiet, she turned to the ledger, flipping through the pages until she found a name listed among the many patrons and their payments. A name written in a bold flowing script, stark black against the yellowing parchment.

Julius Scaeva.

'*You knew, didn't you?*' *Mia asked.* '*The Ministry would have to tell bishops who can and can't be touched, if only to avoid breaches of Sanctity.*'

'*Of course I knew,*' *the old man snapped.* '*They told me as soon as they made me bishop. Why the 'byss do you think I haven't sent one of my Blades to cut the bastard's throat? Standing for a fourth term as consul? He's a fucking king in all but name. And I've said so all along, remember?*'

Mia tapped the entry with her finger.

'*Ten thousand silver priests,*' *she said.* '*Sent to the Church by Scaeva himself, dated three turns after my father's execution. Paid by the man who stood to gain the most from the rebellion's failure. And the name of my father's right-hand man is carved at Niah's feet in the Hall of Eulogies. Explain that to me, Mercurio.*'

The old man stroked his chin with a scowl.

Looked down at the names and numbers, blurring in the dim light.

It couldn't be . . .

Of course he knew Scaeva was secretly paying the Church. Truth told, it made sense for people who could afford the cost to be stuffing Niah's coffers. That was one of the beauties of Sanctity, you see – gift the Church enough money to be considered a patron, you'd be protected under the Red Promise. The King of Vaan had been doing it for years. Stroke of genius, really. Niah's faithful could get paid without lifting a finger.*

Of course, Scaeva went further than just a retainer – he'd used the Church to rid himself of a dozen thorns in his side. But Mercurio had never suspected the Church had been involved with the end of the Kingmakers. Everything he'd ever heard led him to believe Corvere and Antonius had been betrayed by one of their own men.

Could it be . . . ?

'The Red Church captured my father,' Mia said, her voice thick with pain. 'Handed him over to the Senate. They as good as murdered him themselves.'

Mister Kindly tilted his head, purring soft.

'. . . what I do not understand, is why scaeva had remus attack the mountain, if scaeva already has the church in his pocket . . . ?'

'. . . AS IF THAT IS THE ONLY THING YOU DO NOT UNDERSTAND . . .'

'. . . hush now, child, the adults are talking . . .'

'Remus attacked the Mountain without Scaeva's consent,' Ashlinn said.

'Bullshit.' Mercurio turned on the Vaanian girl with a scowl. 'Remus didn't take a squirt without asking Scaeva's permission first. The Senate, the Luminatii, and Aa's Church are the three pillars of the whole fucking Republic, girl.'

'Don't call me girl, you crusty old prick,' Ashlinn snapped. 'My father was the one in league with Remus, remember? The justicus hated Scaeva's guts. O, aye, he took the consul's orders, but Remus was one of Aa's faithful, just like Duomo. Using the Red Church for his dirty work made Scaeva a heretic in Remus's eyes. And shutting down the Church would've cut Scaeva's access to his pack of hired murderers.'

---

*Aye, aye, I can hear your question, gentlefriends. Just as if I were sitting behind you. (No fear, I am not sitting behind you.) But you find yourself wondering, if the Red Church won't murder anyone they're currently employed by, why doesn't everyone simply pay them a retainer and sleep soundly in the nevernight? An excellent question, gentlefriends, with a very simple answer:

It's *fucking* expensive.

A king or consul might afford to keep the Church on permanent retainer. But you must remember, gentlefriends, the Red Church is a cult of assassins, not extortionists. And it'd be quite difficult to maintain a reputation as the most fearsome murderers in the Republic if they spent all their time being paid to *not* murder anyone.

Mercurio scratched his chin. 'I thought Remus and Duomo—'

'Duomo's a patron of the Church too.'

'I know that,' Mercurio snapped. 'I'm not some simpleton fresh in from the rain, I'm a bishop of Our Lady of Blessed fucking Murder.'

'Except our illustrious grand cardinal never hires the Church to blessedly fucking murder anyone.' *Ashlinn flicked through the ledger, showed exorbitant payments from Duomo dating back six years. 'He just pays an annual stipend out of Aa's coffers. Protects him under Sanctity, see? That way, he knows Scaeva can't just have his throat cut while he sleeps. The cardinal and the consul hate each other, and both of them would do almost* anything *to see the other dead.'*

'. . . IT OCCURS TO ME THAT RECORDING THIS IN A LEDGER WAS A FANTASTICALLY FOOLISH IDEA . . .'

'They kept it in a locked vault,' Ashlinn said to the shadowwolf. 'Inside a den of the most feared killers in the Republic. And the only key was hung around the neck of one of the most accomplished assassins the world has ever known. Considering what I had to go through to get hold of it, perhaps it's not as foolish as you think.'

'. . . speaking of which, little traitor, why, pray tell, have we not murdered you yet . . . ?'

'My winning personality?' Ashlinn glanced at the not-cat on Mia's shoulder. 'Or perhaps it's just because I'm the only one with half a clue what the fuck is going on around here.'

'So what is *goi . . .' The old man blinked, looked about the room. '. . . Wait, where the 'byss is Jessamine?'*

Mia and Ashlinn exchanged a long, uneasy glance. Ash's lip was split and swollen from her brawl on the roof, her eye bruised black.

'. . . there was some . . . unpleasantness . . .'

'Fucking wonderful.' Mercurio glared at Ashlinn. 'And you're responsible for it?'

'If it makes you feel better, Jess stabbed me first.' Ashlinn shrugged. 'I just stabbed her last. And . . . repeatedly.'

'So what are you doing here?' the bishop demanded. 'Mia got sent out seven turns ago to kill a braavi and steal a map. She comes back here with the most wanted traitor in Church history. Where do you fit into all of this?'

Ashlinn shrugged. 'I have the map.'

'. . . you *had* the map. it exploded, remember . . . ?'

The girl smirked. 'You don't think I'm stupid enough to let something that valuable go up in flames, do you, Mister Know-it-all?'

'You'd best start talking, then,' Mercurio growled.

'Aye,' Mia nodded. 'Where did you get it? Where does it lead? And who are you working for? The braavi said you were selling the map to Cardinal Duomo.'

'He hired me to get it,' Ash said, leaning against the wall and folding her arms. 'After the attack on the Church went tits up, Da and I spent the next eight months dodging Blades sent to kill us. By the time Da died, we'd burned most of our coin. Duomo and Remus plotted together to bring the Church down, so I knew how to get in touch with the cardinal. Turns out he was looking for someone with my . . . skill set.'

'For what? Back-talking and smart-arsery?' Mercurio spat.

Ashlinn's lips twisted in that maddening smirk. 'Locks. Traps. Dark work. He'd learned of another way he might tip the balance and undo the Red Church once and for all. Without them in the way, he'd be free to take down Scaeva, install a pliant new consul, and have the pot for himself.'

Mia's eyes narrowed. 'What kind of "other way"?'

Ash shrugged. 'He never said. I never asked. My job was to travel with a pack of sellswords and a bishop of Aa's ministry. To a temple ruin on the north coast of Old Ashkah. That's where we found the map. And . . . other things.'

'What kind of other things?' Mercurio asked.

Ashlinn's face was stone, but Mia saw a sliver of fear in her eyes.

'The dangerous kind.'

'What happened to your comrades?'

The girl shrugged. 'They didn't make it.'

'So you came back to the 'Grave alone to sell the map to Duomo?' Mia asked.

Ash nodded. 'The Toffs act as his middlemen. Duomo has the coin to carry a lot of people in his pocket. I didn't know if he'd try to shiv me in the back, but I presumed the worst. I'm a loose end. One of the only people alive who knew the cardinal was working against Scaeva to take the Church down.'

'Well, someone knew Duomo is working with the Toffs,' Mercurio said. 'And that the map was being delivered to them this eve. And that someone hired Mia to . . .'

Mia met Mercurio's stare. The old man's eyes growing wide.

'You don't think . . .' he began.

Mia searched the floorboards as if looking for a truth she'd dropped. Dragging her hair behind her ear. The sinking in his stomach reflected on her face.

'My patron for this offering requested me specifically,' she breathed. '"She *who slew the justicus of the Luminatii Legion". Or so the Ministry said. And I've offered up three others at the same patron's request.'*

'. . . Who did you kill?'

'A senator's son, Gaius Aurelius. The mistress of another Liisian Senator, Armando Tulli. And a Galante magistrate named Cicerii.'

'Black Mother,' Mercurio growled.

'What is it?' Ashlinn asked, looking between them.

'Gaius Aurelius was rumoured to be planning a run for consul against Scaeva,' Mercurio said. 'And Cicerii was organizing an enquiry into the constitutionality of Scaeva sitting a fourth term.'

Mia sank to her haunches, steadied herself against the flagstones. Eclipse coalesced beside her, Mister Kindly licking her hand with his insubstantial tongue.

'O, Goddess . . . ,' she breathed.

'Scaeva is pulling people into line,' Mercurio realized. 'Intimidating opponents or killing them. Making sure he's elected again.'

'And I've been helping him . . .' Mia whispered.

'. . . bastard . . .'

'Which means he knows Duomo is working against him. He knows whatever this map leads to is a threat to the Church, and he's using the Church to eliminate it.'

'Protecting his little cult of assassins.' Ashlinn looked at Mia, shaking her head. 'What did I tell you? Whores, all. And not content with helping to murder your father, the Church made you slit throats for the bastard responsible for his hanging. Solis. Mouser. Spiderkiller. Aalea. Drusilla. They need a killing, Mia. Every last one of them.'

'Scaeva.'

Mia spat the word like a mouthful of poison. Lips peeling back from her teeth. She glared at Ashlinn, slowly shaking her head.

'Scaeva and Duomo first.'

Ashlinn stepped forward, eyes glinting like steel.

'Duomo is probably at the Basilica Grande right now.'

Mia shook her head. 'I can't get in there. I tried once before. The trinities . . .'

'I can get him for you,' Ashlinn offered. 'He might bathe with one about his neck, sleep with one under his damned pillow, there's no trinity that can stop me. I steal inside and cut his throat, then we get Scaeva and the Ch—'

'No,' Mia said. 'They're mine. The pair of them.'

She rose slowly from the floor, black hair draped about a ghost-pale face.

'Those bastards are mine.'

'Hold now,' Mercurio counselled. 'Let's not speak hasty.'

'Hasty?' Mia snarled. 'The Red Church helped kill my father, Mercurio. Just as Scaeva and Duomo did. The Ministry are as guilty as the other two.'

'But why would the Red Church train you if they helped kill your father?'

'Maybe they thought I'd never find out? Maybe Cassius ordered them to train me, knowing I was darkin? Maybe that fucker Scaeva found it amusing? Or maybe they thought once I'd killed enough, grown cold enough, I just wouldn't care any more?'

The old man steepled his fingers at his chin, staring at the ledger.

'Feed someone to the Maw, you also feed it a part of yourself,' he murmured.

'Are you with me?' she asked.

He looked at the ledger. Scaeva's name. The man who'd crafted himself a throne in a Republic that had rid itself of its kings centuries ago. A man who thought himself above law, honour, morality. But truthfully, Mercurio himself had cast most of those aside himself, years ago. All in the name of faith.

'I've devoted my life to the Red Church,' the old man said.

Mia stepped forward, her eyes burning.

'Are you with *me*?'

The bishop of Godsgrave looked at his former pupil. She seemed carved of stone, jaw set, fists clenched in the soft arkemical glow. He searched those dark eyes, looking for something of the girl he'd taken under his wing for six long years. He'd been angry with her after she failed her initiation. After she failed him. But in truth, she'd been his daughter those six years. And she always would be.

The Church had already taken one father from her.

Could he let them take another?

'I'm with you.'

The answer hung in the room like a sword above their heads. Mercurio knew what it would mean, and where it would end. How big the foe they were pitting themselves against truly was.

'We have to do this unseen, Mia,' Mercurio said. 'The Church can't know it's you when you get Scaeva, or they'll retaliate. And you'll have to get Duomo with the same stroke, or else he's going to be ten times as hard to hit.'

'That's the least of our problems,' Mia replied. 'The Church are going to want me back. The Dona is dead. Scaeva could have another offering for me.'

'They still don't have the map,' Mercurio said. 'I can weave a story. Say the map slipped your grasp, but you're chasing it now. Strictly speaking, that could take months.'

'The Ministry won't be pleased with that,' Ashlinn said.

'Fuck them,' Mia scowled. 'The Ministry aren't pleased with me anyway.'

'Wonderful,' Ashlinn said. 'So now all we need do is ponder a way for you to murder a cardinal you can't physically get close to, while at the same time killing the most highly guarded consul in the history of the Itreyan Republic.'

Mia and Mercurio were silent. The old man's brow creased in thought. Mia's eyes were narrowed, roaming the bookshelves and finding no answer along their spines. She turned her gaze to the other wall, Mercurio's collection of weapons. The Luminatii sunsteel blade, the Vaanian battleaxe, the gladius from a gladiatii arena in Liis . . .

Her eyes narrowed farther. The wheels behind them turning.

She glanced to her old teacher, her breath coming quick.

'What is it?' he asked.

Idiotic.

Insane.

Impossible.

'I think I have an idea . . .'

Thirteen gladiatii were gathered in a circle in the training yard. The walls of Crow's Nest rose about them, banners of the Familia Remus fluttering in the rising wind. They'd arrived back from Blackbridge late, and it was near the turn of nevernight. But before evemeal, time would be taken to welcome their new brother and sister into their fold – the most sacred of rites, conducted here on the sacred ground of their collegium.

The *votum vitus*.[*]

---

[*]The origins of the Vow of Blood are shrouded in antiquity, but many believe they lie in the Old Ashkahi Empire, and the mythology of the famed warrior-prince Andarai.

Andarai's exploits were so well known, his legend survived even the fall of the empire itself. He was a typical brand of hero for the age – peerlessly wise, undefeated in battle, and reputedly hung like a mule. He spent much of his time running about rescuing princesses, slaying beasts, and siring bastards, though he also apparently found time to invent the lyre, the loom, and, strangely enough, the birthing stool. His most hated foe was the legendary Thief of Faces, Tariq, who, among his other exploits, stole Andarai's blacksteel sword,

The twin suns beat down on the yard, and Mia felt sweat dripping down her bare belly and arms. She was on her knees in the circle, Sidonius beside her. Arkades stood before them, clad in a gleaming breastplate embossed with twin lions, scratched and scored from years of combat. Dona Leona watched from the balcony in a beautiful silken yellow gown. When she looked down at the executus, she smiled, and the sapphire of her eyes seemed to say, 'I told you so.'

'Gladiatii,' the executus said. 'We stand here on sacred ground, in sacred rite, to welcome these two proven warriors into our fold. We bind ourselves not with steel, but with blood. For blood we are, and blood we shall remain.'

'Blood we are,' came the voices around the circle. 'And blood we shall remain.'

Executus drew a dagger from his belt, drew the blade across his palm, let the red drip upon the sand. And then he passed the blade to his left.

The Butcher of Amai took the dagger. He repeated the ritual, cutting his palm before passing it to Bladesinger. The woman looked Mia in the eye as she cut her palm. And so it went, around the thirteen. To the Vaanian twins, Bryn and Byern, the male Dweymeri, Wavewaker, to the rest of the gladiatii in the circle, until finally, the bloody blade was passed to their champion, Furian, the Unfallen.

The Itreyan watched Mia with dark, clouded eyes, a new silver laurel resting on his brow. She'd watched him fight at Blackbridge, and his victory ('peerless,' the editorii had called him, 'flawless') had only inflamed her curiosity. She felt her shadow tremble as he cut his palm, mingling his blood with his gladiatii familia on the razored edge. He let the scarlet droplets fall to the sand, then walked across the circle to stand before Sidonius and Mia. Glancing from that handsome jaw, those burning

---

and bedded Andarai's mother, sister, *and* daughter, all reportedly on the same evening.

Andarai was somewhat put out about this. Particularly the bit about his mother.

The pair's rivalry spanned decades, and looked surely to end in the death of one or both. But when the daemon-king, Sha'Annu, rose in the north and threatened all the empire, the pair joined forces to defeat him. Bound by the kinship found only in battle, the pair declared themselves brothers, and vowed in blood they would remain so 'til the end of their days. Tariq even refrained from bedding Andarai's mother again.

His daughter, however . . .

eyes, down to the darkness at his feet, she saw his shadow was trembling too.

He stands in your way, she reminded herself.

All of them.

In your way.

'Blood we are,' he said, passing her the blade. 'And blood we shall remain.'

Mia took the knife, her belly thrilling as her fingertips brushed his. And chiding herself for a fool, she turned to the executus, looked him in the eye.

'Not too deep,' he cautioned. 'You will ruin your grip.'

Mia nodded, drawing the blade across her palm. The pain was bright and real, bringing all the world into focus. She was here. A blooded member of the collegium. Before her lay a desert of sand, an ocean of red. But at the end, she saw Grand Cardinal Duomo in his beggar's robes, no trinity about his throat. Consul Scaeva, reaching up to place the victor's laurel upon her brow.

Her shadow, reaching towards theirs . . .

'Blood we shall remain,' she said.

Sidonius took the blade, cut his palm, and repeated the vow.

'Blood we shall remain.'

A rousing cheer went up around the circle. Executus motioned for Mia and Sidonius to rise, and the gladiatii closed in. Bladesinger smiled at Mia, and the Vaanian girl, Bryn, crushed her to her breast, whispering, 'You fought well.' Butcher slapped her on the back so hard she almost fell over, the others offering their bloody hands or giving her friendly thumps on the arm. Only Furian held himself apart – but whether out of his lofty status as champion or the enmity between them, Mia had no idea.

'My Falcons,' came a voice from the balcony.

'Attend!' snapped the executus, and all eyes turned upwards.

Dona Leona smiled at them like a goddess upon her children, arms spread wide. 'Our victories at Blackbridge earn us yet more renown, and berth at the *venatus* four weeks hence in Stormwatch!'

The gladiatii cheered, and Sidonius wrapped his arm around Mia's neck, squeezing as he bellowed. Mia laughed and pushed the big man off, but she couldn't help but find her voice caught up among them.

'The contests shall only grow fiercer as we approach the *magni*. On the morrow, you return to training. But for now, never let it be said your domina does not reward your valour, or the honour you do her each time you take to the sands!'

Leona clapped her hands, and three servants wheeled a large barrel out among the tables and chairs on the verandah.

'Is that wine?' Sidonius breathed.

'Drink, my Falcons!' Leona smiled. 'A toast to your new brother and sister. A toast to glory! And a toast to our many victories to come!'

Three hours later, as she lay down in her cell, Mia's head was swimming.

She'd tried to drink frugally, but Sid had bellowed every time she slacked her pace, and every one of the other gladiatii seemed to drink as though their lives depended on it. It made perfect sense, she supposed – for folk who owned nothing, their lives at risk every time they took to the sands, a moment of respite and a full cup must seem like a paradise. And so, she'd done her best to play her role, drinking hard with her new familia and smiling at their praise.

The Dweymeri woman, Bladesinger, seemed to have taken a particular liking to her, though most of the collegium had a kind word. Her ploy in the arena – wearing the enemy's colours and playing wounded to get close enough to bring them down – had struck most of her new kin as a stroke of small genius.

Bryn, the blonde Vaanian girl, had raised her cup in toast.

'A fine ruse, little Crow.'

'Aye,' her brother Byern replied. 'When I saw you clutching those guts and realized what you were up to, I almost shouted loud enough to give the game away.'

'Crow, my arse.' Butcher had grinned. 'We should call her the bloody Fox.'

'The Wolf.' Bladesinger smiled.

'The Snake.' came a voice.

All eyes had turned to Furian, glowering at the head of the table. Mia had met his stare, watched his lip curl in derision.

'Gladiatii fight with honour,' he'd said. 'Not with lies.'

'Brother, come,' Bladesinger had said. 'A victory won is a victory earned.'

'I am champion of this collegium,' the Unfallen had replied. 'I say what is earned. And what is stolen.'

Bladesinger had glanced at the torc around Furian's neck, the laurel at his brow, nodded acquiescence. The Unfallen returned to his cup, speaking no more. Festivities ended soon after, and in truth, Mia had been thankful. She wasn't accustomed to so much wine, and a few more cups and she'd have been painting the walls.

She sat in her cell now, the bars slowly spinning. She'd heard that same singing from Bladesinger's cell before the lights died, supposing it might be some sort of prayer. But now darkness had descended, all she could hear was the sound of sleep.

Sidonius was on his back snoring like a dying bull, pausing only long enough to fart so loud Mia felt it through the floor. She scowled and kicked the big Itreyan, who rolled over with a grumble.

'Fucking pig,' she cursed, covering her nose. 'I need my own bloody cell.'

'. . . *i seldom find myself ungrateful that I do not need to breathe* . . .'

Mia's eyes widened as she heard the whisper.

'. . . *at this moment, doubly so* . . .'

'Mister Kindly!'

'. . . *she cried, loud enough to wake the dead* . . .'

Two black shapes coalesced from the shadows at the other end of the cell.

'. . . IF THIS LUMP'S SNORING HASN'T DONE SO, NOTHING WILL . . .'

Mia grinned as the pair of daemons bounded up to her, diving into her shadow as if it were black water. A rush of soothing chill washed over her, rippling down the length of her body, leaving an iron calm in its wake. She felt Mister Kindly stalking across her shoulder, weaving among her hair without disturbing a single strand. Eclipse curled around Mia's back, put her insubstantial head in the girl's lap. Mia ran her hands through both of them, their shapes rippling like black smoke. She hadn't realized how badly she'd missed them until she had them back.

'Black Mother, it's good to see you two,' she whispered.

'. . . *I MISSED YOU* . . .'

'. . . *o, please* . . .'

'. . . *I MISSED THE MOGGY LESS* . . .'

Mia ran her hands down the length of the shadowwolf's body. There was no sensation of being able to touch her, but petting Eclipse was like petting a cool breeze.

'When did you arrive?'

'. . . *YESTERTURN. BUT YOU WERE NOT YET RETURNED FROM THE* VENATUS . . .'

'. . . *things went well, i take it* . . .'

'I'm not dead, if that counts for anything.'

Mister Kindly nuzzled against her ear, and Mia's skin tingled. It felt like being kissed by cigarillo smoke.

'. . . *everything . . .*' he whispered.

The trio sat in the gloom for a while, simply enjoying each other's company. Mia curled her fingers through their gossamer bodies, felt any trace of the fear she'd felt over the past weeks fading to nothing. She'd done it, she realized. The first step towards Duomo's and Scaeva's throats was complete. And with her passengers beside her, the remaining steps seemed not so far at all.

'. . . *lovely as this is . . .*'

'. . . ALWAYS WE CAN COUNT UPON YOU TO SPOIL THE MOOD . . .'

'No, he's right,' Mia sighed. 'Is she waiting?'

'. . . AYE . . .'

'Take me to her, then.'

Her passengers faded into the black. Mia felt them coalesce in the shadows of the antechamber, and just as she'd done the nevernight she visited Furian, she closed her eyes, reached into the dark. Perhaps it was the wine, perhaps the practice she'd had, but she found the Step a little easier this time, the sudden rush, the vertigo. Opening her eyes, she found the room spinning wildly, but she was in the shadow of the stairwell beside them.

Bending double, she retched a few cups' worth onto the stone, covering her mouth to stifle the sound. She felt a few gladiatii stirring in the barracks, sinking back into the shadows and fighting the urge to vomit again. She clutched the wall to help it stop spinning. Wiped her hand across her lips, and spat onto the stone.

'Black Mother, remind me not to do that when I'm half-drunk again.'

'. . . COME . . .'

'. . . *the viper waits, mia . . .*'

She glanced to the mekwerk control on the wall, pondering how it worked. On unsteady legs, she stole out through the keep, into the shadows of the verandah. Fang was sitting beneath a table, watching with curious eyes. As Mister Kindly and Eclipse flitted past, the dog's hackles rose. Mia offered her hand to calm the mastiff, but with a low whimper, Fang scampered away.

'. . . *dogs are fools . . .*'

'. . . SAYS THE FOOL WHO GOT LOST ON THE WAY UP HERE . . .'

'. . . *i was not lost, dear mongrel, i was exploring . . .*'

'. . . IT IS AN ENORMOUS KEEP ATOP A CLIFF OVERLOOKING THE WHOLE CITY, HOW DO— . . .'

'Hsst,' Mia hissed, ducking into an alcove. Swift footsteps marked the approach of the magistrae, a serving girl in tow. The pair were in deep discussion about travel arrangements to Stormwatch, the girl marking notes in a wax ledger. Mia waited 'til the pair were out of sight, slowly crept along the corridor to the front doors, open wide to cool sea breeze. Squinting against the sunlight, she peered out at the high keep walls, red stone against a sky of burning blue.

Gathering handfuls of shadows, Mia draped them about her shoulders. Her fingers were a little clumsy from the drink, but finally all the world was shrouded in muzzy black and muffled white, and she was almost as blind as the turn she was born. With soft whispers, her two passengers guided her through the courtyard, past the patrolling guards and into a shadowed alcove just beside the main gates. And from there, she closed her eyes

and Stepped
into the
shadow
across
the road.

Mia fell to her knees, clutching her belly and fighting the urge to vomit with all she had. After a few minutes in the dirt, she caught her breath, wiping tears from her eyes.

'. . . *are you well . . . ?*'

'Next silly question, please,' she whispered.

'. . . WE DO NOT HAVE TO SEE HER NOW . . .'

'No, we should. But we can't be gone too long. They don't rouse us 'til early morn, but if they somehow miss me in the nevernight . . .'

'. . . THE WINE WILL KEEP YOUR CELLMATE DREAMING 'TIL THEN . . .'

'Still, we need to be swift.'

'. . . *it is not far . . .*'

She rose on shaking legs and staggered along the dusty road, winding down the sheer hill upon which Crow's Nest stood. Mia didn't need Mister Kindly or Eclipse as much out here – she knew the road well enough to walk it blind. But she didn't dare risk casting off her shadow cloak just yet. She was still clad as a gladiatii, and the twin circles branded on her cheek marked her as property. Though masters might often walk in the company of armed warrior slaves, it would be a rarity to see one wandering alone. Best to remain hidden, and avoid questions entirely.

Mia could hear the sea to the south, the ringing of port bells below, smell the familiar scents of the town in the keep's shadow. Known as Crow's Rest, it was home to three or four thousand – a bustling trade port that had sprung up under the keep's protection. The buildings were red stone and white plaster, crammed together on the steep hillsides leaning down to the water. The air rang with the song of gulls.

Her passengers led her into the tangled warren of the dockside. She threw off her cloak here, stole down twisted alleys, ripe with garbage and salt air. They arrived at a small alehouse, Mister Kindly nodding to the guest rooms above.

'. . . *second floor, third window* . . .'

Mia glanced about to ensure all was clear, and began to climb. She reached the second-floor terraces, slipped over the iron railing, rapped once upon the glass.

The window opened and she stole inside, quiet as whispers.

Mia's eyes took a moment to adjust after the sunlight outside. But finally she saw a figure dropping herself into an old divan, stretching long legs out before her. She was dressed in black, leather britches and a short leather corset, a long-sleeved shirt of dark silk beneath. She'd dyed her hair to cover the telltale blonde, now as bloody-red as Jessamine's had been. But there was no mistaking those eyes.

The girl leaned back in her chair, looked Mia up and down.

'Hello, beautiful,' she smiled.

'Hello, Ashlinn,' Mia replied.

BOOK 2

BLOOD AND GLORY

CHAPTER 13

EGRESS

Clove-scented smoke curled in the sea air, slipping out in thin trails from Mia's nostrils. She dragged the last breath from the cigarillo, crushed the life out of it against the wall and breathed a contented sigh.

''Byss and blood, I needed that.'

'I knew you'd be missing them.'

Ash smiled, dragged a lock of blood-red hair behind her ear. She'd dyed it for subterfuge – if by some horrid stroke of fate, someone from the Church saw her and Mia together at a distance, Ash might be able to pass for Jessamine. It was a thin ruse, but as Mister Kindly was so fond of telling Mia, this whole game was so thin it was practically translucent.

Still, Mia inclined her head in thanks, and closing her eyes, she leaned back against the old leather divan, listening to the tobacco buzz in her blood.

'It's good to see you again,' Ash said.

Mia opened her eyes, staring at Ash through her lashes. Mister Kindly hopped up onto the divan, tail draped over Mia's shoulder. Eclipse wrapped herself around Mia's waist, head in her lap. Neither of her passengers trusted Ashlinn, and even after setting all this in motion together, Mia couldn't bring herself to either. Ash killed Jess. She'd killed Tric. Killed anyone who stood in the way of her revenge.

Is she so different from you?

She'd not given the Luminatii the location of Mercurio's shop, after all . . .

Ashlinn peered at the rags Mia was clad in.

'Nice to see you dressed up for the occasion.'

'Take you much trouble to get here?' Mia asked.

Ash shook her head. 'Mister Grumpy found us quick enough.'

Eclipse's laughter came from beneath the floor. Mister Kindly tilted his head at Ashlinn and whispered with a voice like smoke.

'. . . *insolence* . . .'

Ashlinn smirked at the shadowcat, slipped a dagger from her belt, and skewered an apple from the bowl of fruit on the table beside her. With a deft flick of her wrist, she tossed it into Mia's outstretched hand.

'We waited at Whitekeep as planned,' Ash said. 'Once Leonides arrived and you weren't among his purchases, I knew something had gone balls up. Though I didn't imagine jewels were facing so proudly skywards until Mister Smart-arse found us.'

'. . . *stop that* . . .'

'. . . *NO, DO CONTINUE, PLEASE* . . .'

Ash ignored the shadows, instead quirked an eyebrow at Mia. The girl took a noisy bite out of her apple, chewing for a good while before she answered.

'I admit, the plan has suffered a few . . . setbacks.'

'You always had a talent for understatement, Corvere.' Ashlinn stabbed another apple from the bowl, began peeling it with deft strokes of her blade. 'Living in the keep that belonged to your father before he was hanged for treason. Under ownership of the wife of the justicus you murdered. In a stable that can only be a half-year old at most, and only has one laurel to its name. How's that faring?'

'I survived the Winnowing,' Mia shrugged.

Ash slipped a sliver of apple between her lips. 'I *had* noticed you weren't dead.'

'And I've taken the blood vow,' Mia continued. 'I'm a full-fledged gladiatii now. The plan remains the same. I'll just have to do it through a different collegium is all.'

'You're going to have to fight twice as hard,' Ash pointed out. 'Leonides has already assured his collegium a berth in the *magni* from previous years' victories. Leona doesn't have anything like the political capital her father does. She needs to win at least three laurels before she can even fight in the grand games.'

'If I need someone to state the bleeding obvious, I already have Mister Kindly, Ashlinn.'

'. . . *some things are important enough to point out twice* . . .'

'Listen, nobody knows better than me how deep the shit we're in is,' Mia snapped. 'But if one of you can think of a better way to get

Duomo and Scaeva at once, without the Red Church getting a whiff of it, I'm all fucking ears.'

'I've told you before, Mia,' Ash said. '*I* can get Duomo for you. I trained at the Church, same as you. We can sail back to Godsgrave right now and—'

'No, I told *you*,' the girl scowled. 'Duomo is mine. Scaeva is *mine*. I want to look those bastards in the eye as they die. I want them to *know* it was me.'

'. . . BLOOD MUST HAVE BLOOD . . .' Eclipse growled.

Ash popped another slice of apple between her teeth, raised an eyebrow at Mister Kindly. The pair might have been at odds about everything else, but as far as the insanity of Mia's plan went, they were of one accord.

'. . . mia, perha— . . .'

'No!' she snapped. 'This is the way. And this was the deal, Ashlinn. You help me get Scaeva and Duomo, Mercurio and I help you get the Ministry.'

'You wouldn't just be getting them for *me*, Mia. Let's be honest.'

'Are you certain you know what honesty even looks like any more, Ashlinn?'

The girl sucked her lip, slowly nodded. 'A fine thrust.'

'I've been practising.'

'I should point out that I *am* here helping you, Mia.'

'I get Duomo. *I* get Scaeva. That was the bargain struck.'

And so it was. Insane as the plan had seemed, sitting for hours in the Godsgrave Chapel, neither Mercurio nor Ashlinn could ponder a better one. Scaeva rarely made public appearances any more, and Duomo spent most of his time in the Basilica Grande. For the pair of them to be together at the *magni*, within striking range, all while Duomo wouldn't be wearing a cursed trinity about his neck . . . No matter how hard it would be to get there, the opportunity was too ripe to waste.

And so, Mercurio had reported to the Ministry that the deal with the braavi had gone south, and that Mia was now pursuing the map on the mainland. The trio had then set about researching the best collegia to see Mia through to the *magni*, although Mercurio wasn't exactly happy about Ashlinn being involved. True, the girl wanted revenge on the Red Church, almost as badly as Mia. True, she was a better liar than Mia; she and her brother had almost brought the Church down all by themselves. But, the fact was, Mia and her old mentor trusted her about as far as they could spit her.

Still, Mia had Eclipse around to keep Ash under watch – the girl couldn't breathe without the daemon there to hear it. And when swimming in drake-infested waters, it never hurt to have company, if only so the drakes had someone to eat other than you.

Ashlinn stretched like a cat, ate another slice of apple.

'Fair enough,' she said. 'I'm just pointing out other options. But the deal was struck, and I'll hold to it. Never let it be said I'm not a woman of my word.'

Mister Kindly scoffed, tail curling about Mia's throat.

'*. . . on the contrary, i feel it should be said as loudly and often as possible . . .*'

Ashlinn flipped the knuckles. 'Nobody was talking to you, Mister Positivity.'

Eclipse raised her head, her whisper echoing through the floorboards. '*. . . AS YOU MAY HAVE GUESSED, DONA JÄRNHEIM AND I HAVE BEEN GETTING ALONG FAMOUSLY IN YOUR ABSENCE . . .*'

'*. . . colour me unsurprised . . .*'

'*. . . HAVE YOU NOT MICE TO CHASE, LITTLE MOGGY . . . ?*'

'*. . . have you not crotches to sniff, dear mongrel . . . ?*'

'All right, enough, enough,' Mia said. 'I need to get back to my lovely stinky cell in Crow's Nest before I'm missed. We need to find out as much about Leona as we can. We knew the book on her father, but the dona herself is something of a mystery.'

'A good thing I've been asking around, then,' Ash smiled.

The girl sliced off another sliver of apple, pressed it to her tongue.

Mia raised an eyebrow. 'Out with it, then.'

'Say please,' Ashlinn smiled.

'Ash . . .' Mia growled.

The girl grinned, leaned back in her chair. 'I've only been here a turn. So there's more to learn. But I know Leona married Remus around three years back. She caught his eye at the last *magni*, and Remus sought her hand from her father soon after. Quite a coup, for the daughter of a mere sanguila to be married off to the justicus of the Luminatii Legion. Shows how much political clout her da has, I suppose.'

Mia took a bite of the apple, spoke around her mouthful.

'Their marriage was arranged?'

'They always are at that level.' Ash sliced a thin wafer, popped it between her lips. 'Though from what I can tell, Leona wasn't forced into it. Remus was rich. Handsome. His political star on the rise. She stood to gain a lot from slipping into bed with him. So I'd not let it slip you slit his throat were I you.'

'O, damnation, because I was planning on it.'

Ashlinn smirked and pressed another sliver to her tongue.

'What about Arkades?' Mia spoke around another noisy bite. 'He was Leonides's champion for years. Why does he serve Leona as executus instead of her father?'

Ashlinn shrugged. 'I've only been here a single turn. Give me time.'

'Well, I need all the leverage I can get.' Mia wiped her lips, stood, and stretched. 'So the more you can find out about my domina, the better.'

Ash nodded to the rags Mia was wearing, staring pointedly at her bare midriff and legs. 'I like her fashion sense, if nothing else.'

Mia ignored the comment, slipped to the window, peered out to look for unfriendly eyes. Finding none, she swung her leg over the sill, made to climb out.

'Mia.'

She turned to look at Ashlinn, one eyebrow raised. The girl's hands fluttered at her sides, picking at the hem of her britches.

'Be careful in there,' she said.

Mia glanced at Eclipse, still curled on the divan in a puddle of black.

'Keep an eye out,' Mia said.

'. . . *AS MUCH AS THE EYELESS CAN* . . .' the not-wolf replied.

And with that, she was gone. Down the wall, to the alley, dragging the shadows about her head. Stealing back up the way to Crow's Nest with Mister Kindly to guide her to her rest.

She thought about the way Ashlinn looked at her. The kiss they'd shared the turn Mia left the Mountain. That had all been for show on Ashlinn's part, she was sure of it. Just a play to further the girl's plan to take down the Ministry. Mia knew it. Everyone knew it. Ashlinn Järnheim was poison. But thinking on that kiss, her mind drifted to that nevernight in Gaius Aurelius's bed, the way that Liisian beauty had tasted on his lips. Wondering if that had been all for show on *her* part – just another ruse to get within striking distance of the senator's son. Wondering if part of her hadn't enjoyed it, or if it mattered, even if she had.

Wondering why she was wondering *at all*.

Eyes on the fucking prize, Corvere . . .

Back at Crow's Nest, she found the portcullis still sealed, the guards watching. The hour was late, and there was little hope a servant might be sent down to the Rest until after the gladiatii were roused for mornmeal. And so Mia reached out to the shadows at her feet, the shadows in the courtyard, and drawing a deep breath, she

Stepped

across

the space

between them.

She fell to her knees in the dust, head swimming, the burning light of the two suns overhead pounding upon her skull. At least the wine had worn off, and she wasn't tempted to spew, but the sensation was still far on the south side of pleasant. The captain of the dona's houseguard, a sharp-eyed fellow named Gannicus, turned at the sound of her hitting the dirt. But with Mia hidden beneath her cloak in the shadow of the wall, he saw nothing of account, and slowly turned back to his watch.

It was several minutes before Mia felt steady enough to rise, creeping slow across the courtyard at Mister Kindly's whispers, down the building's flank to the open verandah at the rear. Stealing down the stairs, groping blind, she finally found the iron bars that sealed off the barracks from the rest of the villa. Taking a moment to ready herself, dreading the incoming vertigo, she felt for the shadows of her dingy little cell. And closing her eyes tight she

Stepped

down into the black

at her feet

and into the cell beyond.

The heat of the suns was nowhere near as intense in the barracks' dark, but still, she was almost sick, puke bubbling up from her gullet and welling in her cheeks. She was getting better at shadow-stepping since the basilica roof – like any muscle, she supposed it grew stronger the more she used it. But a second Step so soon after the first was apparently too much, especially with the suns burning so bright in the sky. She swallowed thickly, crouched upon the straw, clutching the stones beneath to stop the world from spinning. Listening to the cells around her, she heard nothing but soft snoring and sighs.

'. . . *all looks clear* . . .' came a whisper in her ear.

She waited a moment longer, the world slowly steadying itself. And finally, safe inside her cell, Mia threw her shadowcloak aside and blinked around the cellar's gloom, right into Sidonius's opening eyes.

'Fuck me,' he murmured. 'Look wh—'

Mia crossed the cell in a flash, seized the man by the throat, one hand over his mouth. Sidonius clawed her back, muscles bulging, growling as the pair struggled. Sid was bigger, Mia faster, the pair scuffling silently in the straw. Each had the other in a choke hold, veins bulging at their throats, Sid's eyes welling with tears.

'P-pe . . .' he gurgled.

Even as Mia choked him, his own hold tightened. Mia's throat cinched closed, her chest burning, blood cut off to her brain. She was still dizzy from her shadow-stepping, she'd no idea if the big Itreyan would succumb before she did. No idea what he'd do if she did . . .

'P . . . peace,' he managed to gasp.

Mia eased off her hold a fraction, looking into Sidonius's eyes. The big man did the same, letting just a whisper of breath into her lungs. Slow as melting ice, she released her grip, the big man's fingers unwinding from about her neck. Mia rolled off the big Itreyan, retreated to one corner of their cell.

''Byss and b-blood,' Sid whispered, rubbing his throat. 'Wh . . . what was that for?'

'You saw,' Mia whispered.

'So what?'

'You know. What I *am*.'

Sid winced, trying to swallow. He whispered almost lower than she could hear.

'Darkin.'

Mia said nothing, dark eyes locked on his.

'And that deserves a bloody strangling?' he pressed.

'Keep your fucking voice down,' Mia spat, looking about the other cells.

'*. . . advice best followed by everyone concerned . . . ?*'

Sidonius's eyes grew wide as the shadowcat faded into view on Mia's shoulder.

'Bugger me . . .' he breathed.

'*. . . a generous offer, but no, thank you . . .*'

'And thank *you* for telling me all looked clear,' Mia whispered.

The not-cat tilted his head.

'*. . . i can't be perfect in every way . . .*'

Mia and Sidonius looked at each other across the straw. There was fear in the man's stare – fear of the unknown, fear of what she was. But, despite it, Sidonius held his peace, held his tongue, looking her over with curious eyes.

'Shouldn't you be screaming for the guards right now?' Mia asked. 'Blathering that they should be nailing me up for witchery?'

'Witchery?' Sid scoffed. 'Do I look like some addle-witted peasant to you?'

'. . . I admit, you're taking the news better than most.'

'I've seen a lot of this world, little Crow. And you're not the strangest of it. Not by a long ways.' The Itreyan leaned back against the bars, folded his arms. 'It's true, then . . . what they say about you lot?'

'That we spoil milk where we walk and deflower virgins wher—'

'That you walk through walls, you little nonce. I woke up to piss a half-hour ago and you weren't here. Then, *pop*, you appear right out of the fucking air?'

'That's not what happened, Sid.'

'I know what I saw, Crow.'

Sounds of waking could be heard in the villa overhead. The cook's footsteps on the boards, the watch changing outside. Executus would be down here soon, rousing them for their first round of brutal callisthenics.

Mia looked Sidonius in the eye, studying him with care. The man was a smart-arse, a thug, an utter lackwit when it came to women. But he was no fool. She didn't trust him, not by half. But they'd bled together on the sands of Blackbridge, and that counted for something. Still, there was no chance she was willing to share anything of herself without him giving something in return . . .

She looked at the scarred knuckles and heavy muscle that spoke of a man who'd spent a life fighting. The cold blue eyes that spoke of long miles and longer years. The word *COWARD* burned into his skin.

'Just how much of the world *have* you seen?' she asked.

'Liis,' he replied. 'Vaan. Itreya. Anywhere the banner took me.'

Mia raised an eyebrow. Remembering the way Sid had conducted himself during the Winnowing. Barking orders like a man used to command. Thinking tactics, like . . .

'You were in the Itreyan legion,' she said.

Sid shook his head. 'I was *Luminatii*, little Crow. Served the justicus five years.'

Mia's eyes narrowed, belly turning to ice. 'You served Marcus Remus?'

'Remus?' Sid scoffed. 'That treacherous shitheel? 'Byss, no. I served the justicus before him. The *true* justicus, girl. Darius fucking Corvere.'

Mia's heart lurched in her chest. Tongue cleaving to the roof of her mouth. Black Mother, this man had served her *father*.

But that makes no sense . . .

'I . . .' Mia cleared her throat. 'I heard the Kingmaker's army were all crucified . . . on the banks of the Choir. They paved the Senate house steps with their skulls.'

'I wasn't there when Corvere and Antonius's army fell apart.' Sid rubbed the brand at his chest, his voice growing distant. 'Always wondered if I might have done some good had I been . . .'

Sid ran a hand over his dark cropped hair. He nodded at the walls around them. The bars that held them in.

'This used to be Corvere's house, you know,' he sighed. 'He and his familia used to spend summers here, I think. Little girl. Baby son. Before they gave it to that snake, Remus. To think this is where I'd end my turns. Locked in that fucker's basement. Winning blood and glory for his widow until my guts paint the sand.'

So. Sidonius had done more than serve her father. He'd remained loyal, when the whole Republic turned against him . . .

Maw's teeth, she'd never imagined it. To think she'd meet one of her father's men, under this very roof? If she'd felt no kinship before for this man she'd bled beside at Blackbridge, she felt it flooding inside her chest now. The way Sidonius spoke about her father made her want to kiss the stupid sod.

'The true *justicus*,' he'd said.

When everyone else just called Darius Corvere 'traitor'.

Mia rubbed her bruised throat, her shadow rippling as Mister Kindly drank her fear. She'd not spoken of her gift much, not to anyone. People feared what they didn't understand, and hated what they feared. But for all the strangeness of it, Sidonius didn't feel anything close to afraid any more.

He's an odd one . . .

'I can't walk through walls,' she confessed.

Sid's eyes came into focus, looking at her across the cell.

'I just sort of . . . Step. After a fashion. Between shadows, I mean.'

''Byss and blood,' the big man breathed.

'But it makes me want to puke afterwards,' she added. 'And I can make myself unseen. But I'm almost blind when I do. It's not the most wondrous gift, truth told.'

'And your passenger?'

'Say hello, Mister Kindly.'

'. . . hello, mister kindly . . .'

'So you can leave these cells any time you want?'

Mia shrugged. 'After a fashion.'

The Itreyan shook his head in bewilderment. 'Then what in the name of the Everseeing and all Four fucking Daughters are you still doing here, little Crow?'

The portcullis shuddered upwards as a guard pulled a mekwerk lever. Executus marched into the barracks, greying beard bristling, whip curled in his hand.

'Gladiatii!' he barked. 'Attend!'

With a shrug to Sid, Mia rose to begin her turn's work.

CHAPTER 14

BREATHING

Two suns burned the skies clear, Shiih's smouldering yellow and Saan's bloody red against a curtain of endless, beautiful blue.* The heat shimmered against the endless ocean, and Mia cursed the Everseeing for the hundredth time that turn.

She danced across the circle, dodging Bladesinger's strikes, weaving in and out of range. The woman's face was set like stone, her wooden sword whistling as if it knew her name.

'No!' Executus bellowed from the circle's edge. 'You're bouncing like a damned blackrabbit. You'll wear yourself to fainting if you keep dancing in this heat. A shield is a weapon, just like your blade. Batter your foe's strikes aside, send her off-balance.'

Mia raised the great curved rectangle of wood and iron on her right arm. It was heavy as a pile of bricks, affixed with a band of old rope. She hated the fucking thing, truth told, but it was true what Arkades said – she was sweating like a pig from dodging about so much. She tried to mark his tutelage, but as Bladesinger raised her sword and bore

---

* Though the Ashkahi Empire ended in a mysterious magikal calamity millennia previous, remnants of the language survive in the Itreyan Republic to this day. The names of the three suns, Shiih (*the Watcher*), Saan (*the Seer*), and Saai (*the Knower*) are the most obvious example, but it may be of interest to note that the names of the Itreyan pantheon are also Ashkahi words.

Aa is the Ashkahi word for 'all' and *Niah*, Ashkahi for 'nothing'. Itreyan academics spend a great deal of time arguing with each other at dinner parties, debating whether both Aa and Niah were worshipped in Old Ashkah, and whether the religion of the Republic is far older than the Republic itself. Preferably while consuming enormous quantities of wine.

Aa himself has made no comment on the topic, pissed or otherwise.

down on Mia like thunder, the girl instinctively skipped past Bladesinger's guard and slapped her blade against the woman's hamstring.

'Shit,' Bladesinger spat. 'Quicker than a drakeling, this one.'

'*No!*'

Executus limped across the circle, drawing out the steel gladius he always wore to session.

'If you'll not stop dancing like a bride at her wedding, I'll bloody hobble you . . .'

Mia bristled, thinking perhaps Arkades was set to strike her. But instead, he stabbed the sword into the dirt, right in the centre of the ring. He snapped his fingers at Maggot, waiting as always in the shade of the small shed in the corner of the yard.

'Rope,' Arkades commanded.

The girl dashed to the weapon racks, unslung one of the pull ropes the gladiatii used for their callisthenics. Dragging it back to Arkades, Maggot watched with curious eyes as the executus fixed one end around his blade hilt, the other to Mia's leg.

'Dance with that, blackrabbit,' he scowled.

Arkades retired to the circle's edge, barked at Bladesinger to attack. Unable to dodge, Mia was forced to use her shield, Bladesinger's strikes landing like thunderclaps. The impacts jarred Mia's arm, until finally the old rope affixing the shield to her forearm snapped clean in half, snagging up her hand in the knotted leather grip. And with a series of damp, snapping sounds, three of Mia's fingers popped right at the knuckle.

''Byss and fucking *blood*!' she bellowed, dropping her shield.

The other gladiatii in the yard turned to stare, watching as she bent double, clutching her hand. Butcher laughed, Wavewaker broke into a round of applause. Fixing her broken shield in her glare, Mia aimed a savage kick at it ('Fucking thing!'), sent it flying across the yard before dropping onto her backside in the dust.

'Owww,' she moaned, clutching her now-sprained toes with her one good hand.

'Show me,' Executus said, limping over to kneel beside her.

Mia held up her trembling hand. Her smallest finger was jutting out at entirely the wrong angle, her ring and middle finger were both crooked. Arkades turned her hand this way and that as Mia writhed and cursed.

'You broke my fingers!' she said, glaring at Bladesinger.

The woman shrugged, slinging her long saltlocks over her shoulder.

'Welcome to the sand, Crow.'

'Stop whining, girl,' Arkades said, squinting. 'They're just dislocated. Maggot!'

The girl perked up from her shady seat near the shed, dashed over to Mia. Untying the rope at her ankle, Maggot helped Mia up, the older girl rising with a wince. The other gladiatii returned to training as Maggot led Mia by the hand across the yard. She saw Furian sparring with Wavewaker, watching from the corner of his eye. His face was a mask, her belly, as always, a knot of sickness and hunger when he was near.

Do I make him feel the same?

Maggot took Mia into a long room at the rear of the keep, set with four sandstone slabs. The stone was the same burned ochre as the cliffs about them, but it was stained a deeper red, spatter-mad patterns on the surface.

Bloodstains, Mia realized.

'You can sit,' Maggot said in a small, shy voice.

Mia did as she was bid, holding her throbbing hand to her chest. Maggot toddled across the room, fishing about in a series of chests. She returned with a handful of wooden splints and a ball of woven brown cotton.

'Hold out your hand,' the girl commanded.

Mia's shadow swelled, Mister Kindly drinking her fear at the thought of what was to come. Maggot looked her digits over, stroking her chin. And gentle as falling leaves, she took hold of Mia's smallest finger.

'It won't hurt,' she promised. 'I'm very good at this.'

'All riiiiiaaaaaaaaaaaaaAAAGHH!' Mia howled as Maggot popped her finger back into place, quick as silver. She rose from the slab and bent double, clutching her hand.

'That *HURT*!' she yelled.

Maggot gave a solemn nod. 'Yes.'

'*You promised it wouldn't!*'

'And you believed me.' The girl smiled sweet as sugar-floss. 'I told you, I'm very good at this.' She motioned to the slab again. 'Sit back down.'

Mia blinked back hot tears, hand throbbing in agony. But looking at her finger, she could see Maggot had worked it right, popping the dislocated joint back into place neat as could be. Breathing deep, she sat back down and dutifully proffered her hand.

The little girl took hold of Mia's ring finger, looked up at her with big, dark eyes.

'I'm going to count three,' she said.

'All riiiiiaaaaaaaaaaaa*FUCK*!' Mia roared as Maggot snapped the joint back into place. She rose and half danced, half hopped about the room, wounded hand between her legs. 'Shit cock twat fucking *fuckitall*.'

'You swear an awful lot,' Maggot frowned.

'*You said you were going to count three!*'

Maggot nodded sadly. 'You believed me again, didn't you?'

Mia winced, teeth gritted, looking the girl up and down.

'. . . You *are* very good at this,' she realized.

Maggot smiled, patted the bench. 'Last one.'

Sighing, Mia sat back down, hand shaking with pain as Maggot gently took hold of her middle finger. She looked at Mia solemnly.

'Now this one is *really* going to hurt,' she warned.

'Wa—' The Blade flinched as Maggot popped the finger back in. Mia blinked.

'Ow?' she said.

'All done,' Maggot smiled.

'But that was the easiest of the lot?' Mia protested.

'I know,' Maggot replied. 'I'm—'

'—*very good at this*,' they both finished.

Maggot began splinting Mia's fingers, binding them tight to limit their movement. The three circles branded into the little girl's cheek weren't so much of a mystery any more . . .

'Why do they call you Crow?' she asked as she worked.

Mia looked at the girl carefully, trying to ignore the warm, throbbing pain in her hand. Maggot was Liisian; tanned skin and dark, tangled hair, big dark eyes. She was skinny, thin dress hugging her thinner frame.

Perhaps it was seeing her in the keep where she'd grown up. Perhaps it was the mischievous intelligence glittering in those dark eyes, or the way she spoke so brazenly to her elders. But truth told, the little girl reminded Mia a little of herself . . .

'Why do they call you Maggot?' Mia replied.

'I asked first.'

'Crow is a nickname.'

Mia thought back to the first turn anyone had called her by it. Her first meeting with Old Mercurio. The old man had beaten seven shades of shit out of some alley thugs who'd stolen Mia's brooch. The very turn after her father was hanged. She was the daughter of a traitor, wanted by the most powerful men in the Republic. And Mercurio had thought nothing of taking her in, giving her a roof, saving her life.

Black Mother, the things he risked for me . . .

Mia shook her head, thinking about this insane plan of hers.

The things he still risks for me.

'A friend gave it to me,' Mia said. 'When I was a little girl. I had a piece of jewellery with a crow on it. He named me for it.'

'I've never owned jewellery,' Maggot mused.

'I've not owned any since. That one was a gift from my mother.'

'Where is your mother now?'

The dona looked at her daughter, wide eyes and a broken yellow smile, far, far too wide. Mister Kindly materialised on the cell floor beside Mia, and the Dona Corvere hissed like she'd been scalded, shrinking back from the bars, teeth bared in a snarl.

'*He's in you,*' *she'd whispered.* '*O, Daughters, he's in you.*'

Mia stared at the stone floor. The old blood, spattered and brown.

'She's gone,' Mia said.

Maggot looked at Mia, nodded sadly as she tied off the bandage.

'Mine, too,' she said. 'But she taught me all she knew. And so, whenever I stitch a wound or set a bone or mend a fever, she's still with me.'

A fine thought, Mia mused. One no doubt sung to orphans across the world since the beginning of time. But even if there *were* some semblance of her father in the way she fought, her mother in the way she spoke, they were still dead and gone. If they were with her at all, it was as ghosts upon her shoulder, whispering in the nevernight of all that might have been.

If not for *them* . . .

Mia turned her wounded hand this way and that. It was still sore, but the pain had eased. In a week or so, it'd be as new.

'You still haven't told me why they call you Maggot,' she said.

The little girl looked deep into Mia's eyes.

'Pray you never find out,' she said.

The girl walked out of the infirmary, Mia behind her. Maggot retreated to her seat in the shade as Executus limped over to Mia, taking a small pull from the flask at his hip as he came. Grabbing her wrist, he scowled at her wounded hand.

'You'll not be sparring with that for a few—'

'Executus,' came a soft call.

Arkades looked up to the balcony. Dona Leona stood there, auburn hair in long flowing ringlets, her silken dress as blue as the sky above. Beside her stood a rather dapper-looking Liisian man in a frock coat far too fine for the surroundings and far too warm for the weather. He was flanked by two heavyset bodyguards in leather jerkins.

'Attend!' Arkades barked.

The yard fell still at the call, the gladiatii turning towards their mistress.

'Executus, see to Matilius.' The dona glanced to a big Itreyan man, sparring with a Liisian named Otho. 'He is to accompany these men to the home of his new master.'

Arkades's grey brows drew together in a frown. 'New master, Mi Dona?'

'He has been sold to Varro Caito.'

The gladiatii shared uneasy glances, Mia noting the sudden fall in mood. Matilius set aside his practice blades, brow creased as he looked up at Leona.

'Domina,' the Itreyan said. 'Have . . . I displeased you?'

Leona stared at the big man, blue eyes shining. But with a glance at the dapper man beside her, her gaze became hard as the red stone beneath her feet.

'I am no longer your domina,' she said. 'But you still have no right to question me. Know your place, slave, lest I have Executus gift you a parting reminder.'

The big man lowered his gaze, bewilderment swimming in his eyes.

'Apologies,' he grunted.

Leona's cold blue stare fell on Arkades. 'Executus, see to his transfer. The rest of you, back to training.'

Arkades bowed. 'Your whisper, my will.'

Though he hid it well, Mia could still see the confusion in the executus's eyes. Whatever the nature of this 'sale', Leona clearly hadn't consulted him about it.

The big man straightened, looked at Mia, down at her wounded hand.

'You'll not spar for the next three turns, girl.' He nodded to the blond Vaanian twins, working the training dummies across the yard. 'Accompany Bryn and Byern to the equorium amorrow. You can help them with their practice, at least.'

Turning on his heel, the Red Lion limped across the yard. Matilius was speaking swift goodbyes among the other gladiatii in the few moments he had left. He grasped Furian's forearm, squeezed tight. Bladesinger wrapped him in a crushing hug, Butcher and Wavewaker and Otho clapped him on the back. Matilius looked across the yard to Mia, nodded once, and she nodded in reply. She'd not known him well, but he seemed a decent sort. And it was clear he had friends here among the collegium; brothers and sisters he'd fought and bled with, and was now being forced to farewell.

Mia cruised over to the training dummies, slipped up beside Bryn and Byern. The Vaanian girl was short, almost pretty, her blonde topknot drenched in sweat. Byern was taller, better looking, his jaw square and his shoulders broad. His training sword hung limp in his hand as he watched Matilius say his goodbyes. The Vaanians were around Mia's age, but each seemed older somehow.

Something in the eyes, maybe.

'Who is Varro Caito?' Mia asked softly.

The twins startled – they'd not heard Mia's approach. With a scowl, Bryn turned back to the farewells, shooting a poison glance to the dapper Liisian on the balcony.

'A fleshmonger,' she replied. 'He runs Pandemonium.'

Mia raised an eyebrow in question.

'A fighting pit,' Bryn explained. 'Underground. Not sanctioned by the administratii. But the battles are bloody. And popular. Former gladiatii fetch a fine price.'

'So it's a kind of arena?'

Byern shook his head. 'No honour there. No rules. No mercy. Pandemonium is closer to a human dogfight than the *venatus*. And the contests, ever to the finish. Most warriors perish in a few turns. Even the best only endure a month.'

Mia watched Matilius, now being manacled by Executus and handed over to the Liisian fleshpeddler. The bodyguards checked the irons, nodded once. And with one final glance, the man was marched from the yard in the keeping of his new master.

Bryn sighed, shook her head. 'He walks to his death.'

'Then why does he walk?' Mia asked.

'What else would he do?' Byern replied.

'Run,' she said fiercely. '*Fight.*'

'Fight?' Bryn looked at Mia as if she were a child. 'There was a slave revolt down in Crow's Rest. Maybe seven, eight months back. Did you hear tell of it?'

Mia shook her head.

'Two slaves fell in love,' Byern said. 'They wished to wed, but their domini forbade it. So the pair slit their master's throat in the nevernight and fled. They made it to Dawnspear before they were caught. Do you know what the administratii did?'

'Crucified them, at a guess,' Mia said.

'Aye,' Bryn nodded, smoothing back her topknot. 'But not just them. They flogged and crucified every slave in their domini's house beside them to set example. The only one they spared was the slave who told the administratii where the murderers could be found. And for her loyalty to the Republic, that slave was forced to wield the lash during the floggings.'

'Such, the price of defiance in Itreya,' Byern said.

Mia's lips curled at the thought. Sickness in her belly. She'd known the life of a slave in the Republic was cruel, often short. She knew punishment for those who rebelled was horrific. But, Black Mother, the brutality of it . . .

'Did you see?' she asked softly. 'The executions?'

Byern nodded. 'We all did. The administratii commanded every slave from every household in the Rest come and bear witness. The youngest boy they strung up couldn't have been more than eight years old.'

'Four Daughters,' Mia breathed. 'I never imagined . . .'

'As gladiatii, your lot is better than most,' Bryn said. 'Blood. Glory. Be grateful.'

Mia peered at the girl sidelong. 'Are *you* grateful?'

Bryn looked at the wooden sword in her hand. Her brother, Byern, standing tall beside her. She looked to the sky above her head, down to the sand at her feet.

'We endure,' she finally replied.

Mia watched Matilius being marched to the front gate. He paused before the portcullis, throwing one last glance back at his brothers and sisters, raising his hand in farewell. Bryn waved in reply, Byern closed a fist, placed it over his heart. And with a shove in Matilius's back, the man was gone.

Mia shook her head, wondering what she would do in his place. Fight in some futile gesture of defiance and get her brothers and sisters killed? Or march quietly to her death? How would it feel if life in this collegium was truly her lot? If instead of being able to Step outside the walls whenever she chose, she was actually trapped here? No control. No say in her own future?

'How?' she asked. 'How do you endure the unendurable?'

'We have a saying in Vaan,' Byern replied. 'In every breath, hope abides.'

Bryn turned to Mia.

A quick smile to cover her pain.

A slap on Mia's back to break the ugly stillness.

'Just keep breathing, little Crow.'

CHAPTER 15

RIGHT

Evemeal was sullen that nevernight, none of the bawdy jokes or friendly banter that usually marked dinner around the long verandah tables. All minds seemed turned to Matilius's sale. Thinking about the fate that awaited the man in Pandemonium, Mia found herself without appetite, and instead of the usual scraps she gave when Fang came snuffling around, she gave over almost her entire meal.

The big mastiff licked her wounded fingers, his stubby tail all a-wag. She ruffled his ears and tried her best not to dwell on it. To think instead of the contests to come, the revenge awaiting her at the end of them. She was here for one reason, and one alone. And vengeance wouldn't be served by getting too close to any she fought beside. No matter how crushing the thought of it all was.

As if echoing her thoughts, she felt a cool breeze on the back of her neck. Fang whined softly and scampered away from Mia, ears pressed flat, tail tucked. Mister Kindly entwined himself in the shadows of her hair and whispered, soft as shadows.

'. . . *these people are not your familia, and not your friends. all of them are only a means to an end . . .*'

The other gladiatii seemed in no mood to speak on it, chewing their food in silence. Butcher was dark, though, muttering to himself and shaking his head. And near the meal's end, he could keep his tongue in his head no longer.

'This is horseshit,' he growled, pushing his bowl aside.

' 'Tis beef, I think,' Wavewaker said, picking his teeth.

'I mean Mati, you bleeding cunt,' Butcher said, glaring at the bigger man. 'Selling him to that devious shitbag Caito? He deserved better than the damned pit.'

'Mind your language, brother,' Wavewaker waved a warning finger, his baritone growing deeper. 'There are ladies present.'

Bladesinger raised her eyebrow. 'Where?'

'Enough,' Furian growled. The champion stared hard, dark eyes burning. His jaw was set. Muscles taut. 'Eat your food, Butcher.'

'It's not right, Furian.'

The Unfallen slammed a fist down on the table, and all eyes turned to stare.

'It is Domina's will,' he said. 'She is mistress of this collegium. You seem too apt to forget that. But remind me, brother, what were you, before she and Executus dragged you up from the shit?'

'A bodyguard,' Butcher said, squaring his jaw.

'A bloody *mule* is what you were,' Furian spat. 'Carrying bags to market for some wrinkled old dona, and fucking her on command. And what of you, Wavewaker?'

'I was a thespian,' the big man replied proudly.

'Thespian? You were a damned doorman in a two-beggar theatre, bouncing drunks and mopping shit out of the privy between shows.'

Wavewaker looked a little crestfallen. 'I was set to play the Magus Ki—'

'Byern was headed for an Ashkahi copper mine.' The Unfallen gestured about the room. 'Bryn, a Liisian brothel. Aa's bleeding cock, Bladesinger was set to be fucking hanged! And Domina raised all of us up and forged us into *gods*!'

The champion's dark glare roamed the mess, inviting dissent.

'Domina feeds us,' he said. 'Shelters us. Gives us the chance to fight for glory and honour in the *venatus* instead of living on our knees or on our backs. And you name it not right? We all owe our lives to her. Including Matilius. That *makes* it right.'

Mia sat in silence, listening to the Unfallen's tirade. None in the room voiced disagreement. She wondered at the man again; who he was, what made him breathe. She was a good judge of character, but Furian was a mystery. He fought like a daemon in the arena, true enough. And yet, he seemed perfectly content to bend his knee to this life of blood and servitude, and deny the truth of what he really was.

Why, just once, can't I meet a darkin who's not a bastard or a fool?

Evemeal ended, the gladiatii were marched to the barracks and bathed, four at a time. She was often thrown in with Sidonius, Butcher, and Bladesinger, though she preferred bathing with Wavewaker best.

The man had a beautiful voice, and he often sang as he washed – songs learned from his brief spell in the theatre, apparently.

Mia had already abandoned any notion of decency, what with walking about all turn wearing two strips of padded cloth and a pair of sandals. She found it strange, how easily she was becoming accustomed to life in the collegium. No privacy. No modesty. And when she closed her eyes, she could still hear the sound that had lingered in her mind since the games at Blackbridge. The roar, lifting her up on wings of thunder.

The crowd.

Her skin thrilled to think of it, despite herself. The memory burned in the black behind her eyes. Still, she reminded herself she was here for a reason, and that reason was the *magni*. Leona had sold Matilius without discussing the matter with Arkades. If there was some jeopardy for the collegium, she'd best learn the truth of it.

Sid seemed of a mood when Mia returned to their cell after her bath, and she didn't press him. Instead she lay against the bars and snoozed, wondering how she might turn the big Itreyan's allegiance to her father to some kind of advantage. There in the dark, she listened to the soft murmuring under Bladesinger's door, sitting in silence until she was certain the rest of the gladiatii were asleep. She whispered Sid's name, but he didn't stir. Feeling a cool whisper on the back of her neck.

'. . . *where do we go . . . ?*'

'You tell me,' she whispered in reply.

'. . . *i have been roaming the house since evemeal . . .*'

'So tell me a story.'

'. . . *arkades requested a meeting with leona. he was told to come after she had bathed . . .*'

Mia nodded. 'Lead the way.'

Her shadow rippled and Mister Kindly was gone, flitting over to the portcullis, now locked tight for the nevernight. Mia reached out to the shadows in the antechamber, just as she'd done yestereve. They were no easier to grip, her hold slipping for a moment as she scowled in concentration and drew a long steady breath and

      Stepped

            into

                  the shadow

                          beyond the portcullis.

The world turned on its head and she almost fell, biting down on a curse as she steadied herself with her wounded hand. Head hung low, long dark hair draped over ink-black eyes.

'... *come*...'

The not-cat flitted ahead, keeping watch for the houseguards. Slipping through her old home like a knife between ribs, Mia passed the rows of armour, up the wide stairway to the first floor. Her mind swimming with memories of her childhood here.

She remembered her father working his horses in the yard. Her mother reading by the bay windows in her room. She remembered the nevernight her brother Jonnen was born, under this very roof. Her father had wept as he held the babe in his arms.

She could recall him so clearly. The way he smelled. The way he kissed her mother, first on one eyelid, then the other, then finally upon her smooth, olive brow.

A good man.

A loving husband.

A faithful soldier.

What kind of king would he have made?

Mia shook her head, cursing herself a fool. It didn't matter. Her father's kingdom was two feet wide and six feet deep, and two of the men who'd killed him were still talking and breathing. That was all that mattered. *That* was all she should care about.

Up to the fourth floor. The level had been used for storage when Mia's parents had owned the Nest, but with her Falcons kept secure in the basement, the upper level now belonged to the mistress of the house. Quiet as a whisper, Mia stole down the long hallways towards soft voices coming from the bathhouse.

Peering in through the door, she saw Dona Leona emerging from a deep, steaming pool, water running in rivulets down her bare body. Her hair was damp, her face bereft of paint. It occurred to Mia that she was a beauty; full hips and fuller lips. Her eyes roamed Leona's curves, wreathed in steam, and she wondered at the thrill of it. Why, downstairs in the barracks, seeing naked bodies meant nothing, but here, her skin was prickling. Heart beating faster. Thinking, perhaps, of another beauty on Aurelius's bed, her taste on the young don's mouth, her golden kisses sinking ever lower.

She thought of Ashlinn, then. The kiss they'd shared when Mia left the Church. That kiss that lasted a moment too long. Maybe not long enough?

Mia shook her head. Cursing herself for a novice. Ashlinn Järnheim killed Tric. Ashlinn Järnheim betrayed the Church and her sacred vows to avenge her father . . .

She looked across the hall, caught her reflection in a small mirror on the wall.

Remind you of anyone else you know?

Magistrae was waiting faithfully beside Leona's bath, slipping a long robe about her mistress. Leona seemed pensive, chewing her fingernail and staring at the small statue of Trelene that also served as the water spout. She sighed as Magistrae tried to rub the tension from her shoulders.

'What troubles, love?' the older woman asked.

Leona smiled. 'How do you know I'm troubled?'

'These were the hands that delivered you into the world,' Magistrae smiled in return. 'This was the bosom that nursed you. Though I'll not claim to always know your mind, I know when dark thoughts fill it, sure and true.'

Leona closed her eyes as Magistrae worked a knot in her neck.

'. . . I'm having dreams again, Anthea. About Mother.'

'O, love,' Magistrae cooed. 'Long years have passed since then.'

'I know that, as I sit here now. But I'm always a child in the dreams. A little girl, small and afraid. Just as I was when . . .'

Leona chewed a fingernail and shook her head, silence ringing in the bathhouse.

'It's an awful thing,' she finally sighed. 'To live in fear.'

'Then do not, love. Look how far you've come. Look at all you've built.'

'I *do*. But all I've built stands at the edge of ruin, Anthea.' The dona breathed deep, clenched her jaw. 'I need *coin*. Marcus left me with little beyond these walls and the funds I spent reshaping them. He was not a careful man with his money.'

'You two were well suited, then.'

Leona smiled sadly. 'I deserve that, I suppose.'

'Do you miss him, love?' Magistrae asked, swiftly changing subjects.

'. . . No,' Leona sighed. 'Marcus was fair enough, but I never loved him. And . . . I hated needing him. Does that make me awful?'

'It makes you honest,' the older woman smiled.

Silence fell again, Leona gnawing at her fingertips and staring at the wall. The dona seemed younger in here than she did in the yard, her armour cast aside with none but trusted eyes to see. Almost like the little girl she spoke of being in her dreams. Magistrae kept kneading her shoulders, occasionally chewing her lip. When the woman spoke again, it was with obvious trepidation.

'Leona, I know you and your father—'

'No, Anthea.'

'But he has coin aplenty, surely if you—'

'*No!*' She turned on her nurse, blue eyes flashing. 'You forget your place. And I'll not hear another word of it. I will *die* before I accept a single copper beggar from that man, do you understand me?'

The magistrae's eyes found the floor.

'Aye, Domina,' she said.

Watching from the shadows, Mia found herself saddened. She could sense Anthea was truly concerned for Leona, could see the barrier between them had been worn thin over decades. But as much as Anthea cared for her mistress, she'd always be a servant. Though she'd fed Leona at her breast, Anthea would never be her mother.

Still, it was one thing to listen in on a conversation that might decide her fate, entirely another to intrude on such a private moment. Information was power, and power was advantage. But Mia had learned enough here.

Stealing down the corridor behind Mister Kindly, she found the broad dining hall. All the old furniture was still here – the long dining table where her parents had entertained, the wooden chairs she'd crawled and hid among as a little girl. Some of the same tapestries hung on the walls – Goddess Tsana wreathed in flame, Goddess Trelene cloaked in rolling waves.

Footsteps. Approaching. *Clink* thump. *Clink* thump.

Mia and Mister Kindly slipped behind one of the long, heavy drapes. She could have just cloaked herself in shadows and listened to Executus and Leona talk, but in truth she wanted to see their faces. See if the armour Leona wore outside these walls was the same armour she wore for this legend of the arena, who served her instead of the man who'd raised him up a champion.

Arkades limped into the room, found it empty. Jaw clenched, he sat at the long table to wait. Mia saw he'd bathed, brushed his beard and his long salt-and-pepper hair. The scar at his face and his weathered skin made it hard to tell, but she supposed him in his mid-thirties. Life on the sand hadn't been kind, but his physique, the sheer magnetism from a life spent winning victories before the adoring crowd . . .

He'd put aside the leather armour he wore in the yard, dressed in finery instead. His dark doublet was embroidered with the Falcons of Remus and the Lions of Leonides. His walking stick was also set with a lion's head. Mia again wondered at his loyalties. Here he was, serving Leona. And yet he still wore her father's lion on his chest.

Looking about, Arkades lifted a flask from inside his doublet like a thief, took a long, deep pull.

'We have goblets if you prefer, Executus.'

Arkades startled, rising to his feet as Leona appeared in the doorway behind, carrying a bottle of wine and two goblets. His eyes widened a touch at the sight of her, and Mia couldn't help but raise an eyebrow herself. Leona's hair was wet, she was barefoot and still clad in her bathrobe, which was tied only loosely. If one looked hard enough from the right angle, very little was being left to the imagination.

'Mi Dona,' Arkades said, bowing with his eyes to the floor and studiously avoiding looking hard from any kind of angle at all.

Mia noted the small smirk on Leona's face as she walked to the head of the table, flopped into a chair. She poured herself a glass, putting her foot up on the wood. Her robe slipped up, exposing her leg all the way to the thigh.

'Help yourself,' she smiled.

'. . . Mi Dona?'

Leona motioned to the second goblet, the bottle.

'It's awful, I'm afraid. But it cleaves to the task. Here.' Leona leaned forward, poured a glass and pushed it across the table. Arkades kept his eyes fixed anywhere but on her chest, practically writhing as he returned to his chair.

She keeps him off-balance with it, Mia noted. *He's ten years her senior. Twice her size. A warrior of a hundred battles, champion of the* magni, *and the poor bastard doesn't even know which way to look when she walks into the room.*

'So,' Leona said, leaning back and sipping from her cup. 'You have thoughts. Ones most pressing that simply *must* be shared.'

Arkades nodded, his embarrassment evaporating as talk turned to the collegium.

'Matilius, Mi Dona.'

'What of him?'

'His sale to Caito—'

'Was a necessity,' she interrupted. 'The purse at Blackbridge was not enough to cover expenses this month. Our creditors press, and they will have their coin.'

'But Caito . . .' Arkades began. 'Pandemonium is no place for a man to die.'

Leona downed her cup with one swallow.

'Matilius was not a man,' she said, pouring another. 'He was a slave.'

'You do not truly believe that, Mi Dona.'

Arkades stared at the younger woman across the table. Mia could see a moment's softness in her stare, replaced quickly with iron.

'Do I not?' she asked.

'Matilius was gladiatii,' Arkades said. 'He won glory and honour for this collegium. For *you*, Dona. He was not our finest blade, true, but he served you with all he had.'

'It was not enough. I have mouths aplenty and they all cost money. Our debts mount with every turn and my purse is all but empty.'

'And how came that to be, I wonder?' Executus scowled. 'When you spend a living fortune on a single recruit?'

'Ah,' Leona sighed. 'We come to the rub quickly this time.'

'For the thousand silver pieces you paid for that girl, you could have fed this collegium for the rest of the year!'

Mia's ears pricked up at her mention, eyes narrowing.

'Did you watch her at Blackbridge?' Leona asked. 'Did you see the way she ignited the crowd?'

'We have Furian for that!' Arkades all but shouted, rising from his chair. 'The Unfallen is this collegium's champion! That slip can't even lift a damn shield!'

'Then we fight her Caravaggio style. Twin blades. No shield. The crowd will adore it, and her. A girl her size, gutting men twice as big? And looking the way she does? Four Daughters, the crowd won't be able to see for the swelling of their cocks.'

Arkades sighed, pushing his knuckles into his eyes.

'When you started this collegium, Dona, you asked for my aid.'

'I did.' Leona toyed with the neckline of her robe. 'And I am ever grateful for it.'

'So with all respect, my counsel must carry weight. I have known you since you were a child. I know you grew up around the *venatus*. But there is a world of difference between watching from the boxes, and running a collegium.'

Leona's eyes and voice turned cold. 'Think you, I do not know that?'

'I think you wish to spite your father.'

Leona's eyes narrowed, her lips thin. 'You overstep, Executus.'

Arkades raised a hand in supplication at Leona's outrage. 'Daughters know, I remember how he treated you and your mother. And your rage has no lack of merit. But I fear outbidding him on that girl so steeply proves your mind is clouded on matters of familia. Mine is clear. I fought for years on the sand, trained your father's gladiatii years after that. And I tell you now, that girl is no champion. She has a fox's cunning, but she's not half the gladiatii Furian is. There will come a time when guile and wit won't serve her. When it's only she, and a sword, and a man she has to kill.'

Arkades leaned on the table, staring into Leona's eyes.

'And she. Will. Fail.'

Mia's stomach sank to hear Arkades talk so. She thought she'd impressed him with her showing at Blackbridge, but the man seemed utterly blind to her merits.

Leona's eyes fell and Arkades remembered himself, sat back in his chair with an apologetic grunt. The dona downed the rest of her wine, stared into the empty goblet for endless minutes. When she spoke, her voice was so soft Mia almost couldn't hear.

'Perhaps it was ill advised, spending such a sum. But I . . . I didn't want to see him win again. Mother warned me when I was a little girl. "Never stand against your father," she told me. "He *always* wins."'

She looked up at her executus, eyes bright with fury.

'But not this time,' she spat. 'Never again. I want him on his knees. I want him to look up into my eyes and know it was me who put him there. I want to drink his suffering like the finest wine.' She hurled the bottle into the wall just beside Mia's head, shattering it into a thousand splinters. 'Not this fucking slop.'

She hung her head and sighed.

'Even selling Matilius, we owe another dozen creditors.'

'. . . How much?'

'*Much.* And the points accrue by the turn.' Leona curled a fist, knuckles turning white. 'Daughters, if only Marcus hadn't died. Another few years on a justicus's stipend, I'd have had enough to do this properly. If I find the ones who took him from me . . .'

'It matters not,' Arkades said. 'We can pay whatever is owed with the coin we make from the Crow's sale. And from there, we will drive Furian all the way to the *magni*. We have three *venata* between now and truelight, three laurels to win a qualifying berth. You *will* have your victory, Dona,' Arkades vowed. '*If* you let me give it to you. Have faith in me. As I have faith in you.'

Mia looked at the pair of them, each alone, and then together. Leona's robe, the brazen sexuality, the way she used her body to put Arkades off guard – it made a kind of sense, knowing she'd grown up in the home of a domineering father.

But Arkades . . .

The fire in his eyes. The fervour in his voice when he made his vow. He was champion of the most brutal competition the Republic had devised. Ten years her senior. Separated by the barrier between the wealthy born and former property.

And yet . . .

Mia shook her head. Five minutes with them alone and she knew exactly why Arkades had left Leonides and come to serve his wayward daughter.

The poor fool's actually in love with her.

Leona placed her empty goblet on the table and sighed.

I wonder if she knows?

'You are my executus,' the dona said. 'I know you gave up much to come here. And I would see that faith rewarded.'

Leona toyed with the lip of her cup, nodded, as if to herself.

'I will heed your counsel. We will fight the Crow at the *venatus* in Stormwatch at month's end. Not the Ultima, we have our champion for that. Some minor bout, so as not to damage her. With good fortune, she'll comport herself in fashion fine enough to regain some measure of the cost we paid for her.'

Mia's stomach dropped into her boots.

Black Mother . . .

'You will sell her, then?' Arkades asked.

Leona looked to the tapestry on the wall. The goddess of fire, sword in hand, shield raised and wreathed in flame.

'Unless she proves herself Tsana made flesh?'

Leona heaved a sigh.

'Very well. I will sell her.'

Arkades nodded, Leona poured herself another glass.

'Now, if you are well satisfied?' she asked.

The executus grunted apology, stood slow. With a deep bow to his dona, the man limped from the room, his walking stick and iron leg beating a tired retreat down the stone stairs. Leona sat alone, swallowing deep from her cup, clouded eyes fixed on some nothing only she could see. Running idle fingers across her collarbone, down the pale skin of her throat. Taking another draught and licking her lips.

Mia stood silent in the shadows, watching close. Trying to ponder this woman, a way to sway her mind. If she could fashion some way for Furian to lose favour, poison him before a bout, perhaps? If Mia could raise herself in the dona's esteem . . .

One thing was certain – she could *not* be sold.

Leona chewed her lip, blinking as she woke from her reverie. She looked to the open door, stilled herself as if listening, The hour was late, the villa was quiet. Finishing her wine, Leona stood, gathered her robe about herself and, almost on tiptoe, quietly stole out into the corridor.

Mia frowned, narrowed her eyes.

Leona was mistress of this place.

Why creep about like a thief in her own house?

Mia slipped from behind the curtain and crept to the doorway, silent as death. Peering beyond the frame, she saw Leona at the stairs leading down to the third level. She ducked out of sight as the dona looked about, then stole quickly downwards.

'. . . *perhaps we have risked enough this eve, mia* . . .'

Ignoring the shadowcat's warning, Mia followed on whisper-soft feet. Moving like a shadow, she followed Leona down to the third, then second level. Here the dona paused, waiting for Captain Gannicus and another houseguard to walk past, murmuring among themselves. When the guards were gone, Leona crept on, Mia following like a wraith until she reached the first floor.

Mia watched from the stair above as the dona peered about, listening in the still for the guards. Sneaking out from the stairwell, Leona crept to a single wooden door at the far end of the corridor. Out of sight. Out of earshot.

Ah. It makes a kind of sense now.

The tirade at dinner. The insistence that their domina's will alone was what mattered, despite the sale of Matilius. The fervour in his eyes when he spoke of his mistress, his devotion to these walls.

Furian.

Leona reached into a pocket for an iron key, unlocked the door. The Unfallen was waiting on the other side, long dark hair framing his beautiful face, the smile that curled his lips as he saw his mistress. With one last glance the way she'd come, Leona threw her arms around Furian's neck, dragged him down into a hungry kiss. And stepping inside, the dona of the house shut the door behind her.

'. . . *interesting* . . .' came a cool whisper at her ear.

'Aye.' Mia scowled in reply. 'But just once, I'd like to look about and find my life was a little *less* interesting.'

'. . . o, what fun would that be . . . ?'

Mia raised the knuckles to the shadowcat. Mister Kindly only chuckled in reply. And without another sound, the pair stole off into the shadows they so loved.

CHAPTER 16
HONEY

Wsssshhthunk.

The arrow struck the strawman, close to his heart.

Wsssshhthunk.

Another struck closer than the first.

Wsssshhthunk.

A third struck the target, right in its featureless face.

Mia lowered her bow, the fingers on her right hand throbbing.

'Fine work,' Bryn said beside her. 'Where'd you learn to shoot like that?'

'Read about it in a book,' Mia growled. 'When I was done fucking your father.'

The Vaanian girl chuckled, lifting her own bow and drawing back the string.

'Rough nevernight, little Crow?'

Mia set her bow aside, wincing at the pain. 'I've had better.'

'Not with my poor old da, I'll wager,' Bryn grinned.

The blonde let half a dozen arrows fly in quick succession. Three punched through the strawman's heart, two into its throat, the last in its head.

'Maw's teeth . . .' Mia breathed.

'You should see her shoot with her good hand,' Byern said, walking past the pair with a bunch of leather tackle slung over his shoulder.

'Ah, that'd just be showing off,' Bryn replied.

The twins had left Crow's Nest early that morning, just as they did every second turn. Per Executus's command, Mia had accompanied them, trailing behind like a dog with no bone. Arkades limped with them to the gates of the keep, Mia trying to keep the scowl from her face as she remembered how the man had spoken about her the nevernight before. Arkades had made no mention of her impending sale, the sword hanging over her head. It wasn't as if he were offering a chance to prove herself, no. It was clear Executus simply wanted her gone.

It stung her pride, truth told. More than it should have. Mia didn't know why she wanted his approval. But in the intervening hours, hurt pride had turned to burning rage. She didn't have time to waste any more – being sold to another master was a risk she simply couldn't take. She needed to prove herself. Not to Arkades, but to Dona Leona.

The fact that she was bedding Furian aside, Mia suspected the dona still saw some measure of value in her. Mia had ignited the audience at Blackbridge, and the crowd's reaction had set some small ember of respect burning in Leona's breast. Mia needed a way to coax that spark into flame.

The *venatus* at Stormwatch would decide her future, in this collegium, and in the arena. Her plan to murder Duomo and Scaeva hung in the balance.

She'd no idea, yet, how to tip the scales.

Mia, Bryn, and Byern had been escorted by four of Dona Leona's houseguards into the rough scrubland behind Crow's Nest. After half a mile, they'd reached an oblong track, perhaps a mile long, marked in the ochre sand with flat stones. A stable stood to one side, and Byern marched inside with his harness and tackle while Bryn loosed quiver after quiver of arrows into the three strawmen targets.

The houseguards stood in the shade, paying no mind. Mia realized how easy it would be for Bryn and Byern to escape – a few arrows into each guard's chest, two horses, and the pair would be dust on the horizon. But, even if they somehow made their way in the Republic with brands on their cheeks, the twins would be condemning every other gladiatii in Leona's stable to execution in the arena.

She had to hand it to the administratii – the heartless bastards knew their trade.

Mia's fingers were bruising badly, and it hurt to hold the bow for long, so she mostly contented herself watching Bryn's form. The girl could shoot blind, left-handed as well as right. After emptying another quiver, she took off her sandals, clutched her bow between her toes. And, in what might have been the most astonishing display of dexterity Mia had ever witnessed, slowly stood on her hands, arched her spine and loosed a shot with her *feet*, skewering the strawman in the heart.

'Speaking of showing off . . .' Mia said.

Bryn curled smoothly over and stood, brushing the dust off her palms.

'It's child's play when you and the targets aren't moving,' she shrugged. Turning to the stable, she called to her brother. ''Byss and blood, Byern, are you rigging those horses or asking them to marry you?'

'I've asked before, they both said no,' came the reply.

'Well, they have excellent taste.'

Bryn's twin emerged from the stable, carrying a great shield and leading a pair of horses harnessed to a long, sleek chariot. The beasts were white as clouds, muscles carved in marble. Despite herself, Mia felt a small pang at the sight of them, thinking of her own stallion, Bastard. After he'd rescued her from near death in the Ashkahi desert, Mia had set him free rather than lock him up in the Red Church stable. She hoped he was wandering somewhere pleasant, siring as many of his own bastards as he could.

She missed him.

She missed a lot about that time, truth told . . .

'Sister Crow,' Byern waved to the horses with a flourish, 'meet Briar and Rose.'

Mia studied the pair pulling Byern's chariot. Like every horse she'd ever met, the beasts were skittish around her, so she gave them a wide berth. The fact that she called the only horse who'd ever tolerated her 'Bastard' spoke to her feeling about the beasts in general, but she knew a fine specimen when she saw it.

'They're mares,' Mia noted. 'Most equillai I've seen run stallions.'

'Most equillai you've seen are idiots,' Byern replied.

His sister nodded. 'Stallions think with their cocks. Mares know how to keep their heads in a crisis. As with horses, so with humans, eh, brother mine?'

Byern raised a finger in warning. 'Respect your elders, pup.'

'You're *two minutes* older than me, Byern.'

'Two minutes and fourteen seconds. Now, are you coming or no?'

'Stand out in the centre,' Bryn directed Mia, nodding at the dusty track. 'When I give the word, you let fly with the best you have.'

'. . . You want me to shoot you?' Mia asked, eyebrow raised.

Bryn laughed aloud. 'I want you to try. And remember to breathe.'

With that, the Vaanian jumped into the chariot beside her brother. With a snap of the reins and a wink to Mia (met with a punch in the arm from his sister), Byern led the horses onto the track.

The chariot was two-wheeled, broad and deep enough to allow the siblings to trade sides. It was red, trimmed in gold paint, carved with the falcon of the Remus Collegium. The great shield Byern carried was also painted with a red falcon, and its edges were crenellated like the walls of a fortified keep.

Mia walked until she stood in the island of ochre dirt, surrounded by the oblong track. Strawman targets were arranged in a single row down the middle of the island, to Mia's left and right. At a real *venatus*, those strawmen would be *real* men – murderers and rapists set to be executed *e equillai* before the adoring crowd.*

Mia watched as the twins tore around the track, faster and faster. Bryn's topknot whipped in the wind behind her, Byern's bronze skin gleaming in the sunslight.

'Ready?' Bryn called to Mia.

'Aye,' the girl replied.

'Let fly, little Crow!'

Mia sighed, drew a bead on Byern's chest. She tracked the chariot, breathing slow as Bryn had instructed despite the ache in her wounded fingers. And as the pair wheeled around the corner, she loosed a shot right at the handsome Vaanian's chest.

---

*Equillai are a subset of gladiatii, a tradition imported from Liis and adopted by the Itreyan Republic with enormous enthusiasm – equillai races are a highlight at any *venatus*, and the men and women who take to the track can win renown as great as any warrior on the sands.

Equillai fight in pairs: a charioteer, known as the *sagmae* (saddle), and an archer, known as the *flagellae* (whip). Equillai contests are held on an oblong track, marked in the centre of the arena, and traditionally involve four teams. The contest is run over nine laps of the circuit, and the winners decided on points accrued over the entire course.

Points are scored in a number of ways. First, a kill shot on any of the prisoners in the centre of the track. The prisoners are lashed to posts and cannot run, so the points scored are low – only two apiece.

A successful lap of the circuit also earns two points. A wounding shot on a member of an opposing equillai team is worth three points, a kill shot, five. Laurel wreaths, known as *coronae*, are also thrown onto the track at random intervals, and an equillai team scores one point for every *coronae* scooped up from the dirt. However, a shot to the opposing teams' horses is penalized by ten points – the contests are meant to be between the equillai themselves, and the softhearted among you will be pleased to learn attacking their mounts is deemed unsporting.

Murdering fellow equillai as dramatically as possible is perfectly acceptable and, indeed, encouraged.

Byern raised his shield, blocked the shot easily. Firing through the crenellations in the raised shield, Bryn loosed four shots, two of which struck the dirt at Mia's sandals, the other two striking the strawman closest to her.

'I said shoot us, not ask us to dance!' Bryn shouted.

'I can dance with you later, if you wish,' Byern called.

Bryn punctured another strawman, and her brother leaned out of the chariot at a precarious angle, scooping up a small stone off the track with his free hand. Mia scowled, trying to shake the feeling she was being made a fool of.

'All right, fuck this . . .' she muttered.

Mia began firing, shot after shot as the pair galloped around the track. And though her aim was true, she soon realized Bryn and Byern were both masters. Byern's shield was impregnable, and his skill at driving his horses was almost equal to his sister's archery. At the most humiliating point, Byern blocked a shot whistling straight for Bryn's throat, while simultaneously leaning out of the chariot to scoop up a stone, holding the reins in his damned *teeth*. Meanwhile, Bryn peppered every strawman with a dozen shots, pausing occasionally to make Mia dance by loosing a shot at her toes.

Nine laps later, the pair pulled to a stop in front of her. Byern hopped out of the chariot, bowed low. 'Do you prefer the waltz or the Balinna, Mi Dona?'

Bryn punched her brother's arm again, smiled at Mia. 'Fine shooting. You almost got me there, once or twice.'

'Liar,' Mia said. 'I never came close.'

Bryn winced, nodded sadly. 'I was trying to make you feel better.'

'Where did you learn to do that?'

'Our da raised horses,' Byern said. 'And Bryn's been a daemon with a bow since she could walk.'

Mia shook her head. She knew she shouldn't ask. Shouldn't get close. But truth was, she liked this pair. Byern's easy smile and Bryn's self-assured swagger.

'How did you come to be here?' she asked, looking at the track about them, the silhouette of Crow's Nest in the distance. 'This place?'

Bryn sniffed. 'Bad harvest. Three years back. Village didn't have the grain to pay our tithe to the Itreyan administratii. They locked our laird in irons, had him and his whole familia flogged in the stocks.'

'We didn't like that,' Byern explained. 'Me and Bryn were too young for our da to let us go, but anyone big enough to swing a sword marched up to the magistrate's door. Dragged him down to the stocks and gave him a flogging right back.'

'He didn't like *that*,' Bryn said. 'You can imagine what came next.'

'Legionaries,' Mia said.

'Aye,' Byern nodded. 'Five centuries of the bastards. Killed every rebel. Burned every home. Sold everyone left standing. Sis and me included.'

'But you weren't even involved,' Mia said. 'Your da didn't let you rise.'

'You think the Itreyans care?' Byern smiled lopsided. 'This whole Republic, the Kingdom before it, even. It's built on the back of free labour. But now, Liis, Ashkah, Vaan, they're all under Itreyan control. So where do the new slaves come from? When there are no lands left to conquer?'

'They build a Republic that's unfair in its bones,' Bryn said. 'That benefits the few, not the many. But the few have *steel*. And men they pay to wield it, unthinkingly. So, when someone among the many rises against the injustice, the brutality, the system locks them in irons. Makes of them an example for others, and with the very same stroke, sends one more body to be branded. One more pair of hands to build their roads, raise their walls, work their forges, all for a pittance and fear of the lash.'

Mia shook her head. 'That's . . .'

'Bullshit?' Byern offered.

'Aye.'

'That's life in the Republic.' Bryn shrugged.

Mia sighed, strands of raven black stuck to the sweat on her face.

All her life, she'd never questioned the rightness of it. Never stopped to look about her and see the people below her. The folk who'd walked like voiceless ghosts about their home, their apartments in the Ribs. The men and women who'd dressed her, made her meals, taught her numbers and letters. Her mother and father had cared for them, no doubt. Rewarded those who served well. But still, they'd *served*. Not because they wanted to. Because the alternative was the lash, or death.

She felt as if scales were falling from her eyes. The true horror of the Republic she'd been raised inside unveiled in all its awful majesty.

But still . . .

Scaeva.

Duomo.

Their names burned like flame in her mind. Like a lighthouse, ever guiding her way no matter how dark the world became. The injustice, the cruelty of this system, aye, she could see it. But what in truth could she actually do to change it? Without risking all she'd worked for? Closing her eyes, she could still see her father, swinging on the end of his rope in the forum. Her mother in the Philosopher's Stone, light fading in her stare as she pushed Mia's bloody hand away, and with her dying breath whispered:

'*Not my daughter . . . Just . . . her shadow.*'

The memories brought rage, and the rage tasted good. Reminding her of who she was, why she was here. To defeat the greatest gladiatii in the Republic. To stand before her familia's murderers triumphant and open their throats, one by one. And she was going to have a hard time doing that if she was sold off like a leg of beef at market.

Excelling in the *venatus* at Stormwatch. That was her concern.

Her first, her *only* concern.

And so, despite the pain in her injured hand, she nocked another arrow to her bow and nodded at Bryn.

'All right. Tell me what I'm doing wrong. And then, we'll go again.'

'So she's apparently hocked herself to the eyeteeth,' Mia said, dragging on her cigarillo. 'And Arkades has convinced her to sell me to fend off her creditors.'

Ashlinn leaned back in her divan, popped a grape in her mouth. 'Bastard.'

'After I killed a dozen people at Blackbridge. He's got no thought for anyone on the sand, save Furian. "*He* is the champion of this collegium." "*He* will bring you your victory, Mi Dona." O, aye, he'll bring her victory all right, you dozy fuck. Right after he brings her to climax. Should've heard the pair of them going at it . . .'

Mia breathed a lungful of grey smoke as if it were flame.

'Arkades stuck me on a leash in the circle, yesterturn. Near broke my hand with those ridiculous shields. Calling me "girl" as if the word were kin for "dogshit".'

'*Fucking* bastard,' Ash said, eating another grape.

Mia's eyes narrowed at the girl sitting opposite her.

'Look, are you just agreeing to humour me?'

'Mostly,' Ash smirked. 'But it's good to get these things off your tits, Corvere.'

'*. . . i trust you are feeling better now . . .*'

Mia looked at the not-cat curled on her shoulder. 'You're starting in on me too?'

'. . . *moaning or thinking. which is more productive . . . ?*'

'It seems Mister Jolly and I agree on something for once,' Ashlinn said.

'. . . *had i true claws, little viper, i would cut the tongue fr—* . . .'

'Eclipse and I have been snooping about,' Ash continued as if the shadowcat hadn't spoken. 'Your domina's debts certainly aren't common knowledge. She buys the finest at market. Dresses like a queen. I suspect that's half her problem.'

Eclipse raised her head from Mia's lap, voice echoing through the floor.

'. . . *TOO ENAMOURED BY WHAT FOLK THINK OF HER BY FAR* . . .'

'Probably doesn't want word getting back to her father,' Mia said, crushing out her smoke. 'Doesn't want to give him the satisfaction of seeing her struggling.'

Ash tossed a bunch of grapes to Mia, speaking around her mouthful. 'So the way I see it, we have a few options,' she said.

'. . . *THE SIMPLEST IS TO PUT LEONA'S CREDITORS IN THE DIRT* . . .'

'Aye,' Ashlinn nodded. 'It'd take some asking about, but I know for a fact the only place she'd be getting her grain is a merchant named Anatolio. It just so happens he's fond of his whores, and I know exactly where he dips his—'

'We're not going to top some poor bastard whose only crime is extending a line of credit to my domina,' Mia scowled.

'. . . *IT SOUNDS AS IF WE WOULD NEED TO END MORE THAN ONE* . . .'

Ash nodded. 'She's almost certainly in hock to the harbour master. Maybe the builders who worked on the Nest. And her seamstresses wou—'

'Aye, aye, I understand,' Mia said. 'We'd probably need to murder half the Rest. Which we're not going to do. If the collegium puts in a good showing, Leona might be able to secure patronage from some rich marrowborn bastard after the next *venatus*. So for now, it's smarter to just turn our eyes to—'

'Stormwatch,' Ash nodded. 'Aye. The only way to ensure your place in the Remus Collegium is to win at Stormwatch *venatus*. And win grand.'

'We don't even know what shape the *venatus* there will take.'

'. . . *NOT YET* . . .'

Ashlinn nodded. 'That's why you've got me and wolfie, here. There's a ship bound for the 'Watch leaving amorrow. We can be there in a week, can scout the workings at the arena and know exactly what you're in for. Then, we plan accordingly, give you a victory that will outshine even Leona's little fuckboy.'

'I'd never have picked it if I'd not seen it,' Mia sighed. 'She acts far too proper.'

Ash shrugged. 'She wouldn't be the first rich woman to pay for a fine stud to scratch her itches. Having to keep it secret is probably half the thrill.'

Mia chewed her grapes, brow creased in thought. The fruit was delicious, and a welcome change from the endless array of stew and porridge the gladiatii were served for evemeal and mornmeal every turn.*

'Good grapes, these,' she muttered.

'Never let it be said I don't love you, Corvere.'

Mia looked up sharply at that, but Ash was leaning back in her chair, dropping grapes into her mouth. Her boots were up on the divan's armrest, legs crossed, leather-clad. Her hair was getting longer, falling down her back in red waves.

Red. Like the blood on her hands.

And yet, here Mia was. Trusting her. She knew Ashlinn wanted the Ministry dead. And Mia and Mercurio were Ash's best chance back into the Mountain to see the deed done. But was that mutual hatred of the Red Church enough? Was Ash playing a longer game? It wasn't like she hadn't done so before.

Ashlinn Järnheim had lied to her.

Ashlinn Järnheim was poison.

So why had her lips tasted like honey?

Mia ran her hand over her eyes, nodded slow.

---

*In the weeks since Blackbridge, Mia had learned the emaciated cook who served Dona Leona was named 'Finger', though nobody among the stable seemed to know why. Most of the gladiatii assumed he'd earned the name by being finger thin, though Butcher insisted that he'd been a member of a braavi gang whose favoured means of thuggery involved chopping off people's less-essential digits and stuffing them in orifices not usually designed for stuffing.

Whatever the origins of his moniker, Finger's culinary skill was only slightly more impressive than a drunken blind man's skill at finding the pisspot. His porridge had the consistency of runny snot, and one evemeal, Mia found a suspiciously human-looking toe bone in her stew.

Needless to say, Fang, who always nosed about the table looking for scraps, was growing fonder of Mia by the nevernight.

'Head to Stormwatch with Eclipse,' she said. 'The more we know, the better the chance I'll have at a victory Leona can't help but reward. I imagine we'll be arriving a few turns before the *venatus* begins. I'll need to know everything by then.'

Ash nodded, finishing her mouthful and wiping her lips on her sleeve.

'So,' she said. 'Leona's stud. Furian, the Unfallen.'

'. . . THE DARKIN . . .'

'Is he going to be a problem?'

Mia shook her head. 'Nothing you need worry yourself with.'

'But I *do* worry.'

'Because without me, you don't get the Church, aye?'

Dark eyes stared into glittering blue. Looking for the lies behind them.

'Look, I know we've blood in our past,' Ashlinn said. 'But there's more than just red between us. I'm not just here for the Church. And I'm surely not cooped up in this dingy little shithole for the glamour of it. And you must know that, or you'd not be here with me, no matter how many shadowwolves you have watching over my shoulder.'

Mia stared. Ashlinn's eyes. Ashlinn's hands. Ashlinn's lips. The girl simply stared back, letting the silence ask her questions for her.

Mia ignored them all.

'Good luck in Stormwatch,' she finally said. 'Keep an eye on the harbour. Send Eclipse when we arrive and let me know the lie of the games.' She stood swift, dragging her hair over her shoulder and avoiding Ashlinn's stare.

'You're leaving already?'

Mia nodded. 'I'd best be off before I'm missed. Sidonius is a decent sort, but I've no wish for anyone else to find out what I am.'

Ashlinn said nothing, watching Mia walk to the window, climb over the sill and disappear from sight. Without a final word. Without a parting glance.

Shaking her head, Ash dropped another grape into her mouth.

'That much is obvious, Corvere,' she sighed.

CHAPTER 17

STORMWATCH

Mia paced back and forth in her cage, eyes fixed on the sand.

She, Sidonius, Bladesinger, Wavewaker, and Butcher were all locked in cells at the edge of the Stormwatch arena, sunken beneath the floor. Small barred windows let them watch the *venatus* while they waited for their turn before the crowd, Mia stalking about the cage and pondering the events that led her here.

Just as she'd told Ashlinn, the gladiatii of the Remus Collegium had trained another week in the sweltering suns before setting out for Stormwatch. Mia's hand was mended enough to go back to practice after a few turns, though for all the attention Arkades gave, she mightn't have bothered – it was clear all hopes were being pinned on Furian, Bryn, and Byern to win their berth in the *Venatus Magni*. Eavesdropping on Dona Leona and the magistrae, Mister Kindly had learned enquiries were already being made about Mia's sale. There were a few interested parties – a pleasure house in Whitekeep, a local magistrate in need of a bodyguard he could occasionally slip his cock into, and of course Varro Caito and his Pandemonium. Not a real sanguila among them.

Mia's entire plan hung upon victory at Stormwatch.

They'd travelled to the city via the *Gloryhound*, arriving a few turns before the *venatus* was set to begin. The port was abuzz with excitement, and folks had journeyed from miles about for the games; every inn, bedsit, and outhouse was filled to bursting.* Ashlinn had sent Eclipse to

---

* Stormwatch is a port in the northwest of Itreya, and one of the oldest cities in the Republic. Its beginnings were humble – a simple lighthouse on the northern banks of the Bay of Tempests, meant to warn ships away from treacherous reefs.

visit Mia in her cell, and the shadowwolf had spoken of all she and Ashlinn had learned about the upcoming games. Over the next few nevernights, passing messages via the daemon, Mia and Ashlinn had formulated their plan.

Now, all that remained was to execute it.

Mia watched the equillai roar around the track, the percussion of their horses' hooves vibrating through the stone walls. Bryn and Byern were doing well – placed second with five laps to go. But if Mia thought the Vaanians were skilled, she was amazed watching Leonides's team in action. Leona's father fielded only the best, and his equillai were no exception; a Dweymeri *sagmae* whose lion-crested shield seemed impenetrable, and a pretty Liisian *flagellae* whose bowmanship was equal to Bryn's, if not better.

'Stonekiller and Armando,' Bladesinger murmured, standing at the bars beside Mia. 'The b-best equillai in the Republic. The . . . crowd adore them.'

Despite best efforts, enough wrecks still occurred that a community of beachcombers built up on the coast nearby, and eventually raised a city known as Stormwall.

Scandal struck some years later, when Stormwall's lighthouse keeper, Flavius Severis, was accused by his friend, Dannilus Calidius, of steering ships onto the rocks to further his own fortunes. Calidius built a second lighthouse on the southern mouth of the bay, and founded a second city, naming it Cloudwatch.

The rivalry between the Familia Severis and Calidius, and thus, Stormwall and Cloudwatch, was legendary. Several bloody conflicts broke out over the years, and both lighthouses were destroyed. King Francisco I, the Great Unifier, who gave no shits for 'rights' and 'wrongs' but just wanted his 'bloody ships to stop crashing on the bloody rocks', threatened to crucify every Severis and Calidius he could find to ensure peace was restored.

The solution, however, did not lay in violence. Unbeknownst to their parents, a daughter of the Familia Severis and a son of the Familia Calidius met and, in defiance of all common sense, fell madly in lust. Though the story had all the makings of a classic Itreyan tragedy, the tale resolved itself remarkably peacefully, and only one best friend, a second cousin (who nobody much liked anyway), and a small terrier named Baron Woofsalot were murdered in the resulting drama. The pair married, peace was brokered, and many babies were had. Over time, the newly named Stormwatch became one of the wealthiest ports in Francisco's kingdom.

The city stands to this turn – an enduring testament, gentlefriends, to the power of teenage hormones and parents' desire for adorable grandchildren.

Despite a stunning kill shot from Bryn on another team's *sagmae*, the Lions of Leonides simply proved the better, and after nine laps, they stood the victors. Stonekiller and Armando dismounted their chariot together, fingers intertwined and hands held aloft in victory as the crowd around them thundered. It was well known that the pair were lovers, and their astonishing skill coupled with the affection they showed each other made them crowd favourites. The fact that they were undefeated didn't hurt either.

Mia felt bad for Bryn and Byern, worse that the Remus Collegium was still absent its third laurel. But, in truth, her mind was elsewhere. She looked sidelong at Bladesinger, the ghastly greenish hue of the woman's skin beneath her tattoos.

'Feeling better?' she asked.

'Think s-so,' the woman nodded. 'The w-worst seems . . .'

Bladesinger's eyes widened and she fell to her knees, once again vomiting all over the floor. Sidonius lay where he was, barely able to groan as the puke spattered his sandals. Butcher rolled away from the splashback, his own cheeks ballooning.

'At least empty your g-guts outside . . . the cell, sister,' he moaned.

'Fuggoff,' Bladesinger groaned, a long string of drool and puke dangling from her lips. 'Before I s-slap your ugly . . .'

Another fountain of vomit exploded from Bladesinger's mouth, this time hitting Wavewaker, who in turn lunged up onto his knees and aimed a spray of puke out through the bars. The stench rolled over Mia in warm, cloying waves and she stood on tiptoes, pressed her lips between the bars and breathed deep of the comparatively pleasant aroma of blood and horseshit outside.

'Four fucking Daughters,' she swore.

'Pray all you like,' came a growl. 'I fear they're not listening.'

Turning, Mia saw Executus Arkades, standing outside the cell with hands on hips. Surveying the puke-soaked straw, his best gladiatii lying about like wounded after a war. Maggot stood beside him, nose screwed up at the stench as she looked the fallen gladiatii over. Dona Leona hung back, wearing a gown of beautiful scarlet silk and a thoroughly disgusted expression.

'Blessed Aa,' she said. 'All of them?'

'Save Bryn and Byern,' Arkades replied, glancing at Mia. 'And the Crow. Even Furian is bursting at both ends. Everseeing only knows what caused it.'

Mia kept her face as stone, met Arkades's eyes with an expression innocent enough to shame a sister in the Sorority of Flame.* Of course, she knew exactly what had caused the bout of intestinal distress among her brothers and sisters of the collegium. Ashlinn had sneaked rather more Mishap into their evemeal than Mia would have liked – the results didn't need to be quite so explosive, truth told. But Ash had never been Spiderkiller's finest student.

'Food poisoning,' Maggot declared, kneeling by a puddle of vomit. Reaching through the bars, she pressed her palm to Butcher's sweat-filmed brow. 'Not fatal, I think. But they'll wish they were dead before the ending.'

'F-far ahead of . . . you, my d-dear,' Wavewaker moaned, stifling a belch.

'How is it you're not ill?' Dona Leona asked Mia.

'I didn't eat yestereve, Domina,' Mia replied. 'Too nervous about the games.'

''Byss and blood,' Leona spat. 'I should have that cook *flogged*. We're three laurels shy of the *magni*, this is the first *venatus* me and my father pit gladiatii against one another, and my sharpest blades are all sick as sailors with no sea legs?' Her eyes narrowed with a sudden thought, and she turned to Arkades. 'You don't think *he* orchestrated this, do you?'

Executus rubbed his chin in thought. 'Possible, thou—'

Sidonius leaned back against the wall as a spray of puke erupted from his gut, Maggot and Leona both skipping back in disgust. The dona fished a scented kerchief from her dress, pressing it to her mouth as the big Itreyan groaned an almost-indecipherable apology, and promptly shit his loincloth.

'They can't fight like this, Domina,' Maggot said softly.

'Aye,' Arkades nodded. 'It'll be a slaughter. Not a one of them can stand.'

'*I* can stand,' Mia replied.

The trio looked to her silently. Leona's eyes narrowed.

'I can *win*,' Mia swore.

Arkades shook his head. 'Set eyes through those bars, girl. Does anything about this arena strike attention?'

---

*An offshoot of Aa's ministry, fully sanctioned by the Church, devoted to worship of the goddess Tsana. Consisting entirely of women, the sorority's vows include Chastity, Humility, Poverty, Sobriety, and Generally Having No Fun Whatsofuckingever.

Mia peered out to the sands, eyes scanning the walls, the crowd. The remains of the equillai match were being packed up, targets broken down, markers removed. The crowd were stamping their feet, impatient for the next match to begin.

'Broken glass,' Mia said, turning to look at the executus. 'And fire-pots. On the wall skirting the arena's edge.'

'And that tells you what?'

'Either the editorii don't want the crowd getting onto the sand, or they don't want whatever they're about to release on the sand getting into the crowd,' Mia replied.

'Menagerie,' Arkades said. 'The theme for this *venatus*. Beasts from all corners of the Republic, set to do battle with each other and gladiatii for the crowd's amusement.' The big man folded his massive arms, the scar on his face deepening as he scowled. 'Do you have any idea what you'd face out there?'

Mia shrugged, feigning ignorance.

'Whatever the 'byss it is, it can't smell worse than in here.' She looked at Leona, her jaw set. 'Your equillai just lost to your father's men, Domina. And only one of your gladiatii can lift a sword. If you've a thirst for a victor's laurel at all, or anything to prove, it seems you've but one choice.'

Leona's eyes had narrowed at the words 'anything to prove'. But Mia spoke truth – there was only one way Leona would see a victor's purse this *venatus*. Only one way she might recoup some of her costs, win some glory, accrue another laurel for her collegium's berth at the *magni*.

Mia and Ashlinn had orchestrated it that way, after all.

Part of Mia still didn't trust her co-conspirator. She was still waiting for the hammer to drop. But Ash had spoken truth; Eclipse had confirmed it. She'd dosed the other gladiatii, left Mia on her feet, all the better to convince Leona that Mia was the only hope she had of winning the victory she so desperately needed. But still . . .

But still . . .

'Executus,' Leona said, eyes never leaving Mia's. 'Tell the editorii our Crow will fight for Remus Collegium in the Ultima. We will field no other gladiatii this turn.'

'Mi Dona, Furian was slated for the Ultima. A change at this final hour—'

'I paid for berth at this *venatus*,' Leona snarled. 'I will be *damned* if fate's cold hand robs me of my victory. If the editorii take issue with my arrangements, tell them they can bring them to me personally. But, by the Everseeing and all four of his holy fucking Daughters, you'd best warn them to bring an extra pair of balls, because I'll be ripping off the first and wearing them for earrings.' She indicated her gown with a sweep of her hand. 'The red should complement my dress nicely.'

Maggot grinned, and Arkades tried to hide his smile in his beard.

'Your whisper, my will,' he murmured.

With a hand-to-heart bow, the executus limped off in search of the editorii, and Maggot in search of some water to wash away the mess. Leona remained behind in the damp, the stink, staring at Mia through the bars with glittering blue eyes.

'I risk much on you, little Crow.'

'It's only a risk if I don't win, Domina,' Mia replied. 'And in all truth, you've nothing to lose.'

'I'll not forgive it,' Leona warned, 'if you fail me.'

Putting her hand to her heart, Mia bowed low.

'And I trust you'll not forget it,' she replied, 'when I don't.'

The matches had been brutal, bloody, beautiful. The crowd were drunk on it – the wine, the slaughter, their roars reverberating through the stone above Mia's head. The guards were already proclaiming the *venatus* the finest that Stormwatch had ever seen, that the editorii had outdone themselves again.

Spectators had thrilled as a mob of gladiatii hunted a three-ton sabrewolf through a sea of long grass that had grown up from the sands upon command. They'd howled in delight as gladiatii from the collegia of Leonides, Trajan, and Phillipi clashed upon a web of shifting wires hung over the arena, while a pack of Vaanian whitebears prowled below, tearing any warrior who fell into bloody pieces. Prisoners of the state had been tied to stakes and executed by a flock of starving Ashkahi bloodhawks; gladiatii with tridents and nets had fought an actual live sand kraken before the bellowing mob.* And now, as nevernight winds blew in from the ocean and the turn drew near its close, they were ready for the Ultima.

None knew what could possibly top the sand kraken, though all were salivating at the prospect. They stamped their feet in time, the rhythm echoing down into the mekwerk pits beneath the sands. And

---

* Only a twelve-footer, but the beast still killed seven men before being sent to its grave.

then, as if in answer, rumbling up from the depths, came a shuddering, spine-chilling roar.

'Citizens of Itreya!' came the call across the arena horns. 'Honoured administratii! Senators and marrowborn! We give thanks to our honoured consul, Julius Scaeva, for providing the funds for the Ultima to close this most glorious *venatus*!'

The crowd roared approval, and Mia gritted her teeth to hear them chanting Scaeva's name. She pushed thought of the consul from her mind, focusing only on the task ahead. None of the fighters in the staging cell around her had an inkling, but Mia knew exactly what awaited them beneath the floor. And even with the advantage she'd bought herself, she still knew this would be a fight for her very life.

She wore a sleeve of mail rings on her right arm, iron spaulders and greaves to protect her shoulders and shins, a leather skirt and breastplate. The armour would count for next to nothing against the foe she'd face, but still, it was better than fighting bare-arsed with a grin on her face. Her helm was plumed in red – the colour of her domina's standard. *Remus's* standard. The thought chafed, but again, she pushed it aside. No place for pride here. No place for pain. Only steel. And blood. And glory.

The swords in her hands felt like home – good Liisian steel, sharp as razors. She'd need them, and all her strength, if she was to survive what was to come.

'Citizens!' came the cry. 'Behold, your gladiatii! Chosen from the finest collegia in the Republic, here to fight and die for the glory of their domini! From the Tacitus Collegium, we present to you, Appius, bane of the Werewood!'

The portcullis before them shuddered upwards with a metallic groan. A huge man strode past Mia, up into the arena, raising his spear and shield to the din of the roaring crowd. His helm was fashioned like a wolf's head, sunslight glinting on his sleeves and breastplate of steel.

'From the Livian Collegium, Ashbringer, Terror of the Silent Sea!'

A Dweymeri gladiatii strode up to the sand, raised a twin-handed mattock longer than Mia was tall. He prowled about the arena's edge, stamping his feet upon the sand, and the crowd fell in time until the entire world seemed made of thunder.

And so it went. Each collegium was announced, fearsome gladiatii with equally fearsome titles marching up to take their places, riling the crowd with their theatrics. Mia noticed with interest that Leonides wasn't fielding a warrior in the Ultima – unusual for a collegium of stature. She wondered if he had some inkling of the nature of their foe . . .

More than two dozen warriors stood on the sands before Mia heard the editorii call, 'From the Remus Collegium . . .'

'Furian!' came a cry.

'Unfaaaaallen!' came another.

'. . . the Crow!' roared the editorii.

Mia marched up into the sunlight, raising her twin swords above her head. She was met by bemusement, scattered applause, a few jeers from folk who'd been expecting the Champion of Remus Collegium rather than some skinny girl half his size. Not a one of them had any clue who she was.

Soon.

Mia gritted her teeth, silently vowing to herself.

Soon, the sky itself will know my name.

In a grand booth on the arena's edge, Mia saw the governor of Stormwatch, the city's elite gathered about his chair. An editorii stood in a separate booth, clad in the traditional blood-red robe trimmed with golden daggers. A smoke-grey cat was curled on his shoulder, eyeing proceedings with an air of distinct boredom. The man spoke into a great horn, voice amplified across the vast space.

'And now!' he cried. 'Gentlefriends, steady your hearts. Children, avert your eyes! Dragged from the depths of the Ashkahi Whisperwastes at the command of our glorious consul, a horror polluted by the corruption that brought the old empire to its knees. Behold, citizens of Stormwatch, your *Ultima*!'

Mia felt the floor tremble, heard the great mekwerk beneath the sand begin to move. Rocky outcroppings rose from the sand like teeth, tall and wicked-sharp. The arena's heart split apart, sand cascading into the depths as a pit opened wide. And, as if from the abyss itself, up rose a horror unlike anything Mia had ever seen.

''Byss and blood . . .' said a voice beside her.

Mia looked to the Dweymeri gladiatii; the man named Ashbringer. His eyes were wide. His great mattock trembling in his hands.

The monster roared, shaking the very earth. The crowd answered, rising to their feet, cheering, howling, giddy. Not a one among them had ever seen the like, but all had heard the tales. Nightmare of the deepest deserts. More terrifying than the sand kraken. More fearsome than a hundred dustwraiths. A word that struck panic into every caravaneer and trader who ran the Ashkahi wastes.

'Retchwyrm . . .' Ashbringer whispered.*

The beast roared again, raising the end of its body that Mia supposed was its head. Its skin was pitted, cracked and browned like old leather. It moved like some obscene caterpillar, lunging towards the crowd as they screamed. But an iron collar and thick lengths of chain bound the monster to the arena floor, prevented it from getting anywhere close to the audience. Once they realized they were in no danger, the crowd burst into applause, cheering and chanting.

With all eyes on the beast, Mia turned and strode across the sand, thirty more steps, until she stood beneath a statue of Tsana on the inner wall. Stabbing her swords into the earth, she knelt, bowed her head as if in prayer to the goddess. But with her right hand, she began searching beneath the sand at the arena's edge.

She felt nothing at first. Her shadow rippling as her stomach ran cold, as the thought that Ashlinn had betrayed her rose like a dustwraith behind her—

No.

Her fingers felt softness. Leather.

----

*Although commonly considered the apex predator of the Ashkahi wastes, the sand kraken *does* run a poor second to the true masters of the deepest desert. A creature so awful that it almost defies belief, the retchwyrm does its level best to shatter the illusion that there is any kind of benevolence in the creator of the universe at all.

Stretching up to two hundred feet long, the retchwyrm is a serpentine creature with no discernible eyes or nostrils, and only the most rudimentary of ears. Loresmen at the Grand Collegium in Godsgrave have theorized the beasts sense prey by vibration, or perhaps through a kind of echolocation, similar to various breeds of flying mice. However, since any bastard foolish enough to study them usually ends up dissolved in a pool of concentrated sulphuric acid, this theory has largely remained untested.

The retchwyrm has two puckered mouths, one at each end of its body, which also serve as its backsides (which orifice serves which purpose at any given time seems to be entirely arbitrary, and dependent on the mood of the retchwyrm in question). It has no jaw or teeth, and is incapable of seizing prey in its mouth. Instead – in what may be the most disgusting method of consuming nourishment in the entire animal kingdom – the retchwyrm projectile-vomits its *entire stomach* out of its mouth, engulfing its prey in a tangle of writhing tendrils and corrosive acid, then noisily sucks the entire mess back up again, hapless prey included.

Do you see what I mean?

Honestly, what kind of sick *bastard* thought this thing up?

There it is.

She pulled the object from the sand – a leather pouch filled with spherical objects – tucking it beneath one of her spaulder.

The editorii raised his hands, calling for silence.

The crowd fell still as a millpond.

The man drew a breath, heard across the arena. His cat simply yawned.

'Ultima!' he cried. *'Begin!'*

The crowd roared, deafening and rapturous. The beast chained in the arena's heart writhed in response, its blind head swinging side to side as its stomach bubbled up in its throat, desperate to consume the prey it could sense but couldn't reach. And in answer, it let out another sky-shaking roar.

And not a single gladiatii

moved

a

single

muscle.

'*. . . can't blame them, really . . .*' came the whisper in Mia's ear as she took her place back alongside her fellows.

The crowd began to get restless, several starting to boo as the gladiatii all stood paralysed, a few circling the retchwyrm as it thrashed and growled.

'*Kill it!*' someone roared.

'*Fight, cowards!*'

Standing beside Mia, Ashbringer prickled at the word 'coward'. He looked about the bleachers, up to his domini in the sanguila's boxes. And hefting his mattock, he bellowed, 'With me!' at the top of his lungs and charged the beast with weapon raised. Several other gladiatii took up the call, Mia among them, rushing forward with bloody cries. They attacked the wyrm from four sides, hewing and stabbing with spear and sword. Preferring the flank, Mia darted out from behind one of the fangs of stone, burying her blades to the hilt. Ashbringer charged head-on, swung his mattock, pulping a great hole in the beast's hide. And with a revolting wet burping sound, the retchwyrm reared up and spewed its stomach all over the men in front of it.

The flesh was a rotten pink, almost liquid, splashing on the ground and stretching out with finger-like tendrils. Appius was completely buried under the deluge of guts, Ashbringer was engulfed to the waist, screaming as his flesh began to burn in the acid slicking the wyrm's insides. He swung again with his mattock, pounding on the spongy mass. The stomach continued to crawl over the ground, almost like a thing with a mind of its own, stretching out sticky strands and snaring the gladiatii about it. And finally, with a hollow, rushing slurp, the beast inhaled its guts back inside itself, dragging half a dozen screaming men with it. The crowd roared in delight and disgust.

On the beast's flank, Mia stabbed one of her blades hilt-deep again, feeling the monster shiver. Its blood was deep red, almost black, slicking her to the elbows. As the behemoth rolled and bucked, she reached up to her spaulders – the pouch Ashlinn had hidden in the sand. Groping inside, she grabbed a handful and drew it out; three spheres of bright red glass in the palm of her hand.

A gift from Mercurio before they'd departed.

Wyrdglass.*

Dragging her sword free, she pushed her fist into the wound, burying the spheres into the beast's muscle. The retchwyrm roared in pain, rolled over on its side to crush Mia. The girl dived free, narrowly avoided getting pulped against one of the stone fangs as the wyrm whipped its tail. Wyrdglass was activated by pressure, usually by throwing it at the wall or floor, but Mia hoped the press of the beast's own muscles and weight would be enough to break the arkemical bonds that held the glass in solid state. As she stumbled to her feet, dashed away, she heard a dull pop, almost lost beneath the crowd baying, the monster's roars. A bubbling gout of blood and flesh burst up from the retchwyrm's side as her wyrdglass exploded.

The crowd cheered – they'd no idea what the girl had done, only

---

* One of Shahiid Spiderkiller's finest inventions, you may remember wyrdglass comes in three variants:

Black creates smoke, useful for diversions.

White creates a cloud of the toxin known as Swoon, useful for knocking people unconscious.

Red simply explodes, useful for making people dead.

Three colours, three flavours. All rather simple, though you'd be surprised how often a novice Blade has reached into the wrong pouch and grabbed the wrong colour in the heat of the moment. It can be a little embarrassing when you realize the black wyrdglass you threw at your feet to cause a distraction is actually white, and you've accidently knocked yourself cold – although not quite as bad as throwing down a handful of red glass and realizing you've accidentally blown your own legs off.

It does tend to be the kind of mistake Blades only make once, however.

that she'd wounded the beast. The retchwyrm howled, gullet bubbling in its throat, the stench of blood and ashes and acid washing over Mia in waves.

'. . . *I THINK YOU MADE IT ANGRY . . .*'

'. . . *ever the observant one, dear mongrel . . .*'

'. . . *EVER THE SMART-ARSE, LITTLE MOGGY . . .*'

'. . . *flattery will get you nowhere . . .*'

The retchwyrm turned its blind head towards Mia, let loose a terrible howl. The girl dashed back towards the cluster of other gladiatii, seeking cover among the rocks, trying to get beyond the reach of the retchwyrm's chain. The monster snaked after her in pursuit, slamming its massive bulk onto the dirt in an attempt to crush her. The ground shook, Mia stumbled. Other gladiatii were hacking and chopping at the beast, but it seemed largely intent on the girl who'd wounded it worst. In desperation, Mia turned, held up her hand as she scrambled backwards, trying to snare the monster with its own massive shadow until she was beyond the reach of its chain.

The reaction was instantaneous. Terrifying. The behemoth stilled, as if its every muscle went suddenly taut. With a spine-chilling roar, it lunged across the sand right at Mia, mouth distended, corrosive spittle hissing as it thrashed against its bonds. And with a shriek of tortured metal, the bright sound of shattering steel, the chain binding the beast to the floor snapped clean in two.

'. . . *o, shit . . .*'

'. . . *O, SHIT . . .*'

'O, *shit!*'

The beast whipped about, far too huge for Mia to hold it still with her shadow-werking. The girl dived aside as its tail swept across the arena in a great scything arc, crushing stone to splinters and the gladiatii about it to pulp. Mia was clipped as she dived free, smashed into an outcropping, black stars bursting in her eyes. She lost her grip on the shadows as she collapsed, the retchwyrm roaring in incandescent rage.

'It . . .' Mia blinked hard, spitting dust off her tongue. '. . . It heard me?'

'. . . *WHEN YOU CALLED THE DARK . . .*'

'. . . *interesting . . .*'

The beast howled again, seemingly furious, skin rippling as its guts bubbled and burped in its throat. But with no shadows now to distract it, and realizing it was suddenly free of its bonds, the retchwyrm turned its blind head towards the vibrations of the chanting, roaring crowd. And as the audience also realized the behemoth's chain was broken, they broke into screaming, frothing panic.

Mia reached up to her spaulder, blood running cold as she realized the pouch of wyrdglass was no longer there. She searched the sand about her as the retchwyrm snaked towards the arena wall, the broken glass and firepots ringing the enclosure now seeming pitiful in the face of the monster's sheer size and rage. A cadre of half a dozen Luminatii legionaries rushed into the arena, sunsteel blades drawn, crying, 'For the Republic!' and 'Luminus Invicta!' as they charged. Seemingly giving no shits for Republics, Light, or Anything Much at All, the beast vomited its gullet again, engulfing the entire cadre in a tangled mess of rotten pink and burning acid.

Sweat burned Mia's eyes, the screams of the crowd almost deafening. The arena around her was sheer bedlam now, people rushing for the exits, others sitting paralyzed in their seats and crying out in terror.

The retchwyrm reared up and bellowed, its broken collar hanging loose about its throat. Twenty fresh legionaries with swords and shields charged out from one of the iron portcullises, but with a single sweep of its massive tail, the monster smashed them all to pulp against the arena wall. Its thick, leathery hide was pierced in a dozen places by spears and blades, dark blood dribbling from the wounds.

'. . . *well, this is going splendidly . . .*'

'You know, it's very easy to sit back and criticize,' Mia gasped, rolling onto her belly, her head still ringing.

'. . . *strangely satisfying, too . . .*'

'. . . TELL THAT TO THE PEOPLE ABOUT TO BE DEVOURED . . .'

'. . . *what would be the point of that, exactly . . . ?*'

The retchwyrm had reached the arena wall, its eighty-foot length undulating like some grotesque moth spawn. It loomed over the ten-foot barricade easily, featureless head swaying above a pack of terrified spectators, its gullet burbling as it inhaled. Mia dragged herself up out of the dirt, skull throbbing, the bodies of dead gladiatii spattered and smeared all about her. Searching among the corpses, she found a long-spear, its haft still intact. Her damned helmet only interfered with her vision, but she dare not remove it on the off chance some random servant of the Church saw her face. And so, with a silent prayer to the Black Mother, she drew back her arm and hurled the spear with all her strength.

The weapon sailed through the air in a perfect arc, steel head gleaming in the sunlight as it pierced the retchwyrm's throat. The monster bellowed, shaking its head to dislodge the toothpick, black blood spraying. And reaching out once more to the dark puddled beneath it, Mia seized hold of the monster's shadow.

'Oi!' she yelled. '*Bastard!*'

The retchwyrm shuddered, a deep, rumbling whine shivering its entire length. The people in the bleachers forgotten, the beast turned its blind head towards Mia and split the air with a hollow, deafening roar.

'*. . . now you have its attention . . .*'

'Excellent.'

Mia picked up two swords from the bloody dirt around her.

'But what the fuck do I do with it?'

CHAPTER 18
GLORIA

Try as she might, Mia couldn't hold the beast still.

Like a giant pushing aside a helpless infant, the retchwyrm broke free of Mia's shadow-werking, swung its massive bulk away from the crowd, and snaked towards her. Its mouth yawned wide, a trembling roar rolling up from the dark of its belly. The twin swords of Liisian steel in Mia's hands might well have been butter knives, and her shadow rippled as her passengers drank down her fear.

Leaving her cold.

Hard.

Unafraid.

Mind racing. Eyes scanning the arena walls, the broken rocks, the bloody sand, the monster bearing down on her. And finally, there, she saw it, half-buried in a tumble of shattered stone and dirt between her and the charging monstrosity.

Her bag of wyrdglass.

A thought took seed – insane, suicidal. But with no fear, no pause, no breath to waste, the girl raised her swords. Sweat in her eyes, hair stuck to dusty skin, lips peeling back from her teeth, Mia charged with a bloodcurdling cry, right *towards* the enraged retchwyrm.

The panicked crowd fell still in amazement, watching the tiny speck of a girl running headlong at the horror of the deepwastes. The beast reared back its colossal bulk, a horrid belch spilling up from its gullet. Mia sprinted through a mash of broken bodies, broken stone, broken weapons littering the sand, leaping carefully over her small leather sack of 'glass, half-buried in the dust. And the retchwyrm opened its maw, spewing its guts all over the floor.

Completely engulfing her.

In turns to come, the next few moments would be the topic of countless taverna tales, dinner table debates, and barroom brawls across the city of Stormwatch.

There were those who swore they saw the girl dive aside, simply too swift to mark, entirely avoiding the spray of the beast's innards. There were those who claimed that with all the dust and blood and chaos, it was simply too hard to tell *what* happened, only that she moved quick as silver. And there were those – discounted as madmen and drunks, for the most part – who swore by the Everseeing and all four of his Holy Daughters that this little slip of a girl, this daemon wrapped in leather and mail, simply *disappeared*. One moment buried in the retchwyrm's guts, the next, standing ten feet away in the long shadow cast beside it on the sand.

Mia swayed on her feet, the rush of vertigo almost sending her to her knees. Only adrenaline and stubborn will kept her upright, half staggering, half running, chest burning as her head spun. The beast inhaled its innards, slurping up the mashed gladiatii corpses and fallen weapons and the small leather pouch full of shining wyrdglass globes. Mia stumbled up a broken outcropping of stone and launched herself onto the thing's back, burying her swords in its flesh to steady herself. The behemoth thrashed beneath her as she groped her way upright, stumbled along the creature's length, up towards its rearing head. The crowd bellowing, the retchwyrm roaring, her own pulse thundering and beneath it all, through that cacophony, that deafening chaos, she thought perhaps she heard it, deep inside the monster's belly.

A series of tiny, wet pops.

The retchwyrm paused, a tremor running through its body. Mia scrambled onto its neck, throwing one of her blades aside, clinging to a broken spear embedded in its leathery hide. Gripping the beast with her thighs and fingernails and sheer bloody-mindedness, she drew back her Liisian steel and with a cry, plunged it into the flesh behind the monster's tiny ear.

The creature bellowed, a bubble of blood welling up from its gullet and bursting at its mouth. The crowd had no inkling about the 'glass it had swallowed; no clue the explosion had turned a goodly section of the retchwyrm's gullet to bloody soup. All they knew was that as they watched dumbfounded, mouths open in awe, the girl plunged in her blade, the beast swayed back and forth like a drunkard at the privy, and with a bubbling sigh, crashed dead and still to the ground.

The *thuddd* echoed across the arena, dust rising as the creature collapsed. But as the nevernight winds blew across the bleachers, across the blood-soaked sand, the pall cleared to reveal a single figure, standing alone on the dead beast's head.

Panting, bleeding, Mia bent down and dragged her blade free. And turning to the dumbfounded spectators, she slowly raised it to the sky.

Silence rang across the sands. Hollow and still. No one in the crowd could believe their eyes, let alone speak. Until finally, a small boy in his mother's arms pointed at the bloodstained girl at the arena's heart, his brown eyes grown wide.

'Crow!' came his tiny cry.

A man beside him looked to the boy, then shouted to those around him.

'Crow!'

The word began repeating, like an echo, more and more folk taking up the call. Dozens, then hundreds, then thousands, all chanting in time like a vow, like a prayer, 'Crow! Crow! Crow!' as Mia limped the length of the retchwyrm's carcass, sword held high, the audience stamping their feet in time with their chant, faster and faster now, the word and the thunder of their feet blurring into 'CrowCrowCrowCrowCrow!'

Mia roared with them, elation and bloody pride welling inside her chest.

'What is my name?' she screamed.

'CrowCrowCrowCrowCrow!'

'WHAT IS MY NAME?'

'CROWCROWCROWCROWCROW!'

Mia closed her eyes, drinking it in, letting it soak into her skin.

Sanguii e Gloria.

She turned to the sanguila boxes, saw Dona Leona on her feet, cheering. She looked to the gladiatii cells, saw Sidonius and Bladesinger and Butcher at the bars, howling her name and pounding the iron. And finally, up in the crowd, amid the sea of smiling faces, she saw a girl. Long red hair. Eyes as blue as empty skies. And with her smile beaming bright as the suns overhead, Ashlinn raised her hand, fingers spread.

And she blew Mia a kiss.

The Remus Collegium dined like marrowborn that night. A long table in the cells beneath the arena was laden with food and wine, Mia's gladiatii brothers and sisters toasting her victory like the lords and ladies of old. Furian sat at the table's head like a king, as was his place as champion. But if this was a kingdom, it now had a queen. Sat at the table's foot, a silver victor's laurel crowning her long dark hair, Mia Corvere raised her wine and grinned like a madwoman.

The gladiatii were recovered enough from their poisoning, and buoyed by the adrenaline of Mia's victory. They drank a great deal and ate very little, recounting the battle again and again. Sidonius crowed so loud about it, you'd think he'd defeated the beast himself, wrapping his ham-hock arm around Mia's neck and declaring it the greatest triumph he'd ever seen on the sands.

'This magnificent little bitch!' he roared.

'Get off me, you great oaf,' Mia grinned, pushing him away.

'I've never witnessed the like!' Sid bellowed. 'Have you, 'Singer?'

'Nay,' the woman smiled, raising her cup. 'Never the like.'

'Wavewaker?'

'A victory worthy of Pythias and Prospero!' the big man declared.*

---

* *The Tragedy of Pythias and Prospero* is a saga penned by the famous bard, Talia. Though banned by the Ministry of Aa, it remains one of the oldest and most renowned plays in history, predating the Itreyan Kingdom by centuries. The play is based on an ancient myth and is set in the time before the Mother of Night had been banished from the Itreyan sky.

It follows the adventures of two lovers: Pythias, captain of the guard, and Prospero, son of the Sorcerer King, who are separated by Prospero's father when he learns of their affair. Pythias is banished to the far corners of the earth, and in their quest to be reunited, the pair conquer armies, nations, and finally the Sorcerer King himself to be together again.

Sadly, when a tale has the word 'tragedy' in the title, it's probably folly to expect a happy ending; Pythias is poisoned in the final confrontation. Dying in his lover's arms, he delivers a stirring speech on the enduring power of hope, fidelity, and love – widely regarded as the finest monologue ever put to vellum. Prospero, inheritor of his father's magiks, sets his lover's body in the heavens as a constellation, and names it in his honour.

Not a dry eye in the bloody house, gentlefriends.

Though banned by the Ministry, and most copies of it destroyed in the Bright Light book burning of 27PR, Pythias's monologue is still quoted in modern times. A few complete versions of the play are rumoured to exist in secret – handwritten from memory by actors who performed it, or secreted away from the puritans of Aa's church. The copies are rare, however, and have almost become myth among Itreyan theatre groups. Any actor claiming to have read one is more than likely just a lying tosser.

Although now I think about it, most actors I've met were lying tossers anyway . . .

'And you, Butcher? What about you, Otho?'

'Nay,' they replied. 'Never.'

'To the Crow!' Sid roared, and the room raised their cups in answer.

Only Furian was silent, sipping his wine as if it were poisoned.* His eyes never left Mia's, filled with accusation and cold fury. Sick as he'd been, she knew he must have watched her battle, probably felt her calling the dark. But still, there was no denying her victory had been glorious, and no matter how much the sight of that silver laurel on her brow burned his craw, the Unfallen wisely kept his bile behind his teeth.

Occasionally, Mia would stare across the feast with ink-black eyes, boring into the champion's own, the illness and hunger she felt whenever she was around him swelling in her belly. Glancing at his seat at the table's head, she silently promised.

Soon.

'Attend!'

The gladiatii fell silent, rising to their feet as Executus Arkades marched into the room, along with Magistrae. Dona Leona walked behind them, beaming.

'Domina!' the gladiatii barked.

'Be still, my Falcons,' she raised her hands, urged them to take their seats. 'I'll not part you from your revels. The streets ring with the name of the Remus Collegium, and you've earned this moment's joy, all of you.'

The dona smiled as they raised their cups, toasted her health. She'd taken time to change into an off-the-shoulder dress and matching corset in beautiful crushed velvet, the same rust-red as her hair. Mia wondered exactly how much silver the woman had spent on it. How many dresses she'd hauled here from the Nest. How much this damned celebration feast was costing her and where the 'byss she got the coin. For someone who was so strapped she'd been willing to sell Mia to a pleasure house a mere turn ago . . .

Mia glanced at Arkades, saw the Executus eyeing the food and wine with the same concern. Mia looked at the jewels about the dona's throat, the gold at her wrists, the realization only sinking deeper.

She's awful with money. Raised rich, so she's never learned the real value of a coin, or truly understood the life that awaits you when you run out of them. All she cares about is how she appears to others.

To her father.

---

*To be fair, the last wine he'd drunk *had* been.

Mia looked Leona up and down, sighing inside.

Could I have grown up the same way, if mine hadn't been killed?

Mia saw Furian look to his domina from the corner of her eye, perhaps seeking some gesture of acknowledgement. But true to her ruse, tall and proud and O, so *proper*, Leona did not even grace him with a glance.

'My Crow,' the dona said, smiling at Mia. 'A word.'

'Domina.'

Mia followed Leona from the room, conscious of Furian's burning gaze on her back. Arkades and Magistrae followed, the older woman shutting the door as Sidonius started recounting the battle again, using a jug of wine and a toothpick for props.

'You are well?' Leona asked.

'Well enough,' Mia replied. 'My thanks, Domina.'

''Tis I who should be thanking you,' Leona said, her eyes dancing. 'Our collegium is the talk of the entire *city*. The governor of Stormwatch, Quintus Messala himself, has declared this the finest contest the Republic has ever seen, and *you* – Leona squeezed Mia's shoulders – 'you, my bloody beauty, are the heart of it all.'

'I live to honour you, Domina,' Mia said.

Arkades narrowed his eyes at that, but Leona seemed almost giddy.

'Governor Messala holds a traditional feast the nevernight after the *venatus*,' the dona said. 'Every marrowborn and administratii attends his palazzo, and he invites every sanguila who fields gladiatii in the games, along with their champion.' Leona's eyes twinkled with fierce delight. 'But he has sent personal missive, asking that in addition to Furian, I bring *you*, that all may gaze upon the Saviour of Stormwatch.'

'. . . The Saviour of Stormwatch?' Mia murmured.

'It has a fine ring to it, neh?' Leona chuckled. 'The minstrels are already singing of your victory in taverna across the city. You will be the pride of the feast, the jewel in my crown. And we'll be showered in coin – the elite of the city will be throwing offers of patronage at my *feet*. The eyes of every sanguila upon you, *burning* with jealousy.'

Every sanguila . . .

'Messala has always favoured fighters from my father's collegium,' Leona said. 'For years, he has heaped accolades upon the Lions of Leonides. How badly it will burn, to see me in the seat of favour at Messala's right hand.'

The dona pressed her fingers to her lips, smothering her mad grin.

'Imagine the look on the old bastard's face.'

'Mi Dona,' Magistrae warned, glancing at Mia. 'You should not speak so . . .'

'Mmm, aye.' Leona remembered herself, nodding and smoothing down the lines of her dress. 'I keep you from your revels, my Crow. Go and celebrate your victory. But not too much wine, neh? I want you looking your best at the feast amorrow.'

Like a prized pet, Mia realized. *Like a dog at her mistress's feet. To be sold in an instant if she fails to bark on command.*

Sit.

Roll over.

Play dead.

Be dead.

Mia pressed her lips tight. Thinking of her father, swinging at the end of his rope. Her mother bleeding to death in her arms. Her baby brother, taking his first steps in some lightless pit and dying there in the dark.

Thinking of Duomo.

Thinking of Scaeva.

Eyes on the prize, Corvere.

And looking into Leona's eyes, she bowed, hand to her heart.

'Your whisper, my will,' she said. 'Domina.'

B lack fucking Mother, you were *brilliant*!'
       Ashlinn crashed into Mia as soon as she climbed through the taverna window, arms wrapped around her tight. Mia nodded, 'Aye, aye,' and extricated herself from the girl's grip, drew the curtains behind her. She was the most well-known person in Stormwatch, after all, and the streets were still filled with revellers celebrating the *venatus*. The suns were burning her eyes, the beating she'd taken that afternoon was leaving its bruises, and after the feast with her brother and sister gladiatii, Mia was feeling more than a little drunk. Looking about the tiny room, she saw there were no chairs to sit in – just a single cot with a mattress as thin as a slice of fine cheese.

'Not exactly the consul's villa, is it?'

'Every inn, outhouse, and brothel was full because of the *venatus*,' Ash shrugged. 'The Mother smiled on me to even get a berth in this hovel. Don't ask how much we're paying for it. Good thing Mercurio gave us so much coin. But anyway, to the 'byss with the room, you just killed a colossus! The whole city is talking about you!'

Mia slumped down on the bed, massaged her aching ribs.

'Aye,' was all she mustered.

''Byss and blood, Corvere,' Ash said, flopping down on the mattress beside her. 'You slew a retchwyrm! Saved the lives of hundreds of people in front of ten thousand more! Leona would have to be three shades mad and five bottles drunk to even think about selling you now! Aren't you happy?'

Mia had asked herself that same question on the way here, sneaking out from the arena cells and Stepping through the shadows. She *should* be happy. Aside from the retchwyrm breaking its chain, all had gone more or less to her design. Leona's favour won. Patronage for the collegium assured. Her name ringing in the streets. One laurel closer to the *magni*, Scaeva's and Duomo's throats.

But the wrongness of it was creeping on her like a cancer. Every turn she spent with this brand on her cheek made it harder and harder for her to ignore the folk who couldn't just skip away from their chains through the shadows like she could. Not just gladiatii. The whole Republic was oiled by the machine of human misery. Now that her eyes were opened to it, she couldn't unsee it. Didn't *want* to.

But she also knew she couldn't fix it. She couldn't even help the other members of the collegium without dooming her plan to failure. She'd gambled too much to be here already. And not just her. Mercurio. Ashlinn, too. And all for the greater good, aye? Couldn't she truly say that? That the Republic would be better off without a tyrant in the consul's chair?

That *everyone* would be better off once Julius Scaeva was dead?

But what would happen to her brothers and sisters in the collegium, if somehow her plan succeeded? Two slaves kill their master, and the administratii murder every slave in their house. What would they do to the ones she left behind in Crow's Nest, if she killed a cardinal and a fucking consul? Even if she managed to pull off her miracle, Sidonius, Bryn and Byern, Bladesinger . . . they'd all be executed.

Mia looked at the girl, staring back at her with those bright blue eyes.

'A long turn is all,' she sighed. 'Got a smoke?'

Ash grinned, fished inside her shirt and produced her thin silver cigarillo case. It was embossed with the sigil of the Familia Corvere – a crow in flight over two crossed swords. It had been a present from Mercurio, the nevernight Mia turned fifteen. The metal was warm from the press of Ashlinn's skin.

Mia lit the cigarillo with a flintbox, sighed grey.

'Where are Eclipse and Mister Know-it-all?' Ash asked.

'Eclipse is watching the street. Mister Kindly is trailing Dona Leona. There's a big soirée at the governor's palazzo amorrow. Leona's attempting to secure patronage, end her money troubles once and for all. The governor asked to bring me with her.'

'Of course,' Ash nodded. 'You should've seen yourself. Damned retchwyrm looked set to devour half the crowd, and you call it a rude word and it just turns on you like a snake. Unbelievable.'

'Aye,' Mia muttered. 'I can scarce believe it myself.'

She took another drag of her cigarillo, shaking her head. Ash was still grinning, blue eyes shining with the memory of her victory. She reached across, rubbed at the scowl between Mia's brows as if attempting to erase it. Mia batted her hand away.

'Maw's teeth, what's wrong?' Ash sighed, exasperated. 'You're the toast of the city. You won a laurel, gained your dona's favour, and guaranteed the future of the collegium. Everything went your way, and you're scowling up a summer storm.'

Mia chewed her lip. Debating if she should say anything at all. She looked at Ashlinn, dark eyes picked out with a pinprick of flame as she dragged on her cigarillo. The wine in her belly had loosened her tongue, but the distrust in her veins was keeping her jaw firmly clenched.

'. . . 'Byss and blood, Mia, what is it?' Ashlinn asked.

'The retchwyrm,' Mia finally said.

'What of it?'

'. . . In the desert outside the Quiet Mountain, back when was I chasing you and Remus to Last Hope . . .' She exhaled grey, waiting for some kind of reaction at talk of their confrontation last year, but Ashlinn was only listening. 'A sand kraken attacked the Luminatii wagon. Killed scores of Remus's men.'

'I remember.'

Mia drew a deep breath, held it for a long, pregnant moment.

'I made it do that,' she exhaled at last.

Ashlinn blinked. 'How?'

Mia shrugged. 'I've no idea. I just know that any time I called the shadows in the Whisperwastes of Ashkah, sand kraken would come, and they'd be angry. And that retchwyrm in the arena reacted the same way. I tried to hold it in place with its own shadow, and it near lost its fucking mind.'

Mia shook her head, took another drag on her smoke.

'Loresmen say that sand kraken and other beasts of the Ashkahi wastes were twisted by the magikal pollutants left over from the empire's destruction.'

The Crown of the Moon.

The fall of the Ashkahi Empire.

The monstrosities left in its wake.

'I'm wondering . . . could all of it be connected?'

'To the empire's fall?' Ashlinn asked. 'The darkin?'

Mia shrugged, a now-familiar frustration welling up inside her. Cassius hadn't learned a thing of himself. Furian didn't want to. Mercurio and Mother Drusilla had told her she was Chosen of the Mother, but what the 'byss did that actually mean?

No one she'd ever met had any real answers for her. But that thing in the Galante necropolis . . . it seemed to know more.

'*YOUR TRUTH LIES BURIED IN THE GRAVE. AND YET YOU PAINT YOUR HANDS IN RED FOR THEM, WHEN YOU SHOULD BE PAINTING THE SKIES BLACK.*'

'I'm just fucking sick and tired of not knowing what I am, Ashlinn.'

'Well, that's easy,' the girl declared, reaching across and squeezing Mia's hand.

'O, aye?'

'Aye,' Ashlinn smiled. 'You're brave. And you're bright. And you're beautiful.'

Mia scoffed, shaking her head and gazing at the wall.

'I mean it,' Ashlinn said, leaning in and kissing Mia's cheek.

Mia turned to stare, dark eyes fixed on sunburned blue. Ashlinn was still close, drifting closer, ever so slow. The scent of lavender coiled on her skin, red hair cascading around her lightly freckled face, Mia's stomach thrilling as she realized the girl was about to kiss her.

'You're beautiful,' Ash whispered.

And closing her eyes, she leaned in and—

'Don't,' Mia said.

Ashlinn stopped, lips just a breath from Mia's. Looking from her eyes, down to her mouth.

'Why not?' she whispered.

'Because I don't trust you, Ashlinn,' Mia replied. 'And I don't want you thinking you can drag me into bed just to get me in your pocket.'

Ashlinn leaned back on her haunches, looked at Mia in disbelief.

'You think I'd—'

'Do anything to get your way?' Mia asked. 'Lie? Cheat? Fuck? Murder?'

Mia took a long drag of her smoke, eyes narrowed. Her tongue felt a little too thick for her mouth from the wine she'd drunk at dinner, but she'd set it loose now.

'Aye, Ash, that's the problem,' she said. 'I think I do.'

Ashlinn reared up off the bed like Mia had struck her. She walked across the room, far as the tiny space would allow. Hands on hips and staring at the wall. She was silent a long moment, finally turning on Mia with a snarl.

'Fuck you, Mia.'

Stamping back across the room, she raised the knuckles in Mia's face.

'Fuck *you*!'

'Get your hand out of my face, Ashlinn,' Mia warned.

'I should knock that cigarillo out of your mouth!' she yelled.

Mia shook her head, taking another drag. 'Have you ever noticed how people start to shout when they've nothing worthwhile to say?'

'Maw's teeth, you've got some stones. In case you haven't noticed, there's one person in the entire world right now who's on your side, and—'

'Mercurio's on my side, Ashlinn. Long before you.'

'I don't see him anywhere around here, do you?' Ash shouted. 'I don't see him dragging his arse from Godsgrave to Whitekeep to Stormwatch. I don't see *him* sneaking into arenas and planting wyrdglass in the sands and sending you warning about the monstrosity set to melt the flesh off your damned bones. He did nothing but try to talk you out of this, and I've done nothing but fucking help you!'

Mia shook her head, grinding her cigarillo into the wall. 'Not because you hate the Ministry as much as I do. Not because you stand to gain from all this, O, no, Mother forbid. Because you care *so much* about me.'

'And that just fucking terrifies you, doesn't it?'

Mia scoffed. 'I have two shadow daemons who quite literally eat my fear, Ashlinn. I'm not terrified of anything.'

'Mister Shithead and Wolfie aren't in the room,' Ash snapped. 'It's just you and me, now. And for all your bluster, that thought scares you witless. By the smell of you, you had to smash a bottle of goldwine just to muster the courage to send them away. But you *did* send them away. And you're too much a coward to admit why.'

'Fuck you, Ashlinn.'

'I thought you'd never ask, Mia.'

Mia tensed, springing up off the bed, hands in fists. Ashlinn stood her ground, staring Mia down, jaw clenched. Their faces were only a few inches apart, the air between them crackling with arkemical current.

'Don't pretend you don't feel it,' Ash said. 'Because it's written in your every line and curve. You might know me, Mia Corvere, but I know *you* just as well. And I know what it is you want.'

Mia gritted her teeth, one hand curling into a fist. She didn't know whether she wanted to punch the girl or . . .

There was an ocean of lies between them. Ash's betrayal. Tric's murder. The certainty the girl *would* do or say anything to get what she wanted. But there was truth in her words too. Of every person she knew in the world, the only one here helping her in her darkest need was Ashlinn Järnheim.

Ashlinn Järnheim was made of lies.

Ashlinn Järnheim was poison.

And Ashlinn Järnheim was beautiful.

Mia couldn't deny it. Soft lips parted in the smoky light. Long red hair spilling about her shoulders in waves. Her skin was smooth, a hint of anger in her cheeks, turning them to rose. Big blue eyes framed by dark curling lashes, the look in them making Mia's fingers tingle, her belly flip. Wine humming in her veins, she stared into those pools of sunburned blue and saw her reflection, saw the same thing in her eyes as she saw swimming in Ash's own.

Want.

Want.

But . . .

. . . without her passengers beside her, Mia *was* afraid.

Not of wanting a girl, like perhaps Ash suspected. She'd had one before, after all. Even though that golden beauty in Aurelius's bed was simply a means to an end, Mia could admit she might have found a way to kiss the senator's son sooner. Might have ended him quite some time before she felt those golden lips between her legs, tasted the girl on Aurelius's tongue.

No, if Mia was afraid, it wasn't of wanting a girl.

It was wanting *this* girl.

Ashlinn Järnheim.

Thief.

Liar.

Killer.

Traitor.

'How can I trust you?' Mia asked. 'After all you've done?'

'If I wanted you dead, Mia . . .'

'I'm not talking about trusting you with my life, Ashlinn.'

Mia looked at Ashlinn's heaving breast, pictured the heart beneath it. Wondering if it thundered as hard as hers, or if all this was simply a means to an end.

Ashlinn lifted her hand, bringing it up to Mia's face. Her fingers brushed Mia's skin, eliciting a dizzying rush of warmth that had nothing to do with the sunlight or the wine she'd drunk. She inched closer, eyes flitting from Mia's own, down to her lips. Breathing harder, moving closer, just an inch away now, just a heartbeat. And Mia looked across the room and

Stepped

to the shadow

of the curtains

pulling them aside, throwing the window open, her head spinning from the drink, from the shadow-walking, from all of it. Ash called her name, but she ignored it, scrambling over the sill and climbing down the wall, swift as a morning-after goodbye.

Calling Eclipse to her side, she dragged the darkness about her shoulders and over her head, stealing off into the nevernight streets. Celebrations of her victory were still ringing from taverna windows, from smokehouse doors, echoing in the very air. The fear draining from her like poison from a wound as Eclipse coiled inside her shadow, leaving her cold and hard and unafraid.

She couldn't trust Ashlinn Järnheim. That much was certain. But the thought of standing over the corpses of the men who'd destroyed everything she loved? The feel of cold steel in her hand and warm blood on her face and the knowledge that everything she'd worked for over the past seven years was now finally within her reach?

That she could trust.

And nothing else mattered.

She ran her hand down her cheek where Ashlinn had touched her, her skin still tingling.

Nothing at all.

CHAPTER 19

YIELD

They called for Mia before dessert.

Dona Leona had commanded her to wait in a small antechamber, down in the servants' wing of the governor's palazzo. A guard was posted at her door, she was given a simple meal and some watered wine, while the guests in the banquet hall enjoyed aperitifs of stuffed quail hearts doused with brandy butter, followed by a main of roasted honeyfish and kingclaw braised in goldwine.

Mia knew Quintus Messala had served as governor of Stormwatch for six years – he'd been appointed soon after the Kingmaker Rebellion. As a childhood friend of Consul Scaeva and a scion of one of the twelve great familia of the Republic, his wealth and power were the envy of everyone who met him, and it seemed Messala lived to stoke that envy. Mia couldn't recall an affair as lavish, or a house quite as opulent. The antechamber she sat in was decorated with intricate stucco reliefs, gold leaf, and Dweymeri crystal chandeliers. The man who served her meal was dressed in clothes most marrowborn dons would envy.

She'd sat in the room brooding about her argument with Ashlinn until Arkades had come to fetch her. He was dressed in his finery, falcons and lions on his doublet. Mia was dressed in the armour she'd worn yesterturn, though it had been polished to within an inch of its life. They'd not given her helmet back, but there was little she could do about that. The chances of a Red Church servant being at the feast were low, but still, walking towards the banquet hall, Executus in front and two guards at her flanks, Mia felt as if she were buck-naked and strolling into a scabdog's den.

'Hold,' Arkades told her, stopping at the door to the dining hall.

The big man turned to look at her, raised a finger in warning.

'Do not speak unless you are spoken to. Remember that all eyes are upon you. You may never have seen the like before, but the people in this room are *serpents*, girl. They slay with a whisper. Bestow fortunes or end reputations with a word. If you shame your domina's name, I swear by the Everseeing, I'll see you suffer for it.'

Black Mother, the torch he's carrying for that woman could light up truedark . . .

Truth was, Mia knew the machinations of the marrowborn all too well – she'd seen her mother play their power games for years. The Dona Corvere could reduce men to hollow shells and women to tears when she put her mind to it. But Mia wasn't about to let Arkades know that. Instead, she simply bowed her head.

'Aye, Executus.'

Satisfied, the man opened the door to the dining hall and limped inside. Mia waited, hands clasped. She could hear string music, voices in the room beyond.

'Fine match yesterturn,' one of the guards beside her murmured.

'Aye,' the other said. 'Bloody spectacular, lass.'

Mia nodded thanks, grateful word of her victory was still spreading. If there had been any chance of Leona selling her off before the *venatus*, it was as dead as that retchwyrm now. Her domina would have to ponder some other way to pay her creditors – though if all went well this eve, that should prove no difficulty. Wealthy marrowborn often offered patronage to favoured collegia, and with the Falcons of Remus the toast of the city, Leona should have no trouble securing investment.

The future of the collegium was assured.

All that remained was securing her place at the *magni*.

Mia soon heard the clinking of a ring upon a crystal goblet, a lull in conversation. A voice called out in the room beyond; a silk-smooth baritone Mia guessed must belong to Governor Messala.

'Esteemed guests, honoured friends, I thank you for visiting my humble home this nevernight. It gives me and my good wife no end of pride to see so many of you here. May the Everseeing watch over you, and the Four Daughters bestow their blessings.'

Messala waited for the polite applause to die before continuing.

'We hold this feast every *venatus*, to give thanks to friends who grace our city but rarely, and yet, leave their mark indelibly on the hearts and minds of our citizens. It is with no hyperbole that I declare yesterturn's *venatus* the greatest seen in our fine city, and I thank each and every sanguila here present who toiled to make it so!'

Messala paused again for applause. It was a rarity for sanguila to be invited to a governor's home – blood masters could never hold the status of the true marrowborn. But Mia could see Messala's acumen in arranging it. The sanguila were popular with common folk, and the love of the citizenry had seen Julius Scaeva flout all convention and sit in the consul's chair for three terms. It made sense for Messala to court the men who owned the favour of the mob.

A snake this one, sure and true.

'Now,' Messala continued. 'Each sanguila has brought their champion, that we may marvel. But for you, dear friends, I've arranged a gift more marvellous still. Through the generosity of Dona Leona of the Remus Collegium' – Mia heard a murmur ripple through the guests – 'I am pleased to present the victor of yesterturn's Ultima, and one of the finest warriors to set foot upon the sands . . . Crow, the Saviour of Stormwatch!'

The doors were flung wide, and Mia looked out into a sea of curious faces. Hundreds of people were in attendance – the cream of society, gathered in pretty knots or lying on divans around the vast room. The hall was marble, frescoed, tall windows thrown open to let in the cool nevernight breeze. Plates were laden with food, goblets overflowed with wine, wealth dripping off the walls.

Mia recognized this world. She'd grown up in it, after all. Daughter of a marrowborn familia, raised in opulence just like this. So much wealth held in so few palms. A kingdom of the blind, built on the backs of the bruised and the broken.

And nobody born to it ever questioning a thing.

Governor Messala stood at the centre of the room – a handsome Itreyan man with dark, piercing eyes. The divans were arranged about his own, and guests were seated according to their status. Mia saw Dona Leona at a place of honour on Messala's right side, Arkades beside her. Furian loomed behind, dressed in a breastplate of iron, bracers and shin guards crafted like falcon's wings. The champion was practically seething, staring at Mia with hatred in his eyes.

But when she looked at him, still . . . that hunger . . .

That *want.*

Mia noted other sanguila around the room, recognizing their sigils. A heavyset man wearing the sword and shield of the Trajan Collegium. A one-handed man that could only be Phillipi, a former gladiatii who'd started his own stable. And there among them, Mia saw an overweight man wearing a frock coat embroidered with golden lions. She recognized him immediately – the man who'd offered to buy her for a thousand silver priests, and been bested by a single coin.

Leonides.

He was still sat close to Messala, Mia noted, even though he hadn't fielded a fighter in the Ultima. She wondered again at that, and at Leona's revelation that the governor had long favoured the Lions of Leonides. Looking about the room, another might have seen a simple banquet. But Mia saw a spider's web, sticky strands spun among the guests, vibration thrumming to the centre of the web. And at the heart of it was Dona Leona, a goblet to her lips, sitting blithely at the spider's right hand.

Leonides himself seemed unremarkable in many ways. Too fond of his food and drink perhaps, but no kind of monster. He sipped his wine and affected a yawn, pretending not to notice Mia had entered. But she saw how he watched, the glittering blue eyes he'd gifted his daughter not missing a thing.

Thus, the greatest monsters get their way, she realized.

By looking just like the rest of us.

Beside Leonides stood his hulking bald executus, Titus, the girth of his arms straining his silken shirt. And behind Titus, Mia saw an ominous figure, at least seven feet tall, cloaked and cowled despite the heat.

. . . His champion?

'Good Crow.'

The governor's voice snatched Mia from her reverie.

'Come forward,' he beckoned. 'Let Stormwatch see its saviour.'

Mia marched into the room as commanded, the guards in step beside her. The guests weren't so crass as to applaud her presence – Mia was property, after all, and quality didn't clap when a pet successfully performed a trick. But she could feel an arkemical current in the air nevertheless; curiosity, admiration, even desire. Just a turn ago, she'd had tens of thousands of people on their feet, roaring her name. That gave her a kind of gravity, she realized. The same kind of magnetism Arkades wore like armour, the other gladiatii in the room fought to attain. Primal, perhaps. Steeped in blood.

But power nonetheless.

'I commend you, good Crow,' Messala said, 'and give thanks on behalf of the citizens of our city. Not only did you treat us to a spectacle unlike any other, but through skill and courage, the lives of no few of our citizens were rescued from calamity.' The governor raised his goblet, joined by the many guests around the room. 'Aa bless and keep you, and Tsana ever guide your hand.'

Mia bowed. 'You honour me, Governor.'

'You honour *us*, as does your domina.' The governor turned with a smile to the woman at his right, raised his goblet to Leona. 'My thanks to you, gracious Dona, for allowing the opportunity to see our saviour up close.'

Leona inclined her head. 'I am your humble servant, Governor.'

'She *is* quite magnificent, aye?' Messala said to his guests, walking around Mia and admiring the view from every angle. 'The goddess Tsana made flesh. 'Tis one thing to bear witness from the boxes, quite another to see her here, neh?'

Leona smiled. 'Who'd have thought one so fair could be so fierce?'

'I'd wager she could best any three of my houseguards.'

Leona smiled wide, basking in the adoration. She shot a poison glance at her father, Mia noting Leonides's face was flush with anger. And as a thought seized her, Mia saw the dona look to her executus, lips curling in a devious smile.

'Perhaps you and your guests desire a demonstration, Governor Quintus?'

The man tilted his head, playful. 'Would you indulge us, Mi Dona?'

'It would be my honour to pit my Crow against your finest man,' Leona said. '*E navium*, of course."

---

*Matches in the calendar leading up to the *Venatus Magni* are often fought *e mortium*, or to the death. Little else will satisfy the appetites of the crowd, and it's not as if anybody could talk a sand kraken out of their breakfast anyway. But many gladiatii matches are fought *e navium*, or to submission.

Though real steel is still employed, a wounded gladiatii may appeal to the editorii for the match to end at any time by holding out a palm in supplication, and death blows aren't meted out to a fallen foe at the match's end. Injuries still abound, but accidental fatalities are rare in *e navium* bouts. Thus, sanguila can test the mettle of their opponents' stables and build a reputation for their collegia while avoiding the inconvenience and expense of losing a fighter every time they lose a match.

In times past, crafty sanguila employed bladders of chicken's blood and fake blades in order to give appearance of fatalities, even in official *venatus* matches. But such subterfuge can only last so long – the crowds tended to notice when their slaughtered favourites kept returning from the grave. Such cheap theatrics were banned by the editorii in 34PR, and relegated to the realm of mummers

Messala raised an eyebrow, looked among his guests. 'What say you, friends?'

Arkades frowned at the suggestion, obviously displeased. Mia herself didn't much fancy the thought of performing for the elite's amusement – she was black and blue from her battle against the retchwyrm yester-turn. But the marrowborn were well charmed with the dona's suggestion, and impressing with a simple bout *did* seem a sensible way for Leona to secure the patronage she so needed.

Still . . .

Mia looked to Leonides. Back to Messala. Trying to shake the ill feeling crawling on her skin.

The governor turned to one of his guards – a burly lump with biceps as thick as his neck. 'Varius, perhaps you'd be kind enough to oblige?'

The big man nodded, took a gladius from the guard beside him, and tossed it to Mia. Snatching it from the air, she looked to Dona Leona, who simply gave an encouraging nod while Furian – obviously incensed at being overshadowed – glowered in the background. Space was cleared by the governor's servants in the centre of the room, and Mia took up her place, sword raised, trying to shake her misgivings. The guard drew his own blade and bowed to the governor, set his eyes on Mia.

'I beg pardon, honoured Governor,' came a voice. 'If I might inter-ject?'

All eyes turned to Sanguila Leonides, standing by his divan and bowing low.

'Good Leonides?' Messala asked.

'Gracious host, I mean no offence to your man,' Leonides said. 'But if we are to see the Saviour of Stormwatch at her finest, might I suggest she cross steel with one trained in the arts of the sand?' Leonides turned glittering eyes to his daughter. 'Unless the Crow's sanguila feels she is not fit for the task?'

Leona stared at her father across the crowd, her face a mask of perfect calm. But Mia's hackles were raised. She could see the trap now. With a few buttered words, Messala had manipulated Leona into putting a sword in Mia's hand, and Leonides could make his daughter look the coward if the challenge was refused. And yet, Mia knew the man wasn't fool enough to propose a match without some advantage.

---

and theatres where they belong. If one attends a death match of the *venatus* these turns, gentlefriends, if you can be assured of one thing, it is this:

The dead stay fucking dead.

It seemed finally the dona had a sense of the danger herself now, eyes flickering to her host, back to her father, remaining mute a moment too long.

'She hesitates?' Leonides smiled to the other guests. 'Understandable, of course. Remus Collegium has only three laurels to its name, and our Crow here is but a babe upon the sands. Perhaps our saviour needs a few turns to rest her wings before she is fit to fight again, neh?'

Mia saw Arkades whisper in his dona's ear. But Leona raised her hand in annoyance, and the man fell silent. She glanced once more about the room, the faces of the assembled marrowborn – folk she might have sat among as an equal were she still married to a justicus. Patrons she now needed to keep her collegium afloat. Mia could see that desperate need to impress in her eyes. The same desire that saw her bid at the Gardens without thought, spend beyond her means, dress as if she were attending a gala every turn. And as Mia's heart sank to see her so easily goaded, warning trapped behind her teeth, Leona inclined her head and smiled.

'I thought only to spare you embarrassment, Sanguila Leonides. But I gratefully accept your offer. My bloody beauty will meet any man from your stable, steel to steel.'

'Man? O, no, my dear, you misunderstand.' Leonides motioned to the robed and hooded figure looming beside him. 'I'd thought to keep my Ishkah here in lieu until the next *venatus*, as I've only just secured her purchase. But in honour of good Governor Messala, and fighting *e navium*, I see no risk in a small preview to whet appetites now.'

He turned to the figure, speaking softly.

'Be gentle with her, my lioness.'

A murmur of excitement rippled across the room as Leonides's fighter stepped forward into the sparring space. This was a treat no one had expected – to see champions cross blades for the marrowborn's own private amusement. The guests smiled wide, teeth stained dark with wine, pulses quickening at the thought of blood in the water. Mia raised her sword, sunlight glinting on the edge.

'Ladies and gentlefriends, honoured hosts,' Leonides said with a dramatic sweep of his hand. 'May I present the latest addition to my pride. A foe fiercer than the Black Mother herself, a terror among her kind, whose very name means "death" in the tongue of the Dominion. It has taken me years to secure a prize like her, but in all my time beside the sand, I have never seen her equal. I give you my next champion, and the next victor of the *Venatus Magni* . . . Ishkah, the Exile!'

Leonides dropped his hand. And as the crowd gasped in wonder, his challenger sloughed off its robe to reveal the figure beneath.

'Four Daughters . . .' someone breathed.

'Almighty Aa . . .' another whispered.

Maw's teeth . . .

Mia swallowed thickly, shadow rippling at her feet.

A silkling.

Mia had read about the denizens of the Silken Dominion in Mercurio's books as a child, but she'd never thought to see one in the flesh. Looking at Leonides's fighter, Mia could see she was almost certainly female, hips curved beneath her studded leather skirt, six arms folded over the subtle curve of her breasts. She was seven feet tall, her skin chitinous, a green so dark it was almost black. Her lips were painted white, two large, featureless orbs set in a smooth, oval face, six smaller eyes scattered across her cheeks like freckles. She had no eyelids with which to blink. From her readings, Mia guessed the silkling was young, but in truth, she had no real way to tell.*

The silkling reached up to her back, drew forth six glittering blades, each gently curved and razor-sharp, etched with strange glyphs. As the assembled marrowborn murmured in astonishment, she wove the

---

*Native to the Drakespine Mountains bordering Vaan and Itreya and, despite their rather pretty name, the arachnid silkling are a species renowned as . . . somewhat un-neighbourly. The Silken Dominion is scattered over thousands of miles of inhospitable crags, and its conquest by the Itreyan legions proved extraordinarily costly; it was only after every War Walker in the Iron Collegium was brought to bear that the silkling BroodQueen was brought to heel.

Though the silkling have ostensibly sworn loyalty to the Itreyan Republic, their seat in the Senate House has remained empty since it was explained that only males can hold the title of Itreyan senator (male silkling are smaller than their counterparts, and venomless). The Senate themselves are content to leave the silkling mostly alone, and the threat of a posting as Itreyan ambassador to the Dominion is often used as a stick to keep unruly younger members in line. As a general rule, the silkling have nothing to do with the Republic or its citizenry if they can help it.

Silkling females mark their cheeks with ritual scarification for every brood they've hatched. They murder their mates postcoitus with alarming regularity. And if you're tempted to ask how it is the species continues to thrive under such circumstances, I can only assure you that, yes, the females possess vaginas, and yes, the males have penises.

The rest should be self-explanatory.

weapons through the air in an intricate, twisting dance, the steel whistling as it sliced the air. Finishing her display, Ishkah spread her arms like fans, blades poised and pointed directly at Mia.

The girl glanced to Leona, Arkades, Furian. The dona's face was stone, but her eyes were dark with fear, seeing now how simply she'd been played. And yet, with the marrowborn now awash with excitement, she dare not make an overture to end the bout prematurely. Leonides looked to his daughter and smiled like a cat who'd stolen the cream, the bucket, and the maid to boot.

He played her like a lyre. If I lose here, the people of the city might still sing my name. But the people of influence and power . . . they'll sing only of the Lions of Leonides. And Leona's chance of patronage goes up in flames.

Mia saw the trap revealed. Paused a moment to admire its simplicity. She saw the strands of the web between the governor and Leonides, the invitation that had brought Leona here with her guard down. Plying her with a wine or two and a bevy of compliments from folk above her station, manipulating her into a fight she couldn't afford to lose, and yet supposing she couldn't ever win.

We'll see about that, bastards . . .

'. . . *are you certain about this* . . . *?*' came a whisper from her hair.

'Are you certain you could shut up for the next few minutes so I don't get killed?' she muttered.

'. . . *ah* . . . *probably not* . . . *?*'

'Exactly.'

Truthfully, Mia had never been less certain about anything in her life, but she had no choice – to lose here would mean the collegium would still be up to its neck in debt, all her work still at risk. And so, she turned to one of the guards who'd praised her victory before they entered the hall, glanced to the blade at his waist.

'Might I trouble you for a loan, good sir?'

The guard drew his sword, handed it over dutifully. 'Tsana guide you, lass.'

Mia took the blade with a nod of thanks. And cutting her swords through the air, Mister Kindly doing his level best to shut up for a few minutes, Mia took her place in the sparring ring, eyes locked on the silkling's.

'This contest will be fought *e navium*,' Governor Messala reminded them. 'A hand raised in submission will signal an end to the bout. Fight with honour, and for the glory of your collegium. Aa bless and keep you, and Tsana guide your hand.'

The crowd hushed, the music stopped, and all Mia could hear was the thunderous beating of her own heart.

'Begin!' Messala cried.

Quick as silver, Mia struck with both blades, steel ringing as the silkling parried with four of her own. Dancing forward, she struck again at head and chest, but her foe blocked again with ease. Countering this time, the silkling launched a flurry of strikes at Mia, the air a whispering blur. Mia was pushed back, desperately blocking the incoming blades, until she was forced beyond the edge of the sparring circle. The marrow-born around her skittered aside, eyes on her swords. But the silkling didn't press, returning to the centre of the ring and waiting with her weapons poised in a glittering fan.

Mia tilted her head, felt her neck pop. Tossed her hair from her eyes. And stepping up to her foe, she launched another salvo.

She'd always prided herself on her skill with a blade – she'd trained hard under Mercurio, and harder still in the Red Church, her natural speed combined with utter fearlessness and an uncanny aim. But even her best foes had only met her with two blades of their own – never six of the cursed things. Wherever she struck, the silkling's steel was waiting. Whenever she left a gap, Ishkah forced her back. The silkling had the size, the reach, the speed. And worse, Mia knew she wasn't giving her all. Just as Arkades had warned the first turn she set foot on the sand in Crow's Nest, Ishkah was studying her form in readiness for her final assault.

And so, seeking to even the scales (how is six blades against two fair? she reasoned), Mia reached out to the shadow at the silkling's feet.

None in the room would have noticed it – the dark shivered only a little. But as the silkling stepped forward to strike, she found her boots fixed fast to the mosaic tile at her feet, the long shadows cast by the sunlight outside. A moment's hesitation from her foe was enough, and Mia struck hard, a blinding series of strikes that broke through Ishkah's guard and opened a long, ragged wound on her shoulder, just shy of her throat. The crowd gasped in astonishment, blood as green as poplar leaves sprayed from the wound. Mia knocked another silkling's sword flying, and aimed a blow low to sweep her foe off her feet.

And then, just like the first turn she set foot on the sand in Crow's Nest,

she lost her grip on the shadows

and her foe stepped aside.

Mia's strike went wide, the silkling's blades flashed, opening up a

shallow cut across the girl's knuckles and sending her sword spinning
from her hand. Mia tried to counter with her other blade, but was met by
a wall of steel, Ishkah striking with an empty fist, driving the breath from
the girl's lungs. Mia staggered, the silkling twirled behind her, smashing
her across the back of the head with the flat of her blade. Cathedral bells
rang in Mia's skull, the whole world blurring to double as her legs were
knocked out from under her and she crashed senseless to the floor.

The silkling stood above her, blades poised to strike.

'Yield,' she demanded, with a voice like dry cicada wings.

Mia's brow had split on the tile, her head still ringing. Fingernails
clawing the ground, she blinked the blood from her eyes and struck
out with her feet, trying to knock the silkling down. Ishkah sidestepped
like a dancer, pressing her blades to Mia's throat.

'Yield,' she said again.

Mia looked to Leona's crestfallen face. To Arkades, shaking his head
in disdain. And finally to Furian. Staring into his dark eyes, she knew,
sure as she knew the turn she'd faced Arkades – the bastard had wrested
her grip on the shadows, allowed her foe to slip free.

Teeth bared.

Rage boiling in her belly.

'Even a dog knows when it is beaten,' came a voice from among
the sanguila.

'Perhaps the fault lies not with the dog,' Leonides replied, 'but with
its mistress?'

Leona's cheeks were spotted with rage as she looked at her father,
stepped towards him with clenched fists. Arkades whispered – some
word Mia couldn't hear – and the woman fell still, face flushed, eyes
burning.

'Yield,' she commanded.

'. . . yield, mia . . .'

Just a turn ago, she'd stood triumphant among tens of thousands
of people, every one of them chanting her name. And now, she lay on
her belly like a whipped pup, the marrowborn around her tittering
with amusement. Mia looked to Furian, hate boiling in her chest, the
edges of her shadow rippling. She could feel the dark in her, the black,
wanting to stretch out towards the Unfallen and tear him limb from
bloody limb. But the blades at her throat, the memory of her familia,
the thought that none in this room could know what she truly was – all
of it helped her to fight down the rage, stow it in her breast to cool.
Not forgotten, no. Nor forgiven. Never.

And slowly, Mia raised one trembling, bloodstained hand to the governor.

'. . . Yield,' she whispered.

Satisfied, the silkling removed her blades from Mia's throat, sheathed them at her back. Governor Messala looked among his guests, the mood now shifted, tinged with red. Tension was thick in the air, not just from the bloodshed in the circle, but the obvious enmity between Dona Leona and her father. If there was one thing that entertained the rich and idle more than bloodshed, it was scandal. To see it played out in front of them was better sport than any *venatus* under the suns.

'You deceived me,' Leona said, voice trembling.

'You deceived yourself,' her father sneered. 'When you started that backwater collegium. I warned you, Leona. The sands are no place for a woman, and the sanguila's box is no place for you.'

Leona glanced to the silkling. 'Don't look now, Father, but your champion appears to have breasts.'

The crowd tittered as Leona scored her point. Emboldened, she continued.

'But perhaps you don't intend to field her on the sand at all? I noted your collegium's absence yesterturn in the Ultima, when mine was claiming the victor's laurel. All the better to unveil her like some cheap mummer in a two-beggar corner show, and cheat me of my glory behind closed doors?'

Leonides's face darkened.

'If you think yourself cheated,' he declared, 'let Aa and Tsana decide. The next *venatus* is at Whitekeep, five weeks hence. I will field my Ishkah against your Crow. And since you so desperately need it, dear daughter, I shall wager one of my berths in the *magni* against the winner. But a fight to the death this time, neh?'

Leona looked to the marrowborn about her, opened her mouth to sp—

'I fear the contest unbalanced,' said a voice. 'And the crowd would cry the same.'

All eyes turned at the growl. Arkades, the Red Lion of Itreya, stood by his mistress's side, glaring at his former master. His face was twisted in a scowl, his scar cutting a deep shadow down his features. Mia could see the cold enmity in his eyes, looking at the man he'd once fought and bled for.

'I commend you on your find, Sanguila Leonides,' Executus continued, glancing at the silkling. 'I have never seen her equal either.

Not in all my years *upon* the sand. But six blades against two? What honour lies in contest such as that?'

Arkades looked at Mia still sprawled on the floor, then to Furian behind him.

'Especially when our collegium's best is absent the match.'

Leonides looked his former champion over with a calculating smile.

'A fair point. Never let it be said Leonides does not know the will of the crowd.' Glancing around the assembled marrowborn, the showman in him rose to the fore. 'Bring your best *three* champions to Whitekeep, then. Ishkah will face them all. Six blades to six. No quarter, no submission. A match for the ages, neh?'

Arkades shook his head. 'I wou—'

'Done.'

The marrowborn looked to Leona. The sanguila stood still as stone, glare locked on her father. Mia could see the hate there, pure and blinding. She knew that hatred well. The fire of it. Keeping you warm when all else in the world was black and cold. Keeping you moving, when all else in the world seemed simply to drag you down.

She wondered what Leonides had done, exactly, to earn it.

'Done,' Leona repeated. She glanced about the smiling marrowborn, the wine-stained teeth, eyes glittering. 'I will see you in Whitekeep, Father.'

Leona swept from the room, Furian following close behind. Arkades and Leonides stared at each other a moment longer, former champion and former master, now bitter rivals. The executus limped over to Mia, loomed above her expectantly. The girl struggled to her feet with a soft groan, blood gumming her lashes shut, her head pounding with pain. Stumbling behind the big man as he strode from the room.

'Arkades,' Leonides called.

The man stopped, turned to look at the smiling sanguila.

'When next you speak to her, thank your domina for sparing me the mistake of your little Crow's purchase. If your mistress seeks to recoup some of her losses, I've a pleasure house in Whitekeep always looking for new quim.'

Leonides looked Mia up and down with a sneer.

'Perhaps she'd fare better with a different kind of sword in hand.'

An amused ripple flowed through the crowd. Arkades turned and limped from the room without a word. Mia followed, head hung low, dark hair draped about her bloodstained face. She knew it was foolish, that she shouldn't let this pompous fool get to her. That in winning the *magni*, she'd have to defeat Leonides's best fighters and see him taste the shame of defeat anyway. But still . . .

But still . . .

Rubbing this prick's face in his own shit had now become a burning priority.

Personal now, bastard.

CHAPTER 20

THREE

'Furian, certainly,' Arkades said.

'That goes without saying,' Leona replied. 'He is our champion.'

'Are you certain, Mi Dona? I thought perhaps you'd forgotten him.'

Leona steepled her fingers at her chin and glowered at her executus.

'I forget nothing, Arkades. And I forgive even less.'

The pair were sat in a small cabin aboard the *Gloryhound*, the ship rolling and creaking with the ocean's swell. They'd set sail the turn after the banquet at Governor Messala's home, and four turns out from Crow's Nest, Leona and Arkades were still trying to decide who would stand against his silkling. Magistrae sat behind her mistress, weaving Leona's hair into artful plaits while the pair argued. And below her chair, puddled in the shadow, sat a cat who was nothing close to a cat at all.

'We could refuse the match,' Arkades said. 'Throw our dice in the Ultima.'

'We need two laurels between now and truelight, Executus,' Leona replied. 'And Whitekeep is the last *venatus* in the calendar before the *magni*.'

'Our equillai could win us a laurel. Bryn and Byern ran a close second t—'

'Aye, and if they lose?' Leona asked. 'Even with victory in the Ultima after that, we'd find ourselves a laurel short. We wager twice by refusing challenge against my father. We wager but once if we accept. The only way we can be *assured* of fighting in Godsgrave is to best that fucking silkling.'

'Language, Domina,' Magistrae warned.

'Aye,' Leona sighed. 'Apologies.'

The older woman's brow creased in thought as she went back to work on Leona's hair. 'Beg pardon, Domina, but even if you win contest against your father's champion, will the editorii honour the wager?'

'Precedent has long been set,' Arkades replied, toying with the handle of his walking stick. 'Well-established collegia often lure more inexperienced sanguila to compete in one-sided matches with the promise of a seat at the *magni*.'

Leona aimed a withering glare. 'Well, that was unusually tactful.'

'He is *playing* you, Mi Dona,' Arkades replied. 'This berth the bait, and those games the noose. Not content with denying you patronage, your father wants you to send your three best gladiatii to be butchered, and with them, this collegium's future.'

'Without the *magni*, we have no future!' Leona snapped. 'Our Crow was flogged in front of every marrowborn in Stormwatch! No one with a purse will touch us now!'

Silence rang in the room, broken only by the creak of timbers, the incessant pounding of waves upon the hull. Mister Kindly yawned and licked his paw.

'Furian, then,' Arkades sighed.

'Aye,' Leona nodded. 'And the Crow beside him.'

Executus leaned forward, shaking his head. 'Mi Dona—'

'Unless the next words to leave your mouth are "that's a splendid notion, Mi Dona, and by the by, your hair is looking magnificent", I do not wish to hear them, Arkades.'

Executus scratched his beard, tried unsuccessfully to hide his smile.

'Ah, he can still laugh,' Leona preened. 'I thought perhaps you'd forgot how.'

'All due respec—'

'She is the Saviour of Stormwatch,' Leona sighed.

'That silkling almost cracked her fucking skull open!'

'Language!' Magistrae scowled.

Arkades mumbled apology as Leona continued.

'She was bested in Messala's palazzo, aye, but the common folk don't know that. The citizenry will expect to see her draw steel under our banner. Four Daughters, Arkades, she butchered a retchwyrm almost single-handed. You yourself declared the match against the silkling unbalanced. Crow won a laurel for this collegium, and did honour to my name in front of the entire arena. She deserves *some* credit, surely?'

The big man hung silent a moment, finally gave a grudging nod.

'She can't lift a shield to save herself. But her Caravaggio was . . . passable.'

'Such praise,' Magistrae sighed. 'Pray, don't let the girl hear you sing like that, she'll never get her head through the door.'

Leona and Arkades shared a smile as the older woman began a new braid.

'So,' the big man finally sighed. 'Furian and the Crow. Who shall be our third?'

Leona pouted, tapping her lip.

'. . . Butcher?'

'He plays badly with others.'

'Wavewaker?'

'He's a fine blade, but I fear he's too much the brawler.'

'If you'll permit me an opinion, Domina?' said Magistrae.

'O, aye, here's a turn,' Arkades sighed. 'Advice from the nurse. And who shall we seek counsel of next? The cabin boy?'

Leona shot him a withering glance. 'Speak, Magistrae.'

The old woman raised one greying eyebrow at Arkades before continuing. 'Granted, I am no expert. But the Crow's strength seems to lie in her speed. It seems you need someone to bridge the gap between her pace and Furian's brawn.'

Leona and Arkades looked at each other, spoke as one.

'*Bladesinger.*'

Arkades leaned back in his chair, staring into space.

'She has the reach Crow lacks, the speed Furian needs. It could work.'

Leona leaned forward, squeezed his hand.

'It *must* work,' she replied.

Arkades looked down at her hand in his. Her skin was pale, her fingers tapered and delicate, soft as silk. His hand was browned by the suns, cracked like old leather, callused from sword grips and the press of life on the sands.

He swallowed thickly. Pausing, as if gathering his nerve. And wrapping her hand in his own, he leaned down and placed a soft kiss on her knuckles.

'It *will* work, Mi Dona,' he murmured. 'I vow it.'

Leona blinked, hand trapped at Arkades's lips, uncertain where to look. Magistrae simply looked aghast. But without giving his dona a chance to respond, Arkades released his mistress and stood, took up his cane, and limped towards the door. Stopping at the threshold, he turned towards Leona.

'Your hair *is* looking magnificent, by the by.'

Executus turned on his heel and left the room.

'**N**o!' The practice blade slammed into Mia's side, sending her to her knees. Bladesinger lunged with a fierce cry, but Arkades was already twisting aside, bringing his second blade down on the woman's forearm. She stumbled back into Furian, and a second thrust from Arkades sent the pair of them sprawling.

The trio lay panting in the dirt, drenched to the bones in sweat.

'You listen, but you do not hear!' the executus bellowed, limping back and forth between them. 'The Exile is unlike any foe you have faced. Six blades wielded with a single purpose. Eight eyes to track your every move. I have but a pair of each and you cannot best me. How in the name of the Four fucking Daughters do you hope to stand the victors against her?'

They had been drilling all turn, every turn since they'd arrived back at Crow's Nest. The other gladiatii trained around them, but in truth, all eyes were on the four in the circle, watching Arkades kick his opponents' arses up and down the sand. The two suns hung heavy in the sky, blistering with all the heat of summersdeep, burning gold and bloody red. And if one looked hard enough, a subtle hint of brighter blue could be seen on the horizon, heralding the slow arrival of the third eye of Aa.

Truelight was approaching, and with it, the *magni*. And the Falcons of Remus Collegium were only a little closer to those sands than they'd been three months ago.

'Get up,' Arkades barked. 'Move with resolve and strike as one.'

'A difficult task,' Bladesinger growled, 'when two of us attack at cross-purpose.'

Mia wiped the sweat from her brow, glowered across the sand at Furian. The Unfallen stared back at her, black eyes gleaming like obsidian. He dragged himself to his feet and offered his hand to Bladesinger, pulling her up from the dust. Ignoring Mia completely, he gathered his sword and shield and took up a ready stance.

Mia stood, practice blades in hand.

'Attack!' roared Executus.

Without waiting for the others, Furian launched his assault on Arkades, battering him back across the sands. In practice, Executus had always held his own, teaching his sparring partners their weaknesses without seeking to punish them. But over the last few turns, Mia began to realize how much the former champion had held himself back. Arkades was a god on the sand – even with his missing leg, he moved like water, struck like thunder, stood like a mountain. His blows left the air bruised behind them, his guard knew no flaw, and he punished every mistake with a blow close to bone-breaking.

Battering Furian's attack aside, Arkades smashed the champion onto his backside and turned on Bladesinger and Mia. The pair moved well together, Mia weaving below the taller woman's blows and striking at Arkades's belly and legs. She landed a passing blow to his gut, but as she twisted aside from the Red Lion's riposte, she crashed right into a charging Furian, who'd dragged himself to his feet and thrown himself back into the fray.

'Watch your fucki—'

A wooden blade cracked across Mia's temple, sent her flying. Arkades disarmed Bladesinger and locked up Furian's guard, toppling the man with an elbow to the jaw. Rolling across the sand to scoop up her weapons, saltlocks flying, Bladesinger cursed as Arkades hurled both his weapons and struck her in the throat and above the heart.

He stood, empty-handed, chest heaving as he glared at the vanquished trio.

'Pitiful,' he spat.

'That stupid bitch got in my way,' Furian growled.

'O, Furian,' Mia sighed, fixing him with a withering stare. 'If I've learned anything in this life, it's how not to care when a dog calls me bitch.'

'Dog, am I?' Furian rose out of the dust, Mia standing just as swift.

'Enough!' Arkades barked.

The pair hung still, eyes locked and poised to strike. Mia could feel her shadow straining at its edges, like water behind a dam. If she weren't holding it in check, she knew without a doubt it would be reaching across the sand towards Furian's own, hands twisted to claws. Her teeth were gritted, and she fought for calm, blinking the sweat from her eyes. For her to lose her grip here, for everyone to mark her for what she was . . .

'Enough sparring for one turn,' the executus declared. 'Crow, Bladesinger, go work the woodman. You must strike harder if you're to break the silkling's guard. Furian, attend your footwork. You need better pace to best this foe.'

Mia and Furian glared at each other, not moving a muscle.

'Move!' Arkades roared.

Bladesinger gathered up her fallen swords and marched across the yard, began furiously battering the training dummies. Mia followed slower, narrowed eyes still aimed at Furian, feeling cold hate burn along with the sickness and hunger she felt in her belly whenever he was near.

Pigheaded fucking idiot . . .

Taking up position beside Bladesinger, Mia pictured Furian's head atop her woodman, started beating it mercilessly. Sweat soaked her skin, bangs hanging in her eyes as she smashed her blade into its belly, chest, shit-eating face.

'You're going to get me killed,' Bladesinger muttered, shaking her head.

'It's Furian sowing discord, not I.'

'It's the pair of you,' the woman spat. 'I don't know why you don't just find a nice dark corner to fuck in and get it over with.'

Mia scoffed. 'I'd rather have Butcher slip his cock into me.'

'Then what lies between you two?' Bladesinger paused to bind her floor-length saltlocks up. 'Your tongues spit venom but your eyes never stray far from the other.'

Mia knew the woman spoke truth. She'd have bested that silkling if not for Furian's interference. Instead she'd taken a public beating and Leona had lost all chance at patronage among the Stormwatch marrowborn. And yet . . .

She couldn't deny it. Despite her tangle of feelings for Ashlinn, she was *drawn* to Furian. And though the Unfallen was doubtlessly attractive, this was something beyond desire. Something bone-deep. The same thing she'd felt when Lord Cassius was near her. Something beyond lust and more like . . . longing. Like an amputee for her missing limb. Like a puzzle, searching for a piece of itself.

But why?

Cleo had spoken of it in her journal. Walking the earth, being drawn to other darkin as a spider to a fly, and then . . .

. . . then eating them.

But what the 'byss did that mean?

'*The many were one. And will be again; one beneath the three, to raise the four, free the first, blind the second and the third.*

'*O, Mother, blackest Mother, what have I become?*'

Mia shook her head, spat into the dust.

'I've no fucking clue,' she said.

'Well, you'd best ponder on it, and fashion a solution,' Bladesinger warned. 'Because if we step into a contest for our lives the way we are now? All three of us will be sitting by the Hearth before truelight, little Crow.'

The woman began beating the strawman again, eyes narrowed. Mia stared at Furian across the yard, her belly tangled in hateful knots.

'There's no reasoning with him. I've tried before. He's an ignorant fool.'

Crack! went Bladesinger's sword against her target.

'Furian is many things,' she grunted. 'Stubborn, perhaps. Arrogant, most definitely. But never a fool.'

'Bollocks.' Mia struck her woodman's neck. 'Have you ever tried talking to him?'

'O, aye,' Bladesinger nodded. 'Like bashing your head against a stone wall. Honour.' *Crack!* 'Discipline.' *Crack!* 'Faith. These are the principles that define him. But above all, the Unfallen is a champion, and you are a threat to that.' The woman shrugged. 'The greatest gulf between people is always pride, little Crow.'

Mia sighed, glanced over at Furian.

'That sounds suspiciously like wisdom to me.'

Crack! went Bladesinger's sword against her target.

'Not mine,' she grunted. 'It's from the Book of the Blind.'

Mia stabbed at her woodman's chest. 'Isn't that old Liisian scripture?'

'Aye,' Bladesinger nodded. 'I know it by heart. We had to read holy texts from all over the Republic.' *Crack! Crack!* 'The suffi at Farrow like you to have a worldly perspective before you're inducted into the order. Know the world, know yourself.'

Mia tilted her head, looked sidelong at her comrade. It made sense now. The full-body tattoos. The singing she occasionally heard under Bladesinger's door.

'. . . You were a priestess?'

'Just a novice.' *Crack!* 'Never got to take my final vows.'

'Then what the 'byss – *Crack! Crack!* – 'are you doing here?'

Bladesinger shrugged. 'Pirate raid. A quick sale. A common tale.'

Mia shook her head, sickened. 'Too fucking common.'

'The suffi named it so' – *Crack!* – 'when I was born.'

Mia bent double, hands to her knees as she panted.

Black Mother, this heat . . .

'Named it so?'

Bladesinger stopped drubbing the woodman, wiped the sweat from her brow. 'Do you know how Dweymeri are named, little Crow?'

Mia nodded, remembering Tric's tale to her in the Quiet Mountain.

'You're taken to Farrow when you're young,' she replied. 'To the Temple of Trelene. The suffi holds you up to the ocean and asks the Mother about the path before you, and gives you a name to match it.'

'Bladesinger, she named me,' the woman said. 'Not Hymnsinger. Not Prayersinger. *Blade*singer. And I'll be damned,' she said, pointing her practice sword at Mia's face, 'if the last my blades sing is because you and Furian can't agree on the colour of shit. Fuck him. Stab him. Stab him while you fuck him, I don't give a damn. But get it sorted before you get us all killed.'

Mia looked across to Furian, speed training in one corner of the yard. As Mia stared, he glanced up, meeting her eyes with that burning black gaze.

The greatest gulf between people is always pride.

'You two!' Arkades roared. 'Back to work!'

Mia sighed. But as always, she obeyed.

I suspected I'd be seeing you, witch,' Furian said.

Mia looked up and down the hallway, just to be safe. Mister Kindly was trailing the guard patrol – there was no chance they might catch her. But without her passenger, her belly was a tangle of hunger and trepidation, made all the worse by the presence of the man she'd come to see. She tucked her stolen forks/lockpicks into her loincloth and stood expectantly on the threshold of the Unfallen's room.

Waiting.

Wait

ing

'Can I fucking come in or not?' Mia finally snarled.

'If it please you,' Furian said with a sour look. 'Though if the breath were mine, I'd not trouble myself in the wasting of it.'

Mia scowled and stepped inside, closing the door behind. Looking around the room, she saw it was the same as when she'd last visited – the shrine to Tsana, the crude trinity of Aa scribed on the wall.

Furian was at least dressed this time, though within these walls, that didn't count for much. His torso was bared, rippling with muscle, his skin bronzed from working beneath the suns. He was a golden god, fresh from the forge. And he was an intolerable prick, spat from the depths of the abyss.

She hated him. She wanted him. Neither and both at the same time.

Mia looked to her shadow, saw it drifting like smoke across the wall, reaching out with translucent hands towards Furian's own. The Unfallen's shadow trembled in response, but with visible effort, he held it in check, glowering at Mia with those bottomless black eyes.

'Take hold of yourself,' he growled.

Mia clenched her jaw, pulled her shadow into check. It retreated reluctantly, hair blowing as if in a breeze, hand stretched out like a lover saying farewell. She thought of Ashlinn, then. A pang of momentary, inexplicable guilt. Wanting two people, and wanting neither, promises made to none. But in comparison to Furian, a traitor and her honeyed lips and her poison tongue seemed a downright simple proposition . . .

'What do you want, witch?' the Unfallen asked.

'I'm no more a witch than you are, Furian.'

'I hold no truck with the darkness,' he spat. 'I do not step between the shadows and sneak about our domina's house like a thief.'

'No, you just threaten to bring the walls down about her ears, you dozy shit.'

'You dare . . . ?'

'O, I dare,' Mia replied. 'That's the difference between me and most.'

'I fight for the glory of this collegium. The glory of our domina.'

'You cost our domina her patronage at Stormwatch!' Mia hissed. 'All you needed to do was keep your cock in your loincloth and let me drub the silkling, and Leona would have been up to her tits in gold.'

'You werked the darkness in your match against the Exile,' Furian said, folding his arms. 'If I'd allowed you to win at Messala's palazzo with your devilry, you'd have set a taint at the heart of this place. I'd starve before I ate food bought with dishonest coin, and die before I claimed a laurel I'd not earned.'

'Didn't earn?' Mia was incredulous. 'Fuck *you*, you arrogant prick. How many retchwyrms have you slaughtered lately?'

'A victory without honour is no victory at all,' he replied. 'I'll not allow you to win more false accolades for this collegium with your witchery.'

'So you use the same witchery to fuck with me?' Mia caught herself raising her voice, tried to pull her temper into check. '*You* called the dark when you stopped me besting the silkling. That doesn't strike you as the least bit hypocritical?'

Furian stalked towards her, fists clenched.

'Get out of here, Crow.'

His shadow flared, slithering across the wall towards her own. Mia's shadow rose to meet it, twisting and rearing up like a serpent, hands twisted into claws. She swore the room turned chill, hackles rising on the back of her neck, hunger flaring in her belly and threatening to swallow her whole . . .

'No.'

She closed her eyes, shook her head. Forcing the darkness back inside herself. This wasn't going the way she'd planned it. She was meant to be holding her temper, speaking sense. She didn't know what Furian's presence was doing to her, why he made her so eager for violence, what any of it meant. All she knew was . . .

'We must come to accord,' she said, opening her eyes, palms out in supplication. 'Furian, listen to me, if we fight together on the sands as we are now, you, Bladesinger and I will all be butchered. How will that avail our domina?'

'You may hold yourself of no account without witchery to aid you, girl,' the man said, thumping his chest. 'But I am the Unfallen. I fought for almost an hour in the burning suns at Talia, slew two dozen men to win my laur—'

'Ishkah isn't a fucking man! You saw her fight at Messala's palazzo. With two blades in her hands she'd be a match for any one of us. With six? Fighting to the death? She'll cut us to bloody pieces!'

'How is it you live with yourself?' The Unfallen shook his head. 'No faith in the Father or his Daughters, no faith in yourself? Only shadows and darkness and deceit.'

'Don't make the mistake of thinking you know me, Furian.' She glanced at his trembling shadow and shook her head. 'You don't even know yourself.'

'Get out.'

'Expecting another guest, are you?' Mia glanced to his bed.

Furian's eyes widened at that, rage darkening his brow. He raised his hand to shove her backwards, and Mia moved, batting his hand aside and locking up his arm. He seized her wrist, slammed her back against the door, the pair snarling and cursing as they struggled. This close, Mia could smell his fresh sweat, feel the warmth of his skin pressed against hers, rage and lust and hunger all intertwined. Through his loincloth she could feel the heat of his cock, hardening against her hip. She wanted to kiss him, bite him, hold him, choke him, fuck him, kill him, teeth bared in a snarl, heart hammering in her chest, his lips just an inch from—

'Merciful Aa . . .' Furian breathed.

She followed his eyeline to their shadows on the wall, breath catching in her throat. The shadows were tangled like serpents, twisting and writhing and curling like smoke. They'd lost their shapes utterly, two amorphous slivers of blackness, each entwined in the other. Mia realized they were twice as dark as they should have been, just as when Mister Kindly or Eclipse rode with her. The room was noticeably colder, her skin prickling with goosebumps, desire making her tremble.

Furian pushed her back, stepped away, horror on his face. Their shadows continued to tie themselves in knots, and the man held up three fingers – Aa's warding sign against evil. Like locks of knotted hair, the shadows slowly tore themselves apart, resuming their human shapes. They clung to one another, arms, hands, then fingertips, Furian's shadow snapping into place as he backed farther away. Mia's shadow ebbed and pulsed on the wall, like the ocean in a swell.

'What are we?' she breathed.

Furian's chest was heaving, his long dark hair moving as if of its own accord. He snatched it up, tied it in a knot behind his head, snarling.

'We are nothing, you and I.'

'We're the *same*. This is who we *are*, Furian.'

'*That*,' Furian spat, pointing to the trinity on the wall, 'is who I am. A faithful, god-fearing son of Aa. Bathed in his light and taught by his scripture. *That*,' he said, pointing to the wooden swords, 'is who I am. Gladiatii. Undefeated. Unbroken. Unfallen. And so I would remain, if a thousand silklings stood between me and the *magni*.'

'So the *magni* is all that matters? If freedom is so important to y—'

'This is not about *freedom*,' he spat. 'And that is just one more difference between you and me. Being gladiatii is a masque you wear. For me, the sand, the crowd, the glory, it is a reason to wake. A reason to breathe.'

Furian marched across the room, and listening briefly at the door, he opened it. He glared at Mia, seemingly unwilling to touch her again.

'Get out of here, Crow.'

She'd not convinced him. Not even come close. His stupid pride. His idiotic sense of honour. His fear of who and what he was. She didn't understand any of it. And though they were both darkin, in truth, Mia realized they were completely different people. That whatever kinship they might know in the shadows, this here, this life, this flesh, they were as alike as truelight and truedark.

If you can't see your chains, what use is a key?

And so, with a sigh, she stepped beyond the threshold of his room, into the corridor beyond.

'What made you so?' she asked softly. 'What were you before this?'

'Exactly what you will be when the *magni* is done, girl.'

Furian shut the door in her face with a parting jab.

'Nothing.'

Chapter 21

Please

'Well, well,' Sidonius said. 'Look what the shadowcat dragged in.'

Mia crouched on the cell floor, still dizzy from her Stepping. The barracks were almost pitch black, the quiet broken only by the soft snoring and fitful murmurs of the gladiatii around them. Sidonius lay on his side in the straw, eyes open only a sliver. Mister Kindly had warned Mia that the man was awake, but he knew her secret anyway. Well, *some* of her secrets . . .

No sense in hiding what he already knew.

'You pinch me some grub, or what?' Sid asked.

Mia smiled, tossed the man a hunk of cheese she'd stolen from the kitchen. He grinned, tearing off a bite and speaking around his mouthful. 'Sneakier than a fart in Church, you are.'

'Were you waiting up for me? Awfully sweet of you.'

'No, in fact I'll have you know you interrupted a lovely dream involving me, the magistrae, a riding crop, and a featherdown bed.'

'The magistrae?' Mia raised her eyebrow.

'I've a penchant for older women, little Crow.'

'You've a penchant for anything with two tits, a hole, and heartbeat, Sid.'

'Ha! You know me well.' The big man grinned, raising his cheese in toast. 'But, Four Daughters, I do like your style.'

'A pity Furian can't say the same.'

'Ah, that's where you were. How's he hung? A man swaggers around with that much bravado, he's usually compensating for the peanut in his britches.'

Mia remembered the feel of Furian's cock against her hip, pressed her thighs together to heighten the ache. She was feeling edgy after her encounter with the Unfallen. Restless and overflowing. Trying to ignore all of it and think clear.

'I wasn't bedding him, Sid,' she scowled. 'I was trying to convince him not to get me fucking murdered.'

'Well, speaking as a former world traveller, you'd be surprised how far a quick wristjob will go towards mending strained foreign relations.'

Mia kicked the straw at her cellmate and grinned despite herself. 'You're a pig.'

'As I say, you know me well, little Crow.'

'If Furian and I don't learn to fight together, that silkling is going to be using my lower intestines to make her sausages.'

'She that fearsome?'

'I'm not afraid of her, no. But she's the best I've ever seen with a blade.'

'O, aye? And how many others have you seen with a blade?'

'My fair share.'

'Mmf,' Sid grunted, leaning against the wall and looking Mia up and down. 'Secrets within secrets with you. Not eighteen years old, I'd wager. Skinny slip of a thing, and better with a sword than I am. But you do realize there's always an alternative to becoming a silkling's suppertime, don't you?'

'And what's that?' Mia sighed. 'Murder Furian in his sleep and hope Leona pairs me and Bladesinger with someone who's not an insufferable cockhead?'

Sidonius lifted his hands and made the motion of flapping wings.

'Fly awayyyyy, little Crow.'

'Not an option.'

Sid scoffed. 'You step in and out of this cell more often than a fourteen-year-old boy spanks his chaplain. You can leave this place anytime you choose. So if Champion Cockhead is going to get you stone-cold murdered, why don't you just escape?'

Mia sighed. 'If I did, every one of you would be executed.'

'Bollocks,' Sid said. 'I watch you, Crow. I watch you watching *us*. Arkades. Leona. Furian. Me. Those little wheels behind those shady eyes always aturn. And though I don't think you're quite the coldest fish in this pond, you can't honestly say you give a damn whether any of us lives or dies. Especially when we're all likely to perish in the *venatus* anyways. So what's your game?'

'Believe me, Sidonius,' Mia replied. 'The last thing I'm doing here is playing.'

'Have it your way, then.' Sid took another bite of cheese, shook his head, wistful. 'I tell you true, you remind me of a woman I used to know. It's bloody uncanny. Same eyes as you. Same skin. Secrets within secrets on her, too.'

'Some old flame? Break your heart, did she?'

'Neh,' Sid shook his head. 'I never loved her. But most men who knew her did. She almost brought the Republic to its knees. But in the end, she and her shady eyes and her secrets within secrets got her whole familia killed. Husband. Young daughter. Baby son. And a lot of my friends besides.'

Mia's stomach turned cold. Eyes narrowing.

'Who are you talking about?'

'Former dona of this house, of course,' Sid said, gesturing to the walls. 'Wife of the true justicus. Alinne Corvere.' He shook his head. 'Stupid fucking whore.'

Afterwards, Mia couldn't remember moving. All she could recall was the satisfying crunch as her fist landed on Sidonius's jaw, the sharp crack as his head bounced off the wall behind him. The big man cursed, tried to batter her away as she clawed at his throat, punching his cheek, his temple, his nose.

'Have you lost your—'

'Take it back,' she spat.

'Get off me!'

Mia and Sidonius fell to struggling, the bigger man wrestling her onto the floor as her knuckles played a tune on his face. *'Take it back!'* she roared, the pair rolling about in the straw, flailing and punching. A few other gladiatii woke up at the commotion, Bladesinger peering out from the slit in her cell door, Otho and Felix cheering as they realized a brawl had erupted, straining at their cell bars for a better look.

'Shut the fuck up in there!' Butcher bellowed from the cell across the way.

'Peace, Crow!' Sidonius cried.

'. . . *mia, stop this* . . .'

'Take it back!'

'Take *what* back?'

Sidonius cracked Mia across the jaw, Mia punched him in the throat. Choking, the big man grabbed a fistful of Mia's hair and slammed her head into the bars, ringing all the world like a gong. Lashing out blind, stars in her eyes, she landed a brutal kick to his bollocks. Both gladiatii fell to the stone floor, gasping, bleeding, the cut on Mia's brow from her silkling brawl split anew, Sid groaning and clutching his jewels.

'*. . . mia, stop, arkades will hear . . . !*'

Mister Kindly's whisper cut through the red haze in her head, dragged her to her senses. The not-cat spoke truth – if they kept brawling, Executus would surely hear the commotion, and they'd likely be flogged. She aimed one last kick at Sidonius, who rolled away across the floor with a curse. The big man dragged himself into a corner like a whipped dog, Mia into the opposite, the pair gasping and glaring at each other across the bloodstained stone.

'What th-the 'byss . . . was that?' Sid managed, his voice almost an octave higher.

Mia dragged bloody knuckles across her bloody nose.

'*Nobody* talks that way about her.'

'About wh—'

Sidonius blinked. Ice-blue eyes narrowing as he looked across the cell to the girl panting and wheezing in the corner. Dragging her long dark hair away from her dark eyes – the eyes that reminded him of . . .

'Can't be . . .' he breathed.

Sidonius looked to the walls around him. Back to the girl. Mia could see the slow puzzle of it, the impossible maths, all of it falling into an insane kind of place in his eyes. This girl who wouldn't escape these walls, despite being able to leave whenever she chose. This girl who seemed determined to fight in the most vicious contest yet devised in Republic history, just to attain a freedom she could have anytime she chose. So, if it wasn't about the freedom . . .

'The Crow,' he breathed. 'And here we sit, in Crow's Nest.'

. . . it must be about the winning.

'You're . . . You're their . . . ?'

She felt it welling up inside her. Behind the pain of Sid's beating, the pulse throbbing in her head and spilling blood into her eyes. The weight of it. Being surrounded every turn by reminders of who she'd been, what might have become, all that had been taken from her. The frustration and hunger she felt around Furian, the confusion and desire she felt around Ashlinn, the sheer magnitude of the task before her. She didn't feel fear in the face of it all, no, the thing in her shadow wouldn't allow that. But she did feel sorrow. Regret, for all that was and might have been.

And just for a second, just for a moment, the weight of it felt too much.

The other gladiatii had realized the show was over, shuffled back to their places in the straw. Mia sat hunched, hugging her scuffed knees, glaring at Sidonius through her ragged fringe. Lip trembling. Eyes burning in the dark.

'Take it *back*,' she whispered, tears welling in her lashes.

'Peace, Crow,' the man murmured, swabbing his bleeding lip. 'If offence was given, I beg pardon. I didn't . . . I *couldn't* . . .'

He stared at her bewildered, once more glancing at the walls around them. Red stone, iron bars, rusty chains. None could hold her. And yet, here she still was . . .

'Four Daughters, I'm sorry . . .'

Mia sat there in the dark, feeling his eyes, feeling his pity, crawling like lice on her skin. She couldn't stand it, the weakness she'd shown, the sorrow in Sid's gaze, dragging her bleeding knuckles across her eyes and feeling her temper swell once more. Feeling angry felt better – far better than feeling sorry for herself. The adrenaline from her brawl tingled in her fingertips, left her legs shaking. She wanted to run, wanted to fight, wanted to close her eyes and still the tempest inside her head, for time to stand still for just one second.

Is that what she wanted?

What do *you want?*

It had been stupid to let it slip. To let her rage get the better of her, let Sid guess who she was. But had it been a mistake?

He'd known her father. Served him loyally. Still revered him, after all these years.

Maybe she'd *wanted* him to know?

Maybe she wanted to know someone who knew them too? Who understood a fraction of what being here must be like.

The future loomed before her, the empty sands of Godsgrave arena. All the blood that awaited her, all the blood behind her. Every moment of her life had led her to this path, this vengeance, this unbending, unbranching road.

But what did she want, besides revenge?

It was still hours until nevernight's end.

She didn't want to sleep.

She didn't want to dream.

She didn't want to lay her head down in this place that had been her home, and now served only as a fading reminder of all that could have been.

So what do you want?

'Crow?'

She looked up at Sid, quietly bleeding in his corner.

'Blessed Aa, I'm sorry, girl,' he said.

She didn't want him looking at her, that much was certain. And as he rose from his straw and sat down beside her, wrapping one of those big, ham-hock arms around her shoulder, she realized the last thing on earth she wanted was him consoling her. She didn't want pity. She didn't want to fall into some lump's clumsy, slightly uncomfortable hug and cry like some frightened child. That time was long behind her. Dead and buried like her familia. She was a Blade of the Red Church now. Not weak and fragile glass. She was steel.

But she didn't want to be alone, either.

She thought of her time as an acolyte. The forgetting and solace she'd found in Tric's arms. But he was dead and buried too, now. An empty tomb in a hollow hall, carved with the only memoriam he'd ever know. She'd told Shahiid Aalea that she missed him, and there was truth in that. But more, she realized she missed the clarity of it; the simple joy of wanting and being wanted in kind. The lingering ache from her visit with Furian wasn't helping any.

The brightest flames burn out the fastest, Aalea had told her. *But in them, there is warmth that can last a lifetime. Even from a love that only lasts the nevernight. For people like us, there are no promises of for ever.*

Looking up into Sidonius's eyes, she finally realized what she wanted.

Not for ever, perhaps.

But for now.

'. . . Why're you looking at me like that?' the big Itreyan asked.

And without a word

she looked over his shoulder

to the shadow in the stairwell

and disappeared right out of his arms.

Sounds of the harbour. Soldiers calling 'all's well' as they patrolled the nevernight streets. The wind blowing in off the ocean into Crow's Rest was blessedly cool, Mia shivering after the dank heat of the barracks. Her hand hovered above the window glass, just shy of knocking.

'. . . *this is unwise* . . .'

'Go back to the keep,' Mia whispered. 'And tell Eclipse to watch the street.'

'. . . *mia, i—* . . .'

'Go.'

Without a sound, the not-cat left her, her shadow growing thin and pale. As soon as Mister Kindly departed, she felt it, sneaking and creeping inside her belly – the fear she'd have *always* felt without him beside her. Fear of being here. Fear of what it meant, or where it could lead. Fear of who and what she was. And before it could sink its cold claws too far into her skin, she knocked, once, twice, knuckles striking sharp upon the glass.

No sound from the room inside. Mia felt a deepening dread, thinking perhaps she wasn't in there, that she'd stolen away after their argument, betrayed her and left her behind, proved that all the mistrust and sus—

The window opened. Ashlinn Järnheim stood beyond the sill, pillow-mussed and befuddled by sleep. Her eyes were the blue of sunburned skies.

'Mia?' the girl asked, stifling a yawn. 'What time is it?'

Those blue eyes widened as she saw the scrapes on Mia's knuckles, the split above her bruised eye, the bruise at her jaw.

'Black Mother, what happened to . . . ?'

The question trailed off as Mia reached out, pressed a finger to Ash's lips. They hung there a moment; two girls, barely touching, all the world around them holding its breath. The confusion in Ashlinn's eyes began to melt as Mia moved her finger, gentle as feathers. She traced the smooth bow of Ashlinn's upper lip, the plump softness of her lower, slow and soft. The arc of her cheek, the line of her jaw, Ash's breath coming quicker as she came fully awake, aware, awonder, the skin on her bare arms prickling. And as she parted her lips to speak, perhaps to protest, Mia leaned in and silenced her with a kiss.

She'd not kissed a girl before. At least, not like this. The kiss between them in the Mountain had been of farewell – lingering perhaps, but still a goodbye. This kiss was an invitation; a gentle, desperate plea for a beginning, not an ending. A question without words, Mia's mouth open and melting against Ashlinn's own. And as she felt Ashlinn shiver, the feather-light brush of her tongue in kind, Mia had her answer.

She climbed in through the window, their lips never parting. Arms entwined, hands exploring, Mia breaking the kiss only long enough to drag Ashlinn's nightshirt up over her head. She was naked beneath, stripped gloriously bare with a single gesture. Mia paused a moment to drink in the sight; the sunslight caressing the line of her throat, the swell of her curves, the shadow between her legs.

'Mia, I . . .'

Mia sank back, pressing her mouth to Ashlinn's neck. The girl's chest was heaving, her cheeks flushed, whispering soft nothings and letting her head drift back as Mia sank lower, down to her breast, teasing one pebble-hard nipple with her tongue.

The pair collapsed onto the bed, Ash's hands tearing at the bindings about Mia's chest, her hips, groaning as Mia's teeth nipped at her neck. Any questions she might have had were drowned now, breath coming too quick to speak, lips parted as she crushed Mia to her, skin on skin, every sweet secret at her fingertips. Down her ribs, over the swell of her hips to the curve of her arse as Mia wrapped one leg about her, dragging her in closer.

Mia felt Ash's fingers brushing the inside of her thigh, an arkemical thrill sizzling up her spine and sparking in the dark behind her eyes. Her own hand quested lower, down across Ash's taut belly to the downy blonde between her legs. Their hands found their marks at the same time, their kiss deepening, their sighs smothered. Mia's back arched as she felt Ashlinn drawing tight, firm circles on her with clever fingers. She kneaded a breast with her free hand, the other setting to work between Ashlinn's legs, mimicking her slow, agonizing rhythm and listening to her moan in time.

It was like nothing she'd ever known. Jolting current and sweet softness and kisses, endless, paralyzing kisses that filled her with a warmth all the way to her fingertips. Time stood still, nothing but teasing tongues and breathless sighs, a heat building between her legs, setting her whole body aflame.

'O, Goddess, yes,' Mia whispered.

'Don't stop,' Ashlinn pleaded.

Her lips were honey, warm and soft, her body writhing as Mia's fingers rolled back and forth across her swollen bud. She was so hot down there, slick and shivering, the hunger in Mia rising until she could stand it no more.

'I want to taste you,' she breathed, nuzzling Ashlinn's neck.

'O, yes . . . yes . . .'

Descending, slow as melting ice. Running her tongue down the line of Ashlinn's throat, smiling as the girl's back arched, toes curled. Down to the swell of her breasts, Mia took one in her mouth, licking, suckling, her hand still strumming between Ashlinn's thighs. A thirst was burning inside her, desert-dry, and Mia could think of only one way to sate it. Dragging her like some sweet, dark gravity. Down.

Always down.

Ash was splayed on the mattress, groaning as Mia continued her descent, long, languid kisses running over her ribs, her belly. Mia paused, tracing slow, burning circles around her navel with the tip of her tongue, fingernails tracing gentle lines across Ashlinn's skin. Inhaling a soft hint of lavender and the dizzying scent of Ash's desire.

'Please, Mia,' the girl breathed.

Down, down to the smooth length of Ashlinn's parted legs, running her tongue closer to that intoxicating heat. There was a small dark mole at the divot of Ash's thigh and her sex, and Mia licked it slow, smiling dark.

'Please, what?' she whispered.

'*Please*, Mia . . .'

She pursed her lips, blew softly on her mark as Ashlinn shivered. She'd been tasted before, but never done the tasting, anticipation curling in her belly and making her tremble. She wanted to take her time, to savour every second, the thrill of it all, but Ash snarled her fingers in Mia's hair, and with a shivering gasp, dragged her in.

Silken softness, drenched with lust, parting under the press of her kiss. Mia moved slow, running her tongue through Ashlinn's folds, flickering in and out. Ashlinn mewled and sighed, hips grinding in time, the hands in Mia's hair pulling her in tighter. Mia found herself consumed by it, thirsty, starving; the taste of her, the flood of warm nectar across her tongue. Delighting in Ashlinn's moans as she pinched her swollen nipples, ran her hands down the girl's breasts, clawed her arse.

Ashlinn lost herself as Mia went to work in earnest, eyes rolling back in her head, half hanging off the bed as she urged Mia on, *Don't stop, don't stop*. Mia had never felt so much power; her every movement, every flick of her tongue or touch of her lips eliciting a groan, a whispered plea, a tremor running the length of Ashlinn's entire body.

Time lost all meaning, each second a year, each year a heartbeat, the heat building between them, dragging Ash ever higher, hotter, brighter, her moans growing louder, longer, until she went tense as a bowstring, spine arching, thighs clamped either side of Mia's head, every muscle taut and straining as she pointed her toes skywards and screamed as if the world were ending.

Ash's whole body went limp in the breathless aftermath, Mia tracing light circles, still savouring her taste, the power of her little triumph. She grinned as she sank her tongue deeper into Ash's petals, making her groan, 'Enough, Goddess, enough,' relenting as the girl gently pulled her up. Ash enfolded Mia in her arms, their bodies melding into one, slender legs wrapped around Mia's waist as they sank into another long, hungry kiss. Ash's taste mingled upon their tongues, and Mia found herself drowning in it, eyelashes fluttering against her cheeks, so right and sweet and heaped in bliss she never wanted it to end.

But then she gasped, Ashlinn smacking her arse, biting her lips, almost hard enough to draw blood.

'Ow,' Mia flinched. 'What was that for?'

'Making me beg,' Ashlinn scowled.

'O?' Mia smiled, lips brushing Ashlinn's own. 'I heard no complaints at the time.'

'Don't get a big head on me now, Corvere. That was beginner's luck.'

'O, really?'

Soft laughter turned to warm shivers as Ash nuzzled her neck.

'Really,' the girl breathed, teeth brushing her skin.

'Then . . . perhaps the dona would give the novice a demonstration?'

'Say please.'

'I— ah!'

Mia gasped as Ashlinn dragged her head back by her hair, landed another firm smack on her backside. The girl's lips drifted along Mia's throat, teeth grazing her jugular, fingernails tracing lines of fire and ice up her soaking thighs.

'Say,' Ash whispered, nipping Mia's throat, 'please.'

In her heart, Mia had never bowed to anyone. Not in the Church, not in the arena, not in the bedchamber. And though she'd delighted in the control of a moment ago, her every touch, her every move setting the girl in her arms aflame, Mia wondered if there might be a deeper joy found in some small moment of surrender.

Ash's fingers danced over her, light as the breeze. Mia's belly tightened as the girl sank lower, her tongue drawing a tightening spiral around her heaving breast.

'Say it,' the girl whispered, flicking Mia's nipple with her tongue.

Smoky light filtered through the curtain, and Mia closed her eyes as Ashlinn descended, not wanting to see or hear or speak, but only to *feel*. A waterfall of kisses, cascading down her body, Ash's hands seemingly everywhere at once. Mia found her legs parting of their own volition, the ache between them a sweet agony, her breath growing ragged, heart pounding with anticipation. A feeling like nothing she'd ever known was budding inside her – not with Tric, not with Aalea, not with Aurelius and that golden beauty, desire swelling to a burning pitch as she felt Ashlinn kneel between her legs, hot breath against her swollen lips.

'Say . . .'

A brush of the girl's tongue, impossibly light, making Mia buck and shiver.

'. . . please.'

Mia lifted her head, looking down the length of her body to Ashlinn, poised to devour her. Heart hammering, not enough breath in her lungs, dizzy. And eyes fluttering closed once more, she let her head fall back and the tension flee from her bones as she gave herself over to it utterly.

'*Please*,' Mia breathed.

A long, low moan escaped her lips as Ashlinn went to work, lips and tongue dancing in the dark. She'd no idea where the girl had learned her skills; Aalea, some new lover, some old flame. But Goddess, it was blinding. Ash was a maestro, the tune between them, older than time. The heat in her pulsed hotter with every brush of the girl's tongue, Mia barely able to breathe, bedsheet twisted in her tightening fists. She almost lost her mind when she felt Ashlinn slip a finger inside her, curling, coaxing, stoking that smouldering heat, arkemical current crackling to the tips of her toes.

'O, Goddess . . .'

Helpless before it, caught up and swept away, a hurricane of lust and longing, the heat inside her almost impossible to bear. Ashlinn was merciless, the rhythm of her tongue matched by her touch, Mia's back arching, lifting her hips high off the bed, mouth in a perfect O, fingers snarled in the red river of Ashlinn's hair and dragging her deeper, harder, more, *more*. She was shaking so hard she couldn't breathe, couldn't think, couldn't speak save to wordlessly beg an ending to it all. And as she felt Ashlinn's hand move, a second finger joining the first, Mia's hips bucked uncontrollably, black stars blooming behind her eyes, the heat inside her bursting into ravenous flame, and she lost herself, screaming soundlessly, blinded by the fire of a thousand suns.

She felt soft lips on her own, wet and darkly sweet. Mia opened her eyes and saw a girl above her, beautiful, smiling.

A girl she shouldn't trust.

A lover she shouldn't love.

She tried to find her breath, heart hammering against her ribs.

'That was . . . impressive . . .'

'That was overdue,' Ashlinn grinned.

Mia dragged her in for a kiss, their lips crushed together, the ripples of her climax still tingling in her bones. Breaking apart after a long, sweet for ever, Ashlinn flopped back on the mattress, breathing a contented sigh.

Mia climbed out of the bed, legs still shaking. Atop the drawers, she found her silver cigarillo case, lighting one with her flintbox before slipping back between the sheets. Ashlinn threw her arms around her, took her hand and kissed her wounded knuckles before snuggling closer, nuzzling her neck. Mia took a drag of the cigarillo, inhaling deep and feeling the sweet, heavy grey fill her lungs.

'You smoke a lot,' Ash murmured.

'Settles the nerves,' Mia replied.

'Make you nervous, do I?'

Mia held out her hand in answer. She was usually rock-steady, never a tremor to weaken her swordgrip. But her hands were shaking now.

'O, you're all aquiver, love,' Ash cooed. 'First times will do that to a girl, neh?'

'Let's see yours then, smart-arse.'

Ash held up her own hand, and though she tried to hide it, Mia could see she was shaking too. She could feel the girl's breast pressed against her, the heart beneath running to the same thunderous tune. Threading her fingertips through Ashlinn's own, she sensed the current crackling between them. Realizing she was still thirsty.

'Perhaps *you* should take up smoking.'

Ash made a face. 'Don't enjoy the taste, I'm afraid.'

'I can make it sweeter . . .'

Dragging deep on the cigarillo, Mia inhaled another warm lungful. And tipping up Ashlinn's chin with her fingertips, she leaned in close and kissed her, lips parted, breathing into her mouth. Her lips were sugared from the cigarillo paper, the clove-scented smoke drifting around their tongues as the kiss deepened. Ash tilted her head and sighed, pressing the length of her body against Mia's own. Mia's hands roamed her back, feeling the goosebumps rising on Ashlinn's skin, the sweet ache rising once more between her legs. Ashlinn closed her mouth, sucking on Mia's tongue before breaking the kiss.

'Not bad,' she smiled, exhaling grey. 'But I'm still not taking up smoking.'

Mia shrugged, taking another drag. Ashlinn settled in against her side again, Mia's arm around her shoulder. They lay in silence for a time, listening to the sounds of the nevernight outside. She took a good look at the girl in her arms, the slender curves, the twin divots at the base of her spine, fingers pushing the long tresses of blood-red aside and exposing . . .

. . . the inkwerk crawling across her back.

'. . . What's that?' Mia whispered.

Ashlinn tensed, sitting up and tossing her hair back over her shoulder. She'd only caught a glimpse, but Mia had seen intricate lines and shading, a hint of strange writing, the shape of a curved blade on Ash's left shoulder . . .

'One stipulation,' Solis said, holding up his finger. 'An item of import to your patron. A map, written in Old Ashkahi and set with a seal shaped like a sickle's blade.'

. . . *Goddess.*

'The map,' Mia realized. 'Duomo's map.'

'Is that why you came here?' Ash asked softly.

Mia frowned, cigarillo bobbing on her lips. 'What?'

'Eclipse is always skulking about. Maybe she caught a glimpse.' The girl fixed Mia in her blue-sky stare. 'So you figure the only way you'll get a better look is to get my clothes off? Smart play, Corvere.'

'. . . Is that what you think?'

'I don't think anything.' Ash squared her shoulders, making sure the tattoo was hidden from sight. 'That's why I'm asking.'

'Ash, I had no idea. Why do you have Duomo's map tattooed on your back?'

'Not tattooed,' she said, nodding to the double circles marked on Mia's cheek. 'It's arkemical, just like your brand.'

Mia blinked as realization struck her. 'So if they kill you . . .'

'The brand disappears. No map for them.' The girl shrugged. 'People who play with fire do better if they expect to get burned.'

A dozen questions burned in Mia's mind. What was so important about this map that Ashlinn had it indelibly branded on her skin? What did Duomo and Scaeva want with it, that they were set to move so openly against each other to obtain it? Where did it lead? Where did the girl she'd just been holding in her arms fit in with all of it?

'There's a lot about this you're not telling me, Ashlinn.'

'I could say the same for you, Mia.'

'Such as?'

Ashlinn looked deep into her eyes, swallowing hard.

'Why did you come here? Why now?'

'Because I wanted to be with you.'

'But why?'

Mia took a drag of her cigarillo, mulling it over.

'Because I was thinking. About all the things that brought me to this point. The things that made me what I am, and all the things I could've been if I'd been given a choice. And then I didn't want to think any more.'

'So that's all this was?' Ashlinn kept her face steady, her voice cool, but Mia could see the storm building in that sunburned blue. 'Just a distraction?'

'The sweetest distraction,' Mia smiled.

'No jesting,' Ashlinn said. 'You run hot and cold as a faulty bath-house, and if this was just a quick roll to fuck unpleasant thoughts away, that's fine. I'd rather that than a ruse to see the ink on my skin. But whichever it was, I need to know.'

'It was neither, Ash.'

'I know a lie when I taste it, Mia.'

Mia sighed, shook her head. She'd pondered it on the way here, stealing down through the nevernight streets. Why it hadn't been right before, why it felt right now. Her fight with Furian had left her inflamed, her fight with Sid had done nothing to sate it. But it wasn't simply that, wasn't the thought of her parents or the painful reminders of being locked up in that place or the thought of where she'd been or what was to come.

'I thought about all the things I could've been if I'd been given a choice,' she finally said. 'And I realized that mostly I've never had one. Ever since my father was killed, my feet were set upon this course. No denying it. No escape. So I wanted to choose something for myself. Something that could just be mine. *My* choice.'

Mia looked at Ash, running trembling fingertips across her cheek. 'And I chose you.'

Ashlinn simply stared, bee-stung lips parted as she breathed, and Mia found herself falling, down into a long, sweet kiss. Ashlinn surged against her, hands cupping her face, lost in the sweetness of a kiss that seemed to shiver all the way to Mia's soul. She pulled away only with reluctance, dark eyes searching Ashlinn's own.

'Do I taste like I'm lying?' she asked.

Ashlinn smiled soft, shook her head.

'No. Do I?'

Did she? Had anything changed here? Wasn't everything still the same? The question of this map – where it led, why Duomo wanted it, what it all meant – still hung between them. Ashlinn Järnheim was still a girl who'd do anything to get what she wanted. Lie, cheat, steal, kill. She had secrets. She was *dangerous*.

But was Mia so different?

The more time they spent together, the more kinship she saw with this girl she supposed she should despise.

'You taste like honey,' Mia whispered.

Ashlinn smiled, pressed her forehead to Mia's. Mia closed her eyes, listening to the sounds of the streets outside, to the cool nevernight winds, now slowly dying. She had questions. Too many questions. But the turn would soon begin, Executus would rouse them for another session of sweat and beatings and bloody Furian, and all of it – for a blessed moment forgotten in the arc of this girl's arms – came flooding back. Mia remembered who she was. What she was. Opening her eyes and sighing.

'We need to talk on this some more. But I have to get back.'

'I know,' Ashlinn said, leaning in for another brief kiss.

'I want to stay.'

'I know,' Ash breathed, nibbling her lower lip. 'Just promise to return.'

'Say please.'

Ashlinn's nibble turned into a painful bite.

'Fuck you, Corvere,' she smiled.

'Thought you'd never ask.'

'I *didn't* ask, remember?'

Grinning, she kissed Ashlinn's eyes, Ashlinn's cheek, Ashlinn's lips, steeling herself against the moment. And then she rose from the bed, *their* bed, wrapping herself in her scraps of cloth, dreading the sunslight that awaited her just beyond the curtain. But still, she pulled the fabric aside, squinting against the brightness, turning to take one last look at the beauty she was leaving behind.

Has anything changed here?

With a sigh, she climbed out into the waiting light.

Nothing would ever be the same again.

CHAPTER 22
QUIET

''Byss and blood, that's *hot*.'

Mia sighed, closing her eyes and sinking farther down into the steaming heat. The water closed over her head, sounds of the bathhouse momentarily muted, all the noise of the world falling away.

She hung there in the dark and the warmth, enjoying the sensation on her aching muscles. The last two weeks had been spent training under the blazing suns with Furian and Bladesinger, and the trio were no closer to learning to fight together as a unit. Knowing the silkling would give no quarter, Arkades was showing no mercy in the circle, and Mia ached in muscles she never even knew she had. She was black and blue all over, and growing more frustrated with Furian by the turn.

Holding her breath beneath the water, she floated weightless. She was reminded for a moment of Adonai's pools, and blood walks from the Quiet Mountain. Thinking of Solis, Drusilla and the others. The role they'd played in her familia's fall.

What were they doing right now? Helping Scaeva secure his fourth term, no doubt. Rolling in their coin like hogs at trough. But the consul, and thus the Ministry, must be growing impatient at her lack of progress recovering Duomo's map. How was Mercurio fending them off?

Not for the first time, she realized what a risk her old mentor was taking for her. Thinking of it, she found herself ashamed she'd ever thought Mercurio might betray her. She missed him, truth told. Missed his counsel, his smoker's growl, even his bastard of a temper. But soon enough, she'd be back in Godsgrave, standing on the sands of the arena. She'd see him then. And after, when the deed was done.

Presuming I don't get murdered at Whitekeep first . . .

Mia surfaced with burning lungs, shrouded in steam. Blinking the

water from her eyes, she was greeted by the sight of Wavewaker walking
into the bathhouse. The man was gleaming with sweat from his turn's
training, dusted with dirt and grime from the circle. He was singing a
duet called 'Mi Uitori' all by himself; the female's lines in falsetto, the
male's in his traditional baritone.* Stripping off his loincloth at a suit-
ably dramatic *noooooooooote*, he stepped into the bath and Mia gave
him an impromptu round of applause.

'Too kind, Mi Dona,' the big man bowed.

'Quite a set of pipes you've got on you there.'

'I studied at the feet of the best.'

'Were you *really* an actor in a theatre?' she asked, head tilted.

'Wellll,' the big man said. 'I worked in one, on the door. In happier
turns. I always wanted to stride the stage, marvelling the crowd, but . . .'
He shrugged at the walls around them. ' 'Twas not to be.'

---

*An infamous Itreyan opera commissioned by King Francisco XII (known by
his subjects as 'the Proud' in life, and 'the Wanker' in death). Francisco was an
enthusiast of musical theatre, and after his triumph during a rebellion by King
Oskar III of Vaan, he commissioned an ode to his glory. His court's premier
composer, Maximillian Omberti, toiled for over a year on the composition,
naming it 'Mi Uitori' (My Victory).

Francisco was convinced his opera was a path to everlasting fame and
popularity with his subjects. He spared no expense in assembling the production,
and fancying himself as something of a singer, decreed he would play the role
of himself at the premiere. Held at Godsgrave arena, every member of the
nobility was in attendance, along with ninety thousand citizens. To ensure the
crowd would appreciate every moment of his masterpiece, Francisco XII ordered
the arena exits locked as the overture began.

Sadly, though the opera does feature the aforementioned titular 'Mi Uitori'
in its final act – considered Omberti's finest piece, and still played centuries later
– the king had demanded the composer include *every detail* of his Vaanian triumph.
The premiere performance was over seventeen hours in length, its duration made
all the worse by Francisco's singing voice, which was described by the historian
Cornelius the Younger as 'akin to two cats fucking in a burning bag'.

The performance went on so long, two women gave birth during it, and
several hundred citizens risked broken legs and execution by leaping from the
arena's walls to the street outside. A particularly wily baron of the king's court,
one Gaspare Giancarli, faked a heart attack so that the guards would permit
his familia to remove his lifeless corpse from the premises.

Francisco was reported to be 'quite disappointed' with the opera's reception.

Omberti committed suicide shortly after the premiere.

There was no repeat performance.

She looked the man over with a critical eye as he reached for the soap. Wavewaker was a daemon on the sand, a little undisciplined perhaps, but strong as a bull. She'd wager those hands of his could encircle her throat easily, crush her skull if he squeezed hard enough, and she could no more imagine him wearing tights and mumming in some pantomime than she could imagine herself sprouting wings.

'Let me guess.' He raised an eyebrow. 'I don't strike you as the theatre type.'

'Forgive me,' she chuckled. 'But not at all.'

'You're forgiven,' Wavewaker grinned. 'My father said much the same. He raised me in the art of steel, you see. Taught me from the time I was a boy how to break men with my bare hands. He intended me to be an honourguard of the Bara, like his father before him. Called me a fool when I told him I wanted to be a thespian. The suffi hadn't named me "Stagestrider", after all. But I didn't fancy the thought of being told what I could or couldn't be. So I tried anyway. It was my dream. And one best dreamed awake.'

Mia found herself nodding, admiration budding in her chest.

'So I travelled to the City of Bridges and Bones,' Wavewaker continued, with dramatic flair. 'Found a troupe who'd take me in. A little theatre called the Sanctuary.'

'I know it!' Mia gasped, delighted. 'Down near the Nethers!'

'Aye,' Wavewaker smiled broad. 'Grand old place. I had no training, so they started me slow. I was only standing the door and cleaning up after shows at first, but it was still magikal to me. Listening to the great old dramas, watching poetry float in the air like gossamer, and scenes come alive before the crowd's wondering eyes. That's the power of words: twenty-six little letters can paint a whole universe.' Wavewaker's voice grew wistful. 'They were the happiest turns of my life.'

Mia knew she shouldn't open her mouth. Shouldn't let herself know more about the man. But still . . .

'What happened?' she heard herself asking.

Wavewaker sighed.

'Aemillia, one of our actresses. She caught the eye of some rich man's son. Paulus, his name. The dona made it clear she was uninterested in his affections, and I was forced to see him off a few times after he'd had too much goldwine, but that wasn't so unusual. It was a rough part of town. All was going well, really. The troupe was making coin, crowds were growing. I'd studied hard, and was set to play my first role in one of the productions – the Magus King in *Marcus and Messalina*, do you know it?'

'Aye,' Mia smiled.

'It was the turn of my maiden performance. But it seemed even after Aemillia's refusals and the drubbings I gave him, little Paulus wasn't used to taking no for an answer.'

'Rich men's sons often aren't,' Mia said.

'Aye. I found the bastard backstage after dress rehearsal, trying to force himself on Aemillia. Her costume torn. Her lip bloodied. You can guess the rest. Father taught me from the time I was a boy how to break men with my bare hands, after all.'

Wavewaker looked down at his sword-callused palms.

'But he was a rich man's son. It was only the testimony of my fellow players saved me from the gallows. I was sold into bondage instead, the price of my sale paid to Paulus by way of compensation for the broken hands I'd gifted him.'

'Four Daughters,' Mia breathed. 'I'm sorry.'

'Don't be sorry, love,' Wavewaker smiled. 'I'm not. State I left him in, he'll never place those hands anywhere without invitation again.'

'But this is the price you pay?' Mia waved to the stone walls, the iron bars.

'A man must accept his fate, little Crow. Or be consumed by it. As gladiatii, our lot is better than most. A chance to win our freedom. *Sanguii e Gloria*, and all that.'

'But it's not fair, Wavewaker. You didn't do anything wrong.'

'Fair?' The big man scoffed. 'What Republic are you living in?'

Shaking his head and smirking as if Mia had said something funny, the big man kept on soaping himself like all was right in the world. Mia reached for another perfumed bar as Bryn and Byern walked into the bathhouse, stripping off their loincloths and kicking their sandals loose. It'd been their turn to train down by the equorium, and Mia could smell the sweat and horse on the pair of them at ten paces.

'Ah, our brave equillai,' Wavewaker smiled. 'The twin terrors, unequalled on the track, welcome. The Crow and I were just discussing the theatre.'

'Four Daughters, what for?' Bryn scowled, sinking below the water.

'I knew an actress once,' Byern said, his voice wistful.

'What, that sugargirl who'd come through the village in the summers?'

'She wasn't a sugargirl, sis, she was a thespian.'

'If she tugged you for beggars, she was a sugargirl, darling brother.'

Byern glanced at Mia and Wavewaker. 'She's talking rot now.

Smearing my good name to make me look bad. I've never paid for it in my life, and the lass in question was as at home on the stage as a fish in water, I assure you.'

'The only acting she did was pretending that she fancied you,' Bryn scoffed.

'Respect your elders, pup!' Byern said, splashing his sister in the face.

The twins engaged in a brief water fight, Mia and Wavewaker backing away across to the other side of the bath so they didn't get caught in the crossfire. Byern dunked Bryn's head below the surface and she punched him in the stomach. The pair retreated to opposite corners, Bryn raising the knuckles at her brother and scowling.

'Are you two done?' Wavewaker asked.

'Aye,' Bryn said. 'No, wait . . .'

She snatched up a bar of soap and bounced it off her brother's head. 'Ow!'

'Now I'm done.'

'One turn,' Wavewaker declared, once hostilities had died, 'when we're out of this hole, I'll take you all to a proper theatre. Show you some culture.'

'Daughters know some of us could use it,' Bryn said.

'Keep it up, and I shall see you before the magistrate for slander,' Byern warned, splashing his sister again. Bryn retaliated with a sweeping arc of her hand, a great scythe of water hitting her brother and Wavewaker in the face.

'Sorry,' she smirked.

'O, you will be,' the big man replied, wiping his chin.

Wavewaker curved his massive hand and slung a shot of bathwater right into Bryn's eyes. Byern stepped in to defend his sister, slapping water back and catching Mia in the crossfire. The girl joined in, and soon all four were going at it, fierce as whitedrakes, splashing and cursing and laughing. Wavewaker slung Mia clear across the bath into Byern's bare chest, grabbed Bryn in a headlock, and proceeded to dunk her below the surface as she kicked and flai—

'What in the Everseeing's name goes on here?'

Mia slung her sodden hair from her eyes, looked up to find Magistrae standing at the bathhouse door, hands on hips. She was dressed immaculately as always, long grey braid swept over one shoulder. Her voice bristled with indignity.

'You are gladiatii of the Remus Collegium, and here I find you, caterwauling and fooling like a pack of brats. This is how you honour your domina?'

'Apologies, Magistrae,' Wavewaker said, releasing Bryn's neck. 'A moment's jest, is all. The weather grows hot and the turns long, and—'

'And there are only a handful of those turns left before the Whitekeep *venatus*, and from there, the *magni*,' Magistrae snapped. 'Do you know what it will cost your domina if you fail? The shame she will endure? Perhaps you think it wise to spend your time jackanaping, but were I you, I would set mind to the games, and what awaits you all if this collegium falls.'

The smile on Mia's face died, the momentary joy she'd felt evaporating. The gladiatii hung their heads like scolded children. It was true what the magistrae said, and all knew it – if the collegium failed, they'd probably be sold off like cheap meat, and only the Everseeing knew who to. New sanguila perhaps, but more likely to Pandemonium. All their lives hung in the balance.

Maw's teeth, it had been grand to forget it all for a moment. But Mia clenched her jaw. Hardened her resolve. She was growing soft here. Not physically – under Arkades's training, she'd grown harder and fitter than she'd ever been in her life. But letting herself grow close to her fellow gladiatii was a mistake. Likeable as they might be, the men and women in the collegium were only pawns on a board. Pawns that would likely be sacrificed before she got to the king.

These people are not your familia, and not your friends, she reminded herself.

All of them are only a means to an end.

'Harder.'

Leona braced her palms against the wall and pushed her knees into the mattress, head thrown back. Furian had hold of her waist, his grip slippery with their sweat, her whole body shuddering with every thrust of his hips. The bedframe shook from the force of it, stone dust drifting off the wall and down to the floor.

'*Harder*,' Leona groaned again.

Her champion complied, bucking like a stallion. The dona reached back, clawing his skin, urging him deeper as he took a handful of her auburn hair and pulled her back, farther onto his burning length. Leona closed her eyes, rocked to her core and quivering, mouth open wide.

'Fuck me,' she breathed.

'Domina . . .'

'O, Daughters, yes.'

'Domina, I can't . . .'

'Yes, finish it,' she gasped. 'Fuck me, fuck me, *fuck me.*'

Furian slammed himself home a few more times then dragged himself free, his whole body rigid as he spent himself across her buttocks and back. Leona hung her head, fingernails digging into his skin, biting her lip to stifle her cry. Breathless, she collapsed facedown onto the bed, purring like a cat.

The Unfallen lowered himself down beside her, chest heaving, his body drenched. Though the bed was small, he took care not to touch her – it seemed the dona had little taste for postcoital affections. Leaning his back against the wall, he licked his lips and sighed, heart pounding.

'A fine performance, my champion,' the dona murmured.

'Your whisper, my will,' he replied.

Leona chuckled, rolled over onto her back. Wriggling her hips, she arched her spine and looked up at the man above her.

'Four Daughters, I needed that,' she sighed.

'No less than I,' Furian said. 'I'd begun to suspect you'd forgot me.'

Leona cooed, smoothing his long dark hair away from his face, running her fingertips down his rippling abdomen. 'Did you miss me, my champion?'

'It has been weeks, Domina.'

'No need to fear, lover,' the dona smiled. 'Ever I'll return.'

'Until you find favour in another?'

'Another?' Leona's lips twisted. 'And who would that be, pray?'

'The Saviour of Stormwatch,' he muttered with mock theatricality.

'Ah,' Leona sighed, rolling her eyes. 'We arrive at spear's tip. But I've no taste for women, Furian. And even less for jealousy.'

'You fight her on the sands beside me,' he muttered. 'As if she were my equal. But she has no honour. She has—'

'She has a victor's laurel,' Leona said. 'She has the favour of the crowd. And she has one-third the key to unlock the gates of the *magni* for us.'

'I can best your father's silkling alone, Domina,' Furian growled. 'I need help from no one, least of all some conniving slip that my enemy has already defeated.'

Leona sighed. Rising from the bed, she gathered up the sheet and casually wiped his seed off her skin.

'This conversation bores me.'

Furian reached out his hand. 'Leona . . .'

'Leona?' The dona glanced up sharply. 'You forget yourself, slave.'

'O, slave, aye,' Furian nodded. 'Until you've a thirst again. And then it's all "lover" and "my champion" and honeyed words until you've had your fill.'

'And you complain so bitterly at the time?'

'I've a mind to be more than just your stud.'

'And what more would you be?' Leona asked. 'You may stand a champion in the arena, but other laurels, you've far from won. I am domina of this house. Think not that simply because I bed you, I hold you in my counsel. Or that when command is given, I do not expect it to be obeyed.'

'When your nightmares wake you from your sleep, do you think I comfort you because I'm commanded to do so? Do you think I hold you because—'

'You overstep, Champion.'

Furian pressed his lips together, anger darkening his brow. But he spoke no more. Looking at him a long, still moment, Leona's face softened. She sank down onto the bed beside him, pressed her hand to his cheek.

'I care for you,' she murmured. 'But I cann—'

A knock sounded at the door.

'Champion?'

Leona's eyes widened as she recognized the voice.

'Almighty Aa . . .' she hissed. 'Arkades!'

Furian rose off the bed, his face running pale. 'I thought he was in his cups?'

'He was! Passed out in the dining room, dead to the damned world.'

Another knock. 'Furian?'

Leona searched the room desperately. The shrine to Tsana. A small chest. Wooden swords and a practice dummy. Nowhere to hide. Finally, the dona of the house dropped to her knees. Crawling under the bed with Furian's aid, she drew her legs up and hugged them to her chest. Satisfied she was out of sight, the Unfallen tied his loincloth and opened the door.

Arkades stood on the threshold, his face blotched from drink. He was swaying slightly, goldwine thick on his breath as he looked the champion up and down.

'Apologies,' he said. 'Were you asleep?'

'Only resting, Executus.'

'Mmf.'

Arkades shouldered past and limped into the room, his iron leg ringing on the stone, *clink* thump, *clink* thump. He looked about for somewhere to sit, finally thumping down on the bed. The straw mattress sagged under his weight, Leona smothering her cry as it smacked into the back of her skull and bounced her head off the floor. Cursing under her breath, she hunkered lower, like a disobedient child hiding from her parents.

Arkades sniffed the air, raised an eyebrow, his voice thick from drink. 'Stinks in here.'

'The heat, Executus. Saai crawls closer to the horizon every turn.'

Arkades wrinkled his nose. 'I'll have a word to the magistrae. That soap she's got you using smells like a woman's perfume.'

Furian's eyes widened slightly, and looked to the shadow below the bed. The executus didn't notice, pulling out his trusty flask and taking a long pull. He offered it to the Unfallen, who declined with a silent shake of his head.

'Mmf, good man,' Arkades said, stowing the drink away. 'Makes you soft on the sands.'

'But it makes you forget the blood that stains them, too,' Furian replied softly.

Arkades nodded, almost to himself, a faraway look in his eyes. Staring down at his hands. Up into the Unfallen's dark stare.

'I like that about you, Furian. You see. You *understand*. The pain we endure. The red rivers we must wade through.'

'On our way to glory.'

'A heavy weight.'

'I welcome it. If it brings me victory.'

Arkades scoffed softly. 'I like that about you, too.'

'Forgive me . . . But do you need something, Executus?'

Arkades sighed and shifted his weight, the sagging mattress pushing Leona into the floor. The dona was breathing soft and thin, chest pressed hard to the stone, panic on her face. If she made a sound, if her executus discovered her there . . .

'I need you to stop working at odds with the Crow,' Arkades replied, slightly slurred from the drink. 'I need you to fight beside her, not against her.'

Furian scowled. 'That girl is on every tongue this nevernight, it seems.'

A blink. '. . . What?'

'She is a liar and a cur, Executus. Her glory is undeserved.'

'How can you say so?' Arkades frowned. 'Aa's cock, I hold no more fondness for her than you, but you saw her fight at Stormwatch. Her victory over the retchwyrm—'

'Was steeped in treachery. She is not a victor, she is a thief.'

Arkades sighed, reaching for his flask before he caught himself. He stood, unsteady for a moment, Leona sighing in relief now she could breathe again. Regaining his balance and limping around the room, Arkades motioned to the walls around them.

'What do you see?'

'My domina's house,' the Unfallen replied.

'Aye. The walls that shelter you, the roof that keeps the suns off your back. Know you what will happen, if we fail to secure berth at the *magni*?'

'I need no aid besting the silkling, Executus,' Furian growled, bristling. 'And I will not fight alongside an honourless dog who steals what should be earned.'

'Because you'd know all about being an honourless dog, neh?'

Furian's eyes grew wide. 'You dare—'

'Spare me your indignity,' Arkades growled, raising one callused hand. 'You forget I was the one who found you, brought you here. I alone know where it is you came from, what it is you *did* to find yourself in chains.'

Furian glanced to his bed. The figure lurking beneath it.

'That was many a turn ago,' he said. 'I am that man no longer. I am a god-fearing son of the Everseeing, and a gladiatii who lives to honour his domina.'

'You live to honour *yourself*,' Arkades replied, shaking his head in exasperation. 'To prove yourself better than the man you were. And I see to the heart of that. But say not that you fight for your domina. If you truly thought for one moment of Leona, if you felt one drop of what I feel for h—'

Arkades blinked and caught himself. Swaying on his feet. Glancing up at the champion, Executus cleared his throat, rubbed at bleary eyes.

'You have the skill and the *will* to see us all the way to the *magni*, Furian. I did not pluck you from the mire to redeem you from the sins of your past. I did it because I see in you a *champion*, just as I was. You can win your freedom. Walk among us as a man once more, not the animal you were. But those who stand for nothing die for the same. And if you stand only for yourself, you fall alone.'

'Stand for myself?' Furian repeated, incredulous. 'I stand for these walls!'

'Then prove it,' Arkades growled. 'Fight *with* the Crow, not against her. And when the silkling is bested and our berth assured, when you face the Crow in the grand games *e mortium*, you can prove yourself the man I know you to be.'

Arkades placed one hand on the champion's shoulder.

'Or fall alone,' he repeated. 'And bring this house down with you.'

Executus swayed like a tree in a storm, the grip on Furian's shoulder more to steady himself than prove a comfort. But though the goldwine hung heavy on his breath, though he could barely stay upright, it seemed he'd aimed true.

Furian clenched his jaw. But finally, he nodded.

'I will stand with her at Whitekeep,' he said. 'But in Godsgrave, she dies.'

Arkades nodded, limped towards the door, *clink* thump, *clink* thump, turning at the threshold to look Furian over once more.

'Perhaps before? Who can say?'

Executus smiled, closing the door behind him. Furian stood still, listening to the sound of his limping tread fade down the hallway. Sinking to his knees, he offered a hand to Leona, helped her drag herself out from under the bed. Once standing, the dona snatched her hand away from his, dragged her dress over her head to cover herself. Indignity written in every movement.

'So,' she glared. 'You'd disobey my command to fight beside the Crow, but Arkades speaks a handful of words and you see the right of it?'

'Domin—'

'You told me you were a trader before this,' she said, fixing the champion in her glittering blue stare. 'A merchant.'

'I was,' Furian replied.

'Arkades did not make it sound so. He named you animal. How many sins can a simple merchant accrue, that he fights so fierce to redeem them?'

The Unfallen made no reply.

'What did you do, Furian?' she asked. 'What lies have you told me?'

The champion only stared at the trinity of Aa on the wall, refusing to meet her gaze. She stood there long moments, searching his eyes, looking for answers. Finding only silence. And with a disgusted harrumph, she turned, stomped towards the door. Listening for a moment, she tore it open, almost heedless, and strode out into the hallway, slamming it behind her.

The Unfallen slumped his shoulders and softly cursed.

Sitting on the bed, he saw Leona had left her underslip behind. Gathering it up in his hands, he stared at it for long moments, lost in thought. Running his fingers across the silk, the lace. Inhaling her perfume. And finally, he bent down and stuffed it under his mattress, hiding it in the shadows beneath his bed.

The shadows where a not-cat sat and listened.

Trying terribly hard not to roll his not-eyes.

'... *sigh* ...'

CHAPTER 23

WHITEKEEP

The crash of waves on a stony shore.

The screams of gulls in sunsburned skies.

The roar of seventy thousand voices, joined as one.

A lone gladiatii stood in the arena's heart, bathed in thunder. The blinding scorch of the two suns glittered on the twin lengths of razored chain he twirled about his body. He was clad in gleaming steel, arm wrapped in scaled mail, greaves at his shins. His face was hidden behind a polished helm, fashioned like a roaring drake's maw.

The prisoners around him wore no such protection – a few scraps of piecemeal leather, rusty swords in hand. Execution bouts were meant to entertain the crowd between the major events, but there were a dozen condemned men and women in the arena, fighting against a single gladiatii; it wouldn't do to give the criminals much of a chance at surviving. They were meant to die here, after all.

A convicted rapist charged with a cry, the gladiatii whipping his spike chain across the man's belly, spilling coils of purple guts onto the now-scarlet sand. The crowd roared in approval. An arsonist and a murderer struck at the gladiatii's rear, but both were met with a whistling wall of steel, slicing their sword arms off at the elbows and their throats to the bone.

As the mob's cheers swelled louder, as the walls of Whitekeep arena near shook with the stomping of their feet, the gladiatii went to work in earnest. Opening windpipes and stomachs, severing hands and legs, and as a thrilling finale, taking the last prisoner's head clean off his shoulders.

'Citizens of Itreya!' came the call across the arena horns. 'Honoured administratii! Senators and marrowborn! Your victor, Giovanni of Liis!'

The gladiatii roared, raising his bloody chains. As he strode about the sand, whipping the crowd to a frenzy, the criminals' mutilated corpses were dragged away for disposal. Only an unmarked grave and the abyss awaiting them.

Mia stood in her cell, staring out through the bars to the sands beyond. The games were almost done – only the equillai race and their feature match against the silkling remained between now and the Ultima. Butcher had fought earlier in the turn, but he'd been soundly thrashed by a swordsman from the Tacitus Collegium – only a plea for mercy from the editorii had seen his life spared. Wavewaker and Sidonius had fought in a bestiary match with two dozen other gladiatii and a pack of Vaanian scythebears. The pair had slain three beasts between them, though they'd been bested in the final points tally by a pair of stalkers from the Trajan Collegium. Only two marks shy of victory.

So close to a laurel, yet so far away.

The pair sat in the cell with Mia now, nursing their wounds and stung pride. Butcher was with Maggot, getting his head and ribs stitched up. Bladesinger sat with her back to the sand, listening to the furore die outside. She was busy tying a handful of hooked knives into the ends of her saltlocks, humming to herself. The blades were three inches long, razor-sharp. She was clad in a boiled leather breastplate, spaulders and greaves of dark iron. A helmet with the crown cut away sat on the bench beside her.

'Bryn and Byern will be up soon,' Mia said.

Bladesinger nodded, saying nothing.

'Nervous?' Mia asked.

'Always,' the woman replied.

'Courage, sisters,' Wavewaker smiled. 'This match is yours.'

Bladesinger nodded slow. In the weeks leading up to their departure from Crow's Nest, their training with Furian had improved no end, and in the long sessions beneath the burning suns, the trio had reached a kind of synchronicity. Moving as one, they'd begun to best Arkades regularly. Mia's speed. Furian's brawn. Bladesinger the bridge between. Though the Unfallen was kept apart from them in his champion's cell, as was tradition before the match, they were as close to a team as they would ever be.

'We have a chance,' Bladesinger admitted.

Truth told, they had more than one. Ashlinn had arrived in Whitekeep a week before the gladiatii of the Remus Collegium, and had been skulking about the arena ever since. Passing messages through

Eclipse, she'd told Mia exactly how the editorii planned to spice up the spectacle of the clash between the champions of the Leonides and Remus Collegia. But moreover, Ash had arranged a special gift to tip the scales further in their favour.

Mia closed her eyes, listened to the sound of the distant ocean.*
Godsgrave was just across the water – if she climbed the city walls, she'd be able to see it from here. She was just one step away from the *magni*.

One match away from revenge.

Trumpets sounded, the crowd roaring in response. The stone beneath her feet trembled, the great mekwerk apparatus beneath the arena floor churning. Mia looked out through the bars, saw the centre of the sands split apart, an oblong island rising in the heart of the arena. Almost forty crucifixes were lined up in a neat row along the island's length, convicted prisoners lashed tight to the crossbeams.

'It's starting,' Mia said.

Bladesinger joined her by the bars, Wavewaker beside her. She glanced at Sidonius as he muscled up next to her. They'd not spoken about the revelation of her parentage since the nevernight they'd fought in their cell – Sid seemed a man content to wait until Mia approached him, to talk when she was ready. But she noted he never strayed far

---

*The city of Whitekeep is a sprawling metropolis on the southern shores of Itreya, and sister city to Godsgrave. The City of Bridges and Bones can be seen from its shoreline, and the mighty aqueduct that feeds water to Itreya's capital runs from the mountains at Whitekeep's back, down through the metropolis, over the bay, and on to Godsgrave.

Set with statuary of Aa and his Four Daughters and guarded at either end by the towering figures of Itreyan War Walkers, the aqueduct is a marvel of engineering, and one of the wonders of the Itreyan Republic. Its chief architect was a resident of Whitekeep named Marius Gandolfini, who was commissioned to oversee the project by King Francisco II, the Great Builder.

The aqueduct allowed the Itreyan capital to blossom from a squalid cesspool into a water-rich marvel, overflowing with fountains, a complex sewer network, hundreds of public baths, and all manner of waterworks. Though Gandolfini died of old age before the aqueduct was complete, his name is still venerated in the City of Bridges and Bones to this turn. A statue of him stands proudly in the Visionaries' Row of the Iron Collegium, marble busts of his likeness are found in bathhouses across the city, and certain specialist brothels offer a 'Gandolfini' to their more . . . adventurous clientele.

Use your imagination, gentlefriends.

from her any more. Sitting next to her at meals, training nearby, never more than a few feet away. As if he felt protective of her now. As if the news she was the daughter of Darius Corvere—

'Citizens of Itreya!' came the editorii's booming call. 'We present to you, the equillai race of this, the Whitekeep *venatus*!'

The crowd roared in answer, waves rippling across the mob. The Whitekeep arena wasn't quite the size of its sister in Godsgrave, but Mia reckoned there were at least seventy thousand people in the stands. The clamour of them, the heat, the pulsing rhythm of their chants swept her up, back to the sands of Stormwatch as she prowled up and down the retchwyrm's corpse.

'*What is my name?*' she screamed.

'*CrowCrowCrowCrowCrow!*'

'*WHAT IS MY NAME?*'

They knew it now, sure and true. Word of her victory had spread across the Republic; Ashlinn had heard pundits telling tales in a taverna just two nevernights ago. 'The Bloody Beauty', they called her. 'The Saviour of Stormwatch'.

She looked in the direction of Godsgrave. Listening to the sound of the ocean above the crowd's clamour.

Soon, all will know my name.

She clenched her fists.

My real *name . . .*

'And now, our equillai!' the editorii called. 'From the Wolves of Tacitus, the Colossi of Carrion Hall, Alfr and Baldr!'

Two huge Vaanian men rode out from the rising portcullis at the southern end of the arena. They stood astride a chariot embossed with snarling wolves, the wings on their helms and the blond of their beards gleaming in the sunlight as they raised their hands to the cheering crowd.

'From the Swords of Phillipi! Victors of Talia, the Eighth Itreyan Wonders, Maxus and Agrippina!'*

---

*Despite claims to the contrary from enthusiastic editorii, there are only seven Itreyan Wonders:

- The Ribs of Godsgrave.
- The Godsgrave Aqueduct.
- The Mausoleum of Lucius I – the final resting place of the first Liisian Magus King, this ziggurat looms near five hundred feet tall, and baffles contemporary engineers with the genius of its construction.

A second chariot rode out after the first, drawn by chestnut stallions. The equillai were mixed sex like Bryn and Byern, but by the bow in his hand, the male looked to be the *flagellae* of the pair. In an impressive acrobatic display, he stood astride the horses, arms spread wide, whipping up the crowd.

'From the Falcons of Remus Collegium . . . !'

'Here we go,' Sidonius breathed.

'. . . the twin terrors of Vaan, Bryn and Byern!'

The siblings burst forth on their chariot, hooves thundering on the packed dirt. Not to be outdone by the Phillipi's *flagellae*, Bryn was astride Rose's and Briar's backs in a handstand, her bow in her toes. She loosed her arrow into the air, the shaft falling to earth and piercing the track right at the finish line.

Mia and her fellows whooped as Bryn and Byern's chariot swooped past their cell. Byern flashed them a winning grin, Bryn blowing a kiss as they passed, Wavewaker reaching out as if to snatch it from the air.

'Trelene ride with you, my friends!' he bellowed. 'Ride!'

'And now, from the Lions of Leonides, Victors of Stormwatch and Blackbridge, the Titans of the Track, your beloved . . . Stonekiller and Armando!'

The equillai charged forward onto the track to deafening applause,

---

- The Dust Falls of Nuuvash – a series of massive cliffs found in southern Ashkah, which spill vast avalanches of dust off the Whisperwastes into the oceans below.
- The Statue of Trelene at Farrow – found in the high temple of the Dweymeri capital, this marble-and-gold sculpture of the Mother of Oceans performs miracles when credible sources aren't looking.
- The Thousand Towers – a series of natural stone spires, rising hundreds of feet from an ancient riverbed in Ashkah. In truth, there are only nine hundred and sixty-four. 'Thousand Towers' just sounds better.
- The Temple of Aa in Elai – constructed by the Great Unifier, Francisco I, to commemorate his conquest of Liis. At its heart stands a ten-foot statue made of solid gold – the material acquired by melting the personal fortunes of every nobleborn Liisian familia who stood against Francisco in battle.

Honourable mentions to the List of Wonders include the Great Salt; the Tomb of Brandr I; a courtesan named Francesca Andiami, who can do extraordinary things with a bowl of strawberries and a string of prayer beads; and my own personal astonishment that any of you took the time to read this when they're about to start the bloody horse race.

smiles wide. Their hands were joined, held aloft. They wore golden armour, their shoulders draped with the pelts of mighty lions. Armando reached into the quiver at his side and began firing arrows into the air. Through some arkemy, the arrows exploded into confetti and ribbon, falling in rainbow-coloured showers among the delighted audience.

Rhythmic chanting filled the stands as the equillai took up their positions, each at an opposite point of the oblong. Mia watched Bryn and Byern with no fear in her heart, but she knew their odds were long. With Leona fielding no one from her stable in the Ultima, even if the twins won, the Falcons would still be one laurel short of a berth at the *magni* – only Mia's feature match with the silkling could guarantee them a place now. Bryn and Byern were competing simply for the purse, and perhaps for their own glory. But it was a great deal to risk for a handful of coin and some pride.

Mia wasn't the only one who knew the odds. Bladesinger stood beside her, tense as steel. Wavewaker was gripping the bars tight, Sidonius holding his breath. Mia recalled Bryn and Byern's words to her back at the Nest. The saying from their homeland they'd shared.

'*In every breath, hope abides.*'

She reached out, squeezed Sidonius's hand.

'Keep breathing,' she whispered.

'Equillai . . .' came the editorii's call. '*Begin!*'

The crack of reins. The percussion of hooves. Mia gritted her teeth as the race began, each of the teams building up a swift head of speed. As the chariots roared around the track, gaining speed, the archers released shot after shot at the helpless prisoners, trying to kill as many as possible in order to rack up points. The crowd bellowed, the condemned screamed, scarlet painted the sands.

Editorii stood in the crowd with spyglasses, marking the different-coloured feathers from each team and noting who scored the kill shots. Two tally boards stood in the west and eastern stands, spry children marking each team's total by slotting stones into divots in the board. Sidonius pointed to the score.

'We're in the lead.'

The crowd roared, dragging Mia's attention away from the points. The Phillipi team had adopted an aggressive early strategy, neglecting the prisoners and quickly engaging instead. Their archer was firing at Bryn and Byern, black-feathered shafts whistling through the air. Byern protected his sister behind his shield as she put a shot into one of the last prisoners, and spinning on her heel, she returned fire, forcing the

Phillipi archer back into cover. Meanwhile, the Lions of Leonides were trading shots with the Wolves of Tacitus, the crowd thrilling as Armando landed a clever shot into the Wolf archer's thigh.

'First blood to the Lions of Leonides!' cried the editorii.

Trumpets sounded.

Eight laps to go.

Four *coronae* were randomly flung onto the track, the silver wreaths gleaming in the dust. They were worth a single point, but with only a few points between first and last place, every one would count. Bryn loosed three shots at the Phillipi archer as her brother leaned out of their chariot, scooping up one *coronae*. The Swords took the second, the Lions another. The riders thundered about the track, arrows cut the air, Mia and her fellows watching on, cheering with the rest of the mob.

Six laps to go.

More *coronae* fell. Trumpets rang, the ground rumbled as the sands split apart. Wooden barricades rose out of the sands along the track, set with vicious tangles of razorvine. As if the risk of collision weren't enough, the barricades simultaneously burst into flame. The *sagmae* were now forced to focus more on steering their chariots and less on protecting their partners, and with the pace lessened, it was easier to close distance. The arrows flew thick and fast, Mia cursing as Bryn was grazed by a shot that Byern failed to deflect in time. And as the crowd thrilled, the Wolves of Tacitus managed to score a hit on Stonekiller, a white-feathered arrow sinking deep into his shin.

Stonekiller staggered, sinking to his knees and lowering his shield as their chariot skidded wildly. The Wolf archer fired again, the crowd howling as Armando was struck in the shoulder. With the skill that had made them champions, Stonekiller brought the chariot back under control, Armando tearing the arrows from his arm, his *sagmae*'s leg. But the blood was flowing thick, and the Wolves used the time to scoop up three *coronae*, putting them in the lead.

Mia shook her head, watching Bryn and Byern falling further behind.

Four laps to go.

More wreaths were showered onto the track – half a dozen this time. The Wolves held first place, the Falcons and Lions tied for second. Bryn was like a woman possessed, firing shot after shot at her foes. The Swords were coming last in the tally, their situation desperate. In his haste to scoop up a *coronae*, the Sword *sagmae* ran their chariot too close to a barricade, their wheel clipping the burning razorvine with a hail of sparks. Off-balance, the *sagmae* fell to his knee, and Bryn loosed a stunning shot, her red-feathered arrow swishing right through the driver's throat.

The man gurgled, a second shot thudding into his chest. The horses clipped another barricade, snapping the crossbar clean, and the chariot flipped over and crashed into a tangled ruin.

'First kill for the Falcons!' the editorii crowed. '*Sanguii e Gloria!*'

Bryn raised a fist in triumph and Byern scooped up another *coronae*, Mia and her fellows hollering. With those five points, the Remus Collegium was back in first place. Victory in sight.

'Two laps remain!' came the call.

Smoke from the burning barricades drifted over the track, the sands red with blood. With the foes that had dogged them all match now dead, Byern whipped his mares into a burst of speed, closing in on the Lions from behind. Armando was pressed low behind Stonekiller's shield, the pair bleeding heavily. The crowd howled, wondering if the beloved Lions were being set up for the kill, but Mia's eyes were narrowed. Armando and Stonekiller were no fools, and a big cat is never more dangerous than when wounded.

'Be careful!' she shouted as the Falcons wheeled past their cell window.

Bryn raised her bow and took aim, the Wolves' archer did the same from their lead. The crowd was on their feet, thinking Stonekiller and Armando were about to fall in the crossfire. But with astonishing skill, Stonekiller seized one wheel with his bare hands, locking it tight. The drag whipped the chariot sideways, their enemies' shots going wide. Armando rose up from cover and loosed a shot at the Wolves, the arrow whispering right past the surprised *sagmae*'s shield and into his archer's neck. The mob howled, the archer staggered, toppling into the dirt.

'Third kill, Lions!' came the cry.

The Wolf chariot clipped a barricade, rocking it sideways. As three of Bryn's shots thudded into Stonekiller's shield, Armando fired again, striking the Wolf driver in the knee and chest. He collapsed, his leg catching as he fell from the chariot, dragged for a few hundred feet before he was torn loose.

'Lions, Fourth kill! *Sanguii e Gloria!*'

The mob bellowed, drunk on the carnage. Byern scooped up another *coronae*, Briar and Rose both drenched in sweat. Stonekiller whipped his stallions, trying to keep distance from the Falcons. With their two kill shots against the Wolves, the Lions were now in the lead – all they needed to do was maintain distance and keep pace with the Falcons in scooping up wreaths, and victory would be theirs.

'Final lap!'

The entire arena was on its feet, the noise crawling on Mia's skin and down her spine. Sidonius was muttering beneath his breath, urging the twins on, Bladesinger quietly praying, Wavewaker silent as stone. Horses frothing, crowd baying, flames crackling, Mister Kindly swelled in Mia's shadow as fear tried to take root in her belly, her jaw clenched tight. She watched Byern whipping his horses hard, trying to close distance so his sister could score a kill shot. Desperation on their faces. Blood on their skin. Death in the air.

Watching the crowd, Mia felt sick to her stomach. The euphoria, the red glaze in their eyes. Four people were out there on the sands, fighting for their lives. But the crowd didn't see men and women with hopes and dreams and fears.

She wanted Bryn and Byern to triumph. Despite knowing better than to think of them as friends, she *knew* them. She *liked* them. She didn't want them to die. But she was surprised to realize she didn't want Stonekiller and Armando and all their hopes and dreams and fears to die either. Just for the sake of a laurel that didn't matter anyway?

The Lions were closing on the finish line. The crowd, all open mouths and shapeless howls. Rounding to the final straight, Stonekiller leaned down to scoop up another *coronae*. The Falcons flew around the corner behind, running so hard their chariot went up on one wheel. Bryn fired through the dust and smoke and flame – a miracle shot, slipping past the man's shield and into his arm. Stonekiller slipped in the blood, dragging the reins. The chariot slewed sideways, the crowd bellowing as it collided with a barricade, smashing the equillai inside like glass. The axle shattered, one wheel snapping loose from the ruin and bouncing back down the track.

Right at the Falcons of Remus.

Byern hauled on the reins, trying to steer his horses left, but their momentum was too much. The tumbling wheel sheared through Briar's legs, the mare screaming as she toppled. The chariot's crossbeam struck the sand, and as Mia and her comrades gasped

O, no . . .

the whole rig crumpled like dry vellum and flipped high into the air.

Bryn and Byern were tossed like rag dolls, the crowd groaning as the twins crashed to earth. Bryn landed shoulder first in the sand, but her brother wasn't as lucky. Byern flew headfirst into one of the burning barricades, Mia wincing at the wet crackle of shattering bone. The Vaanian crashed clean through the obstacle and tumbled to a rest twenty feet down the track, lying in a tangled heap just beyond their cell window.

'Mother of Oceans,' Bladesinger breathed.

The crowd was stunned – both equillai teams had crashed before the finish line. Stonekiller and Armando lay motionless in the wreckage of their chariot, the young archer's back twisted at a ghastly angle, his partner motionless beside him. But in the ringing aftermath, the mob soon began to cheer.

'Almighty Aa, look!' Sidonius cried.

Mia squinted through the smoke, realizing that Bryn was moving. Slow at first, the girl stirred, pushing herself up onto her knees and slinging off her plumed helmet. As Mia watched, as the crowd began roaring again, the archer swayed to her feet.

Bryn stood perhaps fifty feet from the finish line. All she needed to do was walk across, and the Falcons would have their victory. She began limping towards it, holding her ribs and hobbling, stumbling, the mob began chanting, 'Bryn! Bryn! Bryn!' The young archer spat blood onto the sand, face twisted, eyes locked on the line.

Until she caught sight of her brother.

Mia held her breath as the girl stopped, the entire arena falling still. Confusion flitted across Bryn's face. And then she was stumbling, limping, gasping towards Byern. He lay facedown, just a stone's throw from where Mia and the others were caged. Bryn fell to her knees beside him, rolling him over gently.

'Byern?' Bryn asked, her voice trembling.

Mia saw blood at his lips. Blue eyes open wide to the burning sky above. Bryn reached out with bloody hands to shake him.

'. . . B-brother?'

'O, Daughters . . .' Sidonius breathed.

'Keep breathing,' Mia prayed.

Bryn leaned close, pressed her ear to her brother's lips. Hearing nothing, she shook him again, face twisting as she screamed.

'Byern?' she cried, shaking him. '*Byern!*'

Guards marched into the arena, arrayed all in black. As they checked the bodies of the fallen Lions, Bryn gathered her twin up in her arms and started wailing, weeping, howling. Mia felt her heart aching, tears slipping down her cheeks. Sidonius was as still as a statue. Wavewaker hanging his head as Bryn screamed.

'*BYERN!*'

The guards marched to where the girl knelt in the dust, dragging her up by the arms. Coming to her senses, Bryn fought back, kicking and screaming, 'No! *NO!*' It took four men to drag her off the sand, thrashing and howling her brother's name.

'Citizens of Itreya!' came the call across the arena horns. 'We regret to declare . . . no victor!'

Mia closed her eyes. After all that, it was for nothing. No laurel. No glory. Just nothing. And then, as her belly burned, a chill creeping across her skin, she heard the crowd begin to boo. Staring out through the bars, she saw the mob on their feet, throwing food and spitting on the sand. That sand stained with the blood of eight men and women, seven of whom had just died for their amusement. Seven people with hopes and fears and dreams, now, nothing but corpses.

And the crowd? They cared not a drop.

All they wanted was a victory.

Mia took a deep breath. Clenched her jaw. Sidonius and the others remained at the bars, but Mia turned her back, walked away. Stare fixed on the stone at her feet. The path before her. The vengeance awaiting her at the end of it.

'*. . . i am sorry, mia . . .*'

'You?' she whispered. 'Why?'

'*. . . he was your friend . . .*'

'They're not my *familia*, remember?' she replied. 'They're not my friends.'

She looked down at her hands. Blurred almost shapeless by her tears.

'All of them are only a means to an end.'

CHAPTER 24

OBSIDIAN

Hollow.

That's how Mia felt inside. Listening to the mob stamping impatiently on the bleachers as Byern's corpse was dragged away. Long hair hanging about her eyes, she busied herself strapping the leather breastplate to her chest, the iron greaves about her shins. Every movement cold.

Methodical.

Mekanical.

'. . . ARE YOU WELL . . . ?'

A whisper in her ear, beneath the shadows of her hair.

'. . . mia . . . ?'

Guards arrived at their cell door to collect them, dressed all in black. Furian stood behind them in his gleaming armour, a Falcon helm on his head, his silver champion's torc glittering around his neck. Arkades limped beside the Unfallen, his face a masque. Dona Leona walked before all of them, resplendent in a long, sky-blue gown, tears smudging the kohl about her eyes. As the guards unlocked the cell door, Mia met her domina's stare, trying to weigh her grief.

Was it sincere? Or as hollow as her chest felt at that moment?

'Domina?' Bladesinger asked quietly. 'Is Bryn . . . ?'

'She is with Maggot,' the dona murmured. 'She is . . . not well.'

'Her brother died out there, Domina,' Sidonius said. 'How else should she be?'

'I . . .'

'Enough,' Arkades growled. 'Byern died with honour, as gladiatii. Set your mind to the match and troubling thoughts aside. Your foe will not be hindered by them.'

Mia still stared at Leona. Pondering all she knew of the woman.

The dona had grown up around the violence of the arena. But though she kept a stable of men and women to fight and die for the amusement of the mob, some humanity might remain in her breast. She'd seen hints of it in the bathhouse with the magistrae, even perhaps in her backward affections for Furian. There was more to her than a simple thirst to best her father. Would the dona show true grief now, or urge them to 'avenge their fallen brother', and just happen to win her berth at the *magni* besides?

Leona took Mia's hand. Bladesinger's also.

'I . . .'

She shook her head, trying to speak. Tears welling in her eyes.

'Be careful out there,' she finally whispered.

Bladesinger blinked in surprise. Looking to Arkades.

'. . . Aye, Domina.'

'The match awaits, Mi Dona,' the guard captain warned.

Leona nodded, wiping her face. 'Very well.'

They were marched through the arena's bowels, the thrumming clamour of the crowd echoing in the rafters overhead. They reached a large staging area, black stone and an iron portcullis, four broad steps leading down to the arena floor. The sounds of the crowd washed over her and Mia clenched her jaw, eyes to the sand.

'This is the hour,' Arkades said. 'Immortality within your grasp. A chance to carve your name into the earth, to honour your domina, and win your freedom. Only one foe stands between you and the *magni*. A foe who can bleed. A foe who can die.' He fixed each in his ice-blue stare. 'You are gladiatii of the Remus Collegium. Stand together, or fall alone.'

Furian nodded. 'Executus.'

'Aye, Executus,' Bladesinger murmured.

Mia only stared, remembering what Mister Kindly had told her of Arkades's words to the Unfallen in his room. Knowing that she was only an inconvenience to this man, a stone to be stepped upon on the way to the *magni*. He was only using her to see Furian elevated, his ends attained.

All right then, bastard. Let's use each other.

Mia spoke, her voice cold as wintersdeep. 'Executus.'

Leona said nothing more, and the pair left the staging area, the door locked behind them. Furian looked at her sidelong, expression hidden behind his Falcon helm. Bladesinger's eyes were fixed on the arena as she threaded her saltlocks through her helmet's crown, slipped it over her head. Hefting a heavy iron shield embossed with a red falcon, she tossed her head, the razor-tipped blades she'd woven at the tips of her locks glinting in the sunslight.

Mia clenched and unclenched her empty hands, shadow trembling, all the hunger and desire and breathless energy she felt when she was near Furian rising to her surface. She didn't bother grabbing a shield – she was useless with them anyway. Mister Kindly and Eclipse swelled in her shadow, pouncing on the butterflies trying to take wing in her belly and murdering them, one by one.

She knew this would be the hardest fight of her life.

Trumpets sounded, hushing the crowd, anticipation dripping from the very walls.

'Hold . . .' Furian said, looking to the guard captain. 'Where are our swords?'

'Waiting for us,' Mia answered softly. 'Out there.'

'Citizens of Itreya!' The editorii's words echoed in the quiet. 'Honoured administratii! Senators and marrowborn! We present to you, a feature bout between the Lions of Leonides and the Falcons of Remus!'

An excited murmur rippled through the crowd.

'This match shall be fought *e mortium*, no surrender, no quarter given! Sanguila Leonides has placed a berth in the *Venatus Magni* in ante! Should the Falcons of Remus stand the victors, his daughter, Sanguila Leona of the Remus Collegium, shall be permitted to enter her gladiatii in the grand games at Godsgrave, six weeks hence.'

The murmur became a rising swell.

'Entering from the Coast Gate for the Falcons of Remus, we present to you, Bladesinger, the Reaper of Dweym! The Bloody Beauty and Saviour of Stormwatch, Crow! And the Champion of Talia, the Unfallen himself, Furiaaaan!'

The crowd came to their feet, roaring in approval. The portcullis drew up, and with a final glance to each other, the three Falcons strode out into the sand, guards marching beside them. Bladesinger and Furian raised their hands in greeting, the crowd bellowing in response, thousands upon thousands. Mia only scowled. She remembered not so long ago, when that applause had thrilled her soul. Now, she knew they cheered not for *her*, but the bloody spectacle she provided. It mattered not who swung the blade. Only that someone's neck was there to meet it.

She wanted to be done with this, wanted this bloody gala ended and Duomo and Scaeva gone and a thousand years in a hot spring to wash the blood and stink of it away . . .

The great island that had marked the equillai track had sunk back down into the mekwerks beneath the arena floor. The sand before them was featureless, off-white, streaked with fresh red.

'Wait here,' the guard captain commanded. 'Do *not* move until commanded by the editorii, or you will be disqualified.'

The guards marched back to the portcullis, and sealed them in.

'What the 'byss is happening here?' Bladesinger muttered.

'Just hold still,' Mia replied. 'And brace yourself.'

'Do you know something we do not, Crow?' the Unfallen growled.

'Furian,' she sighed. 'The things I know that you don't could just about fill the Great fucking Salt.'

'Entering from the Tower Gate for the Lions of Leonides, we present a terror from the Drakespine Mountains! A pariah among her own kind, her very name, death in the tongue of the Dominion! Behold, Ishkah, the Exiiiiile!'

A wondering murmur rolled through the crowd, the portcullis in the arena's northern wall grinding open. Out of the shadow walked Leonides's silkling, flanked by a half-dozen guards. She was decked in a suit of magnificent golden armour, highlighted with emerald green. A lion's pelt was draped about her shoulders, its head and great mane fitted around her helm. As the crowd cheered wildly, the silkling strode into the arena. The guards marched back in formation, the portcullis slamming behind them.

Mia stared across the sand to their enemy, dust blowing in the rising wind. Ishkah stood seven feet tall, all gleaming chitin and muscle, her lips painted cloud-white. She sloughed off her lion's pelt, six arms unfolding like a flower in bloom. Her dark green skin gleamed in the sunlight, those featureless eyes staring down her foes.

'Mother of Oceans,' Bladesinger murmured. 'She's a sight.'

'Just brace yourselves,' Mia said.

'Citizens, behold!' cried the editorii. 'Your battleground.'

A deep rumbling sounded beneath the sands, the grinding of colossal gears. The floor shuddered, but Mia's comrades held steady as a large, wedge-shaped section of the floor they stood on began to rise. Sand cascaded down, Mia looking over the edge into the massive mekwerks below. She smelled oil, sulphur, salt.

Other sections of the sand were moving, the entire arena floor breaking up into a series of wedged platforms. Differing heights and dimensions, the platforms began slowly rotating around the central plinth, spinning, twisting, passing above and beneath one another like the interlocking pieces of some enormous clockface. Furian, Bladesinger, and Mia exchanged glances, Bladesinger whispering a prayer to Trelene.

'You can't say they don't know how to put on a show,' Mia muttered.

The gobsmacked crowd were cheering for all they were worth. Mia and her comrades were perhaps twenty feet above ground level now. She glanced down again into the arena's mekwerk guts – to slip off the edge would be to tumble into those great, grinding gears, and be mashed to pulp between greasy metal teeth.

'Weapons!' cried the editorii.

The great circular platform in the centre of the arena groaned, and Mia saw a dozen blades of differing lengths rise hilt-first from the sands. There were shortswords, longblades, and the cruel, curved scimitars that the Exile favoured. All of them were black, razor-edged, gleaming in the sunlight.

'We have to run for our swords?' Bladesinger muttered.

'Aye,' Mia nodded. 'But be warned – they're all made of obsidian, not steel. They'll be sharp as glass, but they're fragile. You'll only get a few swings before they're useless. Block with your shields, not your blades.'

'How do you know this?' Furian demanded.

'Does it fucking matter?' she snarled. 'Let's just get this done.'

'No witchery, Crow,' he warned. 'We will earn this laurel, or a glorious death.'

Bladesinger looked between the pair. 'Stand together or fall alone, remember?'

'Gladiatii!' the editorii called. 'Prepare!'

Mia coiled like a sprinter, eyes on a pair of twin swords in the centre of the ring.

'Good luck, sister,' Bladesinger said. 'Brother. Lady of Oceans protect you.'

'Aye,' Furian nodded. 'Aa bless and keep you, Tsana guide your hands.'

Mia blinked the sweat from her eyes. The crowd was thunder in her ears. She looked out into the seething mob, searching for a girl with dyed red hair and eyes blue as sunburned skies. Her shadow was trembling at its edges, ebbing like water towards Furian's own.

'Mother watch over us,' she whispered.

'Gladiatii!' the editorii roared. 'Begin!'

Mia took off, sprinting hard as she could. Breath burning in her lungs, glare fixed on those swords, the silkling sprinting at them from the opposite end of the arena as the crowd bellowed. Bladesinger charged just a few steps behind her, long legs pumping smoothly, Furian bringing up the rear.

Mia reached the edge of their platform, vaulting the gap to the next. The wedge shifted under her feet, swinging clockwise, those colossal gears grinding below her. Sand crunched under her boots and she leapt across to the next tier of smaller wedges, closer to the arena's heart. Her eyes were on the silkling, running hard, drawing ever closer to those gleaming, black blades. Heart sinking as she realized . . .

. . . *she's going to get there first.*

Mia reached out across the shifting platforms, the swirling sands, the mighty gears. Her shadow trembled as she took hold of the silkling's own, snarled it in her boots. Ishkah hissed, stumbling momentarily as Mia dashed towards the central plinth. But with a curse, she felt her grip on the shadows break, and Ishkah's feet slip free.

Fucking Furian . . .

'No witchery!' he shouted behind her.

Ishkah made the central platform, six hands snaking out and seizing the hilts of six cruelly curved scimitars. The crowd roared, sunslight gleaming on obsidian. The silkling wheeled about as Mia leapt onto the plinth, three of her swords glittering as they scythed through the air, right at Mia's throat. With a gasp, the girl dived left, hit the sand with her shoulder and rolled, under the whistling blades and behind Ishkah. Mia seized hold of two swords and dragged them free.

She turned just as Ishkah struck, her blades a blur. Mia dare not block the strikes edge on edge – the obsidian might shatter if she struck at the wrong angle, and Ishkah had swords to spare. Instead she danced away, sand flying, twisting left and right and bending backwards, spine extended, one of the strikes whipping just over her chin. Tumbling back, she rolled up into a crouch right at the platform's edge, wobbling precariously over a shifting sea of grinding metal cogs.

Bladesinger roared as she barrelled into Ishkah from behind, shield crunching into the silkling's back and sending her flying. Ishkah fell forward, off the platform and onto another passing below, rolling up to her feet. Those pale, featureless eyes glinted as she watched Mia regain her balance, Bladesinger snatch up an obsidian longblade. Ishkah took a few steps towards Furian, but he was too far out of reach, finally vaulting up to the central plinth and snatching up another obsidian sword. The Unfallen raised his blade in the air, the crowd bellowing in reply. The race was over, the competitors all armed. Now, the battle could begin in earnest.

Ishkah opened her arms, scimitars poised in a glittering fan, and without a sound, leapt back across to the central plinth. The three Falcons moved to meet her, Mia dashing out first, quick as silver and striking low. Bladesinger struck mid, her shield guarding Mia, while Furian swung at the silkling's head. Ishkah moved with stunning grace, slipping aside from Bladesinger and Mia's strikes. But as she raised one of her blades to counter Furian, the haft shattered like the thinnest ice.

The silkling rallied, scimitars cutting the air. She put a savage kick into Bladesinger's shield, knocking the smaller woman off-balance. Her swords opened up a shallow cut on Furian's arm. One of her blades whistled past Mia's throat and scraped her breastplate, splitting the leather wide. And drawing a breath, Ishkah parted those cloud-white lips in a snarl, and spat a mouthful of bright green venom right at Mia's face.

'. . . *beware . . . !*'

Mia gasped, twisting desperately and turning her head. The liquid hit the side of her helm, spattering thick. As it touched the metal, the venom hissed, eating through the iron like a heated blade into snow. Mia rolled out of reach, tearing her helm loose and blinking hard. None had got in her eyes, on her skin, but Goddess, that was close . . .

The Unfallen struck back with a furious cry, swinging his sword in a brutal overarm strike. Ishkah raised a blade, but it simply shattered against the Unfallen's. Mia shielded her eyes from the obsidian shards as the silkling hissed in frustration. Bladesinger swung her own sword, her strike glancing off Ishkah's armour. As Mia climbed to her feet, Furian pummelled Ishkah with his shield, forcing her back towards the platform's edge as another of her scimitars fractured on Bladesinger's armour. Mia lunged, feinting high and striking low, the crowd bellowing as she opened up the silkling's thigh. Green blood sprayed on the sand, obsidian splinters flying as Ishkah parried one of Mia's blades into the dirt and stomped on it with her boot. She swung her scimitar and Mia rolled aside, the silkling's fourth sword splintering on the dirt.

Furian's blade was still intact, Mia had one blade left, and Bladesinger's was only slightly fractured. Ishkah had but two swords remaining, and three foes. She struck simultaneously, forcing the Falcons back, the air hissing where she struck. Furian was on the defensive, bashing away with his shield where he could. Bladesinger and Mia fought side by side, the woman catching one of Ishkah's strikes on her shield and driving the sword into the ground, snapping it in half. Ishkah struck with her last blade, the broken haft of another, the blows whistling towards Bladesinger's belly and throat. Furian blocked the high strike on his shield, Mia parried the low, breaking Ishkah's final blade off at the hilt. With a furious war cry, Bladesinger charged, striking the silkling in the belly with her shield and knocking her backwards off the platform. Ishkah made a desperate clicking noise, seizing the lip of a passing platform to halt her fall, and dragging herself up to safety.

The three Falcons stood together, gasping for breath. The silkling revolved around the central plinth on her own platform, featureless eyes locked on theirs. She still held the hilts of her broken swords, pale eyes fixed on the weapons of her enemies. Obsidian was fragile, but it wasn't supposed to be *this* fragile. Though the Falcons' weapons were chipped and scratched, Ishkah's scimitars had proven to be delicate as autumn leaves. Almost as if . . .

As if . . .

A slow smile curled Mia's lips.

'She looks upset.'

'. . . *the viper managed it, then . . .*'

'I wish you wouldn't call her that.'

Mia risked a glance into the crowd, heart swelling in her chest, looking once more among the mob for blood-red hair, a pair of pretty blue eyes. She didn't truly know the concoction she'd devised – one part calcite acid, two parts boric oxide – would prove as effective on the silkling's weapons as it had. Didn't know whether Ashlinn would be clever or quick enough to sneak down into the arena's bowels and treat Ishkah's scimitars with the solution before the match began. But looking at the shattered blades in the silkling's hands, the relatively unscathed sword in her own, she knew somehow Ash had done it. The silkling was all but disarmed, and now, even with the venom and the frightening speed, the scales between them were somewhere close to even.

The crowd roared, urging the Falcons in for the kill.

Furian scowled at Mia. 'The match proves easier than any supposed.'

'Fancy that,' Mia replied.

'*Crow* . . .' Furian growled.

Mia looked at Furian sidelong, and winked.

'Enough talk,' Bladesinger spat. 'Let's just gut this ugly bitch.'

The Falcons raised their weapons, made ready to charge.

'Blades!' cried the editorii.

Mia heard a rumble, turned to a platform at the arena's edge. Her heart sank as the sand shivered, and ten new obsidian blades rose up out of the dirt.

'Shit . . .' she breathed.

'. . . i take it you and the viper didn't know about those . . .'

'Shit, shit, *shit*.'

'. . . o, this is maaaarvellous . . .'

The crowd bellowed as Ishkah dashed towards the fresh swords, leaping from one shifting platform to the next. Mia took off after her, her comrades sprinting behind. The platforms wheeled and turned, a great mekwerk dance that was hard to judge, sweat burning Mia's eyes.

She supposed Ashlinn should've suspected there'd be backup plans in case every competitor broke their weapon, but there was no time to whine about it now – those new scimitars hadn't been weakened by her concoction. If Ishkah got her hands on them, the fight might end up being fair, and *that* couldn't happen. But as she ran, Mia realized with a sinking heart that again, the silkling would reach the blades before her.

'Furian?' she gasped.

'No!' the Unfallen spat, leaping across a rumbling chasm.

Spitting dust from her mouth she shook her head, and despite the burning heat of the two suns above, reached out towards Ishkah's shadow anyway. She felt it in her grasp, cool and tenebrous, slipping up like snakes to entwine itself with Ishkah's feet. The silkling stumbled, fell to her knees, her helm tumbling off her head and into the mekwerks below. But with a sharp, tearing sensation, Mia found her grip ripped away, the darkness slithering through her fingers.

'Mother fucking damn you!' she spat, face twisted.

'Victory is earned!' Furian shouted in reply. 'Not stolen!'

Ishkah reached the swords, casting her chipped blades into the abyss and drawing six new ones – longblades this time, not scimitars. Turning to face the trio as they tumbled and leapt across the platforms towards her, she cut an awesome sight, blades whistling through the air in an almost hypnotic pattern. Mia reached the platform first, tumbling and hurling a handful of sand into Ishkah's face. She had only one sword, so as the silkling staggered back, pawing at her eyes, Mia dived towards the remaining blades to snatch a second, replace her first. She rolled aside as the silkling's swords struck the sand, the crowd gasping as her boot collided with Mia's ribs. The impact was thunderous, Mia feeling her ribs crack, burning fire in her chest. Spit spraying from her lips, Mia's face twisted as Ishkah raised her blades and—

Crack! came the sound as Bladesinger hurled her shield into the silkling's face. Ishkah shrieked, staggering, the audience bellowing as they saw the shield's edge had struck one of the silkling's eyes, smashing it like an eggshell. Green fluid dribbled from the wound, Mia dragging herself to her feet with a pained gasp and snatching up a new pair of blades. Bladesinger leapt across the chasm and Ishkah *screeeeeeched*, the Dweymeri raising her cracked sword and meeting her charge.

Bladesinger's blade shattered with the first blow, the enraged silkling scoring deep wounds on her shoulder, and shattering one of her swords on the side of Bladesinger's helm. The woman fell to her knees, skull ringing. But as Ishkah raised her blades to strike the deathblow, Furian arrived, leaping across the gulf with a howl and crashing shield-first into his foe. The pair fell to the ground in a tangle of limbs, Furian's shield skidding across the dirt.

The Unfallen sat atop the silkling, fingers hooked into her bleeding eyehole, pounding his knuckles on her face again and again.

'Fucking bitch!' *Crack!* 'Do you know who I am?' *Crack!* 'I am the Un—'

Ishkah shrieked, and spat a mouthful of venom. The bilious green fluid spattered over Furian's breastplate, up his unprotected throat, the man screaming as it began to burn. He fell backwards, clawing at his neck, rolling in the sand as the crowd bellowed. Ishkah scrambled to her feet with a gargling growl, snatching up her blades and raising them above her head to end him.

Mia's sword flashed, striking Ishkah's blow aside. Ishkah struck back, cracking Mia's sword at the hilt and lashing out at her head. The girl pulled back, crying out as the blow sliced down through her brow, opened up her cheek, blood in her eyes. Staggering backwards, she fell to one knee, and Ishkah kicked her savagely in the chest again, the fire in Mia's broken ribs burning white. Winded, she tumbled backwards along the dirt, barely stopping herself from plummeting off the platform's edge.

With a shapeless cry, Bladesinger whipped her neck, her long saltlocks scything through the air. The razored blades she'd woven at the ends of her braids tore into Ishkah's face, her forearms. Bladesinger charged, a sword in each hand, clashing toe to toe with the towering silkling over Furian's prone body. Her blades cut the air, whistling, whirling, *singing*, shattering one of Ishkah's weapons and plunging deep into the silkling's side. Bladesinger *twisted* her wrist, shattering the obsidian sword inside the wound, green blood spraying. Ishkah screeched, stabbing back, opening up Bladesinger's forearm to the bone as she tried to ward off the blow. An empty fist pummelled the woman's face, a blade scythed at her throat, and as Bladesinger ducked, the silkling brought her knee up into her foe's face.

Bone crunched, Bladesinger's spine arching as she flew back, helm flying from her head, nose pulped. Holding her sundered guts in with one hand, Ishkah followed through, driving a brutal kick into the woman's solar plexus and sending her rolling back across the platform. Mia rose to her feet, blood drooling from her split cheek, gasping as she realized Bladesinger was about to tumble over the edge.

'. . . *MIA, NO* . . . !'

It was foolish. Idiotic, really. Victory was her goal here, not heroics, and Bladesinger was not her friend. But with a desperate cry, Mia hurled herself across the platform, plunged her remaining sword deep into the sand and seized hold of Bladesinger's wrist. Bladesinger cried out as she went over the edge, dragging Mia with her. The girl screamed as she arrested their fall, holding tight to Bladesinger with one hand, the sword hilt with the other, the fire of her broken ribs blooming inside her chest. The crowd roared in amazement, Mia's bleeding face twisted in agony. Her ribs were pressed against the side of the platform, the colossal gears churning ten feet below as it continued its revolution around the arena's heart. Her grip was slippery with blood, her body drenched in sweat.

'Hold on!' she cried.

Bladesinger gasped in agony, her face a bloody pulp. She glanced down to the shifting mekwerks below, up to Mia, shaking her head.

'Let me go!'

'Are you mad? Climb!'

'I'm too heavy, you skinny little shit! Let me go!'

'Stand together or fall alone!'

Ishkah was on her knees, two hands pressed to the terrible wound Bladesinger had carved in her side, green ichor dribbling from her shattered eye, her slashed face. Features twisted, she scrabbled in the dust, took hold of a fallen sword. And with the strength of a mountain, crowd murmuring in awe, she rose.

'Kill!' the crowd roared. 'Kill!'

'O, shit . . .' Mia breathed. 'Bladesinger, *climb*!'

Ishkah began stalking towards her, sunslight gleaming on her sword. Mia winced, trying to keep her grip as Bladesinger pulled herself up. Her ribs were screaming, face throbbing, teeth gritted at the pain. Her hands were full, she couldn't clutch the shadows, couldn't reach out to the dark as she'd done so many times before . . .

'. . . *mia, look* . . . !'

Beyond the silkling, stalking closer, Furian was stirring. Sloughing off his helmet, the flesh of his chin and jaw and throat a bubbling, weeping ruin, breath rattling in his chest. The crowd's cries became a chant, a rhythm, pulsing with every beat of her heart.

'Kill! Kill! Kill!'

'Furian!' Mia screamed.

The Unfallen looked up, saw Bladesinger trying to drag herself up Mia's shoulder, the girl's face smeared in blood, the silkling a few steps away from ending them both.

'Furian!' Mia roared. 'The dark!'

Ishkah snarled, needle teeth bared as she stepped closer.

'Kill! Kill! Kill!'

'*Do it!*' Mia screamed.

Bladesinger dragged herself up over the edge, reached out to Mia. Ishkah raised her blades, only two steps away. And fingers curled, teeth bared, the Unfallen reached out to the shadow beneath her, and tangled up the silkling's feet.

Ishkah stumbled, hissing in confusion. The crowd ceased their chanting, held their breath. Mia dragged herself up over the platform's edge, face twisted in agony. Furian gasped, collapsing onto his belly as he lost his grip on the darkness, Ishkah stepping up and slashing Bladesinger across her back, splitting the leather, blood spraying. Bladesinger collapsed with a cry, and with a desperate gasp, Mia dragged her obsidian sword from the earth, twisted away from Ishkah's sword, and hacked the silkling's arm off at the elbow.

Ishkah screamed, green blood fountaining. The crowd were alight, howling their fury. Mia twisted, dropping low and hewing at the silkling's leg, bringing her to her knees. The arena erupted, the noise deafening, seventy thousand voices rising in crescendo, '*Kill! Kill! Kill!*,' the suns burning overhead, blood thrumming in her veins, heart thundering in her chest as Mia screamed and swung her sword double-handed, all her strength, all her fury, all her pain, taking Ishkah's head clean off her shoulders.

Blood sprayed, spattering Mia with warm, sticky green. Ishkah's body trembled, six arms twitching as she toppled off the platform's edge and down into the grinding gears below. Mia winced at the bubbling crunch, averted her eyes, bloody obsidian still clutched in her hand.

But still . . .

. . . *I did it.*

Trumpets blared, silver and bright, the platforms ground to a shuddering halt. The editorii's voice rose over the blood-mad roar of the crowd, bouncing off the arena walls.

'Citizens of Itreya! Your victors! The Falcons of Remus!'

The crowd went wild, the applause deafening. Bladesinger staggered to her feet, face alight with pain and triumph, blood streaming from her wounds. But still, she grinned, throwing her good arm around Mia's shoulder and kissing her bloody cheek.

We *did it* . . .

Turning, Bladesinger grasped Mia's hand in her own, raised it high into the sky, bellowing at the crowd.

'What is her name?'

'Crow!' they roared.,

'*What is her name?*'

Feet stamping, hands clapping, the word reverberating across the sands.

'Crow! Crow! Crow! Crow!'

Mia looked down at the bloody sword in her hand. Over to Furian, curled in a ball in the dirt, hands to his savaged throat. She raised her eyes to the sanguila's box, saw Leona on her feet, horrified stare locked on Furian. Arkades stood beside her, hands raised in sombre applause.

She thought of Godsgrave, of the *Venatus Magni*, the berth her victory had now assured. She thought of Bryn, her dead brother cradled in her arms as she wailed. She thought of her father, holding her hands as he whisked her around some glittering ballroom, her feet atop his as they danced. Her mother, making her watch as he was hanged, as she whispered the words that would shape Mia for ever, as the hope children breathed and adults mourned withered and fell away, floating like ashes on the wind.

'Never flinch. Never fear. And never, *ever* forget.'

What is my name?

'Crow! Crow! Crow! Crow!'

What is my name?

'CROWCROWCROWCROW!'

Dark delight in her belly.

Warm blood on her hands.

Mia closed her eyes.

Raised her blade.

O, Mother, blackest Mother, what have I become?

BOOK 3

THE GAME

CHAPTER 25

ROT

'Hold him still!'

'*Almighty God, it burns!*'

'Hold his legs, damn you!'

'*Aa, help me! Help me!*'

Mia sat in a dark corner of the cell, ribs burning, a blood-soaked rag held to her split cheek. She could feel the adrenaline from the match souring in her veins, hands trembling. The crowd bellowed above, the Ultima in full swing, the stone beneath her vibrating with the fury of the final bout. Bladesinger sat beside her, arm swaddled in red-soaked cloth, Mia pressing a sodden bandage to the ragged wound across the woman's back. The pair of them were in need of stitching, blood pooling on the stone around them. But Maggot's hands were more than full.

'Tie him down!' the girl yelled. 'He's only making it worse!'

Furian screamed again, full-throated and trembling, his agony echoing through the arena's bowels. He was laid out on a stone slab, Executus and three of Leona's houseguards trying to keep him still. The flesh of his throat, jaw, and chest was blistered and weeping from the touch of the silkling's venom. He seemed to have gone mad from the agony, muscles corded in his arms and chest as he screamed.

Dona Leona stood by the door, horror in her eyes.

'Almighty Aa . . .' she whispered.

'Tie him down!' Maggot cried again.

Arkades snapped heavy iron manacles about Furian's arms, feet, and waist, securing him to the slab. But the Unfallen continued to thrash, cutting his wrists and ankles on his bonds, smashing the back of his head against the stone. Mia had seen pain before – the blood scourging in the Mountain, her branding in that cell in the Hanging Gardens. But she'd never seen agony the likes of this in her life.

'You need to put him under, Maggot,' she said.

'I don't have any slumberweed!' the little girl cried, pointing to a chest of herbs and remedies. 'It all spoiled on the way here!'

'Do you have any Swoon?'

'I used it all on Butcher!'

'Four Daughters,' Leona cursed. 'Did you only bring a thimbleful?'

'All respect, Domina, but you've not given me coin to restock in months!'

'Well, you must do something!' Leona cried. 'Listen to him!'

Furian screamed again, mouth open wide, his throat bleeding with the force of it. With a wince at her cracked ribs, Mia rose and limped to Maggot's herb chest. Fingers sticky with blood, she rifled through the phials and jars of powder and liquid, all the lessons from Spiderkiller's hall buzzing in her head.

'What the 'byss are you doing?' Arkades growled.

Mia ignored the executus, handed Maggot a half-dozen jars. 'Grind the scalpweed with the maidenhead and a pinch of allroot, mix it with some goldwine.'

'No,' Maggot frowned. 'The alcohol will calcify the maidenhe—'

'That's what the mireleaf is for,' Mia interrupted. 'Steep the leaf in the . . . in fact, let me do it. You go stitch up Bladesinger. She's bleeding all over the fucking floor.'

'Crow?' Leona asked.

Mia turned to the woman by the door. 'Trust me, Domina.'

Leona looked to Furian, still writhing in agony. Eyes brimming, she nodded, and Mia set to work mixing her concoction. Maggot took a needle and silken thread, set to work stitching the awful wound on Bladesinger's forearm. The silkling's blade had sliced the woman down to the bone, and the blood was flowing like cheap wine at a truelight feast. Bladesinger gritted her teeth, eyes locked on the Unfallen.

'Can you save him?'

'I can make him sleep,' Mia replied. 'Executus, I need your flask.'

Arkades raised an eyebrow as Mia held out one bloody hand.

'Your goldwine, now!'

Arkades reached into his tunic, pulled out his silver flask. Mia poured her concoction into the whisky, shook the mixture thoroughly.

Furian was still bucking, screaming, begging. And as Mia stepped closer, flask in hand, his shadow began bleeding over the stone, reaching out towards her own. It was only the dim light of the cell and the drama unfolding on the slab that prevented any from noticing right away, and Mia moved quickly, shouldering one of the guards aside. The Unfallen's shadow melted into her own, all the sickness, all the hunger she felt when she was near him rising in her gullet and almost making her vomit. She staggered, nearly dropped the flask, Arkades grabbing her shoulders to stop her fall.

Black Mother, I can feel him . . .

'Are you well?'

. . . as if he were part of me.

'Hold his m-mouth open,' Mia said.

The pain from her split cheek and broken ribs was awful, but she could feel pain at her throat and chest, too; Furian's agony was somehow bleeding into her, worsening her own.

'Furian, you must drink!' Mia shouted. 'Do you hear me?'

A gurgling wail of agony was his only reply, and so Mia upended the flask into the man's mouth. He gargled, tried to spit the dose out, but Mia clamped her hand over his blistered lips and roared, 'Swallow!'

Furian bucked, straining against his bonds, tears spilling from his eyes. But finally he did as commanded, his mangled throat bobbing as he drank the burning draught. It took a few minutes for the herbs to take effect – Mia wasn't working with the finest materials, after all. But slowly, the Unfallen's struggles slowed, his screams became moans, and finally, after what seemed an age in the lightless bowels beneath that bloody sand, Furian's bloodshot eyes fluttered closed.

Mia fell to her knees, hair plastered to her split brow and cheek, head swimming.

'Where did you learn to do that?' Maggot asked, bewildered.

Mia hung her head, vision swimming.

'. . . Crow?' Leona asked.

'. . . *mia . . . ?*'

'. . . *MIA . . . !*'

Blood on her hands, in her eyes, the taste of bitter medicine she'd never drunk on her tongue. She looked down to her shadow. The shadow that should have been dark enough for three. But as the room swam before her eyes, as the pain of her wounds and the trauma of her ordeal in the arena and the shuddering aftermath rose up to sweep a black curtain over her eyes, she realized . . .

Dark enough for four . . .

'. . . *Mia . . .*'

She woke in the hold of a ship, creaking beams above and the sound of the waves all around. As she opened her eyes, she felt a cool, featherlight touch on the back of her neck, a whispered sigh of relief in her ear.

'. . . *at last . . .*'

The hammock she lay in ebbed and rolled, her mouth dry as dust. Garish light filtered in through a small glass porthole, a glimpse of two blues framed beyond; sunburned bright and ocean deep. Her ribs burned like a dying fire. Mia reached up to her face, felt a bandage over her cheek and brow, crusted with dried blood.

'Don't touch it,' came a voice. 'It'll heal best when let alone.'

Mia looked up and saw Maggot, her dark eyes and pretty smile. She was hovering over Furian, the man swinging in a hammock beside her. Glancing to her shadow, Mia saw Furian's had apparently left hers somewhere as they slept. But still, that sickness lingered, the ache of a missing piece of herself swelling in her chest.

She took a deep breath, signing in Tongueless so only Mister Kindly might understand.

Where?

'. . . *the gloryhound . . .*' came the whispered reply. '. . . *bound for crow's nest . . .*'

Eclipse? Ashlinn?

'. . . *they follow, a handful of turns behind us . . .*'

Furian?

'. . . *not good . . .*'

Mia nodded to herself, looking about the cabin. She'd not been up here before – every trip she'd taken had been spent locked down in the hold. The room was cramped, a chest full of Maggot's implements and herbs and some wooden crates were the only decor. Three hammocks hung from the ceiling, Mia in the middle. Bladesinger was belly-down to her left, eyes closed, swordarm and back swathed in bloody bandages. To her right, the Champion of Remus Collegium lay unconscious, soaked through. Furian's torso and throat were swabbed with a greenish salve, but the wounds from the silkling's venom still looked awful. Above the bilge and the sea and the sweat, Mia could smell the beginnings of a high, ripe decay.

Maggot held a cup of fresh water to her lips, and Mia drank all she was given despite the pain, sighing with relief.

'Bladesinger . . . ,' she began, licking at dry lips. 'H-how does . . .'

'Passing fair,' Maggot whispered, so as not to disturb the sleepers. 'The tendon and muscle in her swordarm are badly cut. But she stitched up well. I think she'll wake.'

'And . . . F-Furian?'

Maggot sighed, looking the Unfallen over. 'Not so well. Infection is taking root, and I fear it will turn to blood sepsis. I need to get him back to the Nest.'

'We sail as fast as Lady Trelene and Lady Nalipse allow.'

Mia looked up to see Dona Leona at the doorway, eyes locked on the Unfallen. Magistrae stood beside her, ever the dutiful second.

As usual, the magistrae's appearance was immaculate, but Mia was surprised to see the turn Leona had taken. The dona usually dressed as if she were attending some grand salon, but now, she wore only a simple white shift. Mia could see her fingernails were chewed down to the quick. In her right hand, she held the silver torc that had once encircled Furian's neck. The metal was melted slightly by the silkling's venom.

'Domina,' Mia nodded.

'My Crow,' the woman answered. 'I am heartened to see you wake.'

Mia sat up with a wince, head swimming. Her cheek felt swollen, and she could feel the pinch of sutures in her skin. Ribs aching, she took a second cup from Maggot, drank until it was empty.

'H-how long did I sleep for?'

'Three turns since your triumph,' Leona said.

'It is ours, then?' she asked, stomach thrilling. 'The *magni?*'

'Aye,' the dona replied, stepping into the room. 'It is ours. My father is many things, little Crow. A snake. A liar. A bastard. But no sanguila would dare renege on a wager made so publicly. With the laurels he has won, he had berths to spare. He can afford to lose one to us. But now, thanks to Bryn and Byern's sacrifice, he has no equillai. And thanks to your valour, he has no champion.'

The woman fixed her eyes on Furian.

'All we have desired is now within our reach.'

'How is Bryn?' Mia asked.

The dona's haunted glance was Mia's only reply. But Bryn had lost her twin brother, right before her very eyes. Crushed and bled out before a booing mob. And all for nothing. No purse. No glory. Nothing at all.

How the 'byss do you expect her to be?

'How are your wounds?' Leona asked.

Mia gingerly touched the bandages at her cheek, looked to Maggot. 'You tell me.'

'Your ribs are cracked,' the young girl replied. 'The bruises will be awful, but you'll mend. The cut to your face is healing well. Though I'm afraid it will scar.'

Mia focused on that thought, briefly burning hotter than the pain of her wounds. She'd never been pretty when she was a girl – she'd only discovered what beauty was once Marielle wove her face into a portrait in the Quiet Mountain. And truth was, she'd revelled in the power it bestowed.

She wondered what Ashlinn might say. How the girl might look at her now, and whether she'd hate the reflection she saw in those pools of sunburned blue. For a moment, she wished she were back in the Mountain, where Marielle could mend all hurts with a wave of her hand. She supposed that option would be for ever denied her now she'd set herself against the Church. That this scar, the brand beside it, would be hers to cherish until she died.

Mia pictured her father, swinging and choking before the mob. Her mother, weeping and bleeding out in her arms. Her brother, dying as a babe in a lightless pit.

And, hand falling away from her face, she shrugged.

'The choice between looking plain and pretty isn't really a choice at all. But any fool knows looking dangerous is preferable to both.'

A mirthless smile curled Leona's lips, and she slowly shook her head.

'I like you, Crow. Everseeing help me, but I do. I know not what you were before this, but for the assistance you offered our champion and your courage in the arena, I will be for ever grateful.'

'I wonder if your champion will say the same, Domina . . .'

The dona's eyes returned to Furian, fingers clasped so tight about his silver torc that her knuckles were white. Mia wondered how often the dona had visited his side since they left Whitekeep. Wondered if perhaps she did truly care for him. Wondered what Arkades would be making of it all if he knew . . .

'Perhaps we should head back up to the deck, Domina?' Magistrae murmured, squeezing the woman's hand. 'Let them rest.'

Leona blinked as if waking from a dream. But she nodded, allowed herself to be led away. As she reached the cabin door, she stopped, turned to Mia.

'Thank you, Crow,' she murmured.

And with that, she was gone.

Turn after turn, the *Gloryhound* cut through the Sea of Swords, a trader's wind at their backs. The Lady of Oceans was merciful, and the ship pulled into the harbour at Crow's Rest a good twenty hours before schedule. But even with Mother Trelene on his side, it seemed Furian the Unfallen's luck was all but spent.

Just as Maggot predicted, his wounds had turned septic. By the time they arrived at Crow's Rest, the flesh about his chest and throat was dark and weeping, and the sweet stink of rot hung over him like fog. Maggot and Mia did their best to keep him sedated, though he slipped in and out of consciousness frequently. He was barely lucid when awake, and murmured fever-dream nonsense while sleeping. What it would mean for the collegium and Leona if he died, Mia had no idea.

A waiting wagon rushed them up to Crow's Nest, hooves pounding on the hillside. Mia's knowledge of herbcraft seemed to have impressed the dona, and she rode with Maggot, Bladesinger and the dazed and groaning Furian, Leona and Magistrae beside her. Arkades and the other gladiatii were left to tromp up the hill on foot.

Captain Gannicus met them at the gates, Leona's houseguards carrying Furian to the rear of the house. Despite the ache of her broken ribs, once inside Maggot's infirmary, Mia began looking for ingredients that might quell his blood poisoning. Maggot herself disappeared into the shed in the corner of the yard. Leona hovered like a mother hen, a kerchief pressed to her nose and mouth to stifle the stench, pale with worry.

'Can you save him?' she asked.

Mia only scowled, sighing as she rifled through Maggot's chests and cupboards. It was true what the girl had said – it looked to have been months since Leona allowed her to restock. Even with all she'd learned from Spiderkiller and her beloved, dog-eared copy of *Arkemical Truths*, there wasn't enough to work with.

'We need hollyroot,' Mia declared. 'Maidenhead. Something to kill the swelling, like tinberry or pufferfish bladder. And ice. Lots of ice. This fever is burning him out like a fucking candle.'

'Can you write?' Leona asked.

Mia raised an eyebrow. 'Aye. I can write.'

'Make a list,' Leona commanded. 'All you need.'

Maggot returned from the shed, waddling under the weight of an old tin bucket. She thumped it on the bloodstained slab beside Furian's head, tied up her hair and began peeling off the pus-soaked bandages from his throat and chest.

'What are you doing?' Mia asked.

'You remember when you asked how I got my name?'

'You told me to pray I'd never find out,' Mia replied.

The girl dragged her nose along her arm, wincing at the stench of Furian's wounds. 'Well, you didn't pray hard enough.'

Mia peered into the bucket and saw a great wriggling mass; hundreds of tiny white bodies, black heads, chewing sightlessly at the air. She put her hand to her mouth, gorge rising at the sight of those crawling, squirming . . .

'Four Daughters,' she gagged. 'Those are . . .'

'Maggots,' the little girl replied. 'I breed them in the shed.'

'. . . What the 'byss for?'

'What do maggots eat, Crow?'

Mia looked at the flesh of Furian's neck, his torso. The infection was dug deep; the wounds streaked with pus, muscles and skin gone putrid with decay. The veins about the wound were dark with corruption, every heartbeat only spreading it farther.

'Rotten meat,' she whispered. 'But what stops them eating . . .'

'The good bits?'

'Aye.'

'Two jars on the shelf behind you. Bring them here.'

Mia did as she was bid, peering at the spidery writing on the sides. She looked at the little girl, a smile creeping to her lips despite herself.

'Vinegar and bay leaves. You *are* very good at this.'

Maggot offered a mirthless smile and began applying the larvae to the wounds, sprinkling them like salt onto the rancid flesh. Sickened despite the genius of it, Mia began writing on a wax tablet, making a list of all they'd need to keep Furian sedated, stop the sepsis spreading, kill his fever. She showed the list to Maggot, who looked up long enough to grunt assent, then handed the list to Leona.

The dona looked over the tablet once, gave it to her magistrae.

'Anthea, head to town,' she commanded. 'Gather all that Crow bids you.'

Magistrae looked over the list, raised her eyebrow. 'Domina, the cost of—'

'Hang the bloody cost!' Leona snapped. 'Do as I command!'

The woman glanced to Mia and Maggot, pursed her lips. But still, she looked to her mistress and bowed low. 'Your whisper, my will, Domina.'

Magistrae marched out into the yard, wax tablet in hand. Dona Leona remained behind, eyes locked on Furian, chewing her tortured fingernails.

'He must live,' she whispered.

A command.

A hope.

A desperate prayer.

But whether it was because she cared about the man, or cared about the *magni*, Mia had no idea.

They worked into the nevernight, Maggot applying the squirming flyspawn over Furian's wounds, smearing the edges with vinegar and bay leaves to repel the larvae from the hale flesh, and then gently wrapping it all in gauze. Mia stood by, helping when she could, but mostly observing with a churning belly.

Finger brought their evemeal to them, the emaciated cook peering at Furian as if he were already dead. Fang came snuffling about looking for scraps soon after, and with the pain of her ribs, the nausea at Maggot's treatments, Mia fed the mastiff most of her meal, scruffing him behind his ears as he wagged his stubby tail. Dona Leona also refused to eat, sitting and staring at the Unfallen, not saying a word. Her eyes were wide and bloodshot. Her cheeks hollow.

The other gladiatii arrived back at the Nest, marching down to the barracks accompanied by the houseguards. Arkades limped into the infirmary, dusty and sore from his long walk. He looked Furian over, pressed a hand to the man's sweat-slicked brow, watched the rapid rise and fall of his chest. The long scar bisecting his cheek deepened as he scowled. Mia touched the bandage at her own face. Once more thinking of Ashlinn.

Wondering.

'How does he fare?' Arkades asked.

'We've done all we can 'til Magistrae returns,' Maggot replied. 'The herbs and brews she's fetching will help. But it's no sure thing, Executus.'

Arkades nodded. 'Crow, return to the barracks. Maggot will call if she has need.'

'I'd prefer to sta—'

'And I'd prefer a villa in southern Liis and my real leg back,' Arkades growled. 'It is after nevernight. Your place is under lock and key in the barracks.'

Mia glanced to Dona Leona, but the woman was paying no attention at all, stare fixed on Furian. Touching Maggot's shoulder in farewell, Mia limped out into the yard, flanked by two houseguards. Arkades remained, staring at his mistress, brow creased in thought. A small, cat-shaped piece of Mia's shadow stayed behind also.

'Mi Dona, you should rest,' Arkades said.

'I will stay.'

'Maggot can inform you if there is any cha—'

'I will *stay!*' Leona snapped.

Maggot glanced up at the shout, returned quickly to work. The executus looked between his mistress and the fallen gladiatii on the bench. Nodding slow.

'Your whisper, my will.'

Turning on his heel, he limped out from the infirmary into the yard. Staring up at the nevernight suns, the blue glow budding ever deeper on the horizon. Truelight was close now – just a few weeks until all three of the Everseeing's eyes burned bright in the sky. Scorching the world pure. Exposing all their sins.

Sins.

Arkades glanced back over his shoulder to his mistress, watching her watching her champion, lips pursed. And then he was walking, into the keep and along the halls, *clink* thump, *clink* thump, the tune of his tread. His brow was a dark scowl, his lips a thin line, those mighty, sword-callused fists clenched.

He did not notice the small, dark shape following him, flitting from shadow to shadow behind. Silent as cats.

Arkades limped past paintings on the walls of old gladiatii battles, the suits of armour and gleaming helms, the marble busts of Marcus Remus's ancestors, paying them not a moment's mind. And finally, he arrived at a single door at the end of the hall, unlocking it with an iron key.

Arkades walked into Furian's room. Folding his arms and surveying the scene. The shrine to Tsana beneath the small window. The trinity of Aa on the wall. A practice dummy and some swords. A small chest for the Unfallen's meagre belongings.

Closing the door behind him, Arkades limped to the chest. Kneeling with a wince, he began rifling through it – two silver laurels won at Talia and Blackbridge. The hilt of a broken sword. A mouldy deck of cards and some dice. Spare loincloth. A fishbone comb. A handful of copper beggars.

Arkades stood, scowling about the room. His face was darkening, eyes glinting with anger. He limped to the bed, searched inside the pillow and threw it to the floor, tore off the sheets, pawed at the straw mattress. With a frustrated curse, he flipped the mattress over and hurled it against the wall. And there, on the bedframe, he saw it.

A silken underslip.

The executus stooped, lifted the slip to his nose and inhaled. The faint scent of jasmine perfume. The same scent he'd inhaled when he'd visited here before the *venatus*, warning the Unfallen that his soap was making him smell like a woman.

'You fucking bastard . . .'

Arkades clenched the slip in one white-knuckled fist.

'You ungrateful . . .'

Arkades returned the room to its former state, remaking the bed, smoothing the sheets. His face was pale, jaw clenched. With the bedchamber as it was, he turned and stormed from the room, *clink* thump, *clink* thump. Limping down the corridor, storm clouds over his brow, he arrived at his bedchamber and slammed the door.

Enraged as he was, the Executus failed to notice Magistrae standing by the storeroom, her arms laden with the remedies she'd fetched from town.

But the old woman certainly noticed the silk slip clutched in his hand.

'. . . *interesting* . . .' the shadows whispered.

CHAPTER 26

SILVER

They gathered in the yard after mornmeal.

Seven turns had passed, and little had changed – Furian's fever burned the lesser, but still hadn't burned out entirely. The fly larvae were doing . . . well, they were doing exactly what maggots do. The process was beyond disgusting, the sight when Maggot pulled back those bandages was almost more than Mia could stomach. And there was still no telling whether it was doing any good.

The gladiatii were of a mood. Buoyed by their victory in the arena and the berth the Falcons of Remus had won in the *Venatus Magni*. But the price they'd paid . . .

Bryn stayed in her cell, speaking to no one, even at mealtimes. Bladesinger might never fight again. Furian hovered close to death's door, and Byern was simply dead. If this was the tithe they paid for a chance at freedom, it was drenched in more blood than most would have preferred.

Arkades had summoned them at the command of their domina, the suns beating down on the sand like hammers as the gladiatii of the Remus Collegium assembled. Mia's ribs ached abominably, the slice on her face itching beneath the crusted gauze. It was odd seeing the world with one eye under a bandage, the lack of depth, the loss of balance. She knew she should go see Ashlinn – Eclipse had appeared in her cell late last nevernight, informing her that their ship had arrived back in Crow's Rest. But with the situation in the keep the way it was, Mia dare not risk a visit. Furian might wake at any moment, and if Maggot called on her to help with some herbcraft in the middle of the nevernight and the guards discovered her missing . . .

She touched the bandage at her face. She'd not yet mustered the will to look underneath it in a mirror. Wondering what she'd see when she did.

Wondering what Ashlinn would see.

Butcher stood with hands clasped behind his back, shifting his weight from one foot to the other as always. Despite losing his match at Whitekeep, he seemed pleased that he'd earned himself a few more scars to add to his collection.

Sidonius waited silently, arms crossed over the COWARD branded on his broad chest. His cropped hair was getting longer, his blue eyes sparking in the sun. As always, he stood right beside Mia, never straying far if he could help it. He'd sung her praises in their cell, declaring her match against the silkling the greatest he'd ever seen. And still, he didn't press about her parents. Didn't ask questions she wasn't yet prepared to answer. For all his bluster and thuggery, for all his foolery around women, he knew when to talk, and when to keep his mouth shut.

Mia liked him more and more with every passing turn.

But he is not my friend.

Wavewaker stood at Sidonius's other side, feet planted in the earth like the roots of mountains. He'd fought like a daemon against those scythebears in the arena; he and Sid had fallen shy of their own laurel by only two points. Again, Mia found it hard to imagine the man strutting about the stage in silken hose, talking in rhyming couplets. Standing tall, skin gleaming in the sunlight, he seemed a warrior born.

And he is not my friend.

Bryn stood beside Otho and Felix, looking as though she'd not slept a wink since Whitekeep. It was so strange to see her without her twin – Mia actually caught herself glancing about for Byern. The Vaanian girl walked like a ghost. Bloodshot and empty stare, arms wrapped about herself.

And she is not . . .

Bladesinger leaned at the door to the infirmary. Her face was bloodless beneath her tattoos, swordarm slung around her neck with blood-soaked gauze. The slice to her back had been vicious, but the gouge to her arm had been horrendous. None knew if the woman would ever wield a sword again. Mia could see fear in her eyes.

But she is . . .

And Furian?

He lay sleeping on the infirmary slab, Maggot by his side. Mia could feel his pain whenever she strayed too near, as if it were bleeding through the dark at her feet. She had no idea why. Even with all her herbcraft, with Maggot's remedies, none knew his future, save perhaps the Mother.

'Gladiatii!' Arkades barked. 'Attend!'

The assembled warriors straightened, fists to their chests. Leona and Anthea marched out from the verandah, the dona one step ahead of her magistrae.

Leona looked tired, but at last she'd dressed in a manner more like her usual self. She was clad in a flowing white dress, the fabric rippling about her sandals as she took her place on the burning sands. Her hair was plaited about her brow like the victor's laurel she held in her right hand.

'My Falcons!' she called, raising the laurel high. 'Behold!'

The assembled gladiatii cheered, but circumstances being what they were, Mia felt their enthusiasm rang a little hollow.

'Though the tithe we paid was steep, we have the victory we have so long sought. With this laurel comes a berth in the *Venatus Magni*, five weeks hence. Freedom is within your reach, and soon, the City of Bridges and Bones shall ring with the name of the Remus Collegium!'

A second cheer rang in the yard, much louder than the first. It seemed no matter how deep they ran, the promise of liberty could make any gladiatii forget their sorrows. Wavewaker clapped his hand on Sid's shoulder, Butcher slapped his thighs and roared. The thought of fighting in the *magni* was enough to thrill their hearts, and Mia found her blood quickening along with the rest. Picturing Scaeva and Duomo in her mind's eye.

Soon, bastards . . .

'Three among you stand tall,' Leona declared. 'The best and bravest yet trained within these walls under the careful eye of our noble Executus.'

Leona inclined her head to Arkades, who responded with a stiff, formal bow.

'And yet,' she continued, 'there was only one who struck the killing blow against the Exile. Only one whose valour and skill have paved our way to glory.'

Leona looked to Mia.

'Crow, step forward.'

Mia glanced to Bladesinger, but did as she was bid, bowing before her mistress. Leona fixed her in that glittering blue stare.

'Kneel,' she said, curtly.

Mia gritted her teeth at the reminder of her station, but did as commanded, wincing at the pain of her broken ribs. Taking care not to snag her bandaged brow, Leona placed the silver laurel on Mia's head. And reaching inside the folds of her dress, she held out Furian's silver torc on her open palm. It was slightly melted, the metal discoloured from the kiss of Ishkah's venom.

'This is yours now,' Leona said.

Mia frowned towards the infirmary, looking up into the dona's eyes.

'If we are to have victory in the *magni*,' Leona continued, 'if the Falcons of Remus are to claim the glory that is rightfully ours, I think it shall be by your hand, no other. But in all truth, regardless of what comes, you have earned this, Crow.'

Leona fixed the torc about the girl's throat.

'My Champion,' she declared proudly.

Sidonius roared, and the other gladiatii followed suit, stamping their feet and pounding their hands together. Mia looked once again to Bladesinger, struck by the injustice. 'Singer and Furian had fought just as hard as she, risked just as much – she'd not have triumphed over Ishkah without them. But only Mia was being named in the glories. Only Mia was being called Champion.

This is what you worked for, she reminded herself.

You only need play the game a few weeks longer.

She bowed her head, her voice soft.

'You honour me, Domina.'

'You honour us, Crow. And you will continue to do so in the City of Bridges and Bones. But you'll not do it clad in leather scraps and offcuts of steel, no. You fight beneath our banner a champion now. And you should look the part.'

Leona clapped her hands.

'Behold.'

Two of the dona's houseguards wheeled out a wooden dummy from inside the keep, out onto the verandah. The figure was wearing one of the suits of armour that had stood in the entry hall, but Mia realized it had been refitted to her size.

The iron was almost black, polished to a dark lustre. The breastplate was engraved with a soaring falcon, and the greaves and spaulders were also crafted like falcons in flight. The breastplate was trimmed with a pleated skirt and sleeves of plated iron, and a cloak of blood-red feathers was draped about its shoulders. The helm was fashioned in the likeness of the warrior goddess Tsana, her expression fierce and merciless. Twin blades were sheathed at its belt; Liisian steel, by the look. A double-edged gladius and a long razored dagger, ideally suited for fighting Caravaggio style.

It was one of the finest suits of armour Mia had ever seen, sure and true. But it must have cost a fortune. A fortune Leona could ill afford.

'*You fight beneath our banner a champion now.*'

Mia glanced at Leona, holding back her sigh.

'*And you should look the part.*'

'I thank you, Domina,' Mia said.

'You may thank me in the *magni*,' Leona replied. 'By bringing me the vic . . .'

The dona's voice trailed off as a houseguard marched into the yard, a young boy in a feathered cap beside him. The lad's cheek was branded with the single circle, but he wore expensive livery, a little dusty from the road. His doublet was embroidered with the Lion of Leonides.

'Messenger, Mi Dona,' the guard said. 'The boy claims the matter urgent.'

'I bring missive from my master, your father, gracious Dona,' the boy said bowing low. 'I am instructed to read it aloud, under pain of the lash.'

'Speak, then,' Leona commanded.

The boy produced a sheaf of parchment set with Leonides's seal. He glanced at the assembled gladiatii, clearly unnerved. But with a loud, clear voice, he began to speak.

'*Beloved Daughter,*

'*It is with a happy heart that I congratulate you upon your victory at Whitekeep. I confess surprise that you did not seek audience to gloat afterwards, and it gladdens me to think that the humility I sought to teach you in your childhood has begun to take root. Would that I had . . .*'

The boy faltered, glancing up at Leona and swallowing thickly.

'Continue,' she demanded.

The boy stammered a moment before he found his voice.

'*. . . W-would that I had beaten you harder, and more often.*'

Several of the gladiatii stirred, glowering at the boy. Mia felt her fingernails cut into her palm, her eyes on the dona. Leona's expression didn't change at all.

This is why she hates him so . . .

The lad was sweating now, pawing at the collar of his doublet as if it choked him. Desperate to finish, his cleared his throat and plunged on.

'*I have been reliably informed by my business acquaintances that*

Remus Collegium is in serious arrears with its suppliers. To spare myself the humiliation of seeing a daughter of my line dragged before the debtor's court, I have taken the liberty of purchasing all debts from your creditors, and consolidating them into a single sum, which is now owed to Leonides Collegium and accrues points weekly.'

Leona's eyes widened. 'What?'

'Your first repayment of three thousand two hundred and forty-three silver priests is due at the turning of the month, three weeks hence. Should you fail to deliver the required sum, I will have no choice but to seek punitive compensation through the magistrate's court, and claim possession of your collegium, properties, and other financial holdings by way of reimbursement.

'Please do not think I hold wrath or rancour in my heart for you, my dearest. This is, as you once told me, just business.'

The boy glanced up at Leona, voice trembling.

'If only your dear mother were here to see just how far you have come,' he finished. *'With all the respect you are due, your loving f-father, Leonides.'*

The courtyard was so still, Mia could have heard Mister Kindly breathing. Looking at the messenger, she realized the poor bastard had no idea about the contents of the letter he was delivering. Glancing at Wavewaker and Otho's faces, the lad probably fully expected to be dragged down to the cliffs and thrown into the sea.

'H-he also wished me to convey you a gift, Mi Dona,' the boy said. 'To celebrate your victory.'

Reaching into his pack, the boy produced a bottle of goldwine and placed it on the sand. A blood-red label denoted the vintage on the side.

Albari, seventy-four.

As Leona saw the label, her entire body stiffened with rage. Mia had no idea why, but to the dona, the sight of that bottle was like blood to a whitedrake. With clear effort, Leona drew a deep breath, only the trembling of her clenched fists to bely her fury. And standing tall, she addressed the boy with customary formality.

'Convey all thanks to my father,' she said. 'Inform him the magistrate's involvement will be unnecessary. He will have his coin by month's end. I do here vow it.'

'Yes, Mi Dona,' the boy bowed, relief flooding his features.

'You may go,' she said, her voice turning to cold steel.

The boy doffed his cap and scurried away as fast as his legs could carry him.

'O, and, boy?' Leona said.

The messenger turned, half wincing, eyebrow raised. 'Y-yes, Mi Dona?'

Leona ran her hand over Mia's new armour, her fingers lingering at the dagger's hilt. 'Please convey condolences to my father at the slaughter of his champion. Tell him that I look forward to watching my Crow butcher his next offering in Godsgrave.'

'Y-yes, Mi Dona,' the boy stammered, and scampered out of sight.

Silence reigned in the yard, only the call of distant gulls and the faint song of the sea to break it. Leona walked across the sand, picked up the bottle of goldwine and held it in her hand, staring at that label. She looked among her gladiatii, fury spotting her cheeks. They had fought so hard, come so far, and even now, on the brink of victory, they still stood at the precipice of disaster. Where in the Daughters' names would she get that kind of money?

'Back to training, my Falcons,' she commanded. 'We have work to do.'

The gladiatii marched to the racks, took up their practice weapons. The dona turned and walked back into the keep.

Arkades watched her leave.

His eyes were narrowed.

His hands, fists.

L eona sat in her study, bent over her ledgers, bathed in sunslight spilling through the bay window. The shadows were long and dark, and if one beneath her desk was of a peculiar shape, the dona was too intent on her work to notice.

A guard knocked softly on the door, stepping inside at her command.

'Mi Dona,' the guard said. 'Executus begs a word.'

'Send him in,' Leona replied.

Arkades entered, *clink* thump, *clink* thump, the guard closing the door behind him. Leona's gaze didn't stray from her bookwork, a quill poised in her fingers, scribing figures in her neat, flowing hand. The Albari seventy-four was sat on the desk beside her, unopened. Arkades stood before her, staring at that bottle, shifting his weight.

'What is it, Executus?' the dona asked, not looking up.

'I . . . I wished to see if you were well, Domina.'

'And why would I not be?'

'Your father's missive . . .'

Leona stilled, finally looking up.

'I thought his gift was a lovely touch.' The dona glanced to the bottle beside her. 'I'm surprised he remembered the vintage.'

'I knew him to be the cruellest of men, but . . .' Arkades sighed, his voice soft with sorrow. 'Your mother was a fine woman, Mi Dona. You do not deserve such insult. And she did not deserve what he did to her.'

'He beat her to death with a bottle of goldwine, Arkades,' Leona said, her voice beginning to tremble. 'Because she knocked over his glass at dinner. Who exactly *does* deserve that?'

The executus searched the floorboards as if looking for the right words. He might be a god on the sands, but here, in the privacy of his dona's chambers, under her saphire blue stare, he seemed as helpless as a newborn.

'If ever . . .'

He paused, swallowed hard. Drawing a deep breath, as if before the plunge.

'If ever you seek comfort . . . that is to say, if ever you wish to talk . . .'

Leona tilted her head, looking her executus in the eye.

'That is very kind of you, Arkades. But I do not think it appropriate.'

He glanced out of the window into the yard, to the infirmary where Furian lay.

'. . . Appropriate?' he repeated.

'I am no longer the girl who spent her childhood on tiptoe, for fear of what might set the monster she lived with off next. I am not the girl who cowered beneath the table as that bottle fell, again and again and again. I am sanguila. I am domina of this collegium. You are my executus. And my father's cheap theatre serves in only one regard: to harden my resolve to stand victorious in Godsgrave.'

Arkades simply stared at her, grief and anger plain on his face.

'I need no comfort,' Leona continued, rage shining in her eyes. 'I need that bastard on his fucking knees. If you'd serve me, Arkades, I pray you, serve me in the matter I pay you for. Bring me my victory.'

Leona bent back over her bookwork, resting her head in one hand.

'You may go,' she said.

Arkades stood for an empty moment, utterly mute. But finally . . .

'Your whisper,' he murmured. 'My will.'

The big man turned and limped from the room, shutting the door behind him. Leona dropped her quill as soon as he was gone. Pressing her lips together and drawing one shuddering breath after another. Swiping a hand across her eyes in rage.

Her tears bested, she turned her stare to the bottle on her desk. The sunslight glinting on the glass. The label, painted in blood red.

Leona hung her head, waves of auburn hiding her eyes.

'*Father*,' she spat.

A knock came at the door.

'Four Daughters, who is it now?' Leona demanded.

'Apologies, Mi Dona,' the guard said, peering inside. 'Magistrae seeks audience.'

Leona sighed, smoothed her hair back from her face.

'Very well.'

The older woman entered, pushing the door closed behind her. Leona sat tall in her chair, quill in hand, a fresh picture of poise. Her magistrae stood before her, twisting her braid of long grey hair and bowing her head.

'What is it, Anthea?'

'. . . Domina, you know that ever I have served you faithfully.' Trepidation shone in Magistrae's eyes as she glanced to that bottle of goldwine. 'And I would never seek to do you hurt.'

'Of course.'

'I know your father presses your finances. I did not wish to place one more trouble upon your brow. I've struggled with whether or not to bring this to you, bu—'

'Anthea,' Leona said calmly. 'Speak your piece.'

'. . . It is Arkades, Domina.'

Leona looked to the door her executus had just left by.

'What of him?'

'He knows.'

Leona put aside her quill and sat back in the chair, frowning.

'Knows what?'

'Leona,' Magistrae said. 'He *knows*.'

M ia sat in the infirmary, listening to the nevernight winds blowing off the ocean. The turn in temperature was a welcome relief, but not nearly enough to let her breathe easy. Squinting at the horizon earlier, she'd fancied she could see the third sun, poised at the world's end. Soon it would rise, truelight would begin; awful heat and thrumming crowds and oceans and oceans of blood.

The sounds of the other gladiatii at evemeal filtered through the stone walls, and Mia could hear Butcher complaining about the quality of Finger's 'stew'. To the hoots and cheers of their fellows, the emaciated cook loudly informed the Butcher of Amai where he could stick said stew if he didn't like it.*

Mia's smile became a wince as Maggot swabbed her cheek with aloe and evermint, the vague sting crawling in her wound. Maggot nodded to herself, wrapping Mia's face in fresh bandages and tying a gentle knot.

'It's healing well,' she said. 'We can leave the wrappings off next time.'

'Aye,' Mia said. 'My thanks.'

'Cheer up, little Crow,' came a groggy voice behind her. 'Pretty as you were, you're not true gladiatii without a few scars.'

Mia turned to Bladesinger, yawning and sitting up on the slab beside her.

'Well, if that's the case,' the girl smiled, 'you're the truest gladiatii that ever walked the sands, 'Singer.'

'Aye,' the woman smirked. She held up her swordarm, still wrapped in bandages. 'It's going to be a beaut, that much is sure.'

'Can you move it yet?' Mia asked softly.

Bladesinger looked to Maggot, shook her head.

'It's early turns,' the little girl declared. 'Far too early to tell.'

Mia and the older woman exchanged an uneasy glance, but said nothing. Finger shuffled into the infirmary, carrying steaming bowls on a wooden tray. As he set down his burden with a flourish, Mia looked the cook up and down, wondering how many people parts he'd used in his creation this time.

'Dinner,' he declared. 'Eat it while it's hot.'

'Scrumptious,' Maggot smiled. 'Thank you, Finger.'

The man scruffed the girl's hair and shuffled back out. Mia raised an eyebrow.

'*Scrumptious?*' she said, once the cook was out of earshot. 'Of every word in creation, the last I'd use to describe Finger's cooking is "scrumptious", Maggot.'

'Depends how you grew up,' the girl shrugged. 'Once you've eaten raw rat with your bare hands, you become far less choosy about cookery, believe me.'

Mia nodded, sucked her lip. Again she was struck by how much

---

*I am not a physician, nor an expert in anatomy. However, Finger's suggestion would seem to require an unearthly amount of flexibility on Butcher's part.

this little girl reminded her of herself. Growing up rough and brash, just as Mia had done after her parents were taken. Unafraid to speak her mind. Maybe a touch too clever for her own good. She knew she shouldn't. Knew it was weakness.

But Mia liked her.

'Fair point,' she smiled. 'Apologies.'

'You want any or not?'

'Give it over, then.'

Maggot passed Mia a bowl, raised an eyebrow at her second patient. 'Bladesinger?'

'My thanks.'

The woman set the bowl on the slab beside her. Mia watched her carefully spoon a mouthful with her off-hand. Wondering what would become of her if she never regained use of her swordarm. How quickly would this world dispose of a gladiatii who couldn't lift a blade?

Fang wandered into the infirmary, the big mastiff looking up at Mia's bowl and wagging his tail hopefully. She leaned down and scruffed his ears, but kept her dinner to herself.

'How does Furian fare?' Mia asked.

Maggot nodded at the Unfallen, speaking around her mouthful. 'Take a look.'

Mia set her bowl aside and rose with a wince – her ribs were still bothering her, and there was no real remedy save working them as little as possible. She stepped to the sleeping Furian's side, shadow trembling, a familiar hunger rising in her belly that had nothing to do with her waiting meal.

Truth told, the Unfallen looked a little better. Colour was returning to his face, and touching his brow, Mia found his fever lessened. Wincing with trepidation, she pulled back the bandages to take a peek. The injuries were ghastly, no doubt about it; the silkling's venom had burned through muscle and skin across his chest and throat. But instead of the rotten, weeping mess she'd last seen, the wounds were clean, healthy, pink. The sight of fat, wriggling maggots crawling over the fissures in Furian's skin still made Mia sick to her stomach, and the smell was far from roses. But Black Mother be praised, the blighted flesh was all but gone.

'It's incredible,' Bladesinger murmured.

'It's disgusting,' Mia said.

Utterly nauseated, she finally surrendered her bowl of dinner to Fang, who wuffed and began chowing down with relish.

'But, aye, it's incredible,' Mia admitted. 'Fine work, Maggot.'

The girl waved her wooden spoon like a queen. 'Too kind, Mi Dona. Too kind.'

'What comes next?'

'It's more an art than a science, aye?' Maggot replied, wiping her nose on her arm. 'I think in a few turns we might rid him of the larvae. My ma told me to drown them in hot vinegar, but I feel bad about that with all the work they've done. After that, we keep it clean, keep it salved, keep him dosed. His fever is still fluxing, and the infection could creep back with bad luck. He's a long way from out of the desert, but between you and me, his odds are passing fair.'

'Will he be able to fight in the *magni*?' Bladesinger asked.

'Steady on,' the little girl said. 'I'm not a bloody miracle worker.'

'Seems like a miracle to me.' Mia shook her head in admiration, smiled at the girl. 'Your ma really taught you all this?'

'Aye. She could have taught me more, if she was given time to. Sometimes I wonder about all the knowings she took to her grave.'

'Aye,' Mia sighed. 'I know what you mean.'

Maggot spooned her stew around the bowl, sucking her lip. 'It's funny, but I was thinking . . . when you take a person out of the world, you don't just take *them*, do you? You take everything they were, too.' The little girl squinted at Bladesinger. 'Do you ever think about that? When you kill someone in the arena?'

'No,' the woman said. 'That way lies madness.'

'What do you think about, then?' Maggot asked, taking another bite.

'I think better them than me,' Bladesinger replied.

The little girl turned to Mia, talking with her mouth full. 'What about you, Crow? Do you think about the things you're taking away?'

Mia parted her lips, but found no words to speak.

Truth was, she *did* think about those she'd ended. More and more, it seemed. The Luminatii she'd killed at the Mountain, those she could justify easily. But everyone after that? The senator's son and magistratii she'd unwittingly murdered in Scaeva's employ? Those men in the Pit at the Hanging Gardens? The gladiatii she'd killed in the arena? In some way, they all paved the way for her to be here, just a few weeks from the consul's and the cardinal's throats. But did that truly vindicate her?

'I think the end justifies the means,' she replied. 'As long as the end isn't mine.'

'Do you truly believe that?'

'I have to.'

'Well,' Maggot smiled sadly. 'Better you than me.'

Fang whined, licked at Mia's fingers with his flat, pink tongue.

'I'm sorry, boy,' she said, kneeling to scruff the dog's chin. 'You already ate it all. Surprised you've got room for more.'

The mastiff whined again, deeper this time, licking at his chops. He snuffled Mia's hand, walking in a small circle with his stubby tail between his legs. Sitting on his haunches, he made a hacking noise, as if from a hairball. And looking at Mia with his big brown eyes, the dog coughed a spray of bright red blood all over the floor.

'Maw's teeth,' Mia cursed, flinching away.

Maggot's bowl of stew fell from her hand, spattered over the stone. 'Crow . . .'

Mia looked up, saw a trickle of blood spill from the girl's lips.

'I don't feel w-well . . .' she whispered.

'O, shit,' Mia breathed.

Maggot coughed a mouthful of blood. Mia rushed to her side, caught her before she fell. She looked to Bladesinger, the woman wiping at her lips and bringing her knuckles away red. As she watched, the woman clutched her belly and coughed a spatter of blood onto the stone.

Mia looked at Fang, curled up in a puddle of gore.

The empty bowl the dog had eaten her dinner from . . .

'O, *shit* . . .'

Poison . . .

'Help me!' she roared. '*Help!*'

She heard cries of pain from the verandah, bewildered curses, hacking coughs. Clutching Maggot in her arms, Mia staggered to the infirmary door and saw every gladiatii in the collegium on their knees or on their backs, mouths and hands smeared with blood, bowls of stew spilled over the tables and floor. Maggot moaned, coughed another mouthful of blood onto Mia's chest. A gobsmacked Finger was staring at the carnage, several guards standing around dumbfounded.

'Don't just stand there, fucking *help me*!' Mia roared.

Finger saw Maggot in Mia's arms, hobbled to her side. Somewhere in the house, someone began clanging the alarm. Between the pair of them, Mia and Finger carried Maggot back into the infirmary, laid her on a slab. Bladesinger had collapsed, blood leaking from her mouth. Mia looked about the room, mind racing. Kneeling by Maggot's bowl, she dipped her finger into the stew, tasted and spat. Beneath the seasoning, she could sense a bitterness, a metallic tang. Her mind racing, all the knowledge that had made her Spiderkiller's favoured student spinning in her memory, repeating the four principles of venomcraft to herself, over and over.

Delivery: Ingested.
Efficacy: Lethal.
Celerity: Five minutes or less.
Locality: Stomach and intestines.

Mia's eyes widened, the answer coming to her in a flash.

'It's Elegy,' she said, turning to Finger.

'Are you—'

'Yes, I'm fucking sure. Do you have cow's milk in the kitchen? Or cream?'

'. . . I've goat's milk for the dona's tea.'

'Set it boiling. All of it. Now.'

'But I—'

'*Now, Finger!*'

The cook hobbled off, and Mia started sorting through Maggot's jars and phials. Elegy was a deadly poison, relatively difficult to concoct unless you knew what you were about. But it was one of the first toxins Mercurio had taught her how to brew, and while the antidote wasn't well known, it was easy enough for a Blade of Our Lady of Blessed Murder to fix. Grateful the dona had allowed Maggot to restock, Mia ransacked the shelves, grabbing the ingredients she needed.

Brightweed. Lopsome. Milkthistl—

'Four Daughters . . .'

Mia turned and saw Dona Leona in her nightshift, standing by the infirmary door. Magistrae stood beside her, horror on her face as the alarm continued to ring.

'What in the Everseeing's name . . .' Leona breathed.

'Poison,' Mia said. 'Elegy, mixed with their evemeal. We don't have much time. I can't find the fucking silver nitrate . . . Do you have a mirror?'

The dona's face was fixed on Maggot's, watching the blood leaking from her lips.

'Leona!' Mia barked. 'Do you have a looking glass?'

The woman blinked, focused on Mia. 'A-aye.'

'Bring it to the kitchen. Now!' She turned to the guards hovering beside their mistress. 'You, carry Maggot, you two bring Bladesinger. Hurry!'

'Do as she says!' Leona barked.

Mia gathered her armful of phials and jars, rushed across the yard with the guards in tow while Leona dashed up to her room. She could hear Maggot coughing again, Bladesinger groaning. The verandah looked like a war zone, gladiatii laid out in pools of blood. Wavewaker was facedown, Bryn leaning on a table, thick ribbons of gore and mucus spilling from her lips, Sidonius on his back. Executus stood amid the carnage, wide-eyed and horrified.

'Arkades, turn Sidonius on his side,' Mia shouted, rushing past. 'Roll everyone off their backs or they'll drown in their own blood!'

In the kitchen, Finger was leaning over a large pot, stirring the steaming milk inside. Mia pushed him out of the way, began adding her ingredients, measuring carefully despite her haste. She had no seconds to waste – every moment would drag Maggot and the others closer to death. But as always, the passenger in her shadow kept her nerves like steel, her hands steady. First rule of venomcraft: a poorly mixed antidote was as bad as no antidote at all.

The guards placed Maggot on the kitchen bench behind her. The girl was ghastly pale, moaning and bringing up another gout of blood.

'Keep her throat clear, she needs to breathe!'

Sweat in her eyes. Pulse hammering under her skin. Maggot coughed again, a bubble of bright red popping at her lips.

'Maggot, you keep breathing, you hear me?'

Leona arrived with a large oval looking glass from her bedroom wall. 'Will this d—'

Mia grabbed it off her, seized a kitchen knife and prised the mirror's frame away. Taking the blade to the back of the glass, she began furiously shaving away the reflective layer of silver nitrate, gleaming flakes of metal spilling onto the kitchen bench. Maggot coughed again, head lolling on her shoulders as if her neck were broken.

'Crow, she's stopped breathing!' Magistrae cried.

'Maggot, don't you die on me!' Mia shouted over her shoulder.

She gathered the flakes of nitrate, crushed them to powder with a mortar and pestle. Shoving Finger aside again, she added the powder to the boiling concoction on the stove, the scent of burning metal in the air. She looked over her shoulder, saw Maggot convulsing in Leona's arms. Prayers to the Black Mother, the Four Daughters, whoever was listening spilling over her lips.

'Please,' she whispered. 'Please please *please* . . .'

It was ready, the concoction set. Mia scooped a healthy dose into a clay cup, turned to the girl behind her. Maggot was pale as death, still as a millpond. The dona's eyes were wide, her nightshift and hands spattered in the girl's blood.

'Take a cupful to everyone affected,' she told Finger. 'The unconscious ones first. Make them drink at least three mouthfuls, take a funnel if you have to, go, *go*!'

Mia wrangled Maggot from Leona's arms, breathing quick. Laying the girl on her back, Mia wiped the bloody foam from Maggot's lips, forced her mouth open. Holding the cup in steady hands, she poured a goodly dose into the girl's mouth.

'Swallow it, baby,' she whispered, massaging her throat. 'Swallow.'

Maggot wasn't listening. She surely wasn't swallowing. Mia pulled her up to a sitting position, the antidote spilling from the little girl's lips. Leona and Magistrae helped prop up Maggot between them, and tilting her head back, Mia poured more of the draught into her open mouth.

'Swallow, Maggot,' she begged. '*Please.*'

Mia massaged the girl's throat, shook her gently. Maggot wasn't responding, wasn't moving, wasn't breathing. Hanging limp in their arms like some broken doll. The Blade in her had seen all this before. But the girl in her, the girl who looked at Maggot and saw a pale reflection of herself, she refused to believe it. Praying for some miracle, like in the books she used to read as a child. Some prince to ride in on a silver charger to wake Maggot with a kiss. Some fae godmother with her pockets full of magik and wishes to spare.

Mia felt hot tears in her eyes, a crushing weight on her shoulders. A scream was building in her belly, but her voice was only a whisper.

'Please, baby.'

'*It's funny, but when you take a person out of the world, you don't just take* them, *do you?*'

Leona looked at Mia, eyes wide with shock, tears spilling down her cheeks.

'. . . Crow?'

'*You take everything they were, too.*'

'*Please,*' Mia begged.

'*Do you ever think about that?*'

The cup slipped from Mia's fingers, shattered on the floor.

Do you ever think about that?

CHAPTER 27
SERVING

Mia couldn't remember the last time she really cried.

She'd spilled a tear or two here and there along the road, but it was never the primal kind of grief. The kind where the sobs are being torn out of you, shaking you to your bones and leaving you hollowed out inside. She hadn't cried when she failed her initiation. Hadn't cried when Ashlinn murdered Tric. Hadn't cried when the Ministry said a quiet mass and sealed the boy in an empty tomb in the Hall of Eulogies.

She wasn't very good with grief, you see.

Mia preferred rage instead.

She stood in the infirmary over Maggot's lifeless body, belly knotted with fury. The girl's hair had been combed, the blood wiped from her face. She looked almost as if she were asleep. Otho lay beside her, just as peaceful. The big Liisian's eyes were closed, the lines of care that had creased his features as he fought upon the sands now smoothed away.

It was a miracle only two of them had died – as if 'only' had a place anywhere in that thought. Maggot was simply too small, and had imbibed too much toxin. Otho was a grown man, strong as an ox. But he'd wolfed his entire meal down and been on the way for seconds before the effects kicked in, and by then, it was too late. More of the Falcons would have succumbed – all, in fact – if Mia hadn't been there. She supposed whoever poisoned their meal wasn't expecting a trained assassin to be on hand to boil up the antidote. As it was, most of the gladiatii suffered varying degrees of internal haemorrhaging, but the remedy she'd mixed had saved them all from death.

Almost all, anyway . . .

Fang lay on a bloodstained blanket, the dog's eyes for ever closed. Executus had almost wept when he found the mastiff curled up in a pool of blood on the infirmary floor. He sat beside Fang now, running one callused hand over the dog's flanks. His fingers were shaking. From anger or grief, Mia couldn't tell.

'How in the Everseeing's name did this happen?' Leona demanded, looking over the bodies with her hands on her hips.

'Simply enough,' Mia murmured, eyes never leaving Maggot's body. 'Somebody dosed the onions in the pantry with Elegy, and Finger used them in the stew. Onion is porous, acts like a sponge. And the smell and flavour does a fine job of masking the toxin's. Good delivery method. The killer knew what they were doing.'

Leona turned to Finger. The cook stood trembling between two houseguards, steel grips on both his arms. His lank hair hung over his eyes, his body shaking.

'What do you know of this?' the dona asked.

'N-nothing, Domina,' the cook replied. 'I serve you faithfully!'

'Any snake would hiss the same,' Leona snarled.

Finger shook his head, his voice shaking.

'Domina, I . . . Ever you've treated me well and fair. I've no cause to harm your flock. Nor would I ever hurt the lass. She was like kin to me. I served the meal to her with my own hands.' Tears filled his eyes, snot at his lips as he looked to Maggot's lifeless corpse. 'You think me cold enough to look in her eyes and smile as I p-passed the blade that would end her?'

The man's chest heaved, face twisting as tears spilled down his cheeks.

'Never. By the Everseeing and all his Daughters, *never*.'

Leona's eyes narrowed, but she could see it in his face, plain as Mia. His thin frame trembling. Eyes swimming with grief. Either Finger was an actor worthy of the greatest theatre in all the Republic, or the man was genuinely gutted at Maggot's death.

'Who had means to get into the larder?' Leona asked.

Finger pawed his eyes, sniffled hard. 'Anyone with access to the keep could get to the provisions, Domina. They're not locked of a nevernight . . . I-I'd have kept them with more care, but I had n-no inkling a serpent lived among us.'

'Nor I,' Leona said. 'But I've suckled one at my breast, sure and true.'

'Elegy isn't easy to make,' Mia said. 'Dangerous. Messy. But in a city as big as Crow's Rest, there's bound to be a way to buy it, if you've the coin.'

'And how do you know this, exactly?' Arkades growled.

'I've made no secret of my knowledge of herblore,' Mia replied. 'The difference between a remedy and a requiem can be as little as half a dram. And if we're taking tally, my meal was dosed too.'

'Then how comes it you were not poisoned with the rest of your fellows?'

'I didn't eat my dinner,' Mia spat.

'The second time in as many months you've dodged a suspicious meal.'

'Have you looked under Furian's bandages?' Mia demanded. 'It's fucking sickening. The smell would put a scabdog off its meal, let alone the sight.'

'And so you just happen to give your draught to *my* dog and watch him die? Then just *happen* to have the ingredients to save the lives of your fellows?'

Mia turned to fully face Arkades, teeth clenched. 'You accuse *me* of this? Poisoning an eleven-year-old girl?'

Arkades ignored her, turned to Leona. 'I say if we seek a serpent among us, begin with the one who best knows poison, neh?'

Rage took Mia then, bright and blinding, and she took a step towards Arkades with her fists clenched. The big man rose with that surprising speed, shoulders squared, chin low. She could feel his growl in her chest.

'Try,' he said. 'Just *try . . .*'

'Executus, enough,' Leona snapped. 'Crow is champion of this collegium. She already stands atop the mountain. What in the Everseeing's name would she gain by murdering all my Falcons, let alone Maggot besides?'

'What would *anyone* gain?' Magistrae asked, looking around the room. 'If we seek the killer, first we must find the motive. How does *anyone* profit from this?'

'Your father would profit, Domina,' Mia said.

Leona shook her head. 'He would not dare . . .'

'Think on it,' Mia replied. 'He owns all your debts. You owe him coin that you simply don't have. How have you made up your shortfalls to creditors in the past?'

'. . . I am still working the figures,' Leona replied.

'Aye,' Mia nodded. 'But even with the Whitekeep purse in consideration, have you pondered any way to conjure over three thousand silver pieces that doesn't involve selling at least a few of your gladiatii to Pandemonium?'

Leona looked to Arkades, then to Magistrae.

'No,' she admitted.

'So what happens if all your gladiatii are dead and you've none to sell?'

'Then I lose everything,' Leona said. 'The *magni*. This collegium. Everything.'

'Is your father the kind of man who murders to get his way? And would it be so hard for a man with that much money to hold sway over one of your guards? Or perhaps someone even closer to you?'

'Impertinent wretch,' Arkades spat. 'Just what are you implying?'

'Only that there's two kinds of loyalty,' Mia replied. 'The kind paid for with love, and the kind paid for with silver.'

'Domina, this—'

Leona held up her hand, cutting her magistrae's objection off at the knee. She turned to her houseguard captain, her voice cold with command.

'Gannicus, I want every bedchamber in the keep searched. Every chest, every cupboard, every crack. You and your fellow houseguards will search by threes, and you will not search your own belongings, am I clear?'

The captain slapped a fist to his chest. 'Aye, Domina.'

Gannicus spun on his heel, gathered the other houseguards and marched across the yard. Scowling dark, Arkades cast one last look at his murdered dog, the murdered girl, and began limping after them.

'Where are you going, Executus?' Leona asked.

'. . . To assist the search, Domina.'

'Gannicus has the matter in hand. Take Finger and gather firewood for a pyre.' She glanced briefly at Maggot's body. 'It would not do to allow them to linger in this heat. They must be sent to the Hearth, and the gentle keeping of Lady Keph.'

Looking Arkades up and down, Mia could see his pupils were dilated, his breathing quickened. Fight-or-flight instinct kicking in.

'. . . *he fears* . . .' came the whisper in her ear.

But finally, as always, the executus bowed.

'Your whisper, my will.'

Mia had never smelled a burning body before.

She'd smelled death, certainly. The noxious stench of sundered bellies. The sweet, high perfume of decay. But until she stood in the courtyard of Crow's Nest, listening to dry wood crackle and snap over the song of the sea, she'd never smelled a funeral pyre. She'd read stories as a child – grieving lovers or orphaned children, sending their loved ones off to the hereafter atop a pillar of flame. There was a kind of romance to it, she'd thought. Something fierce and bright and enduring. But the books never talked about the smell. The burning hair and boiling blood and blackening skin.

It was hideous.

They'd laid Maggot atop the firewood that Arkades and Finger had gathered, Otho beside her. It wasn't the grandest bier ever created, but they'd used all the fuel the kitchen had, stacked in neat rows over three feet high. The pair were wrapped in simple cotton shifts, faces uncovered to the sky. Dona Leona spoke quiet prayers to the Everseeing over their bodies. A wreath of flowers was placed upon their chests. A small mahogany coin beneath their tongues.*

And then, they were set aflame.

Most of the gladiatii held their grief back, but Bryn was weeping openly – this was the second funeral she'd attended in a week, all the wounds from her brother's loss torn open and bleeding fresh. Sidonius was the only other gladiatii to let tears fall, those big brawny shoulders heaving up and down. Mia wondered at the riddle of him, that brand on his chest, the lecherous buffoonery, all at odds with the fellow who'd spoken with such adoration of her father, and tried to comfort her in the dark.

The flames burned brighter, the smoke rising into the blinding sky. The crash of distant waves. The cry of circling gulls. Dona Leona's plaintive prayer to Aa.

With the rites spoken, Leona hung her head, walked solemnly from the pyre. Mia watched her trudge across the yard, the smoke stinging in her unbandaged eye. She knew now Leona was a product of the violence

---

*Known as *reparii*, these coins are paid to the Goddess Keph in return for succour by her Hearth in the hereafter.

Since the Earth Goddess has been slumbering for aeons and has no use for currency, the wooden coins are thrown into the Hearth to keep it burning. The fire within the Hearth was a gift from Keph's sister, Tsana, the Lady of Flame, who thought it unfair that their mother, Niah, be given sole dominion over the dead. Thus, she created the fire to give righteous souls a place to gather and warm themselves against the chill of the hereafter's endless night.

Tsana hates her mother, you see. Almost as much as her father does.

One is forced to wonder if she was hugged enough as a child.

she'd grown up with, that at their hearts, the two of them weren't so dissimilar. If Mia's childhood had been a different one, it could just as easily have been her sitting as mistress of this keep. But a part of her couldn't help but blame the dona for this. If only this collegium didn't exist, if only Maggot had never been sold here . . .

No. You have no time for 'if only' . . .

Leona stepped up to the verandah, just as the guard she'd placed in command of the search returned from inside the keep. Mia watched them sidelong, Gannicus speaking softly, glancing to Arkades. He handed what looked to be a folded piece of fabric to his mistress, and Mia's stomach turned.

'Arkades?' Leona said, turning to her executus.

The man looked up from the burning pyre. The same fear she'd seen in the infirmary lingered in the man's eyes.

'Mi Dona?'

'Explain this,' the dona said, holding out her hand.

Clutched in her fingers was a silken underslip, edged with fine lace. The gladiatii turned to stare, the pyre still blazing in the background. Arkades looked to the warriors he'd trained, his expression darkening. He could barely meet Leona's eyes, his voice edged with shame.

'Mi Dona, if we could speak in private—'

'It was found in your room,' Leona said. 'Beneath your mattress. Now I see why you were so eager to aid Gannicus and his guards in their search. But tell me, noble Arkades, how comes it that my under-clothes are found among your possessions?'

'Mi Dona, I—'

'And what is this?'

Leona held up a small phial of clear liquid, gleaming in the sunlight. Arkades blinked. 'I have never seen that before in my life.'

'It was found wrapped inside my underslip. Hidden among your little trove. Perfume, perhaps? Or a little liquor to make the nevernights easier?' Leona turned to Mia, held out the phial on her palm. 'Crow?'

Glancing at Arkades, seeing the fear swelling inside him, Mia took the phial from the dona's hands. Unstopping it, she sniffed, dabbed her finger and tasted, immediately spat once, twice. Lips curling as she looked to Leona.

'It's Elegy, Domina. No question.'

Leona's glare welled with tears as she looked at Arkades, lip trembling, her entire body shaking with rage.

'*You.*'

Horror welled in Arkades's eyes. 'Mi Dona, I would never . . .'

'Then how comes it to be in your room?' Leona demanded. 'Wrapped in the underslip you stole from me? Or do you deny the keeping of that, too?'

'I do not deny it, I fou—'

'You have known me from a child, Arkades! I thought you a man of honour, who saw the righteousness of my cause. I thought your infatuation harmless, but now I see it turned to poison before my eyes.' She shook the silk in his face. 'Now I see to the heart of you! *Now* I see the reason you have walked with me all these years!'

'Infatuation?' Arkades was pale, his voice trembling.

'How much does my father pay you?'

'. . . What?'

'How much?' she screamed. 'Ever I wondered at the lions you wore on your doublet, the lion's head on your cane. I thought it simple homage to where you'd been and who you were, but now I see it for truth! You were *always* his man! *Always!*'

Magistrae placed a gentle hand on her mistress's shoulder. 'Domina, please.'

Leona snarled, threw off the woman's grip. 'Did he promise me to you, perhaps? Some broken trophy to hide beneath your mattress with all your other dirty little secrets? You'd poison my flock, murder an eleven-year-old girl to have your way? After what he did to my mother? Smiling like a snake and offering me your *comfort?*'

Tears gleamed in Arkades's eyes. 'You think me capable . . .'

'I think you a liar,' Leona spat. 'I think you a murderer. I think you a sad old man ruled by lust and accursed drink and memory of past glory gone wrong and rotten.' Leona dragged ragged breath through gritted teeth. 'I think you every inch the bastard my father is. I want you out of my collegium.'

'Leona, I—'

'Get *out!*' Leona roared. 'Or I swear by the Everseeing and all four of his Daughters, I will show you the mercy you showed the child on that pyre!'

The woman stood trembling, tears pouring down her cheeks. But her jaw was set, teeth bared in a snarl. Arkades hung like a broken mirror, chest heaving, his face pale. Looking among the gladiatii, he found only disdain and rage. He turned back to Leona, agony in his eyes, one final, desperate plea on his lips.

'Please—'

'GET OUT!' Leona screamed, launching herself at him and flailing with her fists. Scratching his face, clawing at his eyes. 'GET OUT! GET OUT!'

Arkades staggered back, and Magistrae pulled the flailing, screaming Leona off him. The guards stepped forward to separate them, hands on their swords, glowering at the executus. Gannicus placed a hand on his chest and shoved him farther away, warning plain on his face. The captain obviously had no wish to draw, but the wishes of his mistress were clear, and the smell of that burning child hung heavy in the air.

Arkades looked around the yard and found no friends. Tears brimming in his eyes. He opened his mouth to speak, but found no words to save him. He searched the faces of his former charges, and found none to vouch for him. Mia could see words struggling behind his teeth, but looking into Leona's eyes, he found only hatred and rage. And with no other real choice, he turned and began limping for the gate.

'Take this!' Leona cried, flinging the slip at his back. 'May it keep you warm in the nevernight!'

The executus paused, looking back over his shoulder. But without a word, he hung his head and simply kept walking. Mia watched him leave, uncertain what to think. Jealousy could drive a man to any lengths, and Arkades *did* still wear the lions of his former master on his chest. To discover the woman he so clearly loved was bedding Furian must have been an awful blow, and love could turn to cancer when watered with betrayal. But a part of Mia found it hard to believe he'd betray Leona so cruelly . . .

Leaning on her magistrae, the dona left the yard, still weeping. Mia looked to the pyre once more, watching the flames rise higher. Heat caressing her skin. Smoke kissing her tongue. So much in the balance. So close to the end. So much to risk before she got there, and so keen to arrive.

She couldn't wait 'til this was all over.

'Goodbye, Maggot,' she whispered. 'I'll miss you.'

And she still couldn't remember the last time she cried.

The bathhouse swirled with steam, the heat of it scalded her skin. Mia sank into the water with a sigh, the ache in her ribs soothed by the warmth. Slipping below the surface, she tried to shush her thoughts, silence her doubts and rage and enjoy a moment's silence. For just a breath. Just a second.

Bryn entered the bathhouse, walking like she were sleeping. Her eyes were bloodshot, her cheeks red raw. Without looking at Mia, she stripped off her clothes and sank into the water, washing the tears from her skin. She stayed under almost a breath too long, Mia about to reach out towards her, when Bryn finally surfaced, sodden blonde framing her face. Drifting to the corner, the girl sat still as stone, as a statue, as a corpse, staring at the ripples on the surface and saying nothing at all.

'A hard turn,' Mia said.

'Aye,' Bryn murmured.

'Domina spoke the service well.'

'Aye.'

'. . . How are you feeling?'

Bryn looked up a moment, eyes gaining focus.

'How do you think?' she whispered.

Mia hung her head, stared at the swirling steam.

'. . . Aye.'

Wavewaker trudged into the bathhouse, unwrapped the cloth from his waist. Mia couldn't remember a single turn where they'd bathed together and the big man hadn't gifted her a song, but Wavewaker didn't hum a note this time. His uncharacteristic silence hung heavy in the air, sorrow welling in Mia's chest. Thinking of the water fight they'd had, here with Byern, just a few weeks ago. Thinking of that little girl burning on that pyre, and all that had been lost along with her.

These people are not your familia and not your—

'Four fucking Daughters . . .'

Mia looked up, saw Sidonius stride past the guards posted on the bathhouse entrance. Shutting the door behind him, he stripped off and sank into the water, eyes wide, breathing quick.

'You seem of a mood,' Wavewaker said.

'There's no "seem" about it, brother.'

'What troubles?'

'Our fucking domina,' the big Itreyan growled. 'I just heard from Milaini, one of the serving lasses. Leona has sent missive to Varro fucking Caito, invited him for evemeal tomorrow.'

'Why does she dine with a fleshpeddler?' Wavewaker asked.

'She's planning to sell us to Pandemonium, why do you think?' Sidonius spat. 'She's already drawn up a list, apparently. Milaini saw it on her desk.'

'. . . Who's on it?' Mia asked.

'Bryn, for starters,' Sid said, nodding at the Vaanian girl.

Bryn blinked, as if hearing the conversation for the first time.

'. . . Domina would sell me to Varro Caito?'

'She needs coin,' Sidonius growled. 'She can't afford a new charioteer to form a new equillai team. But after your showing at Whitekeep, you'll fetch a fortune.'

'Who else?' Wavewaker growled.

'Bladesinger,' Sidonius spat. 'Felix. Albanus. Butcher. And me.'

'She's going to sell 'Singer?' Mia breathed.

'She's going to sell anyone with a fucking pulse,' Sid replied. 'She needs three thousand silver priests, and she's thrown all in on you winning the *magni*, Crow. The rest of us are just sacks of coin to her.'

Bryn shook her head, whispering, 'Shit.'

'That's all you've got to say?' Sidonius whispered, gobsmacked.

'And what else would you have me say?' the girl growled.

'Say you'll not be sold like chaff to die in Pandemonium,' Sidonius growled. 'Because by the Four fucking Daughters, I won't be.'

'And what choice do we have?'

Sid cast an eye to the closed door, lowered his voice further.

'There's always one other choice,' he said.

A chill ran over Mia's skin as she looked Sid in the eye. 'Meaning what?'

'Meaning Executus is gone, and his lash along with him,' Sidonius replied. 'Meaning these houseguards are softer than baby shite, and we're fully fledged gladiatii. We could beat them to death with practice swords if we'd a mind to. Especially with surprise on our side.'

Wavewaker scowled, rubbing his chin.

'Aye,' he muttered. 'We could at that.'

Bryn's eyes widened, voice dropping to a furious whisper. 'You speak of rebellion? Have you lost your mind? You want to end up executed at the *magni*?'

'You'd rather die in Pandemonium?' Sidonius demanded. 'In case you've no eyes to see it, sister, this house is coming down around our fucking ears. I've a mind to absent myself before the roof falls in.'

'This isn't right,' Wavewaker agreed. 'Bladesinger fought with honour. Crow would be the first to admit she'd not have stood victor against the Exile if not for 'Singer, aye?'

Mia nodded slow. 'Aye.'

'And now she's to be sold like meat? Because her swordarm is ruined?' The big man looked to Bryn. 'Your brother gave his life for this house.

And this is how Leona honours that sacrifice? By hocking his sister to a bastard like Varro Caito? I'll not stand by for this,' Sid spat. 'I can't. I won't.'

Wavewaker looked to Sidonius, shook his head.

'Nor I.'

Mia licked her lips, spoke soft. 'Hold now.'

The three gladiatii looked to her, waiting for her to speak. After the showings she'd put in at the arena, there wasn't a one among them who didn't respect her. And while she could see the injustice of it, while she knew that if she were in their position, she'd almost certainly be arguing for the same . . .

If the gladiatii of the Remus Collegium rebelled, she'd never see the *magni*. Never have her revenge. If she aided them, at best, she'd be a fugitive, on the run in a Republic where such rebellion was brutally punished. At worst, she'd simply be killed in the attempt. And if she didn't participate, but allowed it to happen, she'd probably still be crucified by the administratii for belonging to a house in revolt.

But to sit back and do nothing while Bryn and 'Singer and Sid were sold . . .

'Hold?' Sidonius asked. 'Hold for what?'

'. . . Let's not speak hasty,' Mia said. 'The wounds from Maggot's funeral are fresh. I say think on it a few turns before we do anything rash.'

'Rash?' Sidonius scowled. 'We're talking about our lives here!'

'It may be fine for some,' Wavewaker said. 'But not all of us are champions in the dona's favour.'

'And that favour changes like the wind, Crow,' Bryn said, seemingly warming to the idea. 'Look how swift she casts Arkades aside.'

'I only counsel patience,' Mia insisted. 'Leona and Caito dine on the morrow, but no sale will be brokered for a turn or two. Domina's blood is running as hot as the rest of us. Perhaps in time, she'll see her folly and seek another way. Perhaps she'll find some trick in her ledger that yet avoids anyone's sale. I'm certain she has no wish to part with any of us.'

'If you think that woman has a hint of loyalty inside her,' Wavewaker said, 'you are the fool I never took you for. Leona thinks of her own glory, none other's.'

'Patience,' she begged. 'Please.'

The three gladiatii looked among each other, scowling. But it seemed there'd be no more argument for the moment, each falling into a sullen, scowling silence. And with little else to say and no comfort to offer, Mia finally climbed out of the bath and towelled herself off, tying her wraps about herself and padding softly from the room.

Stalking down the hall to her cell, her mind was whirling. She knew she couldn't allow a rebellion against Leona to happen – her entire plan would be undone if she did. But if she allowed the dona to have her way, if Leona couldn't be swayed, Sid and 'Singer and Bryn were as good as dead. Nobody survived Pandemonium. Even the greatest warriors lasted a few months there, at best.

A slow quiet settled over the barracks, the gladiatii bedding down for the nevernight. Sidonius returned from the bathhouse, sitting opposite Mia in their cell. She'd not been moved upstairs yet – with all the drama of the last few turns, she supposed Leona had more pressing concerns than finding her new champion's quarters. And so, Mia was still stuck in her cage. Feeling Sid's eyes on her as the arkemical lamps were turned down, as the talk of the other gladiatii softened and then stilled, finally replaced by the sounds of sleep.

As always, the man stayed quiet when they were alone. Never pressing.

Simply staring.

Minutes ticking by like days. His blue eyes fixed on her.

Unblinking.

Mute.

'Black Mother, what?' she finally hissed.

'I said nothing,' Sidonius whispered.

'So you plan to sit there and stare at me all nevernight?'

'Would you rather me speak?'

'Yes, damn you, say your piece. You weren't shy about it in the fucking bathhouse. We're alone and all of a sudden the cat has your tongue?'

'And what would we speak of? You've made your feelings clear enough.'

'You've been following me like a fucking bloodhawk since you found out who I was. And you've never asked me of it, not once. Yet at the first whisper of . . .' – Mia glanced about, lowered her voice – '. . . of *rebellion*, your tongue is all aflutter.'

'The action we take about my impending sale concerns me direct, Crow. But as far as your parentage goes, it's not my place to speak. And if you were wondering, all you needed do was ask. I follow you out of respect for your father. He'd have wanted me to look after you.'

'And what do you know of what my father would have wanted?'

Sidonius laughed softly. 'More than you realize, little Crow.'

'You were a soldier. Branded for cowardice and kicked out of the legion. You weren't in his counsel. You didn't know him.'

Sidonius shook his head, hurt shining in his eyes.

'I know he'd be ashamed of what this house has become.'

Mia fell quiet at that. Took a deep, shivering breath and looked to the walls around her. The iron bars and the human misery. She'd scrubbed herself hard in the bath, but she could smell the smoke from Maggot's funeral pyre in her hair.

'Your name is Mia, aye?'

She looked up sharply, eyes narrowed.

'It took me a while to remember it,' Sid said. 'The justicus spoke of you sometimes, but he kept talk of his familia mostly to himself. I think he felt closer to you all that way. Not sharing you with others. Not staining thoughts of you with all the blood and shit we saw on campaign.'

'Aye,' she finally answered. 'Mia.'

'Your little brother was Jonnen.'

'. . . Aye.'

Sid nodded, sucking his lip, saying nothing.

'Daughters, spit it out,' Mia sighed.

'Spit what out?'

'The rebuke so obviously churning behind your fucking teeth. "*You can leave these walls anytime you like, Crow, you've no right to stop us trying the same. Even if we fail, the administratii will never catch you. No cell can ever hold you.*"'

'Is that what I was thinking?' Sid asked. 'Or what *you* were thinking?'

'Fuck you, Sid.'

'It took me a while,' the big man said. 'To ponder it. Why you were here, why you'd want to fight in the *magni*. And then I remembered who'd be standing on the sand with you when you were declared the victor. The same men who stood in judgement over him, aye? The same men who smiled as he hanged.'

Mia said nothing. Simply stared.

'I wasn't there when it happened,' Sid said. 'I was already in chains by then. But I heard about it, afterwards. Heard the Dona Corvere stood on the forum walls, above the howling mob. A little girl in her arms. Must have been you, aye? Quite a thing to make your daughter watch.'

'She wanted me to see,' Mia said. 'She wanted me to *remember*.'

'Your mother.'

'Aye,' Mia spat. 'What was it you called her? The *stupid fucking whore*?'

'Aye, that was unkind of me,' Sid sighed. 'But it's hard for me to find too many kind words for your ma, Mia. Knowing what I know of her.'

'And what is it you think you know?'

'Just that Alinne Corvere had more ambition than Justicus Darius and General Antonius put together. Half your father's centurions were in love with her. She had a third of the Senate wrapped around her finger.' Sid steepled his hands at his chin. 'How do you suppose she did that? She wasn't quite the swordswoman her daughter grew up to be. She was a politician. You think a woman like that could almost bring a Republic to its knees without dropping once or twice to her own?'

Mia glowered at Sidonius. 'Don't you dare.'

'I know you're trying to avenge them,' Sidonius said. 'I know you think it righteous. I just wonder if you'd think the same if you knew the kind of woman your mother was. Or, the kind of man your father was.'

'I *know* what kind of man he was. He was a *hero*.'

'We all think that of our parents,' Sid said. 'They give us life, after all. It's easy to mistake them for gods.'

'You speak one ill word of my father,' Mia whispered, 'and I swear by the Black Mother I will fucking end you right here in this cell. He was doing what he thought was best for the Republic and its people. He was a man who followed his heart.'

'I loved your father, Mia. And I served him as well as I could. He had that way about him. The loyalty he inspired in his men . . . I think all of us loved him in our own way.' Sid fixed Mia in his stare. 'And aye, he was a man who followed his heart. Just not in the way you think he did.'

'. . . What are you talking about?'

Sid sighed.

'Your father and General Antonius were lovers, Mia.'

Mia flinched as if she'd been slapped in the face.

Breath trembling.

The whole world shifting under her feet.

'. . . What?'

'Everyone knew it,' Sid said. 'All their men, anyway. Nobody cared. Not even your mother, so long as they kept it quiet. She'd married the position, not the man. Their marriage was one of friendship. Perhaps even a strange kind of love. But first and foremost, it was one of ambition. Your father commanded loyalty among the Luminatii. It didn't bother us that the would-be king and the Kingmaker occasionally slipped into each other's beds. Some even found it romantic.' Sidonius leaned closer, his voice heavy and hard. 'But don't tell me the rebellion was about Darius Corvere's love of liberty or the people, Mia. It was about his love for Antonius. The general wanted to be a king. And your father wanted to be the man who placed that crown upon his head. Plain and simple.'

Mia remembered the nights in Crow's Nest when the general would visit. She'd always called him 'Uncle Antonius'. Her mother and father and he all dining together, the wine flowing, their laughter echoing down halls of long red stone.

And afterwards . . .

Perhaps under this very roof . . .

'Lies,' Mia whispered. 'You're speaking lies.'

'No, Mia,' Sid said. 'I'm just speaking difficult truths.'

Mia sat still, silent, heart pounding in her chest. Blinking hard. She couldn't rightly remember the last time she cried . . .

'Hurts, doesn't it?' Sid sighed. 'When you find out the ones who gave you life are just as mortal and frail as the rest of us? That the world isn't what you thought it was?'

Mia wiped at her tears with shaking hands. Remembering the way her father kissed her mother. First on one eyelid, then the other, then finally upon her smooth, olive brow.

But never on the lips.

Could it be true?

. . . *Did it matter if it was?*

If there was no deceit between them, why did she care who her parents lay with? Though they may not have loved each other, they'd both loved her; she knew that, if nothing else. They'd taught her to rely on her wits, to be strong, to never be afraid. And she missed them both, even now, like a hole had been carved in her chest the turn they were taken away.

But if her father hadn't been the hero of the people she supposed him, if he'd only been trying to overthrow the Senate for his own selfish ends . . .

. . . what was all this murder and blood for, exactly?

No.

No, Scaeva and Duomo still deserved a killing. They'd still imprisoned her mother and brother, left them to die in an oubliette inside the Philosopher's Stone.

'*I will give your brother your regards . . .*'

'I know what it will cost you,' Sidonius whispered. 'To let rebellion happen under this roof. But think of Bryn. Of Bladesinger. Of Butcher and me. Do we truly deserve to die in some godless pit because Leona hates her father, and you love yours too much?'

Silence between them, heavy as lead. Mia looked the man over; this man she'd mistaken for a lecherous fool, a thug, perhaps even the coward his brand told the world he was. She saw he was none of those things. But still . . .

'Why weren't you there when my father and Antonius were captured?' she asked, her voice hollow. 'Why aren't you dead with the rest of their men?'

Sidonius sighed deep, hung his head.

'The Luminatii centurions and their Second Spears were informed of Darius and Antonius's plan the nevernight after we mustered. Antonius made a grand speech, spoke of corruption, of hubris, of the Republic being under the control of weak and impious men. And when all the shield beating and chest thumping was over . . . I just couldn't do it. The Republic is rotten, Mia, I'll brook no argument there. A cancer eats at the bones of this place, and Godsgrave is the heart of it. Julius Scaeva is twice the tyrant Antonius would have been. But we were the Luminatii Legion. Soldiers of God. The war that would've come if we marched on our own capital, the suffering that would have ridden in our wake . . .

'Thousands would have died. Tens of thousands, maybe. And for what? So one man could wear a crown, and another could place it on his head? I couldn't do it. I went to my centurion and told him so. He listened patiently as I tried to tell him the wrong of it. And when I was done, he had me beaten near to death, branded a coward, and sold off to the first bidder on the blocks.'

Sidonius shook his head.

'Six years in chains for one moment of principle. That's the tithe I paid. But you know what I learned in all the years between then and this, little Crow?'

'. . . No.'

Sid fixed Mia in his ice-blue stare.

'There's no softer pillow than a clear conscience.'

Mia sat in the dark, trembling head to foot. Tears spilling down her cheek. And without another word, Sidonius lay down in the straw, rolled over onto his side, and closed his eyes.

'Sleep well, Mia.'

CHAPTER 28

SCARS

'... *this is unwise* ...'

'As you're so fond of reminding me.'

'... *if i don't, who will? that fool eclipse* ...?'

'If I didn't know better, I'd say you were jealous of her and Ashlinn.'

'... *it is a good thing you know better, then* ...'

Mia knelt in the alleyway, found the cloak Ash had left for her and wrapped it about her shoulders. Though skulking about Crow's Rest in this heat while wearing a hood and cloak wasn't exactly the best way to avert suspicion, it was easier than blundering around blind beneath a mantle of shadows.

'I need to talk to her, Mister Kindly,' Mia said, pulling the hood up over her head. 'She's been back two turns and things are moving quick at the collegium.'

'... *once upon a time, you used to talk to me* ...'

'I still talk to you.'

'... *mmm* ...'

Mister Kindly hopped up onto her shoulder, curled his tail about her throat. Mia made her way out of the alley, stalking down Fisher's Row towards the inn. The hour was late, the winds blowing in off the ocean almost pushing her hood off her head. A few scattered folks ran about on their errands, and she could hear bells tolling down in the harbour, but aside from ne'er-do-wells like her, the streets were all but empty.

'All right, then,' she muttered. 'What do you want to talk about?'

'... *where to begin* ...' came the whisper in her ear. '... *that thing that saved your life in galante? your theory that the darkin are somehow connected to the fall of the ashkahi empire? the map inked on ashlinn's back?*

and let us not forget your match with the silkling, and the second set of blades she so conveniently forgot to weaken . . .'

'Anyone could have made that mistake, Mister Kindly.'

'. . . you are a fool to trust her . . .'

'If Ash wanted me dead, she could have ended me ten times over by now.'

'. . . be that as it may, her involvement is clouding your judgement. there are so many questions about what is happening here, and you seem to be looking for answers to none of them . . .'

'There's only so much I can do behind the walls of the bloody collegium,' she hissed. 'The *magni* comes first. We have one chance at this.'

'. . . do you remember what that shadowthing in galante told you . . . ?'

'That I should be painting the skies black. Whatever the fuck that means.'

'. . . it said your vengeance serves only to blind you, mia . . .'

'Are you saying I should forget what Scaeva and Duomo did?'

'. . . i am saying there may be larger things at play here . . .'

'You think I don't know that?'

They rounded the corner to the inn's back alley, the scent of garbage and rot in the air. Mia threw off her hood and Mister Kindly hopped down onto a broken crate, began cleaning his translucent paws as Mia continued.

'Look, I've felt like a pawn that can only see half the board for months now. And the questions in my head are near deafening. But all those questions will still need answers when truelight is over, and the chance to end Scaeva and Duomo will be gone. Our plan is one rebellion shy of ruin. Everything hangs on the next few turns.'

'. . . well, if thought of the gladiatii rebelling is all that troubles you, the answer is obvious . . .'

'O, aye? Pray tell, then.'

'. . . you cannot allow it to happen . . .'

'It's not that simple, Mister Kindly.'

'. . . it is that simple. if you still wish your vengeance, you must win the magni. *and you cannot win the* magni *if you have been executed for rebellion against the republic. you talk constantly of how much you have given up to get this far. you cannot fall now, at the last few feet . . .'*

'So I'm just to let Sid and the others perish?'

'. . . they are not your friends, mia . . .'

'Who are you to tell me that?'

The not-cat tilted his head.

'. . . *i am your friend. your oldest friend. who helped you when scaeva ordered you drowned? who saved you on the streets of godsgrave? who stood beside you through your trials in the church? and in all that time, have i ever steered you wrong . . . ?*'

Mia felt a rebuke rising on her lips, but before she could speak it, she sensed her shadow rippling, a familiar chill prickling her skin. A dark shape coalesced at her feet, sleek and lupine, weaving around and in between her legs.

'. . . *YOU RETURN . . .*'

'. . . Hello, Eclipse.'

'. . . *I MISSED YOU . . .*'

'. . . *o, please . . .*'

Eclipse snarled, shadowclaws digging into the dirt.

Mister Kindly affected a yawn.

'. . . *stop, you're frightening me . . .*'

'. . . *I THINK YOU TOO STUPID TO BE FRIGHTENED OF ME, LITTLE MOGGY. BUT ONE TURN, I SHALL TEACH YOU THERE IS A PRICE FOR OWNING TOO MUCH MOUTH AND NOT ENOUGH TEETH . . .*'

'. . . *tell me, dear mongrel, do you practise these blunt little threats when you're alone, or do you simply improvise . . . ?*'

Mia frowned, her tolerance of the not-cat's sarcasm at an all-time low.

'Mister Kindly, go watch the Nest. Come fetch me if Furian stirs.'

'. . . *you send me away . . . ?*'

'. . . *O, MY HEART BLEEDS . . .*'

'. . . *we have no hearts, you idiotic mutt . . .*'

'. . . *BE SURE TO REMIND ME OF THAT, WHEN I AM EATING YOURS . . .*'

The shadowcat hissed, and the shadowwolf growled. But with a ripple in the black about her feet, Mia felt her passenger depart. She knelt and ran her hands through Eclipse, fancying the slightest whisper of cool velvet beneath her fingertips.

'All is well?'

Eclipse's hackles were still up, but under Mia's touch, she slowly quietened. Licking her mistress's hand with a translucent tongue, the shadowwolf spoke softly.

'. . . *IT IS WELL. BETTER NOW THAT YOU ARE HERE. HOW ARE YOUR WOUNDS . . . ?*'

Mia touched the bandage at her face, grimacing. 'Well enough.'

'. . . *YOU SEEM SAD . . . ?*'

'Perhaps a little.'

'. . . *DO WE NEED TO HURT ANYONE . . . ?*'

'I need you to stay here, Eclipse. Keep watch on the street, aye?'

'. . . *AS YOU WISH . . .*'

Mia smiled, began trudging down the alleyway, glad at least one of her daemons was content to do what it was told. As she walked farther and farther away, climbed up the downspout to the balcony outside Ashlinn's window, she felt Eclipse's hold on her begin to fade, and butter-flies begin creeping into her belly. It was still an unfamiliar sensation, cold and sickly and slick. It made her feel small. It made her feel weak.

Black Mother, she loathed being afraid.

She crouched by the window, fist poised over the glass. The hateful sensation of lice crawling in her belly. Cold sweat stinging in the stitches at her cheek. Gritting her teeth, she dragged up the nerve from the bottom of her feet and knocked softly.

The window opened and Ashlinn stood there, bathed in the burning sunlight. For a moment, Mia forgot the blood, the death, the fear, simply drinking in the sight of her. This girl who'd risked her life again – gathering information in Whitekeep, weakening the Exile's blades to even the odds, following Mia across the Republic and back without flinching.

'O, Goddess,' Ashlinn breathed, pressing her lips to Mia's own.

Mia closed her eyes, slipping her arms about Ashlinn's waist, letting the girl shower her face with kisses. Taking her by the hand, Ash led Mia to the bed, pulled her down and threw her arms about her, squeezing tight. Despite the ache of her cracked ribs, the pain of the last few turns, Mia breathed easier, inhaling lavender and the scent of henna in Ashlinn's hair. Simply being held and holding in turn.

'I missed you,' Ash breathed.

'. . . I missed you, too.'

They kissed again, long and blissful and soft. Ashlinn pulled her closer, face buried in her neck. They lay like that for an age, bodies fitting together like the strangest of puzzle pieces. Of all the places she expected to find herself on her road, wrapped up in this girl's arms was the last. The warmest. The sweetest.

After a long, peaceful nothing, Ash finally pulled back from Mia's arms, looked her over, from the top of her head to the shadow beneath her.

'Where's Mister Mockery?' she asked.

'I sent him back to the keep,' Mia sighed.

'He didn't like that, I'll wager.'

Mia shrugged, toying with the end of one of Ashlinn's braids. 'He was pissing me off. He's always got something sarcastic to say. Always questioning. Always pushing. He's never just . . . nice.'

'Sounds like someone else I know,' Ash smiled.

Mia raised an eyebrow, fixed Ashlinn in a withering stare. 'O, really?'

'Truth is the sharpest knife, Corvere,' Ash grinned.

'You wound me, Dona. I'm fucking lovable, I'll have you know.'

Ash grinned. 'I've been thinking about that, actually.'

'How fucking lovable I am?'

'No,' Ashlinn rolled her eyes. 'About your passengers. How different they are. Spending all this time travelling with Eclipse, I've got to know her quite well. She and Mister Congeniality are like truelight and true-dark. He's sarcastic, mean-spirited, a fucking pain in the arse. Eclipse is simpler, more direct. She doesn't question. And I realized those traits are a lot like you and Lord Cassius. You said yourself he never sought the truth of what it was to be darkin.'

'You think . . .'

'I don't think anything,' Ash shrugged. 'It's just interesting. Maybe a passenger inherits the mannerisms of the darkin they first imprint upon?'

Mia chewed on that for a moment, and it tasted like sense. Thinking on it honestly, her two passengers *were* an awful lot like the ones they'd first rode with. The shadowcat's bitter, black humour and biting wit. The shadowwolf's unquestioning loyalty, her propensity for violent solutions to any situation.

Could it be Mister Kindly was just a dark reflection of her?

And if that were true, weren't his thoughts the best measure of what *she* thought?

. . . *they are not your friends, mia* . . .

'I was worried about you,' Ashlinn whispered. 'During the *venatus* at Whitekeep. I'm sorry I missed that second set of blades. That was stupid of me.'

Mia blinked, thoughts coming back into focus. Looking into Ashlinn's eyes.

Wondering . . .

'Sneaking around down there unseen can't have been easy,' she finally said. 'And it turned out well enough in the end.'

Ash sucked her lip. 'She hurt you.'

'I'm all right,' Mia sighed. 'Cracked ribs. A few scratches.'

Ashlinn leaned up on her elbow, ran gentle fingertips over the bandage on Mia's brow and cheek.

'Didn't look like a scratch when she opened you up.'

'It's fine, Ash.'

'. . . Show me.'

Mia shook her head, belly churning. 'Ashlinn, I don—'

'Mia,' Ash said softly, taking her hand. 'Show me.'

The fear. Welling in her belly like poison. She wanted Mister Kindly and Eclipse back, right now. Life was so much easier with no regard for consequence, no thought for pain. Her passengers were what made her strong, allowed her to be a terror of the sands, to spare no thought for hurting or being hurt in kind. She was steel when they were inside her. Without them . . .

Without them, what am I?

For all her talk of preferring to look dangerous rather than pretty, she was still afraid of what she looked like beneath that bandage. Of what she'd see in Ashlinn's eyes when she took it off. But just as swift, she felt her old temper rising. The anger that had been her companion through all the years between the turn her father was killed and this one. What did she care how she looked?

What difference did it make to who she was?

Mia reached up to the bandage, untied it from her brow. It was stuck to the wound, dried blood crusted in the gauze, and she had to tug it free, wincing at the pain. Ashlinn sat still, staring with those beautiful blue eyes. Mia glanced at her reflection in the looking glass. The gash cut down through her brow, curling in a cruel hook shape along her left cheek, laced with stitches by Maggot's iron-steady hands.

'It's not that bad,' Ashlinn murmured.

'Liar,' Mia replied.

'I am at that,' Ashlinn smirked. 'But not about this.'

The girl leaned forward, and with featherlight lips, she kissed Mia's brow. Sinking lower, she placed a half-dozen gentle kisses along the line of Mia's wound, and finally, she pressed her lips to Mia's own.

'Our scars are just gifts from our enemies,' Ashlinn whispered into her mouth. 'Reminding us they weren't good enough to kill us.'

Mia smiled faintly, entwining her fingers in Ashlinn's own.

'You fought bravely in the arena,' Ash said.

'It's easy to do that with Mister Kindly and Eclipse by my side.'

'And yet you come here alone. That couldn't have been easy.'

Mia shook her head. 'It wasn't.'

'So don't sell yourself cheap, Corvere. There's no one alive who can do the things you do. You're the bravest person I know. Goddess, when you leapt after Bladesinger, I was so afraid . . .' Ashlinn shook her head, gave Mia a playful slap on the leg. 'Don't do anything that stupid again, you hear me?'

'I couldn't let her fall, Ashlinn.'

The girl's gaze softened, a slow frown forming between her brows. 'Why not?'

'She saved my life.'

'And in saving hers, you risked your own.' Ash shook her head, blue eyes glittering. 'That's not why we're here, Mia. This is bigger than the life of one gladiatii. This is the future of the entire Republic. The end of a tyranny that's been allowed to fester for far too long. The end of the Red Church, the end of—'

'I know why we're here, Ashlinn. I'm no hero. I'm no fucking saviour. This is *my* plan, remember?'

'. . . I don't seem to be the one who needs reminding.'

Mia scowled, pulled herself free of Ashlinn's embrace. Prowling to the bureau, she found her cigarillos, struck her flintbox. She inhaled deep despite the pain in her ribs, feeling the sugared warmth spread over her tongue, tingling on her lips.

'Maggot's dead,' she sighed.

'. . . What? How?'

'Arkades apparently dosed our evemeal with Elegy. He was working with Leonides. Leona has to sell a bunch of gladiatii to stave her father off long enough to fight me at the *magni*. But the gladiatii have caught wind of their sale.'

'. . . And how do they feel about that?'

'How the fuck do you think?' Mia folded her arms and leaned on the wall, cigarillo hanging from her mouth. 'They're set to rebel. Sidonius is trying to convince me to help. He knows I can escape the cells, let the rest of them out. If they struck in the nevernight, they'd cut through Leona's guards like piss through snow.'

'Shit,' Ashlinn breathed. 'How are you going to stop them? Tell Leona?'

Mia looked at Ash, dragging hard on her smoke.

'Who says I'm going to stop them?'

'. . . What?'

'They don't deserve to die, Ash. Not a one of them. Not for this.'

'Mia,' Ashlinn said. 'I know you feel a kinship for these people, believe me, I do. But you were always too mindful of others, even as an acolyte. I warned you then, and I'm warning you now.'

Mia scowled at the girl on the bed. That old, delicious anger eating all her fear.

'Ash, if I'd not spared that boy's life in my final trial, I'd have been there when you poisoned the initiation feast. I'd have been trussed up like Hush and the others, completely at the Luminatii's mercy.'

'I wouldn't have let that happen.'

'You couldn't have stopped them,' Mia replied. 'Remus would have gutted me as soon as he got his hands on me. So don't fool yourself. If I'd not shown mercy and failed my trial, I'd be dead just like Tric.'

Ash flinched. Drew a long, shaking breath.

'You throw that at me every time we argue. It's not fair, Mia.'

'O, and what you did to him was?'

'Look, I'm sorry Tric had to die,' Ash said. 'I know you cared for him. I liked him too. But that's my *point*, Mia. *Everyone* has someone who cares for them. The gladiatii you've killed in the arena, the Luminatii you slaughtered at the Mountain – each of them was someone's daughter or someone's son. Each of them had someone to mourn them. This is bigger than one person, or even a thousand. This is the future of the Republic. And this is *everything* you've worked for.'

Mia scowled, dragging hard on her cigarillo. Ashlinn climbed off the bed, walked to Mia, and took hold of her hand.

'You were born for this. And I think you know that. The moment your father chose to rise against the Republic, you were fated for great and terrible things. But fate wouldn't have chosen you if you weren't strong enough to bear the weight of it. I know you're frightened. I know you're hurting. But we're *so* close now. You can do this. You're the strongest person I know. That's one of the reasons I love you, Mia Corvere.'

Clove-scented smoke curled through her fingers, floating into the air and weaving with the words that still hung heavy about her head.

'. . . What did you say?'

Ash leaned in and entwined her hands with Mia's. Pressed her body to Mia's. Placed her lips on Mia's. The kiss was soft and sweet and dizzying, the floor falling away from her feet, wrapping her up in the scent of lavender and burning cloves and an aching, sighing want. All the world stopped spinning. All of time stood still.

'I said I love you, Mia Corvere,' Ash whispered.

For people like us, there are no promises of for ever . . .

'. . . mia . . .'

Mia caught her breath, heart pounding in her chest. Tearing her gaze from Ashlinn's eyes, she saw a familiar shape sitting on the window-sill. A not-cat, cleaning his paw with his not-tongue.

'What is it?' she asked.

'. . . *furian* . . .' Mister Kindly replied.

She'd run like a mad thing back up the hill, cloak flapping behind her, not even bothering to hide beneath her mantle of shadows. If someone from the Rest marked her, so be it, but the repercussions from the collegium's champion being spotted by some random stranger in the street would pale in comparison to what would happen if the guards found her missing from her cell. She'd been a fool, risking a visit with so much in flux. Cursing herself an idiot and trying to forget the fact that Ashlinn Järnheim . . .

Ashlinn Järnheim said she loves me.

Mia pushed the thought aside, pain jarring her ribs every time her foot struck the road.

'He's awake?' she gasped.

'. . . *he is stirring. if they call on you* . . .'

'I know.'

'. . . *you risk too much, mia. all now hangs in the balance* . . .'

'I *know*.'

'. . . *do you really* . . . ?'

Mia gritted her teeth and ran, cursing herself again. Mister Kindly was right. Ashlinn, too. She *was* growing soft. The Mia she knew had been driven. Single-minded. Burning with desire for one thing, and one thing alone. She couldn't afford these kinships any more. The risks they made her take, all that would be undone if she failed here . . .

A safe distance from the Nest, she slung on her mantle of shadows, Stepping across the portcullis as she'd done a dozen times now and feeling her way down to the barracks. Reaching out to the dark, she Stepped across to the shadows of her cell, falling to her knees and clutching her burning chest. Her breath was fire, head swimming, skin filmed with sweat. But after her desperate dash, all seemed quiet – if Furian had woken, it seemed Leona or her guards hadn't yet seen a need for her.

Goddess, that could have been bad . . .

She threw aside her mantle, faded into view there in the dark of the barracks, amid the sighs and snores and sounds of sleep. Lying in one straw-lined corner, Sidonius slowly opened his eyes – the man seemed to have an uncanny knack for sensing when she'd returned. Or perhaps when she'd left.

'Trouble sleeping?' he murmured, pawing at his lashes. 'I've just the cure.'

Mia scowled and didn't reply, not feeling like another lesson on the benefits of a clear conscience. She heard heavy footsteps coming down the stairs, the keys being turned in the mekwerk beside the barracks gate. Sidonius sat up a little straighter, eyes narrowed as three guards approached, fully armed and armoured.

'Rest easy,' she said. 'They're here for me.'

'I rest easy enough, Mia,' he whispered. 'And I've faith you will too.'

The trio of guards arrived at her cell, led by Captain Gannicus.

'The Unfallen has woken,' the guard said. 'He is in pain. Dona Leona left orders you were to be roused if he did, and afforded all courtesy. With Maggot gone . . .'

'Aye, I'll see to it,' Mia sighed. 'Take me to him, if it please you.'

The guards unlocked her cell and Mia stood. Sidonius watched as she was marched out through the barracks, up into the keep and out to the infirmary. Her mind was still whirling, trying to ponder what to do about Sidonius's budding rebellion, the right and wrong of it all. Ashlinn's and Mister Kindly's words swimming in her head. Her heart was torn – the vengeance that had driven her all these years weighed against the thought of allowing Sid and the others to die.

What was more important?

Revenge for a mother and father it turns out she barely even knew? Or the lives of folk who, try as she might to deny it, had become her friends?

The hour was late, but as she approached, Mia could hear choice cursing from within. Stepping inside, she saw Furian on his slab, damp with sweat. His arms and legs were strapped down, the bandages around his chest spotted with blood.

'Fool tried to tear off the dressings,' Gannicus muttered. 'We had to bind him.'

'There's fucking *maggots crawling on me*!' Furian moaned.

'Leave me with him,' Mia told Gannicus. 'I'll see to his hurts. If you could tell Finger to set some vinegar boiling, I'd be indebted.'

'Aye, Champion,' the guard said.

Nodding to his cohorts, Gannicus left a pair stationed outside the infirmary door, and strode off to wake the cook. Mia walked into the infirmary, noted that Bladesinger wasn't lying on her slab. She must have been moved back down to her cell sometime in the nevernight – it was still too soon for her to have been sold off to Caito. Which meant she and Furian would be alone . . .

The man looked her up and down, a dark scowl on that handsome brow. The hunger in her surged as it always did when he was near. He still looked on the south side of awful, his long hair lank with sweat, his skin sallow. But he was awake, alert, dark eyes fixed on the silver torc around her neck.

'She named you champion?' he whispered.

'I didn't ask her for it,' Mia replied. 'But truthfully, none knew if you'd awaken.'

'So she gives away my torc before I'm even cold, and leaves me here to rot?'

'You're not rotting,' Mia sighed.

'I've fucking flyspawn crawling all over me!'

'The maggots are removing flesh turned septic by the Exile's venom. They saved your life. And if you don't calm down and stop thrashing against those straps, you're going to start yourself bleeding again.' Mia poked among the shelves, collecting ingredients. 'The pain can't be pleasant, though. I'll fix you something for it.'

Furian's head sank back against the slab, voice heavy with fatigue. 'Has Domina named you nursemaid, as well as champion? Where is Maggot?'

Mia pressed her lips together, grinding the ingredients with a mortar and pestle.

'Maggot's dead.'

Furian's scowl softened, bewilderment in his eyes. 'How?'

'Arkades slipped a dose of Elegy into everyone's evemeal. Maggot and Otho both succumbed before I could brew an antidote.'

'. . . Arkades?'

'Aye.'

'Horseshit,' Furian whispered. 'Arkades was gladiatii. A man like him looks his enemies in the eye and delivers them with a sword, not a bitter mouthful.'

Mia shrugged, and carefully sniffing a cup of water, mixed her powder into it. Carrying the cup to Furian, she put it to his lips, watching his shadow tremble and ripple about its edges. Her own shadow edged closer, like iron to a magnet. All the questions swimming in her mind. What am I? What are we? Why? Who? How?

'It's only fadeleaf and a bit of ginwort,' she said. 'It will ease the pain.'

The Unfallen stared with narrowed eyes.

'You saved my life, Furian,' Mia said. 'That's a debt not soon forgot. If I wanted you dead, I could have fixed it so you never woke. Now drink.'

The former champion grunted assent, and swallowed the draught as Mia poured. His head drifted back to the slab and he sighed, staring at the ceiling and flexing his wrists against his restraints.

'I remember . . . after the match . . . you took my pain away.'

'A home remedy,' Mia shrugged. 'Easy enough to brew.'

'No,' Furian said, shaking his head. 'Before you gave me the sleeping draught. When I was on the slab, screaming. When your . . . when our shadows touched.'

Mia frowned, remembering that moment beneath Whitekeep arena. As her shadow had darkened, she'd felt *more* pain, not less – Furian's agony mixed in with her own. She supposed that she might somehow be sharing his burden, but apparently she'd lessened his pain by taking it upon herself?

Why?

Who?

How?

'I didn't know I could do that,' she confessed. 'I've never done it before.'

Furian said nothing, watching her with those dark, pretty eyes. She could see the draught she'd given him taking effect, smoothing the lines of pain away from his face.

'I . . . wanted to thank you, Furian,' Mia said. 'For calling the dark in the arena. The Exile would have ended me and 'Singer if not for you.'

'You cheated,' he replied. 'You did something to the silkling's blades.'

'You twisted her shadow. I suppose that makes us both cheaters, neh?'

The Unfallen remained mute for an age, simply staring. When he finally spoke, it was with hesitation, as if compliments didn't sit well upon his tongue.

'You risked your life for a sister gladiatii,' he said. 'You risked your life for *me*. Trickery aside, you still showed loyalty to this collegium. Only fitting that it be repaid.'

'Was that a compliment?' Mia asked. ''Byss and blood, perhaps I mixed too much fadeleaf in with your tea?'

Furian allowed himself a small smile. 'Don't let it swell your head, girl. I'll be reclaiming my torc as soon as I'm able to lift a blade. When I fight at the *magni*, make no mistake – it will be as champion of this collegium.'

Mia shook her head, again trying to figure out the puzzle of this man. He'd treated her with nothing but disdain, spoken of their gifts with the darkness as witchery. But when push came to shove, he'd werked the shadows so that the Falcons could best the Exile. Morality aside, it seemed he was prepared to sacrifice anything for victory.

'Why is all this so important to you?' she asked.

'I have told you before, Crow. This is what I *am*.'

'That's no kind of reason,' Mia sighed. 'You weren't *born* gladiatii. You must have had a life before all this.'

Furian shook his head. Blinking slow.

'I'd not call it such.'

'So what were you? Murderer? Rapist? Thief?'

Furian stared, hidden thoughts swirling behind those bottomless eyes. But the fadeleaf was kicking in now, and the sliproot she'd mixed in with the concoction was loosening his tongue. She felt guilty about dosing him in the hopes he'd open up, but she wanted to understand this man, try to gauge where he'd stand if Sidonius and the others rose in rebellion.

'Murderer, rapist, thief,' Furian replied, his voice thick. 'All that and more. I was a beast who lined his pockets with the miseries of men. And women. And children.'

'What did you do?'

Furian looked to the walls around them, the rusted steel and iron bars.

'I filled places like this. Flesh, my bread, and blood, my wine.'

'. . . You were a slaver?'

Furian nodded, speaking soft. 'Captained a ship for years. The *Iron Gull*. Ran the Ashkah coast all the way to Nuuvash, eastern Liis from Amai to Ta'nise. Sold the men to the fighting pits, women to the pleasure houses, children to whoever wanted them.' A heavy shrug. 'If that turned out to be no one, we'd just put them over the side.'

''Byss and blood,' Mia said, lip curling in revulsion.

'You judge me.'

'You're fucking right I do,' she hissed.

'No harsher than I judge myself.'

'I find that hard to believe,' Mia said, her voice turning to steel.

'Believe what you will, Crow. People always do.'

'So how came you to be here, then?'

Furian closed his eyes, breathing long and deep. For a moment, Mia thought perhaps he'd drifted off to sleep. But eventually he spoke, his voice heavy with fatigue and something darker still. Regret? Shame?

'We raided a village in Ashkah,' he said. 'One of the men we brought aboard was a missionary of Aa. Rapha, his name. I let the men have their sport with him. We weren't really that fond of priests, you see. We beat him. Burned him. In the end, we chummed the water for drakes, and I told him to walk the plank. Looking down into that blue, you see the measure of a person in their eyes. Some beg. Some curse. Some don't even have the legs to carry them. You know what Rapha did?'

'I'd not guess,' Mia shrugged. 'I'm not that fond of priests either.'

'He prayed Aa would forgive us,' Furian said. 'Standing on that plank, a thirty-foot stormdrake circling beneath him. And the bastard starts *praying* for us.'

The Unfallen shook his head.

'I'd never seen the like. So I let him live. I didn't really know why at the time. He sailed with us almost a year. Taught me the gospel of the Everseeing. Taught me that I was lost, nothing but an animal, but that I could find my humanity again if I embraced the Light. But he also told me that I must atone for all the evil I'd done. And so, after a year of it, of reading and arguing, of hating and blustering and crying to myself in the long hours of the nevernight, I accepted the Everseeing into my life. Turned my back on the darkness. I sailed us to the Hanging Gardens. And I sold myself.'

'You . . .' Mia blinked.

'Seems mad, doesn't it? What kind of fool would choose this?'

Mia thought of her own plight, her own plan, slowly shaking her head.

'But . . . *why?*'

'I knew Aa would give me a chance to redeem myself if I placed myself in his keeping. And he put me here. A place of tribulation, and purity, and suffering. But at the end, on the sands of the *magni*, when I kneel before the grand cardinal drenched in my victory, he will not only declare me free, but a free *man*. Not an animal, Crow. A *man*.

'And there, I will be redeemed.'

Furian nodded, took a deep breath, as if he'd purged a poison from his blood.

Mia folded her arms and scowled.

'So that's it?' she demanded. 'You think you can atone for selling hundreds of men and women by murdering hundreds more? You can't clean your hands by washing them in other people's blood, Furian. Trust me, that only gets them redder.'

Furian shook his head and scowled. 'I do not expect you to understand. But *magni* is a holy rite. Judged by the Hand of God himself. And if Rapha taught me anything, it was that the things we *do* are more important than the things we've *done*.'

Mia heard footsteps behind, a knock at the infirmary door. Gannicus marched into the room, two more guards beside him, carrying a steaming pot between them.

'Your vinegar, boiled as requested.'

Mia nodded, turning to Furian.

'I'm going to get rid of the maggots now. This is going to be painful.'

'Life always is, little Crow. Life is pain, and loss, and sacrifice.'

Furian gritted his teeth and closed his eyes.

'But we should welcome that pain. If it brings us salvation.'

S he returned to her cage, flanked by two of the houseguards. Sidonius opened his eyes as the cell door closed behind her, the mekwerk lock twisting closed. Mia had watched carefully from beneath her lashes on the way in here, noting which key on the iron ring opened the barracks gate, controlled her cell door.

Was this the right thing to do?

Would they understand, at the end, that she'd done it all for the best?

'I spoke to Furian,' she whispered once the guards were gone.

'About what?' Sidonius muttered.

'Who he is. How he thinks. Where he's from.' She shook her head. 'He dreams only of the *magni*. He'd never do anything to put it at risk. I think he's still too ill to stand in our way, but when we rise, there's no chance he'll stand with us.'

'When *we* rise?'

'Aye, brother.'

Mia reached out in the dark, squeezed Sidonius's hand.

'We.'

CHAPTER 29

RISE

It was a lot to risk on a single girl.

Sidonius's belly was a knot of raw nerves, his appetite a distant memory. Four turns had passed since Mia proposed her plan in the gloom of their cell, and Sid hadn't slept much since. Instead, he'd paced back and forth in his cage through the nevernight, staring at the mekwerk lock on the door and counting the hours until it began.

Mia had been moved into her champion's quarters three turns back, so Sid found himself alone for the first time since moving to Crow's Nest. Alone with the fear of what was to come, the risk they were all taking, the fate that awaited them if they failed. He was placing so much faith in Mia, and so much rode on her shoulders. He'd served Darius Corvere faithfully, saw the traits he'd admired in the man looming large in his daughter. Courage. Intelligence. Ferocity. But Mia had lost her father when she was only a child, and since then, fallen into the company of shadows and killers.

Sidonius liked her. But could he truly say he knew her?

Could he *trust* her?

Dona Leona had met with Varro Caito three nevernights back, and skulking beneath their table as they drank and dined, Mia's daemon had overheard their every word. Leona had apparently plied the fleshpeddler with honeyed words and honeyed wine, brokering sale of Bryn, Butcher, Felix, Albanus, Bladesinger, and Sidonius himself. The price was a rich one, and Leona would be able to meet the first of her father's repayments, but the cost was steep. The collegium would be gutted, with only Mia, Wavewaker, and Furian remaining. Leona would risk all on one final throw at the *magni*. But she hadn't reckoned on her Falcons throwing dice of their own.

Evemeal had been quiet, the gladiatii subdued. Whispers of the plan had been passed on in the bathhouse, around the practice dummies. All agreed the chances of success were so thin they'd fall through a crack in the cobbles, and Sid could smell fear in the air. It was one thing to risk death in the arena, another thing entirely to pit yourself against the Republic. The administratii. The Senate itself. Every one of them knew this was a step that could never be taken back. The brands on their cheeks would begin to fade only a few minutes after their deaths, so there was no hiding who and what they were if they wanted to keep breathing. To be an escaped slave in the Republic was to be for ever on the run.

Still, better to run than die on your knees.

Even with the few extra turns' rest, Bladesinger was still wounded, her back and arm wrapped in heavy gauze. Mia's ribs were yet bruised, but at least she could use both eyes again. Wavewaker and Sidonius had yet to fully recover from their last arena bout, and Butcher was still limping – they weren't the most fearsome fighting force ever arrayed, to be sure. But they'd have surprise on their side if all went well, and they were trained gladiatii, each and every one.

Their sale was set to happen on the morrow.

Caito had already paid the deposit.

Truth told, it was now or never.

Nevernight had fallen, cool winds kissing ochre walls, dust devils dancing in the yard. After Arkades's betrayal, Dona Leona had doubled the patrols around the house, and the guards were omnipresent. But still, whispers and secret nods were exchanged among the gladiatii, and all seemed in readiness.

But Daughters, the waiting . . .

They sat in the dark, no one speaking, no one moving. Watching the arkemical globes slowly dim, the sounds of the keep above gradually fading. Sid could hear Bladesinger chanting inside her cell – some final prayer to Mother Trelene for good fortune, no doubt. Looking at the cell across the passage, he saw Butcher on his haunches, rocking back and forth and raring to go.

He was reminded of his time in the legion. The nevernight before a battle was always the worst. He'd had his faith in Aa to sustain him back then. His loyalty to his justicus. The solace of his brother Luminatii, and the certainty that what they did was Right. All that was gone now – just a clean conscience and a coward's brand upon his chest to show for it. Instead of brother Luminatii, he had brother and sister gladiatii.

Instead of faith in the Everseeing and the commands of his justicus, he was placing all his faith in his seventeen-year-old daughter.

It was a lot to risk on a single girl.

Sidonius heard a soft thud, the faint ring of metal on stone. Butcher heard it too, rising to his feet, hands wrapped around the bars of his cell. Mia had two options to break them free once she stole out from her room: either somehow brute force the mekwerk controls to release the inner cell doors, or acquire the master key from the guard patrol. Sid had no idea which way she'd go. But his stomach thrilled as he saw a silhouette creeping down the stairs to the cellar antechamber, a wooden truncheon clutched in one hand, and what looked to be an iron key in the other.

''Byss and blood, she did it,' Butcher grinned.

Twisting the key in the mekwerk, Mia unlocked the cell doors, raised the portcullis, Sidonius wincing at the soft grinding of stone on iron. The gladiatii stole out of the barracks, gathering in the antechamber, all fierce grins and bundled nerves. Sidonius gave Mia a quick embrace, his voice a whisper.

'No trouble?'

Mia shook her head. 'Five guards down. The other two are in the front yard.'

'Let's be about it, then,' Wavewaker whispered.

'Aye,' the girl nodded. 'And quietly, for fucksakes.'

Mia led the group up the stairs, where the bodies of five of Leona's houseguards were laid out on the tiles. The men were armoured in black leather, falcon feathers pluming their helms, Captain Gannicus among them. Each had been bludgeoned into unconsciousness. The gladiatii quickly stripped their armour, Sidonius, Bryn Wavewaker, Butcher, and Felix donning the garb instead. Not only would the boiled leather protect them if things turned ugly, but the high cheek guards would do a fine job of covering the brands on their cheeks.

Weapons were handed out – wooden truncheons and shortswords. In the far distance, Sid heard fourbells being rung down in Crow's Rest, the crash of waves upon a rocky shore. The garish light of the two suns streamed in through the open windows, silken curtains rippling as the rebel gladiatii stole through the keep.

They moved quietly as they could, down the entrance hall to the locked front doors. Butcher and Wavewaker lifted the bar aside, the gladiatii gathering in a small knot at the threshold.

'Ready?' Sidonius asked.

'Aye.' Bladesinger raised her sword in her off-hand.

Mia opened the door, and the gladiatii charged soundlessly towards the front portcullis. It took a few moments for the guards to process what they were seeing, and by then, it was too late. One reared back gurgling as Sidonius clubbed him square in the throat. Wavewaker crashed into the other guard, smashing him into the guardhouse wall. The man raised his truncheon, his shout becoming a muffled whimper as Mia clapped her hand over his mouth and buried her knee in his bollocks. He dropped like a stone, and the girl snatched up his club as it fell, cracked it across his head and laid him flat out in the dirt.

Butcher ratcheted up the portcullis as Bladesinger and Albanus stripped the last two guards, began strapping on their breastplates. Mia was too small to wear any man's kit, and besides, there weren't enough unconscious guards to go around. Instead, she threw a cloak she'd got from only Aa knew where about her shoulders, pulled the hood low over her eyes.

'Right,' she whispered. 'We make for the *Gloryhound* in the harbour.'

'Walk tall, look folk in the eye,' Bladesinger reminded them. 'We win this game by appearing as if we belong, aye?'

The gladiatii nodded, and calmly as they could, marched out from the portcullis in neat formation and started tromping down the road. Mia brought up the rear, hood pulled low. Wavewaker's armour didn't fit too well across his broad shoulders, Bladesinger's arm was still swathed in bandages and spotted with blood – under scrutiny, their disguises wouldn't last. But the hour was late, and the port below the Nest was quiet. Hopefully the subterfuge would hold long enough for them to get aboard.

Marching out in front, Sidonius tried to keep his nerves in check. This die was cast, and whatever happened now was in the hands of fate, but Daughters, it was hard not to just break into a run, get as far as he could as fast as possible. The troop walked down the dusty road encircling Crow's Nest, Sid staring out at the blue waters of the Sea of Swords. Marching into the town, they passed a few farmers on the way to market, a messenger rushing about on his master's business, a handful of urchins gathered around a loaf of stolen bread. Not a one of them paid any mind.

He could see the tall masts of ships looming over the harbour now, his heart beating faster. Thinking of that vast blue ocean, the places they could sail, any place but here. He looked to the other gladiatii, risked

a smile, Bryn grinning back, Wavewaker whispering, 'Hold steady.'
Marching closer, the smell of salt in the air, the screeching of gulls like
music in his ears, every step bringing them ne—

'Look alive,' Bladesinger muttered. 'Soldiers ahead.'

Sid gritted his teeth but didn't break stride, noting the quartet of
legionaries from the Crow's Rest garrison marching down the other side
of the street. He'd no clue if the local soldiery mixed with Leona's
houseguards – men of the sword had a tendency to gather and gripe
no matter who they worked for. But at a distance, their disguises should
pass, and it was only a few hundred feet to the harbou—

'I know you,' said a voice.

Sidonius stopped, looked behind them. A young red-headed girl
wearing the feathered cap and pack of a travelling pedlar had stopped
in the street, pointing at Mia.

'Four Daughters, I *know* you,' she repeated. 'You're the Saviour
of Stormwatch!'

Mia shot a warning look to the others, gave the girl a small smile.
'Aye, Dona.'

'I saw you slay the retchwyrm!' the girl cried, her blue eyes shining.
'Merciful Aa, what a fight! I've never seen the like!'

'My thanks, Mi Dona,' Mia muttered. 'But I've ma—'

'Look here!' the pedlar cried to the street. 'The Saviour of
Stormwatch!'

'Here they come,' Wavewaker muttered.

Sid's stomach flipped as he realized the legionaries had overheard
the pedlar, and all four were now crossing the street. Their centurion
saw the ornate plume on Sidonius's helm and called out in greeting.

'Ho, Gannicus! What brings you lazy bastards down here at this . . .'

The centurion stopped, squinting at Sidonius's face through the slits
in his helm.

'. . . Gannicus?'

'Go!' Mia cried.

The gladiatii charged, weapons drawn. The centurion and his men
fumbled with their swords, faces bleached with panic. It had been
truncheons and fists for Leona's houseguards, but there was no room
for mercy here – these were fully armed and armoured Itreyan legionaries,
trained to kill. Wavewaker drove his blade through the centurion's chest,
skewering him like a pig at spit. Butcher smashed another's blade aside,
spun, and took his throat clean out, scarlet spraying in the air with the
salt. The pedlar started screaming, running down the street crying,

'Murder! *Murder!*' as Sidonius finished off another legionary with a flash of his sword. Albanus ended the last of them, cutting the legionary's legs out from under him before burying his blade in the join between the man's shoulder and neck.

'Make for the harbour,' Mia cried. 'Go! Go!'

They broke into a run, all semblance of propriety gone. Sid's sandals pounding the cobbles, folks turning to stare as they dashed past, the cries of *Murder!* from up the street growing louder. They reached the docks, barrelling past sailors and merchantmen unloading their stock, fishermen on the wharf. Wavewaker was running beside him, Bryn out in front, Mia bringing up the rear, all of them splashed with blood. He could see the *Gloryhound* at anchor, perhaps a hundred yards out in the bay.

'There she is,' he gasped.

Sid dropped over the side of the wharf into the *'Hound*'s longboat. The other gladiatii jumped in beside him, Butcher and Wavewaker taking up the oars and rowing as if their lives depended on it. Sid could hear bells ringing now, the alarm spreading through Crow's Rest and waking the residents from their sleep, the fearful cry echoing up and down their quiet streets.

'Rebellion!'

'The Falcons in revolt!'

Butcher and Wavewaker leaned hard on the oars, each stroke bringing them closer to the *'Hound*. Bladesinger shielded her eyes against the water's glare, nodding at the empty masts.

'Sails are stowed.'

'We can set them swift enough,' Wavewaker grunted.

'Are you certain?' Butcher gasped.

'Rest easy, brother,' Wavewaker nodded. 'I was learning to sail while you were still suckling at your mother's teats.'

'You only learned to sail last year?' Bryn grinned.

'Let's leave my mother's teats out of this, aye?' Butcher growled.

'Talk softer, row harder,' Sidonius said.

They reached the *'Hound*, scrambling up the rope ladder and onto the deck. The ship rolled and swayed with the sea, sunlight burning in that endless blue sky. A lone watchman came down from the bow, demanding to know what they were about, but a backhand from Wavewaker sent him to the boards, moaning and bloodied. From up on deck, Sid could see movement around the docks; a handful of legionaries, mariners pointing in their direction.

'We need those sails up now, 'Waker.'

'Aye,' the man nodded. 'They'll be down in the hold. All of you, with me.'

Wavewaker threw aside the large oaken hatch that sealed the 'Hound's hold, climbed swiftly down the ladder into the ship's belly. Bladesinger hopped down second, Sidonius and the other gladiatii following while Mia and Bryn remained on deck to keep watch. Sunslight filtered through the timber lattice above their heads, illuminating the ship's belly, and the gladiatii spread out, searching for the great sheets of canvas that would see them under way. Crates and barrels, coils of salt-crusted rope and heavy, iron-bound chests. But . . .

'I can't see them,' Bladesinger said.

'They must be here somewhere,' Wavewaker growled. 'Keep looking.'

'Why the 'byss would they stow the sails anyw—'

Sid heard scuffling footsteps, a soft curse above their heads. Squinting up through the lattice, he saw two struggling figures, silhouetted against the light. Bryn was one of them – he could tell from the topknot. But the figure behind her, arm wrapped around her neck, looked like . . .

'Mia?' he whispered.

He heard a gasp, a wet thud as Bryn toppled into the hold and landed atop a great coil of rope with a groan. And as Sid opened his mouth to shout warning, the trapdoor above them slammed closed, sealing them all in the 'Hound's hold.

'What the 'byss?' Wavewaker hissed.

Sidonius was kneeling beside Bryn, the girl barely conscious, red marks at her throat. He looked up through the latticework hatch, belly churning, his mouth suddenly dry as dust.

'Crow?' he called. 'What are you playing at?'

'I'm sorry, Sidonius,' he heard the girl reply, voice thick with sorrow. 'But I told you once already. The last thing I'm doing here is playing.'

Butcher climbed the ladder, pounded at the hatch with his sword, trying to break it open. 'What the fuck goes on here?'

The gladiatii met each other's eyes, confusion and dread in every stare. They were sealed in the 'Hound's belly like fish in a barrel, no one to fight, no way out.

'This is how you repay me?' came a voice.

Sidonius looked up, drawing a shivering breath as he saw Dona Leona walking the deck above his head. Instead of nevernight attire, she was dressed in black, her eyes kohled, hair braided as if for war.

'After all I have done for you,' Leona said, staring down at the gladiatii trapped in the hold. 'Raising you up from the mire. Feeding and sheltering you beneath my roof. Drenching you in glory and the honour of my collegium's name. This is my thanks?'

'Crow,' Wavewaker spat, prowling in circles and looking up at the deck. 'Crow, what have you *done?*'

'She has done what no other among you had the courage to do,' Leona said. 'She has remained *loyal* to her domina.'

'You bleeding fucking *cunt!*' Butcher roared, slamming his arm against the hatch. 'I'll fucking *kill you!*'

'You'll do no such thing,' Leona answered. 'You will languish in that hold until I decide your fate. And I fear it shall be an unpleasant one, traitor.'

'You call us traitors?' Bladesinger shouted. 'I brought you honour at Whitekeep. Crow would *never* have stood victor if not for me! And you give me thanks by selling me to that shitheel Varro Caito before my wounds are even healed?'

The woman spat onto the wood at her feet.

'You faithless fucking bitch.'

Leona sneered, shook her head.

'All I hear are treacherous rats, squeaking in a hole of their own making.'

Butcher was smashing at the hatch with his sword. Wavewaker pushing at the timbers above their head. A half-dozen houseguards spilled out from the *'Hound*'s main cabin to surround the dona – the second shift, all of whom should have been slumbering right now in their bunks. There could be no doubt now that Leona had known this was coming, that all the faith they'd put in the daughter of Darius Corvere . . .

Sidonius clenched his fists as he looked up through the lattice. Mia met his stare, dark eyes clouded, her expression grim and bloodless. The scar cutting down her cheek lent her a vicious air, a cruelty and callousness he'd never noticed until now. But still, he fancied he could see tears in those dark lashes, her long dark hair caught up in the nevernight winds and playing about her face like some black halo.

'Crow?'

'It just meant too much to me, Sid,' she whispered.

She shook her head, hands fluttering helplessly at her sides.

'I'm so sorry . . .'

It had been a lot to risk on a single girl.

But he'd never thought for a moment they'd actually lose.

'Aye, little Crow.'

Sidonius hung his head, pawing at his aching chest.

'I'm sorry too . . .'

CHAPTER 30

INTERLUDE

Two passengers met in a dirty alley, in a little city by the sea.

The first was small, thin as whispers, cut in the shape of a cat. It had worn the seeming for over seven years now. It could barely remember the thing it had been before. A fraction of a deeper darkness, with only enough awareness to crawl from the black beneath Godsgrave's skin and seek another like itself.

Mia.

She'd lost her father, the turn they met. Hanged and dancing before the hoi polloi. She'd screamed, and made the shadows tremble, and he'd followed her call until he found her at her mother's side. The image of her father burned bright in her mind as he reached out and touched her. But she'd lost her kitten, too. Its neck broken in the hands of the justicus who'd stolen her father's title along with his life. A tinier wound. The kitten seemed a far more sensible shape to steal, in the end. Far better than the father. Far easier to love a simple thing.

She'd named him Mister Kindly. It fitted well enough. But somewhere deep inside, the cat who was not a cat knew that was not his name.

The second passenger was larger, had worn its shape for longer. She'd found her Cassius when he was but a boy. Beaten. Starving. Abused beyond reckoning. A child of the Itreyan wilds, dragged to the City of Bridges and Bones in chains, and there, almost drowned in misery. The boy's folk had hunted wolves – he'd remembered that much, even in his nadir. And the boy remembered wolves were strong and fierce. So she became a wolf for him, and together, they'd hunted all who stood in their way.

He'd named her Eclipse. It was close to the truth. But somewhere deep inside, the wolf who was not a wolf knew that was not her name either.

She missed him.

'. . . HELLO, MOGGY . . .' the not-wolf said, resting on the wall of a lean-to inn.

'. . . hello, mongrel . . .' the not-cat replied, atop a stack of empty barrels.

'. . . IT IS DONE, THEN . . . ?'

'. . . it is done . . .'

The shadowwolf turned her not-eyes to the ocean, nodded once.

'. . . I WILL TELL ASHLINN SHE CAN REMOVE THAT RIDICULOUS TINKER'S PACK, THEN . . .'

'. . . if you could convince her to drown herself in the ocean at the same time, i would sincerely appreciate it . . .'

'. . . YOUR JEALOUSY FASCINATES ME, LITTLE MOGGY . . .'

'. . . careful, dear mongrel, i do believe you just used a three-syllable word . . .'

'. . . HOW COMES IT THAT ONE WHO FEASTS ON FEAR CAN BE SO AFRAID . . . ?'

'. . . i fear nothing . . .'

'. . . YOU REEK OF IT . . .'

'. . . be a darling and fuck right off, would you . . . ?'

'. . . NOTHING WOULD PLEASE ME MORE . . .'

The wolf who was not a wolf began to fade, like a whisper on the wind. But the not-cat's plea held it still.

'. . . wait . . .'

'. . . WHAT . . . ?'

Mister Kindly hung still for a moment, searching for the words.

'. . . are . . . are you not afraid . . . ?' he finally asked.

'. . . OF WHAT . . . ?'

'. . . not of. for . . .'

'. . . YOUR RIDDLES BORE ME, GRIMALKIN . . .'

'. . . are you not afraid for her . . . ?'

The shadowwolf tilted its head.

'. . . WHY WOULD I BE . . . ?'

The not-cat sighed, searching the horizon.

'. . . i wonder sometimes, what we are making of her . . .'

'. . . WE ARE MAKING HER STRONG. STEEL. RUTHLESS AS THE STORM AND THE SEA . . .'

'. . . the thing we take from her . . . i wonder if she does not need it . . .'

'. . . YOU SPEAK OF FEAR . . . ?'

'. . . no, i speak of fashion sense . . .'

'. . . WHAT NEED HAS SHE OF FEAR, MOGGY . . . ?'

'. . . those who do not fear the flame are burned. those who do not fear the blade are bled. and those who do not fear the grave . . .'

'. . . *ARE FREE TO BE AND DO WHATEVER THEY WISH . . .*'

'. . . *she is different than she once was. she was never this cold. this reckless . . .*'

'. . . *AND YOU BLAME ME FOR THAT . . .*'

'. . . *two of us feast where only one once fed. perhaps we take too much. perhaps we* make *her like this. callous. conniving. cruel . . .*'

'. . . *AND I AM CERTAIN THAT RECENT REVELATIONS ABOUT THE RED CHURCH, HER FAMILIA, HAVE NOTHING TO DO WITH HER CHANGE IN DEMEANOUR . . .*'

'. . . *three-syllable word again . . .*'

'. . . *ARE WE FINISHED HERE, LITTLE MOGGY . . . ?*'

The not-cat looked to the sky, burning red and brilliant gold and blinding blue.

'. . . *a reckoning is coming, eclipse. it waits for us in the city of bridges and bones. i can feel it. like that accursed sun on the horizon. drawing closer with every breath . . .*'

'. . . *A GOOD THING, THEN, THAT WE DO NOT BREATHE . . .*'

Mister Kindly sighed.

'. . . *i hate you . . .*'

Eclipse laughed.

'. . . *GOOD . . .*'

And without another sound, she was gone.

A lone passenger sat in a dirty alley, in a little city by the sea.

It could barely remember the thing it had been before. A fraction of a deeper darkness. A larval consciousness, dreaming of shoulders crowned with translucent wings.

And she who would gift them.

Mia.

CHAPTER 31

TRUELIGHT

Godsgrave.

Mia stood on the deck of the *Gloryhound*, the ocean wind in her hair, staring out at the City of Bridges and Bones. The harbour was full, hundreds of sails scattered across that carpet of rolling blue, folk travelling from all corners to celebrate the greatest of Aa's feast turns in the glorious capital of the Republic.

Truelight, at last, was upon them.

Saai had finally crested the horizon as they sailed from Crow's Nest, that pale blue globe joining its gold and red siblings in the sky. The heat was blistering, and Mia was sickened by it, Mister Kindly curled up in her shadow, just as miserable as she. She could feel all the Light Father's fury, beating down upon her like hammers to the anvil. Bowing her head and walking the decks above people who'd once called her friend.

Sidonius and the others were chained in the hold, manacles about their wrists and ankles. They'd put up a courageous front, vowing to kill any of Leona's guards who came down into the hold to get them, but after three turns with no water in this awful heat, they were too weak to resist. The guards stormed the hold on the fifth turn, shackled them in irons. They'd been fed and watered every turn since then; they needed to be fit enough to wield weapons in their execution bouts, after all.

Mia had only avoided arrest because she'd aided in the insurgents' capture, and Furian, only by dint of his sickbed and Leona's sworn testimony before the administratii. The dona had taken a deposit from Varro Caito for the sale of her crop, but with word spreading through Crow's Rest about the uprising, she couldn't actually complete the transaction – no one would be fool enough to buy a pack of gladiatii who'd rebelled against their mistress.

And so, the dona had simply stolen Caito's deposit and put out to sea, taking the scenic route to Godsgrave and fixing to worry about the outraged fleshpeddler when she returned from the capital in triumph. With the coin she'd filched, along with the purse from Whitekeep and the small stipend she'd be paid for the execution bout, she had enough to manage the first repayment to her father. But if she didn't leave Godsgrave with the *Venatus Magni* won, she'd be utterly ruined.

Everything rested upon that single match.

Everything.

Mia rested her hands against the 'Hound's railing, the sunlight blazing on the ocean's face. She tried twisting the shadows at her feet, but it was near impossible; her grip on the darkness was weak, and trying to hold it was like holding smoke. It made sense, she supposed. Her powers had been at their height at truedark, and it was logical they'd be weakest when the Father of Light was strongest in the sky. But that didn't make her feel any better about her chances in the *magni*.

She stared out at the great Itreyan capital, heart in her throat. It had been months since she'd laid eyes upon it. Months of sweat and blood and tears. All the city was laid out before her, the broken archipelago shimmering in the sunlight. Every square foot was encrusted with tenements and shanties and graceful villas, clinging to the shoreline like barnacles on an old galley's hull. Above the cathedral spires and the looming War Walkers and the Senate House, rose the Ribs – those great, ossified towers stretching high into the sky, their bleached white glare almost blinding.

She'd spent much of her childhood inside her parents' apartment there. Far more than in Crow's Nest, truth told. Sitting with her mother and their servants, playing with her baby brother. If Crow's Nest had been their refuge, Godsgrave had been their world. She'd never managed to escape its pull for long.

The thought of her familia made her chest hurt, her eyes mist, all she'd broken and stolen, all the lives she'd taken and miles she'd run and years she'd studied, all of it would soon be justified. In two short turns, the *magni* would begin. In two short turns, she'd fight for her life and stand before Duomo and Scaeva upon that bloody sand, and scream her name as she slit their throats, ear to fucking ear.

It will be worth it.

She looked over her shoulder, down in the shadows of the hold beneath her feet. She could feel their stares upon her. The ones who'd called her friend.

All of it will be worth it.

'I knew you were a cold one, Crow,' said a voice behind her. 'But I never knew just how much ice flowed in your veins until now.'

Mia stared at the Godsgrave skyline as Furian joined her by the rails. The Unfallen's long black hair blew in the sea breeze, bronzed skin glistening with a faint sheen of sweat. His chest was pitted and scarred, the flesh still scabbed, but with the three weeks he'd rested aboard ship, he was almost hale. Despite the three suns burning above, Mia's shadow trembled as he leaned closer. Glancing to their feet, she saw Furian's did the same.

'What do you mean?' she asked.

Furian looked out at the City of Bridges and Bones, dark eyes narrowed against the light. 'I'm told you're to wield the blade in the execution bout.'

'Domina needs the purse.'

'O, I know it,' Furian nodded. 'And I know it is Domina's right to designate their executioner. I just didn't think you'd be willing to put Sidonius and the others in the dirt.'

'We're the only two gladiatii Domina has left standing, Furian. Your wounds are barely healed enough to risk you in the *magni*. Unless Domina wants the execution purse to go to another collegium, who is she going to field? Should she stick a sword in Magistrae's hand and ask her to do the deed?'

Furian smiled. 'Now, that would be a sight.'

'Aye,' Mia sighed. 'It would at that.'

Furian's smile died slow on his lips, his voice dropping to a murmur. 'Why did you do it?' he asked. 'I've been meaning to ask.'

Mia glanced at him sidelong, lips pursed. 'Do what?'

'You know what I mean,' he growled. 'Bladesinger and the others thought of you as a friend. Yet Domina tells me that as soon as you got wind of their plan, you brought it straight to her. And not only did you foil their escape, but you fashioned a way they'd be captured *alive*, so they might be brought before the mob for justice.'

'If they'd just been killed in their escape, Domina wouldn't have recouped a single coin for their loss,' Mia said. 'Leonides would have shut down the collegium. We wouldn't *be* here. But now, between the Whitekeep purse and the execution bou—'

'Aye, aye, I know all that,' Furian growled, his temper fraying. 'What I don't understand is why you didn't *help* them.'

'Because I'm not a fucking hero, Furian. They want help, they can help themselves.'

Mia turned to walk away, but the Unfallen grabbed her arm, teeth bared.

'Who the 'byss *are* you?' he demanded. 'No nameless slip from Little Liis, that much is sure. I look in your eyes and I see intent. I see *design*. Ever since you set foot in our collegium, I've felt your hand at work. Like some shadow puppeteer ever pulling the strings, and we, the marionettes.'

Mia snatched her arm free with a snarl. 'Don't touch me.'

'You've no loyalty to Leona,' Furian growled. 'I know it now. Even in our match at Whitekeep, risking your life to save Bladesinger, all of it was to further your own ends. You've betrayed those who called you sister. Murdered and lied and stole, all to stand here on the sands of the *magni* when you could just slip between the shadows and claim freedom anytime you choose. So *why in the Everseeing's name are you here?*'

Mia stared into those bitter, chocolate eyes, the darkness trembling at her feet. She'd once thought she and Furian were as much alike as truelight and truedark. But she saw that was a lie now. Saw the similarities between them, as deep as blood and bone. Both prisoners of their past. Both obsessed beyond reason with winning the *magni*, Furian for the sake of redemption, and Mia for revenge.

Mia clenched her jaw, shook her head. Tempted to speak. To look into his eyes and see if he'd grant her some measure of understanding. He of all people should. But this was pointless and she knew it. Furian sought absolution for his sins from the hands of a god. Mia sought to strike down the hands of that same god for their own sins. For one of them to stand the victor, the other would have to fall. And neither would be willing to step aside so that the other might win. This was no storybook. There was no love between them. No fellowship. Only rivalry.

And there was only one way it would end.

'Get your rest, Furian,' Mia said.

She turned her eyes back to that blinding skyline.

'You're going to need it come weeksend.'

———

D*rip.*
　　Silver at her throat.

Drip.

Stone at her feet.

Drip.

Iron in her heart.

Mia sat in the dark beneath the arena, simply listening. Salt water fell from the ceiling above, splashing on the cell floor. All the years. All the miles.

On the morrow, one way or another, it would all end.

They'd been brought ashore yesterturn, once the administratii had sent approval for the execution bout. The calendar was packed – there had already been five full turns of games, and hundreds of prisoners had already been murdered by the state. The editorii were hard-pressed to find room for another execution bout in the morrow's festivities, but an entire gladiatii stable turning rotten could set a vile example for other collegia. And so, the Falcons of Remus were to be delivered to justice in a five-minute window after the final equillai race. Their lives snuffed out as folk waited for food, or dashed off to the lavatory before the main event.

And after midmeal, after their murders, the *magni* would begin.

Drip.

Drip.

Mia had sat alone in her cell and listened to the festivities, the roar of the colossal crowd shaking the very stone at her feet. Champions of each collegium were afforded a little privacy – her walls were stone, her bed was clean, two small arkemical globes shedding a warm, constant light. A small hatch in her heavy oaken door let in a whisper of fresh air, the smell of the kitchens, of blood, of oil and iron. She wondered what kind of conditions Sidonius and the others were being kept in. How much more they'd be forced to suffer before they walked onto the sand for the final time. Mister Kindly sat in her shadow, watching her with his not-eyes. Whispering that soon, one way or another, all this would be over.

She made no reply.

As she and Furian had been marched through the crowded marrow-born district and into the belly of Godsgrave Arena yesterturn, she'd been awed at the sheer size of the structure. She'd seen it as a younger girl, of course, but never this close. The arena's great oblong was carved directly out of the Spine itself, stretching a thousand feet, concentric rings of bleachers reaching four tiers high. Graceful arches and fluted buttresses, solid marble and gravebone throughout, statuary of the Everseeing and his Four Daughters encircling the outer ring. It was a marvel of engineering, testament to the ingenuity of the folk who'd designed it, the suffering of the slaves who'd built it, a monument to the awesome power, vision, and, above all, cruelty of the Itreyan Republic.*

The *venatus* was done for the turn, the crowd pouring out into the street with bright smiles and wide eyes. Cathedral bells tolled all over the city, calling the faithful to mass. With all three of the Everseeing's eyes open in the sky, the more devout citizens of the Republic were preparing for a nevernight of prayer and public piety, and the less religious sorts, an eve of private debauchery.

The excitement was arkemical, anticipation for the *magni* at a dizzying high. Mia could hear the thrum of the great mekwerks beneath her, as the priests of the Iron Collegium tested all would be ready for the morrow. This was the greatest event in the Itreyan calendar, a celebration of the Republic, and the God of Light. Tomorrow, the grandest spectacle beneath the suns would play out before the crowd's wondering eyes, the consul himself would crown Itreya's mightiest warrior with a laurel of gold, as the Hand of God himself granted that warrior their freedom.

---

* Godsgrave Arena was commissioned late in the reign of the Great Unifier, King Francisco I, though construction was not completed until his grandson, Francisco III, took the throne some thirty-six years later.

The principal architects were a husband and wife: Don Theodotus and Agrippina of the Familia Arrius. Theodotus was a man of sheer brilliance when it came to mekwerk, but his wife was simply a genius. The pair toiled their entire lives on the structure – it was rumoured that Agrippina gave birth to their son, Agrippa, at her draughting table.

Agrippina died three turns after the final stone was placed in the arena's outer ring. Heartbroken at his love's passing, Theodotus joined her barely a week later. Statues of the pair stand side by side in the Visionaries' Row of the Iron Collegium, hands entwined, testament to the power of persistence, ambition, and passion.

The script at the statues' base reads, 'In love and stone, immortal'.

That's the story, gentlefriends.

No punchline.

No sarcasm.

I thought you might want to hear something sweet, given what's about to happen . . .

It was the stuff legends were made of.

Drip.

Mia stared at nothing.

Drip.

Saying nothing.

Drip.

Listening instead to the echoes of the retiring crowd, the legionaries patrolling the arena's bowels, the swish of a broom as a slave made his way up the corridor outside. And most of all, to the thoughts inside her head.

This is not where I die.

She shook her head, clenched her fists.

I've far too much killing to do.

The broom stopped outside her door. She heard a whisper of cloth, the soft tune of metal on metal, the gentle click of the mekwerk lock at her door. A man entered, sweeping as he came, his back bent with age, grey hair standing in an unruly shock above a pair of piercing, familiar eyes.

'Well,' the old man said, closing the door. 'The accommodations are nothing to write home about, but the residents in this place are downright deplorable.'

'Mercurio!'

Mia rose from the floor and crashed into his arms. The bishop of Godsgrave grinned wide, wrapped her up in a fierce embrace. She almost sobbed, feeling all the sorrow and pain of the last few turns suddenly weigh a little lighter. The tension bleeding out through her feet into the uncaring stone beneath her. She held on to him so tight he struggled to breathe, and he patted her on the back until she eased her grip, dragged her knuckles across her eyes.

''Byss and blood, it's good to see you,' she breathed.

'And you, little Crow,' her old mentor smiled.

'You look good,' she said.

'You've looked better,' he replied, touching the scar at her cheek. 'How you faring in here?'

'Well enough,' she shrugged. 'Truelight is making it hard to werk the shadows. The food is shite. And I'm dying for a smoke.'

'Well, the first two, I've no remedy for,' the bishop said. 'But the third . . .'

Mercurio reached into his threadbare tunic, pulled out a thin silver case. Mia's face lit up as he pulled out two cigarillos, lit them with a small flintbox. She practically snatched the offering out of the old man's hand, dragging the smoke into her lungs as if her life depended on it. Groaning, she leaned against the wall and tilted her head back, breathing a plume of clove-scented grey into the air and licking the sugar from her lips.

'Black Dorian's,' she sighed.

'Best cigarillos in the 'Grave,' Mercurio smiled.

'Maw's teeth, I could kiss you . . .'

'Save your gratitude for the morrow,' he said. 'You can thank me by not getting your fool self killed.'

'That's the trick of it,' she replied.

'Our young Dona Järnheim has filled me in on the particulars of your adventures while you've been absent the 'Grave,' Mercurio said. 'Thank the Black Mother she wasn't sending me regular updates or I'd have had a fucking heart attack.'

'I'll admit the plan went slightly . . . awry . . .'

'Awry? It's all over the shop like a madman's shit, Mia. Solis has been on me like cheap silk on a two-beggar sweetboy. I've fended him off well enough 'til now, but his patience is worn thin.' Mercurio grimaced, dragging on his cigarillo. 'You're travelling in northern Vaan as we speak, just so you know. You missed catching the map bearer in Carrion Hall by a single turn.'

'That was sloppy of me,' Mia murmured.

'Aye, well, you were never my brightest student.'

Mia smirked, inhaling another lungful of warm, sweet grey.

'I received a visit a few turns after you left, by the by,' Mercurio said. 'A friend of yours came poking around the necropolis.'

'. . . I don't have friends, Mercurio, you know that.'

'A girl named Belle? She said to say you sent her.'

Mia blinked, a slow remembering creeping up on her like a thief. She recalled the fourteen-year-old girl in the braavi pleasure house, with the bruise on her lip and too much hurt in her eyes.

'She came looking for you?' Mia smiled. 'Good for her.'

'I'm not in the business of taking in every stray that walks in off the street, Mia,' he growled. 'I'm a bishop of Our Lady of Blessed Murder, not a fucking charity worker.'

Mia folded her arms, fixed Mercurio with her dark stare.

'I recall a stray who walked into the parlour of Mercurio's Curios not so long ago,' she said. 'A girl without a friend in the world, and a whole Republic arrayed against her. You took *her* in. You gave her a place to belong. You gave her love in a world where she'd thought there was nothing left but shit. And thinking on it now, I don't ever think she said thank you.'

Mia placed a gentle kiss on the old man's cheek.

'So, thank you. For everything.'

'Get off,' he muttered, pushing her away.

'I know what it's cost you to help me,' she said. 'I know what you've risked to get me here. Scaeva and Duomo took my familia away, but I found another in you.'

The old man cleared his throat, scowling.

'You're not going soft on me, are you, little Crow?'

'Wouldn't dream of it.'

The old man blinked furiously, wiped his face.

'Fucking dusty in these cells.'

'Aye,' she smiled, pawing at her eyes. 'It is at that. Is Ashlinn ready?'

'All's prepared. Do you still trust her?'

'With my life.'

'I think she's got a soft spot for you.'

Mia grinned around her cigarillo. 'She always had bad taste.'

Mercurio sighed, looked her deep in the eye.

'Are you certain you know what you're doing?'

'If I'm not, it's a little late to switch the song now,' she shrugged. 'I'll just dance until the music stops, and see where the steps take me.'

'It's *not* too late, Mia. You can still change your mind.'

'But that's the thing, Mercurio,' she said. 'I don't *want* to. Even if Mister Kindly and Eclipse weren't with me, I wouldn't be afraid. Every turn of the last seven years has been leading to this moment. I'll play the role that fate has given me. And amorrow, when the curtain falls on the final act, Scaeva and Duomo fall with it.'

'Just remember,' Mercurio scowled, 'the play's final act needn't be your own.'

'I've no wish to die,' Mia sighed, crushing her smoke out against the wall. 'To be honest, it sounds far more interesting to be the most wanted murderer in the Republic.'

'A noble goal for any lass to aspire to,' Mercurio smiled.

Mia grinned. 'Well, you told me once I'd never be a hero.'

Mercurio's eyes filled with tears. He wrapped her up in a tight embrace, pulled her close to his chest. And there in the dark, just the pair of them, holding the girl he thought of as his own, the old man whispered.

'I might have lied.'

CHAPTER 32

GENTLY

Furian followed the path of a twisting canal through the marrowborn district, flanked on all sides by houseguards of the Remus Collegium. The hour was late, the heat only slightly eased by the cool nevernight winds blowing off the Sea of Silence. Revelry spilled from every taverna, smokehouse, and bordello, handsome dons and donas walking arm in arm, song and merriment ringing in the air.

The Unfallen had stomach for none of it.

The guards escorted him over the Bridge of Solace, along the edge of the Spine to a row of fine villas. They stood in the shadow of the fifth Rib, pale stone and ochre tile, flowers on the windowsills. Not the finest abodes in all of Godsgrave, to be sure, but closer to a palace than any place he'd slept in his life.

The guards escorted him to the front door, where Magistrae awaited in a flowing gown of ocean blue, a sour look on her face.

'The domina requests your presence,' the old woman said. 'If it please you.'

With a last glance at the guards, Furian stalked into the villa, up the winding stair. The walls were polished white marble, silken curtains rippling in the breeze, rich red carpet beneath his feet. He walked slow, unsure of the way, finally arriving at a set of double doors at the end of the hall.

She lay on the bed inside, long auburn hair streaming in delicate ringlets about her face. Her lashes were kohled ink black, her lips blood red. She was dressed in a gown of white silk, thin as gossamer, her soft curves and the delicious shadow between her thighs visible through the sheer fabric. Her wrists were wrapped in thin gold chains, her eyes glittering like the face of the ocean.

Leona opened her arms, beckoned him to the bed.

'Hello, lover.'

M ia sat in the dark of her cell, on a simple cot made of straw, the gloom lightened only by a small arkemical globe. The hour was late, the heat only slightly eased by the cool nevernight breeze blowing in through the bars in the door. She could hear the distant sounds of steel on steel, mekwerk churning beneath the arena sands, the thunder of the crowd still echoing up in the bleachers.

Mia had stomach for none of it.

Guards patrolled the corridor outside, walking the row of champions' cells. They weren't the finest abodes in all of Godsgrave, to be sure, but the cells allowed a moment's privacy before the turn that would decide their occupants' lives.

Mia heard the mekwerk lock twist on her cell door, looked up to see a female guard standing upon the threshold.

'A moment of your time,' she said. 'If it please you.'

The guard walked into the cell, closing the door behind her. The light was dim, her features hidden, but Mia still recognized her at once. The guard pulled off her helm, long red hair tumbling about her face. Her lashes were unpowdered, her lips bereft of paint. She was dressed in a black leather breastplate and skirt, the triple suns of the Itreyan legion on her breast. Her wrists were wrapped in thick leather bracers, her eyes as blue as sunburned skies.

Mia opened her arms, beckoned her to the cot.

'Hello, lover.'

L eona pressed her lips to Furian's, mouth open, hungry. Her hands roamed his back, arkemical thrills running down his spine as she explored the troughs and valleys of muscle. Hands tangled in his long dark hair, Leona dragged him down onto the bed, sighing into his mouth. Her hands were everywhere, stroking, teasing, burning, Leona's sighs on his skin, hot as the sunslight outside.

'I want you,' she breathed.

She straddled him, hair tumbling about his face, her kiss deepening as she moved her hips, grinding against him. Taking his hands, she placed them on her breasts, the heat of her skin, the scent of her perfume, the music of her sighs filling the room.

'I need you,' she whispered.

Her kisses drifted lower, hands descending to unbuckle his belt, whisk off his loincloth. She left a trail of burning kisses down his scarred chest, across the rippling muscle at his belly, her tongue lapping at the sweat on his skin as she sank farther and farther down.

'I own you,' she sighed.

'Stop,' he whispered.

He took hold of Leona's chin, and gently pushed her away.

'*Stop.*'

Ash pressed her lips to Mia's, mouth open, hungry. Her hands roamed her back, arkemical thrills running down Mia's spine as she explored the smooth lines and graceful curves. Hands tangled in her long red hair, Mia dragged her down onto the cot, sighing into her mouth. Her hands were everywhere, stroking, teasing, burning, Ash's sighs on her skin, hot as the sunlight outside.

'I want you,' she breathed.

Ash straddled her, hair tumbling about Mia's face, their kiss deepening as they moved their hips, grinding against each other. Taking Mia's hands, Ash placed them on her breasts, the heat of her skin, the scent of her sweat, the music of her sighs filling the cell.

'I need you,' she whispered.

Her kisses drifted lower, hands descending to unbuckle Mia's belt, whisk off her loincloth. She left a trail of burning kisses down her heaving breasts, across the taut muscle at her belly, tongue lapping at the sweat on Mia's skin as she sank farther and farther down.

'I love you,' she sighed.

'Don't stop,' Mia whispered.

She took hold of Ash's hair, and gently pulled her in.

'*Don't stop.*'

Leona blinked up at Furian, confusion clouding her eyes.

'. . . What's wrong?'

Furian climbed off the soft bed, the thousand-thread sheets, wishing for all the world he were back in his cell. He tied his loincloth about his waist, avoiding her gaze.

'Slave,' Leona demanded. 'I asked you a question.'

He spoke gently then, his words sharp as steel.

'This was a dream. And I was a fool to dream it.'

He met her eyes then.

'This is not love,' he said.

And without a backward glance, he turned and stalked from the room.

A sh lay in Mia's arms, drenched in sweat, looking up into her dark eyes.

'. . . What's wrong?'

Mia only shook her head, held Ashlinn tighter. They lay together on the tiny straw bed in that gloomy pit, the taste of the other still lingering on their lips. Ash's cloak beneath them. Stone and iron around them. All the world against them. Death looming large on a vicious horizon. And for that single, simple moment, none of it mattered.

None of it mattered at all.

'This feels like a dream,' Mia whispered. 'And I don't want to wake.'

She met her eyes then.

'This is love,' Mia said simply.

And leaning in, she closed her eyes and gifted Ash a gentle kiss.

CHAPTER 33

BEGIN

The sound was impossible.

A living, breathing, colossal thing, pressing on Mia's skin, so real she felt she could almost reach out and touch it. A weight on her shoulders, rooting her to the earth. A tremor in the stone around her, a physical sensation in the air. In all her years, even in Stormwatch, even in Whitekeep, she'd never heard the like of it.

She sat in her cell, listening to the song of murder above, the verse of steel on steel, the percussion of hooves, the chorus of the blood-mad crowd. Mister Kindly and Eclipse both swam in her shadow, rippling at the edges, trying to devour the fear swelling in her chest. It was hard not to feel it now, try as she might. The daemons did their best, but still, she could sense it, like those hateful suns above her. The scent of Ashlinn's sweat lingering on her skin. Reminding her of all she now had to lose.

'I'm afraid,' she whispered.

'. . . WE ARE SORRY, MIA . . .'

'. . . *we try, but the suns . . .*'

'. . . THEY BURN US . . .'

She clasped her hands together to stop them shaking. Reminding herself of who she was. Where she sat. All that would be undone if she failed.

'Conquer your fear,' she whispered, 'and you can conquer the world.'

The mekwerk lock clicked, the door swung aside. Dona Leona stood there, tall and proud, surrounded by her houseguards and Itreyan legionaries. She was clad in shimmering silver, the gown flowing off her shoulders like summer showers. Her plaited hair was interwoven with metallic ribbon, like a victor's laurel about her brow.

'My champion,' she said.

'Domina,' Mia replied.

'You are prepared?'

Mia nodded. 'Are you?'

Leona blinked. 'Why would I not be?'

'These are your gladiatii about to die, Domina,' Mia replied. 'I wondered if perhaps you felt some regret about that.'

Leona raised her chin, pride tightening her jaw. 'My only regret is that I fostered a nest of traitors for so very long. Next season, it shall be different, I vow it. With the coin I make from the *magni*, I shall stock my collegium with only the finest gladiatii, and an executus who may be counted upon to forge them into true gods.'

'Arkades forged Furian, did he not? Arkades forged me.'

'Arkades was a cur. An honourless dog who—'

'Arkades was in love with you, Domina.'

Leona lips parted, but she found no words to speak.

'Surely you sensed it?' Mia pressed. 'He was champion and then executus of one of the richest, most accomplished collegia in the history of the *venatus*. Why else would he have followed you to Crow's Nest, if he wasn't following his heart?'

'Arkades *betrayed* me,' Leona hissed.

Mia shook her head. 'Arkades was gladiatii. A man of the sword. Even if he discovered you were bedding Furian, do you honestly think he'd look to poison the whole collegium? Knowing how he felt about you, and what it would cost you if your father got his way?'

'. . . I scarce know where to begin,' Leona said, blustering. 'First of all, how dare you imply—'

'Look to your own house, Leona,' Mia said. 'Look to those closest to you, and ask yourself who truly stood to gain if you were forced to limp back to civilization and beg forgiveness at your father's feet. Who encouraged you to ask him for coin? Who was the first to object, whenever you spoke ill of him in public?'

The dona stood rooted to the stone, a small frown forming on her brow.

'Sanguila Leona,' said a legionary in the hall. 'The Crow must be prepared for the execution bout.'

Mia stepped closer to her mistress, speaking so only they could hear.

'I might have been like you, if fate were kinder, and crueller. I know what happened to your mother. I know what kind of childhood you had. All the things you are, you are for a reason. Vicious and generous.

Courageous and pitiless. I like you, and I hate you, and I couldn't have done this without you. So when the turn is done, I'll give you all the thanks I can muster. You won't think it nearly enough, I'm sure. But it's all I can fashion for you, Leona.'

The dona's eyes were narrowed to papercuts, filled with indignant fury. 'You will address me as Domina!'

The crowd roared above them, trumpets rang bright and clear in the air, signalling the end of the equillai race. Mia looked to the older woman, and slowly nodded.

'Aye,' she said. 'But not for much longer.'

She stood before a portcullis of iron, wrapped in black steel. Falcon wings at her shoulders, a cloak of red feathers at her back. The face of a goddess covered her own, only her eyes visible through the helm's façade.

She was glad no one would be able to see if she wept.

The temperature was soaring, the audience baking in the suns. Many had taken the opportunity after the final (spectacular) equillai race to seek some shade or refreshment. But there was still no shortage of eyes to watch her. Tens of thousands in the stands, stamping their feet and waiting for the main event to begin.

'Citizens of Itreya!' The editorii's words echoed across the blood-stained stone. 'We present to you, our final execution bout!'

The crowd's reaction was tepid, some applause, no shortage of jeers from those who simply wished the *magni* to get under way. After five turns of ceaseless butchery, the thought of a few more reprobates sent to slaughter seemed positively pedestrian.

'These are no common criminals!' the editorii insisted. 'These are the basest cowards, the vilest wretches, slaves who betrayed their masters!'

The crowd perked up at that, resounding boos echoing around the arena.

'We give thanks to Sanguila Leona of the Remus Collegium, for providing the cattle for this righteous slaughter! Citizens, we present to you . . . the condemned!'

A portcullis opened in the northern end of the arena, and Mia's heart sank to see seven figures stagger out into the sunslight to the crowd's jeers. Sidonius and Wavewaker. Bladesinger and Bryn. Felix and Albanus and Butcher. They'd not been treated kindly in their captivity – all looked weak and starved. They were armed with rusted blades and dressed in piecemeal armour. Just a few scraps of leather on their chests and shins that would avail them not at all against someone even half skilled with a blade.

They were meant to die here, after all.

The guard beside Mia handed her a razor-sharp gladius and a long, wicked dagger, polished to a blinding sheen. Mia looked into the guard's eyes, blue as the sunburned sky.

'No fear,' Ash whispered. 'Strike true.'

Mia nodded, turned her gaze back to the sand. Sickness in her stomach. Horror at the thought of what was to come. Certainty that it was the only way, that everything she'd sacrificed would soon be worthwhile, that all the death, all the blood, all the pain would be justified once Scaeva and Duomo were in the ground.

This was the end of a tyranny. And the ends justified the means, didn't they?

As long as the end isn't mine?

'And now,' the editorii cried. 'Our executioner! Champion of the Remus Collegium, victor of Whitekeep, the Saviour of Stormwatch, citizens of Godsgrave, we present to you . . . the Crow!'

The crowd rose to their feet, curiosity finally alight. All had heard the tales of the girl who slew the retchwyrm, who saved the citizens of Stormwatch from certain doom, who'd bested a warrior of the Silken Dominion.

The portcullis rose and Mia marched out into the merciless heat, her shadow shrivelling as both Mister Kindly and Eclipse hissed in their misery. The crowd roared at the sight of her, blood-red feathers and armour black as truedark, her beautiful, pitiless face wrought in polished steel. On cue, the sands around her spat forth rippling flame, the crowd bellowing in approval. She followed the pillars of fire, out into the centre of the arena, awestruck by the scale of it all.

The pale sands stained red with blood. The gravebone walls rising into the blinding sky. The barrier separating the crowd from the arena floor loomed over twenty feet high, hung with banners of the noble houses, the collegia, the trinity of Aa. In the premium seats at the barrier's lip, Mia could see a collection of ministers and holy men arrayed in their bloody red robes and tall, pompous hats, her heart thrilling as she spied the grand cardinal among them. Duomo sat at the heart of his flock, solid as a brick shithouse, looking as ever like a thug who'd beaten a holy man to death and stolen his kit. His robe was the colour of heart's blood, his smile like a knife in her chest.

Beside the church, she could see the ringside marrowborn and the sanguilas' boxes. Mia spied Leonides and his hulking executus, Titus. She could see Magistrae in a dazzling scarlet gown. But of Leona, she saw no sign. She turned her eyes upwards to the stands, to the rippling, roaring, swelling ocean of people.

'Crow!' they roared. 'CROW!'

She looked to the consul's box, set with fluted pillars and shaded from the suns. The Senate of Godsgrave were seated about it, old men with twinkling eyes, white togas trimmed with purple. A small army of Luminatii surrounded it, sunsteel swords blazing in their hands. She could see a great chair, trimmed in gold, dangerously close to what might be called a throne. But the chair stood empty.

No Scaeva.

Trumpets sounded, dragging Mia's attention back to the sand. Sidonius and the others were stalking towards her, rusty swords in hand. These matches weren't supposed to be even, but the former Falcons of Remus were still gladiatii. And though they were beaten, bruised, starving, they were seven, and she was one. A rusted blade could still cut to the bone if wielded with enough skill, and a poisoned tongue could cut deeper still.

'So,' Wavewaker said, stopping twenty feet away. 'They send you to swing the axe, Mi Dona? Fitting, I suppose.'

'Almighty Aa,' Sidonius breathed. 'Where is your heart, Mia?'

'They buried it with my father, Sidonius,' she replied.

'You treacherous fucking cunt,' Bladesinger spat.

Mia looked the seven over, the faces of folk who'd once called her friend. Mouth as dry as dust. Skin drenched with sweat.

Soon, all of this will be worth it.

'I'd tell you exactly why I consider that word a compliment and not an insult,' she said. 'But I'm not sure we've time for a monologue, 'Singer.'

She drew her gladius, her razored dagger, saluted the consul's box.

'Now let's get this over with.'

Trumpets blared, the crowd roared, and Dona Leona made her way to her seat in the sanguila's box. Her magistrae greeted her with a smile, lifting a parasol over her mistress's head to shield her from the Light Father's burning eyes.

She looked about the seats around her, saw Tacitus, Trajan, Phillipi, the other usual suspects. Surrounded by their executi and staffers, decked in the bright colours of their collegia, their sigils emblazoned on banners at their backs. And in the box directly to her left, beneath a roaring golden lion, dressed in an extravagant frock coat and popping a grape between his teeth . . .

'Father,' she nodded.

'Dearest daughter.' Leonides smiled, raising his voice over the thrum of the crowd. 'My heart gladdens to see you.'

'And you,' she nodded. 'My first payment arrived, I trust?'

'Aye,' Leonides called. 'It was received with gratitude and, I confess, no small degree of surprise.'

'You'll find I'm full of surprises, Father,' she called back. 'Your Exile could testify to that, I'm sure, had my Crow not separated her head from her body.'

The sanguila around them smiled and murmured, updating the score in their mental ledgers. But Leonides only scoffed, popped another grape into his mouth.

'We didn't think we'd be graced with your presence for the execution.'

'I'm sorry to disappoint you.'

'I'm used to it by now, my dear,' he sighed. 'But I was just saying to Phillipi here, I'm not certain if shame wouldn't keep me from showing my face, if the best portion of *my* collegium were to be executed for rebellion.'

'Have you still shame, Father?' Leona asked. 'I thought it buried with the wife you beat to death.'

The mood around them dropped, sanguila exchanging uncomfortable glances. Leonides's face darkened, and Magistrae put a restraining hand on Leona's arm.

'You go too far, Domina,' she whispered. 'Is it wise to insult him so?'

Leona looked to Anthea, the slow frown that had been planted in the Crow's cell returning to her brow. But a peal of trumpets dragged her eyes to the sand, and she found herself squinting at the preliminaries through the awful glare. The Crow and her traitorous gladiatii were exchanging poisoned words, but she could only hear scraps.

She knew it was a risk, fielding her champion to mop up some traitorous dregs. But she simply needed the coin too badly to allow another sanguila to wield the axe. Crow was one of the finest she'd seen on the sand, and the traitors had been beaten and starved to the point of exhaustion. With Aa's grace, the Crow would still stand with

Furian in the *magni*, still bring the glory and coin Leona so desperately needed.

Craved.

Trumpets blared again, the match began, the Crow moving swift as her namesake. She had to even the numbers quickly, weed out the weakest of the Falcons before sheer numbers overtook her. Thus, the girl went straight for Felix, skipping under his broad, scything blow and slipping inside his guard. The man was clearly the worse for his captivity, slow to react, and with the speed that had made her the collegium champion, the Crow plunged her dagger into his leather breastplate and the heart beyond.

The crowd roared, Felix clutched his skewered chest and toppled to the sand, the blood spraying bright and red. The Crow moved in a blur, kicking a toeful of sand up into Wavewaker's face and charging at Bryn. The Vaanian girl might have been a daemon with a bow and arrow, but with a sword, she was less the prodigy. The Crow smashed aside her strike with her heavy gladius, opened a small cut on her thigh. As Bryn cried out, staggering, the Crow spun behind her and plunged her blade under the Vaanian girl's spaulder and up into her back.

Blood. Gushing from the wound. Glinting on the Crow's steel. Reflected in the crowd's eyes. They roared as the Vaanian toppled forward in a pool of scarlet, Wavewaker bellowing and running at the Crow like a madman. He swung his rusty blade in a terrifying overarm strike, the steel whistling as it came. But the weeks of starvation in the *Gloryhound*'s hold had weakened his legs, left him slightly off-balance and late to recover, and a swift strike sent him to his knees, hands to his chest, blood welling between his fingers.

'*No!*'

Bladesinger charged, the crowd thrilling as her strike opened up a shallow cut on the Crow's arm. Sidonius struck from the side, Butcher and Albanus from behind, Crow rolling aside and rising again with shocking speed. Her dagger flashed, Butcher cried out, fell back in a spray of red, Bladesinger falling on the Crow in a frenzy. The girl rolled back across the sand, flinging a handful of dirt into the woman's eyes. Flipping to her feet, she met Sidonius's blade on her own, her legs almost buckling under the bigger man's strength. But as every man in the stands winced in sympathy, the Crow drove her knee up into Sidonius's bollocks, dropping him to the sand with a high-pitched wail. Her counterstrike whistled past Albanus's guard, her dagger buried to the hilt under his armpit, the blood a scarlet waterfall.

Blinking the grit from her eyes, Bladesinger struck again, the Crow bending backwards as the blow skimmed past her chin. The woman's long saltlocks seethed as she followed through, knocking the Crow's gladius flying. Armed only with her knife now, the Crow struck back, punching the woman in the face with her free hand, ducking beneath another strike and snatching up one of Bladesinger's long locks. Dragging the woman off-balance, she pulled Bladesinger backwards and onto her blade. The audience howled in approval, Bladesinger stumbled to her knees, blood spilling from her ruptured breastplate and down her belly, collapsing face-first on the sand.

Only Sidonius remained. The man was bent double, clutching his jewels. The Crow moved towards him, merciless, the bigger man trying to fend her off. He was screaming at her, but the pair were so far away, Leona only caught a handful of words.

'. . . traitor . . .'

'. . . father . . .'

'. . . *no* . . .'

And the Crow?

She said nothing at all.

Instead, she feinted sideways and slashed at his wrist, his sword spinning to the sand. She kicked out at his legs, sending him onto his knees. And as the crowd roared, she spun around to his back, long hair streaming behind her, plunging her dagger past the collar of his breastplate and down into his spine. Sidonius's face twisted in agony, a gout of glittering scarlet spraying from the wound. He toppled forward, red spilling across the sand, the mob bellowing in delight.

Leona saw his lips move.

A whispered prayer, perhaps?

A curse for the girl who'd slain him?

And then, his eyes closed for the final time.

Leona sat still, peering at the Crow. The bloodstained blade in her hand.

That slow frown deepening on her brow.

The sanguila about her gave polite applause. Tacitus glanced at her and offered an approving nod at her champion's form. She looked to her father, but couldn't catch his eye. Instead, Leonides was staring at that blood-soaked slip of a girl out there on the sand. The girl who'd bested his Exile. The girl who'd just murdered seven gladiatii and barely got a scratch. His scowl was black. His eyes, narrowed.

He turned to his executus, Titus. Whispering in the big man's ear.

Leona's frown only deepened.

'Citizens of Itreya!' the editorii called. 'Your victor!'

The Crow retrieved her fallen gladius, pointed the bloody blade to the empty consul's chair, then held it to the sky. She was wrapped in black steel. Falcon wings at her shoulders, a cloak of red feathers at her back. As she walked a circuit of the arena, the corpses of the murdered gladiatii were dragged off the sands. The face of a goddess covered her own, only her eyes visible through the helm's façade.

No one could tell if she wept.

CHAPTER 34

MAGNI

Not long now.

Mia had been ushered off the sand after the execution bout, taken straight to a large staging cell, still drenched in blood. Her wound was dressed, she was given a ration of water, then told to wait. Though her mouth was bone dry, instead of drinking, she wasted her water trying to wash the gore from her shaking hands.

By the end of the cup, her fingers were still sticky.

She watched a cadre of Ironpriests scurry past, guards delivering gladiatii to the staging cell a few at a time. She recognized a few from Governor Messala's palazzo: Ragnar of Vaan, Champion of the Tacitus Collegium; Worldeater, Champion of the Swords of Phillipi. But soon there were dozens, then hundreds of others, standing about the chamber, clad in leather and steel.

The temperature was stifling, the walls dripping with sweat. Attendants moved about with buckets and ladles of water, the fighters drinking greedily, but Mia only asked for more water for her hands. Scrubbing away at the stains of the execution, refusing to look at her reflection in the red puddling beneath her.

She could hear mekwerk groaning under her feet; some colossal engine ever hungry for blood. Trying not to think of Bladesinger and Bryn, Wavewaker and the others. They'd chosen their fates. Written them in red. She couldn't afford to spare a thought for them. Their trials were over now, where Mia's greatest lay before her. She could still hear Sidonius's parting words as he lay facedown in the sand.

Eyes fixed on hers.

So quiet, none but she could hear.

'*Good luck, Mia,*' he'd whispered.

Her hands were still sticky.

'*. . . we are with you . . .*'

'*. . . WE WILL ALWAYS BE WITH YOU . . .*'

'You fought well.'

She didn't look up. Didn't need to know who it was who stood before her. The sickness in her belly told her that. The lust and the hunger, the ache of longing. Her shadow moved, inching ever closer to his, like iron to the lodestone. Her lips twisted in a bitter smile as she replied.

'I fought against seven starving prisoners who could barely swing their swords.'

'Such, the price of defiance in Itreya,' the Unfallen replied.

'So they tell me.'

'I was not sure . . . how I would feel watching you. They were my brothers and sisters too. When they fell beneath your blades . . .' Furian sighed. 'I could scarce believe it. I think I expected some ruse. Some ploy or play or last-minute reprieve.'

'Play?'

Mia shook her head, bewildered.

'Why is everyone still acting like this is a fucking game?'

'Gladiatii!' a guard cried. 'Attend!'

The eyes of the assembled warriors turned to the iron portcullis. Mia saw three editorii, silhouetted against the glare outside. The eldest of the trio stepped forward, peering among the gladiatii. His long dark beard was plaited, his eyes mismatched, one brown, one green. A banded python was draped around his neck.

'Gladiatii of the collegia of Itreya,' he said. 'Each of you and your masters have earned, through right of trial and combat, your place upon the sands of the *Venatus Magni*. The greatest spectacle in the Itreyan calendar is about to unfold, and you shall fight and die for the glory of the Republic before an adoring crowd. Those who fall shall still stand as legends. And the one among you who remains at *magni*'s end shall be granted freedom by the Hand of God himself.

'This *magni* is a battle grand; every warrior will begin the match upon the sands. Each will be given a coloured armband, to designate initial loyalties. Gladiatii from the same collegia will be grouped together, though you are under *no* obligation to adhere to these allegiances throughout the match. Never forget; all must fall so one may stand.'

The man let his words hang in the air a moment, iron-hard and cold.

'Once this portcullis opens,' he continued, 'proceed to your designated starting position, and await instruction from the grand editorii. May Aa bless and keep you, and Tsana guide your hands.'

Mia sheathed her blades, still trying to rub the red off her fingers. As the guards roamed among them, handing out strips of cloth in red, blue, gold, and white, she could feel it. The fear. Welling in the hearts and minds of the warriors around her, leaking through the stone and hanging thick in the air. Every one of them was staring into the eyes of death, and all knew only one would survive. Some stalked up and down, pounding their chests, muttering to themselves. Some stood mute, battling their fear in silence. Others looked to comrades for some moment of solace, knowing all loyalties would fail before the final trumpet sounded.

Not long now.

A guard muscled through the mob, tied a strip of fabric around Furian's arm to show his allegiance. Demanding that Mia stand, he bound another strip around her bicep. Both were as red as the stains she'd failed to wash away.

Trumpets sounded, the floor rumbling beneath their feet. The call of the editorii echoed across the arena, the crowd roaring in answer.

'Citizens of Itreya! Honoured administratii! Senators and marrowborn! Welcome to the *Venatus Magni* of Godsgrave! From the finest collegia in the Republic, we present to you the mightiest warriors beneath the three suns! Here to do battle before your wondering eyes, to bathe themselves in blood and glory to honour the Everseeing, almighty Aa. We present, the Drakes of Trajan!'

The iron portcullis ratcheted open, and the first group of gladiatii strode out onto the sand, escorted by a cadre of Itreyan legionaries. There were perhaps two hundred and fifty warriors assembled in staging cells by now – far too many to call out individually. Stables were being marched out en masse: the Wolves of Tacitus; the Swords of Phillipi; the Lions of Leonides, one after another striding forth to the welcome of the crowd. As each collegium took their places in the arena, punters in the stands recognized favourites and honoured champions, the volume steadily rising.

'The Falcons of Remus!' came the announcer's cry.

'So it begins,' Furian whispered.

'And so it ends,' Mia replied.

She walked out into the blinding light, the Unfallen beside her. The crowd cheered, some for the Saviour of Stormwatch ('*Crow! Crow!*

Crow!'), others for the Champion of Talia ('*Unfaaaaaaaallen!*'). As the pair took their places among the other red armbands, the editorii's voice rang in the air.

'Citizens of Itreya, please be upstanding!'

A bright peal of trumpets sounded as the crowd rose to their feet, the fanfare thrilling along Mia's skin.

'Seven years have passed since the traitorous Kingmakers sought to bring our glorious Republic to its knees! Seven years of a glorious peace, seven years of reason and prosperity, seven years of justice and light!'

Mia's heart beat quicker, her mouth suddenly dry. She knew what was coming, *who* was coming. Seven years since he'd destroyed her world, standing over her father's scaffold like a vulture on a cairn. Seven years of bloodstained promises, of murder and steel, of wondering and praying. Furian looked to her, his shadow rippling as hers ebbed and flowed, reaching out with black tendrils towards the Senate, towards the Luminatii, towards . . .

'Your saviour! Your consul! Julius Scaeva!'

It was like a punch to her stomach. The sight of him. After all this time, she thought perhaps it might have dulled. But the pain was a knife in her chest, making her stagger, her shadow ripple and seethe despite the three suns burning above.

He was tall, painfully handsome, his dark hair now shot through with the faintest streaks of grey. He wore a long toga of rich purple, a golden laurel at his brow. When he smiled, it seemed the suns shone brighter, the crowd roaring in rapture. Beside him stood a beautiful woman, dark of hair and green of eye, dripping in fine silk and golden jewellery. In her arms, she held a boy, six or seven years old. He had his mother's dark hair, his father's bottomless black eyes. He wore the emblem of the Luminatii Legion embroidered on his chest, though no trinity around his neck.

Scaeva put one arm around his bride, three fingers outstretched in the sign of Aa. The crowd returned the gesture, a hundred thousand people raising their hands and calling his name. Mia felt her jaw clench so tight her teeth ached. Holding her breath because it was simply too painful to breathe. To see him smiling beside his familia when he'd so casually put hers in the ground . . .

Surrounded by that sea of Luminatii, iron and sunsteel, Scaeva stepped forward to a pulpit in the consul's box.

'My people!' he called, his words reverberating among the human sea. 'My countrymen! My friends! On this most holy feast, we gather beneath the eyes of the Everseeing in this, the greatest Republic the world has ever known!'

The consul paused for a burst of giddy applause.

'My friends, these are troubling times. When I announced my intent to stand for a fourth term as consul, I was plagued with doubt. But continued attacks against our magistrates, our administratii, even the *children* of our noble senators overseas, have convinced me the threat to our glorious Republic is not yet ended. And I will not abandon Itreya, or *you*, in such an hour of need.'

Scaeva called louder as the crowd erupted.

'We must stand together! And with your support, we *shall* stand together! From myself, my beloved wife Liviana, my son Lucius . . .' – Scaeva was forced to pause as the cheers overwhelmed his voice – '. . . from my familia to yours, friends, we thank you for your vigilance, your courage, but most of all, your faith! In God, and us!'

Mia's eyes were locked on Scaeva, boiling with hatred. Her fingers slipping unconsciously to the gravebone dagger hidden beneath the iron encircling her wrist. The gravebone dagger Alinne Corvere had once pressed to Scaeva's throat, the turn he took Mia's world away.

Patience.

Mia's fingers slipped away from the dagger. She could taste blood in her mouth.

Patience.

Scaeva beamed in the crowd's adoration, playing the part of the humble one, the grateful one. Reaching out to his wife, the consul placed his son Lucius on his shoulders, held out his three fingers again in blessing. Mia watched the little boy lean down, whisper in his father's ear.

'My son says ever I speak too long,' he smiled, laughter rippling among the crowd. 'He reminds me we are here at purpose. So, shall we begin?'

The crowd roared as one.

'My friends, I asked, *shall we begin?*'

A single, deafening cheer, rising all the way to the sky.

'I will now hand over to our beloved grand cardinal, and my dear friend, Francesco Duomo, to lead us in prayer.'

All eyes turned to the ministry of Aa in their ringside seats. Grand Cardinal Duomo stood at another pulpit, dark eyes fixed on Scaeva, glittering with veiled malice as he bowed low. He spoke into a mekwerk horn, his voice ringing across the arena, thick as toffee, sweet and dark.

'My thanks, glorious Consul,' he said, bowing deep. 'May Aa ever keep you in the Light. May your *reign* be long and fruitful.'

Scaeva's smile turned sharper as he returned the bow.

'Beloved citizens, please bow your heads,' Duomo said.

The entire arena fell still, silence ringing in the air and on the wind.

'Almighty Aa, Father of Light, creator of all, on this your most holy feast, we thank you for your love, your vigilance, and your many blessings upon us. Remain ever watchful of our hearts, and bless those who here die for the glory of our Republic.

'In your name, this we pray.'

The crowd replied as one.

'*In your name, this we pray.*'

Duomo spread his arms, a smile brightening his eyes.

'Let the *magni* begin!'

The crowd roared, stamping and hollering as Duomo returned to his flock of cardinals and bishops, smug as a groom after his wedding night. Mia's gaze returned to Scaeva, watching as he took his seat, the consul's dark eyes fixed on Duomo. The pair watched each other like a pair of vipers over the corpse of a single mouse. But Scaeva's son whispered something in his ear, and the consul suddenly laughed, bright and loud. His bride leaned over, kissed him on the cheek. Scaeva broke his gaze from Duomo's, instead beaming at his familia. Mia felt her legs trembling.

They didn't deserve to be so happy. For Scaeva to have a wife and child when he'd left her with nothing. For Duomo to play at piety and speak of love when he'd destroyed her entire world. She looked to the gladiatii around her, every one of them an obstacle, every sword a hindrance, every throat a stepping stone on the way to those bastards' hearts.

'I can feel it . . .' Furian breathed. 'Your hatred . . .'

Mia blinked, looked to the man beside her. Furian was looking at her with a mix of horror, fear, pity. Glancing down to the shadow at her feet.

'Almighty Aa . . . what did they do to you?'

'Citizens of Itreya!' came the cry. 'Behold, your battleground!'

The crowd stilled as a great, trembling groan ran the length of the entire arena. The four groups of gladiatii, red, white, gold, and blue, were positioned at opposite points around the arena's oblong, clustered together in mobs of sixty or so. As Mia watched, the ground before her split apart, sand cascading down into the arena's mekwerk belly. The crowd were on their feet, straining for a better look as four great shapes loomed up from beneath the floor. Fifty feet long, heavy ironwood hulls, fantastical beasts carved at their prows, their flanks studded with dozens of gleaming oars.

'Those are war galleys,' one bewildered gladiatii murmured.

'But . . .' another said. 'But . . .'

'Gladiatii, attend!' the centurion barked, pointing at the rope ladders dangling from their ship's flank. 'All of you, climb! Now! Move!'

Mia did as she was told immediately, and Furian followed without question, scrambling up the ladders to the deck above. Others climbed along behind, but yet more gladiatii simply stared at the centurion in undisguised bafflement.

'Ships?' one asked. 'Almighty Aa, we're standing on fucking sand!'

The ground groaned again, trumpets blaring.

'I'd do as commanded, were I you,' the centurion said.

The man turned, and with the rest of his cadre, beat feet back across the sand. Some gladiatii began climbing onto the galleys, others looking about in bewilderment. Mia heard another mekwerk moan, the groan of metal under pressure. Heavy iron shutters clanked down over the cells skirting the arena's edge, a series of circular grates rose from beneath the sand. And as the crowd watched in wonder, those grates shivered and, with a last hollow metal cough, began spewing water high into the air.

The mob sighed, cheered, water vapour caught on the swirling breeze and bringing a merciful cool to the arena's oppressive heat. But within moments, those sighs became delighted roars as the water began gushing forth harder, higher, flooding over the arena floor and swirling about the ships. Soon it was six inches deep. Eight. A foot, rising up the gladiatii's shins in an inexorable flood.

'This is salt water,' one said.

A Lion of Leonides leaned over the railing, shouting at the top of his voice.

'It's a naval battle, you stupid bastards, climb, climb!'

The gladiatii obeyed now, dashing to the ladders and scrambling up the sides. Mia stood at the prow, watching the water rushing and crashing around their keel. Ten feet deep and still rising, their ship beginning to rock in its wooden scaffold as it was buoyed up on the flood. Thanks to Ashlinn's reconnaissance, Mia had some inkling of what was in store for her on the sands, but to stand among it all . . .

The girl shook her head, simply awed by the power on display. The ingenuity. The sheer fucking hubris. Instead of sending its citizens to the ocean, the great Republic of Itreya had brought the ocean to its citizens.

'Citizens of Itreya!' cried the grand editorii. 'The Senate and Iron Collegium of our glorious Republic are proud to present to you, the Battle of Seawall!'*

The water was fifteen feet deep now, growing deeper. A great plinth rose in the centre of the arena, a stone keep atop it – presumably representing the mighty fortifications at Seawall itself. Mia could see mekwerk catapults atop the crenellated walls, loaded with burning pitch. And looking down into swirling eddies below, Mia saw dozens of dark shapes cruising around their hull.

Furian peered over the railing, squinting at the serpentine shadows. 'Are those . . . ?'

The crowd roared as one of the shapes breached the surface, all blunt snout and dead black eyes and row upon row of razored teeth. Almost fifteen feet long, it cut the water with its massive forked tail before disappearing below the surface.

'Stormdrakes,' the Unfallen breathed.

Mia shook her head. Catapults ahead. Enemy ships around. Monsters below.

And as she looked to the sigils on breastplates and shields on the gladiatii around them, she realized she and Furian were surrounded by Lions of Leonides. At least a dozen, all as big as houses and hard as the iron at her chest.

'Well,' Mia murmured. 'Isn't this cosy.'

'Foes on all sides,' Furian whispered.

'At least my life is consistent.'

'If it comes down to you and I . . .'

'I know.'

'But until then?' He glanced to the blades in her hands, still stained

---

*An infamous clash in the earliest years of the Republic, and probably the largest sea battle ever fought under the three suns. The Battle of Seawall involved four massive fleets; the Itreyan Navy under command of the Great Unifier, Francisco I, and a tithed fleet from the vassal state of Vaan clashed with Dweymeri clan ships under command of Bara Sundancer of the Threedrake clan, and an armada of pirate lords who had sworn to resist Itreyan dominance of the seas.

As you might have guessed, resistance lasted about as long as a bottle of top-shelf goldwine in a brothel full of pissheads.

with the blood of those who'd called her friend. 'You had duty enough to defend the collegium, put those who betrayed it in the ground. I am hoping perhaps I was wrong about you. That you have learned something of honour, and the way of the gladiatii. Need I worry about your blade at my back?'

Mia looked at him sidelong, the water about them rising ever higher.

'There's only one way this ends,' she said. 'And you and I both know it. But I'll come at you frontways. I can promise you that, at least.'

The Unfallen nodded, tightened his grip on his blade.

'So be it. *Sanguii e Gloria.*'

Mia shook her head. 'You can keep the glory, Furian.'

She turned her eyes to the consul's chair.

'I'm just here for the blood.'

Down in the arena's belly, Mercurio finished loading the wheel-barrow, dragging the heavy bucket into the tray with a wince. Truth was, he was too old for this kind of rot. His bloody arthritis was playing up again, and walking about down here dressed in rags for the past two turns wasn't helping his shingles any, either.

'Next time, *I* get to dress up in the guard's kit,' he growled.

Ashlinn rolled her eyes.

'Who the 'byss is going to believe you're a guard, you grumpy old prick?'

The girl was lurking by the antechamber door, eyes on the hallway outside. She was still dressed in her stolen armour, black leather breastplate and skirt, a plumed helm to cover her face. Mercurio could hear the audience roaring above his head, belly filling with ice and butterflies as he realized the *magni* was under way.

Though she kept her face like stone, Järnheim's daughter seemed to share his concern. She looked to the arena above their heads, sighing.

'I should be up there,' she whispered.

'This is important to her,' Mercurio replied.

'Be that as it may, this whole plan is fucking lunacy.'

Mercurio sighed. 'I'm not sure if you've noticed yet, girl, but Mia Corvere and lunacy go together like cigarillos and smoke.'

Ashlinn smiled. 'O, aye, I noticed.'

The bishop of Godsgrave joined her by the doorway, peered out into the corridor.

'I realize this isn't the time or place,' he muttered. 'But just know, if you hurt her, there's no place under the suns you can hide that I won't find you.'

Ash raised an eyebrow, looked the old man up and down.

'You know, you really are very sweet for a grumpy old prick.'

'Fuck off,' Mercurio growled.

'Sounds like a plan to me. Shall we?'

'Aye. But as you're so fond of noting, I'm a senior citizen.'

'So?'

'So you push the bloody wheelbarrow.'

Applause echoing on the stone about them, Ashlinn pushing a barrow before them, the pair stole off into the dark.

The crowd thundered as the trumpets rang, every man, woman, and child on their feet. After five turns of slaughter, five turns of blazing sunlight, five turns of blinding spectacle, the *Venatus Magni* was under way.

Leona watched as the catapults in the Seawall keep loosed their barrels of flaming pitch. The first rounds were simply warning shots, tumbling through the air before plunging into the water with a vicious hiss. But the threat of immolation was enough to send the gladiatii scrambling, chaos breaking out on the decks as brief struggles for command got under way.

Ragnar of Vaan quickly took leadership of the Gold ship, the crowd thrilling as he ended a brief mutiny from another Wolf of Tacitus by putting his sword through the man's throat and kicking him over the side. The water beneath the railing turned to foaming red as at least four stormdrakes tore the man to screaming pieces. Roaring to the oarsmen, Ragnar took the helm and steered his ship for the keep.

Worldeater of the Phillipi took command of the Blue ship soon after, the crew also bending their oars for the fortifications. The deck of the White ship had broken into complete chaos, with the Drakes of Trajan fighting for dominance with gladiatii from three other collegia. The crowd roared as the vessel became a slaughterhouse, blood slicked over the boards.

Looking to the Reds, Leona saw their galley was under way, the Bloodhawks of Artimedes at the helm. She could see the Crow and Furian at the bow, blades drawn, their ship headed for the fortifications. But as she watched, she saw more than a dozen Lions of Leonides forming up at their backs. Not content to wait until they'd reached the keep, Leonides's gladiatii looked set to end Leona's hopes of victory here and now.

The dona looked to her father, found the man staring back at her, smiling.

'Just business,' he whispered.

They come,' Furian murmured.

'I know,' Mia replied.

'Don't die before I can kill you.'

'This is not where I die.'

The Lions charged without ceremony, and Mia and Furian turned to meet them, steel crashing against steel. The crowd thrilled at the sudden and bloody betrayal, Mia and Furian forced across the deck until their backs were to the figurehead at the bow.

Though outnumbered, they'd chosen their battleground well – the prow was narrow, bottlenecking the Lions and making their numbers count for less. Mia reached out to the shadows at a charging Lion's feet, but simply couldn't hold them with all three suns blazing overhead. She was forced to rely on her speed instead, the training she'd endured under Mercurio, Solis, and then Arkades, the turns, weeks, months she'd spent with some kind of blade in her hands.

That, and the measure of Swoon that Ashlinn had mixed in with the gladiatii's water supply, of course.

It hadn't been a huge dose; not enough to send them dreaming. But she knew anyone who'd swallowed a ladleful would be feeling it by now, and it seemed the Lions charging them had been thirsty before the match. Mia feinted left, the Lion stumbled, cursed as Mia opened up a deep gouge on his thigh with her gladius. He lunged, but she slipped sideways, her blows glancing off his shield, his blade knocked from clumsy fingers and sent clattering to the deck.

Furian moved like water, long black hair flowing behind him as he battered the charging Lions backwards with his broad shield. He met a thrust with his own blade, his counter sending the sword spinning from its owner's grip and off into the water. The catapults loosed another round, flame streaming through the air and striking their ship's flank. Fire bloomed, a thunderous boom drowning out the crowd. Men fell screaming to the deck, wailing into the water, drakes' teeth flashing and gnashing in the foaming red. Black smoke drifted among the dancing sparks, the stench of burning oil and meat. And Mia raised her sword and struck again at her foe.

The man stumbled, just a touch drunk from the Swoon, but it was enough to give her the edge. A whistling slash from Mia's blade opened up his windpipe, just as Furian ended his foe with a short, deadly thrust. Despite the carnage, despite the fear, she felt elated, her blood thrilling, her skin prickling. And as she glanced down to the deck, Mia realized her shadow was moving of its own accord, creeping like molasses across the blood-slick wood towards Furian's. And more, his own was reaching out to hers.

Like lovers parted.

Like a puzzle, searching for missing pieces of themselves.

Mia shook her head. Breathless. Hungry. The deck around them had erupted into chaos, gladiatii turning on each other as the Lions attacked Mia and Furian and their brief allegiance collapsed. Steel crashed against steel, agonized cries splitting the air, another barrel of burning pitch exploding overhead and raining liquid fire down onto the deck. The Lions were beset from behind, Furian and Mia fighting for their lives up against the bow. She realized the Gold ship had reached the fort, the gladiatii seizing control of the mekwerk catapults. The White galley was almost entirely ablaze, the Blue ship almost as bad, timber shrieking and men screaming as it crashed headlong into the keep. The Blues charged with a bloody cry, scrambling up the rope ladders and onto the battlements, the Golds meeting them head-on.

Another fire barrel hit the Red galley, this time onto the aft deck, immolating the gladiatii at the helm. The oarsmen rowed hard, desperate to reach the fort and escape their burning coffin. But with none to steer and the helm ablaze, the ship sailed wide, oars crushed to kindling against the plinth. The vessel shook, Furian stumbling to his knees, Mia almost following.

'Come on!' Mia cried, sheathing her blades and taking a running leap over the rails. Hands outstretched, she clutched a rope ladder hanging from the battlements, dangling precariously over the water. Furian followed, leaping onto a ladder beside her, oarsmen and other gladiatii following swift suit. A Lion made a desperate leap, seizing the ladder below Furian, only to have the Unfallen's boot send him down into the churning waters with a scream. Smoke burning her eyes, Mia scrambled up the rope, onto the keep's walls, the stink of burning oil and sundered guts almost overpowering.

The crowd was chanting, cheering, awestruck at the slaughter and spectacle. Mia blinked the sweat from her eyes, felt Furian leap over the battlements behind without turning to look at him. Just as when they fought in his room, Mia felt the pull in her own shadow, the hunger inside her swelling like a living thing.

And looking to her feet, she saw their shadows were completely entwined.

'What the 'byss is happening?' she gasped.

L eonides spat a black curse, on his feet and roaring. It was difficult to tell through the pall of smoke, but it seemed the great sanguila had very few warriors left in the battle at all. Leona watched as the Red and White galleys began sinking, oarsmen leaping over the side to take their chances with the drakes rather than burn to death. The water was a churning soup of dorsal fins and forked tails and wails, the crowd baying as the tiny ocean turned red.

Leona watched the Crow through narrowed eyes. A wrongness chewing at her insides. There was something about the girl . . . something amiss that she couldn't quite place. Watching her move among the Lions, she'd proved herself every bit the champion Leona had named her. But there was something off about the way she fought. Hacking, slashing, punching, kicking . . .

. . . *but never stabbing* . . .

Leona rose to her feet, squinting through the black haze, watching the Crow fight upon the battlements alongside Furian. The pair were devastating, cutting down all before them and slowly advancing from the fortifications' edge. But her suspicion was right. Even when presented an opening for a thrust with her dagger, the Crow was only using it to block her opponent's strikes. She'd used the smaller blade with bloody abandon in the execution bout, but now the *magni* was under way . . .

'She only strikes with her gladius . . .' she whispered.

Magistrae turned to her mistress. 'Domina?'

Leona felt a chill in her belly. Remembering the turn she presented Crow with her armour, the gladius and dagger of black Liisian steel to match it. Watching the sunslight flash on the silvered blade in the Crow's hand, and knowing with dread certainty . . .

'. . . That is not the dagger I gifted her.'

———————

Ashlinn and Mercurio walked through the arena's belly, down wending corridors and beneath archways of stone, following the trail of sticky scarlet. They passed patrols of soldiers, cleaners, attendants, but almost anyone with eyes was upstairs watching the *magni*. They could hear the sounds of the conflict raging above, hollow booms and the howls of the crowd.

At the end of the hall, they saw a set of broad wooden doors, a pair of distinctly frustrated legionaries standing watch, heads tilted as they listened to the carnage upstairs. The taller one straightened as he saw Mercurio approach, looking the old man up and down before fixing Ashlinn in his stare.

'You hav—'

Ashlinn bent low and sent a small white glass globe bouncing across the stone. The pair had time enough to register the wyrdglass before it popped with a hollow bang, a cloud of pale gas filling the air. Ash and Mercurio waited to see if any came running at the sound, but the volume of the crowd and the conflict above seemed to have successfully drowned out the explosion.

Tying heavy kerchiefs about their faces, the pair entered the room, sealing it behind them, the carved plaque on the doors now clearly visible.

MORTUARY.

Blood on her hands and on her tongue.

Blood on her blades and in her eyes.

Mia fought atop the battlements, the stone slippery with gore. Knots of gladiatii hacked and stabbed at one another, steel ringing on steel, war cries filling the air. Worldeater, Champion of the Phillipi, was drenched head to foot in red, swinging a mighty two-handed mattock and crushing armour and shields like paper. Ragnar of the Tacitus Collegium was still standing, howling like a madman as he bent low and flipped a charging gladiatii over his shoulder, down into the water below.

The carnage was awful, the bodies piled high, perhaps only twenty gladiatii remaining where almost three hundred had begun. Mia had never seen bloodshed like it in her life. Furian fought beside her, painted to the armpits.

Their shadows were fully entwined now, all four of them, Mia, Mister Kindly, Furian, Eclipse, coalescing in the black beneath their feet. She could hear the crowd dimly, watched her blades dancing in the air almost as if they had minds of their own. But more, she could hear Furian, his heartbeat, his breathing, and beneath that, beneath the blood and the smoke and the deafening roar of the slaughter-drunk crowd, she realized she could hear . . .

. . . not his thoughts, but . . .

His hunger. His longing. His thoughts for Leona, edged with sorrow and bitterness. His desire for the victor's laurel, echoing in every beat of his heart. For a moment, she felt it so truly, so much a part of herself, that she was tempted to simply throw down her sword and let him best her. For his own part, Furian seemed to feel her, also, sparing a glance for the consul's box, the grand cardinal among his craven flock, his jaw clenching with hatred.

'Almighty Aa,' he breathed. 'Those bastards . . .'

Her breath was burning, eyes stinging with sweat, pulse drumming beneath her skin. Her blade sang in the air, her arms aching, and somewhere in the distance, ever so faint, beneath the roar of the crowd, the roar of the flames, the roar of those three suns burning the sky blind overhead, she heard it.

The darkness.

Beneath the water.

Beneath her skin.

Beneath the marble crust over this city's bones. Her shadow entwining with Furian's, bleeding into his own like the gore slicked across the stone.

'. . . mia . . .'

'Do you feel it?' she breathed.

Furian buried his blade in another chest, blood slick on his hands. 'I feel *you*,' he gasped.

Twisting and turning, feinting and striking, time crawling.

'I feel *us* . . .'

'. . . MIA, WHAT IS HAPPENING . . . ?'

'I don't know,' she whispered.

She felled another gladiatii, ducking beneath his strike and slicing his hamstring clean through. 'Black Mother help me, I don't know . . .'

Worldeater raised his mattock and charged at Mia, feet pounding on the stone. From behind, she could feel Ragnar and Furian locked together, blade to blade. Even with the Swoon in their veins, the men were champions, veterans of a dozen slaughters, hard as steel. But Mia could still sense Furian, their shadows utterly enmeshed, coiling across the stone, dancing in the blood. It was as if she had two sets of eyes, two hearts, two minds, twice the strength, twice the will, twice the fury. Worldeater swung his mattock at her head and she felt Furian's hand on her own, guiding her counter. Furian struck at Ragnar, and he felt Mia's grip on his blade. Coalescing, unending, no sense of where she ended and he began. There beneath those burning suns, if only for a moment, the puzzle seemed to have found its missing piece.

Her gladius sliced the flesh behind Worldeater's knee, severing tendon to the bone. Furian disarmed Ragnar with a lightning thrust, but the Vaanian crash-tackled the Unfallen to the ground, the pair clawing and punching on the red-slicked stone. As Ragnar's hands closed about Furian's throat, Mia felt her own windpipe constrict. She gasped, choking, felt Worldeater's mattock crash against her ribs. Both she and Furian cried out in pain. Mia lost her grip on her dagger, the blade ringing bright as it skidded across the stone, coming to rest beside Furian and Ragnar.

Ragnar's hands tightened on Furian's throat, Mia gasping for breath. Worldeater dragged the girl to the ground, slammed his fist into her head, knocking her helm loose, her gladius flying. She couldn't breathe, couldn't see, Ragnar's grip on Furian making her choke. Reaching out across the stone, the crowd roaring at the top of their lungs, Furian's fingers scrabbled at the hilt of Mia's fallen knife. Worldeater slammed Mia's head into the ground, again, again, again, sunlight burning in her eyes.

Furian's fingers closed on the hilt of Mia's dagger.

'Furian,' Mia gasped. 'It won't—'

With a desperate cry, the Unfallen drew back the knife and plunged it into the gap between Ragnar's breastplate and spaulders.

The crowd gasped.

Furian cried out in triumph.

And Mia's spring-loaded blade slid right up into the hilt.

'Oi.'

Sidonius felt a light kick to his arm. His belly lurched sideways, but the gladiatii kept his eyes closed, holding his breath.

Another kick from a particularly bony toe.

'I can still see your slavemark, deadman. Good thing the folks who dragged your corpse down here didn't bother to pull off your helmet. Time to go.'

Sidonius opened his eye the tiniest crack, saw an old man in tattered rags leaning over him. He had bright blue eyes, a shock of grey hair, a lit cigarillo on his lips.

'You're . . . Mercurio?' he whispered.

'No, I'm the grand cardinal's mistress. Now get up.'

Sidonius sat up on the mortuary floor, surrounded by hundreds of dead bodies. He could see a slender girl in guard's armour leaning over Wavewaker's 'corpse', tapping him on the shoulder.

'You're Ashlinn,' Sidonius whispered.

'Pleased to meet you,' the girl nodded. 'Now seriously, get the fuck up.'

Bladesinger was standing, dragging off her helmet, still drenched in gore. With a grimace, Sidonius pulled off his own helm, reached behind his neck, pulled the punctured bladder out from under his breastplate. He could feel the chicken's blood down his back, coagulating into a slick, greasy mess.

'Bucket's in the wheelbarrow,' Mercurio said. 'Get washed, get dressed. We need to be gone before the *magni*'s done. And that won't be long.'

The Falcons of Remus collegium took turns, scrubbing off the blood as best they could and changing into the outfits they were given. Armour from the unconscious doormen, rags for the rest of them. Sidonius pulled on a guard's steel helm, leather breastplate, looking to the stone above as the crowd roared in delight.

'How you suppose she's doing up there?' he murmured.

Wavewaker patted him on the shoulder. 'Have faith, brother. She got us this far.'

'With more than a little help from you.' Bryn grinned.

'Aye, but did it have to be chicken's blood?' Butcher grimaced. 'It stinks.'

Wavewaker shrugged. 'That's the way they taught me back in the theatre.'

Mercurio scowled, stubbed out his cigarette.

'I realize the odds of the administratii sending out a search party to look for a pack of dead gladiatii are slim, but if you lot are finished chatting, we have a daring escape to undertake.' The old man gestured towards the door. 'So if you wouldn't fucking mind . . . ?'

'Apologies,' Ashlinn muttered. 'He's always like this.'

Straightening his helm, Sidonius squared his shoulders. His comrades behind him, he marched out into the corridor. The arena's innards were virtually empty, all eyes on the spectacle above. They made their way swiftly through the hallways, Ashlinn out in front, until they came to a small servants' entrance, locked and barred.

Ashlinn opened the door onto a small alleyway. Two guards were slumped outside it, dead or sleeping, Sid couldn't tell. But he also saw a small merchant's wagon, and a pretty blonde girl sitting in the driver's seat. She looked at them and smiled.

'This is Belle,' Mercurio said. 'She'll take you across the aqueduct. A slaver named Teardrinker is waiting for you on the mainland.'

'A slaver?' Bladesinger growled.

'She owes Mia a favour,' Ashlinn said. 'The largest kind of favour there is. She has the papers verifying that you've purchased your freedom. And contacts with the administratii to get your brands removed. Now go.'

'Mia . . .' Sid began.

'*Go.*'

Bryn and the others were already in the wagon. Wavewaker clasped Sidonius's arm, hauled him up into the flatbed. The girl snapped the reins and they were moving, bouncing across the cobbles and off through the Godsgrave streets.

'Fine horses,' Bryn said, nodding at the beasts leading the wagon.

'The black stallion is Onyx,' the girl smiled. 'The white mare is Pearl.'

Sidonius climbed into the driver's seat beside her, trying to look officious in his uniform. But he found his hands were shaking, his knees weak, the ordeal leaving him hollow. After weeks of plotting, playing the part, praying they might somehow pull it off, the adrenaline was souring in his veins, leaving him exhausted and . . .

'Don't be afraid,' the girl said, squeezing his hand. 'All will be well.'

Sidonius looked her up and down. Dark, wide eyes. Barely more than a child.

'. . . How do you know?' he scoffed.

'Because the voices in your head that say otherwise are just Fear talking. Never listen to Fear.'

The girl smiled, turned her eyes back to the open road.

'Fear is a coward.'

Mia gasped as Worldeater cracked her skull back into the stone again, his thumbs pressed into her eyes. And slipping her gravebone dagger out from the bracer at her wrist, she slammed the blade up under the champion's chin, right into his brain.

Worldeater gurgled, toppled aside. Rolling to her feet, she snatched up her gladius and charged across the battlement, lips peeled back in a snarl. Ragnar had his hands about Furian's throat, looking up as the girl ran him down. He raised his arms to ward off her blow, but the Swoon still hummed in his veins and her blade of Liisian steel sheared through his wrists, cleaving his helmet and splitting the flesh and bone beyond. Mia tore the blade free, the champion's body falling back in a spray of red.

Furian kicked free of the corpse, rolled up to his feet. Mia's spring-loaded dagger was still clutched in his hand, dark eyes burning into hers. The crowd was roaring with bloodlust. Of the hundreds of men and women who'd taken to the sand, only two now remained. Though they couldn't hear the words the Falcons spoke over the distance, the howls of their fellows, the blood pounding in their veins, all knew the match would soon be ended. The fact that these two were comrades from the same collegium made no difference. There was only one way this could end.

'*All must fall so one may stand!*' came the cry.

Mia and Furian stared at each other across the carnage, shadows seething at their feet. Where once they'd been entwined, coalescing to a perfect black, now they were coiled, writhing, clawing at each other with fury.

'So,' Furian spat, hurling the false dagger at Mia's feet. 'A liar to the last.'

The crowd was a distant roar. The arena a faded backdrop, pale and translucent. Mia could feel the city of Godsgrave around them, sweltering beneath those awful suns. Feel it like a living thing, feel the rage and hatred nestled in its bones, like the truedark so long ago when she'd failed to kill Scaeva in the Basilica Grande.

Feel it like she felt herself.

'Furian . . .' she began.

'You've learned *nothing* of honour, have you? I thought you claimed you weren't a hero? That if they needed help, they could help themselves?'

'They *did* help themselves, Furian,' Mia replied. 'We helped each other.'

'And why?'

'Because they're my friends. And they didn't deserve to die.'

'But die they will,' he spat. 'Like the traitors they are. When I am named victor, the first thing I will do is tell the editorii of your ploy. And all your lies will be for naught.'

He stooped and picked up a bloody sword from the carnage about them.

'You can't wash your hands clean with more blood, Furian,' Mia said.

'I give myself to the Everseeing.'

'Furian, can't you feel it? Look at our shadows! Listen!'

'I hear nothing,' he spat. 'Save the witch I am about to kill.'

'Don't!'

The Unfallen charged across the stone, bloody sword raised high. The roar of the crowd came crashing back down around her, a deafening tidal wave ringing in her skull. Time crawled, second by second, Furian's mouth open in a roar, his blade raised high.

She didn't want to kill him.

But she didn't want to die.

'. . . *mia . . . ?*'

'All must fall so one may stand!' came the cry.

'. . . *MIA . . . !*'

All must fall so one may stand.

And so she moved, gentlefriends. Moved like wind. Like silver. Like shadows. Slipping beneath the blow scything towards her throat, steel whistling past her skin. The dark beneath them clawed and tore at each other, ink black upon the bloody stone, hate and hunger and something close to sorrow. The shadowcat hissed and the shadowwolf growled and the girl, the Blade, the gladiatii struck, the tip of her sword catching the Unfallen in the neck as he rushed past.

A spray of red. A breathless gasp. She felt pain, hand pressed to her throat as if she'd been dealt the blow herself. No bladders filled with chicken's blood now. No ploy. No play. His blood as real as the sunlight on her skin.

Furian looked to her, eyes wide with surprise. Clutching his throat, he turned to the sanguila's box, looking towards his domina. Mia felt it all. Regret. Sorrow. Bidding Mister Kindly and Eclipse to reach out across the stone, and in his final breath, to take his fear away.

And with a final gasp, the Unfallen fell.

A hammerblow to Mia's spine. A rush of blood in her veins, skin crawling, every nerve ending on fire. She fell to her knees, hair billowing about her as if in some phantom breeze, her shadow scrawled in maddened, jagged lines beneath her, Mister Kindly and Eclipse and a thousand other forms scribbled among the shapes it drew upon the stone. The hunger inside her sated, the longing gone, the emptiness suddenly, violently filled. A severing. An awakening. A communion, painted in red and black. And face upturned to the sky, for a moment, just for a breath, she saw it. Not an endless field of blinding blue, but of bottomless black. Black and whole and perfect.

Filled with tiny stars.

Hanging above her in the heavens, Mia saw a globe of pale light shining. Like a sun almost, but not red or blue or gold or burning with furious heat. The sphere was ghostly white, shedding a pale luminance and casting a long shadow at her feet.

'THE MANY WERE ONE.'

'*Crow! Crow! Crow! Crow!*'

'AND WILL BE AGAIN.'

A scream ripped up and out of her lungs, long and thin and keening. The sky crashed closed, the scorch of the suns bringing burning tears to her eyes. She was on her knees on the bloody stone, the arena ringing, the crowd on their feet, '*Crow! Crow! Crow! Crow!*' Arkemical current dancing on her skin, sweeping her up on their wave of euphoria. Blood on her hands. Blood on her tongue.

Furian dead on the stone before her.

She hung her head. Gasping. Breath burning in her lungs. Full and empty all at once. Triumphant. All the miles, all the years, all the pain, and she'd done it.

She'd won.

But something . . .

. . . something was different.

And looking down, she saw her shadow, now still as a millpond, pooled on the bloodstained stone beneath her.

Dark enough for four.

CHAPTER 35
GONE

Leona cried out with the rest, heart in her throat. Something between elation and agony, watching Furian topple and the Crow fall to her knees over his corpse, triumphant. She'd done it. She'd won. Victory for the Remus Collegium. All Leona's dreams realized. All her sacrifice vindicated.

But the dagger the Crow used during the *magni* was wrong.

Which meant the execution bout . . .

'Mi Dona, a glass?'

Leona blinked, turned to a slave who'd materialized beside her. An old man with a silver tray, goblets, and a bottle of top-shelf goldwine. He was one of a dozen bondsmen now roaming the sanguila boxes, handing the blood masters fresh drinks as they stood and offered Leona grudging applause. The *magni* had been hard fought, but it had been glorious, and it was time for the men who profited most to honour the games and their victor with a traditional and well-earned drink.

The old man's circular brand looked fresh, a touch too dark on his cheek. His blue eyes twinkled like razors, and something about him put Leona distinctly ill at ease. She looked to the goblet he offered, shook her head.

'No,' she murmured. 'My thanks.'

Leona turned her eyes back to the arena's heart, saw the Crow standing amid the carnage. The girl held aloft her bloody gladius, and the audience erupted. Everyone was on their feet – from the ministers of Aa's church to the commonfolk, all the way up to the consul's box. Scaeva himself was standing, his boychild on his shoulders, cheering loud.

Could none of them see?

Were they all blind?

'Mi Dona?' the old man asked again.

'I said no,' Leona snapped. 'I am not thirsty, begone!'

'I'm not suggesting you drink, Dona,' he said, forcing a goblet into her hands.

The dona snarled, ready to berate the old fool for his temerity. But then she caught sight of the vintage on his bottle. A label she recognized from her childhood, the memory burned into her mind's eye. That bottle clutched in her father's hand, splashed blood red as her mother screamed.

'Albari,' she whispered. 'The seventy-four.'

'Fine drop, that one,' the old man replied.

'Be off!' Magistrae snapped. 'Before I have you beaten for your impertinence!'

The old man turned to the magistrae, fixed her in his ice-blue stare. He pushed his laden tray into the woman's arms as she blustered, and, reaching into his tunic, he pulled out an expensive clove cigarillo, propped it on his lips.

'You know,' he growled, 'there's a special place in the abyss reserved for those who murder little girls.'

Leona's heart stilled. She looked to Anthea, then to her father. Never the type to waste a fine vintage, the man was raising his glass of Albari seventy-four with the rest, glittering blue eyes locked on her as he and his colleagues drank deep. Perhaps he thought it chance. Perhaps he simply didn't care. But after he'd drunk deep from his cup, he looked at his daughter and gifted her a dark smile.

Leona stared at the goblet the old man had given her. A thin strip of parchment was nestled in the bottom, six words scribed in black ink.

'*All the thanks I can muster.*'

Below it, she saw a sketch of a crow in flight above two crossed swords.

The sigil of the Familia Corvere.

Leona looked up into the old man's eyes. Her own wide with realization. The old man pulled out a flintbox, lit his cigarillo, and dragged deep.

'Should you want him, you'll find Arkades in Blackbridge,' he said. 'I'd not return to Crow's Nest if you value your pretty neck. They'll take everything from you. Your house. Your collegium. Your wealth. And you'll have to leave your name behind. But you'll still have your life if you scamper away now. That's all she was willing to leave you, I'm afraid.'

The old man scowled once more at Anthea, then turned and shuffled away, up through the sanguila's boxes and down the stairs. Leona

looked again to her father, turning to her magistrae. The perfume of a
funeral pyre in her nostrils. Mia's voice echoing in her head.

Look to those closest to you . . .

'. . . I need to use the privy,' she said. 'I feel ill.'

'But, Domina . . .' Magistrae began. 'Your honours? They will be
presen—'

'. . . I'll only be a moment. Wait here until I return.'

Magistrae frowned, but bowed low. 'Your whisper, my will.'

Leona nodded to her houseguards, gathered up her dress, and began
marching up the stairs. Pausing, she turned back to her magistrae.

'O, and Anthea?' She nodded to the tray in the woman's arms. 'Pour
yourself a drink while I'm gone.'

'Yes, Domina,' the woman frowned. '. . . Thank you, Domina.'

'Not at all,' Leona replied, turning away. 'I believe you've earned it.'

*P*atience.

Mia stood on the central plinth, steady as the stone around her.
The memory of that single, softly glowing orb in the heavens etched in
her mind. That voice, echoing in her skull. Despite the three suns
burning overhead, her grip on the dark felt stronger with Furian dead.
Deeper, *richer* somehow, the shadow at her feet rippling, rolling, bleeding
out across the flagstones towards . . .

Scaeva.

Duomo.

'. . . THEY COME . . .'

'. . . *ever the observant one . . .*'

She could see them, making their way down to the arena's edge. The
crowd about them parting like a sea before the wave of Luminatii
preceding them. Mia heard a mekwerk groan, the drake-infested waters
churning as a large stone archway surfaced from the arena floor. Seawater
pouring from its flanks, it slid into place, forming a broad bridge from
the arena's edge to the central plinth. Scaeva stood on one side, his son
on his shoulders, raising three fingers to bless the adoring crowd.

'. . . *he brings the boy . . .*'

'. . . AND? HE THOUGHT NOTHING OF MURDERING MIA'S FATHER IN FRONT OF
HER . . .'

'. . . *so thirsty for blood, dear mongrel . . .*'

'. . . GIRD YOURSELF, CUR. TIME FOR YOUNG LUCIUS TO LEARN LIFE'S HARSH
REALITIES . . .'

Mia fixed her eyes on Scaeva in his rich purple toga, Duomo behind him in his blood-red cardinal's robes. As she watched, a half-dozen attendants took the cardinal's staff from his hands, slipped off his vestments. Beneath, the great holy man was clad in a shift made of threadbare sackcloth, barefooted. He removed his rings, his golden bracelets, and finally, the blessed trinity of Aa hanging about his neck.

Stripped bare.

The holiest man in the Republic. The Hand of God himself, reduced to a beggar, just as the Father of Light had been in the old parable when he granted the generous slave his freedom. And soon, the champion of the *magni* would know that same freedom, bestowed by the voice of the Everseeing upon this earth.

But first came the Luminatii and a bevy of arena attendants. Marching across the stone span, fat and sated stormdrakes cruising below. An entire century of soldiers, clad in gravebone armour, their sunsteel blades rippling with holy flame. Reaching the fortifications, they surrounded Mia, the attendants setting to work, tipping the bodies of the slaughtered gladiatii off the battlements and into the churning waters below. She spared a glance for Furian's body, watching it tumble and splash down into the blue, the black at her feet rippling. A Luminatii centurion stood before Mia, wordlessly held out his hand, glancing to her bloody gladius. Mia gave over the blade without blinking.

As the crowd chanted, cheered, the attendants quickly washed away the blood, gathered the fallen weapons and tossed them into the water beside the corpses of their owners, and scurried back across the bridge. Mia was left surrounded by Luminatii, flanking her on all sides, a hundred to her one.

'Kneel, slave,' the centurion commanded.

Mia did as she was told, knee and knuckles pressed to the stone, head bowed.

Her gravebone dagger hidden back inside the iron bracer at her wrist.

Trumpets rang. The procession began, Duomo first, his broad shoulders squared, beard bristling, three fingers raised as he marched across the bridge surrounded by yet more legionaries. Next came Scaeva, waving to the jubilant crowd, his son atop his shoulders holding the golden victor's wreath. Mia kept her head down, glaring through her lashes as the cardinal approached, the Luminatii around her parting to allow him through.

Duomo stopped before her, looked down with a gentle smile. It had been years since he'd seen her last. She had a new face and new scars to show for her time. But looking up into his eyes, she searched for recognition. Some sliver of understanding about who it was kneeling before him. Some acknowledgement of all he'd done.

Nothing.

He doesn't even know me.

More Luminatii, Scaeva marching behind, taking his time. Waving with his son to the crowd. And as he and his retinue drew nearer, closer, above the stubborn butterflies flitting about her belly, Mia felt it. A now-familiar sensation.

Hunger.

Want.

The longing of a puzzle, searching for a piece of itself.

Maw's teeth . . .

Her eyes widened. Mouth dry as ashes.

Someone here is darkin . . .

She searched among the soldiers, felt no hint of hunger. Heart hammering, she looked to Duomo, but no . . . that would be impossible. She'd seen him wielding a blessed trinity in his hand – if he were darkin, sanctified sigils of Aa would repel him, just as she . . .

O, Black Mother . . .

. . . *Scaeva?*

Her stomach sank. Eyes wide. But again, she'd seen him the truedark she attacked the Basilica Grande. There among the pews in Aa's holy house, no ill effects among the Light Father's faithful or his blessed symbols. But . . .

O, Black Mother . . .

The boy . . .

Scaeva's son.

She looked at him, found him looking back, brow creased in puzzlement. He was dark of hair, dark of eye, just like her. And as her stomach sank towards her toes, in his face, the line of his cheeks, or perhaps the shape of his lips, she saw . . .

'*Luminus Invicta, heretic,*' Remus said, raising the blade above her head. '*I will give your brother your regards.*'

. . . she *saw.*

'*You have what is yours,*' Alinne said. '*Your hollow victory. Your precious Republic. I trust it keeps you warm at night.*'

Consul Julius looked down at Mia, his smile dark as bruises. '*Would you like to know what keeps me warm at night, little one?*'

No . . .

Mia blinked in the gloom. Eyes searching the cell beyond.

'Mother, where's Jonnen?'

The Dona Corvere mouthed shapeless words. She clawed her skin, dug her hands into her matted hair. Gritting her teeth and closing her eyes as tears spilled down her cheeks.

'Gone,' she breathed. 'With his father. Gone.'

Not 'dead'.

Only 'gone'.

With his . . .

. . . no.

O, mother, please no . . .

'Father,' the boy on Scaeva's shoulders asked.

'Yes, my son?' the consul replied.

The child narrowed his ink-black eyes. Looking right at Mia.

'I'm hungry . . .'

Mia turned her eyes to the stone. Her heart was thundering now, despite all Mister Kindly's and Eclipse's efforts. Pulse rushing beneath her skin. The thought was too repulsive to believe, too awful, too horrifying, but glancing up again into the boy's face, she saw it. The shape of her mother's eyes. The bow of her lips. Memories of the babe she'd played with as a child, seven years and a lifetime ago, flooding back into her mind and threatening to spill from her throat in a scream.

Jonnen.

O, sweet little Jonnen.

My brother lives . . .

Mind racing. Heart pounding. Sweat burning. Mia curled her hands into fists and pressed her knuckles into the stone as Cardinal Duomo stood before her and spread his arms wide, face upturned to the sky.

Patience.

'Father of Light!' Duomo called. 'Creator of fire, water, storm, and earth! We call you to bear witness, on this, your holy feast! Through right of combat and trial before your everseeing eyes, we name this slave a free woman, and beg you grant her the honour of your grace! Stand and speak your name, child, that all may know our victor!'

Patience.

'Crow!' the crowd roared. 'CROW!'

The name echoed on the arena walls.

Reverberation.

Admonition.

Benediction.

'*Crow! Crow! Crow! Crow!*'

The girl rose slowly, standing like a mountain beneath those burning suns.

'My name is Mia,' she said softly.

Hand slipping to the gravebone blade at her wrist.

'Mia Corvere.'

Duomo's eyes widened. Scaeva's brow creased. The blade whistled as it came, slicing through the cardinal's throat, ear to bloody ear. He staggered back, dark blood fountaining from the wound, fingers to his severed carotid and jugular. The spray hit her face, thick and red, warm on her lips as she moved, as the Luminatii moved, as everything around her moved. The crowd roaring in horror. The cardinal collapsing to the stone. The Luminatii crying out, raising their blades. And the girl. The Blade. The gladiatii. The daughter of a murdered house, child of a failed rebellion, victor of the greatest bloodsport the Republic had ever seen . . . she charged.

Right at Julius Scaeva.

Fear bleached his handsome features, his dark eyes wide with horror. The Luminatii moved to intercept her, but she was quick as shadows, sharp as razors, hard as steel. Scaeva cried out, lifting the boy off his shoulders, the child's eyes wide with fear. And as Mia's belly rolled, the consul held his son out like a shield, and coward among cowards, he threw the boy at Mia's face.

She cried out, hand outstretched, the child's arms pinwheeling as he flew. The world slowed to a crawl, the suns pounding at her back, the heat of sunsteel flame rippling on her skin. She caught the boy, clutching him tight in her free arm, pulling him close. And rising up on her toes, she spun like a dancer, long dark hair streaming, arm outstretched in a glittering arc.

Perfection.

Her blade sank into Scaeva's chest, buried all the way to the hilt. The consul gasped, eyes open wide. Mia's face twisted, scar tissue pulling at her cheek, hatred like acid in her veins. All the miles, all the years, all the pain, coalescing in the muscles of her arm, corded and pulled tight as she dragged her blade sideways, splitting his ribs and cutting his heart in two. She left the gravebone blade quivering in his chest, the crow on the hilt smiling with its amber eyes, dark blood fountaining from the wound. And with the boy clutched tight to her chest, still spinning like poetry, like a picture, she twisted backwards, over the edge of the battlements.

And she fell.

In turns to come, the next few moments would be the topic of countless taverna tales, dinner table debates, and barroom brawls across the city of Godsgrave.

The confusion arose for a number of reasons. Firstly, it was around this moment when Magistrae, Leonides, Tacitus, Phillipi, and virtually every other sanguila and executus in the ringside boxes began vomiting blood from the poisoned goldwine they'd drunk, which proved more than a little distracting. The central plinth was a fair distance from even ringside seats, so it was difficult for many in the audience to see. And last, and most important, the grand cardinal and the consul had just been brutally murdered by the champion of the *magni*, which left everyone in the crowd a little shocked.

Some said the girl fell, the boy in her arms, right into the mouth of a hungry stormdrake. Some said she hit the water, but avoided the drakes, making her escape through the pipes that had vented the ocean out onto the arena floor. And then there were those – discounted as madmen and drunks, for the most part – who swore by the Everseeing and all four of his Holy Daughters that this little slip of a girl, this daemon wrapped in leather and steel who'd just murdered the two highest officials in the Republic, simply *disappeared*. One moment, falling towards the water in the long shadow of the battlements, the next, completely vanished.

The arena was in an uproar, fury, dismay, terror. The blood masters collapsed in their seats, or fell to the stone, Leonides and Magistrae dead among them, every gladiatii stable in the Republic beheaded with a single stroke. Duomo lay on the battlements, his face bled white, throat cut to the bone. And beside the grand cardinal, his purple robe drenched with dark heart's blood, lay the saviour of the Republic.

Julius Scaeva, the People's Senator, the man who had bested the Kingmakers and rescued Itreya from calamity, had been assassinated.

CHAPTER 36

GODSGRAVE

Ashlinn stole through the City of Bridges and Bones like a knife through a consul's chest. The sounds of panic were swelling in the arena behind them, the girl's heart singing as cathedrals all over the city began ringing a death knell.

'Black Mother, she did it.'

She chewed her lip, stifling a fierce grin.

'She *did* it.'

Ash moved quicker, over canals and through the twisting thorough-fares of the marrowborn district. The three suns blazed above, the heat relentless, sweat soaking her through. She would have stopped for a breather, but truth was, she had no time to breathe. From the sounds of chaos rising from the distant arena, word of Scaeva's death was spreading across the city like a brush fire. Soon the Red Church would know their beloved patrons were dead, and all the fury of the acolytes of Our Lady of Blessed Murder would be raining down on their heads.

She had to meet Mercurio at the necropolis, then Mia in the harbour. From there, they could slip out into the blue where no Blade or member of the Ministry could find them. Then she could rest. Breathe. Sink into Mia's arms and never, ever let go again.

Ashlinn made her way in the shadow of the Ribs, over a broad marble span to the Sword Arm. The air was slowly filling with the song of tolling bells, panicked shouts ringing through the city behind her. A boy ran past, eyes wide, waving his cap and yelling in a shrill voice.

'The consul and cardinal slain!'

'Assassin!' came another distant shout. '*Assassin!*'

She reached the wrought-iron fences surrounding the houses of Godsgrave's dead. Slipping through the tall gates, Ashlinn made her way to a door carved with a relief of human skulls, and down into the dank shadows of the necropolis. Swift and silent, she stole through the twisted tunnels of femurs and ribs, to the tomb of some long-forgotten senator. Pulling a small lever to reveal a hidden door in a stack of dusty bones, and finally, slipping into the corridors of the Red Church chapel.

Dark.

Quiet.

Safe at last.

She dashed to Mia's sparse bedchamber, snatched up a small leather pack and Mia's precious gravebone longsword. The crow's eyes on the hilt glittered red in the low light, Ash sparing a glance for the empty bed, the empty walls, the empty dark. And turning on her heel, she dashed back down the corridor to Mercurio's office.

'Are you ready t—'

Ashlinn's heart stilled in her chest. Sitting behind Mercurio's desk, fingers steepled at her chin, was an elderly woman with curling grey hair. She seemed a kindly old thing, eyes twinkling as she looked Ashlinn up and down. Though she sat in the bishop's chair, she wouldn't have seemed out of place beside a happy hearth, grandchildren on her knee and a cup of tea by her elbow.

'Revered Mother Drusilla,' Ashlinn breathed.

'O, no, young Dona Järnheim,' the old woman said. 'I've not been Revered Mother since your treachery saw Lord Cassius murdered. Now, I am Lady of Blades.'

Ashlinn looked about the room. Four other figures, swathed in gloom – the entire Red Church Ministry, waiting for her. Aalea with her death-black stare and blood-red lips. Spiderkiller, glowering in a gown of emerald green. Mouser with his old man's eyes and his young man's smile. And finally, Solis, blind gaze upturned to the ceiling, glowering at her nonetheless.

Ashlinn's grip tightened on Mia's gravebone sword.

'. . . Where's Mercurio?' she demanded.

'The bishop of Godsgrave is already back at the Quiet Mountain,' Solis said.

'He put up some resistance,' Mouser said. 'We had to hurt him, I'm afraid.'

Spiderkiller looked at Ashlinn with black, glittering eyes. 'There are some among us who are dearly hoping the same can be said of you, child.'

'Please,' Drusilla waved to the chair in front of her. 'Sit.'

'Or what?' Ashlinn said, her anger rising. 'You can't kill me like you killed my da, you old bitch. The map's branded on my skin. If I die, it's lost for ever.'

'Please sit, Dona Järnheim,' said a voice.

A man stepped out from Mercurio's bedchamber, and Ashlinn's belly filled with cold ice. He was tall, painfully handsome, dark hair shot through with the faintest streaks of grey. He wore a long toga of rich purple, a golden laurel at his brow.

'No . . .' Ashlinn breathed.

'If we wanted you dead, you'd have been so long ago,' Consul Scaeva said. 'So please, sit before we are forced to resort to . . . unpleasantness.'

'You're dead,' Ashlinn whispered. 'I *saw* you die . . .'

'No,' Scaeva said. 'Although I admit the likeness *was* uncanny.'

Ashlinn's eyes grew wide as realization sank home . . .

'The Weaver,' Ash whispered. 'Marielle. She gave someone else your face . . .'

'You always were a clever one, Ashlinn,' Aalea smiled.

'You'll forgive the appertaining drama, I hope,' Consul Scaeva said. 'But such subterfuge is necessary for a man with as many enemies as I.'

Ashlinn searched their faces, mind awhirl.

They'd known.

They'd known this whole fucking time . . .

But why would they let us . . .

. . . Unless they wanted *us . . .*

Like a puzzle box with no more missing pieces.

All of them falling into place.

'You wanted Cardinal Duomo dead,' she whispered. 'But you couldn't just have the Church kill him. He was protected by the Red Promise. Only a Blade would be good enough to end him . . . but it had to be a Blade willing to betray the Ministry. That way, the Church's reputation stays intact, and you still see your enemy dead.'

'And once I reveal myself miraculously alive to Godsgrave's adoring citizens . . .'

'. . . They'll adore you all the more.'

'And be left with *no doubt* of the continuing danger our Republic faces.'

'Buying you a fourth term as consul . . .'

'O, no,' Scaeva said, smiling wide. 'That laurel is already bought. But the brutal assassination of a grand cardinal in front of the entire capital on Aa's most holy feast? Say it with me, young Dona Järnheim. Perpetual. Emergency. Powers.'

Ashlinn's lips curled in derision.

The ego on this tosser...

The girl tossed her pack away with an almost casual contempt, plopped herself into the offered chair, and put her feet on Mercurio's desk, right in Drusilla's face. The old woman glowered, but Mia's gravebone blade was still in Ash's hand, her fingers drumming on the hilt.

'Foresaw everything, neh?' she asked the consul.

'I foresaw enough.'

'Except the part where Mia stole your son?'

The smile slowly faded from Scaeva's lips.

'That was . . . unfortunate,' the consul said, a muscle twitching at his jaw. 'The boy should never have been allowed to accompany my doppel-gänger to the presentation. My wife . . . she cannot have children, you see. So she indulges, perhaps too much.' Scaeva's lips curled in a smile again, small and deadly. 'But no matter. I have the beloved teacher. And now I have the beloved. And cold as she is, I think not even my daughter would harm her own brother.'

The floor dropped away from beneath Ashlinn's feet.

'. . . Daughter?'

Ashlinn felt movement behind her. A quick glance showed a thin, pale boy with stunning blue eyes in the chamber doorway, dressed in a dark velvet doublet. He was mute as always, but the knife in his hands looked sharp enough to cut the sunlight in six. The last time she'd seen him, he'd been trussed up in Luminatii chains, thanks to her betrayal. She'd wager he was the type to bear a grudge.

'All right, Hush?' Ashlinn asked.

She saw other figures behind him, scowling, glowering – Blades, all, no doubt.

'Time to go, Ashlinn,' Drusilla said.

'O, no,' Ashlinn mewled. 'Can't I stay a little longer and listen to the consul gloat? I do *so* enjoy hearing the wanker tell me how he's thought of everything.'

'You disagree, Dona Järnheim?' Scaeva smiled.

'I fear I must, Consul Scaeva,' Ashlinn smiled in reply. 'Because a person who'd thought of everything might have thought to look in my pack before I dropped it. And a person not so fond of his own fucking voice might have heard the fuse on the tombstone bomb inside.'

Drusilla's eyes widened. Ashlinn threw herself aside as her pack exploded with an ear-splitting boom. Solis was blasted across the room, smashing into the wall. The Ministry were caught in the arkemical fireball. Hush was smashed out through the chamber doors, his doublet aflame, the rest of the Blades tossed about like straw.

Ashlinn was up and running, ears bleeding, clothes smoking, head swimming from the blast. Mia's gravebone sword in hand, she dashed through the necropolis, at least three Church Blades on her heels. Sprinting through the twisting labyrinth, she made it to the upper levels, bursting out into the graveyard, suns beating down on her back. She had to make it to the harbour, had to—

The dagger took her in the back of her thigh, scraping the bone. She screamed and stumbled, mincing her palms and knees on the flagstones as she hit the ground. Teeth gritted, she rolled over, tore the dagger loose. Staggering to her feet, she saw four Church Blades bearing down on her. Silent and grim, dark eyes hardened to flint. Killers one, killers all. Each a storm, with no pity for the one they were to drown.

Ashlinn raised Mia's gravebone sword.

Looking among the killers and smiling dark.

'I'm guessing you're supposed to take me alive,' she grinned. 'Apologies in advance . . .'

'Aye,' said the woman leading them. 'We're sorry too.'

Ashlinn blinked. Vision swimming. World spinning. Looking at the blood on her shaking fingers, spilling over her wounded thigh, down to the dagger that had struck her, and finally noticing the discolouration on the steel.

Poison.

'S'pose I should've expected that . . .' she muttered.

A chill stole over her, dark and hollow. Goosebumps rippling on her bloodied skin. The suns burned high overhead, but here in the necropolis, the shadows were dark, almost black. A shape rose up behind the Blades, hooded and cloaked, swords of what could only have been gravebone in its hands. It lashed out at the closest killer, hacked his head almost off his shoulders. The other Blades turned quick as flies, raised their steel, but the figure moved like lightning, striking with its gravebone once, twice, three times. And almost faster than Ashlinn could blink, all four Blades were left dead and bleeding on the flagstones.

'Maw's teeth,' she whispered.

It wasn't human. That much was clear. O, it was shaped like a man beneath that cloak – tall and broad shouldered. But its hands . . .'byss and blood, the hands wrapped about its sword hilts were black. Tenebrous and semitranslucent, fingers coiled about the hilts like serpents. Ashlinn couldn't see its face, but small, black tentacles writhed and wriggled from within the hollows of its hood, pulling the cowl lower over its features. And though it was truelight, three suns burning high in the sky, its breath hung in white clouds before its lips, Ash's whole body shivering at the chill.

'. . . Who are you?'

The thing peeled back its hood. Pallid skin. Saltlocks writhing like living things. Pitch-black and hollow eyes. But even with the poison swimming in her veins, all the world around her fading to black, Ashlinn would recognize his face anywhere.

'HELLO, ASHLINN,' he said.

''Byss and blood,' she breathed.

The darkness closing in.

'. . . Tric?'

DICTA ULTIMA

No.

I hear you say the word, as if I sat in the room beside you. I see you, bent over the tome in your hand with a frown on your face and a curse on your lips, as if I were puddled in the shadow at your feet. The realization that there are no more pages is sinking in now. I hear it. I see it.

No, you say again.

What of Mia and Jonnen? Of Scaeva? Mercurio and Ashlinn and Tric? The secrets of the darkin? The Crown of the Moon? I promised ruins in her wake. Pale light glittering on waters that drank a city of bridges and bones. All these questions unanswered, and yet the book is at its end?

No, you say. It cannot end like that.

Fear not, little mortal. The song is not yet sung. This is but the calm before the crescendo. This tale is only two of three.

Birth. And life. And death.

So patience, gentlefriends.

Patience.

Close your eyes.

Take my hand.

And walk with me.

here he fell

ACKNOWLEDGMENTS

Thanks as deep as the Dark to the following:

Amanda, Pete, Jennifer, Paul, Joseph, Hector, Young, Steven, Justin, Rafal, Cheryl, Martin, and all at St. Martin's Press; Natasha, Katie, Emma, Jaime, Dom, and all at Harper Voyager UK; Rochelle, Alice, Sarah, Andrea, and all at Harper Australia; Mia, Matt, LT, Josh, Tracey, Samantha, Stefanie, Steven, Steve, Jason, Kerby, Megasaurus, Virginia, Vilma, Kat, Stef, Wendy, Marc, Molly, Tovo, Orrsome, Tsana, Lewis, Shaheen, Soraya, Amie, Jessie, Caitie, Nic, Ursula, Louise, Tori, Siân, Caz, Marie, Marc, Tina, Maxim, Zara, Ben, Clare, Jim, Rowie, Weez, Sam, Eli, Rafe, AmberLouise, Caro, Melanie, Barbara, Judith, Rose, Tracy, Aline, Louise, Adele, Jordi, Kylie, Iryna, Joe, Andrea, Piéra, Julius, Antony, Antonio, Emily, Robin, Drew, William, China, David, Aaron, Terry (RIP), Douglas (RIP), George, Margaret, Tracy, Ian, Steve, Gary, Mark, Tim, Matt, George, Ludovico, Philip, Randy, Oli, Corey, Maynard, Zack, Pete (RIP), Robb, Ian, Marcus, Tom (RIP), Trent, Winston, Andy (RIP), Tony, Kath, Kylie, Nicole, Kurt, Jack, Max, Poppy, and every reader, blogger, vlogger, bookstagrammer, and other breed of bookpimp who has helped spread the word about this series.

The people and city of Rome.

The people and city of Venice.

And you.

BONUS CONTENT

Hello, and welcome to the bonus bits.

When the wonderful folks at Barnes & Noble decided to do an exclusive edition of *Godsgrave*, they asked if I had any deleted scenes they could include to make their edition extra shiny. Now the good news is, every writer has a bottom drawer full of deleted scenes. The bad news is, there's a reason those scenes get deleted, and that's because they're usually bloody awful.

But it just so happened I had a deleted scene I rather liked.

Confession time: I know you're never supposed to show people how the sausage gets made, but the awful truth is, I usually start writing my books in the wrong place. Once I wrote eighty thousand words before I realized I'd done it. True story.

I wrote a first chapter for *Godsgrave* back in 2014, with a clear vision of how the book would flow. The idea was that Mia would begin the novel undercover, lying in wait for Ashlinn Järnheim or her father to contact an old ally, but a well-meaning buccaneer would throw her plan into disarray. But by the time I sat down to work on the book in earnest, the plan for the novel had totally changed, and that first chapter didn't fit any more.

But still, I liked it. I worked hard on it. And now you get to read it. It has pirates and sword fighting and witty banter, and a few of my other favourite things. The more observant among you might notice I even recycled a few of the jokes for the final book. And though it was consigned to the bottom drawer, I still hope you find it extra shiny.

Enjoy.

Jay K

CHAPTER 1
DAMSEL

It wasn't the name his mother gifted him, but to friend and foe alike, he was known as the Storm of Galante. And he was having a bastard of a nevernight.

His rapier of Liisian steel, having sent more than a dozen men to the Hearth, now weighed heavy in his grip. The gilded stiletto in his off-hand gleamed in the light of two swollen suns, yellow and shimmering red. It'd be truelight in a few months, and the Storm of Galante couldn't help but wish Earl Gunnar's daughter could've got herself kidnapped in a cooler time of year.

He was at serious risk of breaking a sweat.

The three hüsguards sizing him up across the windblown battlements probably knew the Storm by reputation if not by sight. In the seven years his ship, the Bloody Maid, had sailed the Sea of Stars, the Storm had amassed notoriety like a dockside sweetboy amasses crotch lice. He was known as a peerless swordsman, unabashed rake and all-round buckler of swashes. And though he made his living as a privateer, he was still the sort of scoundrel who liked to ensure a fellow knew his name before he murdered the shit out of him.

'Do you know who I am?' he asked the guards, eyebrow raised.

'Aye,' a short one replied.

'You're the Storm of Galante,' said a brutish second.

'Bravo, gentlefriend. And do you know why they name me so?'

The hüsguards glanced among each other, shrugging.

'Allow me to demonstrate,' the Storm smiled.

Watching him lunge across the battlements to skewer the first hüsguard, it would've been easy to believe the Storm was named for his swordarm. He moved just like his namesake, his blade swift as lightning. His boot met *the short hüsguard's groin like a thunderclap, dropping the man with a whimper. The last guard mounted a valiant defence with a sharp battleaxe, but with a flick of the Storm's wrist and a bright flash of arkemical powder, the guard was sent reeling backwards, and the Storm's rapier signed the poor fellow's death note in red.*

The Storm looked down from the battlements into the courtyard below. The keep's alarm had been raised, and more hüsguards would be on their way. Kael Three Eyes and Windseer were blocking off the lower stairwells, but trouble would be on the Storm's heels soon enough. He'd only a few minutes before he'd have to turn this daring rescue into a daring escape, with the Earl's daughter in hand or no. The Storm had hoped this job might be seen through with a little luck and a lot of guile, but with Brightstone Keep now on full alert, he and his merry crew had a shorter life expectancy than a bottle of top-shelf goldwine in a brothel full of pissheads.

'Ahoy!' he called. 'Windseer!'

Now, swordsmanship aside, some said the Storm was named for his voice – a booming, honey-smooth baritone. Oftentimes as the Bloody Maid *sailed the Sea of Stars, the Storm would stand at her prow, harp in hand, and simply sing. His songs were so bewitching, it was rumoured even rayfolk and deepweres would swim up from the gloom to listen. Old Stomper swore blind that one turn, he even saw a craykith weeping when the Storm put his harp away.*

'Windseer!' the Storm called again.

Down in the courtyard, a hulking Dweymeri man turned from gutting some hapless hüsguard. 'Aye, Cap'n?'

'The game is up! Make for the skiff!'

'What about the girl?' his first mate shouted.

'You mean the dona*?' The Storm flashed a handsome grin. 'Leave her to me.'*

'There's a hundred more of these bastards, Cap'n, I'll not leave—'

'And I'll not have your lives put to forfeit without need! Go, brother! If I'm not back aboard in half an hour, tell your wife I love her!'

The first mate cursed, but the loyalty of the Maid*'s crew was unshakeable. The Storm of Galante wasn't the sort of captain who hung at the wheelhouse and let his men do the fighting, gentlefriend. When the* Maid *had been becalmed for seven weeks in the Sea of Sorrows, it'd been the Storm who'd gone without rations that his men might eat. When half a dozen of his crew had been snatched by fleshrunners in the Straits of Tsana, it'd been the Storm who led the charge into the fenpits to rescue them. Time and again, this captain had bled for his men. His command was the word* of Aa himself. And so Windseer and the rest of the Maid's crew broke out, fighting their way back to the wall and escape into the ocean below.

The Storm turned from the battlement, kicked through the doorway into Brightstone tower. The keep crouched atop vicious bluffs along the coastline of southern Vaan, known as the Boneyard. Approach from land was only possible across a single narrow drawbridge, guarded by the best of Hüslaird Kustaa's men. Approach from the sea was an even dicier proposition – it'd taken the Storm and his band the best part of a turn to make the climb, and they'd lost three of their number on the ascent. Now, those damned bells seemed set to finish what the Boneyard had started.

He met another pair of hüsguards on the stairs, shooting the first through the throat with his hand crossbow and flinging the last of his arkemical powder at the second, cutting him down in the flash's aftermath. Reloading as he dashed up the stairwell, he found himself in a long hall, run with rich red carpet and crowned with an ornate, gilded mirror. The Storm peered down the stairs for pursuit, and satisfied none was forthcoming, stopped to check his reflection in the glass.

He was about to rescue nobility, after all.

The privateer was clad all in black; leather jerkin and suspiciously tight britches spattered with blood. Sapphire-blue eyes gleamed beneath the brim of his feathered tricorn. Short whiskers dusted a jaw you could break a shovel on, and a perfect smile completed a portrait that didn't so much turn heads as break necks.

It was said by some of his crew that he'd seduced one of the baphomantii, and pleased the she-daemon so thoroughly she'd gifted him a face all would love. Others whispered he'd out-riddled one of the betweenfolk and stolen her glamour. Whatever the truth, his first mate, Windseer, claimed that here was the source of his captain's moniker. For it was said that wherever he travelled, much like his namesake, the Storm left members of the fairer sex somewhat . . . damp in his wake.*

The Storm of Galante peered at his reflection.

Adjusted the ruffled cuff of one black sleeve.

And he winked.

He dashed along the corridor, crashing between servants with hurried apologies and sprinting up more stairs, thinking he'd left the last of the laird's men dead behind him. And finally reaching the landing outside the keep's master bedchamber, he was disappointed to find a dozen elite hüsguards in heavy plate armour waiting for him.

---

*I confess I don't know whether to love him or hate him either.

The men were lumps of scar and muscle, armed with short, double-edged pigstickers and curved rectangular shields. And handsome though he might be, every one of the bastards looked like he'd gleefully pick his teeth with the Storm's shiny rapier of Liisian steel, right after eating the rest of him for breakfast.

The Storm skidded to a stop twenty feet from the mob.

'Good turn, gentlefriends. Do you know who I am?'

'Aye,' said a towering lump of beef. 'You're the soon-to-be-dead Storm of Galante.'

'The same,' the Storm replied, sweeping off his tricorn with a bow. 'But do you know why they name me so?'

'Because you're soon to be dead?'

The mob advanced, axes raised. Seemingly unfazed, the Storm reached into his doffed tricorn, and produced a bulb of polished glass. With a twist of his fingers, he tossed the bulb into the group, stuffing his hat back onto his head before diving back down the stairs he'd charged up from.

White flame scorched the walls as an explosion bloomed, and a deafening boom tore across the landing. Glass splinters and the occasional unidentifiable body part bounced down the stairwell to smoke at the Storm's feet.

The privateer uncovered his ears, picked himself up from his crouch, and propping his hat at a jaunty angle, skipped back up to the landing. Stepping over the minced wreckage of Kustaa's elite, the Storm drew his rapier and stepped through the now-open bedchamber door.

'Dona Astrid?' he called.

The shutters were sealed, the room beyond shrouded in gloom. The scent of candles and overcooked meat hung thick in the air. Black smoke from the arkemical bomb billowed about the Storm's shoulders, his silhouette outlined against the summer blue outside.

'Dona Astrid?'

'Bastard!'

A thin cry tore the air as a man flew at the Storm from out of the dark. The privateer lashed out with his blade, heard a gasp of pain. Grabbing the fellow's collar, the Storm saw that his foe was old and feeble, clad in a robe as red as the blood now gushing from his chest.

'Laird Kustaa, I presume,' the Storm murmured.

'You d-dare . . .' the laird wheezed.

'O, I dare, old man. That's the difference between me and most.'

The freebooter released his grip, let the laird sink to his knees. Kustaa clutched his chest and set about turning the stone beneath him as red and sticky as possible.

'O, no!'

A figure in a thin white gown stumbled across the room, falling to her knees at the laird's side. She was barely more than a girl, winter pale and slender, loose dark hair flowing down to her waist, sharp bangs over her eyes. She rolled Kustaa onto his back, stripping away his robe to inspect the wound.

'My Laird?' The girl shook the old man's shoulder. 'My Laird!'

'Dona Astrid?'

The girl blinked up at him, hair strung like black cobwebs about her face. She was beautiful, he realized. Cherry, bee-stung lips and kohled eyes, black enough to drown in. Gunnar Svärda's daughter had been imprisoned in Brightstone for over two months – Aa only knew what torments she'd endured at Kustaa's hands. But as she knelt there in the widening pool of the laird's blood, the Storm swore she looked almost grieved at the old bastard's death.

He offered his hand. 'Mi Dona, I've come to rescue you.'

Her ears were bleeding from the arkemical bomb's shock wave, poor thing. It took her a moment to grasp his words.

'. . . Rescue me?'

'Aye, Dona.' He swept his tricorn off in a perfect bow. 'Do you know who I am?'

Gunnar's daughter looked back down at the dead laird's body. Shoulders slumping as she hung her head.

'Aye,' she sighed. 'I know who you are.'

The girl rose from the blood.

The shadows rippled at her feet as she snarled.

'You're an absolute fucking wanker.'